Berkley Prime Crime titles by Lorna Barrett

MURDER IS BINDING
BOOKMARKED FOR DEATH
BOOKPLATE SPECIAL
CHAPTER & HEARSE
SENTENCED TO DEATH
MURDER ON THE HALF SHELF

Anthologies

MURDER IN THREE VOLUMES

Murder in Three Volumes

• • •

Lorna Barrett

BERKLEY PRIME CRIME, NEW YORK

THE BERKLEY PUBLISHING GROUP
Published by the Penguin Group
Penguin Group (USA) Inc.
375 Hudson Street, New York, New York 10014, USA
Penguin Group (Canada), 90 Eglinton Avenue East, Suite 700, Toronto, Ontario M4P 2Y3, Canada (a division of Pearson Penguin Canada Inc.) • Penguin Books Ltd., 80 Strand, London WC2R 0RL, England • Penguin Group Ireland, 25 St. Stephen's Green, Dublin 2, Ireland (a division of Penguin Books Ltd.) • Penguin Group (Australia), 250 Camberwell Road, Camberwell, Victoria 3124, Australia (a division of Pearson Australia Group Pty. Ltd.) • Penguin Books India Pvt. Ltd., 11 Community Centre, Panchsheel Park, New Delhi—110 017, India • Penguin Group (NZ), 67 Apollo Drive, Rosedale, Auckland 0632, New Zealand (a division of Pearson New Zealand Ltd.) • Penguin Books (South Africa) (Pty.) Ltd., 24 Sturdee Avenue, Rosebank, Johannesburg 2196, South Africa

PUBLISHING HISTORY
Berkley Prime Crime trade paperback edition / October 2012
Murder Is Binding Berkley Prime Crime mass-market edition / April 2008
Bookmarked for Death Berkley Prime Crime mass-market edition / February 2009
Bookplate Special Berkley Prime Crime mass-market edition / November 2009

Berkley Prime Crime trade paperback ISBN: 978-0-425-26363-1

An application to register this book for cataloging has been submitted to the Library of Congress

PRINTED IN THE UNITED STATES OF AMERICA

10 9 8 7 6 5 4 3 2 1

CONTENTS

Murder Is Binding

• • •

For Valerie Bartlett.
Thank you for introducing me to
the wonderful world of mystery novels.

ACKNOWLEDGMENTS

Many generous friends (most of them members of my Sisters in Crime chapter, The Guppies), helped me with this first book in the Booktown Mystery series. Deb Baker, Marilyn Levinson, Nan Higginson, and Doranna Durgin were invaluable first readers during the proposal stage of *Murder Is Binding*, and Nan and Marilyn gave wonderful feedback on the final version of the book. My thanks to Elizabeth Becka for forensic information. Michelle Sampson, Wadleigh Memorial Library Director, Milford, New Hampshire, supplied me with local color, as did Nancy Cooper.

Hank Phillippi Ryan volunteered the services of her husband, Jonathan Shapiro, Esquire, for legal advice (any mistakes in that regard are entirely my own). Go Hank and Jonathan! Local bookseller Rebecca Budinger at the Greece Ridge Barnes & Noble was invaluable for sharing information on booksellers. Sharon Wildwind continues to amaze me with the depth of her knowledge and her willingness to share it.

My local critique partners Gwen Nelson and Liz Eng are tireless cheerleaders. They've been with me through thick and thin. (Don't go away, guys, I need you!) Thanks, too, to my tireless IM buddy, Sheila Connolly (also known as Sarah Atwell) for her marvelous brainstorming and cheerleading ability.

Thanks also go to my editor, Tom Colgan, and his assistant, Sandy Harding, for making the process run so smoothly. And most of all I'd like to thank my wonderful agent, Jacky Sach, without whom this book would never have been written.

ONE

"I TELL YOU, Trish, we're *all* victims."

Victims? In the town voted safest in all of New Hampshire? Tricia Miles raised an eyebrow and studied the septuagenarian bookseller before her over the rim of her cardboard coffee cup. *Here it comes,* she thought with dread, *the pitch.*

Doris Gleason would never be called subtle. Everything about her screamed excess—from her bulky frame clad in a bright pink polyester dress, her dyed, jet-black pageboy haircut, to the overlarge glasses that perched on her nose. She leaned closer over the oak-and-glass display case, making Tricia glad she'd taken refuge behind the antique register as a way of guaranteeing her personal space. Too often Doris was in her face.

"If we all negotiate together, we can beat that bastard."

Tricia drained her cup and sighed. "I assume you're referring to Bob Kelly, our mutual benefactor?" President of the local Chamber of Commerce and owner of Kelly Realty, Bob had recruited Doris, Tricia, and all the other booksellers to relocate to the picturesque village of Stoneham, New Hampshire.

"Benefactor my ass," Doris grated, pink spots appearing on her cheeks. She removed her glasses, exhaled on one of the lenses, and polished it with the ribbed edge of her dingy white sweater. Half-moon indentations marred the ridge of her cheeks where they'd rested. "That chiseler owns or has a share in every storefront on Main Street. He controls our rents, tries to control our stock *and* the quality of our customers. I nearly lost my voice after our last shouting match. It was all I could do not to throttle him."

From her perch on a shelf above the register, Miss Marple, the store's resident cat, a regal, gray domestic longhair, glared down at the older woman—disapproving of her temper. Tricia had to agree, yet she understood Doris's anger. Bob Kelly had charged her extra to transform the facade of her shop front even though the changes had incorporated much-needed repairs to the century-old building.

Most of the village revered Bob. Bringing in antiquarian and specialty booksellers—and the tourist dollars they attracted—had saved the little town from financial collapse. His ideas, commitment, and even a bit of sweat equity, had turned a forgotten hamlet on the New Hampshire–Massachusetts border

into a tourist mecca for readers in a world dominated by the Internet and other instant-gratification entertainment. The fact that he could also be the most demanding, insufferable bore on the face of the Earth . . .

Tricia forced a patient smile. "Now, Doris, you know we can't participate in collective bargaining. None of our leases come up at the same time."

Doris pulled off her glasses, set them on the counter as her lips twisted into a sneer. "I *knew* you wouldn't cooperate. The rumors about you must be true!"

Tricia felt her face start to burn. "What rumors?"

"That you're incredibly rich. That you don't *have* to worry about paying your rent. You don't *have* to worry about stock or overhead." Doris glanced around the well-appointed store, the richly paneled walls decorated with prints and photos of long-dead mystery authors, the expensive upholstered armchairs and large square coffee table that made up the seating nook and allowed patrons the comforts of home while they perused Tricia's stock of vintage first-edition mysteries and newly minted best sellers.

A fat lot Doris knew. Tricia struggled to quell her ire. "I have the same worries as you and every other bookseller in the village. This store isn't a hobby for me. I resent the implication that I conspired against you and the other booksellers. I didn't know Bob Kelly before I came to this town, and I'm sure my rent is probably triple or quadruple what you're currently paying."

"That's my point," Doris insisted. "If you hadn't agreed to pay such an exorbitant price, the rest of us wouldn't be in this mess."

It was true Tricia hadn't done much haggling before she signed on as the village's newest bookseller, but then she'd been used to the idea of Manhattan rents and the contrast made the deal she'd been offered seem like a steal.

"I'm sorry, Doris," Tricia said and disposed of her disposable coffee cup in the wastebasket beneath the counter, "but I really don't see how I can be of any help."

Doris straightened, her contempt palpable. "We'll see." She turned and plodded for the exit, wrenched open the door. The little bell overhead gave a cheerful tinkle, an absurd end to an unpleasant conversation.

"Don't tell me the old crab was in here carping about her rent again."

Tricia turned. Ginny Wilson, a lithe, twentysomething redhead and Tricia's only employee, staggered under the weight of a carton of books and dumped it on the counter. "Word is that Daww-ris"—she said the name with such disdain—"has been all over town, badgering the merchants to hop on her 'let's save the Cookery' bandwagon. She claims she's going to have to go out of business if she can't negotiate a better lease." She waved a hand in dismissal. "I say good riddance."

A glance around the area proved at least one of the shop's regular patrons, Mr. Everett, a silver-haired elderly gent who showed up at opening and often

had to be chased out at night, had been eavesdropping on the conversations. Tricia placed a finger to her lips and frowned.

"You never had to work for her," Ginny hissed and removed a sheathed box cutter from the pocket of her hunter green apron, opened it, and slit the tape on the carton. Haven't Got a Clue, the bookshop's name, was embroidered in yellow across the apron's top. Pinned to the neck strap was Ginny's name tag.

Tricia, too, wore a tag, but not an apron. She wanted some distinction made between the owner and the help—not that she didn't do her share of the hefting and carrying around the store, though she tried to do it after business hours. Slacks and sweater sets were her current dress code, and today she'd chosen a raspberry combination, which seemed to accent her blue eyes and complement her light brown hair.

"Oh, before I forget," Ginny said, dipping into her apron pocket once again. "I found this in a copy of Patricia Cornwell's newest release."

Tricia took the small folded piece of paper and sighed: another religious tract. Often visitors would hide them in books, hoping to spread the good word, but as she scanned the text Tricia's eyes went wide. "Nudists?"

Ginny grinned. "Is that weird or what?"

Tricia crumpled the leaflet and tossed it, too, into the wastebasket. "We'd better be on the lookout. If we find one, there's usually ten more hidden amongst the stock."

The circa-1935 black telephone by the register rang. Tricia picked up the heavy handset, noticing Doris had left her glasses on the counter. "Haven't Got a Clue—Tricia speaking. How can I help you?"

"Darling Trish. I'm so glad it was you who answered. I despise speaking to that little helper of yours. She never wants to put me through to you."

The apprehension Tricia had felt when talking with Doris blossomed into full-fledged dread as she recognized her sister's voice. "Angelica?"

"Of course it's me, and I've been trying to get ahold of you for a week. Doesn't that girl ever give you messages?"

"It must have slipped her mind." Which was a lie. Tricia had given Ginny orders to screen calls and to never put Angelica through. It wasn't that the sisters couldn't get along; it was just that Tricia chose not to. Growing up in Angelica's shadow had been painful enough; putting up with her in adulthood was simply out of the question.

"You should give me your cell number," Angelica badgered.

No way! "We're really very busy today, Ange; can I call you back later?" Another lie. The store was practically empty at only ten fifteen on a Tuesday morning.

"Oh no, you're not cutting me off again. I only called to tell you that I've

booked a room in the sweetest little bed-and-breakfast in Stoneham, the Brookview Inn. I hear it's very quaint."

Hardly. The Brookview was Stoneham's finest show palace, boasting a French chef, spa facilities, and catering to a very exclusive clientele. Angelica had the money, of course, but the rest of her personal résumé was definitely lacking. Okay, maybe that was untrue, otherwise how would she have attracted so many husbands? Still, being near her sister seemed to bring out the worst in Tricia.

"What do you want to come here for? It's deadly dull. The shopping isn't up to your usual standards. There's nothing to do here but *read*. You'll only be bored."

"I'm coming to see you, dear—and your *little* shop."

Tricia ground her teeth at the descriptor.

"I had Drew pull up your website on the computer," Angelica continued. "You know how challenged I am when it comes to anything electrical. The pictures are just darling, and you look so stunningly slim and successful, as we all knew you would be."

Tricia cringed at the second dig. On the other side of the counter, Ginny suppressed a giggle. Tricia's gaze swiveled and she pointed to a puzzled-looking patron standing by one of the shelves. Ginny gave a resigned shrug and left the counter. Tricia balanced the heavy receiver on her shoulder and took over emptying the box Ginny had started. "This really isn't a good time, Ange. We're already gearing up for the Christmas rush."

"It's only September," Angelica growled. "One would almost think you're trying to discourage me from coming."

"Don't be silly. I love it whenever you visit." And love it more when you leave. "When are you arriving?"

"This afternoon—I'm already en route." In the back of a limo, no doubt—zooming up I-95 even as they spoke. "I can't wait to see you. I should be arriving before dinner. I'll give you a ring. Now how about that cell number?"

"I'm sorry, I'll be right with you," Tricia said to a nonexistent customer. "Excuse me, Ange—I really have to go."

"Oh, all right then. Kiss, kiss—see you tonight."

Tricia slammed the phone down and turned, startling the handsome, middle-aged man with a full head of sandy hair and dressed in the dark business suit who stood before her. "I'm so sorry, I didn't see you there. How can I help you?"

The man thrust his hand forward. "Mike Harris. I want to be your next selectman and I hope you'll consider voting for me."

"Tricia Miles." She shook hands, immediately noting the absence of a ring on the fourth finger of Mike's other hand. "The general election isn't for another two months."

"It's never too soon to meet my future constituents." Mike's white-toothed smile dazzled, making Tricia feel giddy. She giggled. It had been a long time since a man had inspired that reaction in her. Far too long.

Mike relinquished her hand and passed her a glossy color folder with his left, his expression growing serious. "I understand leases are an issue with the booksellers. I'd like to better understand the problem in case I can be of some assistance. I'm no attorney, but as an independent insurance agent I've read my share of pretty complicated contracts."

Tricia studied his face, noted the fine lines around his eyes, the slight graying of his fair hair around the temples. He was maybe five years older than herself—putting him in his mid-forties, but without the girth so often associated with his age group. She'd escaped middle-age spread herself, thanks to inheriting genes from the paternal side of the family—about the only perk of growing up a Miles. Angelica hadn't fared so well and had never forgiven her for it.

She shook away thoughts of her sister, focusing again on the man before her. How had she gone six months in this town without meeting this feast for the eyes?

"I'm afraid the leases aren't an issue with me. You might want to visit my neighbor to the north over at the Cookery. She can give you all the facts as she perceives them."

Mike frowned. "I've already spoken with Ms. Gleason. She has . . . an interesting perspective on the subject."

"Yes." Tricia left it at that.

"I take it you're new to our little village?" Mike asked.

"I've been here almost half a year. But I can't say I've seen you in my store before."

"I'm not much of a fiction reader," he admitted. "But I've spent a bundle over at History Repeats Itself. I'm fascinated by anything to do with World War Two, military aircraft being my special interest. As a kid I wanted to be a fighter pilot. That is until I figured out I have a fear of heights."

Tricia laughed. "I can recommend some wonderful novels that take place during the war. Books by J. Robert Janes, Philip Kerr, and Greg Iles. And I'll bet I've got most of them in stock." She indicated the tall oak shelves surrounding the walls and their lower counterparts that filled the center of the long, narrow store.

Mike dazzled her with his smile again. "Some other time, perhaps. I'm taking a day off work to introduce myself to all the merchants on Main Street. Very nice meeting you, Tricia. I'm sure I'll be back." He offered his hand again, this time holding on longer.

"I'll look forward to it." Tricia held on, too. Their gazes locked and she dazzled him with a smile of her own.

• • •

TUESDAY NIGHT: THE slowest night of the week. Like most of the other merchants on Main Street, Tricia closed an hour early. That meant that she might actually get a chance to eat a decent dinner or truck on over to nearby Wilton to see a movie if she felt so inclined—which she usually didn't. More often than not she'd retire to her third-floor loft apartment, select a variety of CDs for the player, heat a frozen pizza, settle in her most comfy chair, and *read.* Since her divorce a year earlier, she hadn't often felt a need for male company. Then again, when she thought of Mike Harris's smile . . .

Angelica's arrival in Stoneham, however, had put a damper on her usual Tuesday-night routine.

Ginny had hung up her apron and grabbed her purse to leave. "You're going to be late meeting your sister, Tricia."

"I know," she said and sighed. "I didn't get to vacuum or anything." She retrieved her purse from the cabinet under the display case, slipped past the register, and noticed Doris's glasses still sitting on the counter. "You would've thought she'd miss these," she said and stuffed them into her bag. "I better drop them off on the way to meet Angelica."

"Better you than me—on *both* accounts."

"I'll give you a hundred dollars—cash—if you do both."

Ginny laughed and shook her head. "Maybe for a hundred thousand, but nothing less."

Miss Marple meowed from her perch on the shelf above the register. "Don't worry, you'll get your dinner when I come home." Miss Marple rubbed her head against the security camera. "And stop that. You keep messing up the camera's angle."

Miss Marple threw her entire eight-pound body against it, knocking it out of alignment, and purred loudly.

"I told you so—I told you so," Ginny sang. Yes, she had told Tricia the camera wasn't high enough on the wall. But it would've interfered with the decorative molding if it was mounted any higher.

Tricia scooped up the cat and set her on one of the comfortable chairs. "Stay down," she ordered.

Miss Marple tossed her head, dismissing the command.

Tricia rolled her eyes and headed for the door once again. She locked it, then realized she hadn't lowered the window shades. She'd have to do it on her return.

The lights in the Cookery bookshop were already dimmed, but Tricia could see Doris still standing behind the sales counter.

"See you tomorrow," Ginny called brightly and headed down the street toward the municipal lot where she'd parked her car.

Tricia gave a wave and turned back for the door, giving it a knock. Doris looked up, had on another pair of outsized specs, but motioned Tricia to go away before she bent back over the counter again. Tricia retrieved the glasses from her purse and knocked once more. This time, she waved them when Doris looked up.

The annoyed shopkeeper skirted the sales counter, lumbered to the door, and unlocked it.

"I'm glad you're still here. You left these in my store this morning," Tricia said.

"So that's where they went. I'm always losing them. That's why I keep an extra pair here at the shop." She pocketed them in the same ugly sweater she'd worn earlier in the day, but the rest of her attire had changed. Dressed in dark slacks and a red blouse, she looked pounds lighter, years younger, and, except for the sweater, almost elegant.

Tricia had never actually been in the Cookery before. It seemed like all her encounters with Doris had been in her own shop. Since all the storefronts were more or less the same—give or take a few feet in width—the Cookery was set up in the same configuration as Haven't Got a Clue, except that where the mystery store had a seating area, the cookbook store housed a cooking demo area: a horseshoe-shaped island with a knife block, complete with ten or twelve chef knives, a small sink, burners, and an under-the-counter refrigerator. Overhead hung a large rectangular mirror so that an audience would see the hands-on instruction. A thin film of greasy dust covered the station, which obviously hadn't been used in a while.

"Nice store," Tricia said.

"It ought to be," Doris groused. "I put a lot of money into it, and if Bob Kelly and I can't come to an agreement on it tonight, I'll lose it all."

The cost of doing business, Tricia thought, but didn't voice what would obviously be an unpopular opinion.

Doris glanced at the big clock over the register. "Bob should've been here ten minutes ago—the inconsiderate jerk."

Atop the main sales counter sat an oblong Lucite container that housed what looked like an aged booklet. The little hinged door sported a sturdy lock. "The prize of your collection?" Tricia asked, her curiosity piqued.

Doris's eyes lit up, and for the first time Tricia saw beyond the sour expression to the woman's true passion. "Yes. It's *American Cookery*, by Amelia Simmons, the very first American cookbook ever published back in 1796. A similar copy recently sold for ten thousand dollars at auction."

Calling the little, yellowing pamphlet a book was stretching the definition.

Doris exhaled a shaky breath, her expression akin to a lovesick teen. "I wish I could keep it myself, but—"

Tricia knew that "but" only too well. Like every other collector she, too, had coveted the holy grail for her own collection. She'd been close a few times, but had never been able to obtain an original copy of *Graham's Lady's and Gentleman's Magazine* containing Poe's short story "The Murders in the Rue Morgue."

"What are you asking for it?"

Doris hesitated. "I haven't actually set a price. I only obtained it a couple of weeks ago. The lockbox arrived just yesterday. But I couldn't resist putting it on exhibition." She gazed fondly at the booklet. "Of course I have a facsimile of it at home and have read it many times, but to actually hold an original copy in my hands has been the thrill of a lifetime."

Tricia nodded.

Doris shook her head. "It's sad how few people really appreciate a well-written cookbook. Most of the slobs who come in here are looking for the latest Food Network star's most recent atrocity. And I can't tell you how much money I make on old Betty Crocker books from the fifties and sixties. Not even first editions, mind you. I can sell a tenth or twelfth edition for twenty bucks." She shuddered. Clearly, the woman hated the books, but she'd sell them to pay her rent—it was something else Tricia understood.

"How did you score such a find?" Tricia asked.

Doris's expression curdled. "Private sale."

The fact that she wouldn't elaborate must've meant the former owner had since had an inkling of what the booklet might be worth.

Tricia forced a smile. "I'd better get going."

"Thank you for returning my glasses," Doris said, her tone still clipped.

"No problem."

Doris followed Tricia to the door and locked it behind her without even a good night.

Tricia headed down the sidewalk with no thought to the snub—now to face Angelica. Of the two, she ruefully admitted that she'd probably rather spend time with Doris.

She'd parked her own car in the municipal lot earlier in the day. By this time it was mostly empty. Now that school was back in session, the bulk of the summer tourist trade had evaporated. That would change when the autumn leaves began to turn and tour buses and crowds would return for another few weeks of superior sales. Thank goodness for the cruise ships that moored in Portsmouth and Boston harbors, which often brought in more customers. Once winter arrived they, too, would be gone. Still, the business slowdown

would give Tricia time to establish a storefront in cyberspace, something she'd been meaning to do since she'd opened some five months previous.

Stoneham wasn't very large and it only took a minute or two for Tricia to drive to the Brookview Inn, lit up like a Thomas Kinkade painting with warm yellow light spilling from every window. Soft pink roses flanked steps leading to the entrance, the last of the summer's offerings crowding against white-painted wrought-iron railings. Tricia hesitated, taking in the delicate scent. No doubt Angelica would have doused herself in the latest overpriced perfume with a celebrity's name attached to it.

Stop it, she ordered. Yet she'd spent her whole life finding fault with her older sister. Was it natural that even as an adult she hadn't been able to let go of her childhood animosity? If she was honest with herself, she should blame their mother for fostering such an unhealthy atmosphere.

Then again, Mother never took the blame for anything.

Tricia took a breath to control her anxiety. It was really her own reactions to her sister that upset her. Angelica wasn't likely to change anytime soon. It was up to Tricia to ride out the visit and not let it turn her into the jealous child she thought she'd long outgrown.

The Brookview had given Tricia shelter for three weeks during the time when the apartment over the store was being made habitable. She could've opted for one of the efficiency bungalows behind the inn itself, but had been seduced by the sumptuous bedding and other pampering amenities, finding the inn a serene haven during the demolition and chaos of the store's renovation. And she'd tried to replicate some of that ambiance in her own much more humble abode. So far she'd only managed to acquire the four-hundred-thread-count sheets and fluffy down pillows. Tricia missed the cuisine and the friendly staff, but admitted she still preferred the privacy of her own home and the company of her cat and her precious books.

Bess, the plump sixtysomething night clerk, looked up from her keyboard behind the reception desk, a smile lighting her face. "Welcome back, Ms. Miles. And what brings you to the Brookview tonight?"

"My sister, Angelica Prescott, is a guest."

"No doubt at your recommendation," Bess said and beamed.

Tricia smiled, pushing down the guilt.

"I think you'll find her in our dining room. The special tonight is hazelnut-encrusted salmon." Bess closed her eyes in a moment of pure ecstasy. "It *is* to die for."

"Sounds heavenly. But I've already eaten." Her dinner had consisted of a burger on a soggy bun that Ginny snagged at the Bookshelf Diner down the street from the shop. "I'll just pop in and see if Angie's there."

"You go right ahead, dear." Bess gave a little wave and returned her attention to her keyboard.

Tricia crossed the foyer to the opened double doors at the far end of the lobby. The Brookview's elegant dining room, with its crown molding, traditional furnishings, and lamp-lit oil paintings of Revolutionary War heroes, welcomed her. And at the best table, holding court, sat Angelica, leaning forward, manicured index finger wagging to make a point with her guest. She was blond again, cut short and stylish, and what looked like a recent weight loss was evident in her face. She'd always been the family beauty, and so far age had not worked against her. Even with his back turned toward her, Tricia recognized the man who sat opposite her sister: Bob Kelly. Two of the three people on the planet who irritated Tricia the most, and now she had to deal with both of them—together.

The fact that Bob could've passed as her ex's twin—albeit a decade older—may've been responsible for part of Tricia's dislike for him. Did he have to be so drop-dead handsome? Tall, muscular, with a head full of wavy dark hair that had never seen a colorist, and those deep green eyes. Yes, except for the eyes, he could have been Christopher's double.

Dinner had been cleared and only demitasse cups and crumb-littered dessert plates remained on the linen-shrouded table.

Tricia took a breath, plastered on a smile, and charged forward. "Angie!"

Angelica looked up, a look of true pleasure lighting her expression, reinforcing the guilt Tricia felt. "Darling Trish." She rose, arms outstretched.

The women embraced and Tricia quelled the urge to cough. Angelica did indeed smell like she'd been dipped in a vat of perfume. A couple of air kisses later, Tricia pulled back. "You look fabulous. You've lost weight."

"Twenty pounds," Angelica admitted proudly. "I've just returned from this divine spa in Aspen, and—"

Bob Kelly cleared his throat. Tricia hadn't noticed that he'd also stood. She nodded, dropped her voice. "Hello, Bob. I see you've met my sister."

"Yes, and what a delightful surprise."

Tricia gave the empty chairs around the table a cursory glance. "Where's Drew?"

Angelica scowled. "Obviously not here." She abruptly changed the subject, taking her seat once again. "Order some dessert, Trish, and we'll all have a nice conversation."

Bob remained standing. "I'm afraid I have a business meeting this evening."

"So late?" Angelica asked.

"The downside of being a successful entrepreneur, I'm afraid."

Tricia fought the urge to gag. By now Doris would be furious—and that's probably exactly what Bob wanted.

Bob offered Angelica his hand. She took it. "Thank you so much for the dessert. I'd love to take you to dinner some time during your visit."

"And I'd love to accept. Do call me."

"I will. Ladies." And with a nod, Bob excused himself.

"Isn't he just a doll," Angelica whispered once he was out of earshot.

Tricia took Bob's abandoned seat and forced yet another smile. Her cheeks were already beginning to ache. "What brings you all the way to New Hampshire, Ange? This really isn't your style at all."

Angelica sighed. "I can't keep anything from you, can I?"

Tricia's stomach tensed. Bad news? Angie's twenty-pound weight loss . . .

Angelica played with the chunky diamond ring on her engagement finger. Her wedding band was gone. "Drew and I . . . well, our trial separation proved successful. We're finished."

Tricia relaxed. Not a total surprise. Drew was Angelica's fourth husband. He was a quiet, studious type, whereas Angelica was boisterous and liked fun and crowds of people. Sedate New Hampshire was much more Drew's sort of refuge. "I'm so sorry." And she was. She and Drew could talk books for hours, much to Angelica's chagrin.

"No, actually, I've come to help you with your little store," Angelica charged on. "I'm a successful businesswoman in my own right and quite naturally I assumed you'd need my help."

Tricia gritted her teeth and grimaced. Angelica had worked in a boutique in SoHo for all of five minutes some twenty years before. It had closed within weeks of opening. "No, but . . . thank you anyway."

"Nonsense. I'm here and I'm dying to see the little place." Angelica raised a hand in the air and within seconds a waiter appeared. "Please add the dinner to my account."

"With pleasure, ma'am." The black-suited man bowed and made a discreet exit.

Angelica rose. "Come, come," she ordered and, like a well-trained dog, Tricia jumped to her feet to follow.

Already the evening was not going as Tricia had planned.

Minutes later, Tricia steered her Lexus onto Main Street and under the banner strung across the road that proudly proclaimed Stoneham the Safest Town in New Hampshire. She pulled into the empty parking space in front of Haven't Got a Clue, cut the engine, and waited to hear the inevitable insult disguised as a compliment.

"Oh, Tricia, it's lovely," Angelica breathed, and she truly sounded awed.

All the brick-faced buildings along Main Street sported a different pastel hue, except for number 221. The bottom floor's white stone facade resembled a certain Victorian address in London, while Tricia had had the brick of the top two floors sandblasted to reveal its natural state. The door, beveled glass on the top and painted a glossy black on the bottom, looked impressive with glowing period brass lanterns on either side. The gold-leafed address numbers 221 shone brightly on the Palladian transom above. The plate-glass display window to the right did sort of spoil the effect, but the effort Tricia had made to approximate the beloved detective's home hadn't been lost on the majority of her customers.

"Surely the address is wrong," Angelica said. "Shouldn't it be 221B?"

"I didn't know you'd read Dr. Watson's stories."

"Please! Grandmother bored me to tears with them before you were born."

Tricia had never been bored when Grandmother had read her Sir Arthur's stories. As a child, she hadn't always understood them—but she'd loved the sound of all those wonderful words and her grandmother's voice.

"Come on in and I'll give you the fifty-cent tour."

Tricia opened her car door and stepped out onto the pavement. She held up her keys, selecting the proper one as Angelica got out of the car.

"Do you smell something burning?" Angelica asked.

"No." The truth was, after being sealed in the car with Angie's perfume, Tricia wondered if she'd ever be able to smell anything again.

"Something's definitely burning . . . or maybe smoldering," Angelica insisted. Shading her eyes, she peered into the mystery bookshop's large plate-glass window, then turned her head from right to left and sniffed loudly, her nose wrinkling.

Tricia watched as her sister moved a few steps toward the Cookery. "Trish, I think it's coming from the mail slot next door."

Sure enough, a thin veil of smoke drifted from the painted flap in the door.

Tricia jammed her keys back in her purse, scooped up her cell phone, and hurried to Angelica's side. "Dial 911," she ordered, shoving everything into her sister's hands. She grasped the Cookery's door handle, shocked when it yielded to her touch.

The smoke was thick, but with no sign of flames, Tricia took a deep breath and plunged inside. Grabbing the heavy rubber doormat, she searched in the dim light for the source of the smoke and found a section of carpet glowing red.

Swinging the mat, she beat at the embers until they were extinguished, then rushed outside for a much-needed breath of air.

The Stoneham Fire Department was only a block or so away and already Tricia could hear their sirens.

"Think there's anybody in there?" Angelica asked.

"I didn't see anyone, but I'd better look, just in case."

Back she dipped into the stinking building. The smoke seemed to hover, but already it wasn't as thick as it had been only a minute or so before. "Doris?" she called and coughed. "Doris, are you in here?"

Grateful for the security lighting that hadn't winked out, Tricia searched behind the sales counter. No sign of Doris. But a glance to her right showed that the little Lucite case that less than an hour before had housed Doris's treasured cookbook was no longer perched on the top of the shelf. Had someone tried to burn the place down to hide the theft of the book?

"Doris?" she called again, trying to remember if Doris inhabited an apartment over the shop or if she lived elsewhere.

Tricia stumbled over something and fell to her knees. The air was definitely better down here. Righting herself, Tricia pivoted to see what had tripped her. She gasped as she focused on the still form half protruding from behind the horseshoe-shaped kitchen island, noting the carving knife that jutted from its sweatered back.

TWO

Miss Marple wrinkled her little gray nose, sniffing the cuff of Tricia's slacks before giving a hiss of fear and backing away.

"I couldn't agree more," Angelica said and aimed a squirt of perfume in Tricia's general direction.

"Please, don't—I'd rather smell like smoke," Tricia complained, waving her sister off.

Chagrined, Angelica returned the atomizer to her handbag.

Outside the bubble-gum lights of a patrol car flashed upon the walls and shelves of stock, reminding Tricia of a carnival ride—one that, as a child, had made her violently ill.

"Let's go through it once again," Sheriff Wendy Adams said.

Until that night, Tricia hadn't had an occasion to meet any of the county's law enforcement community. The sheriff's uniform shirt buttons strained against her ample cleavage, her large hips accentuated by the cut of her standard-issue slacks. But it was mostly Sheriff Adams's no-nonsense countenance that made

Tricia feel so uncomfortable. It probably worked well in police work. Good thing the woman's livelihood didn't rely on retail, where a no-nonsense attitude was the kiss of death.

Tricia sighed and repeated for the third time the events leading up to her discovery of Doris Gleason's body.

Sheriff Adams scowled. "Wouldn't you know, I'm up for reelection in two months and now I've got a murder on my hands. Did you know we haven't had a killing in Stoneham in at least sixty years?"

"No."

The sheriff continued to scowl. "How much was that missing book worth?"

Tricia sighed. "My expertise is in mystery novels—not cookbooks. But Doris told me a copy recently sold at auction for ten thousand dollars. It's all subjective: an antique, book or otherwise, will only sell for what a buyer is willing to pay."

"Whatever," Sheriff Adams muttered. "Did Mrs.—or was it Miss—or Ms.—Gleason have any enemies?"

Tricia's eyebrows rose, her lips pursing as she gazed at the floor.

"Is that a yes?" the sheriff asked impatiently.

"Doris was negotiating a new lease for her store," Tricia explained. "She felt the new terms were . . . perhaps a little steep."

"And who was she negotiating with?"

"Bob Kelly."

"Oh," Angelica squealed. "I just had dessert with him at the Brookview Inn. Very nice man, and oh, those lovely green eyes of his are heavenly."

The sheriff turned her attention to Angelica. "What time was that, and for how long?"

"Surely you don't suspect the town's leading citizen?" Angelica said.

"How do you know his status?" Tricia asked.

Angelica shrugged. "Bob told me, of course."

It took all Tricia's resolve not to roll her eyes.

As if on cue, a worried Bob stuck his head around Haven't Got a Clue's unlocked door. "Wendy, what's going on?"

"There's been a murder, I'm afraid."

Stunned, Bob's mouth dropped open in horror. "Murder? Good grief! Ten years of Stoneham being named the safest town in all New Hampshire . . . down the drain." A parade of other emotions soon cascaded across his face: irritation and despair taking center stage. "What'll this do to my real estate business?"

"That's nothing compared to what Doris Gleason lost—her life," Tricia said, disgusted.

"Doris?" he repeated in disbelief.

The sheriff rested a hand on Bob's shoulder, turning him around. "Let's take this outside," she said and led him out the door and onto the sidewalk for a private chat.

Angelica inhaled deeply, bending lower until her nose was inches from Tricia's hair. "Oooh, you stink."

Tricia sniffed at her sweater sleeve. "I was only in the Cookery for a minute at most."

"Believe me. You stink."

Tricia's heart sank. "If I smell this bad, think about all those poor books. I wonder if they can be salvaged."

Angelica shook her head. "Only you would think about such a thing."

"Me and every other book lover on the planet."

The sheriff returned with Bob in tow. "Are you okay, Tricia?" Bob asked.

Tricia nodded, suddenly feeling weary.

The sheriff consulted her notebook once again, then spoke to Angelica. "Mrs. Prescott, you said you're staying at the Brookview Inn?"

"Yes, and isn't it just lovely?"

"For how long?"

Angelica gazed down at Tricia. "I arrived just this afternoon and I'll be in town for as long as my sister needs me."

Tricia rocketed from her chair, belatedly wondering if her clothes had already imparted their smoky scent to the upholstery. "I'm fine, Angie. You don't have to hang around on my account."

"Nonsense. What's family for?"

So far emotional support hadn't been a Miles family trait.

"Ma'am," said a solemn voice from the doorway. A firefighter, his scarlet helmet emblazoned with the word chief stenciled in gold and white, motioned to the sheriff. "All the smoke detectors in the Cookery were disabled. Whoever did this didn't want the crime discovered too quickly. However, it appears there was no accelerant used."

Did that mean whoever murdered Doris hadn't planned the killing? Yet they'd been clearheaded enough to try to cover their tracks—however inefficiently.

"Let's keep this discussion private," Sheriff Adams said, and she and the fire chief moved to stand out of earshot on the sidewalk.

Angelica rested a warm hand on Tricia's shoulder. "Trish, dear, you must come and stay with me at the inn. I won't sleep a wink tonight knowing you're here all alone in such a dangerous place. You could've died if that fire hadn't been discovered."

"If *you* hadn't discovered it. Besides, I wouldn't have died. My smoke alarms work—and I have an excellent sprinkler system."

"You discovered the fire?" Bob asked, zeroing in on Angelica.

She waved a hand in dismissal. "It was nothing, really. I only wish we could've saved that poor woman."

"It wasn't *nothing*," Bob said. "The whole block could've gone up, and then the village would've—" He let the sentence fade, his face blanching. No doubt he was already thinking about the upcoming zoning board meeting, and how he could force through new rules for fire safety. The costs would no doubt be passed on to the lease owners. Tricia knew that, like Doris, several other bookstore owners were already living on the precarious edge of profitability with the possibility of folding. And trust Bob Kelly to care more for the buildings than the potential loss of a human life.

Bob's gimmicky idea of basing the village's economy on used bookstores luring in tourists had been inspired by the town of Hay-on-Wye. That little Welsh town had been in the same financial boat as Stoneham: picturesque but fallen on hard times. The original leases had been written in favor of the booksellers, but as Doris had found out, success came with a price. The signs were already evident that Doris's business was on the slide. Fewer food-prep demonstrations and the fact her best-selling product was at the low end of the profit spectrum.

That will not happen to me, Tricia thought. For years she'd daydreamed about every aspect of her store, from the stock to the décor. She'd written and rewritten her business plan, had goals for expanding the business and a timetable to do it. Her divorce a year earlier had presented her with the money and all the time in the world to pursue her lifelong dream of entrepreneurship. After five months in business, Tricia was exactly where she expected to be: paying her rent, her employee, covering her overhead, and making a modest profit. Only time would tell if word of Doris's murder would have an impact on the whole village's revenue stream. The thought depressed her.

As though anticipating her owner's solemn thoughts, Miss Marple appeared at Tricia's side. She gave a muffled "*yow*," and dropped her favorite, rather ratty-looking catnip sock at Tricia's feet.

"Oh, thank you, Miss Marple," she said, patting the cat's furry gray head. "You are a very thoughtful kitty." Miss Marple purred loudly.

"Darling Trish. You must come back with me to the inn. I'm sure they can move some kind of cot into my room. You're much too upset to drive, so give me your keys," Angelica insisted once again.

"That won't be necessary. This is my home and I'm staying put. And I'm not upset," she lied. "As soon as the sheriff is finished, I'll drive you back to the inn."

"Nonsense," Bob interrupted. "I'd be delighted to escort you back to the Brookview, Mrs. Prescott."

Angelica turned slowly to face Bob. "Call me Angelica," she said, her voice softening, her blue eyes lowered coyly.

Bob smiled, practically oozing with gentlemanly charm.

What was this effect Angie had on men? And what was wrong with these two? A woman had been murdered mere feet from where they all stood. Then again, if Bob managed to get Angelica out of Tricia's hair, she might be inclined to ignore some of his other annoying attributes.

Sheriff Adams returned, looking bad-tempered. "I guess that's all for tonight, folks. But I'll be needing official statements from all three of you. I'll send a deputy by sometime tomorrow to take them. In the meantime, please don't leave town without notifying the sheriff's department."

As if, Tricia was tempted to sniff. Then it occurred to her what Sheriff Adams was really saying: that perhaps she didn't believe their accounts as they'd given them.

Miss Marple hadn't appreciated an early wake-up call, but the image of Doris Gleason with a knife in her back kept Tricia from restful sleep; her dreams had been shadowed by dark menacing images she could only half remember. She'd showered, dressed, and fed herself and her cat before trundling down the stairs to her shop. Next on the list: vacuuming, tidying, and all the other chores she hadn't accomplished before leaving the night before. It was while resetting the security system she noticed the cord from the wall-mounted camera dangling loose, with the unmistakable indentations from feline teeth.

"Miss Marple. Didn't I tell you not to mess with that camera?" she admonished.

The cat jumped to the counter and rubbed her head against Tricia's arm.

"Oh no, you don't. I am not your friend right now."

Miss Marple swished her tail and jumped down, sashaying across the carpet without a backward glance.

Before Tricia could call the security company, the phone rang and she let the answering machine kick in. "The Haven't Got a Clue mystery bookstore's hours are ten a.m. to seven p.m. on Mondays, Tuesdays ten to six; Wednesday through Saturday ten to seven, and Sunday noon to three. Please leave a message at the tone."

Beep!

"Bernie Weston, *Nashua Telegraph.* Looking to interview Tricia Miles about last night's Stoneham murder at the Cookery. Please call at—" He left a number.

That was one phone call Tricia was determined not to return. True, talking

to the press would get the shop's name in the newspaper, but a murder—even next door to a mystery bookstore—was negative publicity, and she preferred not to believe that even negative publicity was good publicity.

She wiped the message from the machine and dialed another number.

"We're swamped," said the harried male voice at Ace Security. "I might be able to get someone out to you by the end of the week, but I can't make any promises. If the rest of your system's intact, you shouldn't have too much of a problem."

Let's see: murder, theft, and arson had occurred just feet from Tricia's doorstep. Why wouldn't she feel secure with a third of her system on the blink? As a small-business owner, she'd wanted to patronize other local businesses, but now wondered if she'd regret that decision.

She hung up the phone, put a soothing Enya CD on low, and commandeered her sheepskin duster. Taking care of her beloved books always had a calming effect on her psyche. And she needed that calm, for in the next half hour the answering machine took four more calls from newspapers, radio stations, and/or television stations in Concord, Nashua, and Manchester. Screening calls was the order of the day. Stoneham's small-town gossip mill was bound to be in full force, and the best source of information showed up ten minutes after Haven't Got a Clue opened.

A bleary-eyed Ginny scowled as she snagged a cup of coffee from the store's steaming pot before she'd even hung up her jacket. "Sheriff Adams was waiting for me when I got home last night. Let me tell you, being interrogated by a cop can really put a crimp in your love life. Brian hightailed it out of my place so fast I almost got windburn."

"What does *he* have to hide?" Tricia asked.

Ginny glowered. "I think his car's inspection sticker might be a little overdue."

"A little?"

"Okay, by two months."

"What did the sheriff ask you about?"

Ginny's answer was succinct. "You."

Tricia started. "Me?"

"Apparently, you were the last person to see Daww-ris"—she again dragged the name out—"alive."

"Except for the killer, you mean."

Ginny shrugged, warming her hands on the store's logo-emblazoned cardboard cup. "I suppose."

Tricia hoped her only employee had been a little more aggressive in defending her when speaking with the sheriff.

"I told her I was in Doris's shop for perhaps five minutes, just to return her

glasses. We talked briefly about her expensive little cookbook, then I went to the inn, picked up my sister, and we were back here within thirty—maybe forty minutes."

"I'm sure you have nothing to worry about," Ginny said, gulped her coffee, and got up to cash out the first of the day's customers.

But Tricia did worry about it—to the point of obsession; it only got worse after she'd given her statement to the young deputy who'd stopped by. She rang up sales incorrectly, punching in three cents instead of thirty dollars for a slightly water-stained dust cover on a first edition of Josephine Tey's *The Singing Sands*, and asked a customer to pay three hundred ninety-five dollars for a laminated bookmark. And still the telephone kept ringing.

"You ought to take a break," Ginny advised, after soothing the latest irate customer. "Go for a drive in the country. Take your sister shopping in Manchester."

"Being with Angelica is the last thing I need. No, here is where I belong."

Ginny shrugged. "You're the boss."

A gray-haired woman with big sunglasses presented a book for purchase. Ginny rang up the sale and Tricia picked it up to place in the store's plastic bag. A slip of paper fell out and hit the floor. Tricia bent to pick it up and silently cursed: another nudist tract. She shoved it into her slacks pocket and handed across the book and bag to her customer. "Thank you for shopping at Haven't Got a Clue," she said cheerfully, hoping her irritation hadn't been apparent. The woman smiled and headed for the exit.

"Another one?" Ginny asked.

Tricia nodded, removing the paper from her pocket. Ginny pulled more leaflets from her apron pocket, handing them over. "You were right when you said we'd find more."

Tricia read over the text extolling the benefits of a natural lifestyle free from restrictive clothing: "a healthy lifestyle that encouraged body acceptance and self-confidence." Still, she wondered how many people caught cold or cut their toes while romping around in the altogether.

Tricia balled up the leaflets, tossing them in the trash. "Let's hope this is the end of it."

The bell over the door jangled and a dark-haired, middle-aged man in faded jeans and a Patriots sweatshirt charged in. He was a couple of weeks late on a haircut, and his Nikes had seen much better days, although Tricia supposed he was good-looking, in a rustic sort of way.

"Looking for the owner, Tricia Miles," he said.

Tricia raised a hand. "That would be me."

The man offered his hand. "Russ Smith, editor of the *Stoneham Weekly News*."

The name sounded familiar. "I believe we spoke on the phone just after my

shop opened. You ran a paragraph or two back in the spring, telling the community about the store."

"Oh, yeah." He'd obviously forgotten. "You probably guessed that I'm here about the murder at the Cookery. It's the biggest news to hit Stoneham in—"

"Sixty years, apparently." Tricia's muscles went rigid. She hadn't counted on the local fish wrapper to come calling. The top story in the last issue had been squirrels chewing through the village gazebo's roof. "Mr. Smith, finding Doris was pretty upsetting. I really don't want to talk about it."

He cocked his head. "Why? Did you kill her?"

Tricia gasped and blinked. "Of course not."

"Then why not take the opportunity to tell the whole village so?" He grasped her by the elbow, maneuvered her around the sales counter, and led her to the nook, where three of the four upholstered chairs were empty. He pushed her into a seat and took the adjacent chair. Tricia hadn't noticed that he'd carried a steno notebook in his left hand, which he now opened. He came up with a pen, too.

He looked at Tricia over the rims of his gold-toned glasses. "I've got the facts from Sheriff Adams. You want to give me your take on the murder?"

"I really don't think I should talk to the press. I mean, what if I say something that compromises the sheriff's investigation?"

Mr. Everett, the shop's most regular customer and seated in another of the nook's chairs, peeked over the top of the book he held unnaturally close to his face. At Tricia's pointed stare, his eyes disappeared again.

Smith read through his notes. "You found the body at approximately six forty-eight p.m. Put out the smoldering fire—"

"It was the other way around. I put out the fire first, then found poor Doris."

"Were you two enemies?" he cut in, his eyes narrowed.

Tricia recoiled. "No."

"Talk is the two of you argued last night."

"We did not! She wanted to enlist me in her crusade to renegotiate the booksellers' leases. I told her I couldn't help her. My lease doesn't come due for more than two years."

"Do you think Bob Kelly is responsible for her death? It's known she argued with him, too," he said.

Tricia took a calming breath and straightened in her seat to perch on its edge. "I was not privy to their conversations. I only know she had an appointment to speak with him again last night. Apparently he was delayed." Gosh, she sounded formal. Would that make her sound even more guilty to this Jimmy Olsen wannabe?

"Kelly was delayed by your sister, an—" He consulted his notes. "An Angelica Prestcott. Was their meeting something you engineered? Something to keep Bob Kelly from meeting Ms. Gleason?"

Tricia stood. "I don't appreciate your inference, Mr. Smith, and I wish you'd leave."

Smith's calculating scowl tempted Tricia to slap him; only her clenched fists and sheer willpower kept her from doing it. He took his time closing his notebook, clipping the pen onto its cover. Finally, he stood. "I think you'll wish you were a bit more candid, Ms. Miles."

"Is that a threat, Mr. Smith?"

He shook his head. "I'm just stating facts." With that, he turned and moved toward the door. It slammed shut behind him.

Tricia glanced down at Mr. Everett, whose eyes were once again peering over the top of his book. Seeing her, he quickly ducked down again.

Too upset to interact with customers, Tricia grabbed her duster and headed for the back shelves, hoping to work off her anger.

As she ran the fleece over the topmost shelf, she puzzled over the sudden void she felt from Doris's death. The woman hadn't been known as the friendliest person on the planet. Her quick-to-judge temperament and an acid tongue hadn't served her well in business and from what Tricia could tell her personal life, either.

What was so special about the cookbook that had been stolen? Yes, it was a rare first edition, but Doris's reluctance to discuss where she'd obtained the book now seemed more sinister than circumspect.

Or was it only paranoia that kept Tricia's thoughts on that circuit? Somebody had killed Doris, had stolen a rare book, and had committed arson to try to hide the crimes.

And just who among the denizens of Stoneham was capable of such wanton acts?

There was only one way to find out. Talk to them. And she knew just where and with whom to start.

THREE

Stoneham's Chamber of Commerce resided in the former sales office of a company offering log homes. Tricia had passed it hundreds of times, and though she'd been a member since before the actual day she'd opened her store, she'd never had time to visit the office.

She stood out on the sidewalk admiring the charming little pseudohome

with its stone chimney, folksy rockers on the front porch, and the double dormers poking through the green-painted metal roof. Someone had a green thumb, judging by the welcoming baskets of magenta fuchsias, pink begonias, and colorful pansies that hung suspended along the porch's roofline.

Tricia climbed the steps and entered through the glossy, red-painted door. Like every other business in Stoneham, a little bell tinkled as she entered. Inside, the cabin was just as charming, with its chinked walls and timbered rafters. The outside had hinted of a second floor, but the cathedral ceiling was a good twenty feet above her and sunlight streamed through the dormer windows. A sitting area, furnished in comfortable leather couches and chairs with a rustic flair, gave way to racks of local brochures, file cabinets, and other utilitarian office equipment.

"Howdy!" came a female voice with a thick Texas twang. "How can I help you?"

Tricia stepped up to a counter, where a thin woman with close-cropped, gray-streaked brown hair, with a face wrinkled by years of smiles, and wearing a baggy crimson-and-white Hawaiian shirt awaited. "I was hoping to find Bob Kelly here. His real estate office is closed and I thought—"

"I don't usually see much of Bob during the workday. He tends to catch up on chamber business on evenings and weekends. Today's an exception. He's been doing damage control; interviews with the media and such. We've got ourselves a little PR crisis here in Stoneham after last night's events."

So now Doris's death was an event?

"Is there something I can help you with?" the woman asked again and went back to chomping on her gum cud.

"My name is Tricia Miles, and—"

"I know you! You're the lady runs that mystery store. Let's see, joined in late March this year. Haven't made one of our luncheons at the Brookview Inn, yet, have you? Best grub in town, that's for sure."

"Uh, no," Tricia said, wondering if this woman was for real or putting on an act.

The woman extended a calloused hand. "Hi. Frannie Mae Armstrong, but folks just call me Frannie. Named after my grandma on Daddy's side."

Tricia blinked, but took her hand. "How nice."

Frannie's handshake was as strong as any man's though not crushing. "How's the book business? Doin' real well, are ya? I read romances myself. Love that Nora Roberts—but not those J. D. Robb ones she writes." Frannie leaned closer, lowered her voice confidentially. "They're set in the future, ya know, and that's just plain weird."

"Can't say as I've ever read any of her work."

"You're missing out on some real entertainment. Since that Have a Heart romance bookstore opened, my TV watching has dropped by half."

"You'd seem to be one of the few locals who patronize us."

Frannie nodded sagely. "Oh, there's a few of us out there. Maybe you should try starting a reader group—maybe team up with the library on that. They supply the warm bodies, you supply the books."

"That's a good idea. Thanks."

"But you're right about one thing: there does seem to be an us-verses-them sort of rivalry going on among the merchants. There's also no doubt that bringing in the booksellers has revitalized Stoneham. Some of the old-timers—that's what I call those businessmen who were around before the booksellers came—resent you newcomers. What for?" she asked, her hands flying into the air. "They didn't want to be located on Main Street anyway—it was falling apart. Most of 'em moved to the edge of town to be near the highway. And the bookstores bring in lots of money. Saved 'em all from bankruptcy if you ask me." She shook her head.

"Have you lived in Stoneham long?" Tricia asked, genuinely interested.

"Must be going on twenty years, now." She laughed and the windows rattled. "It's my accent, huh? I *am* a long way from home," she admitted, "but I've come to love the changing seasons. That is until I retire, then I'll be off to Hawaii. They call it paradise, ya know." She straightened, her face losing some of its animation, all business now. "Now just what was it you wanted to ask of old Bob?"

Tricia had almost forgotten why she'd stopped in. "I had some questions concerning Doris Gleason's murder."

Frannie shook her head, her left hand rising to clasp the side of her face. "Lord, isn't that just awful. And I heard you found her, you poor little thing."

"Yes, I did. Did you know Doris?"

"No. She wasn't a chamber member. I called her several times to ask if she wanted to join, but she was just the most ornery woman I ever did speak to. Told me to stop bothering her or she'd report me to the state's attorney general as a telemarketer."

"But being a chamber member is great, even if you only use it to promote your store."

"I know, and I tried to tell her that, but she hung up on me. I don't see how she stayed in business as long as she did. And now she's dead. Well, I guess she annoyed someone one time too many, don'tcha think?"

Tricia shrugged, afraid to agree—especially as it appeared she was the prime suspect. "Doris told me she had an appointment to meet with Bob last night, but apparently he didn't make it over to the Cookery to see her before she was killed."

Frannie crossed her thin arms across her equally thin chest. "Well, that's

Bob for you. He's always overbooking himself. Thinks he's Superman." Frannie laughed again, and Tricia feared for the window's mullions. "I know he had a dinner meeting at the Brookview Inn. Must've fallen behind schedule."

"I saw him there last night. When he left, he said he was late for an appointment. I assumed he meant with Doris, but he didn't show up for at least another hour after he left the inn."

"Do tell," Frannie said and cocked her head. She paused in her gum chewing, looking thoughtful. "I wonder . . ." But she didn't articulate exactly what it was she pondered. Long seconds went by before she shook herself and seemed to remember Tricia stood before her. "Do you want to leave Bob a message?"

Tricia shook her head. "I'll call him later."

"You want his cell number? He doesn't mind taking calls when it comes to protecting the good name of Stoneham. Business is business, ya know."

"I don't want to bother him." That wasn't exactly true . . .

"Well, I'll tell him you stopped by. If there's anything the chamber can do for you, you just give us a holler, ya hear?"

Discussion over.

Tricia managed a wan smile. "Thank you, Frannie, you've been most helpful." Not.

She headed for the door with Frannie calling a cheerful good-bye behind her. Once outside, Tricia stood on the porch for a few moments, wondering what it was concerning Bob that Frannie hadn't wanted to talk about.

Since she'd gone inside, a crew had arrived to take down the Safest Town banner from the north end of the street. Had they already removed the one from the south end?

A sheriff's cruiser rolled slowly past, its driver taking in both sides of the street. Was it just the cool breeze that made the hairs on the back of Tricia's neck prickle or was it the idea the deputy might be watching her?

Two hours later, Tricia was positive she did not suffer from paranoia. Even Ginny remarked about the sheriff's cruiser making a regular circuit up and down Main Street, and that too often its occupant's attention seemed to be focused on Haven't Got a Clue.

When she ducked out to take the previous day's receipts to the bank, Tricia noticed a patrol car parked in the municipal lot. Inside it, a deputy's gaze was trained on Stoneham's main drag. It made Tricia want to look over her shoulder, keeping an eye out for the real murderer. Then again, Doris's killer could be just about anybody. Since there was no sign of forced entry and the door had been unlocked, it was likely Doris had opened it to let in her killer. Meaning,

she'd probably known the person—and Tricia wasn't about to let anyone think that person might be her.

What would Miss Marple, Hercule Poirot, or any other self-respecting protagonist in a Christie novel do in this situation? Ask questions.

Tricia took a detour on the way back to her shop, stopping at the Happy Domestic, a boutique specializing in new and gently used products, consisting of how-to books, gifts, and home décor. She'd met the owner, Deborah Black, at an auction several months before where they'd shared coffee and local gossip, and they had continued to look out for each other at every other sale. Deborah loaded up on glassware and bric-a-brac while Tricia had scoured box lots for interesting titles.

Thirtysomething Deborah, her swollen belly straining against a maternity smock, wore a plastic smile that never waned until the customer she'd waited on had exited her store. "Oh God," she exhaled and collapsed against her sales counter. "Sometimes I think I'll kill myself if I have to coo over another satin pillow with the words 'Do Not Disturb' cross-stitched on it."

Tricia laughed. "Only a few days more and you'll have a vacation from customers. You're due next week, aren't you?"

"And, boy, am I ready. Jim Roth over at History Repeats Itself has a parlay going. He says I won't make it until my due date on Monday." She looked down at herself and laughed. "And he may be right."

"Hey, nobody told me about the parlay."

"I think there's a few squares left, if you want to get in."

"I may just visit him when I leave here."

Deborah studied Tricia's face. "Betting on my baby's birth is not why you came to visit today—not during work hours. You're here about Doris, right?"

"That obvious, huh?"

"Well, her murder *is* the talk about town." She bent down to pick up a cardboard carton.

"Let me get that," Tricia said and lifted the box onto the counter. "So, tell me what you know about Doris," Tricia prompted.

Deborah untucked one of the box's flaps and withdrew a paper-wrapped package, talking as she worked. "She was a nasty piece of work. The rest of us avoided her at all costs. Never a positive word. Never contributed to the United Way. Never wanted to do anything positive for the village or the community at large. Her view in life seemed to be 'What have you done for me lately?'"

"So the rest of the shop owners won't be mourning her."

Deborah shook her head, tossing her long brown hair back across her shoulders. "You know what she was like."

How pathetic, Tricia thought, not to be mourned at all. Surely Doris had had some redeeming qualities. She voiced that question.

Deborah shook her head, unwrapping the first of the bundles, a delicate pink, etched water goblet. "Not that I noticed. You might want to talk to some of the other booksellers. Most have been around here longer than me. But if you expect heartfelt tributes, you're wasting your time." She held up one of the glasses to the light. "Aren't these just the prettiest crystal?"

Tricia nodded and counted the remaining bundles. "Only seven."

"If nothing else, I can sell them as a set of six. I'll set up a whole new display around them. Lots of pink, girly items. It'll be gorgeous."

"Did you pick these up at the last auction?"

She shook her head. "No. I got them from Winnie Wentworth."

"Who?"

Deborah laughed. "The village eccentric. A combination bag lady/antiques picker. I'm surprised you haven't met her. She sells to all the shop owners."

Tricia inspected one of the goblets. "Is the quality of her merchandise always this good?"

"Gosh, no. She sells mostly junk—but occasionally she comes up with a few prizes. I learned to inspect most items pretty thoroughly for chips, nicks, and repairs before I part with any money."

Tricia set the glass back down on the counter. "I'm sure you've heard the gossip going around town. Doris had an appointment with Bob Kelly, but no one wants to look at him as a possible suspect. You've been here longer than me—what do you know about him?"

Deborah sobered. "Definitely a man who focuses on results. It's no wonder he's been single all these years. He lives and breathes the real estate business. But he has been good for the village."

Another testimonial for Saint Bob.

"Doris complained about her new lease," Deborah continued, "and it's made me look at my bottom line as well. I'm already trying to budget for a substantial increase when it comes time for me to renew."

"Can you afford it?"

"It'll be a stretch, but the village—and Bob in particular—gambled on me and all the other booksellers when we first came aboard. Most of us have done okay. And it may be that Bob was tired of dealing with Doris's complaints. He may have simply demanded a higher price to get rid of her. I don't know, and anyway it's moot. Doris is history. Now he can rent the place to anyone he pleases."

Tricia's thoughts exactly.

The door opened and a couple of women entered the store. "Can I help you?" Deborah asked cheerfully, abandoning the glassware.

"Thanks for the chat." Tricia clasped her leather briefcase and Deborah gave her a quick wave as she headed for the door.

Tricia's next stop was the Coffee Bean, a heavenly shop that sold exotic blends and decadent chocolates, where she bought a five-pound bag of fresh-ground Colombian coffee. Too many customers clogged the shop for her to engage the owner in idle gossip, and she'd intended to head straight back for her own store, but a new enterprise on the block caught her attention. She made one more diversion.

A red-white-and-blue poster, with patriotic stars across the top, heralded Mike Harris's selectman campaign office. Tucked between two shops—Stoneham's Stoneware and History Repeats Itself—it had to be the most narrow storefront on Main Street. No wonder it had remained empty since Tricia's arrival. It really was too small for a retail establishment.

Tricia opened the door and entered the crowded room. Boxes and cartons stacked along the north wall awaited unpacking. Two desks and assorted chairs seemed to be in place, but none of the usual office accouterments yet occupied them. A fake ficus stood in the corner, looking decidedly forlorn.

Footsteps sounded from a back room.

"Hello!" Tricia called.

Mike Harris stepped into the main room. Dressed in jeans and sneakers, shirtsleeves rolled up to his elbows, he looked ready to tackle the towering boxes.

"Looks like we're neighbors," Tricia said.

"Hey, thanks for stopping by."

Tricia glanced around at the freshly painted walls and the stacks of printed literature in one of the only opened boxes. "No offense, but I wouldn't have thought the race for selectman warranted a campaign office."

"Ordinarily I'd agree with you. The lease on my current office is about to run out and Bob Kelly offered me a great deal. Besides, I intended to open shop here in the village after the election anyway."

Tricia glanced around. "By the look of things, you haven't been here long."

Mike nodded. "I moved in last evening."

"Before all the chaos?"

He frowned. "I heard what happened to Ms. Gleason, but I didn't see anything." He shook his head. "Her death could become a campaign issue."

Tricia frowned. "How?"

"Not all our citizens are happy with the way development has been handled in Stoneham. They think the village is growing too fast and want a moratorium on new businesses until an impact study can be done." That echoed what Frannie had said about the unofficial divide between the old-timers and newcomers.

"Sounds like a waste of taxpayer funds. From what I understand, the influx

of money has paid for a new a library and sewer systems—things the village sorely needed. What's so bad about that?"

Mike crossed his arms over his chest, sobering. "When the tax base expands, so does the cost of maintaining it. That new sewer system is just one example."

He had a point, but it didn't make sense. The newcomers had taken over the crumbling Main Street while the old-timers had fled the village for the outskirts of town, presumably building new structures along the way. No wonder there was animosity between the two camps.

Still, how sad was it that Doris had been reduced to a campaign issue.

"I hope you've registered to vote."

"Yes, as a matter of fact I have."

He grabbed a brochure from the stack. "That's what we need in this town. Voters who care about Stoneham's future."

She took the paper from him; he must've forgotten he'd given her one the day before. "I'll read through it carefully. Why don't you stop by my shop for a welcome-to-the-neighborhood coffee later?"

"Sounds great. Thanks."

"See you then," she said and backed toward the door.

Mike waved. "Stop in anytime."

The line at the register was three deep when Tricia arrived back at Haven't Got a Clue. Wispy hairs had escaped the pewter clip at the base of a harassed Ginny's ponytail. "Where have you been?" she scolded Tricia under her breath. "A bus came through and these people have to be back on it in ten minutes."

"Sorry. I had no idea. I had to make a few stops after the bank." While Ginny rang up two pristine early Dick Francis first editions and an Agatha Christie omnibus, Tricia bagged the order, first checking the books for nudist leaflets before tossing in the current week's stuffers and a copy of the bookstore's newsletter. Within a couple of minutes everyone had been served and the door shut on the last customer's back.

Ginny sagged with relief and headed straight for the coffee station and a caffeine fix. She collapsed onto one of the store's comfy chairs and, still feeling guilty for leaving her alone during a rush, Tricia didn't have the heart to remind her it was against store rules for the help to sit in the customers' reading nook.

Ginny took a gulp from her steaming cup and stretched her legs out before her. "Winnie Wentworth stopped by to see you."

"Finally," Tricia said, circling around to face her employee.

"You want to meet her?" Ginny asked, puzzled.

"Deborah Black told me about her just a while ago. I wondered why she hadn't been offering me merchandise."

"Her stock isn't as good as most of our regulars. She only seems to go to tag

sales to find books and other stuff to resell to the shop owners. Her car's a rolling junk mobile. She's been coming around the last couple of weeks. I've tried to discourage her, but today she was adamant; she wants to deal only with the owner—you—and said she'd be back."

"What's she trying to sell us?"

"Mostly crappy old paperbacks—things you wouldn't even put on the bargain shelf. There were too many customers in the store, and I just didn't want to deal with her."

The shop telephone rang and Tricia grabbed it. "Haven't Got a Clue, Tricia speaking."

"Trish, dear, where have you been all morning? That little helper of yours kept saying you were out of the store."

Tricia grimaced, her already haggard spirits sinking even lower. "Sorry, Ange, I was running errands."

"You sound tired. Is everything okay?"

"I got back in time for a rush of customers."

"Good, then you're flush. Let's go shopping. I hear there's an outlet mall not too far from this sleepy little village of yours."

"I can't leave the shop."

"Every time I've called, you've been away from the store. I've been running all over town myself; I'm surprised I didn't run into you." Her sarcasm came through the phone lines loud and clear.

Tricia ignored it. "Yes, well, Ginny was inundated with customers because I have been out most of the day."

"If you can't leave now, can you at least get off early?" Angelica pressed.

"No. Ange, this is *my* store. It's up to me to—"

Angelica cut her off with a loud sigh. "Have you never heard the word *delegation*?"

"Yes, and I'm also familiar with the words *responsibility* and *ownership*. Pride of ownership," she amended.

"No shopping today?" Angelica whined.

"Sorry."

"How about dinner tonight?"

Tricia's turn for the heavy sigh. "At the inn?"

"Goodness no. I'm going to cook for you. I'll come by at seven with everything I need. Have you got a bottle of red in the fridge?"

"Yes."

"Good. I've got loads to tell you. See you then."

The phone clicked in Tricia's ear. She hung up.

First Angelica showed up for an extended visit. Now she wanted to cook

for her little sister. Something about this whole visit didn't feel right. Angelica was a confirmed chatterbox, yet she'd barely spoken of—nor seemed unduly upset about—her impending divorce, merely saying she and Drew would remain good friends. Still, it was unlike Angie to be so *nice* to Tricia. Something was definitely up, and Tricia was afraid to find out just what Angelica might be plotting.

WINNIE WENTWORTH HAD her own car, so she didn't actually qualify as a "bag lady." Then again, from the looks of the contents of the backseat of her bashed and battered 1993 Cadillac Seville, maybe she did live in her car.

Winnie raked a grubby hand through the wiry mass of gray hair on top of her head. Her threadbare clothes were gray, too, either from repeated washings or from not being washed at all. She watched, eagle-eyed, as Tricia sorted through the offerings in her trunk. Book club editions, creased and well-thumbed paperbacks, all good—mostly contemporary—authors, but not the kind of stock Tricia wanted to carry at Haven't Got a Clue.

Desperate to find something of worth, Tricia pawed through the books a second time. "I understand you sell to all the local bookshop owners. Did you ever sell to Doris Gleason?"

Winnie pulled back a soiled scrap of old blanket from around another stack of books. Six copies of different Betty Crocker cookbooks peeked out. "She was my best customer. Now what am I going to do with all these stupid books? Nobody else in this town will touch 'em." Eyes narrowed, she scrutinized Tricia's face. "And you don't want any of my books, either, do you?"

Tricia hesitated for a moment. "Did you see the Amelia Simmons cookbook Doris had in her special little case?"

"See it? I sold it to her. She gave me five bucks for it."

"Did you know it was worth much more?"

"Everything I sell is usually worth more than what I can get for it. But I don't have the overhead you people do." She nodded at Tricia. "I don't wear no froufrou clothes. I don't got no fancy house. Maybe she coulda given me more, but then I was only gonna ask a couple a bucks for it anyway. Most people didn't like Doris, but she was always fair to me."

Perhaps Doris would be mourned after all.

"Do you remember where you bought the book?"

Winnie shook her head. "I don't remember where I get stuff, let alone who I get it from. I buy from tag sales, estate sales, and auctions." She leaned forward, squinting at Tricia, who got a whiff of the woman's unwashed body. "But mark my words—whoever I got it from musta seen it in her shop. Outside of the fancy shops, ain't many books like that in and around Stoneham."

Did Winnie realize the implications of what she'd just said? "Doris was murdered by someone who wanted that book. I think you should be careful. That person may think you can implicate him or her in Doris's death."

Winnie waved a hand in annoyance. "Nah. Everybody around here knows I got a mind like a sieve. I ain't worried. Now are you gonna take any of these books or not?"

Tricia selected three and paid Winnie five dollars in cash.

"Don'tcha wanna see what else I got?" Winnie folded back another end of the blanket. A small white box contained a tangle of costume jewelry: bright rhinestones of every color of the rainbow adorned brooches, clip and screw-back earrings, and necklaces. Other metals glinted dully under the trunk's wan lightbulb. Tricia picked through the offerings. She loved the colorful brooches in the shapes of flowers, butterflies, and snowflakes, but they were out of date, not something she could really wear herself. But one little gold pin drew her attention.

"That there's a scatter pin, and an oldie," Winnie said with pride.

Tricia examined it closely. About an inch long and maybe three-quarters of an inch wide, it was made of gold—solid gold—with an old-fashioned clasp. Its face was etched with delightful leaves and curlicues. A faded memory stirred in Tricia's mind. "My grandmother had a pin like this."

"It'd look real nice on a jacket or a hat," Winnie said, smelling a sale.

Tricia held the little pin in her hand, rubbing her thumb in circles against its surface. Grandmother Miles had worn her scatter pin on the collar of a snowy white blouse. As a little girl Tricia had sat on her grandmother's lap, playing with the pin while Grandmother would read to her. Whatever happened to that plain little adornment?

"You can have it for five bucks," Winnie offered.

Tricia's gaze rose from the pin to the old woman before her. Winnie's wispy hair was rustled by the breeze, her eyes red-rimmed but bright at the prospect of another sale.

Tricia gave her ten.

Back inside the shop, Tricia tossed the paperbacks into the trash barrel and headed for the sales counter and a group of waiting customers. She opened the cash drawer and deposited the scatter pin in the left-hand, empty change hole before ringing up the next sale.

Winnie was foolish if she thought her poor memory would keep her safe from whoever had killed Doris Gleason. It might be something Tricia should report to Sheriff Adams.

And she did.

But her warning came too late to save Winnie.

FOUR

SHERIFF ADAMS SQUINTED down at Tricia, her piercing gaze sharper than a stiletto. "Two people have died in the last twenty-four hours after speaking with you, Ms. Miles. Why do you think that is?"

Tricia exhaled a slow breath through her nose, surprised steam wasn't escaping from her ears. "I talked to a Deputy Morrison in your office only minutes after speaking to Winnie, warning that she could be in danger from the same person who killed Doris Gleason."

The sheriff consulted her notebook. "That was at eleven-oh-three this morning. And have you left the premises since that time?"

"No, she hasn't," Ginny answered curtly.

A flush of gratitude warmed Tricia. Ginny just earned herself a twenty-five-cent-an-hour raise.

Sheriff Adams frowned. "Odd all the same."

"How did Winnie die?" Tricia asked.

"Car accident. She hit a bridge abutment and wasn't wearing a seat belt. No skid marks. I'm having the car's brakes checked."

"You think they were tampered with?"

"It's possible."

"Well, Tricia certainly didn't cut the lines," Ginny said hotly. "Look, there's not even a pill on her sweater, let alone a speck of dirt or grease."

Tricia fought the urge to show Sheriff Adams her grease-free fingernails.

This is ridiculous, she thought. *I am not responsible for anyone's death.* Yet the heat of Sheriff Adams's scrutiny had caused sweat to form at the back of her neck.

"Will there be an autopsy?" Tricia asked.

"To rule out drug and alcohol use. It's also possible she had a heart attack—or simply blacked out while behind the wheel. Who knows if she even ate regularly?"

"Then why come here and practically accuse Tricia of murder?" Ginny demanded.

Tricia laid a hand on her assistant's arm. "Now, Ginny, I'm sure Sheriff Adams is only doing her job." *Which should include clearing me!* "Are there any leads in Doris's murder?"

"Not so far." Sheriff Adams slapped her notebook closed. "I'll be in touch."

Tricia and Ginny, along with the six customers who'd been eavesdropping on the conversation, watched as the sheriff got into her double-parked cruiser and took off.

"The music has stopped," Tricia told Ginny, trying not to focus on all those pairs of eyes. "Let's put on something cheerful. Maybe Celtic?"

"You got it." Ginny crossed the room for the CD player and the customers went back to perusing the shelves.

Miss Marple jumped up on the sales counter, rubbed her little warm face against Tricia's hand. "Good girl," she murmured, and yet even the comfort of petting her cat couldn't ease the knot of apprehension that had settled in Tricia's stomach. Two deaths less than twenty-four hours apart and both connected to that antique cookbook. Had the sheriff started looking for it on online auction sites or had she or one of her deputies called Sotheby's? Would the killer be dumb enough to try to sell it or would he or she now dump the book to avoid drawing attention to themselves? Perhaps a third party would be enlisted to sell it in a year or two.

Tricia's gaze was drawn to the clock on the wall. Twenty minutes until closing, and then Angie would show up to cook her dinner—and no doubt spoil what was left of her day.

With one last scratch behind the ears, Tricia left Miss Marple to begin her end-of-day tasks.

Main Street was bathed in shadows as the last of the customers departed, with Mr. Everett bringing up the rear. "Good. All gone," Ginny said, turning the sign to closed and throwing the dead bolt. She diverted on her way to the register to close the blinds over the shop's window. "Another good day."

"That depends on your point of view," Tricia said, thinking about Winnie, although she knew Ginny meant the cash drawer stuffed with bills, checks, and credit card receipts.

Ginny stopped before the counter and fished in her apron pocket.

"Don't tell me—" Tricia said, dreading what she knew she was about to see.

"Yep. I found a lot more. And I've got a theory," she said, slapping ten or more of the nudist leaflets on the sales counter. "Somebody's been hiding these things in a lot of books. Pretty much everybody who comes in here is a stranger, except for—"

"Mr. Everett?" Tricia said, aghast. She shook her head. "No, I won't believe that sweet old man—"

"Runs around in the buff?" Ginny finished. She thought about it and shuddered. "Have you got any ideas?"

"No," Tricia admitted. "I wonder if we're the only business being targeted."

"We'll have to make some calls tomorrow to find out. If we have time."

Ginny hit the release button on the cash drawer, which popped open. "Look at all that wonderful money!" She grinned.

Tricia took out the day's receipts, counted them, and placed them in the little blue zippered bank pouch. By then Ginny had retrieved her jacket, said a cheery good-bye, and departed. Tricia locked the money in the safe; that left only the nudist leaflets on the counter.

She tried to imagine prim and proper Mr. Everett in his birthday suit and, thankfully, failed.

She trashed the leaflets.

The clock ticked. Miss Marple had parked herself at the door leading to the back stairs and the loft apartment and cried, impatient for her dinner. "I'm hungry, too, but we have to wait for Angie."

Miss Marple turned her back on Tricia, licked the pads on one of her white boots.

The streetlamps glowed and most of the parked cars had disappeared when the sound of an engine drew Tricia to draw back the shade on the front window to see Angie's rental car pull up in front of the store. She got out, waved a hello, and opened the car's rear door, crouching down for something. Tricia headed for the shop's door to intercept.

"Here, take this," Angelica said, handing Tricia a large, heavy Crock-Pot along with funky chili pepper potholders. Tricia set it on the sales counter, heading back to the door to hold it open for Angelica, who juggled her large purse and a big brown grocery bag, with a crusty loaf of Italian bread poking over its rim.

"How much food did you bring?"

"You can freeze the leftovers. Besides, you're much too thin. I'll bet you haven't had a decent meal in months. Now lead me to the kitchen, and then you can tell me how it is you became Stoneham's jinx of death."

MISS MARPLE SAT before her now-empty food bowl, daintily washing her face. After a brief tour of the loft apartment, with its soaring ceiling and contemporary décor, which Angelica had declared gorgeous, she'd commandeered the kitchen, demanding various utensils that had gathered dust from months of disuse. The pasta water was already bubbling on the stove when Tricia located her corkscrew and opened the wine. She poured, handing a glass to Angelica.

"Just who in town thinks I'm a jinx, and how are you privy to that kind of gossip? You've only been in town one day."

Angelica shrugged theatrically. "It's my face. People feel they can unburden themselves to me."

Tricia frowned. She'd never felt so inclined.

"You know, I never saw the appeal of small-town life," Angelica began and took a sip of her wine. "But everyone's just so friendly and they *love* to talk."

"About me, apparently." Tricia said, growing impatient.

Angelica waved a hand in dismissal, put down her glass, and stirred the sauce once more. "It's just an odd coincidence. I'm sure the sheriff's department will take care of everything within a few days and someone else will be the object of everyone's curiosity." She tasted the sauce. "Mmm. Maybe it could use a little more oregano." She started opening cupboards.

"The one by the sink," Tricia said. "And just what is it everyone's saying?"

Angelica squinted at the row of jars. "I told you. That you're a jinx. Don't be surprised if the locals cross the street as you approach. Set the table, will you? The pasta is almost al dente."

Tricia dutifully gathered place mats, plates, and cutlery. "Who did you meet? How did you meet them?"

Angelica sprinkled on the herb and stirred it in. "I took a walk around your new little hometown. It's very cute. I can see why you love it here. Let's see, I spoke to most of the other booksellers, or at least their sales staff. Do you realize there isn't one shoe store in this entire town?" She slapped her forehead. "Like I need to tell you. Look at your feet."

Tricia glanced down at her thick-soled loafers. "What's wrong with my shoes?"

"Honey, between them and those sweater sets, you are in dire need of a fashion intervention. I have not arrived a minute too soon."

"I have to stand for ten hours a day. I need comfortable shoes."

"If you say so. I also noticed that besides the Brookville Inn, there isn't one decent restaurant in Stoneham."

"We've got the Bookshelf Diner."

"As I said, there isn't one decent restaurant," Angelica deadpanned. "Where do regular people go for food that isn't dripping in grease?"

"I eat in a lot."

"Good thing, too. It's a lot healthier." She stirred the pasta. "Now, do you want to hear the results of Doris Gleason's autopsy, or are you squeamish?"

"Give me a break, Ange. I've been reading mysteries and thrillers since I was in grade school."

Angelica snagged her glass and drank. "As expected, the knife wound was fatal—sliced up something terribly vital. She died almost instantaneously, that's why there wasn't much blood."

Hardly a gory account. "Tell me something I didn't know."

Angelica sobered. "The poor woman had pancreatic cancer, which she

either didn't know about or had chosen not to have treated. Without immediate treatment, it's likely she would've died within months."

Doris couldn't have known, otherwise she wouldn't have been worried about renegotiating her lease. "That poor soul."

Angelica frowned. "I suppose that depends on your point of view. A quick death with little fear or pain, or lingering in agony: I'll take the former any day."

Tricia reached for linen napkins from a drawer. "How did you find out about Doris's autopsy?"

Angelica went back to work on the salad as she spoke. "Didn't I tell you? Bess, the Brookview Inn's receptionist, has a cousin who works for the county health department, who has a direct pipeline to the medical examiner's office. Isn't it amazing how already I've met the most eclectic assortment of people here in Stoneham? Not many of them seem to know you."

"That's because nearly all my customers are from out of town."

"And I'm sure the fact that—except for today, apparently—you rarely leave the store also has a lot to do with it." She paused in slicing a tomato and looked over at her sister. "I'm worried about you, Trish. You need to have a life outside your bookstore."

"I'm doing just fine."

"Have you made any friends?" Angelica asked, abandoning her knife to add spices to a little bowl of olive oil.

"Of course I have," she said, thinking of her conversation earlier in the day with Deborah.

"All booksellers, no doubt. They probably work themselves to death, too, with no real social outlets. Then again, you were right; aside from reading, there isn't much else to do in this burg."

"It's the main draw. How I and all the other booksellers make our living. And in a world with so many other distractions, it's getting harder and harder to find new readers."

Angelica shook her head sadly. "How typical you'd choose a dying trade."

Tricia ignored the jab. "Have you spoken to any of the locals about Bob Kelly?"

"Of course. He's a fascinating man and I want to know all about him. Although I've noticed people either seem to love him or hate him."

"And you're choosing to love him?" Tricia asked.

"Don't be silly. I only met the man last night. But it seems something's going on in town."

"Oh?" Tricia thought back to Frannie, who hadn't wanted to let on what she thought about Bob's meeting the night before.

"There's talk of a big box store wanting to open up right on the edge of town."

"And just who's saying this?"

"People." She didn't elaborate. "It's a hot topic, and I wouldn't want to get in between someone who's for and another who's against the idea. You could lose your life. Some of the locals don't like all these tourists in town and don't want to encourage any more change. If a big store came in, they might have to actually add a traffic light on Main Street." She rolled her eyes.

"Is Bob negotiating for the village?"

Angelica checked the wine level in her glass, then topped it up. "He's apparently exploring the idea, although I don't know if he's doing it for himself or the Board of Selectmen."

"Who told you all this?"

Angelica's smile was sly. "I told you, I'm sworn to secrecy."

Tricia frowned, growing grumpier by the moment. "That pasta will be gummy if you don't serve it soon."

"Oh, right." Angelica switched off the burner and drained the penne. She placed the salad bowl, sliced bread, and dipping sauce on the table and within another minute had heaped their plates with pasta, ladling the sauce on thick. Tricia had to admit it smelled divine. Angelica took her seat across from Tricia, sighed, and smiled. "Isn't it great to be back in each other's lives again?"

Tricia's fork stopped inches from her mouth, cold dread encircling her heart. "How long were you planning on visiting?"

"Oh, didn't I tell you? I've decided to move to New Hampshire."

FIVE

TRICIA NEARLY CHOKED on her wine. "You what?"

Angelica picked up her napkin, smoothed out the folds, and placed it on her lap. "I don't like the idea of you living up here all on your own. Murders happening right next to your place of business." She shook her head. "Mother and Daddy would be heartsick if they thought I'd abandon you in such a violent community. I feel it's my duty to stay here with you at least throughout the crisis."

Tricia sat back in her chair. "There is no crisis. This is the first murder in Stoneham in over sixty years. It's not likely to happen again."

"What about that poor woman who crashed her car?"

"You heard about that, too?"

"I told you, people here like to talk."

"Well, there's no proof she was murdered. I'll bet she didn't maintain that old rust bucket she drove."

Angelica picked up her fork, speared a chunk of tomato. "Surely that's what yearly car inspections prevent."

"Let's get back on topic, which is you moving to Stoneham. There's nothing for you to do here. There's no shopping, no art galleries, no museums, no gourmet restaurants—and as you pointed out, no shoe stores."

Angelica toyed with a piece of pasta. "Perhaps it's my destiny to bring culture and a sense of style to this little backwater."

"Stoneham is my home. Don't call it a backwater. It has history and charm and it doesn't need outsiders coming in with an agenda to change it."

"Au contraire. You yourself are an outsider. Bob Kelly told me the majority of booksellers were all recruited from out of state to come here. And you just said yourself that most of your customers are out of towners."

"Yes, but—"

"Most of the villagers don't mind you little guys opening shop, but they don't want malls and big box stores moving in and changing the area's character, not to mention all the people from Boston crossing the state line just because it's cheaper to live here."

"Tell me something I don't know."

"Change happens, Tricia," she said, pointedly. "Whether some people want it or not."

Tricia's temper flared. "You do not need to live here in Stoneham."

Angelica swirled the wine in her glass. "And I may not stay long. Just long enough to see you through this ordeal." And then she did something that totally startled Tricia; she laid one of her hands on Tricia's. "I may not have been the best big sister in the past, but I intend to make up for that now."

Flabbergasted, Tricia could only sit there with her mouth open. Then she shut it. Angelica had never before displayed even a hint of altruism. Something else was behind her visit, and her newfound sisterly love.

How long would it be before she revealed her true intent?

BEING LABELED THE village jinx didn't seem to have an impact on customers at Haven't Got a Clue. A busload of bibliomaniacs on a day trip from Boston had unloaded an hour earlier, and business had been brisk. It was easy to tell the townsfolk from the transients. The villagers paused at the shop's windows, faces peering in to see the jinx on display like at a zoo, judgment in their eyes. Tricia braved a smile for each of them, but the faces turned away.

Tricia rang up a three-hundred-dollar sale for a British first edition of

Agatha Christie's *Why Didn't They Ask Evans?* and carefully wrapped the book in acid-free tissue before placing it in one of the store's elegant, custom-printed, foil-stamped shopping bags. No plastic for an order of this magnitude.

"Please sign our guest book," she suggested as she handed over the purchase to a dapper old gent.

"I will, thank you."

The phone rang and Ginny stepped up to the counter, taking the next customer. Tricia answered on the second ring. "Haven't Got a Clue, this is Tricia speaking, how can I help you?"

"Hi, Tricia, it's Mike Harris." Aha—one friendly voice remained among the locals. "Scuttlebutt about town is that you've developed into the village jinx. How's it feel to be raked over the coals?" Then again . . .

Tricia sidled over to the front window, looked across the street to Mike's campaign office. "I'm feeling the heat but so far haven't been burned."

"How'd you like to escape the pressure cooker for an hour or two? I know a little bistro up on the highway that serves a mean lobster bisque, and their sourdough bread is the stuff of legends."

"Right now that sounds heavenly."

"Fine. I'll pick you up at eleven thirty."

"I'll be here." Tricia hung up the phone and turned to find Ginny at her elbow.

"A date?"

"It's not a date."

"That'll be thirty-seven fifty," Ginny told the elderly male customer. "Then what do you call lunch with a handsome man?"

"An escape. Can I help you find something?" Tricia asked a matronly woman in a denim jumper.

Six sales and fourteen more nudist tracts later, Tricia glanced at the shop's clock. The Care Free tour bus had picked up its passengers and there was sure to be a lull in foot traffic, assuring Tricia she needn't feel guilty for leaving Ginny alone in the shop.

At precisely eleven thirty a sleek black Jaguar pulled up in front of Haven't Got a Clue, its powerful engine revving. Ginny gawked and inhaled deeply. "Ooh! I smell money."

"Behave," Tricia scolded and grabbed her purse. "I'll try to be back within—"

"Take your time. I'll be fine here," Ginny said. "But you'll have to report on everything the two of you talk about."

"No promises," Tricia said, suppressing a smile as she headed for the door. Then on impulse, she stopped, went back to the counter, and fished one of the nudist leaflets from the trash, stuffing it in her handbag. "See you later," she told Ginny as the door closed behind her.

In celebration of the beautiful early autumn day, the Jag's windows were wide open, and Tricia bent down to see Mike's smiling face. "Hop in."

Tricia opened the door and slid onto the cool, black leather seat. "What a beautiful car. The insurance business must be booming."

"Not bad if I say so myself."

Tricia pulled shut the door and buckled her seat belt as Mike eased the car back into traffic. Her gaze momentarily lighted on the Cookery, the yellow crime tape still attached to the door frame reminding her of Doris Gleason's murder. She shook the thought away and concentrated on the Jag's dashboard, with its GPS screen and rows of buttons and switches. It reminded her of the cockpit of a jumbo jet. She wiggled her shoulders deeper into the leather, remembering she had once been used to this kind of luxury in the early days of her marriage to Christopher. She glanced across the seat, caught Mike's eye. He looked fabulous in a gray pin-striped suit, crisp white shirt, and a pale yellow silk tie—and nothing like her ex. "You're dressed to the nines. For my benefit?"

"I'd love to say yes, but I've got a speaking engagement later this afternoon. There's always next time." Again he flashed those perfect white teeth.

Next time. That sounded nice. Maybe Angelica had been right. In pursuing her goals to get the bookstore up and running Tricia had neglected to factor in time to build a social life.

"Is this little restaurant in Milford?"

"Just east of there. It's only twenty minutes down the road. Don't worry, I'll have you back to your store before the Red Hat Society bus comes in."

Tricia stifled a laugh. "Do you have all the tourist bus schedules memorized?"

"I'm making an effort. Stoneham's economy has rebounded thanks to tourism. I want the business owners to know how much I appreciate their efforts to keep the village in the black."

"Happy potential constituents mean a landslide victory?"

"Something like that."

"Forgive me, but I thought the village voted for these kinds of things in the winter—not on traditional election day."

"That's right. This is a special election at the next town meeting to fill the spot left by Sam Franklin, who had a heart attack and died a few weeks back. My opponent and I are pretty much evenly matched."

Tricia couldn't remember seeing any other literature for the selectman campaign, realizing she didn't even know the other candidate's name.

"What made you decide to run?"

"Too many former Stoneham selectmen have been outsiders who came to the area after retiring. They fought against the idea of tourism, wanting Stoneham to remain a quaint little—dead—village. They were also lawyers," he said with con-

tempt. "They didn't have a clue how to bring life back to the village. It was people like Bob Kelly who turned Stoneham around. The board begged him to take the job of village administrator, but he said he couldn't afford to take the pay cut."

"Oh?"

"It's only a part-time job, but Bob felt it would take away from running his real estate empire. Besides, he wields his own power as president of the Chamber of Commerce."

"Yes, he does seem to, doesn't he?"

"We could use a couple more Bob Kellys in Stoneham. I intend to follow his lead in a number of areas. We need to boost the tourist trade by offering more than just the lure of used books. We need more restaurants; maybe attract some kind of light industry."

"And do you insure buildings suited for light industry?"

Mike flashed his pearly whites. "How did you guess?"

"Is there anything in the works?" she asked, thinking about the rumors of a big box store coming to town.

He kept his eyes on the road. "There might be, and that's all I'm at liberty to say about it."

"You're a tease."

"And you're beautiful."

That wasn't true . . . but she liked hearing it anyway.

She cast around for something else to talk about. "I've noticed the locals don't seem too interested in supporting the booksellers. Why do you think that is?"

He shrugged, his gaze fixed on the road ahead. "You don't sell what they need."

"Which is?"

"That's something I need to learn," he admitted. "Rare and antiquarian books and expensive baubles—those are for collectors and people who don't know what to do with their money."

Hurt and irritation suddenly welled within Tricia. "Is that how you feel about us?"

Mike momentarily tore his gaze from the road. "Of course not. But that's what a lot of the villagers think. Surely you've at least considered that."

"Yes," she grudgingly admitted.

The Jaguar slowed and Mike pulled into the parking lot of a little ramshackle building, its white paint peeling, the bands of color on the lobster buoys decorating it bleached to pastel hues. A hand-painted sign with red lettering proclaimed ED'S.

"Oh," Tricia said, trying—and failing—to hold her disappointment in check. "It's a clam shack."

"Don't let the outside fool you. They serve the best chowders and bisques on the eastern seaboard."

Except that they were at least fifty miles from the ocean. Tricia painted on a brave smile. "And I can't wait to try it."

The décor inside Ed's consisted of nets studded with lobster buoys, lobster traps—complete with plastic lobsters—starfish, and shells. Picnic tables were covered in plastic tablecloths with lighthouse motifs, and each had bottles of ketchup, vinegar, salt and pepper shakers, as well as bolts of paper towels on upright wooden holders.

"Nothing too fancy," Mike conceded. "But you won't be disappointed. Sit down while I go order."

Tricia nodded, her smile still fixed.

She chose a table near the rear of the tented patio. Attached to the wall was a large gray hood with a heater inside, presumably used to keep the makeshift dining room habitable during the colder months. Several other couples munched on fried clams and fries served on baker's tissue set in red plastic baskets, washing it down with cans of soft drinks or bottles of beer.

Settling at the table, Tricia ran her fingers across the tablecloth, thankful to find it wasn't sticky. Still, she tore off four sheets of paper toweling, fashioning two crude place mats.

Mike returned with napkins and plastic cutlery. "It'll only be a few minutes." He settled on the bench across from her and tied a lobster bib around his neck, settling it over his suit coat. "Don't want to spill soup on my tie. Have to look presentable for my speech this afternoon."

"What are you talking about? Who are you speaking to?"

"A group of seniors at the center on Maple Street. Thanks to my mother's difficulties, I have a unique perspective on the kinds of problems they have, what with the cost of medicine, health care, and the realities of living on a fixed income."

"You mentioned your mother's difficulties," she began, interested, but not wanting to appear too nosy.

"I probably wouldn't have returned to Stoneham last year if it weren't for Mother. Alzheimer's," he explained succinctly.

Something inside Tricia's chest constricted.

"At first she seemed safe enough to leave on her own, but her mind has really deteriorated in the past year," Mike continued. "I had her moved into an assisted living facility almost six months ago. The next step is probably to a locked ward in a nursing home."

"I'm so sorry." Head bent, Tricia looked unseeing at the table in front of her. Mike's words had triggered a plethora of unhappy memories for her. She'd watched her former father-in-law go from a funny, loving man to a sometimes violent, empty-eyed soul. It had torn Christopher's immediate family apart, putting a strain on her own marriage. A strain that contributed to shattering it.

"Let's talk about something more pleasant," Mike suggested. "Like books. They're your specialty. I've slowly been cleaning out Mother's house, and I don't have a clue about what to do with her lifelong collection of books."

Though not a true change of subject, it was something Tricia was much more interested in discussing. "What kinds of books did she have?"

"A little bit of everything. Strike that: a *lot* of everything. Mother was on the village board when Bob Kelly came up with the idea of bringing in all the used booksellers. I'm sure she was one of the booksellers' best customers."

"Can she still read?"

Mike shook his head, grabbed the pepper shaker, and set it in front of his place.

How sad to lose the thing that means the most to you, Tricia thought. Of course her scattered family was important to her—she even grudgingly loved Angelica, and couldn't forget dainty little Miss Marple—but to be deprived of her favorite pastime would be akin to stealing a portion of her soul.

"Would you like me to have a look at the collection?"

Mike tore his gaze from the paper towel place mat he'd been playing with. "Would you? I'd like to see every one of them go to a good home, but that just isn't practical. I've already called libraries within a hundred-mile radius; they aren't interested. Booksellers are my last hope before I resort to a Dumpster."

"Never say that word to a bookaholic," Tricia warned. "And yes, I'd love to have a look. But it'll have to be on a Sunday. That's the only day my shop has limited hours. What's best for you, morning or evening?"

"Morning. Campaigning has eaten a lot more of my time than I'd planned. I'm afraid I'm falling behind in my work with deadlines looming."

"How does nine o'clock this Sunday sound?"

"Perfect. I'll give you the address later."

A portly, fiftysomething man with a white plastic apron over a stained white T-shirt and a paper butcher's cap covering his balding head approached the table and plopped down a couple of bottles: a Squamscot black cherry soda and a straw for her, and a bottle of Geary's pale ale for Mike. Retrieving a church key from a chain on his belt, he opened Mike's beer. "Be right back with your soup," he grunted.

"Ed?" Tricia guessed.

Mike laughed. "You got it. He's a client of mine. Saved him a lot of money when I took over his insurance accounts. Let me know if you'd like me to take a look at your contracts. I'll bet I could offer you lower rates, too."

Always the salesman, she thought. "I'll consider it."

Mike took a swig of his beer and smacked his lips. "Great stuff."

Tricia wrestled with the cap on her bottle, before giving it up for Mike to

open. Uncovering the straw, she popped it into the bottle and took a sip. "Oh, this is nice." She examined the label. "Ah, a local product."

Mike held up his beer in salute. "I think I've patronized every microbrewery in New Hampshire, Massachusetts, and Maine."

"A real pub crawler, eh?"

Mike dazzled her with another of his smiles. "In my youth. Those wild and carefree days are behind me now."

"But you never settled down."

"With a family? Not yet, but there's still time," he said and winked.

Tricia sipped her soda. A couple rose from a nearby table and walked in front of them to deposit their trash in a bin. The man's pants were slung low around his hips, exposing the top of his rear end and reminding her of the nudist tract in her purse. She'd meant to call other shop owners this morning but hadn't had time. She opened her purse and removed the leaflet. "Have you seen any of these around town?"

Mike took the paper and squinted at the text. Then he laughed. "This is a joke, right?"

"I'm afraid not. I've been pulling them out of books for the last couple of days."

He turned it over and frowned. "My guess is this is the first in a series."

"What do you mean?"

"It's just a basic message to get an idea across. The next in the series will give more information. It's been done hundreds of times. The U.S. and British troops dropped thousands of pounds—probably tons—of leaflets on the enemy back in World War Two. It's still done today in war-torn countries."

"How do you know so much?" she asked, then remembered their conversation the first day they met. "Didn't you say you were a World War Two buff?"

"Yeah. I've even got a few examples of propaganda leaflets that I bought off the Internet. It's a fascinating subject. They tried dropping them by hand—only to be sucked into the plane's air intake—and in bombs that exploded at a predetermined height above the ground. The Brits were famous—and very successful at reaching their targets—by sending them up in balloons."

"You sound like an expert."

He shrugged. "It's just a hobby."

Ed returned with a tray laden with steaming bowls and a basket of chunky bread, which he placed before them. "Eat hearty."

Tricia picked up her plastic spoon and stirred the thick soup, turning up large pieces of lobster, potatoes, and onions. "Smells wonderful."

Mike grinned. "Dig in. I guarantee you'll feel like you've died and gone to heaven."

SIX

THE JAG PULLED smoothly to the curb on the west side of Main Street, and Tricia got out. "See you soon," Mike called and pulled away, heading south. Tricia didn't even have a chance to look for oncoming traffic before her gaze was drawn to the front of the Cookery. The yellow crime scene tape that had been there less than two hours ago was gone. A huge kelly green poster, decorated with shamrocks and screaming FOR LEASE—KELLY REALTY and a phone number, took up several square feet of the front window. The door was wedged open, and the scene of Doris Gleason's death less than forty-eight hours before was now a hive of activity. Double-parked nearby was a Becker's Moving van. Two guys in buff-colored coveralls emerged from the store, carrying boxes and loading them into the van.

Tricia hurried across the street. "What are you doing?" she asked. "You can't take those books. Who said you could—?"

"Don't talk to me, lady. Talk to him." The mover jerked a thumb over his shoulder just as Bob Kelly emerged from the inside of the store. His nose and mouth were covered with a dust mask, and he held a clipboard in his left hand, making notes with his right.

Tricia marched up to him. "What's going on?"

Bob looked up, pulling his mask down below his chin. "I'm clearing out my property. I need to get it professionally cleaned and painted if I'm going to rent it out in the next couple of weeks."

"Doris hasn't even been buried yet and already you're emptying her store? What kind of an unfeeling monster are you?"

Bob's glare was arctic cold. "I am a businessman. This is my property. The terms of the lease were immediately negated at the time of Doris Gleason's death."

"What are you going to do with all her stock?"

"Put it in storage. I've rented a garage over at the self-storage center on Bailey Avenue. I'll bill the cost to her estate."

"But it's not right!" she cried. "If the rent was paid till the end of the month—"

Bob's gaze, and his voice, softened. "You're getting all emotional over nothing,

Trish. Doris is gone. What she left behind has no meaning for her now. The sheriff gave me the okay to enter the premises and I'm well within my rights to take care of my property in any way I see fit."

She had no doubt of that. It was just such a cold-blooded move—and typical of the man. "Those books are smoke damaged, but they're still salvageable if they're taken care of properly."

"That's not my concern."

"Well, it ought to be. You're cheating Doris's heirs out of what's rightfully theirs."

"The sheriff has been unable to locate any heirs. And besides, I'm not taking anything away from the heirs. Just relocating it. According to the terms of the lease—"

"Oh, give it a rest, Bob." Fists clenched, Tricia turned on her heel and stalked into her own shop. Ginny was in the midst of making a fresh pot of complimentary coffee for their patrons, while Miss Marple dozed on the sales counter. The sight of such normalcy instantly lowered Tricia's anxiety quotient by half. That still left the other half to bubble over.

Tricia stowed her purse under the counter. "Did you see what's going on next door?"

"How could I miss it?" Ginny said. "The truck pulled up only a minute after you left for lunch. I guess that means the police have finished their investigation, otherwise Bob Kelly wouldn't be allowed inside."

"I've read a lot of true crime and police procedurals and I've never heard of a law enforcement agency abandoning a crime scene so quickly," Tricia said.

"Wendy Adams will figure it out. She's supposed to be good at her job," Ginny offered.

"Maybe, but she's never had to solve a murder before."

"But as she also pointed out, it's an election year. That'll give her plenty of incentive."

Tricia nodded thoughtfully.

The phone rang. Tricia grabbed it. "Haven't Got a Clue, Tricia speaking. How can I help you?"

"Trish? It's Deb Black. I wanted to let you know a deputy's been canvassing Main Street, asking questions of all the shop owners."

"Let me guess: asking questions about me."

"More like planting suspicions." She sounded worried.

Tricia swallowed. "Thanks for the heads-up." She remembered the nudist tracts. "Deb, have you had a problem with leaflets about—"

"Nudists!" she cried. "Yes, and it's really, really tacky. I offer quality merchandise and these horrid little pieces of paper are just plain vulgar. I called the

sheriff, but she told me she's too busy with a murder investigation to bother with something so trivial. And besides, they're not illegal, just a nuisance."

"That's what I was afraid of."

"I've got customers. See you Tuesday night at the auction—that is if I don't have the baby before then."

"You got it. See you then." Tricia hung up.

"More bad news?" Ginny had obviously been eavesdropping.

Tricia shrugged. Movement outside caught her eye. One of the movers placed another carton in the back of the truck and closed the hinged doors, throwing a bolt. "There goes the first load." Tricia's thoughts returned to the Cookery. "Bob said Sheriff Adams hadn't located any of Doris's heirs. That doesn't mean there aren't any. I'm sure the sheriff has already searched Doris's home for that kind of information . . . insurance policies . . . whatever."

Ginny nodded. "It's not much of a home, really. More like a cottage."

Tricia looked up. "You've been there?"

"A couple of times. Once when we had a celebrity author come in, Doris forgot some paperwork she needed and sent me over to her house." She lowered her voice. "I know where she hid an extra key to the back door."

"And?" Tricia whispered.

"Maybe it wouldn't hurt for an interested party—someone the sheriff seems to want to pin this murder on—to go over there and have a look."

The thought repelled yet fascinated Tricia. "But that would be breaking and entering."

"Not if you've got the key," Ginny said. "You could go tonight."

"You'd have to come with me."

"Can't. Brian's taking me to Manchester for a Red Hot Chili Peppers concert—we've planned it for months. Which reminds me, I'm going to need to leave a little early tonight. Is that a problem?"

Tricia shook her head.

"You could go on your own to Doris's. You can park in the back. No one will see your car from the road. No one will ever know you were even there."

"Maybe," Tricia said.

"Think about it. In the meantime, why don't you have a nice cup of coffee and tell me all about your lunch date." Ginny handed Tricia a cup, just the way she liked it.

"He took me to some little clam shack that served the best lobster bisque in the entire world."

Ginny smiled. "That would be Ed's."

Tricia laughed. "Does everyone know about this place but me?"

"You're still relatively new here."

Tricia sipped her coffee, her thoughts returning to the conversation she'd had with Mike. "You're a lifelong resident of Stoneham; do you know Mike Harris's mother?"

Ginny shook her head. "Not my generation. I suppose my mom or grandmother might. If I think of it, I'll ask." She considered Tricia's question for a moment. "Why do you want to know?"

"Mike wants me to have a look at her book collection. Give him some ideas on disposing of it."

Ginny frowned. "Makes it sound like the books are nothing but garbage."

"I know. The idea seemed to bother him, too."

"What do you expect to find?"

Tricia sighed. "Nothing of particular value. Cookbooks, book club editions of bygone best sellers . . ."

"And no doubt the dreaded *Reader's Digest* condensed books."

Tricia shuddered. "Please—don't blaspheme in the shop."

Ginny laughed.

A gleaming white motor coach passed by the shop on its way to the municipal lot to disgorge the latest crowd of book-buying tourists.

Ginny brightened. "Get ready for the ladies of the Red Hat Society. It's showtime!"

SOON AFTER GINNY left for the evening, the store emptied out as well. All except for Mr. Everett, who sat in his favorite chair in the nook, nose buried in a paperback copy of John D. MacDonald's *The Scarlet Ruse*, being careful not to crease its binding. Tricia lowered the shades, closed down the register, and counted the day's receipts, locking them in the safe before disturbing him. "Closing time," she said.

Mr. Everett looked up, glanced at the clock, which read 7:05. "I'm sorry, Ms. Miles. I was so entranced . . ." He slid a piece of paper inside the book to hold his place, and stood, about to replace it on a shelf.

"Just a moment," Tricia said and took the book from him. As she suspected, his bookmark was indeed one of the nudist tracts. "You wouldn't know anything about these, would you, Mr. Everett?"

Mr. Everett looked both embarrassed and aghast. "Certainly not. But I will admit to finding more than a dozen of them in the last day or so."

"You haven't seen who it was who put them inside the books, have you?"

"No, but I have been watching the customers in an effort to put an end to it. I'm sorry to say I haven't caught the culprit. I know everyone in the village and can't say I've seen any come in, so it must be an outsider."

"My sentiments exactly." Tricia turned for the sales counter and a little basket holding author promotional bookmarks. "We'll save your place with one of these, okay?"

Mr. Everett lowered his head, his cheeks reddening. "Thank you, Ms. Miles."

"See you tomorrow?" she asked.

"Bright and early," he promised, the hint of a smile gracing his lips.

Tricia walked him to the door, closed and locked it, spying a sheriff's cruiser slowing, its driver craning his neck to check out her shop. Her cheeks burned as she lowered the shades on the windows and commenced with the rest of her end-of-day tasks, tidying up and running the carpet sweeper across the rug. With Ginny gone early, every task seemed to take extra time, or maybe she was just dragging her feet. The idea of violating the sanctity of Doris Gleason's home bothered her. Then again, it bothered her more that the sheriff still seemed to think she was the prime suspect in the murder and might be staking out her store.

Maybe the deputy had been checking out Doris's shop, not Haven't Got a Clue. But if that was true the driver should've speeded up when he'd passed the Cookery, not slowed down.

Miss Marple patiently waited at the door to the apartment stairs. Tricia cut the lights and headed for the back of the shop when a furious knock at the door caught her attention. Miss Marple got up, rubbed eagerly against the door, and cried.

The knocking continued.

"Now what?" Tricia groused. Guided by safety lighting, she crossed the length of the shop, ready to tell whoever was at the door that she was closed. Pulling aside the shade, she saw Angelica balancing a tray on her knee, holding on to her huge purse, and about to knock again. Tricia opened the door. "Ange, what are you doing here?"

"I brought you dinner." She bustled into the shop, leaving behind the scent of her perfume. "Why is it so dark in here?"

"The store is closed. And you don't have to bring me dinner every night." She took a sniff—bread? Sausage? Heavenly!—and realized that her bisque lunch had been many hours before. "Let me take the tray. Follow me, and don't step on Miss Marple when we get to the door."

Angelica muttered something about "that damn animal," but followed. Tricia hit the light switch and the little gray cat scampered up the steps ahead of them, with Angelica complaining about the three-flight trek and the lack of an elevator.

Tricia balanced the tray and opened the apartment door, hitting the switch and flooding the kitchen with light. She set the tray down and lifted the dishcloth covering the evening's entrée. It looked like a meatloaf-shaped loaf of bread. "Stromboli?" she asked.

A breathless Angelica nodded. "And a thermos of the most amazing lobster bisque you're ever likely to eat."

Tricia stifled a laugh. "You don't say. Where did you get it? At a clam shack?"

"I made it." Angelica set down her gargantuan purse on the counter and leaned against it, still panting.

"I really appreciate you feeding me, Ange, but I don't want to make you wait until after my shop closes just to eat dinner."

"Darling, on the Continent they don't dine until nine or ten."

"And where are you cooking all this stuff, anyway?"

"At the inn. I've made friends with the executive chef, François. He's learned a few things from me, too." She turned to her suitcase-sized purse and withdrew a bottle of red wine. "Where's the corkscrew?"

"No wine for me. I'm going out later."

Angelica set the bottle down, shrugged out of her suede jacket, and hung it on the coatrack just inside the door. "Where are we going?"

"Not we, *me*. Besides, I'm not sure what I've got planned is exactly legal."

Angelica's eyes flashed. "Ooh, this sounds like fun. What've you got in mind?"

"Someone told me where to find the key to Doris Gleason's house. I'm hoping I might find something the sheriff could use in her investigation."

"And what makes you think you could do a better job than the sheriff?"

"Well, I have read thousands of mysteries."

"That's true. I'll bet you've got so much vicarious experience you could open your own investigation service."

Tricia frowned. "Sarcasm doesn't become you."

Angelica advanced on the stove, turning on the oven. "Well, just listen to yourself. Got a cookie sheet handy?"

Arms crossed over her chest, Tricia nodded toward the cabinet next to the stove. Already acquainted with some other portions of the kitchen, Angelica found aluminum foil in another cupboard, tore a sheet, and pressed it over the tray. "The stromboli should only take ten minutes to reheat. Why don't you set the table?"

Why don't you stop ordering me around in my own kitchen? Tricia felt like shouting. Instead she gathered up plates, bowls, and spoons. Miss Marple sat beside her empty dinner bowl and complained loudly. "And you, too," Tricia hissed and picked up the dish, putting it in the sink to soak.

By the time she'd fed the cat, Angelica had popped the bread into the oven and was pouring the soup into a copper-bottomed pan to reheat as well. "Did you know there was a sheriff's car parked down the street from here? Looks like they've got you under surveillance."

The heat returned to Tricia's cheeks. "That's why I want to go to Doris's house. The sheriff still has an unnatural fixation on the idea that I might've killed her."

"Or they could just be watching her shop—maybe waiting for the killer to return to the scene of the crime."

"There's nothing to return to. Bob Kelly emptied the place out this afternoon."

"I heard about that."

Was there nothing the local gossip mill missed?

The yeasty aroma of bread filled the kitchen, and Tricia's stomach gurgled in anticipation. Angelica leaned against the counter. "You can't go out the front door without the deputy seeing you, so I think it best if I leave first, swing around, and pick you up in the alley behind the store."

"Wait a minute, you're not going with me."

"How much investigating do you think you can pull off with a tail?"

"How do you know so much about police procedure?"

Angelica rolled her eyes. "I do have a television, you know. I've seen enough crime shows over the years to have as much investigative experience as you."

"Television? Please. The scientific blunders alone have every jury in the country believing you can pull forensic evidence out of thin air, and they expect it in minutes when the reality is that most police departments are understaffed, and most labs underfunded and overworked, and—"

"What's that got to do with us checking out Doris Gleason's house?" Angelica turned, plucked a wooden spoon from the utensil crock on the counter, and stirred the soup.

"*We* are not going to do it. *I* am. Do you realize how much trouble I'd be in if I was caught? What kind of sister would I be to put you in that same situation?"

"Then who's going to act as your lookout? You can't search the place if you're looking over your shoulder every minute."

Tricia hadn't considered that. She changed tacks. "I don't know if the house is on a well-lit street, if the neighbors would be watching. I'm not even sure I can go through with it. I just thought I'd drive out there and take a look."

"Then there's no harm in me going with you. Here, try some of the soup." Angelica held out the spoon.

Tricia tasted it, surprised at its robust flavor. She took another taste. It was even better than the bisque at Ed's—something only hours before she would have thought impossible. "Where did you learn to cook like this?"

Angelica shrugged. "Let's get back to the subject of searching Doris's house. Do you have any latex gloves? We don't want to leave a bunch of fingerprints."

"We don't need gloves. It wasn't a crime scene. I have no intension of committing a misdemeanor by breaking in if I can't find the key."

"Party pooper."

"Why are you so hyped to come along, anyway?"

Angelica smiled coyly. "Because it just might be fun."

SEVEN

DORIS GLEASON'S LITTLE white cottage had seen happier days, as evidenced by its peeling paint, rusty metal roof, and the overgrown privet that adorned the west side of the property. As Ginny promised, a gravel driveway circled to the back of the dark house, affording the perfect cover for Angelica's rental car. She killed the lights and the yard was engulfed by the night. The engine made tinking noises as the sisters waited for their eyes to adjust to the darkness.

Angelica spoke first. "The woman didn't have a whole lot in her life, did she?"

Tricia shook her head. "I wonder if she owned the place or if it was a rental. She probably spent more time at the Cookery than here anyway."

"How long are we going to sit here?" Angelica asked.

"Give me a minute," Tricia said, looking over the darkened yard. Now that they were here, poking around the dead woman's home seemed like a bad idea—more than that, creepy. Okay, the house was isolated, its nearest neighbor at least a quarter mile in either direction. With the drapes pulled shut there was little chance they'd be seen by passing cars, but just what did Tricia hope to find? A big red sign pointing to a will or an insurance policy?

Tricia reconsidered their quest. "I think we'd better go."

"Oh, come on," Angelica urged, "where's your sense of adventure?" She reached behind her and dragged out the convenience store bag, extracting the big orange flashlight they'd stopped to buy along the way. She fished out the D batteries and filled the empty compartment, switching it on. An ice white beam of light pierced the car's darkness.

"Not in the eyes," Tricia complained, putting a hand up to shield her face.

"Sorry. Now where'd you say the extra key was hidden?"

"It's supposed to be under a fake rock by the back door."

"Right." Angelica opened her door, but Tricia's hand on her arm stopped her.

"Before we do anything else, here." She reached into her jacket pocket and

pulled out a pair of latex gloves and handed them to Angelica. "I changed my mind. I decided you were right and we shouldn't leave any fingerprints behind."

"Whoa. That's a first. Me, with a good idea? Can I stand the compliment?"

"You're making me paranoid."

"Where did you get them?" Angelica asked, pulling a glove over her left hand and flexing her fingers.

"The hardware store. I bought them for a refinishing job I never got around to doing." Tricia put on her own set of gloves, got out of the car, and marched toward the darkened house. Angelica followed, their feet crunching on the gravel drive. Good thing it wasn't raining. Tricia didn't want to track in any detritus and leave any other evidence that they'd been there.

The flashlight's beam whisked back and forth around the steps. "I don't see any fake rocks. How long ago did your little helper say it was that she used it?"

Tricia went rigid. "I never said it was Ginny."

"Don't give me that look," Angelica chided. "Who else would it be? You don't talk to anybody from around here except her. I'm assuming she either once worked for Doris or moonlights as a burglar."

"Yes," Tricia reluctantly admitted, "she worked for Doris for a couple of months before she came to work for me." She explained why Ginny hadn't accompanied her on this little expedition.

Drooping perennials and overgrown grass along the back of the house made it difficult to search for the pseudorock. "Be careful," Tricia whispered. "Don't step on the flowers. If the sheriff comes out here again, we don't want her to know someone's been snooping around."

"I think I've got it," Angelica said.

Tricia hurried over. Using the flashlight, Angelica held back a swath of grass. A little white plastic rock sat sheltered by the greenery. She lifted it up and a fat worm recoiled at being disturbed.

"Oh, ick!"

"Grow up," Tricia warned, still whispering. The key was embedded in the dirt, bringing a small clod with it as Tricia picked it up. "Nobody's used it for a long time."

"Why are we whispering?" Angelica asked.

Tricia cleared her throat. "Come on."

She wiped the dirt from the key, stepped up to the back door, and inserted it in the lock. She turned it, grasped the handle, and let herself in. Fumbling around the door, Tricia found the light switch, flipped it, and a meager glow emanated from the kitchen's single, overhead fixture.

Angelica crowded against her. "Move over."

The tiny off-white kitchen was tidy with signs of a life interrupted. A newspaper

sat neatly folded on the white painted table. A solitary coffee-stained mug occupied the dry stainless-steel sink. A stack of opened mail on the counter awaited consideration. Dusty footprints marred the otherwise clean, but dated dark vinyl floor—no doubt those of the sheriff and her deputies.

"Prisons look homier than this," Angelica offered.

She was right. Not a picture, an ornamental hanging plate, or even a key rack decorated the bland walls. No curtains, just a yellowing blind hung at half-mast over the room's only window. Tricia fought the urge to pull it down completely.

"Creepy," Angelica muttered.

"My sentiments exactly. And how would I feel if this were my home being violated by a couple of strangers?" Tricia wondered aloud. Still, she swallowed down the guilt and stepped into the darkened, narrow hallway, with Angelica so close on her heel she could feel her sister's breath on the back of her neck.

The light overhead flashed on, and Tricia's heart pounded. She whirled to find Angelica with her hand still on the switch. "Sorry."

Tricia ground her teeth, hoping her glare would scorch.

"Looks like a bedroom here," Angelica said, poking her head into a darkened room. She found that light switch, too. The smell of old paper and leather permeated the space. A twin bed wedged into the corner was made up, the patchwork quilt covering it the only splash of color in the room. On the small nightstand next to it was an open book and a pair of reading glasses, looking like they awaited their owner. The walls were floor-to-ceiling bookshelves stuffed with old tomes, while stacks of homeless books stood in front of the bottom shelves. Tricia stepped closer to examine the titles nearest her.

"Are they cookbooks?" Angelica asked eagerly.

Tricia shook her head. "No. But wow—!" She picked out a dark volume, holding it reverently as her trembling fingers fumbled to turn the pages for the copyright information. She let out a shaky breath, throat dry, making it hard to speak. "It's a first edition."

"Of what?"

"Dickens. *A Tale of Two Cities*."

"Must be worth a few bucks, huh?"

Tricia turned on her sister, ready to lecture, but the passive expression on Angelica's face told her she didn't have a clue about antique books, their intrinsic value, and there was no way she could readily explain it, either. "Yeah, it's worth a few bucks." She drank in some of the other titles, their brittle leather covers and the gold lettering on their spines making her catch her breath. Alcott, Alger, Emerson, Hawthorne, Melville, Thoreau, Twain, Whitman—the quintessential collection of nineteenth-century American authors. The only

author missing was Edgar Allan Poe—and a good thing, too, or Tricia might have been tempted to—

"My God, if they're all first editions, there's a fortune in this room alone."

"I thought you said Doris only sold cookbooks."

"That's what her store was dedicated to, but obviously her taste in literature was much more discerning."

Angelica shrugged. "If you say so," and she trotted out of the room. Tricia fought the urge to touch each and every one of the spines, and backed out of the room, turning off the light and silently closing the door with a respect usually held only for the dead.

A trail of lights led to the living room. Angelica stood in the middle of the worn and dingy, putrid green wall-to-wall carpet, sizing up the space, which, like the bedroom, was primarily a storage place for books, though the shelves here seemed to hold mostly contemporary fiction. "Lousy taste in furniture," she said at last, her gaze fixed on the olive drab sofa, its lumpy cushions and sagging springs declaring it a reject from the 1960s. "You'd think with all those valuable books, she'd live in a space to show them off."

"Maybe that was the point," she said. "She could only afford them if she lived like this."

Angelica shook her head. "Not my life choice."

Nor Tricia's. Still, it was a choice she could understand. "I'll take the desk. You want to investigate the rest of the house?"

"Sure."

Tricia was glad to note the drapes were heavy, effectively blocking the light so it wouldn't be visible from the street. Knowing that gave her more confidence to inspect the cherry secretary that stood defiantly against the west wall. It was tall, topped with a glass cabinet that held an antique glass compote, several more old books, and a silver mercury glass vase with hand-painted roses. Tricia grasped the pulls and opened it. The cubbies inside were stuffed with envelopes, a checkbook, and other assorted papers—not Doris's doing, as evidenced by the tidiness of the rest of the house. Had the sheriff been in a hurry when going over the house's contents? Maybe she'd found what she was looking for and had shoved everything back in the pigeonholes with more speed than efficiency.

Utility bills, bank statements, magazine subscription notices, but no last will and testament. Abandoning the top section, Tricia opened the first drawer. Extra checks, a phone book, pens and pencils, paper clips, scissors—typical desk fare.

The next drawer held more receipts and the minutiae of a busy life. She sorted through the papers and found a stack of five or six paper-clipped statements

from New England Life Insurance Company. Tricia glanced over the information. Policy Number 951493. Insured's Name: Doris E. Gleason. Plan of Insurance: Whole Life, issued six months previous. Nowhere on the statement did it list who the beneficiary was, probably for security reasons. Tricia took the oldest one, folded it, and slipped it into her pocket, then replaced the others.

She opened the last drawer without enthusiasm. In it were a little pink photo album and a bulging string envelope. The album drew her attention. She picked it up and opened to the first page to find a fuzzy black-and-white photograph of a baby. In fact, the book was dedicated to the child, whose features quickly changed from nondescript to the all-too-familiar features of Down syndrome.

The string envelope contained receipts and canceled checks, each of them referencing the Anderson Developmental Clinic Group Homes, located in Hartford, Connecticut. The letters referred to a Susan Gleason as "your daughter."

"Oh boy." If Doris had no other living relatives, who would take on the responsibility for her mentally disabled child? Would the young woman—oh, no longer young, she realized—lose her spot in a group home? End up on the streets, homeless?

"Trish! Come and see all these wonderful old cookbooks," Angelica called.

Tricia replaced the album and envelope, closed the drawer, and wandered toward the back of the little house. She found Angelica, book in hand, in another small room crammed with boxes and shelves.

"Look, it's the *Household Bookshelf*, an all-in-one cookbook from 1936. Grandmother had a copy of this in her kitchen. I remember how I loved to read the recipes in it. See this, they used to call bread stuffing bread *forcemeat*. There must be a dozen variations." Angelica looked up at Tricia, her eyes aglow with the same kind of pleasure Tricia had felt in Doris's other book storage room. "Wouldn't it be a kick to try them all?"

Tricia had thought Angelica's infatuation with meal prep had been a recent development. Why hadn't she known her older sister had been interested in cooking even as a little girl?

Angelica closed the book, replacing it on the shelf before her. "Wow, there's—" She ran her fingers along the row of books. "Twelve copies of it. Where did she get them all?"

"Estate sales, tag sales—pickers. Doris might've been collecting them for years."

"It's too bad she's dead," Angelica said wistfully, "I'd love to buy a copy of it from her. And look at all these others. *The Boston Cooking-School, The Settlement House.* I've always wanted an old copy of the Fannie Farmer cookbook. I've only got a softcover edition." She sighed and looked away, embarrassed.

"Did you find any sign of heirs? Maybe they'll have an estate sale and I can get copies of some of these old books."

"Looks like her only living relative is a retarded daughter living in a group home. I couldn't find anything to the contrary."

"Oh no. That poor woman."

Did she mean the daughter, Susan, or Doris?

"Find anything else of interest?"

Tricia shook her head. "You didn't happen to see a copy of *American Cookery*, by Amelia Simmons, did you?"

"That was the book stolen from the Cookery. Why would it be—? Oh, you think the killer might have brought it back here, hidden it amongst all her other stock?"

"He or she can't very well sell it. Not without drawing attention to themselves. Let's take a minute and look. Then we'd better get out of here before our luck runs out."

It took longer than a minute, more like fifteen, but it wasn't until she'd scanned nearly every title in the room that Tricia was satisfied Doris's precious treasure was not buried among her less valuable stock.

Ready to go, she found Angelica's attention had returned to one of the copies of the *Household Bookshelf.* "You okay, Ange?"

She nodded. "It just seems so sad to leave all these old books here alone, knowing their owner will never come back. They might never be loved again."

Touched, Tricia leaned in closer to her sister. "I've never heard you talk about books that way before."

Angelica's expression hardened. She sniffed and threw back her head. "Ha!" She pushed past Tricia, heading back for the kitchen. "Probably something I picked up from you these last few days. I'm sure it'll wear off."

With one last look around the crowded room, a frowning Tricia turned off the light and pulled the door closed, just the way it had been when they'd arrived.

EIGHT

Deception wasn't Tricia's strongpoint. Not when she'd been seven and blamed Angelica for a vase she'd broken, nor when coming up with excuses to

avoid dating high school jocks who couldn't spell, let alone comprehend, Sherlock Holmes.

She paced her kitchen, cell phone in hand, until the clock on her microwave read 9:01. Did a cell phone number come up on caller ID and would it also reveal her name as well? She didn't think so, which was why she'd decided not to use her regular phone. She punched in the number, listened as it rang three times.

"Good morning. New England Life, this is Margaret. How can I help you?"

No long wait on hold? An actual American, not a native of some foreign land earning pennies an hour?

"I . . . I—" Tricia hadn't come up with a plausible story, so she told the truth. "I need to find out a beneficiary on one of your policies."

"Do you have the policy number?"

"Yes." She read it off, heard the tap of a keyboard in the background. "Doris E. Gleason. Did you wish to report her death?"

"Uh, yes. She died three days ago."

"Are you authorized to act on her behalf?"

"Um . . . yes."

"You'll need to provide us with a copy of the death certificate and copies of letters of administration. Are you Ms. Gleason's executor?"

"Not exactly. I'm a friend. I need to track down her next of kin and I thought—"

"I'm sorry. Privacy laws prohibit our giving out sensitive information of this nature. Please have Ms. Gleason's attorney or executor contact us with the necessary paperwork and we will inform the beneficiary the death has occurred."

"Oh. Okay."

"Thank you for calling New England Life."

Click.

Rats!

No sooner had she turned off the cell when her apartment phone rang. "Hello."

"Trish, it's me, Angelica."

"How did you get this number?" Was it too early to already feel so annoyed?

"I figured you'd never give it to me so I read it off the phone and wrote it down last night." Very smart, and she sounded oh so smug.

Tricia examined her empty coffee cup and poured herself some more. "Isn't this awfully early for you to be up, Ange?"

"I've mended all my evil ways. Age does that to you."

Hadn't Mike said something similar? Always a bookworm, Tricia had never had any evil ways to mend.

"Besides," Angelica continued, "I know you're only free during the hours

the store isn't open. This is my only window of opportunity to talk to you until tonight."

"So what do you want to talk about?"

"Nothing really. I just wanted to tell you I had a great time last night. I felt like one of the Snoop Sisters."

"You remember that old TV show? It couldn't have lasted more than one season, and we are both far younger than any of its characters."

"I do admit I was a mere infant, but it was one of Grandmother's favorite shows. And anyway, you know what I mean." She actually giggled.

Tricia glanced at her watch and sighed. "What else do you need, Ange?"

"When are you going to call Doris's insurance company?"

"I already did. It was a bust."

"You're kidding."

"No, I'm not."

Silence for a few moments. "Give me all the info," Angelica demanded.

"What for? They told me I needed a death certificate and all kinds of other documentation before they'd give me any information. And they only want to talk to Doris's attorney or executor."

"Just let me try."

"Fine. If you've got time to waste, be my guest." She pulled out the old insurance statement and read off the pertinent information.

"Hmm. This could take some time," Angelica admitted, ruefully. "I may have to call in a few favors. I'll get back to you." She hung up.

Tricia drained her cup and replaced the handset. "Good luck."

As usual, Mr. Everett was waiting outside the door of Haven't Got a Clue at 9:55 a.m. on that gray Friday morning. He liked to be the first customer inside the door every day, although "customer" was a misnomer since so far in the five months the shop had been open he hadn't bought a thing. But he usually only drank one cup of Tricia's free coffee and, despite hanging around for most of the day, he ate only one or two of the complimentary cookies that she laid out for the paying clientele. And if she and Ginny were busy with customers, Mr. Everett had been known to make a recommendation or two and could knowledgeably talk about any book they had in stock.

Tricia unlocked the shop's door. "Good morning, Mr. Everett."

"Morning, Ms. Miles. Looks like rain today."

A glance at the sky proved the clouds hung low. "Ah, but rain is good for retail. It brings in customers who spend. And there's no better weather to settle down with a good book."

"Obviously you haven't yet seen one of our winters."

She laughed. "You've got me there."

Mr. Everett didn't share in her mirth, nor did he move to his customary seat in the nook; instead he looked down at the folded newspaper in his hands. "I brought you a present, but I don't think you're going to like it." He handed her an obviously read copy of the *Stoneham Weekly News.* The 72-point headline screamed "A Murderer Among Us?"

"Oh dear," Tricia breathed.

Mr. Everett patted her arm. "Why don't I make the coffee this morning?"

Tricia nodded dumbly and headed for the sales counter. She laid the paper flat and immediately Miss Marple jumped up to investigate. The swishing of her tail and rubbing of her head against Tricia's chin made it difficult to follow the text. By the time she'd reached the end of the first column, Tricia had removed a miffed Miss Marple and set her on the floor. She looked over at Mr. Everett, who'd taken shelter behind the side counter and the coffeemaker. He averted his gaze.

For a moment Tricia wasn't sure if she'd been libeled or slandered. She finished the article, then read it again. And again. Russ Smith was a careful writer, so suing him was definitely out. It wasn't so much what he said, but what he didn't say that inferred her probable guilt. Her lack of answers to his questions and the fact that Sheriff Adams had no other suspects in Doris Gleason's murder painted an unflattering picture.

Bob Kelly hadn't been mentioned at all. The editor knew Bob had an appointment with Doris the night she was killed, knew the two of them had argued about the leases, but instead he'd intimated that Tricia was suspected of murder—no one else.

Ginny arrived just as the phone rang. Tricia had no intention of answering it. She let the answering machine take it as Ginny hung up her coat. Then she folded the newspaper and put it under the counter.

The door opened and a couple of women entered. "Good morning, ladies, and welcome to Haven't Got a Clue."

Dressed in jogging attire, they didn't look like tourists, and they didn't have that *we're here to spend* look in their eyes. One of the women giggled. "This is a mystery bookstore, isn't it? You sell *murder* mysteries, don't you?"

Tricia swallowed, forced a smile. "Yes."

"I hope you don't *murder* your customers," the other woman said and snickered.

Ginny returned in her shop apron with the look of a mother tiger out to save her cub and insinuated herself between Tricia and the women. "Mrs. Barton, Mrs. Grant, thanks for stopping by. This must be your first visit to Haven't Got a Clue. Can I help you find a book?"

"No, thanks, we just came by to look the place over," one of them said, bending to look around Ginny and catch a glimpse of Tricia.

Tricia turned her back on the women and found some busywork at the counter. She tried not to listen to the rest of the conversation, but noted Ginny's words were not delivered in her usual, friendly tone.

Eventually the door opened, the bell tinkled, and the door closed. Footsteps approached. "You okay?" Ginny asked.

Tricia turned, braved a smile. "Sure."

"Everybody's talking about Russ Smith's front-page article. I wouldn't be surprised if more of the villagers dropped by just to have a look at—" She stopped, looked embarrassed.

"Look at what?" Mr. Everett asked, still standing at the coffee station.

"The, uh, jinx," Ginny said in a tiny voice.

The muscles in Tricia's calves ached from being so tense. "We'll just have to welcome them, if they do. Maybe I should get another couple of pounds of coffee." She almost managed to keep her voice steady.

"You're being a lot more generous than I could be," Ginny said.

"I won't let idle gossip run me out of town. I'm here for the long haul."

Ginny's smile was tentative. "You go, girl."

With a small tray in hand, Mr. Everett appeared behind Ginny. "Coffee, ladies?"

Tricia and Ginny each took a cup, and Mr. Everett took one, too. "I propose a toast. To Haven't Got a Clue, the best bookshop in all of Stoneham. Long may we read!"

Tricia swallowed down the lump in her throat.

"Here, here!" Ginny agreed, and the three of them raised their cardboard coffee cups in salute.

LIKE MOST FRIDAY afternoons, this one was busy, and the forecasted rain did bring out paying customers. Stoneham was a favorite day trip for senior groups from Vermont, Massachusetts, and from within New Hampshire itself, a happy happenstance for every business owner in the village. And while most seniors took the trips to alleviate boredom, a lot of them actually were avid readers. However, when four or five buses converged at once, the result was chaos.

Ten or twelve customers hovered like angry bees around the sales counter in Haven't Got a Clue. "Our bus leaves in less than ten minutes," someone from the back of the crowd growled.

"It won't leave without you," Ginny said reasonably, as she stacked wrapped books into a plastic carrier bag.

"Well if it does, you'll be paying my hotel bill for the night," snapped a thin, bleached blonde in a beige cashmere sweater set and pearls. An idle threat. There were no hotels or motels in or around Stoneham. Just the Brookview Inn.

Tricia's fingers flew over the cash register's keys, and not for the first time she wished the store had a laser checkout system. Though tagging the books would be great for inventory purposes, the resale value on the older, most expensive books would plummet.

"As soon as the last bus rolls down the road and out of town, we'll break open that pound of Godiva I've been saving," she muttered to Ginny, who smiled gratefully. Lunchtime had come and gone several hours earlier, but they'd been too busy to even stop and grab a bite.

The shop door opened and the little bell rang as Tricia accepted a copy of Dorothy L. Sayers's *Gaudy Night* from a pair of outstretched hands. She turned to ring it up when from beside her Ginny let out a stifled scream. Mouth covered with one hand, with the other she pointed at the apparition standing just inside the door.

Tricia, too, gulped at the sight of the seventysomething plump, but smartly dressed woman who stood in the doorway. She took in the tailored red pantsuit, white turtleneck shirt, and large red leather purse, designer glasses, and severely short, dyed jet-black hair. Unable to find her voice, Tricia mouthed the name: "Doris?"

The woman charged forward with an energy the living Doris Gleason had never possessed. "Hello, I'm Deirdre Gleason. Doris was my sister." The voice was a shade deeper, her words spoken more slowly. "What on earth happened to Doris's shop? Why is it empty? Where is all her stock?"

"Excuse me, but I was here first," said the woman in a damp trench coat, elbowing her way forward.

Tricia looked from her customers to the doppelganger in front of her. "Can you give us a couple of minutes? We're a little overwhelmed right now, but I'd be glad to tell you everything I know as soon as things calm down." She gestured toward the coffee station. "Help yourself and then we'll talk."

The woman's lips pursed, but she nodded and skirted the crowd at the sales counter.

Once the initial shock had passed, Tricia had little time to think about Deirdre Gleason, who wandered the store during the rush. Nine customers and three hundred dollars later, the shop was nearly empty and Ginny gave Tricia a nudge in the direction of the mystery woman who had finally settled in the sitting nook. "I believe in ghosts," she whispered. "Make sure she isn't one of them, will you?"

A curious Miss Marple had perched on the coffee table in front of the

woman. The cat wasn't spitting or acting odd, so Ginny's fear of specters was no doubt unfounded.

Tricia sat down on the chair opposite Deirdre and offered her hand. "Hello, my name is Tricia Miles. I own this store and—"

"You found my sister's body." A statement, not an accusation.

Tricia swallowed, pulling her hand back. "I'm so sorry for your loss."

The woman shrugged, her creased face ravaged by the effects of gravity and sorrow. "The coroner said poor Doris was sick with cancer and probably didn't even know it. I would've lost her anyway. I'm just sorry I never got a chance to say good-bye."

Tears threatened and Tricia's throat closed. Angelica was a gigantic pain in the butt, but she had always been in Tricia's life. Sometimes lurking, sometimes in her face, but always her big sister. The thought of her suddenly gone . . .

"I'm sorry there's nothing I can tell you that will ease your pain. Someone killed your sister and I believe it had to do with a rare cookbook that was stolen the night she died."

"The sheriff told me all about it. I'm not sure she believes it."

Not good news, but not totally unexpected, either. "I didn't know Doris had a sister, although I did know about her daughter."

Deirdre's left eyebrow arched. "Doris wasn't one to chat about her personal life."

Tricia quickly adopted a wide-eyed and, what she hoped was, innocent expression. No way was she going to say how she knew about Doris's daughter. Deirdre's penetrating gaze was as unforgiving as her late sister's.

"Why is the Cookery empty? What happened to all the stock? I spoke to Doris last Monday and she didn't say anything about closing the shop. In fact, she said she was negotiating a new lease."

"That's true. Uh . . ." Tricia stalled, trying to come up with a tactful reply. "The landlord apparently didn't realize Doris had any heirs. I think he—"

"Jumped the gun at emptying the store?"

"I'm afraid so."

The woman sighed, shook her head, irritated.

Tricia became aware that her palms, resting on her knees, had begun to perspire. She wiped them on the side of her slacks and sat back in the comfortable chair, feeling anything but comfortable. "He had all the books and display pieces moved to a storage unit. I'm afraid they may be smoke damaged."

"Would you happen to know where I can contact this . . . this landlord person?"

"Yes. As a matter of fact, I believe I have one of his business cards."

Ginny, who had been unabashedly eavesdropping, spoke up. "I'll get it. It's

here in the register." She opened the drawer, lifted the cash tray, and came up with the card. In seconds she'd handed it to Deirdre.

"Thank you." She stowed the card in the pocket of her jacket. "It was always my intention to move to Stoneham to help Doris with the shop. Her death has just hastened my entry into the world of bookselling." She opened her purse, took out a tissue, and bowed her head, looking ready to cry. "I've been a very selfish woman. I should've been there for her in her time of need. I knew she was having cash-flow problems; I knew she wasn't feeling well. And I knew she'd had employee problems—"

At this, Ginny stepped back, looking guilty. She'd quit the Cookery to take the job with Tricia. Doris had never replaced her.

Deirdre faced Tricia once again. "I was always too busy, wasting money on travel and clothes when I should've been here helping my sister."

Tricia wasn't sure how or if she should reply. Deirdre made it easy on her and rose from her seat.

"What will happen to Doris's daughter?" Tricia asked, and also stood.

"Susan is now my responsibility." Deirdre pursed her lips, an effort that failed to stop them trembling. "It wasn't Doris's way to let on that she cared—about anything. But she loved that girl. It broke her heart when Susan had to go live in the group home. But apparently she's happy there. Doris told me she has friends and a job. I don't know how I'll tell her she'll never see her mother again."

The three women stood there, all of them fighting tears for several long moments. Finally Deirdre cleared her throat and straightened, her expression once again impassive. "Thank you for answering my questions. It was traumatic to hear of Doris's death. Finding her had to be even more so."

Odd, Tricia thought, except for Frannie, Deirdre had been the only other person to acknowledge that she might've felt traumatized by the experience. This morning's newspaper story had brought it all back in vivid detail, but it had also bolstered Tricia's determination to clear her name. And yet, she had no clue how to go about it.

"Yes, it was. If only I'd arrived a few minutes sooner."

"You mustn't blame yourself. If you had arrived sooner, Doris's murderer might've killed you, too."

Deirdre's words, spoken with such casualness, made Tricia go cold.

NINE

"Good night, Mr. Everett," Tricia said, shut the door, turned the sign on it to closed, and was about to shut and lock it when she saw the familiar rental car pull up in front of the shop.

Ginny was still tidying up, but she, too, saw the car, turned off the vacuum, and began to wind up the cord. "You don't mind if I leave, do you?" she said, already shoving the cleaner toward the utility closet. "Sorry to say, but your sister really hates me for all the times I screened your calls."

"I know, and I'm sorry. I never thought you two would ever face each other." Tricia crossed to the register, opened it, lifted the money tray, and withdrew an envelope—Ginny's paycheck. "I didn't get a chance to tell you before, but I've given you a raise. Sorry it couldn't be more."

Already shrugging into her jacket, Ginny paused, her surprise evident. "But you gave me a raise only last month."

"Well, you've been so supportive these past few days I figured you'd earned another."

Ginny accepted the envelope. "Thank you, Tricia. I've worked for three booksellers here in the village in the past four years, but you are by far the best." She gave Tricia a quick hug.

"Can somebody help me?" came a muffled, annoyed voice from behind the shop's door.

Tricia crossed the store to open the door, letting in Angelica, who scowled as Ginny went out, calling cheerfully behind her, "See you tomorrow."

Once again Angelica was weighed down with a grocery bag full of ingredients. "That girl," she muttered and dumped the sack on the nook's coffee table.

"Ange, I hope you don't think you have to come here every evening and cook for me," Tricia said, although the thought of the leftovers now residing in her freezer was a comfort.

"You work so hard, and it's the only part of the day you have time for me." She patted one of Tricia's cheeks and simpered, "I do so miss my baby sister. We've still got years and years to catch up on."

Tricia didn't reply. It was the memory of Deirdre Gleason's sorrow at the

loss of her sister that made her keep quiet. She would try to be a better sister to Angelica. She would.

She turned for the door.

"I've got it," Angelica said, triumphantly.

"Got what?"

She pulled a piece of paper from her jacket pocket and waved it in the air. "Doris's beneficiary."

With everything else going on, Tricia had completely forgotten her quest from earlier in the day. "Don't tell me. Susan Gleason, but in some kind of trust with Deirdre Gleason in control."

Angelica's face fell. "Who told you?"

"I met Deirdre a couple of hours ago. She came into the shop, wanted to know why the Cookery was empty."

Surprise turned to pique. Angelica exhaled sharply. "If you only knew how much trouble I went through to get this."

"Sorry, Ange. I figured you'd come up against the same brick walls I did." Avoiding her sister's gaze, Tricia reached for the door.

"Don't lock it—I've asked Bob Kelly to join us for dinner," Angelica called, rummaging through the grocery bag. "Oh dear. I hope you've got an onion. I don't think I picked one up at the store."

"I wish you'd asked me first."

"Doesn't everyone keep onions?" Angelica asked, looking up from her supplies.

"I mean about inviting Bob. I told you he isn't my favorite person."

"Like you, that poor man is a virtual workaholic. Why I'll bet he hasn't had a home-cooked meal in ages."

"What are you making?"

"Stroganoff."

Like Pavlov's dog, already Tricia anticipated the aroma of one of her most favorite entrées. "Well, next time please let me know when you're going to invite guests to *my* home."

"That's why I invited him. If I'm going to be staying in Stoneham for the winter, I'll need a place to live. I considered staying in one of the inn's bungalows, but I really want more space and I've heard Bob is the best person to talk to about the local real estate market." And with that, Angelica picked up the sack and headed for the door to the upstairs apartment, where she paused. "Why don't you like Bob, anyway? What's he ever done to you?"

"Have you taken a close look at his face?"

"Yes, and he's a very good-looking man."

Tricia crossed her arms over her chest. "Exactly. And who does he remind you of?"

Angelica thought about it for a moment. "Christopher?"

"Duh! My ex-husband."

"Well, that's certainly not Bob's fault," Angelica said with a shrug and turned. "I'll go get dinner started. Don't let me keep you from whatever you have to finish up."

From her perch on the shelf above the register, Miss Marple looked from Tricia to Angelica. The squeak of the door's hinges promised food, and the little gray cat jumped down to follow.

"Traitor," Tricia hissed, but Miss Marple took no heed and scampered up the steps.

It was another ten minutes before Tricia finished her evening chores, all the while stewing about Angelica's threats to make Stoneham her new hometown. She'd emptied the wastebaskets, cleaned the coffee station, straightened books on the shelves, and aligned the mystery review magazines on the nook's big, square coffee table, and still there was no sign of Bob. They'd never hear the bell from the third-floor apartment, so she was forced to wait until he showed up.

Her irritation escalated to smoldering anger with every passing minute. She peered out the shop windows. Nothing. She wondered if she should give him a call, but then remembered Ginny had given her only copy of his business card to Deirdre. She went in search of the phone book and remembered she'd let the answering machine take at least one call this morning. She'd been too upset to answer it after reading the *Stoneham Weekly News.*

Tricia played the message.

"Tricia? Hi, it's Mike Harris. In case you haven't already seen it, the *Stoneham Weekly News* has a scathing report about the murder at the Cookery. I wanted to let you know that Russ Smith is a jerk, and the whole village knows it. He'll sensationalize anything to sell copies of that rag. Don't take it seriously. My day is pretty full, but I'll try to get over to see you later this afternoon or early tomorrow. We're still on for Sunday morning, right? Talk to you later."

Tricia's finger hovered over the delete button. Well, at least one citizen in the village thought she was innocent.

A knock on the door caused her to look up. It came again and Tricia went to the door. Shoulders hunched inside his jacket, Bob Kelly looked as peeved as Tricia felt.

"Hello, Bob," she greeted without enthusiasm.

"Tricia," he grunted and stepped inside the shop.

"Angelica's upstairs."

He grunted again, waited as she locked the door, then followed her across the shop. "This way," she said and started up the stairs at a brisk pace.

As she hit the top-floor landing, Miss Marple was there to admonish her. "Did you give the cat anything to eat?" Tricia asked.

Angelica looked up from a pan on the stove. "I don't know what to feed a cat."

Miss Marple rubbed against Tricia's ankles, looked up at her with hope in her green eyes.

"Where's Bob?" Angelica asked.

Tricia looked down the staircase. Bob was nowhere in sight. "I thought he was right behind me." Annoyed, she started back down the stairs, with Miss Marple right at her heels. Bob rounded the second-floor landing.

"Sorry. Had to tie my shoe," he said. "What smells so delicious?"

Tricia waited for him to catch up, then turned back for her apartment, with Miss Marple sticking to her like glue. Bob was breathing hard by the time they reached the apartment.

"There you are," Angelica called from her station at the counter. Already a heavenly aroma teased the senses. "Trish, take Bob's coat," she scolded.

Tricia did as she was told, stowing Bob's jacket on the coat tree.

He took in the changes she'd made to the third-floor loft—he hadn't been there since she'd signed the lease. "It's beautiful, Trish. You've done a wonderful job converting the space into a home."

She had. But everything was modular—from the pickled maple cabinets to the granite-covered island that doubled as a breakfast bar. Should she ever decide to relocate she could remove everything, leaving the space as she'd found it—an empty shell.

"Have a glass of wine and relax, Bob," Angelica suggested. "Or would you like something a little stronger?"

"Wine is fine," he said, settling on a stool at the breakfast bar.

Again Angelica proved she knew her way around Tricia's kitchen. She took another couple of glasses from the cabinet and poured, setting the merlot before Tricia and Bob. Then she grabbed a pot holder, took a tray out of the oven, and settled the contents onto a waiting platter.

"The seafood around here is pretty good. I hope you like crab puffs." She offered the plate to Bob, who took one of the golden savory pastries. He popped it into his mouth and chewed.

"These are delicious. Where did you buy them?" he asked, eyes wide with pleasure.

Angelica laughed. "I made them, silly."

Tricia selected one as well. "From scratch?"

"Of course. Have another, Bob," Angelica said, taking one for herself.

"You're going to spoil me," he said, but he took another puff anyway.

Angelica set the platter down within reach of all them, pushed the napkin holder toward her guest, and leaned her elbows against the granite, resting her head on her balled fists. "You look tired, Bob. Tough day?"

Bob snagged a napkin, wiped his fingers. "I've got problems. Who knew Doris Gleason would have a sister bent on keeping the Cookery open?"

Angelica shook her head. "I heard all about it."

From where? Tricia wondered, annoyed. She turned to Bob. "I believe I suggested you wait to take action on the property. It fell on deaf ears."

Bob didn't answer, only glowered at her.

"Tricia, behave," Angelica admonished. "Bob is our guest."

No, he was *her* guest in Tricia's home.

"The worst thing is, this woman—this sister—is making out like *I* might have had something to do with Doris's death, just because I exercised my rights as the building's owner to do some cleanup and maintenance. She as good as accused me of killing Doris so I could lease the Cookery to someone willing to pay a lot more in rent."

Good. At least one other person in Stoneham considered Bob a viable suspect.

"Oh I'm sure she doesn't believe that," Angelica said. "It's just grief. If I lost my only sister"—she looked fondly at Tricia—"I'm sure I'd be just as devastated."

Bob wasn't listening. "She's already called in an attorney. Apparently Doris had sent her sister copies of the current and proposed leases. The sister threatened a lawsuit over my emptying the store. It may be easier for me to cut my losses and extend the current lease—as is—for another year and renegotiate at a later date. That way she would be up and running again in a couple of weeks. No matter what, it's going to cost me." He shook his head. "The damage that woman's death has done to Stoneham's economy will end up being in the millions."

"Don't be ridiculous," Tricia said.

"I'm not. The PR value of being the safest town in all New Hampshire was priceless. Losing it could affect future development here for decades."

Angelica clucked sympathetically, but it took all Tricia's self-control to keep quiet on that account. Instead, she decided to move things along. "How's that Stroganoff coming, Ange? It sure smells good."

Angelica was not about to be hurried and topped both her own and Bob's wineglasses.

Resigned, Tricia tried another topic. "What's this about a big box store coming to Stoneham?"

Bob choked on his wine. Angelica scurried around the island, thumped him on the back. "Are you okay?"

"Who told you that?" Bob asked, anger causing his eyes to narrow.

"I heard it. Around," Tricia offered lamely.

"I did, too, Bob," Angelica said. "Is it true?"

Bob cleared his throat, pounding on his chest before answering. "No. Maybe. I hope not."

"That's not much of an answer," Tricia said.

"All I can tell you is that a nationally known company has put out feelers. That doesn't mean they're actually looking to establish a presence in Stoneham."

"But you are talking to their representatives," Tricia pushed.

"I've been approached, and so has the Board of Selectmen, on a number of proposed projects. That's all I can say."

"Would candidates for selectman know about this interest, too?" Tricia asked. Maybe she could pump Mike Harris for information.

"No," Bob said emphatically and gulped the rest of his wine. Angelica filled his glass again.

So much for that idea.

"Any news on Winnie Wentworth's death?"

"How would I know?" Bob looked up, aggravated.

Tricia shrugged. "You seem to have your finger on the pulse of Stoneham. I wondered if they'd made a determination."

"I have no interest in vehicular accidents unless they pose a threat to commerce."

Talk about coldhearted.

"Winnie was a citizen of Stoneham. Surely, she—"

"She didn't own property. She didn't pay taxes. She was little more than a pest to most of the shop owners, always trying to flog her junk. I had more than a few complaints about her over the years. Everything from vagrancy to harassment."

"Yes, but—" Tricia tried to protest, but Bob cut her off again.

"She was an embarrassment to the village. It's hard to promote tourism when you've got her sort wandering about. She was a nuisance in life and a liability in death. No one's claimed her body. It'll probably be up to the taxpayers to bury her," he finished bitterly and took another gulp of wine. He turned his attention to Angelica. "Now, what kind of house were you thinking about buying or were you just interested in renting?" And Bob launched into his pitch for possible residential rentals and sales.

Taking the hint, Tricia busied herself by feeding Miss Marple and setting the table. Although Bob was her first official dinner guest since moving in, she

decided not to use her grandmother's best china and tableware. For someone like Mike, however, she might be persuaded to pull out all the stops.

She would've liked to have returned Mike's call, thanking him for his support. Hadn't he said his mother's book collection included cookbooks? Deirdre Gleason would need additional titles to restock the Cookery. Perhaps Tricia could broker a deal for the books, which would at least keep the lines of communication open with her nearest neighbor.

When the crab puffs were finally gone Angelica declared the entrée ready to serve. She'd whipped up a romaine salad and homemade poppy-seed dressing as well. The three of them took seats at the table.

Bob dug in, chewed, and swallowed. "Unusual flavor. What is it?"

Tricia took a bite and could tell the meat wasn't beef. "Yes, it's different, but it's delicious," she said and took another bite.

"Venison," Angelica said, smug. "Most people won't eat it, but I know how to take out the gamey flavor."

"And how do you do that?" Bob asked, shoveling up another mouthful.

"It's a secret." She sipped her wine. "I'm sorry I had to use store-bought noodles, but there just wasn't time to make them from scratch," she lamented and sighed.

Tricia watched as Bob stabbed another forkful, then savored the taste. "This is absolutely delicious. Have you ever thought about opening a restaurant, Angelica?"

Angelica brightened. "Well, actually, I have."

Bob leaned in closer, his voice growing husky. "I've got a couple of beautiful properties that could be converted into the most exquisite little bistros."

Tricia cringed. Honestly, he sounded like the worst kind of used car salesman.

Angelica didn't seem to notice and fluttered her eyelashes. "Do tell."

Tricia cleared her throat, afraid they'd forgotten she was still there. She'd never seen Angelica turn on the charm for a man before—and she was sure she didn't want to see a repeat performance.

"Gee, it's too bad Drew isn't here. As I recall, Stroganoff was his favorite. And he has such a vast knowledge of architecture and renovation—which would sure be a big help if you're serious about opening a restaurant."

"Drew?" Bob asked.

Angelica straightened in her chair, her expression souring. "My soon-to-be ex-husband."

"I'm still hoping for a reconciliation," Tricia said, trying to look encouraging.

Angelica put down her fork. "Well, I'm not. More Stroganoff, Bob?"

Tricia studied her sister's face. There was hurt behind her strained smile. Tricia still didn't know why her sister's marriage was about to end, and teasing her now, in front of Bob, really wasn't fair. Although, the last thing she wanted was for the two of them to start a relationship.

Tricia sipped her wine. Then again, why should she stand in the way of her sister's happiness even if she'd find it with someone like Bob Kelly? Wasn't she looking forward to seeing Mike Harris again? The pain of her own divorce was still fresh, and somewhere in the back of her mind she heard her mother scolding, *"If something happens to Dad and me, you're all you've got."* Those words held new meaning for her after finding Doris Gleason's body, and suddenly Tricia found herself looking at her sister with kinder eyes.

"Tell me more about those hot properties, Bob," Angelica cooed, lashes fluttering again.

Tricia's grasp on her fork tightened. If she didn't end up killing Angelica first.

TEN

Tricia lay awake half the night, disturbed by dreams of Angelica, radiant in a long white gown, and Bob Kelly in a tuxedo with a green shirt and tie, making goo-goo eyes at each other as they exchanged I dos, and vowing to live a life of wedded bliss *in* Tricia's home. The rest of the night Tricia lay awake, various scenarios of her future—none of them good—circling through her mind.

Regular coffee might not be enough to get her through the day. A double shot of espresso was what she needed, except there was no place in all of Stoneham to get a cup of that black-as-tar brew at this time of day.

After a half hour of running nowhere on the treadmill, a shower, and a Pop-Tart breakfast, Tricia and Miss Marple headed down to the store, if only to soak up its cozy ambiance on that gray morning. Miss Marple settled down on one of the nook's chairs, ready for some serious napping, while Tricia puttered around the shop.

Mr. Everett must've seen the lights on, because he showed up especially early, with his collapsible umbrella under his arm. Tricia let him in and offered him the first complimentary cup of coffee of the day.

"Thank you," he said, taking his first sip. He scrutinized her face. "Is something troubling you, Ms. Miles?"

She shook her head—definitely in denial—then thought better of it and nodded. "Yes. I keep thinking of all that's happened in the past few days and I can't quite make sense of it all."

"Death is never as easy to handle in person as it is in fiction. Yet that's the fascination that inspired all the books here on your shelves."

"That's true," she admitted, "but it doesn't feel so antiseptic, so remote when you've actually known the deceased."

"I agree." He took another sip. "Death is not a stranger to Stoneham. We lose people all the time to sickness, to accidents. That we've lost one to murder gives us more in common with our big-city cousins. Not something we as a village aspire to."

"You're right. When someone dies of natural causes there's pain, but also a sense of acceptance. But murder and accidents . . ." She studied the old man's gray eyes. "Did you know Winnie Wentworth?"

His gaze dipped and he took his time before answering. "Yes."

"What was she like?"

"In years past she liked honeydew melons, green beans, and pork rinds and malt liquor on a Saturday night."

Not the kind of details Tricia would've expected. She laughed. "How do you know that?"

He shrugged. "Just some things I observed over a number of years. For instance, you don't want customers to know how passionate you are about keeping the work of long-dead mystery authors alive. So you carry the current best sellers and give them some prominence, but when you talk to your customers, you always recommend the masters."

Of course she did. Like the rest of the booksellers in town, Haven't Got a Clue offered used and rare books. He hadn't really answered her question.

"Tell me something else about Winnie," she said, hungry to hear more.

Mr. Everett searched the depths of his quickly cooling coffee. "She had contempt for the written word, or at least reading for pleasure, but she recognized books as a way to stay afloat with the changes that came to Stoneham these past few years."

"Then why didn't she offer me more books?" Tricia asked, puzzled. "I didn't meet her until the day she died."

Again he shrugged. "She was eccentric, didn't trust many people. But I do know one thing: she was always careful with her car. It's all she had. She wasn't one to drive recklessly."

"Do you think her death was an accident or . . . something else?"

He glanced around the shop with its thousands of books. "Perhaps I read too much. Yet unless she was ill, it makes no sense that she crashed and died on such a beautiful, sunny day. Especially when she was the only person who knew where the book stolen from the Cookery came from."

Though Winnie denied remembering, Tricia suspected Doris's killer could've believed the same thing. Hearing that theory from another source gave her no comfort.

"OH DEAR," MR. Everett said within minutes of opening a copy of Carter Dickson's *The Punch and Judy Murders.* Even with a Nicholas Gunn CD playing softly in the background, the tone of his voice caused Tricia to look up from opening the morning mail.

Mr. Everett rose from his chair, headed for the sales counter.

Ginny, who'd been helping a customer, excused herself and intercepted him.

The elderly gent handed a folded piece of paper to Tricia. Another nudist tract, but this one was different. Instead of a generic missive on the health benefits and pleasure of a nudist lifestyle, this one was a blatant advertisement. "Free Spirit Inc. presents Full Moon Camp and Resort," Tricia read aloud. The tract went on to list all the amenities, including a pool, hot tubs, therapeutic massage, and—"Why is it nudists are so intent on playing volleyball?" she asked.

Ginny giggled. "Look, there's a website listed. Maybe they've got pictures."

Tricia made the trek up to her apartment, snagged her laptop computer, and was back down to the shop in record time. She booted up and was connected to the Internet within another minute or two. The three of them gathered behind the sales counter. "If there're naughty pictures, I'm shutting it down," she warned.

"We're all grown-ups," Ginny said sensibly, but Mr. Everett bristled at the notion. Still, he didn't walk away.

Free Spirit's home page flashed onto the little screen. No naked people. So far so good. Instead there was a cute little graphic of a squirrel named Ricky, which was apparently the site's mascot. By clicking on various links, Ricky took visitor 120,043 on a tour of the website. First up, the volleyball court, but there were no naked men and women playing the game, only the photo of a well-groomed court. The pool was Olympic-sized, with scores of white chaise longues lined up around it, each with its own clean, neatly folded white towel. That picture was also devoid of people, as was every other photograph on the website. Instead, like any other camping resort, the text stressed the clean, well-maintained facilities at every Free Spirit location.

"It's a chain?" Mr. Everett asked.

"Apparently so." Tricia clicked on the coming attractions page and found what she'd been looking for. "Aha. Listen to this: 'Our newest Full Moon location is scheduled to open next summer in southern New Hampshire.'"

"You think they mean here in Stoneham?" Ginny asked.

"It can't be." Still, there had been the rumor of a big box outfit wanting to locate in the area. No, retail was a year-round moneymaking concern while a nudist resort would, for the most part, only be seasonal.

"There's no reason it would have to be located near here. Saying 'southern New Hampshire' is rather ambiguous. They'd probably want to be near a larger city to make it accessible for travelers," Mr. Everett said reasonably.

"You're probably right," Tricia agreed.

Mr. Everett stepped away from the counter. "I think I'll go back to my reading. Excuse me, ladies," he said, and off to the nook he went.

"I think it would be cool to have a nudist resort right outside of town. Think of all the new money it would bring to the area," Ginny said wistfully. "All those people might get bored with volleyball after a while. Did you see all those lounge chairs? They'd definitely need something good to read while they whiled away the hours working on their tans."

"One can hope," Tricia said. "But, oh, think about the mosquitoes and all the new places you could get bitten." She shuddered and Ginny laughed. "Better be on the lookout for more of these," she said, crumpled up the tract Mr. Everett had found, and tossed it into the trash.

"Could you help me, miss?" asked the customer Ginny had abandoned only a few minutes before.

"I'll keep an eye out for more of those advertisements," Ginny told Tricia, before skirting the counter. "Now, what can I help you find?" she asked the customer.

Tricia clicked on the button for the website's home page once more. Ricky smiled at her with a toothy grin more appropriate to a cartoon chipmunk. Bob hadn't wanted to talk about big box stores. How eager would he be to talk about the possibility of a nudist resort—if she could even catch him at his realty office to ask?

Tricia didn't have an opportunity to find out. Their slow start of a morning suddenly morphed into a busy afternoon of enthusiastic shoppers looking for vintage mysteries. Tricia was deep in conversation with a Mrs. Richardson, a serious collector from the Hamptons, who had already picked out more than a dozen books with authors ranging from Margery Allingham to Cornell Woolrich. She glanced up as the bell over the door jingled and a damp Mike Harris shook the drops from his raincoat onto the mat just inside the door.

Both Ginny and Mr. Everett were also deeply involved in customer service,

so Tricia gave Mike a be-with-you-when-I-can smile. He waved a no-hurry hand in response and started browsing amongst the shelves.

The Hamptons woman spent close to seven hundred dollars and left the store a happy customer; likewise, Tricia was a very happy proprietor. A Charioteer tour bus rolled down Main Street, which would hopefully mean another influx of customers. A patient Mike had settled into the nook, thumbing through *Mystery Scene Magazine*. Tricia knew she only had minutes before the store would be flooded with potential customers again.

"I'm sorry it took so long," she apologized, taking the seat opposite him.

"No, I'm sorry. I should've called; but then I wouldn't have gotten to see you."

Tricia felt her cheeks redden. "I wanted to thank you for your call yesterday. I didn't grab it because—"

"If it was me, I'd have been screening my calls after that hatchet job in the *Stoneham Weekly News*."

"I'm afraid that's exactly what I was doing. Unfortunately some people believed every word. A few even came here to gawk at me."

"Don't judge the whole village by a couple of jerks." He changed the subject. "We still on for tomorrow?"

"I wouldn't miss it. Just give me the time and place."

"I know you need to open at noon. Is nine o'clock too early?"

"Not at all."

"Great." Mike pulled a piece of paper from his jacket pocket. "Here's the address. Do you need directions?"

Tricia glanced at the paper. "No, I've driven through this neighborhood before. Very nice houses."

Mike's smile was wistful. "Yes. It's a shame I have to sell it. But Mother's care comes first."

Tricia nodded, remembering the pain of losing Christopher's father to dementia.

The bell over the door jangled as a fresh wave of customers entered the shop.

Mike stood. "I'd better make room for the onslaught." They stood for a moment, looking into each other's eyes, then Mike clasped her hands and drew her close, kissed her cheek. "See you tomorrow."

Surprised but pleased, Tricia watched Mike depart, even going so far as to follow his progress as he crossed the street to his new office and campaign headquarters. She did, however, move away from the window in case he turned. She didn't want him to know she'd been watching him.

At the coffee station, Ginny motioned for Tricia, then proffered the pot. "It

isn't even two o'clock and this is the last of the coffee. We're already out of cookies. Want me to go get more?"

Tricia shook her head. "Most of our sales today have been via credit card; we haven't got much cash in the till. I'll go get the supplies and be back within half an hour. Can you manage?"

"I'd be glad to help out if you need me," said Mr. Everett, coming up behind Tricia.

"I can't keep imposing on you."

"I like to feel useful," said the older gentleman.

"Go on," Ginny encouraged. "We'll be fine."

Tricia grabbed her purse, raincoat, and umbrella and ducked past the hoard of customers for a hasty exit. She waited for traffic to pass before crossing the street. Mr. Everett's help these last few days had been a blessing. As he was at the store on a daily basis, she wondered if she should offer him a part-time job. Her balance sheet was already in better shape than what she'd initially projected and as Ginny had Sundays off, he might be willing to help out then. Granted, it was a slow day, but she could always use his help for shelving new stock. It made perfect sense, and why hadn't she thought of it before?

The Coffee Bean was just as busy as Haven't Got a Clue, and Tricia took a number, noting there were at least eight customers ahead of her. Stoneham was really hopping on this bleak, late-summer afternoon.

To pass the time, Tricia distracted herself by examining the store's stock: coffee cups that ran the gamut from artful to sublimely silly, packets of gourmet cookies, petit fours, and chocolate in colorful wrappings, everything so beautifully packaged it enticed customers to spend. But she'd get her cookies from the village bakery—if they had anything left this late in the afternoon.

As Tricia read the list of ingredients on a box of Green Mountain chocolates, she began to feel closed in. Looking up, she saw editor Russ Smith was standing well within her personal space. "Excuse me," she said, stepping aside.

"I understand you weren't happy with my article," he said without preamble.

"Who would be?"

"I owe it to my readers to—"

"Act like a tabloid journalist?"

His eyes flashed. "That's uncalled for."

"So was painting me as a murderer—and without even circumstantial evidence." Heads turned at her words. She lowered her voice. "I don't think this is the place to discuss this."

"Then how about dinner. Are you free tonight?"

Tricia blinked. "You've got to be kidding."

Smith's gaze was level. "No, I'm not. We could discuss the story, and perhaps a follow-up—among other things."

Tricia replaced the box of chocolates on the shelf. "I don't think so."

"I'm not your enemy."

"And after what you wrote about me, you're not my friend, either."

"Number forty-seven," the salesclerk called out.

Tricia glanced down at the crushed ticket in her hand. "If you'll excuse me, Mr. Smith." She elbowed her way through the other customers and placed her order, all the time feeling Russ Smith's gaze on her back.

DODGING THE RAINDROPS, Tricia clutched her bags of coffee and cookies and hurried down the sidewalk. The big, green Kelly Realty FOR RENT sign was gone from the front window of the Cookery. The door stood ajar and the lights blazed. Poking her head inside, Tricia called, "Deirdre?" A woman in a baggy red flannel shirt and dark slacks, with a blue bandana tied around her hair, turned from her perch on a ten-foot ladder. In her hand she clasped a soapy sponge. A six-foot-square patch of wall had already been scrubbed of soot, showing creamy yellow paint once again.

"You shouldn't be doing that," Tricia admonished. A fall for a woman Deirdre's age could send her to a nursing home—or worse.

"It's got to be done," Deirdre said, in the same no-nonsense voice as her dead sister.

"But surely Bob Kelly ought to be paying someone to do it."

Deirdre dropped the sponge into a bucket and carefully stepped down off the ladder. "We came to an agreement on other more important things." The hint of a smile played at her lips. Perhaps she was a harder bargainer than Doris had been, which had been the reason for Bob's sour mood the evening before.

"How soon do you think you'll reopen?"

"Possibly a week. Then I think I'll hold a grand reopening the first week in October. Doris had already lined up an author signing for that week. It should work out nicely."

"But what about the smoke-damaged stock? It'll take weeks to restore them, and surely some of them won't be salvageable."

"I've got an expert coming in on Monday. Meanwhile there're hundreds of boxes in the storeroom upstairs, which thankfully Mr. Kelly neglected to clear out, and there's a room of excess stock at Doris's house. We'll start with that and fill in with newer titles until we replenish our supply of rare and used books."

"We?" Tricia asked.

Deirdre frowned, her gaze dipping. "Excuse me. I can't help talking about

Doris and myself as though we'll always be together. She was my twin. When we were younger we were so very close she used to swear we could read each other's minds."

Tricia felt a pang of envy laced with guilt. She'd never felt that way about Angelica. "It sounds like you've had experience running a shop before."

"I was an accountant until last winter, but I heard so much about the Cookery from Doris I always felt I could step into her shoes and run it at a moment's notice. And now I have." She pursed her lips and swallowed.

Tricia considered carefully before voicing her next question. "Have you made any arrangements for Doris?"

Deirdre's expression hardened. "There will be no service, if that's what you mean. She told me she had no friends here in Stoneham. If there's one thing she hated, it was hypocrisy. I couldn't bear to hear platitudes and regrets from people who had no time for Doris during her life."

Ouch—that stung, but Tricia couldn't blame the woman. No doubt Deirdre would grieve for her sister in her own way and time.

"Have you had a chance to visit with your niece?"

Deirdre shook her head. "Her counselor doesn't seem to think it's a good idea. Doris and I looked so much alike it would only confuse her."

"I was very surprised to hear Doris even had a child."

"How was it you found out?" Deirdre asked.

Again, Tricia adopted an innocent stare. "I can't for the life of me remember. It must've been hard on her—being a single mother with a special child."

"You can call Susan retarded. It doesn't offend me, and it didn't offend Doris."

Tricia wasn't sure what to say.

Deirdre averted her gaze. "Being pregnant out of wedlock was one thing; keeping a Down syndrome child was another. Our family abandoned Doris. All except me," she amended. "I was the only one who cared about poor Doris. The world in general"—she turned back to Tricia—"and Stoneham in particular—always treated Doris shabbily."

"Is that what she told you?"

"It's what I observed. But yes, she did tell me that. We were very close."

"I can't say as I recall seeing you here in Stoneham before this week."

"I was not a regular visitor. We kept in touch by phone." Deirdre turned her back on Tricia, picked up her sponge, and began wiping the grimy wall once again. "Is it my imagination, or is this conversation turning into an interrogation?" She looked over her shoulder with a hard-eyed stare.

"I'm sorry. I was merely curious." Tricia changed the subject. "Tomorrow I'll be looking at a private collection of books; the owner is eager to sell. I'd be glad to look out for any cookbooks."

Spine still rigid, Deirdre gave a curt nod. "Thank you, Ms.—?"

"Call me Tricia. After all, we are neighbors."

Deirdre nodded and stepped closer to the ladder. "I must get back to work if I'm going to reopen next week. Thank you for stopping by."

Tricia knew a dismissal when she heard it. She gave a quick "Good-bye," and headed out the door.

Soft, mellow jazz issued from Haven't Got a Clue's speakers as Tricia reentered the store. Stationed at the sales counter, Ginny flipped the pages of a magazine, while sitting in the nook. Mr. Everett's nose was buried in a book without a dust jacket. Tricia hung up her coat, stowed her umbrella and purse, and headed for the coffee station, where she made a fresh pot and set out a new plate of cookies before heading for the sales counter.

Ginny looked up from her reading, quickly closing the big, fat magazine and turning it over. Tricia leaned close. "What would you think about me asking Mr. Everett to come work for us?"

Ginny's gaze slid to the closed magazine and then up again. "What a great idea. I've always felt bad about you being all by yourself here on Sundays. Business is good and he sure knows his mystery authors. Go for it."

Tricia caught sight of the magazine's name on the spine: *Bride's World.* Was there a wedding in Ginny's future? She nodded and smiled at the thought, also happy Ginny approved of her decision.

Tricia approached the elderly gent. "Mr. Everett?" He made to stand, but Tricia motioned him to stay put and took the seat opposite him. "Mr. Everett," she began again. "You've become a bit of a fixture here at Haven't Got a Clue."

Mr. Everett's eyes widened, his mouth dropping open in alarm. "I don't mean to be a pest, Ms. Miles. I won't take any more of your coffee and cookies, I promise—"

It was Tricia's turn to be alarmed. "Oh no—you misunderstand me. I'm not trying to throw you out. I'd like to offer you a job, Mr. Everett."

Alarm turned to shock. "A job? Me? But what can I do?"

"Sell books. You're very good at it. You know as much as I do—and probably a whole lot more—about our merchandise, and goodness knows you're dependable about showing up every day."

Color flushed the old man's cheeks. "A job?" he murmured in what sounded like disbelief.

"I won't ask you to lift heavy boxes, and your hours would be flexible, but you've already proved to be an asset to Ginny and me when the store is busy. I can't offer you a lot of money, and unfortunately I'm not in a position to give benefits of any kind, but—"

"A job—" he repeated, as though warming to the idea.

"I'd be glad to give you a couple of days to think it over. You wouldn't have to give me your answer until—"

Mr. Everett suddenly stood, a fire lighting his bright eyes. "No need for that. When do you want me to start?"

Tricia laughed. "How about an hour ago?"

The old man's lips quivered, his eyes growing moist. "Thank you. Thank you, Ms. Miles." He shook himself, then his head swiveled back and forth. "What do you want me to do first? The back shelves are in a terrible state. Customers have no sense of order. They take books out and then put them back every which way. Or I could rearrange the biographies in chronological order, versus alphabetical, so that customers would have a better understanding of how the genre grew. Perhaps it should have been done long before this."

Tricia stifled a laugh. "I'm glad you have so many good ideas. But right now I have a different kind of request. Would you be willing to go next door and make sure Ms. Gleason doesn't fall off a ladder? I don't want you to do anything that puts you in a position of getting hurt yourself, but just make sure she doesn't hurt herself in trying to get ready to reopen her sister's store."

"I could do that," he said, sounding less than enthused.

"Great. And tomorrow we'll figure out what your regular hours and duties will be."

Mr. Everett held out his hand. Tricia took it. "Thank you, Ms. Miles. Thank you for making an old man feel useful again. I'll go next door right now and make sure Ms. Gleason stays safe."

"Thank you."

Mr. Everett started for the door, which opened, admitting Angelica, who paused in the entryway, barring Mr. Everett's escape. They did a little dance with muttered "sorry's" and "excuse me's" while they tried to maneuver out of one another's way. At last Angelica stepped over to where Tricia still stood in the nook.

"I've never been here when the store was open," she said, without even a hello. She took in the clusters of browsing shoppers and Ginny at the register waiting on a customer with a stack of books. Angelica nodded approvingly. "You've created a nice atmosphere here, Trish. And it doesn't stink of old paper like some used bookstores do, either."

Trust Angelica to spoil a compliment. "Thank you. I think. What brings you here so early?"

Angelica picked up one of the well-thumbed review magazines. "I wanted to let you know I can't fix dinner tonight."

Tricia hated to admit it, but in only three days she'd come to enjoy and look forward to one of Angelica's delicious entrées. "What's up?"

Angelica actually blushed. "I've got a date."

Tricia's stomach tightened. "Not with Bob Kelly."

"But of course. I haven't met any other eligible men in this burg."

"Where is he taking you?"

"Some divine little bistro called Ed's. I hear they've got the best seafood and that it's charmingly intimate."

"Charming for sure," Tricia admitted. Intimate as in small. But she didn't want to spoil her sister's anticipation.

"You've been there?"

She nodded. "The food is very good." An idea came to her: Bob and Angelica, dinner, a relaxed social atmosphere . . . "Ange, when you're with Bob tonight, see if you can get him to spill where he went after he left us at the Brookview on Tuesday night."

"I will not," she said sharply.

"Why? Don't you want to help prove me innocent?"

"Of course, but I also don't believe Bob killed the woman."

"Ange, please?" Tricia found herself whining.

Angelica turned away, refusing to meet her sister's gaze, and glanced out the front window and at the street beyond. "I'll think about it."

A couple of women walked past, clutching shopping bags, but they didn't enter Haven't Got a Clue.

"I circled the block three times before I gave up and parked in the municipal lot," Angelica said, annoyed. "Who owns that car out front with the Connecticut license plates? They've been hogging that spot all morning. Surely you have parking restrictions along the main drag during business hours."

Tricia hadn't noticed the car. "The sheriff's department is pretty busy these days; at least I hope they're busy trying to solve Doris Gleason's murder."

"Mmm," Angelica muttered, her attention still on the offending vehicle. "That's the third or fourth time I've seen it."

"Excuse me, miss, could you help me?" asked a middle-aged woman, clutching a handwritten list. "I'm looking for *Murder with Malice*, by Nicholas Blake. Do you have a copy?"

Tricia gave the customer her full attention. Angelica mouthed, "Later," and wandered off toward the back shelves.

Ginny popped a more lively CD into the player, and between them she and Tricia waited on four more customers who paid for their purchases. The crowd had thinned by the time a puzzled-looking Angelica stepped up to the counter, slapping a booklet onto the glass top. "What are you doing with an old cooking pamphlet on one of your shelves?"

Awestruck, Tricia gaped at the booklet's title: *American Cookery*, by Amelia Simmons. "Good grief, it's the book that was stolen when Doris was murdered."

ELEVEN

Curious onlookers lurking under umbrellas peered through the plate-glass windows of Haven't Got a Clue, the closed sign and locked door did nothing to deter them from rubbernecking. And despite the lack of customers, the shop seemed crowded with Sheriff Adams, a deputy, Angelica, Ginny, and Tricia, as well as Deirdre Gleason and Mr. Everett, who'd followed along after Ginny had called Deirdre over.

Sheriff Adams's piercing glare was fixed on Tricia. "I thought you said this thing was a book?"

Tricia looked down at the little booklet. "Technically, it is. Its significance is undisputed in the evolution of American cookery books. It's condition and rarity make it extremely valuable."

"This can't be worth ten grand," the sheriff said, poking the pamphlet with the eraser end of a pencil, unconvinced.

"Oh yes, it can," Ginny chirped up. "I looked it up online."

The sheriff shook her head, then took in the four women standing around the sales counter. "Who's touched the *book* since it was found?"

Tricia looked sidelong at her sister, but didn't answer.

The quiet lengthened. "Okay, it was me," an exasperated Angelica said, crossing her arms across her chest. "And what's the big deal anyway?"

"You might've obliterated whatever incriminating fingerprints were on it," the sheriff muttered.

"Oh, don't go all *CSI* on me. Whoever stole that little pamphlet probably wiped it clean before they dumped it here."

"Ange," Tricia warned.

The sheriff turned her scrutiny back to Tricia. "It's very odd that the person who found Ms. Gleason's body should now possess the stolen book."

"And not at all coincidental, if someone is trying to implicate my sister as Doris's killer," Angelica said, her voice rising. "And do we even know this is the same book?"

The sheriff turned to Tricia for the answer. "Given its rarity, it's unlikely there'd be two copies of it in a town this size. And, Sheriff, I assure you I have no idea how it ended up in my store, but I'm not responsible."

"Any ideas on who might be?"

If she had, she certainly would've volunteered that information before now. Tricia shook her head, fought to stay calm. "People wander in and out of here all day long, most of them strangers. Anyone could've planted that book here."

"But it's not likely Ms. Gleason would've let a stranger into her shop after hours."

"She was expecting someone," Tricia reminded the sheriff. "Bob Kelly."

"Trish." It was Angelica's turn to scold.

Sheriff Adams threw back her head and straightened to her full height. "Mr. Kelly has accounted for his whereabouts at the time of Ms. Gleason's death. I'm satisfied with his answers."

It was all Tricia could do not to blurt, "Yeah, but—" The way the sheriff kept glowering at her reinforced her fear that she remained the prime suspect.

"Why wasn't I told my sister expected Bob Kelly on the night of her death?" Deirdre demanded.

"I saw no need to upset you. And as I've just told Ms. Miles here, I don't suspect him."

"And why not? He was determined to force my sister out. The way he cleaned out the store less than forty-eight hours after her death is proof positive."

Sheriff Adams pointed a finger of warning at Deirdre. "This discussion is closed." She looked over her shoulder at the young deputy standing behind them. "Placer, take this 'book' to the office and lock it up. We'll send it to the state crime lab first thing Monday morning."

The uniformed officer stepped forward with what looked like a tackle box, which he opened, and took out a pair of latex gloves. He withdrew a paper evidence bag, shook it open, and picked up the booklet. A yellowed note card fell from it, hitting the carpeted floor.

"What's that?" Angelica asked, bending down.

"Looks like a birthday card," Tricia said.

"Don't touch it," the sheriff warned. "Placer?"

The deputy elbowed his way in and picked up the card, setting it and the booklet back on the counter before stepping aside. The five women crowded around, silently studying the front of the card, with its old-fashioned font and the image of a dozen red roses, the colors muted by the yellowing paper. "Happy Birthday, to my dear wife," Angelica read.

"Open it up," the sheriff said.

Ginny stepped back so the deputy, with his gloved hands, could do so. The text in black was the usual syrupy wishes for a happy day; it was the peacock-blue-inked script that drew them in. "To my dearest Letty, Happy Birthday, love Roddy."

"What kind of a name is Letty?" Ginny asked.

"Letitia comes to mind. Or it could be short for something else," Tricia suggested. She raised her gaze. "Anybody in town named Letitia or Letty?"

The sheriff shook her head. "Not that I know of. And I've lived here my whole life."

They watched as the deputy carefully placed the book into a paper evidence bag, then put the card in another. With a curt nod to his boss, the officer headed out the door to his double-parked cruiser.

"That book is worth a lot of money. With my sister's passing, it now belongs to me," Deirdre asserted.

"It's part of a criminal investigation," the sheriff said.

"Will I ever get it back?"

"Possibly. But these things take time. Sometimes years."

"Years?" Deirdre repeated, appalled.

"Just what are you going to do to the book?" Ginny asked.

The sheriff bristled. "Normal procedure."

"Wait a minute," Tricia said. "Subjecting that book to black magnetic powder or ninhydrin would ruin it. I suppose iodine fuming might work. It develops prints beautifully. They'd just have to be photographed, not lifted, but it should spare the book. Then again, all that humidity." She shook her head. "CrimeScope. That's the book's best option, though on a porous surface like paper, it might not show a viable fingerprint, either."

"How do you know so much?" Sheriff Adams asked, suspicious.

Tricia waved a hand, taking in the thousands of books on the shelves around them. "I deal in mystery fiction. Not only do I read the classics, I read contemporary authors like Patricia Cornwell, Kathy Reichs, and Elizabeth Becka. You can practically get a degree in forensics just by reading these top authors. But that doesn't change the fact that it's likely only Angelica's prints are on the book, anyway."

"I want a receipt for it," Deirdre said. The sheriff just about rolled her eyes, and Deirdre snorted in outrage. "If any harm comes to that book, I will not only sue the county sheriff's department, but you personally."

"Will you at least ask the state lab to take special care with it?" Tricia pressed.

"I'll ask, but I can't make any guarantees."

"And I can't guarantee I won't immediately speak to my lawyer, either," Deirdre said. "Now about that receipt—"

Tricia provided a pen and a piece of paper. The sheriff scribbled a few lines, handing the sheet to Deirdre, who gave Tricia a nod. "I appreciate you calling me over. Otherwise, I'm not even sure I'd have been told the book was found." She turned on her heel and stalked out the door.

Sheriff Adams was the next to leave, following Deirdre without even a good-bye.

Angelica scowled. "I thought people from New Hampshire were supposed to be extra nice. Isn't that the state motto? Be nice or die?"

"That's 'Live Free or Die,' and don't judge all of us by some people," Ginny said, then, "What am I saying? Sheriff Adams is a good person. I've just never known her to be so cold. She must be getting pressure from somewhere else, like maybe the village board."

"What should I do next, Ms. Miles?" asked Mr. Everett, who hadn't said a word during the entire conversation.

"Why don't you go back and help Deirdre? Ginny and I can manage here." He didn't look happy, but nodded anyway. She glanced up at the clock. Two hours until official closing. Although the onlookers had disappeared, there was no reason she had to stay closed. She followed Mr. Everett to the door, turning the sign back to OPEN, and shut the door behind him.

"I guess I should go, too. Have to get ready for my big date tonight," Angelica said brightly. Shouldering her enormous handbag, she fingered a wave, called, "Ciao," and she, too, was gone.

Tricia and Ginny exchanged glances. "I need a cup of coffee," Tricia said.

"I'd go for something stronger," Ginny muttered.

"Not during work hours—but I agree. Put something cheerful on the CD player and hope we get busy so we don't have to think about what we've just been through."

"You got it," Ginny said.

Tricia poured them both a cup of coffee while Ginny sorted through a stack of jewel boxes, selecting a jazz piano CD.

Peace now reigned, but forgetting the significance of finding that wretched booklet in her store wasn't going to be so easily accomplished.

THE HANDS ON the clock finally crawled around to closing time. Despite her hopes otherwise, very few customers had come in during the intervening hours and Tricia and Ginny had completed all their end-of-day tasks, save for counting the receipts. Mr. Everett had checked in, assuring Tricia that Deirdre had left the Cookery for the day, then he, too, departed. Miss Marple sat patiently at the door to the stairs, anticipating her evening routine.

Ginny grabbed her coat and purse from the back closet and headed for the exit. "Night, Trish."

The door opened before she could grasp the handle. Russ Smith stood in the open doorway. "Are you closed?"

"Yes," Ginny said emphatically.

"Not quite," Tricia said. "How can I help you?" Her tone was civil, but cool.

"Want me to stay?" Ginny asked.

Tricia shook her head. "Go on. Have a nice day off. See you Monday."

Ginny looked uncertain, but Tricia waved her off. "It's okay. Now scoot."

As the door closed behind her, Russ walked up to the counter. Shoving his hands in his trouser pockets, he gave the shop the once-over. "I seem to be your last customer."

"Yes, and you're keeping me from my dinner."

"As I recall, I invited you out."

"And as I recall, I turned you down. Come on, you're only here because you heard the book stolen from Doris Gleason's store was found here earlier today."

"Actually, I *didn't* know that, but thank you for sharing. The special over at the diner is meat loaf and real mashed potatoes."

"How do you know they're real?"

"I wasn't always a small-time reporter. I worked the Boston crime beat for years. And besides, I've seen the peels in their garbage."

Tricia's stomach growled, betraying her.

"See, at least part of you wants to go with me. And what's your alternative: a peanut butter sandwich?"

Had he been scoping out her cupboards and fridge? And although she'd neglected her paperwork for days and needed to catch up, the truth was she really didn't want to be alone tonight and cursed Angelica for having a date.

"Okay," she agreed, "but only if we go Dutch."

Russ shrugged. "Saves me eight-ninety-nine plus tax and tip."

Already Tricia regretted her decision, yet she locked the cash drawer, pocketing the keys. "I have to feed my cat before I can go."

"Do what you gotta do," he said and flopped down into one of the nook's chairs. "I'll wait."

THE WALK TO the Bookshelf Diner had been silent. At least the rain had stopped, but a voice in Tricia's head kept up a litany of "big mistake, big mistake" with every step along the damp pavement.

Russ held the door open for her. A sign on the metal floor stand said SEAT YOURSELF. With only two other booths occupied, they had their pick of the place. Heads turned as the village jinx walked down the aisle, but Tricia aimed for the back of the restaurant with her head held high. She slid across the last booth's red Naugahyde seat and shrugged out of her jacket, folding it and placing it next to her. Russ hung his on a peg and sat down.

A college-age waitress with a quick smile, a pierced brow, and a name tag that said "Eugenia" handed them menus and took their drink orders before disappearing.

Tricia eyed her surroundings. The name over the door did not match the décor. The only books in the Bookshelf Diner were of the trompe l'oeil variety—and then on a commercial wall covering. The waitress returned, setting the stemmed glass down in front of Tricia and pouring coffee for Russ. After quickly consulting the menu she did order the meat loaf, then practically gulped the well-deserved glass of red wine.

"Tough day, huh?" Russ asked.

"I've had better. And I don't want to talk about it."

"Why should you? The sheriff suspects you of murder. I'm sure it's just lack of motive that's keeping her from locking you up. She'll have to turn up the heat after finding that book in your store."

"She did not find it. My sister did."

"Then she's not doing you any favors, either."

Tricia snatched up her glass, gulping down the rest of her wine, then let it smack back down on the table. "I barely knew Doris Gleason. She argued with Bob Kelly, had an appointment to see him on the night she was murdered. He wanted her out of that store, which is at least a credible motive for murder. He left the Brookview Inn before Ange and I did, but he didn't show up at the Cookery until more than an hour after I found Doris dead. Where was he during that time?"

"You tell me."

"He could have murdered Doris, then showed up later feigning no knowledge."

Russ sat back, folded his arms across his chest. "If I was you, I'd quit harping on Bob Kelly as a possible suspect. For one thing, he would've never started the fire at the Cookery and put his property at risk just to get rid of a tenant. And even so, it wouldn't matter if he were caught plunging the knife in the victim's back. Most people around here consider him a savior for how he almost single-handedly brought Stoneham back to life."

"So someone like me, who's innocent, should take the blame?"

"I didn't say that. But in the sheriff's eyes, so far you are the only 'person of note.'"

Tricia picked up her glass, signaling the waitress for a refill. "I did not kill Doris Gleason. I had no reason to kill Doris Gleason."

Heads turned at the sound of her words.

"I'd start looking for reasons why others might've wanted her dead."

"That isn't my job. You said you were once a big-time reporter; isn't there at

least a shred of Clark Kent left inside you? Why don't you take up the challenge, or at least direct one of your minions to do it?"

"Honey, I have a staff of two, one of which spends her time soliciting ads to keep us afloat. My chief reporter is a soccer mom who writes most of her copy after her kids go to bed. I do everything else. You own a small business—you know the drill."

"Do I ever."

The waitress returned with another glass of wine and their dinners.

Russ picked up his fork and stabbed at his mashed potatoes. "Besides, you run a mystery bookstore. You've probably read enough of them to get you started. In fact, you may already have bits and pieces of knowledge about the murder you haven't yet put together. I'd be happy to brainstorm with you about it."

"You'd be the last person I'd bare my soul to. I'd see whatever I tell you in next Friday's edition. It's just as likely whoever killed Doris was a transient. Someone who'd canvassed the Cookery, figured any book worth locking up would be of value, killed Doris, and stole it." She took another sip from her glass.

"Is that you or the wine talking? Don't kid yourself. The fact that book was found in your store means someone wants you to take the blame. You can either keep wandering around in denial or ask yourself some tough questions: like who wants you out of the picture and why?"

TWELVE

When the check arrived, Tricia and Russ ponied up their shares, donned their jackets, and headed for the exit. The wind had picked up and the clouds had departed, leaving the sky clear and star-strewn. "Walk you home?" Russ offered.

They stood outside the Bookshelf Diner. Tricia buttoned her jacket. "I'm not afraid of the dark. And besides, Stoneham is safe."

"I believed that a week ago," he said. "Now I'm not so sure."

Tricia looked down the street and saw the flashing lights of a police cruiser. "Now what?" She started walking, heading south down the sidewalk at a brisk pace.

"Looks like it's parked outside the Cookery," Russ said, as he struggled to keep up with her.

It was, but a deputy stood outside Haven't Got a Clue. Tricia broke into a run, crossed the street, and practically skidded to a halt in front of her shop.

The large plate-glass window now sported a gaping hole in its center, with cracks radiating from it in a sunburst array. Inside the shop, what was left of her security system wailed.

"You wanna shut that thing off?" She didn't recognize the deputy, whose name tag read PLACER.

Heart pounding, Tricia fumbled for her key, unlocked the door, and flipped on the light switch. Seconds later, she'd disarmed the alarm and quiet descended. She joined the deputy on the sidewalk. "What happened?" she asked, breathless.

"Looks like a rock," he said, peering into the hole.

Tricia frowned at his blasé attitude. Glass covered Tricia's display of Ross Macdonald's books. Several people had turned up, rubbernecking from behind the back of a parked car.

"So what's the story, Jim?" Russ asked Placer.

"Just what it looks like, petty vandalism."

"How can you be sure?" Tricia asked. "A woman was killed right next door just days ago. This could be tied in."

The deputy shook his head, turned his attention to the clipboard he held and the report he'd already started to fill in. "Probably just kids."

"Did anybody see anything?" Tricia called to the unfamiliar faces in the gathering crowd, but they all shook their heads, huddling in their coats and jackets.

Placer handed Tricia a business card. "These guys can board up the window until you can get it fixed. You want me to hang around until then?" He couldn't have sounded more bored.

"Wait a minute. Aren't you going to check out the shop?"

"The door was locked—you opened it yourself. Did you see any other damage or anything missing?"

"I've hardly had a chance to look."

"So look," he said and turned his attention back to his clipboard.

Tricia threw Russ a glance, as if to ask if this was the way all law enforcement acted in Stoneham. He shrugged.

Tricia reentered her store, doing a quick walk-through. Save for the gaping hole in her window, everything seemed just as she'd left it a little over an hour before. The door to the stairs was still closed. The alarm would've sounded in the apartment, too. Poor Miss Marple was probably hiding under the bed, terrified.

Russ stood inside the doorway. "Want me to go upstairs with you, make sure everything's okay? I got Jim to promise he'd hang around at least another five minutes."

"If you wouldn't mind, thank you."

Tricia opened the door, threw the switch to bathe the stairwell with light,

and bounded up. The door to the second-floor storeroom was locked, just as she'd left it. Still, she took out the key, opened it, and groped for the light switch and entered. Nothing looked out of place in the cavernous room full of stacked boxes—all of them containing books. She closed and locked the door.

Russ was behind her as she started up the stairs once again. The door to her loft apartment was unlocked and she quickly decided to amend her own personal security measures in the future. She'd left a light on for Miss Marple, but the cat was nowhere in sight.

"Miss Marple. Miss Marple!" she called. Sure enough, a pair of frightened green eyes appeared when Tricia lifted the bed's dust ruffle. She reached for the cat, scooping her into her arms. "Oh, you poor little thing," she cooed, as she struggled to her feet.

She found Russ standing in the middle of her kitchen. "Everything okay?"

"Yes, thank goodness." Miss Marple had already engaged her motor and nuzzled Tricia's chin, purring loudly. "She was just frightened."

Russ smiled. "I'll go downstairs and keep watch. Why don't you call the guys to cover the window?"

"Good idea. But first, I think someone deserves a treat." At the sound of the magic word, Miss Marple wriggled to get down and Tricia placed her on the floor. She spilled half a packet of kitty cookies into Miss Marple's bowl, knowing she'd only toss most of them later. But at that moment, she didn't care.

The board-up service the deputy recommended was available twenty-four/seven and promised Tricia someone would be there within the hour. Next up, a call to her security company. They weren't as helpful, saying a service rep *might* be by bright and early Monday morning. No more chances, Tricia decided. It was time to find another security company.

Miss Marple had had her fill of cookies and had settled on one of the breakfast bar's chairs, ready for a nap by the time Tricia headed back downstairs to the store.

Russ had closed the shop's door and the crowd had dispersed. He sat in the nook, reading an article in *CrimeSpree* magazine. He looked up as she approached. "Everything okay?"

She nodded.

Russ stood. "Seems like all I've asked you for the last hour is 'everything okay?'"

For the first time since she'd seen the cruiser's flashing lights, Tricia smiled. "The enclosure company will be here pretty soon. They said not to bother to sweep up the glass, they'd clean up everything. If the window's a standard size, they can have it replaced first thing Monday morning. They'll even take care of the insurance claim."

"Can't beat that for service." He handed her a paper that had been sitting on the nook's coffee table. "Here's the police report. And what about your security system?"

"That's another matter. I may have it back up on Monday, but I'm not going to bet on it."

"Should you stay here without it working?"

"I'll be all right. Besides, I can always hide under the bed with my cat."

"I'm serious, Tricia. Someone's trying to make you look responsible for Doris Gleason's death, and now this."

"There's no proof the two events are connected."

"That's not what you said to the deputy. Do you have a girlfriend or a relative you can stay with tonight?"

Tricia thought about Angelica, remembered she had a date with Bob, and immediately nixed that idea. "I'll be fine."

"I've got a guest room," Russ offered. "It's got a lock on the door."

"That's very kind, but—" She shook her head, thinking of the logistics of moving Miss Marple. Food and water bowls, toys, litter box . . .

The conversation lagged. "You don't have to stay, Russ. I'll be all right until the repair guys get here."

"No way," he said. "I want to prove to you that chivalry isn't dead in Stoneham."

Tricia almost laughed, considering the article he'd published on her only the day before. Still, she wasn't about to turn down an act of kindness. "At least let me offer you a cup of coffee while we wait."

"I'll take you up on it."

Russ retreated to the nook and his magazine while Tricia made coffee. Her gaze kept returning to the broken window, which a gale seemed to be blowing through. The rock, quite a hefty specimen, had crashed through *her* window—no one else's. Whoever had thrown it had had to have the strength to do it. Her chief suspect in Doris's murder was on a date with Angelica.

Who else wanted to frighten her?

LIGHT FROM THE streetlamps outside was all that lit Tricia's bedroom. Sleep had not come and she'd been staring at the glowing red numerals on her bedside clock for almost two hours while Miss Marple, curled beside her on the comforter, snored quietly.

Tricia's thoughts followed a circular track: *Doris dead: someone wants to blame me. Rock through window: someone out to get me.*

She'd taken her security for granted in this quiet little village. Five years ago

she'd led a much different life. Until her divorce, she'd never revealed her desire to open a mystery bookshop. She'd lived the life of a stockbroker's wife, had a gorgeous apartment overlooking Central Park West, spent many an evening at five-star restaurants and the theater, her days filled with . . . not much since the nonprofit agency she'd worked for since college had downsized staff. But she'd loved Christopher and the life they'd shared, even if he worked much too hard.

And then everything changed.

Christopher changed. Wanted a simpler life. A life that didn't include responsibilities . . . or a wife.

And yet . . . somehow they'd remained friends. And right now she wanted to hear the sound of a friendly voice.

On impulse, Tricia picked up the receiver on her bedside phone, punched in the number she'd memorized but so far hadn't used.

The phone rang four times before a sleepy voice answered, "—llo?"

"Christopher?"

Long seconds of silence.

"Tricia?"

She sagged against her pillows. "It's me."

"What time is it?"

"After one. Oh, wait—that's eleven your time. You go to bed early these days."

"It's all that fresh air. There's nothing like it." She could hear the unspoken *should've done this years ago.* "What's wrong?"

"Can't a friend call a friend without something being wrong?"

"Trish," he admonished.

She sighed. "Someone threw a rock through my shop window tonight."

"What?"

"And my neighbor was murdered on Tuesday." She left out the part that she was the main suspect.

"You're not serious," he said, no longer sounding sleepy.

"It's all true."

"All those years in Manhattan without a problem, and you move to a small town in New England to find chaos."

"Could only happen to me, right?" she said, but the laugh that accompanied it was forced.

"I can't just come over and make it right for you."

"I know. I wouldn't expect you to. It's just . . ." She reached out, petted her cat, who began to purr. "Miss Marple misses you."

"I miss her, too."

She dared speak the words she'd been afraid to ask. "Are you with anybody?"

"Nobody could live up to you."

"Then why . . . ?" she asked, the hurt bubbling up once again. He didn't answer, hadn't had a real answer the day he'd announced his decision to leave. "I didn't want a divorce. We could've worked things out."

"No. I wasn't going to drag you down with me. You're too special for that, my girl."

But Tricia knew she would never be his girl again. "Are you happy?"

"Yeah. I am. It's a much different life. It's not something you'd enjoy. You need people. Stimulation. Tell me, were you happy before Tuesday, before all this crap happened?"

"Yes," she answered without hesitation. Admitting that did make her feel a bit better.

"When things calm down, you'll feel happy again."

"Angelica's visiting. She says she wants to move to Stoneham."

"Scratch that, then," he said, which made her laugh. That's why she'd called. Some part of her had known he'd make her laugh.

"It'll be okay, Trish. You're strong and you'll get through whatever's going on. You'll be fine."

"You promise?"

"Yes. Now close your eyes and dream about something wonderful. Like a cheese blintz."

Tricia couldn't help but smile. "I take it they're hard to find in the wilds of Colorado."

"You got it, sweetheart."

She laughed again. "Thank you for picking up the phone. I'm sorry I woke you."

"You know you can call me anytime."

It was time to hang up and actually doing it was proving harder than she'd anticipated. Saying what she had to say would be even more difficult. "Good-bye, Christopher."

"Good-bye, Trish."

Tricia carefully replaced the phone in its cradle, knowing she would never call him again.

THIRTEEN

Tricia inspected her makeup in the mirror over the bathroom sink. After three attempts to cover the dark circles beneath her eyes with concealer, she admitted defeat and set the little tube aside. Talking to Christopher hadn't settled her nerves, and Russ Smith's words of warning the evening before had stayed with her, keeping her from yet another decent night's sleep.

She'd come to no conclusions during her tossing and turning, grateful she could spare no time this morning to ponder the situation. Still, she took another moment to assess herself in the full-length mirror on the back of the door, wanting to look nice for Mike. She'd chosen the peach sweater set over beige slacks. With the days growing shorter, she'd soon put it away for darker fall colors. The idea of winter setting in and the possibility of spending it in the New Hampshire State Prison for Women did more than depress her.

I will not think about it, I will not think about it. And despite his chivalry after the rock incident, she cursed Russ for even hinting at the possibility she could end up in jail.

Out in the kitchen, Miss Marple rubbed her little gray body against the door leading to the stairs and the store below. "It's Sunday," Tricia told her, and took one last sip of her tepid coffee before dumping it in the sink. "You don't need to go to work until noon." But the cat would not be dissuaded.

Tricia grabbed her coat from the tree and snagged her purse and keys.

The phone rang. Who on earth would be calling so early on a Sunday morning?

Miss Marple stood up, scratched the door, and cried piteously. Tricia unlocked and opened it for her. The phone rang again as the cat scampered down the stairs. Tricia snatched it on the third ring. "Hello?"

"Tricia, it's Angelica. What took you so long to answer?"

"I was almost out the door," she said, balancing the phone on her shoulder as she struggled into her jacket sleeves.

"I thought the store opened late today."

"It does. I'm going out to evaluate a private collection. Can this wait until later? I'm going to be late."

"Wait! I just heard about your store being vandalized. Are you okay?"

"Of course," she lied. "I'm perfectly fine. Why wouldn't I be?"

"There's a murderer running around Stoneham, and now someone's targeted you—maybe the same person."

"Don't be so melodramatic. It was only a window; it'll be replaced tomorrow. Besides, I wasn't even in the building at the time."

"Are you opening the store today?"

"Definitely. But as I said, I've got to head out right now or I'll be late."

"I think you should close the store and come house hunting with me today."

"You know I can't. There are at least two buses coming through this afternoon."

"Well, at least you close early, don't you?"

"At three."

"Fine. By then I'll have looked at two or three properties. If I find one I like, I'll want your opinion."

That was a first. Tricia couldn't remember her sister ever consulting her on anything, be it a brand of designer shoes or the ripeness of a banana. For some reason, it pleased her. "Okay. Who's driving, you or me?"

"Me."

"All right. See you at three."

"Be careful," Angelica warned.

Tricia hung up the phone to find an annoyed Miss Marple sitting at her heels. "You know perfectly well there's a door at the bottom of the stairs and that it's closed until I open it."

Miss Marple stood and swaggered back to the open doorway. Tricia grabbed her purse once again and followed.

The Harris homestead was a lovely pseudo-Tudor nestled in a quaint, upscale neighborhood with mature trees and professional landscaping.

Tricia parked her car at the curb, noting Mike's sleek black Jag sat under a massive maple, its highest leaves just beginning to turn gold. The remnants of a now-untended garden rimmed the front of the buff-colored, stucco-faced house. A sense of recent abandonment clung to the property. Mike probably had his own home to take care of, and the house was huge, much too big for one person—especially someone with the beginnings of Alzheimer's disease. Poor Mrs. Harris.

Tricia pressed the doorbell and heard a resounding *bing-bong* from within. Moments later the heavy oak door swung open. "Welcome," Mike greeted, ushering her into an elegant foyer with its polished tile floor and matching floral wing chairs flanking a marble-topped mahogany table. To the left was a mag-

nificent staircase, with ornately carved banisters, that swept up to the second floor. Light streamed in through stained-glass panes of green and yellow diamonds, casting a warm glow on the carpeted steps.

"What a beautiful home," she said, wondering what other delights it might contain.

"Thanks. It was a nice place to grow up in. And as you can see, my parents took good care of it." He held out his hands. "Let me take your jacket. I've got a pot of coffee brewing in the kitchen. Can I get you a cup?"

"Yes, thanks," she said and shed her coat.

Mike took it from her and hung it in a closet off to the left at the base of the stairs. "How do you take it?"

"Milk or creamer only—no sugar."

"Coming right up. Most of the books are in the living room," he said, gesturing to his right. Go have a look—make yourself at home." He gave her an encouraging smile and took off down a dark hallway.

"Thanks," she called after him.

With Mike gone, an unnerving silence enveloped her. She took in a deep breath of stale air and wondered how long the house had been closed up.

Since she was there to see the books, Tricia figured she might as well get started and entered the living room through the opened French doors, where both chaos and order reigned. A stack of mismatched, taped cartons sat beside an empty curio cabinet just inside the doors, bald patches in the dust suggesting the shapes of the delicate objects that had once occupied it. Several seating arrangements compartmentalized the large room. Most of the furniture lay hidden beneath drop cloths, while other pieces, richly brocaded in shades of beige, were not. The carpet hadn't seen a vacuum cleaner in months. Rectangular patches on the walls hinted at where paintings, prints, or photographs had once hung.

Tricia picked her way across the room to the reading nook with its matching wide and inviting pillowed chairs and floor lamps, not unlike what she'd created for Haven't Got a Clue. The adjacent bookshelves stood on either side of a white painted mantel and drew her to them. It didn't take much imagination to conjure up an image of a sedate Mrs. Harris in her declining years, seated in one of the chairs before a roaring fire, book in hand, lost in its pages.

Now the room felt cold, empty. Without its mistress, the room—if not the home—had lost its soul.

Tricia shook away the image and retrieved her reading glasses from her purse, slipping them on to assess the titles. Mrs. Harris had eclectic taste in reading material, from mystery fiction to romances, biographies to travel books, as well as mainstream fiction and the classics, and she'd grouped them as such. Noticeable gaps on the shelves proved that the collection was not entirely intact.

She grabbed a mystery at random, *Deadly Honeymoon*, by Lawrence Block. It turned out to be a first edition with a mint condition dust cover. She'd sold a used, discarded library copy for eight dollars only a week before. This would bring much more. Checking the copyright dates on several other books was just as encouraging. Other titles by authors such as James Michener and Ann Morrow Lindbergh were also first editions. They'd be worth more signed, but were still valuable to die-hard collectors.

Mike reappeared with a tray containing two steaming mugs and a plate of Oreos, which he set on the dusty table in the nook. He handed her a mug. "So what do you think?"

"I'm no expert on most of what's here, but a lot appear to be first editions. That's always a plus."

"Could you give me a ballpark estimate on the whole lot?"

Tricia shook her head. "I shouldn't tell you this, but if you offer them to a dealer, you'll get substantially less than they're worth. Your best bet is to sell them on one of the online auction sites."

Mike frowned. "I figured as much."

"I see some of the books are already missing."

Mike's grip on his coffee mug tightened. "I gave them to friends of Mother's. At first I didn't realize they might be worth anything. I even considered boxing up the lot and taking them to Goodwill just for the tax write-off. Even then, I'd need an estimate on their worth—something I couldn't do."

"A lot of them may end up there anyway; for instance, the travel books and most of the paperbacks she has squirreled away. Unless of course she had some of the old pulp paperbacks from the forties and fifties. They're quite collectible if only for their lurid covers."

"Doesn't sound like Mother's cup of tea."

Tricia remembered her promise to Deirdre. "Did your mother have any cookbooks?"

"In the kitchen. Come on, I'll show you."

Tricia followed Mike down the dark hallway, past a formal dining room, and into a large airy kitchen, which hadn't seen a remodel since the 1970s. The harvest gold appliances and bicentennial patterned vinyl flooring, with 1776 stamped every few squares, seemed stuck in time. Then again, the oak table with stenciled Hitchcock chairs and the dark-stained woodwork were classic. Except for a layer of dust on just about everything, the room was tidy, the counters clutter free.

The hundred or more cookbooks resided in a glass-fronted double-doored cabinet above and between the sink and stove, no doubt to keep them grease free. Like in the living room, gaps on these shelves proved they had also stored

more than were currently there. Would all the other cupboards be empty as well? And what did it matter? Mike had said he was liquidating the estate to pay for his mother's health care. A pity that was necessary.

Tricia opened one of the doors, selecting a book at random and thumbing through to the copyright page. "The Cookery is in need of new stock because of smoke damage after the fire."

"The Cookery? I thought it was closed. I saw it had been emptied out and someone was cleaning the place yesterday. I assumed it was the new tenant."

"Doris Gleason had a sister. She's taking over the business and is looking for new stock. If you're going to dump these books anyway, you might consider offering them to Deirdre. Who knows, she might even vote for you in the election."

He laughed. "Thanks."

Tricia replaced the book, closing the cabinet. She turned to find Mike staring at her, or rather her bust. She pulled her long-sleeved sweater tighter about her, crossing her arms across her chest. "Goodness, our coffee's getting cold."

Mike seemed to shake himself. "Come on." He led the way back to the living room, and they resumed their places before the cold fireplace. Tricia picked up her mug, took a sip, and resigned herself to yet another cup of tepid coffee.

Mike grabbed a book at random from the closest shelf. A yellowed piece of paper jutted out of it, marking a place. He took out the paper and showed it to her: a recipe for Yankee bean soup torn from a magazine. "Still having problems with the propaganda leaflets?"

Tricia nodded, grateful for something else to talk about. "Yes. And you were right. The one I showed you was just the first in a series. They've stepped up to a direct advertising campaign. Ever hear of Full Moon Camp and Resort?"

"Can't say as I have," he said, crumpled the paper, and tossed it into the fireplace's maw. He replaced the book on the shelf.

"It gave a web address that said they were opening a new location next summer in southern New Hampshire, but it didn't specify where. I meant to call Bob Kelly about it, but with everything else that's been going on . . ."

Mike looked concerned. "Such as?"

"Didn't you hear about the rock through my window?"

"No. When did that happen?"

"About eight thirty last night."

"Huh. I was in my new office last night, unpacking. It must've happened after I left."

"What time was that?"

"Quarter after eight, maybe eight twenty."

Interesting.

Mike picked up his cup, swallowed a sip of cold coffee, and grimaced.

The conversation lagged.

"This really is a beautiful house," Tricia said finally.

"If you think this looks nice, you ought to see the bedrooms," he said à la Groucho Marx, and waggled his eyebrows for further effect. "I'd be glad to give you a personal tour."

Tricia's entire body tensed, but somehow she managed a weak smile. "Sorry, I can't stay too much longer."

"Your shop doesn't open for at least another two hours. That's plenty of time for us to get better acquainted," he said and moved a step closer.

Tricia's already tense muscles went rigid. "I have a new employee I'm training today."

"Oh?"

"Mr. Everett."

"Oh, the old coot who's taken root in your store."

"He's a treasure," she said, feeling protective of the old gentleman. "He'll be a great asset at Haven't Got a Clue."

Mike turned away and set his mug back down on the tray. "You seem to be collecting men these days."

Tricia blinked. "Excuse me?"

"Last night when I walked to the municipal lot to get in my car, I saw you at the diner with Russ Smith," Mike said, a slight edge entering his voice. "That surprised me, especially after what he wrote about you. And what will people say about my girl being seen with another man?"

My girl? That's what Christopher always called her, and she'd liked the sound of the words—the emotions behind it. But coming from Mike, the words gave her a chill.

Tricia thought about the gaping hole in her shop window, the strength it had taken to heave the miniature boulder that had shattered it. Unease wormed through her as she realized how isolated the two of them were in the big vacant house. She swallowed down the lump that had suddenly appeared in her throat. "We've been out to lunch exactly one time, that hardly makes me 'your girl.'" She even managed a little laugh.

"Maybe I'd like to change that." Mike stepped closer, putting his hands around her and pulling her against him.

"Mike," she said, squirming in his embrace.

He didn't let go, his face hovering close to her own, his breath warm on her cheek.

"Mike," she said with more urgency.

He leaned in closer, brushing his lips across her neck.

Panicking, Tricia pulled her arms free and pushed against his chest. "Mike, please!"

He stumbled back, puzzled. "I'm sorry, Trish. I thought you were as attracted to me as I am to you."

"That's very flattering. It's just—" How do you tell someone he's just creeped you out?

"Ah," he said, a sympathetic lilt entering his voice. "Too soon after your divorce?"

"That's exactly it. And anyway, it's not like Russ and I are even friends. We only discussed Doris's murder, which quickly became tedious, believe me. And it wasn't a date. We each paid for our own dinners." She didn't mention Russ staying with her until the enclosure guys could show up. And why did she feel she owed him an explanation, anyway?

"Any new developments in the murder case?" Mike asked, with no real interest.

"Just that the stolen book's been found."

He raised an eyebrow. "That is news. Where was it?"

"In my store."

"That's not good."

"No, it isn't." Tricia picked up her purse. "Look, I really have to get back to the shop." She took a step back, but he reached out, capturing her arm in a strong grip.

"Are you sure you can't stay for another cup of coffee?"

Tricia forced a smile as she pried his fingers from her forearm. "Sorry. I really have to get going." She turned and practically ran from the room, then realized it would be bad manners to snatch her jacket from the closet and flee. Yet she stood for long seconds in the empty foyer and Mike didn't appear.

As time ticked on and still he didn't appear, she figured the heck with manners and wrenched open the closet door. She'd expected to find it stuffed with coats, scarves, hats, and boots, but hers was the only jacket amongst the row of dark wooden hangers. She grabbed her jacket, slammed shut the door, and turned to find Mike, hands in his pants pockets, slouched against the wall, watching her.

"Um, thank you," she stammered, "for the coffee."

"I wish you didn't have to leave."

"Me, too," she said too cheerfully, the lie obvious. She inched closer to the front door.

"Thanks for the advice about the books," Mike said, his voice sounding oddly composed.

"You're more than welcome. Glad I could be of help." She had her hand on

the door handle, turned it, and found it locked. Panicked, she pulled at it, fumbling for the lever.

A hand touched hers and she shrieked and jumped back.

"Calm down, calm down," Mike soothed and stepped forward.

Tricia backed away, afraid he might come after her. Instead, he flipped the dead bolt, pulled the door open. Fresh air and the sunny morning poured into the foyer once again. Tricia zipped past Mike and onto the step outside. The tightness in her chest relaxed a bit and she felt like an absolute idiot for her behavior. She turned back. Mike stood in the open doorway, looking concerned.

Tricia forced a smile. "See you in town." Her tone almost sounded normal.

Mike stared at her for long seconds, his face impassive, then nodded and closed the door.

Frozen in time, Tricia stared for long seconds at the barrier between the real world and the stifling air of the lifeless house before she turned and hurried down the steps, letting out a whoosh of air as she went.

It wasn't until she'd driven a block away that she felt anywhere near calm again.

TRICIA WELCOMED THE return to the familiar surroundings at Haven't Got a Clue. True to form, Mr. Everett had been waiting outside the locked door for her. As expected, he was full of questions and concerned about the boarded-up shop.

"We will open today, won't we?" he asked, anxiously, as she unlocked the door.

"Yes, although it does seem awfully dark in here. We'll have to turn on all the lights. Let me hang up our coats and we'll get started."

It soothed the last of Tricia's jagged nerves to walk Mr. Everett through the daily tasks, and it turned out he'd been observant during all the months he'd visited the store as a customer who never purchased anything. He probably knew everything about the daily routine except the combination to the little safe under the counter.

During the three hours the store was open they shelved four boxes of books, waited on fifteen customers, and sold seventeen novels. Not bad for what was usually her slowest day. They also found another twenty-two nudist leaflets. Who on earth had been stashing them around the store, and why hadn't they caught the culprit?

Staying busy kept Tricia from thinking too much about her panic at being at the Harris home alone with Mike. Then again, too often lately she'd been employing a selective memory—especially when it came to what could be her future. And why had she ever agreed to go house hunting with Angelica?

True to her word, Angelica showed up at precisely three p.m., honking the car horn outside Haven't Got a Clue. Anticipating her sister's arrival, Tricia had closed a few minutes early, stuffed the day's receipts in the safe, waved good-bye to Mr. Everett, and was ready to go when the rental car pulled up out front.

"That stupid out-of-state car is still parked in front of your store," Angelica said in greeting, glaring at the offending vehicle.

Tricia buckled her seat belt as a horn blasted behind them.

Angelica hit the gas and the car lurched forward. "The shop looks dreadful. Couldn't you at least have that plywood painted to match the rest of the storefront?"

"It'll only be there another day."

"It's not likely to entice customers. You look dreadful, too, Trish. Those dark circles under your eyes are really unbecoming."

Tricia bit her tongue to keep from blurting a scathing retort.

Oblivious of her sister's pique, Angelica continued. "I have big news. I won!"

"Won what?" Tricia asked, glad for the change of subject.

"The parlay on Deborah Black's baby. He was born last night at eight thirty-seven p.m."

"How did you even know about it?"

"I told you, I visited all the stores in town. The owner of History Repeats Itself, Jim Roth, sold me the square. He's an absolute doll. Too bad he's married."

"Speaking of dolls, how was your big date with Bob last night?"

Angelica snorted. "Some date. He takes me to this little dump of a clam shack on the side of the highway and gives me an hour-long real estate pitch. Although I have to admit the food was pretty good."

A grudging admission if Tricia had ever heard one.

"Still, it reinforces my belief that what this little town needs is fine dining. And I might be just the person to make it happen."

Tricia was determined not to encourage her. "I had dinner at the diner last night and only three tables were occupied. They roll up Stoneham's sidewalks at seven."

"It might have to be a lunch-only establishment. Surely that little diner can't handle all the tourists at midday."

But Tricia didn't want to talk about restaurants. Her window had been broken at about eight thirty. Where had Bob been at the time? "So what time did you invite Bob back to your hotel room?"

Angelica's hands tightened on the wheel. "I did *not* invite him to my room."

"But surely he took you back to the inn. What time was that?"

"Terribly early. Somewhere around eight."

So, Bob could've thrown the rock. The question was, why?

"At least he invited me to the dining room for a nightcap," Angelica continued with disdain. "Otherwise I would've been in bed and asleep by nine o'clock."

"What time did he leave?" Tricia pressed.

"I don't know. Maybe nine fifteen."

Tricia's insides sagged. So much for Bob being responsible, though that still left him a viable suspect in Doris's murder. "The subject of where he went after he left us on Tuesday night didn't come up, did it?"

"It did. But it wasn't easy working it into the conversation," Angelica said, her attention focused on the road. "Bob doesn't like to talk negatively about Stoneham. And the first murder in sixty years is definitely negative."

"And?"

"He wouldn't say. Just that it was 'business.'"

"Typical of him." There had to be other avenues Tricia could explore, but right now she couldn't think of any so she concentrated on the matter at hand. "Did you find anything promising on your house hunt this morning?"

Angelica brightened. "Actually, Bob did steer me toward a darling little cottage that's for rent with an option to buy. The problem is the size. It's much too small."

"Is that where we're going now?"

"Yes. If nothing else, it's got potential."

Stoneham's small business district was already past, and trees and mileposts sped by.

"I'm trying to decide what to do with the money," Angelica said.

"Money?" Tricia asked, confused. "Oh yeah, the parlay. How much did you win, anyway?"

"Four hundred dollars."

"Four hundred dollars?" Tricia repeated, shocked.

"Not bad, huh? I think I'll send Deborah some flowers as a little thank-you."

Tricia sank back in her seat. "And you'll still have enough left for a Louis Vuitton key chain, too."

A number of businesses hugged the road that approached the highway. Tricia spotted the old smashed-up Cadillac Seville sitting beside a service station. "Stop the car!" she yelled, craning her neck as they whipped past.

Angelica slammed on the brakes, the car fishtailing onto the shoulder. "What's wrong? Did I hit something?"

"Back up, back up!"

Angelica jammed the gearshift into reverse and hit the accelerator.

"Whoa—stop, stop!" Tricia called, unhooking her seat belt and bolting from the car. She charged across the sea of asphalt surrounding the closed gas station, halting in front of the mangled mess that had once been Winnie Wentworth's most prized possession. The front end was now a tangle of metal, already rusting

from all the rain they'd had since Winnie's death. The windshield's glass had been reduced to a spider's web of cracks. No sign of blood. With no seat belt, she might have been ejected out the driver's window. The outcome was the same: death.

Angelica was suddenly at her side. "This belonged to the woman who sold Doris the cookbook?"

Tricia nodded and leaned forward to try the rear passenger side door handle. It opened.

"Hey, wait a minute," Angelica said and pulled Tricia's hand away. "This is a crime scene."

"The sheriff said Winnie's death was an accident. There's no crime tape. Poking around inside the car isn't trespassing."

"Says you."

Tricia waved her sister off and climbed into the grimy, damp interior. Various unpleasant odors assaulted her, and it was difficult to discern them: sweat, urine, and possibly mold? She rooted through the pile of gray clothes and blankets on the floor, coming up with a sheaf of yellowing newspaper clippings that had been stuffed under the driver's seat. She backed out of the car, shoving the papers toward Angelica, who stepped away in horror.

"I don't want to touch that. Think of all the germs!"

Tricia slammed the car door, shook her head in disgust, and set the fluttering papers on the right rear quarter panel. They were all the same: pages from the *Stoneham Weekly News* advertising section, listing tag sales, estate sales, and auctions, with a number of entries circled.

"There must be five or six weeks' worth here," Tricia said, flipping through the sheets.

"So what?"

"Maybe we can find the address where Winnie bought that cookbook."

Angelica frowned. "What good will that do?"

"It might lead us to whoever killed her."

"You just told me the sheriff said it was an accident."

"And if you believe her, let me interest you in some swampland in Florida. Oh, Ange, it's obvious Sheriff Adams doesn't care about actually solving Doris's murder. She seems to spend all her time trying to pin it on me!" She gathered up the scraps and started back for Angelica's car.

"You can't take that stuff along," Angelica said, struggling to keep up with her sister's brisk pace.

"Why not? The sheriff apparently didn't want it. It's just garbage now."

"Then throw it away."

Tricia stopped dead, turned, and faced her sister. "Not until I map out where Winnie found her treasures in her last few weeks."

FOURTEEN

ANGELICA STARTED THE car and pulled back onto the highway. "You *are* in a mood today."

Tricia clutched the papers on her lap. "I have reason to be." She let out a sigh and related her encounter with Mike Harris earlier that morning, feeling better for finally having unburdened her soul. "I'm even wondering if he could've thrown that rock through my store window last night."

"Hmm. Sounds more like you had a panic attack," Angelica commented, steering the rental car through the countryside with amazing familiarity. "My friend Carol used to get them whenever she had to face something unpleasant—like a visit with her in-laws. No wonder she could never stay married for more than six months at a time."

"It's never happened to me before."

"You're under stress," Angelica explained reasonably. "Who wouldn't be with the possibility of a murder charge hanging over her head?"

"I did *not* kill Doris Gleason, and I wish everyone would just stop saying that."

"My, we are very, *very* testy today. Mind you, right about now I could go for a tight embrace with a handsome man. And so far I've liked every man I've met here in Stoneham. They seem like the marrying kind."

"You'd be bored silly within a month and you know it," Tricia grumbled.

The idea of Angelica living nearby—and the possibility of Bob Kelly as a possible brother-in-law—was enough to make Tricia physically ill, especially since she still wanted to believe he had a hand in Doris's death. Too bad she didn't have a shred of evidence to prove it.

Time to ask the big question that had been so much on her mind. "Ange, isn't there any hope you and Drew can get back together?"

Angelica's mouth tightened, and she took her time before answering. "No."

"Do you mind if I ask what happened?"

"Oh, it's all so tedious," she said, with impatience.

"You obviously haven't found someone else. Has he?"

Again Angelica's hands tightened on the steering wheel. "If you must know, yes. And she's ten years older than me, with a face full of wrinkles! Some

woman he works with. They talk about math and physics and bonsai, of all things. One thing led to another and . . . he asked me to move out so she could move in."

And that's why Angelica had lost weight and come to Stoneham—to lick her emotional wounds. And Tricia had dropped all those snide comments about Drew in front of Bob the night before. "I'm so sorry, Ange."

"It was his house, after all," she continued, her gaze riveted on the road. "Drew isn't a beast. I'll get a good settlement. He paid for the trip to Aspen, and for storing my things until I find a place to settle. He's really been very kind."

Except for tossing her aside like an old shoe. But then Christopher had been just as generous when he'd announced he'd wanted his freedom, too. Maybe the Miles girls were just doomed to be unlucky in love.

"It's taken me a few months," Angelica continued, resigned, "but now I'm ready to move on. I mean, what choice do I have?"

"There's no chance of counseling, or—?"

Angelica shook her head. "Apparently he's loved that woman for years, but always thought she was unattainable. Then her husband died last year, and Drew figured he wasn't getting any younger. Not that he was unhappy with me, he later told me. But one thing led to another and . . . well, the rest as they say is history."

Tricia let out a breath. At least Christopher hadn't left her for someone else. Freedom for him meant solitude, which he'd apparently found and savored.

"Ah, here we are." Angelica slowed the car and turned off the highway onto a long gravel drive lined with decades-old maples. A little white cottage stood in a clearing, looking like something out of *Snow White and the Seven Dwarfs*, with its forest green shuttered windows, gabled, slate roof, its foundation surrounded by alternating pink and red rosebushes still in bloom.

"Oh, Ange, it's darling," Trish said. "Can we go inside?"

"I wish. But the agent who showed it to me this morning said she couldn't come back today. I just wanted you to see it, to see what you think."

"I love it." And it was far enough away from the village that Angelica might not want to drive into town come winter when the roads were reputed to be icy and treacherous. Bad Tricia wanting to keep her sister at bay! And really, she wasn't sure she felt that way anymore. Well, at least some of the time, and that had to be progress. Didn't it?

"Do you want to walk around the yard?" Angelica asked, hope coloring her voice.

"Sure."

The sisters got out of the car and walked ten or so yards to stand before the cottage. "Isn't that slate roof just incredible?" Angelica asked.

A few tiles looked skewed; did that mean it leaked? Tricia sidled between a

couple of rosebushes, shaded her eyes, and peered in through one of the leaded glass windows. The room inside was bare, but the walls, in neutral tones, looked freshly painted and the floors shone like they'd just been sanded and sealed.

"That's fir flooring, and look at the wonderful fieldstone fireplace. Imagine how cozy it would be on a cold winter's night," Angelica said wistfully.

Tricia stood back. "It's delightful. I had no idea a sweet little place like this was even available locally."

Angelica's smile was tentative. "I'm glad you like it. I thought you might be angry with me for wanting to live near you. It might not be forever, I just—I need you right now. Is that too terrible a thing for a sister to say?"

Touched, Tricia rested a hand on her sister's arm. "No, and I'm happy you feel that way. I just wish I could leave all the baggage from our childhood behind."

"I have none. But then why should I? I was the cherished child they never thought they'd have, and you were . . . well, you weren't expected. By that time Mother had moved on to other pursuits."

Angelica's words were nothing Tricia hadn't considered for herself too many times over the years, yet it did hurt to hear them. She withdrew her hand.

Angelica frowned. "I've spoiled the moment, haven't I?"

Nothing new, Tricia felt tempted to say, instead she turned and walked back to the car. Angelica took the hint and followed. Once inside, she started the engine, backed into the turnaround, and headed down the drive for the highway once again.

"Where to now?" Tricia asked, not caring what the answer was.

"I thought it might be fun to have dinner at the inn tonight. My treat. What do you say?"

Since the idea of cooking for herself was always a turnoff, and Miss Marple wouldn't be expecting her dinner for several hours anyway, Tricia nodded.

As she drove, Angelica gave a running commentary about the cottage's charms and its drawbacks, including the lack of closet space and how she thought she might like to add a patio and lap pool to the backyard and did Tricia know anything about pool maintenance?

"No."

Meanwhile, Tricia turned her attention back to Winnie's newspaper clippings. She must have circled forty or fifty addresses and Tricia wasn't sure she had a detailed map of the area to check them out. Stoneham had no map store, and she wasn't aware of any of the bookstores catering to local history, either. Maybe the Chamber of Commerce had done an advertising map. If she ran into Bob, she'd ask. Other than that she decided to just call Frannie at the C of C office on Monday.

Others must have had the same early-dinner idea as Angelica because the

inn's parking lot was jammed, and though she circled the lot twice, there simply were no empty spaces. "Darn. Now I'm going to have to park behind the inn in the bungalow lot."

"So, there's a back entrance, isn't there?"

"Is there? I don't know."

Once behind the inn, Tricia pointed out the door that led to the building's secondary entrance, and Angelica parked the car next to the Dumpster, the only available spot in the back lot. They got out of the car and she pointed to the white Altima with the Connecticut plates that sat in front of the door. "Look, there's that stupid car that's been taking all the desirable parking places in the village. I've had enough. I'm going to ask Bess who owns it."

Angelica marched ahead, leaving Tricia struggling to keep up.

Bess was once again stationed at the inn's reception desk, but she was helping another guest and the sisters had to wait to gain her attention. Tricia wandered over to a wooden rack that held brochures detailing the local attractions, and much to her delight found a stack of Chamber of Commerce maps of Stoneham. She scooped one up. Dinner now seemed unimportant.

Angelica stepped up to the reception desk.

"I hope you're enjoying your stay, Mrs. Prescott," Bess greeted at last.

"Very much so. In fact, I'm so impressed with the whole place, I'm thinking of moving to Stoneham."

"That's wonderful. Now, how can I help you this evening?"

"There's a car in the back lot with Connecticut plates: 64B R59. Does it belong to a guest?"

Bess's smile faltered. "I'm not sure I should give out that information."

"But I'm about to become a townie," Angelica insisted.

"That's villager," Tricia corrected.

Bess frowned. "I guess it can't hurt," she said, although she didn't sound convinced. Angelica repeated the plate number. Bess tapped a few keys on her computer. "Let's see. Oh, here it is. The car belongs to Deirdre Gleason; she's in bungalow two."

Her words tore Tricia's attention away from the map.

"It can't be," Angelica asserted. "That car was here when I arrived on Tuesday, which was the day Doris Gleason died."

Bess checked the register. "Ms. Gleason checked in on the third."

"And Doris was murdered on the fifth," Tricia said.

"What difference does it make what day she checked in?" Bess asked.

"Until Saturday no one knew Doris even had a sister," Tricia said.

"I did," Bess said. "Deirdre Gleason told me so."

"When did she tell you?" Angelica pressed.

"I don't remember exactly."

"Why didn't you report it to the sheriff after Doris's death?" Angelica insisted.

"I didn't think about it. I mean why would I?" Bess said, sounding defensive.

Bess was right; she wouldn't have known the sheriff was looking for next of kin. Tricia turned her attention back to her map.

"Tonight's Ms. Gleason's last night with us. She's moving into her sister's home tomorrow," Bess said.

Angelica leaned against the counter, bending closer. "Really? Tell me, have you gotten to know Deirdre during her stay?"

Tricia unfolded another section of her map and rolled her eyes, only half listening to the conversation.

Bess shook her head. "Not really. She keeps to herself. Has all her meals in the bungalow."

"Has anything about her changed since her sister's death?" Angelica asked.

"Changed?" Bess echoed.

"Her appearance: clothes, glasses, makeup?"

Bess thought about it. "She got her hair cut real short."

"Did she really?" Angelica said slyly.

Tricia refolded her map and changed the subject. "Bess, do you know what tonight's special is?"

It took a moment for the question to register. "Um . . . seared scallops with tropical salsa."

Angelica glowered at Tricia. "Sounds yummy."

Snagging Angelica's arm, Tricia pulled her away from the reception desk. "Thanks, Bess."

"Trish!"

"Shhh," Tricia warned and steered Angelica toward the dining room. "What was all that about?" she whispered.

"I'm working on a theory. I'll tell you about it later."

The hostess arrived to seat them, and they followed her to a far corner of the crowded dining room. The table was not to Angelica's liking.

"This is outrageous," she grumbled, knocking her elbow against the paneled wall. We deserve a better table than this."

"And there aren't any others, so be quiet and read your menu." But Tricia wasn't looking at her own menu; instead, she squinted at the tiny print on the map's index.

"Aren't you even the least bit curious as to why Deirdre made it sound like she wasn't in town before her sister's death? And how come nobody in town even knew Doris had a sister?"

"Of course I'm interested," Tricia said, setting the map aside and diving into her purse for her reading glasses. "But right now I'm more interested in finding out where Winnie got that blasted cookbook."

It was Angelica's turn to shush Tricia.

"And the reason nobody in town knew Doris had a sister," Tricia whispered, "is because she's not a Stoneham native. Aside from a few people like Mr. Everett, not many of the townspeople frequent the bookstores. Bess probably didn't even know Doris existed until Deirdre came to visit."

"It still seems funny to me," Angelica griped, but focused her attention on the menu. "Especially since the sheriff told you the dead woman had no relatives."

Had the sheriff said so, or had Tricia only imagined she had? Now she wasn't sure.

She thought back. It had been Bob who'd said Doris had no heirs the day he'd cleared out the Cookery. He'd either been in denial or clueless.

"Speak of the devil," Angelica muttered, looking over Tricia's shoulder.

Tricia turned. Sheriff Adams was maneuvering her bulk past the Brookview's dining patrons, bumping into chairs and jostling tables and glasses as she made her way toward the sisters. "Now what?"

Sheriff Adams paused in front of Tricia's table, her thumbs hooked into her belt loops, a stance that would've done John Wayne proud. "Ms. Miles, I'd like to speak with you."

"Now? On a Sunday evening? In the middle of the Brookview's dining room? What about?"

The sheriff surveyed the dining room, as though making sure those at nearby tables could hear her. "Doris Gleason's murder. We can discuss it here, or we can do it in the lobby."

Tricia gauged the interest from her neighbors, who'd suddenly lowered their heads to study their soup courses or were now hiding behind menus. "I have nothing to hide. Ask away."

"I'm going to ask a judge to have your financial records subpoenaed. I contend that you stole that valuable book and killed Doris Gleason for financial gain."

"Interesting that you'd make such an accusation without proof and in front of so many witnesses," Angelica commented, still perusing her menu. "I'm sure you understand the legal ramifications of slander."

"I'm not talking to you," the sheriff growled.

"And you know something, Tricia, I don't think you should talk to the sheriff, either. I mean, not without a lawyer present. You want someone with legal experience who can document just how ridiculously this investigation is proceeding."

"Ange—" Tricia warned.

"I mean really," Angelica continued. "I'm sure you've got more money in

your petty cash fund than the sheriff makes in a year. And since you couldn't give a Kadota fig about cooking or cookery books no matter how old and valuable they are, I don't see that continuing this conversation for an instant longer is going to be productive for either you or the sheriff. Especially when there are other people the law could be investigating."

"Like whom?" Sheriff Adams demanded.

"Bob Kelly, for one," Tricia said.

"We've already been over that territory."

"Then how about Deirdre Gleason," Angelica suggested. "She was in town days before her sister was murdered. Funny she didn't step forward to reveal her relationship with poor Doris until you went looking for her."

"She was out of town at the time of the murder," the sheriff said.

"And you have proof of that?"

"Deirdre Gleason was registered with the inn for three days before the murder. And although she paid for the room, she was out of town at the time of her sister's death. I'm satisfied with the information I've obtained to corroborate her story."

"And why aren't you satisfied with Tricia's answers? Because she's younger and prettier and much, much thinner than you?" Angelica asked pointedly.

Tricia slapped the table. "That's enough, Angie."

Angelica waved Tricia's protests aside, leveling her gaze at a pink-cheeked Wendy Adams. "Now unless you have specific allegations you want Tricia to address, please go away and let us have our dinner in peace. Perhaps you could do something useful, like finding out who broke Tricia's store window, or is even that beyond you?" She looked back down at her menu. "I think the herb-crusted sea bass sounds divine. How about you, Tricia?"

Tricia picked up her menu once again, struggling to keep her voice level. "I was thinking more along the lines of fowl. Perhaps the candied peacock?"

Sheriff Adams stood rooted to the spot, mouth open, eyes bulging, for a full ten seconds before she turned and stalked back across the dining room, jostling more tables as she went.

Tricia turned her menu so it hid her face from the onlookers. "That bit about me being thinner was a real low blow," she whispered. "But thanks for getting in the shot about my window."

"Well, she deserved it. There's no reason for her to keep hounding you. And do you really think she's looked into Deirdre's alibi?"

"I would think she'd have to. What makes you think Deirdre would've killed her sister?"

"Are you really sure it was Doris Gleason you saw lying dead on the floor of the Cookery? You saw her within an hour of her death; did you see her face? What was she wearing when you found her?"

Tricia thought back. "She had on the sweater she'd been wearing all day."

"Are you sure?"

She nodded and shuddered. "I can picture it—bloodstained—with the knife handle sticking out of it."

"What about her hair? Was it the same?"

"I . . . I don't know. It was all mussed—it covered her face, and at the time I was glad of it." She hadn't wanted to see the dead woman's lifeless eyes.

The waiter arrived to take their orders. Angelica took her time, consulting the wine list and asking for recommendations before settling on a sauterne that would go with both the appetizers and entrées. Tricia had plenty of time to think about their conversation.

The waiter departed and Angelica leaned close. "What are you thinking?"

"Suppose Deirdre did kill Doris, she might've hightailed it back to her home in Connecticut to establish an alibi. And she also had plenty of time to plant that cookbook in my shop the day she came in and introduced herself to us. We were swamped and she wandered the store for a good ten minutes before I could stop long enough to talk to her."

"Yes, but you also said Bob could've planted it, or even Mike Harris. Make up your mind, Trish, just who is your prime suspect?"

"That's the problem. I'm as much in the dark as Sheriff Adams."

FIFTEEN

Miss Marple swished her tail, refusing to let Tricia pet her after Angelica dropped her off at Haven't Got a Clue. "Your dinner is only ten minutes late," she explained, but Miss Marple would have none of it.

Tricia gathered up the empty dish and water bowl, chose a can of seafood platter, and set the dish and fresh water down before the cat. Miss Marple sniffed, turned her nose up at the offering, and walked away. "You're just being contrary," Tricia accused, but Miss Marple continued across the kitchen before pausing to wash her front left paw.

With the track lights turned up to full over the kitchen's island, Tricia spread out her C of C map along with Winnie's newspaper clippings and several colored markers. She'd been itching to jump into the task since she'd found the papers in Winnie's car.

It didn't take a genius to figure out that Winnie had circled any sales that mentioned books, which wasn't at all unusual since she had apparently bought and then sold a lot of them to the other booksellers in Stoneham. Too bad Ginny had discouraged her from coming around.

Tricia took the first clipping and started charting the addresses in pink for the week prior to Winnie's death, blue for the week she died. Miss Marple sashayed back into the kitchen, rubbing her head on the backs of Tricia's calves. "Don't try to get back in my good graces," Tricia muttered and squinted at another listing, this from two weeks before Winnie died. "Follow the signs on Canfield Road." That was where Mike Harris's mother's house was located.

The ad didn't specify the house address, but Mike's mother's home had a detached garage. Would he have been so foolish as to sell the valuable old manuscript for pennies at such a sale? Then again, the book had been in remarkably good condition. He might have considered it a reproduction and not given it a second thought.

Tricia eyed the phone. She could try to call Mike, but what would she say? "Sorry I ran out of your house like a raving idiot. Now did you sell a valuable book to an old lady, kill another elderly woman for buying that book from her, and then kill the first old lady to cover your tracks?" That wouldn't go over well, but she would have to find a way to casually run into him and tactfully ask some questions. And maybe hell would freeze over in the next couple of days, too.

Miss Marple levitated onto the island. "Hey, you're not supposed to be up here," Tricia scolded, but the cat merely circled around, rubbed her head against Tricia's chin, purring lustily.

Tricia scratched the cat's head, but kept her gaze on the yellowing ad. "Follow the signs on Canfield Road," she repeated. Russ Smith should be able to check who'd placed the ad. Surely there were no confidentiality issues between a newspaper's ad page and the purchaser of said ad. There'd be no one at the paper at this time on a Sunday night. Another task for the morning, and something law enforcement ought to be doing.

Angelica taunting the sheriff hadn't been wise, and while Tricia appreciated the sentiment behind it, she was still irked at her sister. Then again, why was the sheriff so intent on nailing her for Doris Gleason's death besides clearing up the matter before the pending election? And was that enough of a motive? One thing was certain, Sheriff Adams wasn't interested in finding another suspect. If her name was to be cleared, Tricia was going to have to do it herself.

Tricia leaned against the brick wall beside the door of the *Stoneham Weekly News*, clutching a cardboard tray with two cups of the Coffee Bean's best brew.

The recorded message had said the paper's office hours were from eight until five, but Tricia had shown up at seven forty, anticipating Russ would arrive for work before office hours. And she'd been right.

"Been waiting long?" Russ asked, as he approached from around the corner. He pulled a set of keys from his jacket pocket, selecting one of them. He looked like a farmer in well-worn jeans with the collar of a blue plaid flannel shirt sticking out the neck of his denim jacket.

"About five minutes. Hope you're thirsty," Tricia said, proffering the cardboard tray.

"I am." He unlocked the door. "Come on in."

She followed him as he led her through the darkened office. He hit the main switch and the place was flooded with fluorescent light. Peeling off his jacket, he headed for a glass cubicle in the back of the room. The rest of the office was open landscaping, with two desks with computer terminals. Stacks of the most recent issue sat atop a long counter that separated the public part of the office with the work zone behind it.

Russ took his seat, powering up his computer. "To what do I owe the pleasure?"

Tricia set the tray down and handed him a cup, offering creamer and sugar. "Just a little thank-you for your help the other night."

"What're friends for?"

So now he considered himself a friend. All the better. Tricia took one of the standard office guest chairs in front of his desk. "As you know, the sheriff seems determined to prove I killed Doris Gleason, quite a feat as I didn't do it."

Russ made no comment, but dumped a tub of the half-and-half into his paper cup.

"I'm taking your advice and trying to find out who *did* kill Doris."

"And you want me to help." It wasn't a question.

Tricia leaned forward. "I'm convinced Winnie Wentworth bought Doris's stolen cookbook at a tag sale, and I think I've found the ad right here in the *Stoneham Weekly News*. I was hoping you could tell me who placed it."

Russ stirred his coffee, then leaned back in his chair. "Depends on how long ago it was placed. We purge our system on a monthly basis, otherwise it gets bogged down storing all that data."

"Why don't you just copy it onto a CD?"

"What for? It's not even old news. We don't really care who buys classified ad space. It's the display ads that bring in the money. And we keep bound copies of the paper for posterity—not that I think anyone would ever want to look at an old ad ever again."

"The ad I'm concerned with was printed in the August nineteenth issue."

Russ tapped at his computer keyboard, studied the screen, then shook his head. "Looks like Sherry has already purged the August ads."

Tricia gripped her cup, hoping her disappointment wasn't too obvious. "Well, thank you for looking."

Russ turned back to face her and picked up his cup once more. "Just who did you think placed the ad?"

"I don't think I should speculate, at least not to you, without some other kind of proof."

"How will you find it?"

"I don't know. But I'm not going to give up." Tricia took a sip of her coffee. Since Russ was supposed to be on top of everything that happened in Stoneham, she decided to tap him for more information.

"What's the scuttlebutt on a big box store coming to the area?"

He shrugged. "I hadn't heard about it."

"Is that so?" she said, incredulous.

Russ laughed. "I've got no reason to lie."

"You've at least heard about the nudist tracts someone's been leaving all over the village."

"Nudists?" Either he was clueless or the world's worst reporter.

"You need to get out of your office more often. According to the website listed on the leaflets, a nudist resort is supposed to open somewhere near here next summer."

He picked up a pen, jotted down a note. "Tell me more."

She gave him the name of the business. "Drop by any of the bookstores if you want copies of the tracts. We've all got them."

"I'll do just that."

Tricia stood and picked up her coffee. "The day's getting away from me." She turned to leave, paused, and turned back. "Just one thing: would you have told me who bought the ad if the information had still been available?"

Russ smiled. "Don't you know that a good reporter never reveals a source—be it of information or revenue?"

Tricia swallowed down her annoyance. "I'll remember that for future reference."

Piqued, Tricia discarded her nearly full cup of coffee in one of Stoneham's municipal trash cans and headed back for Haven't Got a Clue. The lights inside the Cookery were already on, and she could see that Deirdre had finished washing the walls and had even made some progress with her restocking efforts. Had Bob opened up the storage unit and let her reclaim the display

pieces? Some of them even had books on them, perhaps from the stock stored on the second floor or from Doris's home storeroom.

Tricia hammered on the door and waited. Deirdre had to be in the back room. She knocked again. Sure enough, Deirdre lumbered out of the back. She looked uncannily like her sister—but then wasn't that the way with identical twins? She even seemed to have lost her glasses.

Deirdre opened the door, her smile of welcome almost convincing. "Good morning, Tricia. You're out early."

"And you're already hard at work, I see."

"I've got a schedule to keep if I want to reopen the Cookery next Monday. Come in." Deirdre stepped over to one of the bookshelves. Several opened cartons sat on the floor. She picked up a book and squinted at its cover.

"Did you lose your glasses?" Tricia asked.

"My what?" Deirdre asked, alarmed.

"Your glasses. You're not wearing them."

Deirdre patted her cheek in panic. "Good grief, you're right. I must have taken them off when I first came in. They're around here somewhere. Now what can I do for you?" she said, changing the subject.

Tricia prayed for tact, knowing there really was no easy way to begin what she had to say. "I'm sorry to say that Sheriff Adams is convinced I killed your sister."

Looking doughy and toadlike without her glasses, Deirdre merely blinked, apparently startled at Tricia's bluntness.

"I did not kill Doris," Tricia asserted.

"I should hope not," Deirdre said.

"But I do have some questions for you."

Deirdre visibly stiffened. "Me?"

"Yes. Within hours of Doris's death, the whole village was buzzing with the news. You were in town, registered at the Brookview Inn. Why didn't you step forward and let the sheriff know you were her next of kin?"

"I was *not* in Stoneham when Doris was killed. Yes, I'd taken a room at the inn, but I'd gone home to take care of some business and collect more clothing. I didn't arrive back until days after her death."

"How many days?"

Deirdre's eyes narrowed. "What are you implying? That I had something to do with my own sister's death?"

Tricia hesitated. If she mentioned the insurance policy, Deirdre would wonder where she learned about it. Likewise if she mentioned anything else about Doris's daughter. "Of course not. I just thought it was funny you didn't come forward sooner."

"Well, I don't think it's funny at all. What if something happened to *your*

sister and people accused you of doing her in? Would you think *that* was funny?"

"No, I—"

"And neither do I." She pointed toward the door. "I think you should leave."

"Deirdre, I—"

"Now, please," she said and grasped Tricia by the shoulders, shoving her across the room and out of the Cookery, slamming the door and locking it before stalking away.

"Deirdre! Deirdre!" Tricia shouted to no avail.

Suddenly Mr. Everett was standing beside her, looking through the Cookery's door as Deirdre disappeared from view. "She's in a bit of a snit, isn't she?"

"With cause." Tricia turned and walked the ten or so feet to the door to her own store, withdrew the keys from her purse, and opened the door. Mr. Everett trotted in behind her, hitting the main light switch. Miss Marple sat on the sales counter, ready for another hard day of sleeping on the stock or perhaps a patron's lap.

Juggling his umbrella, Mr. Everett shrugged out of his coat. "Would you like me to hang up your coat as well?"

"Yes, thank you. Looks like you're ready for rain."

"There's talk we'll get the tail end of Hurricane Sheila later today or perhaps tomorrow, depending on how fast it travels."

"Hurricane?" Tricia asked. Preoccupied, she hadn't turned on the TV or the radio in days.

"Would you like me to finish alphabetizing those biographies, Ms. Miles?"

"Please call me Tricia." Mr. Everett nodded, but she knew he wouldn't. Any more than she could call him by his first name, which he'd written on his official application and she'd already forgotten. He'd always be Mr. Everett to her.

"Yes, go ahead. Oh, but maybe you wouldn't mind dusting the display up front. Should it be a sunny day, it's really going to be obvious it hasn't been touched in days. But be careful; there still may be some glass up there."

"I'll get the duster," he said and started for the utility closet.

Tricia opened the small safe from under the sales counter and sorted the bills for the drawer, settling them into their slots. She caught sight of the little scatter pin she'd bought from Winnie, which had resided in the tray since the day Winnie had died. On impulse, she scooped it up and pinned it on the left side of her turtleneck, wondering why she hadn't thought to take the little brooch upstairs to her jewelry box where it belonged.

She checked the tapes on the register and credit card machine, finding them more than half full, and though the store wouldn't open for more than an hour, she decided to raise the shade on the door and let in some natural light. Mike's office across the street was still darkened, and she wondered when or if

he'd show up today. He'd said he still had some time left on the lease for his last office. Perhaps he started the day there and only came to the campaign office when work permitted.

Mr. Everett had donned one of the extra Haven't Got a Clue aprons and was happily dusting his way along the front window display. Tricia gave him a smile and turned back to stare out the window. If Mike had sold Winnie the Amelia Simmons cookbook, then found out how valuable it was, he might've decided to take back what had once been his property. He could've slipped across the street and done the deed in the thirty to forty minutes between Tricia speaking to Doris and then finding her dead. And then on Saturday morning Mike had also spent time wandering around Haven't Got a Clue when he could have planted the stolen book to avert suspicion. Not that anyone but Tricia suspected him. Or Bob. Or Deirdre.

She thought about her encounter with Mike at his mother's home the day before. What kind of woman had raised him? She looked over at her new employee. "Mr. Everett, what do you know about Mike Harris's mother?"

"Grace?" he asked, not looking up from his task. "She's a very nice woman. Used to be quite friendly with my late wife, Alice. It's a pity she had to go to St. Godelive's."

"I'm sorry?"

He paused in his work. "St. Godelive's. It's an assisted living center over in Benwell. I understand she came down with dementia. Such a pity." He shook his head in obvious disapproval.

Came down with dementia? Okay.

"It used to be only the indigent that ended up there, but it seems they've been trying to upgrade the place and are now taking patients who can pay for their services."

The indigent? Surely Grace Harris had arrived after they'd changed their policies. After all, Mike had said he'd been clearing out her home to pay for her medical expenses. She thought back to the birthday card that had fallen out of *American Cookery* two days before. "Just out of curiosity, what was Mike's father's name?"

"Jason."

And the other name on the birthday card found in Doris's cookbook was Letty. So the book hadn't been a gift from Mike's father to his mother. Scratch that notion.

Still, the possibility of Mike being a murderer nagged at her. Facts were facts. He visited the Cookery the day of Doris's death. If he'd sold the booklet to Winnie for pennies, and saw that she'd sold it to Doris and it was on display, he might have decided to take back the book—by force if necessary.

"Mr. Everett," she called, interrupting his dusting once more. "What do you think about Mike Harris running for selectman?"

His brows drew together in consternation. "I really don't like to participate in idle gossip," he began. "Then again, I do believe I'm entitled to an opinion when it comes to the village's representation."

"So I take it you won't be voting for him."

"Certainly not!"

Tricia hadn't expected such vehemence from mild-mannered Mr. Everett.

"Do you mind telling me why?"

He exhaled a sharp breath. "His reputation as a youth was . . . soiled."

"In what way?"

"It seems to me he was always in trouble. Schoolyard fights, shoplifting, and when he got older, he was a terror on wheels. That's not someone I want to represent me, even in local government."

"I see. And you don't believe he's capable of redemption?"

"I suppose everyone is. However, there's also a saying I've come to believe in: a leopard doesn't change its spots." And with that, he turned back to his dusting.

Thoughts of Mike kept replaying through Tricia's mind like a CD on repeat. Although she really didn't know Mr. Everett all that well, she trusted his assessment of Mike's character. She was also sure Angelica would accuse her of taking out her anger at Mike by making him a possible suspect. Then again, Angelica was convinced Deirdre had killed Doris, taken the book to fake a robbery, and then tried to cover her crime with arson.

Confronting Deirdre was one thing; she had no fear of the older woman. Confronting Mike, with his strong hands and steel-like arms, would be another thing. And what if all her suppositions were wrong? What if Doris had been murdered by a complete stranger? But that didn't make sense, either. Doris had unlocked her door to let her killer in. Someone had planted the stolen cookbook in Tricia's store. Someone still in town.

Someone who didn't want to be arrested for murder.

SIXTEEN

As promised, the men from Enclosures Inc. arrived to replace the broken window at just past ten that morning. The whole operation took a lot longer than Tricia anticipated, and Miss Marple was extremely unhappy to be banished to the loft apartment during the repair. Her howls could be heard by everyone in

the store, and Tricia found herself explaining to more than one person that no one was pulling the cat's tail. Still, the entire ordeal put a damper on business.

After the window was replaced and order once again reigned, Tricia again called her security company. They were still too busy to come out to fix her system, but she suspected her monthly bill would arrive on time with no mention of interrupted service. She documented the call and intended to start contacting other firms when she realized the day was once again getting away from her. And she had to at least try to smooth over the damage Angelica had done between her and Sheriff Adams before attending to other matters.

Tricia drove to the sheriff's office rehearsing her speech. When she got there, Wendy Adams listened, but from the look on her face, she wasn't likely to accept anything Tricia had to say.

"You're beginning to sound like a broken record, Ms. Miles," she said at last and leaned back in her office chair, folding her hands over her ample stomach. "Or maybe someone so desperate she can't wait to point the finger at anyone else to evade suspicion."

"Look, Sheriff, I'm sorry my sister was rude to you yesterday, but I have real concerns that you're not taking this investigation seriously."

"Oh, I'm very serious. And I'm going to prove that you killed Doris Gleason."

"Even if I'm not guilty? That'll be quite a trick."

"Ms. Miles, I've known Mike Harris nearly all his life—and mine. He's no more a killer than I am. Perhaps he had a few run-ins with the law as a teenager—speeding, I believe—but he hasn't had so much as a traffic ticket in recent memory." She picked up her phone, right index finger poised to push buttons on the keypad. "Now if you'll excuse me, I have *real* police work to attend to."

And what would that be? Tricia wondered. Issuing parking tickets? Even that seemed beyond the sheriff's capabilities, as she hadn't issued one ticket to Deirdre for monopolizing the parking space in front of Tricia's store. "Do you have any idea who broke my window, or is it considered too petty a crime to be worth the sheriff's department's time?"

Wendy Adams stabbed the air with her index finger, pointed to the door, her expression menacing.

Tricia turned and left the office, heading for her car. With Ginny and Mr. Everett taking care of Haven't Got a Clue, she had time to pursue her own investigation. Her next stop: a visit with Grace Harris. But first, she dropped in at her store to select a certain book off the shelf.

ST. GODELIVE'S ASSISTED Living Center squatted on a small rise, an older, bland brick building without the flash that seemed to come standard with

newer homes for the infirmed. No retaining pond filled with cute ducks and geese, no water spout, and virtually nothing in the way of landscaping. In fact, all the place needed was a chain-link fence and razor wire to win a prison look-alike contest. The overcast sky only reinforced that notion.

Tricia parked her car and walked along the cracked sidewalk to the main entrance. Pulling open the plate-glass door, she stepped inside and sighed at the sea of institutional gray paint that greeted her. Everything seemed drained of color, from the tile floor to the glossy walls devoid of ornamentation, to the woman dressed in a gray tunic who manned the reception desk. Already feeling depressed, Tricia checked in and signed the guest book, was given a visitor's badge, and was directed to the third floor.

Stepping out of the elevator, Tricia was struck by the starkness around her—that and the nose-wrinkling scent of urine that all the air fresheners in the world wouldn't quite erase. The bland white corridor—wide enough to accommodate wheelchairs and gurneys—had no carpet, no doubt left bare for easy cleaning, with sturdy handrails fixed along the walls to aid those who no longer walked on steady legs.

A hefty woman in blue scrubs, whose name tag read "Martha," manned the nurses' station to her left. She greeted Tricia with a genuine smile. "Can I help you?"

"I'd like to visit Grace Harris."

"Are you a friend? She gets so few visitors. In fact, I think you're only the second or third person to visit her the whole time she's been with us."

Tricia frowned. "And how long is that?"

"Almost six months, which is a shame as she's improved so much in the past few weeks."

"Doesn't her son visit?" Tricia asked, surprised.

The nurse shrugged. "Occasionally. You'd be surprised how many people dump their relatives in places like this and never think to visit them again."

That wasn't the impression Mike had given her. "So you don't think he's a good son?"

The nurse shrugged. "It's not my place to judge." But it was clear she had. Martha rounded the counter. "This time of day Grace will probably be in the community room. Follow me, please."

Tricia noted that most of the patient room doors were open, with too many white-haired, slack-jawed elderly people staring vacant-eyed at TVs mounted high on the walls. They passed a few ambulatory residents shuffling through the hall, or slowly maneuvering themselves aimlessly back and forth in their wheelchairs, barely noticing the stranger in their midst.

Martha paused in the community room's doorway, pointing across the way.

"There she is, over by the window. Let me know if you need anything else." Her smile was genuine.

"Thank you," Tricia said and turned to watch Grace as the nurse's footfalls faded.

She hesitated before entering the nearly empty room. Three old gents played cards at a square table off to the right, and a couple of older women sat together on a couch knitting or crocheting colorful afghans that cascaded across their laps. Except for the TV in the corner droning on and on, it was the only color in the otherwise drab room.

These residents seemed to be functioning on a higher level than those she'd already passed. However, Grace, a mere wisp of a woman dressed in a pink cotton housedress with slippered feet and looking like everybody's great-grandma, stared vacantly out the window at the cloudy sky. Her white hair had once been permed, judging by the flat two inches broken by a part in the middle. Pale pink little-girl bunny barrettes on either side of her face kept the hair from falling into her eyes.

Tricia padded closer to the woman and waited, hoping she wouldn't startle her. "Grace," she called softly.

Slowly the woman turned red-rimmed eyes on Tricia.

"Hello, my name is Tricia Miles. I live in Stoneham and own a bookstore there. I understand you like to read mysteries. I brought you one." She held out a copy of Lawrence Block's *Deadly Honeymoon*. "I understand you used to have a copy of this book."

Grace held out a wrinkled hand, took the book, which no longer had its dust cover, and studied the spine. "Used to have a copy?" she said, her voice sounding small, and looked up at Tricia, confused. "What happened to the one in my living room?"

She remembered! But then wasn't it true that with Alzheimer's disease old memories stayed intact while short-term memory faded? "Yes, that's right," Tricia agreed. "I thought you might like to read it again."

Grace turned her attention back to the book, flipping through its pages. "That was very thoughtful of you . . ." She looked up in confusion. "Who did you say you were?"

"Tricia Miles. I own one of the bookstores in Stoneham. It's called Haven't Got a Clue."

"Oh yes, the new mystery bookstore. I've been meaning to visit it. When did you open? Last week?"

"Five months ago."

Grace frowned. "That can't be right. I remember reading about it in the *Stoneham Weekly News*. The article distinctly said the store would open on April fourth."

Tricia swallowed down her surprise. "Yes, we did. But that was five months ago."

Grace's brows drew closer together, her face creasing in confusion once again. "Where did the time go?" She looked up at Tricia and her eyes opened wide in recognition, her mouth drooping. "Where did you get that pin? It's mine."

Tricia's hand flew to the gold scatter pin at her throat. "I bought it."

Grace shook her head. "Oh no. I would never have sold it. It belonged to my grandmother."

"Are you sure?" Tricia asked.

"Would you let me look at it?" Grace held out her veiny hand.

Tricia unfastened the pin and handed it to Grace, who held it close to her face, squinted at the curlicues and scrollwork, her right index finger tracing the pattern. "See here, it says Loretta. That was my grandmother's name."

She handed the pin back to Tricia, who also had to squint. She turned the pin around and around again, and finally did see that it wasn't just ornamentation, but a name: Loretta. She gave the pin back to Grace, who immediately fastened it to her housedress.

"Mrs. Harris, did you ever own a cookbook called *American Cookery*, by Amelia Simmons?"

"A book? I'm not sure."

Another sign of Alzheimer's?

"I did have a darling little pamphlet written by someone named Amelia that belonged to my mother. It may have even belonged to my grandmother—it was very old—but I don't think I ever made anything out of it. All that colonial food was so stodgy. Jason, my late husband, he was partial to ethnic food. He loved watching Julia Child on TV and often had me make her recipes."

Julia Child and ethnic food didn't seem to belong in the same sentence.

"Did friends call your grandmother Loretta, or did they have a pet name for her?"

Grace frowned. "Hmm. Seems to me they called her Letty."

"Was your grandfather Roddy?"

"Rodney," Grace corrected. "Why do you ask? Are you a long-lost relative?"

Tricia saw an unoccupied chair across the way and pulled it across the floor so that she could face Grace instead of towering over her. She sat. "I have some unhappy news for you. I believe the cookbook and that pin you're now wearing were sold. Probably many more items from your home have been sold, too."

"That can't be. My son, Michael—" But her eyes widened and her words trailed off. Slowly, her face began to crumple as tears filled her eyes. "Not again," she crooned, nearly folded in half, and began to rock. "Not again."

Tricia placed a hand on the old woman's arm. "I'm so sorry I had to tell you."

"If what you say is true, it isn't the first time he's stolen from me. I was a good mother. We gave him everything. Why would he keep doing this to me?"

"He said he needed the money so that you could stay here and be taken care of."

Grace turned sad eyes on Tricia. "But I have insurance. There should've been no need to sell my things—and especially without telling me."

"Does Mike have power of attorney?"

Grace shook her head. "No. There's no way I would ever give him that. My lawyer has instructions for my care when I can no longer make decisions; they specifically say that Michael is never to be permitted to represent my affairs."

"Are you aware that your son placed you here? He's been telling everyone you have Alzheimer's disease."

"I admit my memory hasn't been as good as it was, but lately I've felt so much more like my old self. I've been wondering how I ended up here and why no one comes to see me. I have many good friends . . ." Her voice trailed off again as her hand grasped the pin on her housedress, and her gaze slipped out through the window.

Tricia waited for a minute or two for the old woman to continue, but Grace seemed to have lost interest in the conversation.

"Mrs. Harris? Mrs. Harris?"

"How is it you came to buy this pin?" Grace said at last.

"I bought it from a woman named Winnie Wentworth. I believe she got it at a tag sale at your home. She sold it to me last week. She was killed in a car accident the very same day."

"Killed? Oh my. An accident?"

"I'm not sure."

A tear rolled down Grace's cheek, and her gnarled hand still clasped the pin on her chest. "I love this pin. It meant so much to my grandmother. She gave it to me when I was a bride. I have her wedding band hidden with some of my other jewelry. It would break my heart to know it, too, was gone."

Feeling the need to ease the old woman's pain, Tricia found herself patting Grace's back. "Do you remember the last time you saw your son?"

Grace stared straight ahead again, her gaze unfocusing. "At my home. We argued over . . ." She shook her head. "We argued."

Probably over money, or Mike's pilfering. And shortly afterward, Grace had ended up in St. Godelive's.

"I've asked about leaving here," Grace said, "but they won't give me a straight answer, and I must get to my home to stop Michael from stealing from

me. I don't know you, but—" She glanced up at Tricia with worried bloodshot eyes. "Would you help me?"

Despite the need to clear her own name, Tricia had no hesitation in answering. "Of course. What do you want me to do?"

"Please make sure the rest of my jewelry is safe. I had two beautiful jewelry boxes in my bedroom, but I've also hidden some of my most valuable items just to keep them out of Michael's reach. Gifts from my husband, and some that belonged to my mother and grandmother. Then there's Jason's coin collection. It's worth tens of thousands. Michael helped himself to some of it after his father died."

"Where should I look?"

"There's a small trapdoor on the floor at the head of the bed in the master bedroom. I don't think Michael knows about it."

"How will I get into the house?"

"You'll find a spare key inside the garage. It hangs on the back wall on a nail under a little framed picture of flowers . . . if he hasn't sold that, too," she added bitterly.

"I'll try to get there either tonight or tomorrow, and I'll come back and tell you what I've found."

Grace clasped Tricia's hand. "I'm trusting you—a stranger. Please help me."

Tricia swallowed down a lump in her throat and nodded. "I will."

SEVENTEEN

TRICIA STOOD AT St. Godelive's third-floor nurses' station, trying to make sense of what she'd just learned. "And you say Grace's memory just seems to have returned—like magic?"

"More like a miracle," Martha said, and grinned. "I've worked with the elderly for over twenty years, and you don't see it happen often, but when it does, it truly is a gift from God."

Miracle my foot, Tricia thought cynically. Something had to have changed for Grace, but Tricia wasn't about to speculate in front of someone working for St. Godelive. Could she trust any of them? Mike would had to have had help in keeping Grace senseless. But who? A staff member? Maybe her own physician? No one else came to visit Grace, so that seemed most likely.

"I'd like to come visit Grace again. You don't see any problem with that, do you?"

"Not at all. In fact, stimulation is the best thing for her at this point in her recovery."

Tricia gave the nurse a smile. "Thank you."

Dressed in a neon pink Hawaiian shirt, Frannie Mae Armstrong stood on the porch outside the Chamber of Commerce's offices, watering the fuchsias as Tricia drove past. She slowed and honked the horn. Frannie bent down, squinted, recognized her, and waved.

Tricia parked her car in the village's municipal lot and hiked the half a block to the C of C office. With no sign of Frannie outside, she entered the log cabin to find the secretary-receptionist attending to her indoor plants. "Hi, Frannie," she called.

"Well, how-do, Tricia. What brings you back to the chamber?"

"I've been admiring your flowers on the porch," she lied. "They're beautiful."

"I feed 'em liquid plant food. Works like a charm. But they won't last much longer. First frost and—" She made a slashing motion against her throat. "Then again, the porch roof might protect them for another week or two, unless the remnants of Hurricane Sheila washes them away in the next twenty-four hours. It's always a crapshoot with those babies." She retreated to the counter and set down her watering can. "I saw your window had been broken when I drove by yesterday. Did the sheriff figure out who did it?"

"Not yet."

Frannie clicked her tongue. "It's just terrible what's been going on here in Stoneham this past week. I would've never believed it. Maybe in Honolulu, but not here."

"Honolulu?" Tricia asked. Talk about a non sequitur.

Frannie smiled broadly. "Where I plan to retire. It's a big city compared to Stoneham. Mighty expensive, too. But my heart's set on it." She pulled at the lapel on her shirt and winked. "I've already got my wardrobe."

Tricia could do little more than gape at the woman.

"Now," Frannie said, all business. "What can I do for you today?"

Tricia struggled to change mental gears. "I'm still trying to figure out where Bob Kelly could have been last Tuesday night after he left the Brookview Inn. Any chance you can tell me?" she asked brightly.

Frannie's lips tightened. "He had a business meeting."

"With a representative from a big box company?"

"I can't tell you that," Frannie said. "I can't tell you any more."

"Oh, come on," Tricia chided. "It's no secret. Everyone in the village is talking about it."

"Who?"

Tricia shrugged. "Everybody."

"Now, Miss Tricia, you wouldn't want me to blab my boss's business, risk my job, just to satisfy your curiosity, now would you? Surely you'd expect that kind of loyalty from your own employees."

Tricia blinked. "Well, yes, of course. It's just that—" She realized that no matter what she said, she already looked a fool. "I'm sorry, Frannie. I didn't mean to put you in a compromising position."

"Well, of course you didn't," Frannie said in all sincerity. "I can understand where y'all are coming from. Things don't look good for you right now." She lowered her voice confidentially. "We all read the story in Friday's *Stoneham Weekly News.*"

Tricia's cheeks burned, but she kept her lips clamped shut.

"It's been said you think Bob might have killed Doris Gleason. Now, I don't know about you, but I prefer to believe in the good in people. My daddy always said hearsay and gossip is just not nice. And I know in your heart of hearts that you don't believe Bob would hurt anybody. He's a good man, and I know you're a good woman. I just know these things."

"Thank you," Tricia managed, feeling even smaller.

An awkward silence fell between them.

The phone rang and Frannie picked it up. "Stoneham Chamber of Commerce. Frannie speaking. How can I help you?"

Tricia inched away from the counter, reaching behind her to find the door handle.

"Hold on just a sec," Frannie told the caller. "Now you have a good afternoon, Miss Tricia."

Tricia forced a smile. "Thank you," she said and hurriedly left the office.

An impatient Ginny stood at the door when Tricia returned to Haven't Got a Clue. "Thank goodness you're here. I've nearly been jumping out of my skin for the last hour waiting for you."

"What's happened?" Tricia asked, concerned. "Why didn't you call me on my cell phone?"

"You've got it turned off," she said with disdain. "Again!"

Tricia waved her off and headed for the sales counter to stow her purse. "So what's the big news?"

"We caught her!" Ginny said with triumph.

"Caught who?"

"The mad leaflet dropper!"

Tricia's head whipped round so fast she was in danger of whiplash. "Who is it?"

"You mean today? Just some tourist."

Tricia waved her hands beside her ears, as though brushing away a pesky fly. "Run that by me again. A tourist?"

Ginny's smile was smug. "It's a racket." She signaled for Mr. Everett to join them. "I got her to tell me her part, but it was Mr. Everett who tracked down the whole story, and I think he should be the one to tell you."

"You give me too much credit," the older gentleman said as he approached. "Ms. Miles, the customer told me which bus she came in on, and I went in search of it to talk to the driver. It seems he's seen this happen several times over the last week or so. A man in a business suit approaches one of the tour members, someone who doesn't appear to be with friends. He offers that person money if they'll hide the leaflets in books or other merchandise when they visit the booksellers in Stoneham. He pays them in cash—as much as fifty dollars."

Tricia crossed her arms over her chest. "Where did the tour originate?"

"In Boston."

She exhaled a long breath through her nose. "It was probably a representative from the Free Spirit chain of nudist camps and resorts. It's helpful information, but unfortunately it doesn't help us stop the problem."

"Perhaps we could ask for the sheriff's help," Mr. Everett suggested. "These people are in a sense littering. Perhaps if a deputy met each bus and warned them—"

"It's a good idea—if it can be worked out. But I'm afraid I have no pull with the sheriff's office," Tricia said, her unpleasant visit with Wendy Adams still too fresh in her mind.

"Why don't you ask Mike Harris to deal with it?" Ginny proposed. "He's running for selectman."

Tricia fought to keep a grimace from pulling at her mouth. "Mike and I . . . aren't exactly on friendly terms today." And she wanted to keep it that way.

"I see," said Mr. Everett. "Then perhaps we could enlist one of the other booksellers to approach the sheriff. I'd be glad to speak with Jim Roth over at History Repeats Itself."

"No, that would be my responsibility, but thank you just the same, Mr. Everett."

He nodded. "Very well," he said and turned back for the bookshelves.

"Did all your errands go all right?" Ginny asked.

Much as she liked her employee, Tricia didn't feel comfortable sharing with Ginny everything that was happening. Instead she forced a smile. "Just great."

Ginny nodded. "We're slow right now if you want to go see Jim."

"Yes, perhaps I'd better," Tricia said, although after her encounters with the sheriff and Frannie, all she really wanted to do was pull the shades and hide.

"I PUT AN offer in on the cottage," Angelica said offhandedly. It was almost eight o'clock, and she stood at the stove in Tricia's loft with her back to her sister, stirring a pot of Irish lamb stew.

Tricia paused, about to lay a fork down on the place mat. "Oh?" Was she supposed to sound happy? Maybe she should be. The two of them had actually been getting along for most of the past week, but that couldn't last. At least it never had before.

"Did you bid high or low?"

"Low. I mean, it does need a lot of work. It's much too small for my needs, and it's really much too far out of town."

Tricia struggled to keep her voice level. "It doesn't sound like you really want it."

"Oh, but I do. It's just . . . I don't know. I guess I really didn't think you'd approve."

"It's not a question of my approval," she asserted once again. "You've decided to live in the area. You're the one who has to actually stay there . . . if you get it."

Angelica turned back to her pot. "I could just 'flip' it—you know, fix it up a little and sell it off quickly. Or turn it into a shop. Or maybe a restaurant. If it weren't for the location, it would make a sweet little tearoom." Angelica peeked at her sister over her shoulder.

"Are you really thinking of opening a restaurant?"

Angelica turned back to her stew. "I don't know. I just know that my life hasn't worked out so far and it's time for a major change."

No doubt about it, moving to the outskirts of a small village like Stoneham was going to be a tremendous change for life-of-the-party, shopaholic Angelica. And yet, if Tricia was honest with herself, Angelica hadn't annoyed her half as much as in years past. Tricia was even beginning to anticipate their nightly meals together, knowing it would end sooner rather than later.

Angelica seemed to be waiting for some kind of comment.

"I think it's great," Tricia said at last. "And, if nothing else, I think you'll have a lot of fun fixing it up and decorating it."

Angelica's smile was small, but pleased. She changed the subject. "And what did you do today?"

One thing she wasn't about to disclose was her talk with Frannie. Never had she been shamed so thoroughly and sweetly.

"I made a trip to Benwell, spoke to Mike Harris's mother at the assisted living center."

"The poor woman with Alzheimer's?" Angelica asked.

"I don't think she has dementia of any kind. She even remembered the date my store opened."

"Then what's she doing in an old folks' home?"

"Good question. And as I suspected, it looks like her son has been selling off her assets without permission."

"The rat. Why are half the men I meet rats?" Angelica asked.

"Grace is concerned about her jewelry and her late husband's coin collection. Apparently Mike has stolen from her before."

"Then I don't blame her for being upset."

"She wants me to check out her house and make sure those items are still there."

"And you want to do that tonight?" Angelica asked, her eyes gleaming with delight.

"I thought about it. You busy?"

Angelica planted her hand on her left hip. "Would I be here with my sister if I had a man to cook for?"

"You tell me."

Angelica didn't answer, but bent down to peek through the oven's glass door at the Irish soda bread she had baking.

Tricia wandered over to the kitchen island, rested her elbows on the surface, with her head in her hands. "It bothers me that Grace was committed to St. Godelive's for dementia six months ago, but suddenly her symptoms have disappeared. What if she never had dementia? Could Mike have faked the symptoms that put her away?"

"Very easily," Angelica said. "Remember Ted, my third husband? His doctor prescribed some new heart medicine for him that interacted with another drug he was already taking. Suddenly the man I loved was gone. It was a nightmare until I figured out what was wrong—with the help of our local pharmacist, of course. Took more than a month for Ted to get back on an even keel. Of course we broke up six months later when he fell in love with said pharmacist. He felt she'd saved his life." She rolled her eyes.

Poor Angelica. Dumped by at least two of her husbands. And that wasn't fair. She was a woman of worth. What was wrong with these jerks?

Tricia changed the subject. "I also saw Sheriff Adams today. That woman is more stubborn than a terrier. She's determined to prove me guilty of Doris Gleason's murder."

"All the more reason to check out Grace's house. The soda bread will be ready in a few minutes. Take out the butter and let's chow down and hit the road."

Tricia smiled, pleased. "Okay, but only if you insist."

ALL THIS INTRIGUE had Angelica thinking like the heroine in a suspense novel, and she insisted on parking her rental car several blocks away from the Harris homestead. Despite the threat of rainy weather, the clouds remained high, blocking out the moon. They left their umbrellas in the car and prayed the rain would hold off, as Tricia didn't want to leave any wet, muddy telltale footprints in and around the house.

Dressed all in black and armed with the large orange flashlight, Tricia felt like a cat burglar and was grateful for the canopy of trees blocking most of the light from the streetlamps. She and Angelica turned up Grace's driveway and seamlessly blended into the darkness.

Mike hadn't bothered to leave on any outside lights, and none of them appeared to have motion sensors, leaving the yard spooky and uninviting. However, trying to lift the garage door proved it was either locked or was fitted with a door-opening system and effectively locked. They circled the garage and found a door, but it, too, was locked.

"Break the glass," Angelica urged. "You *do* have permission to be here."

"I'm sure the sheriff would disagree with you on that. Besides, Mike would see it the next time he came by."

"Isn't there a window on the side? Break it."

Easier said than done. The window was old, three-over-three panes; she'd have to break the whole bottom level in order to have enough room to struggle through, and then there were the mullions. She'd have to somehow dismantle them, too, and they'd brought no tools. The flashlight proved to be as effective as a hammer, and Tricia was grateful the next-door neighbors' windows were closed, with a good fifteen or more feet away from the sound of breaking glass and splintering wood.

"How am I going to get in without getting cut on all that glass?" she hissed.

"You'll have to go feet first. I'll help you."

Tricia was thankful there was no one nearby with a video recorder to chronicle the deed as she and Angelica hauled a heavy trash can to the window.

"What's in here, lead?" Angelica complained.

Tricia removed the lid and shone the light inside. Paper, stuff that should

have been shredded. Old bills, receipts, and . . . "Photographs?" An old album of black-and-white photos and lots of torn color shots of people Tricia didn't know. As she flipped through the pictures she recognized many of Grace.

"Why would Mike throw away all these pictures?" Angelica asked.

"Maybe he doesn't have a love of family. From what I understand, it's just him and his mother left."

"All the more reason to hold on to your memories of the past."

The thought didn't comfort Tricia, who rescued as many pictures as she could see, piling them by the side of the garage. "I'll save these for Grace. Maybe take a few of them to her tomorrow. Hopefully we'll find a bag inside to make it easier to carry them back to the car."

With half its contents removed, the trash can was considerably lighter and easier to maneuver. But worming through the window was a lot harder than Tricia would've thought. Climbing onto the can, she poked her feet through the window and Angelica huffed and puffed to raise her derriere up high enough to push her torso through and into the garage. Next Angelica held on to her hands as Tricia bent back like a limbo dancer and lowered herself into the garage, her sneakered feet crunching broken glass as she landed. Once inside, Angelica handed her the flashlight. "Be careful."

The bobbing light failed to give adequate illumination, and Tricia's hips bumped and banged against a number of tables haphazardly heaped with kitchen items, old clothes, and glassware, no doubt items that hadn't sold at Mike's tag sale. Tricia sidled her way to the back of the garage. Old dusty rakes, snow shovels, and other garden tools hung on the wall and she waved the beam back and forth, searching for the little flowered print Grace had assured her would be there.

"What's taking so long?" Angelica demanded in a harsh whisper.

Tricia ignored her, and restarted her search, this time painting the light up and down, noticing an old spiderwebbed set of golf clubs, aged, stained bushel baskets, and finally—a little, faded print of pansies. She pulled the framed picture from its nail and just as Grace had said, found an extra set of house keys.

"Eureka!" She replaced the picture, unlocked the door, and turned off the flashlight before stepping back outside and closing the door once more. "Angelica? Where are you?" she whispered into the inky blackness. A tap on the shoulder nearly sent Tricia into cardiac arrest. "Don't do that!"

"Well, you did call me. I take it you have the key?" Angelica asked.

"Keys," she said, and held them up. "Come on, let's get inside before someone sees us."

They walked to the back of the house and Angelica held the flashlight while Tricia tried the first key, which didn't fit. What if Mike had changed the locks?

She tried the next one. Still no luck. “There’s only one left.” She slid the brass key into the hole and this time it turned.

“Thank goodness,” Angelica breathed.

Tricia turned the handle, pushed the door open, and stepped inside, with Angelica close enough to step on her heels. “Give me the flashlight and close the door,” she whispered. Angelica complied and Tricia searched for a light switch, flipping it as soon as she heard the door latch.

Bright white light nearly blinded them and it took a moment for Tricia to realize they’d entered the big house through the butler’s pantry. Dark-stained oak shelves and cabinets lined the ten-foot walls clear up to the ceiling, with a little ladder on a track making the highest regions accessible. The shelves, however, were completely empty. No crystal, no dishes. No cans of peaches or coffee. Just an accumulation of dust. And in that small, enclosed space, Tricia was suddenly aware of Angelica’s perfume.

“What is that you’re wearing?”

Angelica pulled at her jacket. “This little thing?”

“No, your perfume. Do you bathe in the stuff?”

“I won’t even dignify that question with an answer. Now, do you think the neighbors will think something funny is going on if we turn on the lights?” Angelica asked.

“Maybe we’d better close the blinds, just to be on the safe side.” And Tricia did.

“Where does that doorway lead?”

“The kitchen.”

“Why are we whispering?” Angelica asked.

Tricia cleared her throat. “Didn’t we go through this at Doris’s house?”

“It’s you who keeps whispering,” Angelica pointed out.

Tricia gritted her teeth. “Come on.”

They entered the kitchen, and Tricia flicked on a flashlight.

“Whoa! Time warp,” Angelica declared, taking in the color of the dated appliances and décor.

The kitchen looked exactly as it had when Tricia had been there only the day before with Mike—with a couple of small additions. A mortar and pestle sat on the counter, along with a canister of gourmet cocoa.

“This looks suspicious,” Angelica said.

“Yeah. What do you think the odds are that if we looked through the drawers—or maybe the garbage—we’d find some empty medicine vials?”

“I’m game to look,” Angelica said and pulled open a drawer with the sleeve of her jacket drawn over her fingers. “Look, Trish, plastic gloves. I assume you didn’t bring any this time. Maybe we’d better use these. We wouldn’t want to leave any incriminating evidence behind.”

Having read a score of *CSI*-based books, Tricia knew they probably already had. Still, she placated her sister and donned the pair of gloves Angelica handed her. Angelica pulled open another drawer.

"The nurse on Grace's floor mentioned she had made a sudden improvement. I'll bet Mike sent her there with a supply of her favorite cocoa and they ran out in the last couple of weeks. Looks like Mike's concocting a new batch."

"Sounds plausible," Angelica said and shut her fourth drawer. "No sign of any little amber bottles."

"We'll check the rest of the kitchen and the garbage on the way out. We'd better get moving in case Mike shows up."

"It's almost nine thirty. If he was going to steal more of his mother's possessions, wouldn't he do it earlier in the day?"

"Who can fathom the criminal mind?" Tricia took off down the darkened hall, the flashlight beam guiding her way. She paused in the foyer at the base of the grand stairway leading to the upstairs.

"Can't we turn on any lights?"

"Not unless we can be sure they can't be seen from the street."

"What do we tell the paramedics if one of us falls and breaks her neck?"

"Oops?" Tricia aimed the light up the long, dark stairway, wishing she'd taken Mike up on his offer of a house tour. Then again, she might've unwillingly ended up in one of the beds.

They crept up the stairs, with Angelica so close behind Tricia that she could feel her sister's breath on her neck. A stair creaked, Angelica squeaked, and a shot of adrenaline coursed through Tricia.

"If any vampires jump out at us I'm going to lose it completely," Angelica rasped.

They made it to the top of the stairs without any attacking bloodsuckers descending and Tricia ran the flashlight's beam across the floor and into an open doorway. Angelica grabbed her sleeve as she started forward, following her step for step.

The prim and proper formal sitting room had Victorian furniture and décor, from the clunky marble-topped tables, embroidered pillows on the horsehair couches, to the frosted glass sconces on the walls. They found another parlor across the hall, but this was furnished for more masculine tastes, no doubt the domain of the late Jason Harris.

A computer sat on the desk, with neat stacks of papers at its side. Tricia trained the light over one of the pages. "Exhibit one," she said, the light focused on the eBay logo on the top of the sheet. It was a listing for the online auction site, complete with a picture of a Hummel figurine. "I'll bet this is one of the things from Grace's now-empty curio cabinet downstairs. He's been listing her

stuff. This is only dated yesterday. And I'll bet I gave him the idea," she said, angry with herself.

"Don't be ridiculous. Look at that stack," Angelica pointed out. "Nobody could accomplish all that in only a day. See, there are photos for everything, too. Doesn't the background look like the kitchen counter and backsplash?"

She was right.

Tricia folded the paper, stowing it in her pocket. "I'll show this to Grace to confirm it's one of her figurines. Maybe there's a way she can recover it, or at least prove that Mike's been stealing from her."

"We'd better get moving," Angelica advised.

"The bedrooms must be in the back," Tricia whispered and turned away for the doorway, still unable to squelch the feeling they were violating the house with their presence.

The two small bedrooms on the right side of the hall were connected by an old-fashioned bathroom. The first, painted in tones of blue, would've suited a boy, and had probably been Mike's. The other, a tiny guest room with a small empty closet, had only a bed, an empty dresser, and a straight-backed wooden chair.

They crossed to the other side of the hall and Tricia played the flashlight's beam across an unmade king-sized bed. "Aha, the master bedroom."

"Now can we turn on a light?" Angelica asked.

Tricia threw a switch and the lights blazed. Unlike the other rooms that were more or less intact, the once-pretty master suite had been ransacked. What Tricia had taken as a rumpled bed proved to be destroyed—the sheets torn and the pillows shredded. The gold-edged French provincial dresser's drawers had all been dumped, with piles of woman's clothes littering the floor. She didn't see the jewelry boxes Grace had told her about.

"Looks like the result of a lot of anger," Angelica said.

"I hope this means he didn't find Grace's hiding place."

"And you know where it is?"

Tricia nodded. "Help me move the mattress and box springs."

"Do I look like a stevedore?" But Angelica did help Tricia pull the mattress up to stand against the wall, and they hauled up one of the twin box springs against it, too. Grace hadn't mentioned the trapdoor would be under a large area rug. They ended up moving the other box spring, dragging away the heavy headboard and side rails in order to pull up the rug. The trapdoor was exactly as Grace had described it, although much larger than Tricia had anticipated, measuring one by two feet. Tricia knelt in front of the recessed brass ring, pulled it up, and yanked open the door. The hiding space was even bigger than the door to it, and filled with an assortment of little black velvet-covered boxes.

Angelica grabbed one and popped it open. "Trish, look."

It was empty.

It took ten minutes of searching to find that they were all empty.

Tricia's eyes grew moist. She hadn't thought the loss of Grace's treasures would affect her so much. But anguish soon turned to pique. "That stinking rat."

Angelica sniffed. "Maybe you were right. A man who could steal from his own mother probably *is* capable of throwing a rock through a storefront window. Do you think he's already sold everything?" Angelica asked, her voice soft.

"You saw all those eBay sheets." Tricia picked up the first of the boxes and replaced it in the hiding place. "Have you seen his expensive little car? I'm not saying an insurance agent couldn't afford it, but it seems pretty coincidental that he bought it after his mother was put in the home—and her assets started disappearing." She glanced around at the devastation. "This had to just happen."

"How do you know?"

"Just yesterday morning Mike offered me a tour of the upstairs. He wouldn't have if the room was in this shape."

"Unless he was hoping to suddenly discover a robbery with a handy witness in tow."

Tricia frowned. "He did seem eager for me to come up here." Maybe Angelica was right and it wasn't her feminine wiles that had precipitated the invitation.

She shook her head. No, the slimeball had made his intentions well known.

"How did he ever find Grace's hidey hole?" Angelica wondered. "I mean, this isn't exactly the easiest place to find."

"He's been throwing out receipts. There were lots of them in the trash. He could've found one from whoever built this hiding space."

"It's possible," Angelica agreed, but she sounded skeptical. She helped Tricia replace the rest of the boxes before they restored the room to the way they'd found it. Hopefully Mike wouldn't notice if the sheets, pillows, or bedspread weren't in the exact same positions.

Tricia turned the flashlight on and switched off the overhead light. They waited for their eyes to adjust to the darkness before she led the way back down the long staircase, with Angelica at her heels once more.

They'd reached the bottom of the stairs and just started down the hall toward the back of the house when Tricia stopped dead, flicking off the flashlight.

Angelica ran right into her. She opened her mouth but Tricia pivoted and clamped a hand across it. "Shhh!"

Voices.

In the kitchen.

Mike, and he was with another person . . . a woman, whose voice Tricia recognized.

EIGHTEEN

WITH HER RIGHT hand still clamped across Angelica's mouth, Tricia shuffled across the Persian runner and into the dining room, dragging her sister along with her. She plastered herself against the wall of the darkened room, closed her eyes, and listened—concentrating.

Yes, it *was* Deirdre Gleason's voice.

"I can't make out what they're saying," Angelica complained.

Tricia's hand tightened around her sister's arm, silencing her. She closed her eyes again, concentrating on the muffled voices, but caught only snatches of words:

"Books . . . case price . . . wholesale . . ."

"Total—cash only . . ."

Obviously they discussed some kind of financial deal. No doubt after their talk the day before, Mike had contacted Deirdre, eager to dump more of his mother's possessions. And a cash deal left no paper trail.

Although risking detection, Tricia crept forward and peeked through the crack in the door, hoping to hear better. A solemn-faced Deirdre stood beside the counter, a book in hand, looking very much like a professor in mid-lecture. Could she have picked up that much knowledge about cookbooks in such a short time? Then again, Tricia didn't know how much the sisters had discussed the business before Doris's passing. Or perhaps it was her accountant's background that made Deirdre such a hard negotiator.

Finally, a deal was struck and Mike disappeared into the butler's pantry while Deirdre started taking down the cookbooks from the kitchen cabinet.

Tricia grabbed Angelica's arm and hauled her back into the hallway where they crept along, backs pressed to the wall. "We've got to hide."

"Where?"

"There's a closet in the foyer."

"Ooohhh . . . please don't make me hide in a closet," Angelica whined. "I'm claustrophobic."

"We get caught and you'll feel a lot more claustrophobic sitting in a jail cell."

With exaggerated care, Tricia opened the closet door, but the hinges were well lubricated and nothing squeaked except Angelica as Tricia pulled her inside and closed the door.

Tricia was glad she'd donned her good old dependable Timex and not the diamond-studded watch her ex-husband had given her on their tenth anniversary. She pressed the little button and the watch's face lit up: 9:53.

"How long do you think it'll take before they leave?" Angelica whimpered.

"I don't know. I just hope Mike didn't go looking for boxes in the garage. He's sure to see the broken window if he does."

"That doesn't mean he'll come looking for us in here."

"I can't remember if I put the pansy picture back on the wall."

Angelica let out another strangled whine. "I hate this, I hate this. I want to go home. Please let me go home. This isn't fun anymore. In fact, it never was fun. I don't like being a criminal. How did I ever let you talk me into helping you?"

"You volunteered!"

"Keep that light on, will you? I can't stand being in here."

"It'll wear down the battery. Besides, if you can't see you're in a closet, you can't be claustrophobic."

"Do you have to keep reminding me!"

"Shhh!"

Footsteps creaked along the hardwood floor, paused. Tricia thought about Angelica's perfume. Could Mike have caught the scent?

Panic started to grow within her as the seconds ticked by and she heard nothing else. Then, the footsteps moved away, probably heading for the living room. Could Mike be searching for them or had he just gone looking for another empty cardboard box?

Angelica began making small squeaking noises again and Tricia pressed a hand over her mouth once more. But the sounds of anguish were also beginning to tear at her soul and she found herself putting her other arm around her sister's shoulder in hopes of comforting her. Hot tears rolled over Tricia's fingers and Angelica began to tremble. "Not too much longer. You're doing great," she lied.

To prove her wrong, Angelica's knees went rubbery and she started to slide. Tricia struggled to hold her upright, but ended up on the closet floor beside her. Angelica drew her knees to her chest, crossed her arms over them, and rested her head on her hands, her stifled sobs bringing stinging tears to Tricia's eyes. Never had she inflicted such suffering on another human being, and yet she didn't open the door, didn't dare risk their being found.

The footsteps came closer again, then headed down the hall and faded.

Long minutes passed.

The air in the closet seemed to grow staler. Finally Tricia could stand it no longer and reached for the handle, opening the door a crack. Fresh air rushed in, and Angelica hiccupped.

"Shhh!" But this time Tricia's aim was to soothe, not rebuke.

Time crawled. Except for their breathing, no sounds broke the absolute silence.

Eventually Tricia poked her head around the door, listening.

Nothing.

More minutes passed.

Finally Tricia pulled herself up, muscles stiff from their confinement.

Angelica didn't move.

Tricia slipped out of her loafers, crept down the hall, saw no light coming from beneath the door that led to the kitchen. She padded into the dining room, peeked around at the crack around the door to the kitchen. It was dark, silent, and once again empty.

With more speed than agility, she headed back down the hall.

"It's okay, they're gone. You can come on out," she called, but still Angelica didn't move.

Tricia stepped back into her shoes, bent down, and fumbled for the flashlight, which was still on the closet floor. She switched it on and trained the light on her sister's inert form. "Ange. Ange!" She shook her sister's shoulder.

Angelica lifted her head, blinked red-rimmed eyes. "I think I fell asleep," she said, her voice tiny.

Tricia helped her to stand, threw her arms around Angelica. "I owe you big-time, big sister."

"Can we go now? I think I need a really strong drink."

"You're not the only one. Come on."

Linking arms, Tricia steadied Angelica as they made their way back to the kitchen. She pointed the flashlight at the cabinet, which was now devoid of books. "Looks like Deirdre took the lot."

"She can have them."

Tricia ran the flashlight's beam across the kitchen counter. "Hey, look." The mortar and pestle hadn't been put away, but the cocoa container was gone.

ANGELICA UPENDED THE bottle of chardonnay, watching as a single drop fell into her empty stemmed glass. "Got anything else to drink?"

"I think you've had enough," Tricia said, dipping another slice of baguette into herb-laced olive oil. She closed her eyes, leaned back, and let the bread lay on her tongue, savoring the spices of Tuscany.

On the way back from Grace's house, they'd diverted to Milford and a Shaw's grocery store where, despite being an emotional wreck, Angelica had been only too willing to toss together a grocery basket of comfort foods featuring bread, artesian cheeses, fresh fruit, and a couple of bottles of wine. Return-

ing to Haven't Got a Clue, the sisters settled on the sumptuous sectional in Tricia's living room, with mellow jazz on the CD player, a purring cat, and a desire to totally pig out.

Tricia cut herself another slab of St. Agur, a French blue cheese so buttery and mild it made her think of running away from home to forever milk contented cows in lush mountain meadows. She savored the flavor again, closing her eyes and reveling in it—only to open them again to see Angelica's vacant gaze had wandered out the darkened windows that overlooked Main Street beyond.

"Don't think about it," Tricia said.

Angelica shook herself, cleared her throat. "Think about what?"

Tricia didn't have to say. "I'm so sorry, Ange. I had no idea you had a problem with—" The words hung like a wet blanket at a birthday party.

"How could you? I mean, it's not like we were ever close." Angelica's eyes grew moist. "Until maybe . . . now?"

"What happened with us? Why didn't we ever talk? Why couldn't we ever be close?"

Angelica sighed. "I was five when you were born. That's a lifetime to a little girl. I was the star, the loved one. The sun rose and set on me, and then you came along—an intruder, something to tear Mother's and Daddy's love from me."

"But I didn't."

"Of course you didn't. I told you, I *was* the star. And you were this little mousy thing only too happy to stand in my shadow."

Tricia bit her tongue, struggling to hold on to the warm feelings she'd experienced toward her sister, afraid it had all been for nothing.

"Too bad Mother and Daddy didn't just smack my bottom and tell me to get over it. Think of the years we've wasted." She held up her glass, with only a drop or two of wine at its bottom.

"Where did your claustrophobia come from?"

Angelica sighed. "I was locked in a closet when you'd just started to walk."

Tricia's stomach roiled. "I couldn't have locked you in there."

"Of course you didn't. You were just a baby, fussy and sick that day. I was annoyed you were getting all the attention. So I . . . kind of . . . pinched you, made you cry, only I didn't know Grandmother was watching. She threatened to send me to an orphan home. To escape her wrath I fled to Mother's bedroom closet and shut the door—only I couldn't get it open again. They didn't find me for hours and hours, and by then I was a basket case, sure they'd forgotten me and that I'd never be loved again. I've hated small, closed-in spaces ever since. Didn't you ever wonder why I never fly anywhere?"

"I did . . ." But not very hard, Tricia admitted to herself. "How can you drive?"

"When I'm behind the wheel, I'm in control. In other situations . . . let's say

I just don't do as well." She let out a breath. "There, now it's in the open. I'm sorry if I embarrassed you."

"I'm sorry to have made you go through it all again tonight."

Angelica's lower lip sagged. "Thank you. Let's try not to have a repeat performance." She sniffed and sank back into the sofa cushions. "And can we please change the subject? Like what's going on with Mike Harris and Deirdre Gleason?"

Tricia, too, was glad to leave the night's events behind them. "I still say that Mike had the motive and opportunity to kill Doris."

"Or do you only believe that now because he's proved himself to be a lying, cheating son?"

Tricia shook her head, wouldn't back down.

"Okay, give me his motive," Angelica said mechanically, lounging against a stack of pillows.

"Stealing that rare cookbook."

"Give me the opportunity."

"Stoneham's sidewalks roll up at six p.m on a Tuesday. The street was empty, the shops all closed. He could've crossed the street from his campaign headquarters, stabbed her, and fled on foot with the book. It was small enough to hide under his shirt. And he's a known entity with a reason to be on Main Street at that time of night. No one would even think twice about seeing him."

"Yada, yada, yada," Angelica muttered, leaning forward and slathering another piece of baguette with creamy cheese.

Tricia folded her arms across her chest in defiance. "Okay, give me Deirdre's motivation for killing her sister."

"Money. It always comes down to money, same as you figure for Mike. She inherits her sister's business, life insurance policy—"

"Doris's business was on the downslide. She complained to me that if Bob raised her rent, she'd have to close down."

"And isn't it amazing that he's backed off that demand—"

"Only for a year, and only because he fears being sued."

"Every sibling in the world has, at one time or another, wanted to kill his or her sisters and brothers. It's been that way since the days of Cain and Abel."

Tricia opened her mouth to deny it, but closed it again.

"I pinched you when you were a baby. If I'd been a really rotten kid, who knows what I would've done. Of course, after that one incident I rose above such base instincts." She gouged another lump of cheese from the rapidly disappearing slab.

Only the threat of being sent to an orphanage had curtailed young Angelica's homicidal tendencies. And while Tricia had often found her sister as irri-

tating as a thorn imbedded in her skin, she'd never actually harbored feelings of fratricide. Not seriously at least.

"The problem is," Angelica said offhandedly, "nobody but the two of us is even worried about who killed Doris Gleason, or who might be cheating Grace Harris. And there's really nothing we can do about either situation."

"I'm not so sure. We just haven't got enough information."

"And where are we going to find it?"

"I'm going back to St. Godelive's tomorrow to make sure Grace isn't given any more of Mike's cocoa, and I'm going to see what it'll take to get her out of that place."

"Haven't you forgotten something?"

"What?"

"The sheriff is trying to pin Doris's death on you. You may not have much more time before she decides to come after you. I think you should call an attorney."

"I've got a business to run—"

"Which you can't do from jail," Angelica pointed out.

"Then why don't you find me a lawyer? You haven't got anything else to do."

"In this little burg?"

"It might be better than bringing in some hotshot from Boston. A local guy—"

"Or gal—"

"—might know how to manipulate Sheriff Adams," Tricia continued.

"Or deliver you straight into her hands," Angelica warned.

Tricia raised her wineglass to her lips but paused before drinking. "I'll take that risk."

NINETEEN

TRICIA WASN'T EXACTLY sure how Angelica ended up in her bed while she and Miss Marple were relegated to the couch, but she vowed it wouldn't happen again. She'd run four miles on the treadmill, showered, and breakfasted before Angelica even opened an eye.

"Coffee," Angelica wailed, as she shuffled into the kitchen. Her hair stood out at odd angles and Tricia's white terry bathrobe was at least two sizes too small for her. She settled on a stool at the island and allowed Tricia to place a

steaming mug in front of her. "Please, don't ever let me polish off an entire bottle of wine again."

"I've got to get the store ready for the day. Hang out here as long as you want. I left the phone book over on the counter."

Squinting, Angelica peered over the rim of her cup. "Phone book?"

"You said you'd find me a lawyer today."

"Oh yeah." She closed her eyes and took a tentative sip. "I didn't sleep real well last night. Had a lot of time to think. You've got too much going on, what with chasing around and looking for killers, so I've decided the least I can do is help out at Haven't Got a Clue."

Sudden panic gripped Tricia. If Angelica made herself comfortable in the store, she'd never get rid of her. "No need. I've just hired Mr. Everett. Between him and Ginny, and me, we're covered."

"But Mr. Everett has spent a lot of time watching Deirdre, and you've got to go see Grace Harris. And Ginny has to have a lunch break at some point. No, I insist. And I intend to help you as long as I'm here in Stoneham."

Tricia didn't bother to argue. Instead, she turned and marched down the stairs to her shop. As expected, Mr. Everett was waiting at the front door, with his umbrella in hand. She let him in and he immediately went to the coffee station, pulled out a new filter, and measured coffee for the Bunn-o-Matic.

"You're ready for rain again, I see," Tricia said and moved to the counter to watch him, marveling at how easily he'd slipped into Haven't Got a Clue's daily routine.

"Doppler radar shows what's left of Hurricane Sheila sweeping through western New York. We'll see it by the afternoon, I'm afraid."

Tricia nodded. Thinking about the day ahead, she asked, "Mr. Everett, would you mind keeping an eye on Deirdre again today?"

His brow puckered. "It's not as interesting as working here, but if that's what you need me to do, I'm happy just to feel useful."

Time to dig a little deeper. "Has she . . . mentioned her sister much?"

Mr. Everett hit the coffeemaker's start button. "She doesn't really talk to me, except to order me about. I must say I expected her to be a little kinder than Doris. Then again, they are twins."

Were twins, Tricia automatically corrected to herself. "I assume you haven't told her that you're on my payroll."

"Not exactly. I told her that you were concerned about her safety and had asked me to help out."

That being the case, it wasn't likely she'd say anything of any use in front of Mr. Everett. Still, having a mole in enemy territory could be beneficial.

"What time does Deirdre usually show up at the Cookery?"

He consulted his watch. "Right about now."

As if on cue, the white car with Connecticut plates pulled into the parking space in the empty slot between Haven't Got a Clue and the Cookery.

"Why don't you take Deirdre a cup of coffee? And maybe you can find out where she's getting her new stock."

Mr. Everett smiled. "Shall I pretend I'm master spy George Smiley?"

"Why not? It may even make your day go faster."

"I will admit that I'm looking forward to Ms. Gleason reopening her store so that I may come back here and do some real work. Those biographies could still use reorganizing."

"I'm sure it'll only be for another couple of days. And I really appreciate you helping Deirdre out like this. I'm fairly certain she won't voice her gratitude to us directly."

Ginny arrived as Mr. Everett departed. "Grab my coat when you hang up yours, please."

Ginny did as she was asked. "Going somewhere first thing in the morning?"

Tricia finished counting the bills for the cash drawer. "I've got an errand to run that just won't wait."

"No problem. I can handle just about anything that crops up."

Tricia closed the register, remembering something she'd meant to ask Ginny before this. "You worked for Doris Gleason at one time. Did she always have that ugly jet-black hair?"

Ginny laughed. "No. She only started dying it in the past year."

"Do you remember when she started?"

Ginny let out a breath, frowning. "It must've been just before I came to work for you. I thought she looked downright stupid."

"What about that pageboy hairdo?"

"She used to have long white hair pinned up in a bun. I had to bite my lip to keep from laughing the day she showed up with it cut short and dyed coal black."

"Tricia!" came the sound of Angelica's voice from the stairwell to the loft apartment.

Tricia snatched her jacket and struggled into the sleeves. "My sister thinks she might like to help out around the store. But I want to make it clear that *you* are in charge. And whatever you do, don't let her bully you. In fact, if she insists on helping, start her out stocking shelves. Hauling around heavy boxes ought to discourage her from volunteering in the future."

Ginny's grin was positively evil. "This could be an awful lot of fun."

Tricia grabbed the photo album she'd rescued from Grace's trash can,

stuffed it into a plastic bag, snagged her purse, and hurried for the door. "Make it so—and thanks."

"Tricia!" Angelica called again.

The door closed on Tricia's back with the jingling of little bells. She headed down the sidewalk at a brisk pace, but made sure to look through the Cookery's plate-glass window, where she could see Deirdre already bullying Mr. Everett. A big first-week bonus was definitely in store for the patient little man.

TRICIA PARKED HER car, huddled in her jacket, and headed up the long concrete walk toward St. Godelive's main entrance. Just since the day before, a riot of yellow and magenta chrysanthemums had been planted around the entryway, giving the somber brick entrance a badly needed splash of color on this gray day. She walked through the entrance and was surprised that the foyer's drab, institutional gray paint had been replaced by a sunny yellow. New original art, beautifully framed, adorned the walls. A small plaque gave the names of the residents who had made the paintings.

"What happened?" Tricia inquired at the reception desk, taking in the entryway with the wave of her hand.

The receptionist grinned. "New management. The official takeover was almost two weeks ago. So far the changes have been invisible—mainly new client procedures, that sort of thing. I'm hoping we see a lot more physical changes to the building and grounds. It'll make life a lot more comfortable and cheerful for our residents and staff."

"And your visitors, too. I'm here to see Mrs. Grace Harris."

The woman pushed the guest book and pen in front of Tricia with one hand and a visitor's badge with the other.

The elevator doors opened to the same depressing sight Tricia had witnessed on the previous day. It would no doubt take weeks—maybe longer—before the whole building saw a cosmetic makeover. Could the new patient procedures be responsible for Grace's return to her senses?

Tricia made a point to stop at the nurses' station. Martha was once again on duty.

"Hi, Martha. I'm here to see Mrs. Harris again."

"Welcome back. She's either in her room or the community room where you found her yesterday. Would you like me to take you there?"

"No need. I was thinking it might be nice to bring Grace a gift. Maybe some fruit, or candy, or—"

Martha shook her head. "I'm afraid we can't allow that."

"Is that one of your new rules?"

She nodded. "Well-meaning family and friends were bringing in outside food and desserts that played havoc with our clients' medical problems. For instance, there are a number of medications that interact with grapefruit. And a box of chocolates given to a diabetic can mean hospitalization."

"I understand Grace's son often brought her special gourmet cocoa. Do you still have it?"

Martha shook her head. "When St. Godelive's was sold, the staff was given strict instructions to dispose of any contraband that could compromise a client's well-being. That means everything not provided by the parent company was immediately trashed."

And days later Grace's personality emerged from a drugged state.

"Well, I can certainly understand your banning such things. Perhaps I could bring her some flowers or a plant instead?"

"I'm sure she'd love that. And it would sure brighten up her room."

Tricia leaned in closer, lowered her voice. "What would it take for Mrs. Harris to leave St. Godelive's?"

"She'd have to have somewhere to go where someone could watch over her. Although she's made splendid progress, she might even be able to live alone once more, but that would be up to her doctors and her family."

And perhaps the help of a good attorney.

"What do the doctors think caused Grace's remarkable recovery?"

"We're not allowed to talk about our clients' conditions."

"But surely her son was notified when she started to get better."

"Of course. But I can't—"

"—talk about it," Tricia finished for her. "I understand. Thank you." She gave Martha a sweet smile before starting down the hallway.

Once again she found Grace in the community room, in the same chair, staring out the same window, her expression blank. She still clasped the book Tricia had given her the day before, and for a moment Tricia's heart sank. Had Grace's recovery been only temporary? In a scant eighteen hours had she descended back into the maelstrom of fog that had held her captive for months?

"Grace?"

The light blue eyes flashed with recognition as Grace looked up. "Tricia! You came back. Did you bring me another book? Look, I've already finished *Deadly Honeymoon*." She held up the book, opening it to the last page.

"Did you enjoy it?"

"Just as much as the first time I read it. I'd love to reread all of Block's Bernie Rhodenbarr books again. Do you have any of them?"

"I'm sure I do. And I'd be glad to give them to you."

"Oh no. I can pay." She patted the chair next to her, inviting Tricia to sit. "I

could barely sleep last night. So many thoughts circled through my head. First of all, were you able to go to my house?"

Tricia moistened her dry lips before answering. "Yes."

As Grace studied Tricia's face, her expression began to sag. "It's gone, isn't it? All my jewelry. All Jason's coins. Everything."

"I'm afraid so," Tricia said, sadly.

Grace's hand flew to the little gold scatter pin Tricia had given her the day before. "Then this is all I have left from my grandmother." Her bottom lip trembled. "Jason would've been so disappointed in Michael. I can barely think his name without getting angry."

"You need to use that anger to get you out of here."

But Grace wasn't listening. "That boy has been the major disappointment of my life. We tried giving him pets when he was small, but he'd only torment them. A week didn't go by that we weren't called by the principal's office during his school years. In desperation, we sent him to boarding school for his last two years of high school. That seemed to straighten him out for a while. He flunked out of three colleges before he finally managed to graduate. He stayed away for a number of years after that. After Jason died, Michael came back to Stoneham, but it didn't take long before I'd found him helping himself to his father's possessions."

"The coin collection?"

Grace nodded. "And more."

Tricia opened her purse, took out the folded piece of paper she'd appropriated from the computer desk in Grace's house. "Do you recognize this figurine?"

Grace studied the ink-jet photo. "Jason gave me one just like this for my birthday one year. He gave me one every year since the late 1970s. I've got quite a collection." She studied the page, seemed to understand its significance. "They're all gone, too, aren't they?"

"If that's what you kept in your curio cabinet in the living room, then I'm afraid so."

"I only kept a few in there, along with some Waterford crystal," she shook her head, her eyes glistening. "All my beautiful things . . ."

"I'm afraid I have another unhappy piece of news." Tricia explained about the drug-laced cocoa and the fact that St. Godelive's being sold was what had saved her sanity. "Unfortunately, the chocolate Mike provided has been discarded, that means we can't prove what he's done to you, but at least he can't bring in any more."

"You've got to contact my lawyer, Harold Livingston. His office is in Milford." She shook her head impatiently. "I don't understand why he hasn't come

looking for me. Not only is he my lawyer, but we've been friends for over thirty years . . . at least I always thought so."

"I'll give him a call as soon as I get back to my store." And maybe Mr. Livingston could help Tricia protect her own interests, too. "I brought you something." Tricia withdrew the photo album from the plastic bag and handed it to Grace.

"Where did you get this?"

"I found it and a lot of other photos in the trash at your house."

"Oh dear, no," Grace said, and tears began to flow once more.

"It's okay. I rescued all I could find. I've got them safe at my store, and I'd be glad to hold on to them until you're out of here."

Grace turned moist eyes on Tricia. "You've been very kind to me, dear. Why?"

So she could clear her own name and get Sheriff Adams off her back?

Definitely.

Because Grace strongly reminded her of her own grandmother?

Maybe.

Because it was the right thing to do?

No contest.

TWENTY

Hand clutching the office door handle, Tricia paused to wonder if what she was about to do was the right course of action. She'd debated with herself during the twenty-minute trip from St. Godelive's to the county sheriff's office, and the entire hour Sheriff Adams had let her sit in the reception area's uncomfortable plastic chairs waiting for an audience. It was now showtime.

Wendy Adams sat back in her worn gray office chair behind a scarred Formica desk, hand clamped to a phone attached to the side of her head. She waved Tricia to the same straight-backed wooden chair before her that Tricia had taken the day before. Comfort for visitors was definitely not a high priority for Sheriff Adams—and was no doubt a calculated decision.

With ankles and knees clamped together, hands folded primly on her purse, Tricia waited for another five or six minutes for the sheriff to complete her phone conversation, which consisted of a number of grunts and "uh-huhs"

until Tricia was sure there was no one on the other end of the line and the sheriff was merely trying—and succeeding—to annoy her.

Tricia spent those final moments rehearsing her speech. She would not raise her voice. She would not lose her temper.

She hoped.

Finally Sheriff Adams hung up. She sat up, shuffled through some pages on the blotter before her, and without looking up spoke. "Now what was it you wanted to talk to me about?"

"Grace Harris."

The sheriff opened a drawer, rooted through the contents, and came up with a pen, which she tested on a scrap of paper before signing a document before her. "And who's Grace Harris? You going to accuse her of killing Doris Gleason, too?" She laughed mirthlessly.

"Grace Harris is Mike Harris's mother—you know, the guy running for selectman in Stoneham. Your lifelong friend? Grace is currently a resident at St. Godelive's Assisted Living Center in Benwell."

The sheriff looked unimpressed. "What's that got to do with anything?"

"It's rather a complicated story. But it turns out Grace was the original owner of the Amelia Simmons cookbook that was stolen from the Cookery the night Doris Gleason was murdered."

Contempt twisted Sheriff Adams's features. "And how did you come up with that?"

Don't get upset. Don't get angry, Tricia chided herself. *No matter what, you will remain calm.*

"The story begins with a spoiled son who decided not to wait until his remaining parent died before helping himself to what he felt was his inheritance."

She recounted the whole chain of events in chronological order: how Winnie Wentworth had purchased the rare booklet in what was probably a box lot of paperbacks and other ephemera. That Winnie had sold the booklet to Doris Gleason, who was probably murdered in an attempt to recover the book. How days later Winnie sold Tricia the little gold scatter pin and died before she could recount where she'd obtained it and the booklet. How Tricia had examined Grace's book collection at Mike Harris's behest. How her own curiosity compelled her to visit Grace at St. Godelive's, where she found the woman recovering from what had at first appeared to be dementia, but was in all likelihood a drug interaction. If not for the home's new rules and regulations, how Grace would've been sentenced to live out her days in a foggy netherworld, while her son sold off her assets and treated himself to a lavish lifestyle, while bankrolling his campaign for Stoneham selectman.

During the entire recitation, the sheriff's expression remained impassive. When Tricia finally finished, Wendy Adams stood, hunched over, planted her balled fists, gorilla-style, on her desktop, and drilled Tricia with her cold gaze.

"Since day one of this investigation, you have done your best to misdirect my efforts with wild accusations to divert attention from your own guilt," she said, her voice low and menacing. "I will not stand for this any longer. Mike Harris is a longtime resident of this village. If you continue to slander his good name, I will see to it that you face a lawsuit that will strip you of every asset you possess before I arrest you and see you rot in jail for the murder of Doris Gleason."

Stunned, Tricia could only stare at the woman in front of her. Mike's good name? Not according to Mr. Everett. And what possible reason could Sheriff Adams have for hating her so? Then in a flash it occurred to her: Mike Harris had shown interest in Tricia. Had asked her to lunch. Had invited her to his mother's home. Could Wendy Adams possibly have a crush on Mike? Or worse, could she be in bed with him—both literally and figuratively? Mike told Tricia he considered her his girlfriend. As a man skilled in manipulation, he could've said the same thing to Wendy Adams and she, being plain, overweight, and never married, chose to believe him. She wouldn't be the first intelligent woman to fall for flattery and the chance at romance with someone unworthy of her.

Struggling to remain calm, Tricia tried again, this time with Angelica's scenario. "There's also Deirdre Gleason's arriving in town prior to her sister's death. Why didn't she step forward? Why did she wait for you to contact her about Doris's murder before she—?"

For such a bulky woman, Sheriff Adams stepped around her desk with amazing speed, stopping only a foot in front of Tricia, towering over her. "I've had just about enough. If you're smart, you'll get out of here before I call in a deputy and have him arrest you on the spot."

"And the charge?" Tricia asked.

"Obstructing justice."

Tricia swallowed, somehow managing to hold on to her composure, and stood. "Thank you for your time, Sheriff Adams. I'm so glad you approach your job with such an open mind. I would hate to think you let personal feelings influence the way you serve the people of this county."

Wendy Adams straightened, leveled her blistering stare at Tricia, but made no further comment.

All eyes were upon her as, head held high, Tricia exited the sheriff's office and walked through the reception room and out to the parking lot. At some level, she hadn't really believed the sheriff would follow through with her threat of arrest. She did now. Angelica was right. She needed a lawyer, and fast. What

was Grace's attorney's name? Sounded like some old explorer. Stanley? No, Livingston—Harold Livingston.

The sky to the southwest was darkening as Tricia headed back to her car. Her hands were shaking as she withdrew her cell phone from her purse and found that once again she hadn't bothered to switch it on. It promptly announced that she'd missed two calls—both from Haven't Got a Clue. She dialed the number. It rang three times before a cheerful voice said, "Haven't Got a Clue, this is Angelica, how can I help you?"

It took a few moments for Tricia to find her voice. "Aren't you tired of playing store by now?"

"Trish, is that you? You sound funny."

Funny was not the word. "Ginny is in charge. You are not to try to take over," she said firmly.

"Oh, she made that abundantly clear," Angelica said, woodenly. "And she's been working me like a slave—shelving books, vacuuming. My back may never be the same. How did things go with Grace?"

Tricia had to take a calming breath before she could answer. "She wants me to talk to her attorney. It's a firm in Milford. Can you look up the number for me? The guy's name is Harold Livingston."

"Of Livingston, Baker, and Smith? Office on Route 101 A, right off 'the Oval'?"

"Uh, I guess. Why?"

"Because that's the firm I called to help you out." She paused. "What's an 'Oval'?"

"It's a rotary."

"A what?"

"A roundabout." Silence. "A traffic circle?" she tried.

"Oh. Well, anyway, you have an appointment with Mr. Livingston at two p.m."

"Looks like I need him. The sheriff just told me she definitely has plans to arrest me and hopes I rot in jail."

"Well, of course she'd say that. She's facing reelection. Even if the charge doesn't stand, she's got to have someone to pin the crime on. Why should she care if it costs you thousands in legal fees, plus your reputation? I already told you who murdered Doris—it was Deirdre."

"Try convincing the sheriff of that."

"I will. Yikes, look at the time. You'd better get going if you hope to make that two o'clock appointment."

Tricia glanced at her watch. "But I haven't even had lunch yet."

"I'll make you a big dinner. Here's the number," and she rattled it off.

Tricia jotted it down, then heard the tinkle of the bell over the shop door.

"A bus just unloaded another bunch from a cruise ship. I'm going to really push that stack of Dorothy L. Sayers books Ginny made me shelve. Gotta fly," Angelica said and the connection was broken.

Tricia lowered the phone and frowned at it. Angelica seemed to be enjoying playing store clerk a little too much. She called the attorney's office, received the address and directions, and headed for Milford.

The law firm of Livingston, Baker, and Smith was located in a charming Victorian house, a painted lady done in shades of blue, and it was obvious the building had been lovingly restored and maintained. Raindrops were just starting to fall as Tricia parked between a Lexus and a Lincoln Navigator along the south side of the building. She grabbed her umbrella from the backseat but didn't bother to open it, and walked around to the front and up the wooden stairs for the main entrance, with its stained-glass double doors.

The foyer's marbled floor looked freshly waxed. The grand, curved oak stairway directly in front led to apartments on the upper level, disappearing somewhere above the twelve-foot ceiling. The law office was to her right and through another tall oak door. A Persian rug and comfortable tapestry-upholstered chairs ringed what was once a formal parlor, its gray marble fireplace sporting a bushy fern in its maw. A painting of a distinguished older gentleman in a navy suit graced the back wall. Before it stood a counter; behind it, a receptionist looked up from her workspace. "May I help you?"

Tricia approached the desk, noticed the brass nameplate below the portrait read "Harold Livingston."

"My name is Tricia Miles. I have a two o'clock appointment with Mr. Livingston."

The receptionist, a thin, fiftysomething woman in a gray suit, stood, reminding Tricia of a blue heron. "He's waiting for you. Please come this way."

Tricia followed the woman down a brightly lit corridor. Evidently the rest of the first floor had been gutted to accommodate the partners' offices, however, they must have been rebuilt with architectural salvage, the result looking more like an old bank, with oak-and-frosted-glass doors, the occupants' names painted in gold leaf.

The receptionist knocked and opened the door at the far left. "Your two o'clock is here, Mr. Livingston." She turned back to Tricia. "You can go right in."

Tricia stopped at the room's threshold to stare at the man seated at the polished mahogany desk. Instead of a stately gray-haired gent, she found a dark-haired thirtysomething man, the sleeves of his white dress shirt rolled up, looking like he should be on a Hollywood movie set, not in a New England law firm.

"There must be some mistake. I understood I was to see Mr. Harold Livingston."

The younger man stood. "My late uncle. I'm Roger Livingston." He offered her his hand and she stepped forward to take it. Firm, but not crushing. One point in his favor. "Please sit." He indicated one of the client chairs before his desk.

"When did your uncle . . . pass?"

"Just over six months ago." Which would explain why he had never gone looking for Grace. Had Mike known this? Had he been biding his time, waiting for Grace to be especially vulnerable before implementing his plan to pillage his mother's estate?

"I understand you have quite a problem. I've only handled a couple of criminal cases, but I interned at a firm in Boston that took on a lot of pro bono work, defending at-risk youths."

"I'm afraid Sheriff Adams is determined to arrest me for murder, despite the fact there's no evidence or motive for me to have committed the crime. But I was also hoping to talk to your uncle about a client of his, Mrs. Grace Harris."

"Attorney-client privilege would've prevented that," he explained.

"Mrs. Harris is in desperate need of legal protection. If you've taken over your uncle's practice, I'd appreciate it if you could review her file. She told me your uncle had drawn up papers—including power of attorney—that specified who did and who did not have the right to take care of her affairs should she become incapacitated."

"As I said, I'm not at liberty to talk about Mrs. Harris's affairs."

"Would you at least speak to her? She was committed to an assisted living facility under suspicious circumstances. Her son seems to have been selling off her assets and she wants it stopped."

Roger took out a pen, jotted down a few notes. "Where is she now?"

"At St. Godelive's Assisted Living Center in Benwell."

He nodded. "I know the place."

"Will you go see her, today if possible? I'd be glad to pay you up front for your time."

"Are you a friend of Mrs. Harris's?"

"I met her yesterday, but I suspect her problems may be linked to my own legal troubles."

Roger Livingston set down his pen and leaned back in his chair. "I think you'd better tell me everything."

TWENTY-ONE

THE DRIZZLE HAD escalated into a driving rain as Tricia drove back to Stoneham and Haven't Got a Clue. Although it had cost her five thousand in a retainer's fee just to cover her size-eight butt, she felt better about the entire situation. Unless she'd manufactured evidence, the sheriff had no probable cause for an arrest. And Tricia had firm instructions not to even speak to the sheriff again. "Talk to my lawyer, talk to my lawyer," would now become her mantra. Thankfully, Roger Livingston remembered Grace Harris and promised he'd look into her situation as well.

Tricia parked in the village's municipal lot, grabbed her umbrella, and hurried down the empty sidewalk. The rain seemed to have chased away the tourists, and from the look of the weather, the gray skies had settled in for the rest of the day. She glanced at her watch and found it was already 3:40.

Passing by the Cookery, she saw Mr. Everett looking dour as he stood holding the ladder for Deirdre, who placed books on a shelf. From the look on the older woman's face, she wasn't giving him a compliment. Okay, that was enough. As of today, she would free Mr. Everett from his mission and allow him access to his beloved biographies and his rearranging.

She hurried past and backed into Haven't Got a Clue to close her umbrella before entering. At times like these she wished 221B Baker Street had had an awning over the front door so her shop could be likewise outfitted. Ginny looked up from her post at the sales counter; beside her, Miss Marple sat with paws tucked under her, haughty and dignified. "'Bout time, too," Ginny said in greeting and immediately shifted her gaze toward the nook. Eyes closed, and resembling a sack of potatoes, Angelica had stretched out on one of the upholstered chairs, her feet resting on the big square coffee table.

"Ange, we don't sit while the store's open. It's not good for business," Tricia admonished.

Angelica opened one eye, glared at her sister. "You people are slave drivers. You don't even give your help decent lunch breaks. I barely had time to whip up a grilled cheese sandwich, let alone eat it, before Simon Legree here was screaming for me to get back to work."

"I needed help with the customers," Ginny said, her attention dipping back down to the magazine on the counter.

Tricia set her wet umbrella down beside the radiator to dry, then marched straight over to Angelica, grabbing her by the arm and pulling her to her feet.

"There're no customers, why can't I sit?" she wailed.

"It looks bad to potential customers who look through the windows." As if to emphasize her words, the door opened, the bell over it tinkling, but it was only Mr. Everett.

"Ms. Miles, I quit!" he said resentfully, crossed his arms over his chest, and stood firm.

"Why?"

"I simply refuse to be bullied by that . . . that . . . horrible woman next door. I regret I must tender my resignation if I'm not permitted to do the work for which I was hired—"

"It's okay, Mr. Everett," she placated, hands outstretched. "Twice today I saw your expression as she barked at you, and I agree you've gone above and beyond the call of duty."

"That woman verbally abused me. I didn't tolerate that kind of disrespect when I owned my own business, and I can't abide seeing it in others."

"You owned your own business?" Ginny asked.

The older man puffed out his chest. "Yes. At one time I owned and managed Stoneham's only grocery store. We were forced to close when the big chain stores came into Milford."

Tricia stepped forward, touched the elderly man's arm. "Starting right now, you can help us here in the store again."

"What about me?" Angelica demanded.

Tricia turned on her sister. "I can't afford three employees."

Angelica's sour gaze swept across the room to land on Ginny, as though daring Tricia to fire her.

"We can barely squeeze the customers in now," Ginny said, worry creeping into her voice.

"Was that a crack about my weight?" Angelica growled.

"Ladies, please!" Mr. Everett implored, hands held out before him in supplication. "I've heard enough harsh words for one day. Can't we all just get along?"

Tricia lost it, bursting into laughter.

"Now, if you'll excuse me, I'll just get busy with those biographies," Mr. Everett said and turned for the back closet where he retrieved his Haven't Got a Clue apron, donned it, and set off to work.

A tinny, electronic version of Gloria Gaynor's "I Will Survive" broke the

quiet. "Oh, my cell phone!" Angelica said and patted at her waist, finding the offending instrument. "Hello?"

The shop's old-fashioned telephone rang as well. Ginny picked it up. "Haven't Got a Clue, this is Ginny. How can I help you?"

"Really?" Angelica squealed and practically jumped. "Yee-ha!"

"You're kidding," Ginny said, crestfallen.

"What's the rest of it?" Angelica asked, her eyes wide.

"Can't we counter?" Ginny asked, her words caught in a sob.

Tricia's head swiveled back and forth as she tried to follow the two conversations.

"And the tentative closing date?" Angelica asked with glee.

"Are you sure?" Ginny asked. Her shoulders had gone boneless.

"Thanks so much for calling, Bob," Angelica said, bouncing on the balls of her feet.

"Thank you for letting me know," Ginny said, her voice so low it threatened to hit the floor.

Both women hung up.

"I lost my house!" Ginny wailed, closing her eyes in angst.

"I got my house!" Angelica crowed, and pumped her right arm up and down in triumph.

Suddenly the air inside Haven't Got a Clue seemed to crackle as the two women's heads whipped around to face each other.

"You!" Ginny accused.

"Uh-oh," Tricia said under her breath.

"Me?" Angelica asked.

Ginny's eyes had narrowed to mere slits. "What house were you bidding on?"

Angelica eyed her with suspicion. "A little white cottage on the highway."

"Slate roof? Pink and red roses out front?"

Angelica nodded.

Ginny's face crumpled, her eyes filling with tears. She smacked her clenched fists against her forehead.

Tricia wasn't sure what to do. Congratulate her sister or commiserate with her employee?

"Well," Angelica started. "Well . . . I bid low. I really did. You must've bid really, really low."

"It was all Brian and I could afford," Ginny cried, tears spilling down her cheeks.

Tricia stepped forward, captured Ginny in a motherly hug. "I'm so sorry, Ginny."

Angelica's mouth dropped open, her eyes blazing.

"We're getting married next year," Ginny managed between sobs. "We figured it would take us that long to fix the place up. We had it all planned out, right down to the nu—nu—nursery."

"All's fair in love and real estate," Angelica said, defiantly crossing her arms over her chest. "And how was I supposed to know you were even interested in that house?"

"You weren't," Tricia said, looking over at her sister while gently patting Ginny's back. "Come on. Have a cookie. You'll feel better." She led Ginny over to the coffee station, but the cookie plate was empty. Instead, she poured Ginny a cup of coffee.

"How was I to know she was interested in that house?" Angelica groused.

A customer entered the store, and Angelica sprang into action. "Welcome to Haven't Got a Clue. Can I help you find something?" She hurried over to the woman.

"*She* hasn't got a clue where anything is," Ginny growled, then gulped her coffee, setting the cup down with a dull thunk. "I'd better help the customer before your sister helps us right out of business." She wiped her eyes on the back of her hand, straightened, and stepped forward, heading for the customer. "Did you say Ngaio Marsh? Right over here."

Scowling, Angelica backed off and stepped up to the coffee station. "I really didn't know Ginny wanted that house," she hissed.

"She'll get over it. Have a cup of coffee." Tricia poured the last of the pot into one of the store's cups and gave it to Angelica.

Angelica swirled the dregs, then glanced over the assortment of creamers, choosing hazelnut. "How did it go at the lawyer's office?"

"Better than I thought. And he's going to try to help Grace, too."

"That's great. I wonder if he does real estate closings."

Ginny cleared her throat, glared at Angelica. "Have you finished unpacking that case of Dashiell Hammetts yet, Ange?"

"Don't call me Ange. And no, I haven't."

Tricia wasn't about to get caught up in a Ginny/Angie catfight and headed to the back of the store where Mr. Everett was already happily rearranging the biographies. "Mr. Everett, you mentioned Deirdre was grumpy. Just what was bothering her today?"

The older man straightened, holding on to a biography of Anthony Boucher by Jeffrey Marks. "That woman is just as disagreeable as her sister ever was. In fact, if I didn't know she was dead, I would swear I'd spent time with Doris, not Deirdre Gleason."

"Did you know Doris well?" Tricia asked.

"Not well, but I'd observed her enough times. I was a grocer. I knew how to cook a few basic dishes, and when my wife died I attended a number of the Cookery's demonstrations to learn more. Macaroni and cheese from a box palls after a few meals," he confided.

"Would you say the sisters' personalities were interchangeable?" Angelica asked from behind Tricia, who hadn't heard her sister approach.

"Ms. Deirdre puts on airs when she thinks she's got an audience, but in private she's just as irascible as her late sibling."

Angelica gave her sister a jab. "Didn't I tell you? I'd bet my Anolon cookware the woman next door is really Doris, not Deirdre."

"Don't be absurd. We've been over this before."

"And I'm still right. I'll bet when they were kids those identical twins switched personalities whenever it suited them. And if that's so, why wouldn't they do that later in life?"

"Nobody in their right mind agrees to change identities, especially if they're about to be killed."

"Well, of course Deirdre wouldn't agree to the idea—not if she was the victim. But if Doris did take her identity, she'd have it all. The insurance payout would cover her debts and she'd also have access to whatever assets Deirdre, a successful businesswoman, had owned, which would save her failing shop and also help support her daughter. And why should she feel guilt? Her sister had a fatal illness, she would've died anyway. Doris may have justified the act believing she'd saved Deirdre from the horror of a painful death."

The idea made sense, but Tricia didn't want to embrace it. Not only did it negate her own theory that Mike Harris killed Doris, but there was no way on earth she wanted Angelica to be proven right—again.

"Maybe I should go next door and talk to Deirdre. I know a fair bit about cooking. If she does, too, it would only help prove my point."

"Do what you want," Tricia said and waved a hand in dismissal. "Talking about all this isn't getting the work around here done."

Mr. Everett bent over his task once more as Angelica rolled her eyes theatrically. "Says she who's been away from the store all day."

"There won't *be* a store if I can't get Sheriff Adams off my back," Tricia countered.

"Well, even if you do go to jail, *I'm* still here to pick up the pieces. And isn't that what family is for?"

Tricia found her fingers involuntarily clenching—her body's way of saving her from another murder rap by preventing her from choking the life out of her only sibling. Meanwhile, Angelica stood before her, waiting for some kind of an answer.

Tricia turned away. "I'm starving, I haven't had a thing to eat since breakfast. Where's the bakery bag? There must be a few cookies left."

"Sorry," Angelica apologized. "I ate the last one just before you came back."

Suddenly fratricide seemed like a wonderful solution to all life's problems.

TWENTY-TWO

TRICIA TRIED NOT to keep an eye on the clock, but after Angelica had been gone for almost an hour she began to worry. What if Angelica said or did something to tip Deirdre off about her suspicions? What if Deirdre threatened Angelica? The what-ifs in her mind began to escalate and she was glad to wait on the few customers who'd braved the elements to patronize Haven't Got a Clue.

The rain had not let up and the streetlamps had already blinked on. Tricia let a still-distraught Ginny leave early, and she and Mr. Everett were discussing the merits of doing more author signings and the possibility of starting a reading group when Angelica finally returned.

"Well?" Tricia asked.

Angelica pushed up her sweater sleeves and shrugged. "That woman would make a pretty fair poker player."

"What was her attitude?" Mr. Everett asked. "Polite or had she reverted to type?"

Tricia blinked, surprised. That made twice in one day Mr. Everett had shown irritation.

"She was polite, but she has absolutely no clue how to sell a room," Angelica said and made an attempt to fluff up her rain-dampened hair. "Then again, her house was no better."

Mr. Everett frowned, puzzled by the remark.

"That's because she's selling books—not a room," Tricia grated, hoping Mr. Everett wouldn't ask Angelica how she knew about Doris's home.

"Yes, but if you want to be successful," Angelica continued, oblivious of her gaffe, "you've got to have atmosphere, which you've achieved here with your hunter green accents, sumptuous paneling, the copper tiled ceiling, the oak shelves—you've even got great carpet. This room makes you want to sit down with a good book, a glass of sherry, and a cigar."

Mr. Everett blinked at this last.

"Well, not me personally—I don't smoke—but you know what I mean. Whoever that woman is next door—she's clueless when it comes to selling."

"And what would you do to entice a customer to buy old cookbooks?" Mr. Everett asked.

She turned to face him. "I'd offer more than just books. Exotic gadgets—even just as décor. I'd have samples of dipping sauces, tapanades, mustards, relishes, jams, jellies, and chutneys. I'd feature different cuisines, from Indian to Irish to Asian fusion."

"Doris used to have cooking demonstrations. And don't forget, the lure of Stoneham is rare and antiquarian books," Tricia told her.

"So why can't you offer the new with the old? Tricia, people love to eat. For a big segment of the population, food is more important than sex. Why else would there be an obesity crisis in this country? When life hands you lemons, you make a meringue pie or a luscious curd."

Had Angelica found solace in food? Then again, she'd recently lost a lot of weight. Maybe she'd made the effort to appear more attractive to the husband who no longer wanted her.

"My point is," Angelica continued, "her shtick is food. She ought to play it up."

"Did you tell her that?"

Angelica frowned. "Not exactly. I did tell her I was thinking of opening a restaurant, and we had a nice discussion about food prep."

"Did she seem to know a lot about cooking?" Tricia asked.

"She asked a lot of questions. The kind someone might ask if they weren't sure what they were getting into."

"Where does this leave your theory about her?"

"I don't know," Angelica admitted. "She may have been testing me, or maybe just giving me a snow job."

"I didn't know you wanted to open a restaurant, Mrs. Prescott," said Mr. Everett. "I'm an old hand when it comes to fresh produce. I'd enjoy having a dialogue on it with you some time, if you wouldn't mind."

"I'd love to. How about tomorrow? We can unpack books and talk asparagus and Swiss chard."

"I'll look forward to it," he said.

Thunder rumbled overhead. Tricia looked around the empty shop. "Thanks to what's left of Hurricane Sheila, I don't think we're going to have any more customers tonight. Why don't we call it a day? You can head on home, Mr. Everett."

"If the weather were better, I would insist on staying on until our normal closing time, but I think I will take you up on your generous offer. I will be here bright and early tomorrow, however." He took off his apron and went to the back of the store to retrieve his jacket and umbrella. "Until the morning, ladies."

"Good night," the sisters chorused, as the door shut on his back.

"I'd better head upstairs and get that chicken in the oven if we're ever going to eat tonight," Angelica said.

"What chicken?"

"I went out during a lull and got the fixings. If I'd known I'd have something to celebrate, I would've gotten steaks. We can have that tomorrow."

"Isn't roast chicken kind of pedestrian for you?" Tricia asked.

"Comfort food is comfort food." Angelica glanced around the shop. "Miss Marple, are you coming?"

The cat, curled up on one of the nook's comfy chairs, opened one eye, glared at Angelica, and closed it again.

"So much for trying to make friends with *you*." All business, she headed toward the stairs at the back of the shop. "Okay, I'm off."

"I've got things to do," Tricia called. "Be up in a few minutes."

Tricia locked the door and pulled the shades down on the big plate-glass window that overlooked the sidewalk on Main Street, thankful to have a few minutes to herself to decompress. Roger Livingston had made her feel better about her own legal situation, but poor Grace Harris was still alone, still trapped at St. Godelive's.

Tricia crossed to the sales counter. With Angelica gone, Miss Marple decided to be more sociable and hopped down from the chair, trotting over to jump up on the counter and then over to the shelf behind the register next to the still-nonfunctioning security camera.

Tricia planted her hands on her hips. "How many times have I asked you not to get up there?"

Miss Marple said, "Yeow!"

Tricia lifted the cat from the shelf, placing her on the floor. Not one to take direction well, Miss Marple jumped up on the sales counter and again said, "Yeow!"

"Don't even think about getting back up there," Tricia cautioned and turned back for the camera. How could one eight-pound cat continually knock a wall-mounted camera out of alignment? Tricia usually had it pointing at the register—in case someone tried to rob them—but she often thought it made more sense to train it on the back of the shop where shoplifters tended to steal the most merchandise. Now it pointed out toward the street, in the direction of the Cookery, exactly as it had on the night of Doris Gleason's murder.

Tricia peeked around the side of the shade, glancing across the street to Mike Harris's darkened storefront campaign headquarters. She hadn't pulled the shades down on the night of the murder. If Mike had killed Doris, he would've had to cross the street to enter the Cookery during the interval Tricia

had left the village to pick up Angelica at the Brookview Inn and her return some thirty minutes later.

She glanced over her shoulder at the camera still mounted on the wall. Had it been in operation at the time? If so, what would she find if she studied the tape?

Footsteps pounded at the far end of the shop, and Angelica appeared at the open doorway to the loft apartment. “Are you ever coming up? I want you to give me a hand making stuffed grape leaves. My version is just divine.”

“In a minute,” Tricia said, annoyed.

Angelica padded across the shop in her stocking feet. “What’s got you so hyped up?”

“What do you mean?”

“The look on your face. It almost says ‘eureka!’”

“I’m just wondering . . . Miss Marple messed with my security system the night Doris was murdered. I don’t think I reset the system before I left to pick you up at the inn. What if it recorded Mike Harris crossing the street from his new offices and showed him going to the Cookery?”

Angelica frowned. “It might show him crossing the street and heading north, but you couldn’t prove he went next door.”

“No, but it might be something my new lawyer could use to help prove me innocent should Sheriff Adams make good her threat to arrest me.”

“Well, I’m all for that. I’ve got the chicken in on low if you want to play your tape. Do we need to take it upstairs?”

“I only have a DVD player in the loft, but we could play it back on the shop’s monitor.”

“Go for it.”

Always interested in technology of any kind, Miss Marple moved to the edge of the counter to study the operation. Tricia hadn’t touched the cassette since the morning before Doris had been murdered, and the whirr of it rewinding in the player fascinated the cat.

Tricia noticed Angelica’s bare feet. “Where are your shoes?”

“They got wet. Maybe I’ll bring a pair of slippers over tomorrow.”

“Don’t get too comfortable. You’ll soon have your own house here in Stoneham.”

The tape came to a halt with a clunk and Tricia was about to press the play button when someone banged sharply on the shop door. “Ignore it,” Angelica advised. “The store’s closed.”

The banging came again, this time accompanied by a voice Tricia recognized: Mike Harris. “Open up. I know you’re in there, Tricia. The lights are still on,” he bellowed. Miss Marple jumped down from her perch and hightailed it

across the shop and up the stairs to the apartment. Tricia bit her lip, looked back at the door.

"Don't you dare open that door," Angelica ordered. "He sounds ticked."

The banging continued. Then got much louder.

"I think he's kicking it in," Tricia said, alarmed. "What if he gets inside?"

"Call the sheriff's department," Angelica said.

"Are you kidding? They'd probably lock *me* up, not him!"

The wood around the door began to splinter.

"Don't you have any friends in this town you can call?" Angelica asked anxiously.

"Mr. Everett and Ginny."

Angelica grabbed the shop's phone and started dialing. "Why couldn't you have a modern phone?"

"Use your cell," Tricia implored.

"I left it upstairs. Ah, it's ringing. Come on, Bob, answer!"

The door crashed open and Mike burst into the shop, soaking wet, chest heaving, his face twisted in anger. "Where the hell do you get off accusing me of murder?" he demanded.

"Answer the phone," Angelica implored.

"Hang up!" Mike ordered.

A defiant Angelica held on to the receiver.

"I said hang up!"

"Bob, it's Angelica! Get over to Haven't Got a Clue right now. There's a madman—"

Before she could finish her sentence, Mike had charged across the carpet, yanked the phone from her hand, and pulled the cord from the wall. Both she and Tricia darted behind the sales counter, putting it between them and the crazy man before them.

"Why did you visit my mother at the home and fill her head with nonsense?"

"What are you talking about?" Tricia bluffed.

"I just got a call from Sheriff Adams. She said you'd visited Mom, accused me of trying to poison her and steal from her. That's a bold-faced lie!"

"Is it?" Tricia said. "The home changed their practices, stopped serving her the gourmet chocolate laced with who knows what that you brought her. It only took a couple of days for her mind to clear. She filed papers to keep you away from her assets. Winnie Wentworth may be dead, but you left enough evidence to nail you for selling off items from your mother's home without her permission."

His eyes had narrowed at the mention of Winnie. "You have no proof."

"An admission of guilt if I ever heard one," Angelica quipped.

"Ange, shush!" Tricia ordered.

"Come on, Trish, you were all hyped just now to see if he was on that tape."

"Ange," Tricia warned.

"What tape?" Mike demanded.

"From the security camera. It was focused out on the street the night Doris Gleason was murdered," Angelica said.

"Give it to me," Mike commanded.

"In your dreams," Angelica said with a sneer.

"Ange," Tricia said through clenched teeth. "You're going to get us killed."

"I said give it to me!" Mike lifted the heavy phone with both hands and smashed it through the top of the sales counter, sending chunks and shards of glass spraying across the carpet.

Both women jumped back and screamed.

Deirdre suddenly stood in the open door, her big red handbag dangling from her left forearm. "What's going on?" she demanded.

"Call the sheriff! Call the sheriff!" Angelica squealed.

Instead, Deirdre stepped inside the shop, pushed the door so that it was ajar—but it wouldn't shut properly with the doorjamb broken and hanging.

"I said what's going on?" Deirdre repeated.

"They've got something I want," Mike said, then turned. "Now give it to me."

The sisters stole a look at each other. Angelica barely nodded, but it was enough for Tricia to reach down to retrieve the tape from the video recorder. She handed it to Mike and backed up, hitting the wall, nearly cracking her head on the shelf that housed the useless video camera.

Mike dropped the tape to the carpeted floor, stomped on it with his booted right foot until the case cracked. Again and again his foot came down until the plastic gave way and he was left pummeling the ribbon of magnetic videotape.

Breathing hard, he looked up, his eyes wild. "Give me a bag."

Tricia blinked, unsure what he meant.

"I said give me a bag!"

Angelica pulled one of the green plastic Haven't Got a Clue shopping bags out from under the counter and threw it at him.

Mike picked up the largest pieces of tape, shoving them in the bag. "We're safe now, Doris."

"Shut up," Deirdre/Doris growled, moving closer, her expression menacing. "We're not safe. You and your stupid temper. Can't you see you've ruined it all?"

Mike's mouth twitched, but he didn't say anything, just kept picking up the plastic fragments.

Angelica stepped back, bumping into Tricia. "I told you she killed Deirdre," she hissed.

Tricia reached out, pinched Angelica to silence her.

"These two are now a liability. We'll have to get rid of them." Doris opened her purse and brought out a couple of the wickedly sharp kitchen knives that matched those from the Cookery's demonstration area. "Take this," she said, shoving the handle of a boning knife toward Mike. "Ladies, come out from behind the counter. Slowly. No funny business."

Funny business was the last thing on Tricia's mind. She gave Angelica a shove in the small of her back. Angelica stayed rooted.

"Look," Angelica said, her voice relatively level. "I've got a nice roast chicken in the oven. I'm making a wonderful appetizer, too. Can't we all have a glass of wine and talk this over?"

Doris's lips were a thin line. Her cheeks had gone pink, her grasp on the knife handle tightened.

Tricia gave her sister another slight shove. "Ange." Finally, Angelica took a step forward.

"What are we going to do?" Mike asked.

Doris ignored him. "Out in front, ladies, hands where I can see them."

Tricia and Angelica stepped around to the front of the cash desk, Tricia's shoes crunching on glass. Angelica yelped, stepping away from the sparkling shards, leaving a patch of blood on the carpet.

"You." Doris nodded toward Tricia. "Where's your car?"

"In the municipal lot."

She turned to Angelica. "You?"

"My car's there, too."

"So's mine," Mike groused. "Terrific, now how do we get out of here?"

"Deirdre's car is parked just outside." Doris fished inside her purse and came up with a set of keys. She tossed them at Tricia, who caught them. "You'll drive."

"Where?"

Doris nodded toward the street. "Just get in the car."

"Oooohh," Angelica crooned in anguish, and shifted from foot to foot, the patch of blood growing larger on the rug.

Mike grabbed Tricia's arm, pushed her ahead of him, pressing the knife against her hip. "If I'm not mistaken, the femoral artery is near the tip of this knife. You wouldn't want it severed and ruin your beautiful carpet, not to mention your day."

Doris stepped forward, brandishing her shorter vegetable knife. "Don't think I can't do a lot of damage with this," she told Angelica. "I can filet a five-pound salmon in under a minute. Just think what I could do to your internal organs in only seconds. Liver anyone?" she said and laughed.

No one else did.

She shoved Angelica forward, toward the door.

The wind had picked up and the rain came down like stinging pellets as

Tricia led the way to the pavement outside her shop, with Mike practically attached to her. They paused and he looked up and down the dark, empty street. No one stood on the sidewalk. No hope of rescue.

Mike pushed Tricia toward the driver's door. "Get in. Don't try anything—unless you want Doris to slice your sister."

Tricia yanked the door handle. It was like a bad movie, including Doris's and Mike's corny dialogue. *I'll wake up from this nightmare, I'll wake up soon.* But it wasn't a dream.

Already soaked through, she got in, slammed the door, and on automatic pilot, buckled her seat belt. Glancing over her shoulder she saw Doris with one hand on Angelica's shoulder, the knife-wielding one hidden in shadow.

Mike got in the passenger side, brandishing the wicked knife clenched in his left hand at mid-chest—the perfect position for slashing. "You really blew it, Trish. We could've been great together."

"Is that what you told Wendy Adams?"

"We've talked," he admitted, his expression a leer. "And more."

The right rear passenger door opened. Angelica ducked her head, got in, scrambled across the seat with Doris crawling in after her. The door banged shut.

For a long moment no one said anything.

"Start the car," Doris ordered. "And don't try anything funny. You saw what happened to Deirdre. She thought I didn't have the guts to kill. They say it's easier the second time."

"What about Winnie?" Tricia asked.

"Not my handiwork," Doris said and glanced at Mike.

Tricia swallowed, her gaze focused on Doris's reflection in the rearview mirror. "Then it doesn't matter if you kill us here or someplace else."

"Think I'm joking?" Doris lunged to her left and Angelica cried out.

"She cut me, Trish! She cut me!"

Stomach churning, Tricia's neck cracked as she whirled to look, but the heel of Mike's hand caught her shoulder with a painful punch. "Ange?" Tricia shouted.

"I'm okay, I'm okay!" Angelica cried, but the fear in her voice said she was anything but.

Tricia's eyes darted to the rearview mirror. She could just make out Angelica's bloody left hand clutching the slash in her light-colored sweater.

"I'll cut her again, only with more precision, if you don't start the car. Do it now!"

Tricia tore her gaze from the mirror, fumbled to put the key into the ignition, turned it until the engine caught.

"If you don't want to see your sister's throat cut, I suggest you put the car in gear and head north to Route 101," Doris ordered.

Tricia glanced askance at Mike, hoping her pleading gaze would be met with some shred of compassion, but there was none. And why would he show that emotion for her when he'd shown Winnie no mercy and treated his own mother so callously?

Tricia turned her gaze back to the empty rain-soaked street. All the other shops had closed; the only beacon of light was the Bookshelf Diner. Even if she blasted the horn, no one was likely to hear or even pay attention to the car as it passed. Their one ace in the hole was Bob Kelly. Had Angelica reached him or his voice mail, or had she simply been bluffing?

Come on, Bob.

Then again, Mr. Everett knew of their suspicions. If they turned up missing, he could point the law in Mike's and Doris's direction. That is, if Sheriff Adams would even listen to him. And if he spoke, would he become the next murder victim?

Stalling, Tricia fumbled with the buttons and switches on the dash until she found and turned on the headlights. Next, she checked the mirrors before pulling out of the parking space and driving slowly down Main Street, heading out of the village. Within a minute the glow of friendly streetlamps was behind them, the inky darkness broken only by the car's headlights.

"Turn here and go straight until you reach Route 101," Doris directed.

"Then where?"

"You'll head for Interstate 93."

"Where are we going?" Angelica asked, uncomprehending.

Tricia could guess. The interstate cut through the White Mountain National Forest, the perfect place to dump a couple of bodies where they wouldn't be found for months—if ever.

No one spoke for a long minute.

Angelica cleared her throat. "Does anyone have a handkerchief or something? All this blood is ruining my sweater. Not that I could ever find anyone in this town who can repair cashmere, even if they could get the stains out."

Tricia exhaled a shaky breath. Was Angelica's claustrophobia acting up, or was she simply in shock? Either she didn't realize what was going to happen to them, or she was in deep denial.

Time was running out. If they got as far as the interstate, they were as good as dead.

"My foot's still bleeding, you know," Angelica went on. "I think there might be a piece of glass in it."

Mike smashed his fist against the dashboard. "Will you shut up!"

Tricia clenched the steering wheel. Route 101 was only a couple of miles ahead. If she was going to save them, it had to be in the next few minutes—and she could only think of one option: crashing the car.

She'd read too many mysteries to think of disobeying Mike's or Doris's direct orders—Angelica's bleeding shoulder was proof of that. Still, she couldn't remember any fictional scenario from a book that would keep herself and Angelica alive.

The most famous car crash she could recall was that of Princess Diana in a tunnel in Paris. The one passenger wearing a seat belt had lived—the others didn't. Only Tricia wore a seat belt. If she crashed the car, would Angelica survive? How fast did she need to go to incapacitate her captors without permanently maiming her sister?

The headlights flashed on a mile marker.

The dashboard clock's green numerals changed.

Not much time left.

"What happened, Doris? Did Mike witness Deirdre's murder and hit you up for money?"

"None of your business," she snapped.

"He didn't have to see the murder," Angelica said. "I'll bet he planned it."

Collusion! Suddenly, it all made sense. "You sold Doris the million-dollar insurance policy, and when she told you her sister was dying and she'd have to change the beneficiary—"

"All very neat, really," Doris said. "It solved all our problems."

"Not Mike's. His mother has regained her memory."

"I'm having her moved from St. Godelive's in the morning. She'll go right back to loving her nightly mug of cocoa tomorrow night."

Not with Roger Livingston looking after her affairs, but Tricia wasn't going to voice that fact.

"Why did you throw the rock through my window?" Tricia asked Mike.

He laughed. "Just to keep things interesting."

"Did you really think I was going out with Russ Smith?"

"It crossed my mind."

"Oh please," Angelica groused.

Keep them talking, something inside Trish implored. "There's still something I don't get."

"And what's that?" Doris asked.

"Why did you set the Cookery on fire and disable the smoke alarms when you had every intension of keeping it open with 'Deirdre' as the owner? You could've destroyed everything. Or did you have the contents heavily insured as well?"

"The place wouldn't have burned. That carpet is flame-retardant. I know, I paid a small fortune for it."

"Stop all this yapping and turn on the defroster. Can't you see the windshield's steaming up?" Mike carped, and rubbed at the glass with his free hand.

Tricia glanced down, couldn't find the control. Instead, she fumbled for the window button on the door's arm, pressing it. The window started to open.

"I said turn on the defroster!"

"I don't know where it is!" She held the button until the window was completely open. The rain poured in and she eased her foot from the accelerator.

Mike leaned closer, searching the dashboard. "Doris, where the hell is it?"

"I don't know. This is Deirdre's car. Keep pushing buttons until you find it."

With Mike preoccupied, Tricia knew her window of opportunity was short. Headlights cut through the gloom on the road up ahead. If she could sideswipe the vehicle, or merely scare them into thinking she would, they were sure to call the sheriff. If she didn't kill them all first.

"Now or never," she breathed and jammed her foot down on the accelerator.

Mike fell back against his seat, the knife flying from his grasp, disappearing onto the darkened floor.

Tricia aimed straight for the oncoming car.

"What are you, crazy?" Angelica screamed from behind.

Tricia risked a glance in the rearview mirror, but Angelica wasn't talking to her; she wrestled with Doris in the backseat—trying to disarm her.

Mike's hands fumbled around Tricia's legs, yanking her foot from the accelerator, grappling for the missing knife.

The wail of the approaching car's horn cut through the rain pounding on the roof and Angelica's screams. Tricia steered to the right, barely missing the oncoming car.

Mike grabbed the steering wheel, jerking it left, and Tricia jammed her foot on the brake, sending Mike flying. The car hydroplaned on the slick, wet road, sliding sideways.

Tricia wrestled with the wheel, but the car had a mind of its own, hit the guardrail, and went airborne, sailing into the black, rainy night, flipping before it landed in the swollen waters of Stoneham Creek.

TWENTY-THREE

Stunned, for a moment Tricia didn't realize the car had come to a halt. It was only what was left of the deflated air bag hanging out of the steering wheel and in her face, and the rising chilly water swirling around the crown of her head

that brought her back to full consciousness. Blinking did no good, she couldn't see a thing, but finally it sank in that she hung suspended by the seat belt, about to drown from the water that gushed through the car's open window. The sound of rushing water filled her ears as she fumbled for the catch.

The belt released and Tricia plunged into the freezing water. Arms flailing, she pawed for the aperture, found it, and pulled herself through into open air, then fell into the raging torrent. The current immediately slammed her against the car. Winded, she groped for and clung to the undercarriage above the water. Shoes gone, her stocking feet slipped on mossy rocks, and she struggled to find a foothold on the driver's window frame.

Upside down, the car was hung up on the rocks in the creek bed, listing at a forty-five-degree angle. Raking aside the hair flattened around her face, Tricia realized light shone down from above and behind her—the glow of a mercury vapor lamp on the bridge over Stoneham Creek.

"Help! Please help me!" Tricia looked around, realized the weak voice came from inside the car.

Angelica!

Sliding down the side of the car, Tricia sank back into the arcticlike stream, fumbled for the door handle, pulling with all her strength, but the rushing water was too powerful—she couldn't yank it open.

"Help—oh, please help," came the voice, sounding fainter.

Grasping the window frame, Tricia took in a lungful of air, sank down, and pulled her upper body into the black interior. In only a minute or so the car had filled with water; just a pocket of air remained along what had once been the car's floor. Fumbling fingers captured Tricia's hand and she pulled with all her strength, trying to keep her head above water. "Be careful," she gasped. "Come on. I've got you!"

The hands clamped around her forearms in a death grip.

Muscles straining in the numbing-cold water, Tricia pulled and tugged and eventually a dark, bulky figure emerged from the car, coughing and sputtering.

"Thank you, oh, thank you," Doris Gleason cried, clutching at the car to find a handhold.

"Where's my sister?" Tricia demanded, steadying the woman.

"I don't know—I don't know," Doris wailed, inching away from her and toward the car's front tire.

Panicked, Tricia pulled herself back into the driver's compartment. The cockpit's air bubble was half the size. Tricia took a gulping breath and plunged into the black water, fumbling behind the driver's seat, searching, searching for her sister. Angelica was claustrophobic—she'd be terrified! But suddenly the midsized car's backseat area seemed to have expanded.

The back of her hand scraped something sharp and Tricia grabbed, capturing the chunky stone of Angelica's diamond ring. She pulled the hand and the body attached to it toward the driver's compartment with all her might, but Angelica was a dead weight, too large to drag under the driver's seat.

Fighting panic, Tricia groped for a lever, to make the seat recline.

Where in God's name was it?

Finally, her fingers clasped a plastic handle. She pushed it, yanked it.

Nothing happened.

Come on!

She had to let go of her sister, wrenched the lever with one hand while she beat on the saturated seat with the other.

With lungs ready to burst, she was forced to seek out the air pocket, took several painful gulps, and plunged down again.

More seconds flashed by as she struggled with the lever. At last it moved, and so did the seat, but only by inches. It would have to be enough.

Angelica had slipped back into the black abyss. Maddening eons passed as Tricia's frozen hands once again probed the icy darkness.

Her fingers were nothing more than pins and needles from the cold when something brushed against her. She snatched at it—Angelica's sweater. Hanging on, she maneuvered her legs out the driver's window.

Tricia pulled and tugged and jerked until she dragged a lifeless Angelica around the seat and out through the window. She slipped on weedy rocks, plunging into the water, gashing her knees on the rocks. Skyrockets of pain shot through her, but she managed to grab her sister as she tumbled into the torrent. Angelica's foot caught on the window frame and she hung suspended, with most of her body underwater. Tricia captured Angelica's arms, yanking her free, and the force of the water smashed them against the side of the car.

Nearing exhaustion, Tricia struggled to keep her own and her sister's head above water. Mike was still in the car—probably near death, and yet Tricia wasn't sure she had the strength to keep Angelica from drowning, let alone look for another victim.

"Get away! Get away! You'll push me in," Doris screamed.

If she'd had the energy, Tricia would've gladly slapped Doris, the cause of all their problems. Instead, she looked down at her sister. It took a long few moments for reality to register in her brain.

Angelica wasn't breathing.

"Ange. Ange!" Tricia screamed, panicked. She didn't know CPR, had never bothered to take a class.

Why hadn't she ever taken a class?

"Breathe! Breathe!" Tricia commanded, slapping Angelica's cheek, but Angelica's head lolled to one side.

Not knowing what else to do, Tricia shoved her sister's body against the car, pressing hard against her back.

Again. Harder.

Again! Harder still!

"Come on, Ange! Breathe!"

Once, twice, three more times she slammed Angelica into the side the car until she heard a cough, and a gasp, then choking sounds as Angelica vomited.

"Stop, stop! You're hurting me," she cried weakly.

Tricia threw an arm around her sister to hold her up and rested her head against Angelica's shoulder, allowing the pent-up tears to flow.

"Need help?" came a voice from the bridge, one that sounded vaguely familiar.

"She tried to kill me!" Doris cried. "Get me out of here. She tried to kill *us*!"

Tricia craned her neck to look. From the safety of the bridge above them, Russ Smith tossed Doris a rope. "Tie it around yourself. I'll pull you over to the bank."

"Call 911. There's still someone trapped in the car!" Tricia called.

"Already called." Something flashed repeatedly. Tricia glanced over her shoulder to see Russ lower a little digital camera. "This is going to make a great front-page story for the next edition of the *Stoneham Weekly News*," he said with zeal.

"Who cares about that? Get me out of here!" Doris demanded, again, already tying the rope around her chest.

"I want to go home," Angelica sobbed.

Tricia's cheek rested against her sister's shoulder once more and she closed her eyes, ready to collapse. "Me, too."

TWENTY-FOUR

TRICIA BOWED WITH theatrical aplomb, holding the polished silver tray in front of her guest. "Care for a smoked-salmon-and-caviar bite? They're absolutely delicious."

Juggling a martini in one hand and a china plate already heaped with hot hors d'oeuvres in the other, Russ Smith shook his head and laughed. "I already feel like the fatted calf. I'll need to go on a diet after this feast."

"Nothing is too good for the man who saved my life." Ensconced in the plushest chair in Haven't Got a Clue's reading nook, her leg resting on the south edge of the nook's large square coffee table, Angelica toasted Russ with her own glass. Her ankle, encased in a pink fiberglass cast, had been broken in three places, but she'd been getting around in a wheelchair for the last few days. Despite her near-death experience, she looked fabulous in a little black cocktail dress, one black pump, a string of pearls around her neck, and nails polished to match her cast. In comparison, Tricia felt positively frumpy in her usual work clothes.

She handed the tray to Ginny, who took a crab puff and placed it on the table, which had been cleared of its usual stacks of books and magazines. "Excuse me," Tricia said, "but I believe I'm the one who pulled you out of that car and kept you from drowning."

"Yes, but I would've died of hypothermia if this darling man hadn't used his cell phone to call 911. Never complain about paying your taxes, Trish, darling—not when the county employs such cute paramedics."

Tricia wasn't likely to complain at all. Her own cuts and bruises were nothing compared to Angelica's assorted injuries. Crutches weren't likely to be in her future until her two cracked ribs healed—an injury caused by Tricia's clumsy but successful attempt at resuscitation. Makeup had done a reasonable job of covering up Angelica's blackened eyes, but it was the defensive knife wounds on her arms she'd received fighting off Doris that had finally convinced the law that they'd been the kidnap victims—and not the perpetrators. By comparison, Tricia's aches and pains were of little consequence.

Miss Marple sashayed around the nook, her little gray nose twitching at the aroma of salmon and caviar. "Shoo, shoo!" Angelica admonished, and the cat reluctantly retreated to a spot several feet away, her gaze never leaving the food on the table.

"How did you show up in the nick of time?" Ginny asked Russ.

He tipped his glass toward Tricia. "I was on my way back from Milford when your boss aimed her car directly at me."

"It wasn't my car—it's was Deirdre's—or Doris's. Well, it wasn't mine," she defended.

"At the last second, it swerved. I saw the car go out of control and doubled back to see if I could help. The rest, as they say, is history." He popped another canapé into his mouth, chewed, and swallowed. "These are the best finger foods I've ever eaten."

"All my recipes," Angelica bragged. "I had the executive chef at the

Brookview Inn whip them up for us." She picked up a canapé from her own plate. "They're almost as good as I make them."

Tricia clenched her teeth. She'd been doing a lot of that lately, as well as biting her tongue. Angelica had been insufferable since she'd been fished, more dead than alive, from Stoneham Creek exactly one week before. Yet, grateful her sister still lived, Tricia had indulged Angelica's every whim, including this little party at Haven't Got a Clue.

"Could I please have a glass of wine?" she asked Mr. Everett, who stood behind the makeshift bar that had been set up on the newly repaired sales counter. He uncorked a bottle of chardonnay, poured, and handed her the glass. She took a deep gulp.

After Angelica had been released from the hospital, Tricia had temporarily moved into the Brookview Inn to take care of her sister. From her palatial bed piled high with lace-edged pillows, Angelica had taken care of all the party details, from ordering the food and liquor to coordinating the guest list, although so far only Russ had arrived. By the amount of appetizers heaped on platters and crowding the nook's table, Tricia expected an army.

Someone knocked on the shop door, the CLOSED sign apparently keeping them from entering. Tricia leapt up to find her new attorney standing outside. "Come in, Roger."

"I've brought a friend," he said and held out a hand to his companion.

Grace Harris had undergone a dramatic change since the last time Tricia had seen her. White hair trimmed and perfectly coiffed, the elderly woman looked slim and elegant in a long-sleeved, pink silk, shirtwaist dress, accompanied by a single strand of pearls. Several gold bracelets graced her wrists, and the little gold scatter pin Tricia had given her decorated the lace collar at her throat. One of her first stops after leaving St. Godelive's must've been a jewelry shop. Grace allowed Roger Livingston to hold the door for her as she entered the shop.

"Dear Tricia—my savior," she said and rushed forward to pull Tricia into a warm embrace.

Tricia stepped back. "Come inside and meet everyone, won't you?"

Grace took in the others. "I believe I already know two of them. Hello, Russ." The newsman nodded a greeting as she walked past him to join Mr. Everett, who took her hands in his.

"It's been far too long, Grace."

"Oh, William, you don't know how good it is to see an old friend."

Mr. Everett's eyes were shining. "I did visit you several times when you were in St. Godelive's. I'm sorry to say you didn't know me."

Grace smiled. "I know you now. And I thank you."

Tricia introduced Grace to Angelica and Ginny before ushering her into the

chair next to her sister. Mr. Everett, an excellent bartender, soon placed a glass of sherry in Grace's freshly manicured hand.

Grace swept the shop with her gaze. "My, my. I'm so sorry I missed your grand opening, Tricia. You've done a wonderful job reinventing this old building."

Tricia smiled, pleased at the compliment, and settled on the broad arm of Grace's upholstered chair. She took a more reasonable sip from her glass, realizing the inevitable couldn't be avoided.

"I'm so sorry about Mike," Tricia said. She'd spent the last week wrestling with guilt over his death. She hadn't had the strength to enter the partially submerged car a third time to attempt his rescue.

Grace sipped her sherry, her expression thoughtful. "I'm sorry to say I lost Michael a long, long time ago, dear."

"You're torturing yourself unnecessarily, Tricia," Russ said, all business. "The medical examiner ruled Mike Harris's death an accident. He hit the windshield and died on impact. You weren't to blame."

Was that really true? When push came to shove, Tricia hadn't been able to crash the car. More than anything she wanted to believe that fate—and Mike grabbing the steering wheel—had caused the car to careen out of control. She hadn't meant for him or Doris to die; she just wanted to save herself and Angelica.

"Did we miss the service?" Angelica asked, looking to Tricia for guidance.

"Under the circumstances, I thought it best not to have a public memorial," Grace said, her voice subdued. "He was cremated and I scattered his ashes in my backyard yesterday morning. He loved to play there as a small boy. I prefer to remember him that way."

Her admission cast a bit of a pall on the party. No one seemed to know where to look. It was Mr. Everett who broke the ice. "Does the district attorney feel he's got a good case against Ms. Gleason?" he asked Roger Livingston.

"Fingerprints proved that the woman killed at the Cookery was indeed Deirdre Gleason. Her doctors in Connecticut confirmed she suffered from pancreatic cancer and had only a few months—possibly weeks—to live."

Russ picked up the story. "The cops theorized Doris saw her sister's illness as the answer to all her problems. With a successful financial background, Deirdre had invested wisely. Her portfolio was worth at least two million dollars. However, her will stated that the bulk of her estate was to go to a number of charitable organizations. She'd only designated a paltry ten thousand to be paid to her only surviving sibling. I can imagine that didn't sit well with Doris, whose business was on the rocks and she was faced with a new lease she couldn't afford. Killing Deirdre and taking her place had to seem like the answer to all Doris's problems."

"And don't forget," Angelica added, "Doris as Deirdre also stood to inherit at Doris's so-called death, too."

Ginny shook her head. "This is all so convoluted it's making me dizzy."

Russ hadn't brought up Mike Harris's part in Deirdre's death. Out of respect for Grace, Tricia didn't mention it, either. And his excusing her part in Mike's death sounded all well and good, yet the memory of seeing his limp body being pulled from the hulk of Deirdre Gleason's car would haunt Tricia for a long time to come.

Grace patted Tricia's hand. "It's all right, dear. Please don't dwell on what happened. Michael won't hurt anyone ever again, and now no one will ever hurt him, either."

Tricia wondered if she could be so charitable if put in Grace's shoes.

"I'd still like to see Sheriff Adams apologize for hounding you, Tricia," Roger said.

"That'll never happen. Mike was a charmer, and I'm afraid he charmed Wendy Adams. She saw me as a threat to whatever relationship she thought she had with him. And despite the coroner's report, she blames me for Mike's death."

"I'm afraid my son used his charisma to get himself out of many scrapes over the years," Grace said.

Tricia thought back to that awful night. Wendy Adams had stood on the little bridge over Stoneham Creek as the local firefighters had hauled Mike's body out of Deirdre's car. She'd inspected his cold, dead face and then walked up to Tricia, who stood on the roadside shoeless and shivering under a scratchy blanket. Fighting tears, the sheriff had stared at Tricia for long seconds, and Tricia had been sure the woman was going to slap her. Then, abruptly, Wendy Adams had turned away. Shoulders slumped, she'd gotten back in her police cruiser and driven off into that bleak, rainy night.

They hadn't spoken since. A deputy had been dispatched to Haven't Got a Clue to take Tricia's statement, but Tricia had no doubt that Wendy Adams now considered her an enemy—the person who had robbed her of a future of love and companionship.

Still, Tricia felt only pity that the sheriff had been so easily duped, so manipulated by a handsome man with a glib tongue.

The shop door opened, the little bell above it tinkling merrily, and a smiling Bob Kelly stepped inside. "Am I too late for the festivities?"

Angelica's face lit up and she held out her hands. Bob surged forward, clasped both of them, and bent down to draw them to his lips for a kiss.

"You look beautiful as ever," he gushed.

"You're a liar, but after the week I've had, I can use the compliment," Angelica said, a blush coloring her cheeks.

Tricia rose and turned away from the sight, ready to gag.

Angelica patted the arm of her chair and Bob dutifully perched beside her, still holding her hand. Mr. Everett offered him a drink and Bob accepted a Scotch and soda.

Russ set his plate aside and straightened in his chair. "You've been avoiding my calls for a week now, Bob. What's the story on the big box store coming to Stoneham?"

Bob took a sip of his drink. "I hadn't planned on announcing it until later this week, but since the *Stoneham Weekly News* won't be out for another five days, I suppose I can break my silence."

The room seemed to crackle with electricity as everyone leaned forward to listen.

Bob sipped his Scotch, milking the anticipation.

"Come on, Bob, spill it," Tricia said. "What big company is coming to town?"

"None."

"None?" Russ repeated, incredulous.

"The rumors were just that—rumors. But come summer there will be a new business venture opening on a one-hundred-acre site just north of town."

"Some kind of light industry?" Tricia guessed, remembering her lunch conversation with Mike.

He shook his head. "New Hampshire's newest spa and resort."

"Ah, another venture like the Brookview Inn?" Angelica speculated. "Yes, Stoneham is in need of more fine dining."

"No, lovely lady, not an inn."

Spa and resort? "Don't tell me," Tricia began, "a Free Spirit Full Moon Nudist Camp and Resort?"

"The very same," Bob said and tipped his glass back.

"Nudists?" Grace said, appalled.

"It's only the second nudist resort in New Hampshire," Bob explained. "They're very family oriented. Should bring in a lot of tourist dollars."

"Didn't I tell you, Tricia," Ginny piped up. "Nudists get bored and like to read, too."

"How on earth did you convince the Board of Selectmen to go for it?" Russ asked.

"Tax dollars," he explained simply. "That land isn't worth much the way it is, but once they start developing it with their lodge, spa, snack bar, Olympic-sized pool, and other amenities, we'll see a nice surge in the tax base. It's also far enough out of town that none of our residents should be offended."

"But nudists!" Grace protested.

"I hope this means we've seen the last of the nudist tracts in our stores," Tricia added.

Bob cleared his throat, looking embarrassed. "Yes, well, Free Spirit wanted to get the word out to the last of our summer tourists. I've spoken to them about it and they've promised it won't happen again."

"Hallelujah!" Tricia said.

"Can I quote you on this?" Russ asked.

Bob nodded. "I'll have a press release ready for you by Wednesday. And I have more news to share," he said, hoisting his glass as though for a toast. "The Cookery's assets have been sold. You'll soon have a new neighbor, Tricia."

Tricia wasn't sure she was ready to hear what else he had to say.

"Do tell," Ginny said, rolled her eyes, and picked up another crab puff, popping it into her mouth.

"I'd be glad to." But instead of launching into his story, Bob inspected the morsels on the plates and trays before him. He chose the biggest stuffed mushroom on a tray and took a bite, closing his eyes and throwing back his head theatrically. "This has got to be the most delicious thing I've ever eaten in my entire life."

Quelling the urge to throw up grew more difficult. "Come on, Bob, you're obviously dying to tell us," Tricia said.

He chose a piece of the prosciutto-wrapped asparagus from one of the platters and downed it in one gulp. "Heaven. Just heaven."

Tricia tapped her foot impatiently.

Bob took a fortifying sip of his drink before setting down his glass. "It seems Deirdre Gleason's assets have been frozen. Doris needed money to hire a good defense attorney so she's sold the Cookery, lock, stock, and barrel. And I have already rented out the building."

"To whom?"

Bob pulled a set of keys from his pocket and handed them to Angelica, who smiled coyly. "Me."

Tricia's stomach tightened. "But I thought you wanted to open a restaurant."

"All that time lying around got me to thinking about the long hours and the low profit margin associated with owning a restaurant. And—and I thought it would be such a kick to have my own little business right next to yours. Aren't you just thrilled, Tricia?"

Thrilled wasn't the word.

"That little demonstration area Doris devised is absolutely perfect. I can cook all day while my employees run the store. I'll have a steady income and get to do what I love. It's as simple as that."

"But you don't know the business. Where will you get your stock? Have you ever hired or trained an employee? Do you have any idea about the paperwork involved juggling inventory, vendor invoices, and taxes?"

"Trish—" Angelica cut her off. "That's the beauty of having my shop right next door to you. You already have all the knowledge I need and I can tap into your brain anytime I want. What could be better? Now you must tell me who did your loft conversion. Of course, I'm leaning toward French country for my decorating scheme, but I was thinking it would be neat to knock a hole through the bricks and put in a door linking my apartment with yours."

"No way!" Tricia declared, worried she'd never again have a private moment to herself.

"What's going to happen to the house you bought?" Ginny asked, her eyes flashing with interest.

Angelica turned to Bob.

"By canceling the deal, you've forfeited your deposit, I'm afraid. But the house is back on the market. It sat for a long time. I'm sure if you upped your offer by a few thousand, you'd get it, Ginny."

"It would be a stretch, but I think we could do that," Ginny said, her hope restored.

"One more reason to celebrate," Angelica said. "This calls for champagne."

"We don't have any," Tricia said, feeling like a party pooper.

"Yes, we do," said Mr. Everett. And he brought out a chrome champagne bucket on a stand from behind the sales counter.

"If you'll look under that tray on the shelf over there, Ginny, I think you'll find the crystal flutes. Isn't it amazing what you can rent in a wonderful little village like Stoneham?" Angelica said and beamed.

For a small-town grocer turned bibliophile, Mr. Everett would have made a pretty fair sommelier. He popped the cork with style, and Ginny captured the geyser of sparkling wine in a couple of glasses, passing them to Angelica and Bob, and then to the rest of the gathering, including herself and Mr. Everett.

"Who'll make the toast?" Roger asked.

Tricia stepped forward, feeling anything but cheerful. "I suppose it had better be me." She turned her gaze to her sister, exhaled a long breath, forced a smile, and raised her glass. "To Angelica, and her new venture."

"Here, here," chorused the rest of them and sipped.

"I should like to make a toast as well," Angelica said. "To Tricia, who makes all things possible."

Tricia waved an impatient hand. "Like what?"

"Like what? You've given Ginny and Mr. Everett here jobs—that's good for the local economy. Through your efforts Grace has been freed from her impris-

onment at that assisted living center, and your shop brings happiness to all those tourists with nothing to read."

Tricia shrugged. "I guess."

"And because of you I've got a new life. New friends." She eyed the gathering and gave Bob a modest smile. "A new job, and will soon have a new home." Angelica raised her glass, tipping it in her sister's direction.

Tricia raised her glass as well and managed a smile. "Not bad for the village jinx, huh?"

ANGELICA'S RECIPES

SPAGHETTI SAUCE

1–2 tablespoons olive oil
1 large onion, chopped
3 cloves garlic, chopped (I often toss in a lot more)
1 pound country spareribs
1 pound Italian sausage links (I use hot)
1 can crushed tomatoes (28-ounce size)
2 cans tomato puree (28-ounce size)
1 can tomato paste (6-ounce size)
3 bay leaves
1 teaspoon salt
1½ teaspoons sugar

In a large pot, heat oil, brown onion and garlic, sear ribs, and brown sausage.

Empty contents of all the cans (tomatoes, puree, and paste). Add bay leaves, salt, and sugar.

Simmer 3 to 4 hours, longer if you like a thicker sauce. Stir occasionally.

Serve over your favorite pasta with grated Parmesan or Romano cheese, and with crusty bread.

LOBSTER BISQUE

1 lobster (1½ pounds)
2 stalks celery
1 cup butter (½ pound)
2 shallots, minced
1 small onion, chopped
2 cups half-and-half (or whole milk)
1 teaspoon paprika
salt, white pepper
½ cup sherry
1 cube chicken bouillon
1 cup flour

Place lobster and celery in a heavy saucepan and cover with cold water. Bring to a boil; boil for 10 to 15 minutes or until lobster is red and cooked.

Remove lobster, set aside to cool. Strain broth and set aside.

In a large saucepan, melt butter. Sauté shallots and onion until soft and translucent. Add half-and-half plus some of the lobster broth (reserving 3 cups for later). Heat thoroughly, then add seasoning, sherry, and bouillon cube. In a bowl, mix together the flour and 3 cups of lobster broth. Add flour mixture to the saucepan. Heat until thickened.

Remove meat from lobster and add to the bisque. Allow the bisque to simmer (do not boil) for 15 minutes, stirring occasionally.

STROMBOLI

Angelica is a stickler for making things from scratch. Unfortunately, not all of us have the time. Therefore, this recipe uses a shortcut of two loaves of frozen bread dough. But if you'd like to follow in Angelica's footsteps, by all means use your favorite from-scratch bread recipe. Feel free to play with the ingredients and add others to this wonderful bread that makes a meal when accompanied by most soups.

2 loaves (1 pound each) frozen bread dough, thawed
½ pound sliced ham

¼ pound sliced pepperoni
¼ small onion, chopped
¼ cup chopped green pepper
1 jar (14 ounces) pizza sauce, divided
¼ pound sliced hard salami
¼ pound sliced mozzarella cheese
¼ pound sliced Swiss cheese
1 teaspoon dried basil
1 teaspoon dried oregano
¼ teaspoon garlic powder
¼ teaspoon pepper
2 tablespoons butter, melted

Let dough rise in a warm place until doubled. Punch down. Roll loaves together into one 15-inch-by-12-inch rectangle.

Layer ham and pepperoni on half of the dough (lengthwise). Sprinkle with the onion and green pepper. Top with ¼ cup of pizza sauce. Layer the salami, mozzarella, and Swiss cheese over sauce. Sprinkle with basil, oregano, garlic powder, and pepper. Spread another ¼ cup of the pizza sauce on top.

Fold plain half of the dough over the filling and seal the edges well. Place on a foil-lined, lightly greased baking pan.

Bake at 375 degrees for 30 to 35 minutes. Brush with melted butter. Heat the remaining pizza sauce and serve with the sliced Stromboli. Serves 4 to 6.

CRAB PUFFS

1 cup crabmeat (canned will also work)
½ cup shredded sharp cheddar cheese
2 tablespoons chopped chives
1 teaspoon Worcestershire sauce
1 teaspoon lemon juice
1 teaspoon dry mustard
1 tablespoon dill weed
½ cup (1 stick) butter
1 cup beer (can also substitute chicken broth or clam juice)

½ teaspoon salt

½ teaspoon lemon pepper

1 cup all-purpose flour

4 large eggs

Preheat oven to 400 degrees. Line baking sheets with parchment paper or aluminum foil.

In a bowl, combine crabmeat, cheese, chives, Worcestershire sauce, lemon juice, mustard, and dill weed. Set aside.

In a large saucepan, melt butter, add beer, salt, and lemon pepper. Bring to a boil. Add flour, remove from heat, and stir briskly with a wooden spoon. Return to heat. Continue to beat until a dough ball forms. Remove from heat.

Add eggs to dough, one at a time, beating vigorously after each addition until well combined.

Fold crab mixture into dough.

Drop by spoonfuls onto baking sheet.

Bake crab puffs 25 to 30 minutes until crispy and golden brown. Best served warm.

Makes 35 to 40 crab puffs.

BEAST STROGANOFF

3 cups sour cream

1½ tablespoons prepared Dijon-style mustard

3 tablespoons tomato paste—sun-dried in a tube gives the strongest flavor

3 tablespoons Worcestershire sauce

2 teaspoons sweet paprika

¾ teaspoon salt

black pepper, freshly ground, to taste

1 pound medium-sized mushrooms

10 tablespoons butter (1¼ sticks)

2 medium onions, sliced thin

3 pounds beef, veal, or venison, sliced thin on the diagonal (you can use leftover meat if you have it)

In a medium-sized saucepan, combine the sour cream, mustard, tomato paste, Worcestershire sauce, paprika, salt, and pepper and simmer slowly for 20 minutes, then remove from heat, cover, and keep aside while you cook the rest of the ingredients.

After washing mushrooms, slice thin and sauté in 3 tablespoons of butter until tender. Put in a separate container.

Cook the sliced onions in 2 tablespoons of butter until they are transparent and lightly browned, about 10 minutes. Put them in a bowl with the mushrooms.

Cook the meat over high heat in the remaining butter (if using leftover meat, just until warm; if raw meat, 3 or 4 minutes until lightly browned).

Put sauce over medium heat, bring to a simmer, and add the mushrooms and onions; let simmer for another 5 minutes.

Add meat and simmer until meat is heated through, about 2 minutes.

Serve over wide noodles and enjoy!

ANGELICA'S IRISH SODA BREAD

4 cups all-purpose flour
¼ cup sugar
1 teaspoon baking soda
2 teaspoons baking powder
1 teaspoon salt
2 large eggs
1½ cups buttermilk
¼ cup corn or canola oil
2 teaspoons caraway seeds
1 cup golden raisins
1 tablespoon milk

Preheat oven to 350 degrees. Foil-line a baking sheet, lightly grease.

In a large bowl, stir the flour, sugar, baking soda, baking powder, and salt together. In a separate bowl, beat the eggs, buttermilk, and oil together. Make a well in the center of the flour mixture and pour in the buttermilk mixture. Add the caraway seeds and raisins. Stir until a soft dough forms.

With floured hands, shape the dough into a large ball on a lightly floured board or waxed paper. With a sharp knife, make an X across the top of the dough. Place the dough on the prepared baking sheet. Brush the top with milk. Bake in the center of the oven until golden brown (30 to 40 minutes).

Serve warm with butter.

IRISH LAMB STEW

3 pounds stewing lamb
6 large all-purpose potatoes
4 yellow onions
2 tablespoons finely chopped parsley
1 teaspoon thyme
1 teaspoon salt
Freshly ground black pepper
1½ cups chicken broth
1½ tablespoons butter, softened
1 tablespoon flour

Preheat oven to 350 degrees.

Cut the lamb into slices or cubes. Peel the potatoes and onions and cut them into thin slices or chunks.

Mix the parsley and thyme together. Butter a casserole.

Arrange a layer of ⅓ of the potatoes on the bottom of the casserole. Cover with a layer of lamb, then a layer of onions. Season with the herbs, salt, and pepper. Repeat to form 3 layers, seasoning between each layer and ending with the onions. Add the broth (add enough broth so that the contents of the casserole are nearly covered but not submerged).

Cover the casserole and cook in a 350-degree oven for 1½ hours until the lamb is tender.

Combine the butter and flour in a small bowl and add the paste to the casserole (distributing it evenly). Continue cooking 5 minutes until the juices are thickened.

Makes 6 servings.

STUFFED MUSHROOMS

24 large mushrooms
2 tablespoons butter
1 large onion, finely chopped
4 ounces pepperoni, finely chopped
½ cup green pepper, finely chopped
2 small cloves garlic, minced
1 cup firmly crushed cracker crumbs
6 tablespoons Parmesan cheese
2 tablespoons minced parsley
⅔ cup chicken broth

Wash and dry mushrooms. Remove stems, chop finely.

Melt butter in skillet; add onion, pepperoni, green pepper, garlic, and chopped mushroom stems. Cook until tender.

Add crumbs, cheese, and parsley. Mix well. Stir in chicken broth.

Spoon stuffing into mushroom caps.

Bake uncovered at 325 degrees for 25 minutes.

Serve hot.

Bookmarked for Death

. . .

ACKNOWLEDGMENTS

I don't work in a vacuum—at least I hope I don't. Therefore, I'd like to say a public thank-you to my writer chums who've been so generous with their time and expertise. My friend and fellow Berkley Prime Crime author Sheila Connolly is wonderful when it comes to brainstorming. She shared some pictures with me that were the inspiration for two of the subplots within the book. (To see them, check out my website—where you can also sign up for my periodic newsletter: LornaBarrett.com.) She's a great pal and a wonderful critique partner.

Thank you to Sharon Wildwind for sharing her medical knowledge, as well as tidbits on a half dozen other subjects; to Hank Phillippi Ryan for her tips on reporters and how they behave; and to Sandra Parshall and the rest of my Sisters In Crime chapter, the Guppies, for answering so many of my questions—at all hours of the day and night. Jeanne Munn Bracken let me pump her for information on librarians, and her friend Richard Putnam provided local color. Marilyn Levinson, Shawn McDonald, and Gwen Nelson were my beta readers and gave me great input. Thanks, guys!

Thanks, too, to my agent, Jacky Sach, and to Sandra Harding at The Berkley Publishing Group. I couldn't have done it without them!

ONE

Crowded behind a table with her two employees and her guest author, Tricia Miles, owner of the Haven't Got a Clue mystery bookstore, held the left end of the sheet cake and flashed her most winning smile. "Cheese," she called along with the others.

"Oh, darn," Frannie Mae Armstrong said from behind her digital camera. As the only member of the Tuesday Night Book Club who owned such a camera, Frannie had been designated the group's official photographer for all signing events.

Behind her, Tricia's older-by-five-years sister, Angelica, flapped her hands in the air, encouraging them all to smile brightly. Her grin was positively demonic.

Tricia fought the urge to deck her.

A sigh from her near right and the muttered "Get on with it" also grated on Tricia's nerves.

Historical mystery author Zoë Carter turned her head and sighed as well, her patience waning—not with Frannie but with her assistant, who shifted from foot to foot. "Kimberly, please!"

Kimberly Peters, a skinny, bored, twenty-something in a wrinkled gray suit, ran a hand through her shaggy straw-colored hair, and sighed.

Frannie laughed nervously, pressed the button, and the flash went off. Tricia's facial muscles relaxed as Frannie studied the miniature screen on the back of the camera.

"Oh, Mr. Everett, you must've blinked. Let's go for another one." She moved the viewfinder back against her eye.

In his late seventies, William Everett was Tricia's oldest yet newest employee. He gave her an anxious glance.

"Do you mind?" Tricia asked the best-selling author.

"Of course not," Zoë said patiently. "I'm here for all my fans."

"Say cheese!" Frannie encouraged in her strongest Texas twang.

Dutifully, Tricia, Zoë, Mr. Everett, and Tricia's other employee, Ginny Wilson—at twenty-four the baby of the group—complied. The flash went off and Frannie inspected the results. "Perfect!"

A round of applause from Angelica and the members of the Tuesday Night Book Club greeted her announcement. Zoë's talk had gone well, if not spectacularly. Though she'd spoken in little more than a monotone, the twenty or so shoppers who'd crowded into the narrow bookstore for what was the last stop on Zoë's first and only national book tour had listened politely. Most of them had also picked up more than one copy of the book—for friends, family, and, in some cases, to put away and never be read. Signed first editions could be valuable, even for *New York Times* best sellers like Zoë Carter.

Stoneham's master baker, Nikki Brimfield, and her assistant, Steve Fenton, took charge of the eats table, assembling napkins, plates, and plastic cutlery.

Zoë sat down behind the stack of books on the larger of the two tables, away from the frosting and punch, and picked up her gold Cross pen, ready to sign. Kimberly leaned back against a bookshelf and folded her arms over her chest, looking aggrieved.

Frannie was the first in line, clutching three copies of Zoë's last book, *Forever Cherished*. She thrust her free hand forward, shaking Zoë's arm so forcefully the petite woman was nearly pulled from her chair. "I sure am glad to meet you at last, Miz Carter. I'm the receptionist over at the Chamber of Commerce. My boss, Bob Kelly, has spoken to you a number of times."

"Uh, yes. I believe I remember him," Zoë said, with a hint of scorn in her voice.

Frannie missed it. "I just started reading mysteries a few months back, after meeting Tricia," she said, flashing a grateful smile in Tricia's direction. "Of course, my very favorite author is Nora Roberts. What a storyteller, and you're guaranteed at least three books a year from her—not counting the ones she writes as J. D. Robb."

Kimberly rolled her eyes. "That hack? A reader can get dizzy from all that head hopping. And her prose—? Don't get me started."

Frannie's jaw dropped, and Tricia stood by, both aghast at this assault on one of the romance genre's icons.

"Kimberly, why don't you go outside for a cigarette break?" a tight-lipped Zoë suggested.

"It's cold. And, anyway, you know I'm trying to cut down."

"But—but—" Frannie sputtered around the wad of gum in her mouth. "But I like Miz Nora's books. And millions of other people do, too."

"There's no accounting for taste," Kimberly said. She indicated the bright green palm fronds on Frannie's long Hawaiian shirt over a turtleneck and slacks. "And what's with the getup?"

Frannie looked down at herself. She longed to retire to the Aloha State one

day, and her attire was the closest she could get to it while living in the great state of New Hampshire. "Getup?" she echoed, puzzled.

But Kimberly had already forgotten about her and rummaged through the handbag hanging off her shoulder, turning up a crushed pack of smokes. She moved away.

Frannie's jaw tightened, her mouth a thin line. She glanced down at the books still cradled in her left arm.

"I apologize for my niece's deplorable behavior," Zoë said. "Kimberly's been with me since her mother died, about ten years. I'm sad to say she never left her rebellious teen years behind her." She reached for the first of Frannie's books. "Here, let me sign that for you. Could you spell the name, please?"

Frannie sniffed. "Frannie—with an I-E, not Y."

Zoë bent down, picked up her pen, opened the book to the title page, and wrote: *To Frannie, I hope you enjoy Jess and Addie's last adventure. Fondly, Zoë Carter.* The words were written in tight cursive script. No flourishes, no embellishments. Just like Zoë herself.

"Thank you," Frannie said, a wan smile crossing her lips. She handed over the other two books. "Could you make the second one out to my sister? It's her birthday next month."

"I'd be delighted."

Tricia looked up to see Ginny at the register, ringing up a sale. She tossed back her long red hair and gave Tricia a wide grin and a thumbs-up. The event promised to be the best author signing Haven't Got a Clue had hosted since it opened exactly twelve months before.

As the next person in line offered Zoë a book, Tricia caught a whiff of perfume as a hand on her elbow pulled her away. Angelica.

"What are you doing just standing around?" she hissed. "This is your opportunity to sell the rest of your stock. Make the most of it."

Tricia's jaw clenched. Her sister had been in the bookselling business only five months; her own store was next door. Under Angelica's ownership, the Cookery had never held a book signing. In fact, in the six months since she'd moved to Stoneham, this was the first book signing Angelica had bothered to attend at Haven't Got a Clue.

"Why don't you just back off and take notes, and we'll compare strategies later," Tricia suggested.

Angelica shook her head, not a moussed hair on her blond head moving. "These events are supposed to boost sales."

"And they do. Go help Ginny at the sales counter and you'll see for yourself."

Angelica frowned. "I was really hoping to speak to Zoë for a few minutes."

"What about?"

"Oh, you know, the craft of writing. The publishing world. Stuff like that."

Angelica had never been interested in those subjects before. Tricia looked back toward her guest, who was signing a book for Tuesday Night Book Club newcomer Julia Overline. "I'm sure Zoë would be glad to talk to you for a few moments, but can't it wait until the end of the signing? I'd rather she give the most attention to paying customers. That is, after all, what she's here for."

"Oh, all right," Angelica groused. She and Ginny were not the best of friends. In fact, Tricia had had to break up more than a couple of spats between them. Still, Angelica turned and headed toward the cash desk. Ginny looked up, saw her approach, and glowered.

Tricia turned her attention back to her guest author and the line of fans awaiting her attention. Elderly Grace Harris, her short white hair perfectly coiffed and always as poised as her first name, stepped up to the table with two copies of the book nestled in the crook of her left arm, offering her right hand to Zoë.

"It's nice to meet you once again, Ms. Carter—this time in happier circumstances." She didn't elaborate, and Zoë continued to smile sweetly. "I've read every one of your books at least three times. You deserve every award you've received," Grace said, her voice carefully modulated.

"Thank you so much. Believe me, I feel so honored to have those two Edgar statuettes and my three Agatha Award teapots. Historical mysteries usually aren't as popular as, say, a Tess Gerritsen thriller or the forensic novels of Kathy Reichs and Patricia Cornwell, but I don't mind being in such good company."

"I was disappointed to hear you've decided to retire the series. Isn't there anything your fans can do to change your mind?"

"I'm afraid not. It's time to move on, literally and figuratively speaking. I'm selling off the old Stoneham homestead. My winter residence in North Carolina will be my permanent home base."

"I'm surprised a woman your age still lives in this climate," Kimberly cut in, returning pink-cheeked from her smoke break outside.

"I have ties here," Grace said, taken aback. "And I like the changing of the seasons."

"Highly overrated. And a fall on the ice could be fatal for someone your age. That's why I can't wait to get Aunt Zoë out of this backwater. And what is it with all the goose poop around here?" She lifted her right foot to examine the bottom of her shoe, where some of the offensive goop still clung, then wiped her feet on the carpet, staining it.

Tricia stepped forward. "I'm terribly sorry. Lately the geese have gotten out of hand. We make an effort to clear the sidewalk several times a day, but—"

"Obviously, you're not doing a very good job of it."

Tricia clamped her teeth together, trying to hold onto her patience. Kimberly could have wiped her feet on the natural bristle doormat just inside the entrance, instead of grinding the droppings into the rug.

Zoë turned in her chair, lowered her voice. "If you're going to continue to be this disagreeable, Kimberly, why don't you just go home?"

"It's my job to take care of you, Auntie dear. To see to your every need," Kimberly simpered.

The cords in Zoë's neck distended alarmingly, and Tricia was afraid she was about to lose her temper when a voice rang out from behind her.

"Shall we cut the cake?"

Tricia turned, grateful for the interruption. Nikki held a cake knife in one hand, a stack of paper napkins in the other. Though younger than Tricia by ten years, at thirty-one Nikki looked older—probably because she worked so hard. As manager of the Stoneham Patisserie, her baking prowess was renowned. She'd insisted on bringing the cake, her contribution as a member of the book club. And who in their right mind would turn down one of her fabulous creations?

But Zoë hadn't finished with Kimberly. "Go. Now."

Kimberly's cheeks flushed. "I'll go. But how will you get home, Auntie dear? You can't walk the dangerous streets of Stoneham—all four blocks of it—back to the house." She bent lower, but her words were still audible to a handful of onlookers. "Not with your blackmailer lurking out there."

The color drained from Zoë's face. "I'm sure I can prevail on someone to take me home."

"Y-yes, of course," Tricia stammered. "I'd be delighted."

"I'd be glad to take Ms. Carter home," Mr. Everett volunteered eagerly. "She'll be quite safe with me."

Zoë looked as if she was about to protest, but Kimberly spoke again. "I may not be there when you get back. And you forgot to take your medication earlier, so you'd better take it by at least eight o'clock. I wouldn't want you to keel over and get hurt." She turned on her heel, marched to the door, and yanked it open. Tricia was glad she didn't slam it—otherwise she'd probably need to replace the glass. Twenty or so pairs of eyes stared at the exit.

Embarrassed for Zoë, Grace turned away, and the next person in line held out a book for the author to sign.

Tricia turned to Nikki and found her looking at the door where Kimberly had exited, her expression thoughtful. "She's a nasty piece of work."

"And how." Tricia let out an exasperated breath. "Thanks for breaking the tension."

"No problem. But I didn't mean to rush the evening along, either," Nikki said, making the first cut. "It's just that I really need to get home and get to bed. Three thirty comes awfully early. I already told Steve to head on home."

"Three thirty? Is that when you guys have to get up?" Tricia asked.

"It's the only way to have fresh bread and pastries available for our customers at eight a.m."

"Then it's well worth it—at least for your customers. Any news on the bank loan?"

"Not yet. I've got my fingers crossed it'll be either tomorrow or Thursday. Then the Stoneham Patisserie will be mine, all mine." The power of her grin could have lit a hundred lightbulbs.

"I'll keep my fingers crossed, too. What does Steve think?" Steve Fenton was well known around town as "the weirdo who doesn't drive." He had a reputation as a loner who was often seen riding his bike or jogging around the village—and sometimes hitched a ride to nearby Milford and surrounds. Maybe ten years older than Nikki, he was also her only employee and as knowledgeable about baking as Ginny was about bookselling—and just as valued.

"He says he'll rough up the bank manager if I don't get it."

"You're kidding."

"Steve is. He's all bluff and bluster, but I'm glad he's on my side."

Steve could be called scary. Tall, brawny, head shaved bald, sporting a do-rag and gold earring, and his muscular arms covered with tattoos, he fit the description of a biker, but without the motorcycle.

Tricia glanced down at the sheet cake. Zoë's book cover had been reproduced in exact detail, but now was marred by the cake's dissection. "Too bad cutting the cake ruins the picture. Just how did you transfer the cover onto the frosting?"

Nikki shrugged. "I snatched the picture off her website. It's much the same process as an ink-jet printer—only with edible inks. Not my favorite way to decorate a cake, but for occasions like this it works well."

"And what's the surprise?" Tricia asked knowingly.

Nikki's eyes sparkled, subtracting a few years from her face. "Mocha chocolate cake with rum-infused white ganache filling."

"Sounds heavenly," Tricia said. Her stomach growled. She hadn't had dinner, and although cake wasn't her favorite food, she was willing to eat just about anything to stave off hunger pangs.

Already the book club members and the others who'd shown up for the signing were lining up in front of the eats table, their eyes wide in anticipation. "Let me get out of your way," Tricia told Nikki, just as the little bell over the entrance jingled. Russ Smith, editor of the *Stoneham Weekly News*, entered the

store. A Nikon digital camera dangled around his neck, and he grasped it in anticipation of taking a shot. He looked across the crowded shop, found Tricia, and made his way through the throng.

"Am I too late?"

"Nikki's just cutting the cake."

"I mean to interview the big-time author." He didn't roll his eyes, but his tone suggested he'd thought about it. He glanced in Zoë's direction. "Not much of a looker, is she?"

Tricia, too, had been surprised by the author's appearance. A plain Jane dressed in what could've been a nun's habit—black skirt and shoes, and a white blouse. No headgear, of course, and the chain around her neck was unadorned as well—no gold cross hung from it.

"Now, Russ," Tricia chided, reaching up to straighten the collar on the plaid flannel shirt beneath his denim jacket. His brown hair curled around the base of his neck. No matter how often he got a haircut, it always seemed like he needed another in short order.

"No, really, Tricia. I don't need to be here."

They'd been over this before. She had to agree that in a town full of booksellers, another author signing was hardly breaking news, although Zoë was perhaps the biggest name to come through town in quite a while. Still, despite his budding relationship with Tricia, it was only the enticement of a slice of Nikki's cake that had sealed the deal and lured Russ away from his evening with ESPN. "You told me that the last few times you've written about Zoë, you've received a lovely thank you note, and even a couple of review copies over the years."

He nodded, resigned. "You're right."

The cake line snaked around the table, and a number of people clutched their signed copies as they oohed and aahed over Nikki's to-die-for confection. What was left of the book's icing cover now looked like a mosaic, and Nikki heaped another slice onto a waiting plate.

"I saw Frannie leaving. She wasn't exactly happy," Russ said.

"No, and I'm afraid she's not my only unhappy customer. Zoë's been great, but that assistant of hers should have her mouth washed out with soap."

"Assistant?" Russ asked, looking at those assembled.

"Zoë's niece. She sent her home a few minutes ago. That young woman was really obnoxious." Tricia caught sight of Grace speaking to Mr. Everett, pointing at where Kimberly had stood, and frowning. "Despite the fact this is probably the best author-signing I've hosted, I'm afraid Kimberly may have spoiled the evening for more than a couple of people, and that could be a bad reflection on the shop."

"Time will tell. What is this, your fourth, fifth signing?"

"Thirteenth."

"Well, that explains it," Russ said and laughed. "Thirteen is an unlucky number. And you are—"

"Don't even mention that 'village jinx' business to me again." A few unfortunate events some six months before had saddled Tricia with that irritating label.

Russ shrugged, his gaze wandering over to the rapidly diminishing cake.

"Tricia?" The timbre of Ginny's voice conveyed her growing annoyance.

"Get your cake—and be nice to Zoë," Tricia told Russ.

"If you say so."

Tricia hurried over to the register to save her employee from her sister. "Ginny, why don't you help Nikki with the cake," she suggested. "She's got to get up awfully early tomorrow morning and really needs to leave."

"Gladly," Ginny grated, scooted around the counter, and stalked away.

"Ange," Tricia admonished.

"I was just trying to help Ginny with that last customer. Honestly, she has no marketing savvy at all."

"Ginny is the best assistant in the entire village, and you know it. Why don't you go pester your own help?"

Angelica threw back her head and sighed theatrically. "Samantha quit this afternoon." Which would account for Angelica's sour mood. "She wasn't of much use, but I don't know what I'm going to do tomorrow at the store."

Stay busy and out of my hair, Tricia hoped.

Bursts of light drew Tricia's attention back to Zoë, who posed, pen in hand, for Russ. Again and again the camera flashed. Printing one of the shots in the *Stoneham Weekly News* wasn't going to bring in a horde of customers after the fact, but it wouldn't be bad for business, either.

Another customer stepped up to the counter. Tricia took Ginny's vacated spot at the register while Angelica bagged two copies of *Forever Cherished* and a couple of paperback thrillers from the bargain shelf.

"That'll be fifty-seven thirty," Tricia said and finally looked up. "Deborah!" She'd been so preoccupied she hadn't even noticed her customer was also her best friend in Stoneham, Deborah Black. "Thanks for coming."

"Believe me, it's my pleasure. Little Davey's teething. I had him with me all day at the shop—it's his dad's turn to deal with him." Deborah ran the Happy Domestic, a boutique specializing in new and gently used products, how-to books, gifts, and home decor. Her son had been born some seven months before. Between running her shop and taking care of the baby, the poor woman had been worn to a frazzle. For the past few months, Tricia had been consulting

her on redecorating—softening the industrial-looking exposed-brick walls—in her loft apartment. At least that was the excuse Deborah had given her husband for her Wednesday "girls' night out" dinner with Tricia.

"We still on for lunch tomorrow?" Deborah asked. Unfortunately, she couldn't make dinner this week and they'd already made alternate plans.

"I wouldn't miss it."

"Lunch?" Angelica piped up hopefully. "Mind a straggler joining you?"

Yes, Tricia was tempted to blurt, but instead said, "You can't go anywhere. You lost your sales force this afternoon."

"Darn."

"See you at the diner at noon—or as close to as possible," Deborah said, picked up her purchase, and headed for the exit.

Deborah's departure seemed to trigger a mass exodus of guests, who'd abandoned their paper plates and plastic forks on just about every flat surface, and headed for the checkout or exit, some having escaped without purchasing a book.

The crowd had thinned by the time the rush was over, leaving just Ginny, Grace, Mr. Everett, Russ, and Angelica on hand.

Ginny glanced at her watch. "Eight fifteen. People didn't stay as long as we thought they would."

"No." Tricia took in the stacks of unsold books still sitting on the author's table. Zoë was nowhere in sight. "Nor did they buy as many copies of Zoë's backlist as I'd hoped."

"I told you so," Angelica piped up. "And I haven't had a chance to talk to Zoë yet. Where is she, anyway?"

Ginny ignored her, turning back to Tricia. "How much stock will you have her sign?"

"All of it. Besides being a best seller she's a local author, even if she is abandoning Stoneham."

"Let's hope you can sell them to tourists. Her handler turned off a number of the locals we'd managed to lure in here tonight."

Tricia sighed. "What did Kimberly say to you?"

"Nothing too insulting. Just implied my career aspirations must be pretty low to 'settle' for a job in retail. I had to bite my tongue to keep from mentioning that I didn't have to depend on nepotism to keep me employed."

Tricia looked around the shop. "Where is Zoë? As soon as she signs that stock, I can shut the door and scrounge some dinner." She hadn't even managed to snag a piece of Nikki's cake, of which only crumbs remained—not that she was often seduced by sweets or desserts. Too hard on the figure.

"I didn't see her go," Ginny admitted.

Mr. Everett and Grace were rounding up icing-stained forks and plates, depositing them in a big black plastic trash bag. "Did Zoë leave?" Tricia asked them.

Mr. Everett shook his head, pointed to the coat still slung over the back of one of the signing table's chairs.

"I think she went to the restroom," Grace said. She frowned. "Didn't that awful niece of hers say she needed to take her medication at eight o'clock?" She glanced at the diamond watch on her wrist. "Oh, my, she's been in there quite a while."

They looked uneasily at each other. "I'll go see," Tricia said.

Tricia had sacrificed her utility closet to add the small washroom a couple of months before. Most of her clientele arrived via bus tours, and one of the first stops the mostly elderly ladies and gents wanted to make was a bathroom. Since the front of her store had been outfitted to look like the Victorian facade of Sherlock Holmes's beloved 221B Baker Street, Tricia had carried out the decoration of her restroom in the same manner, with an antique pedestal sink and an oak mirror overhead, a high-tank toilet, dark beaded board, and reproduction hunter green flocked wallpaper. Unfortunately, she was the one who got to clean the little room every evening after the shop closed. Not the most glamorous part of owning her own business. In lieu of the closet, she'd had a wall erected to hide the boxes of stock and dollies, and had added shaker pegs higher on the wall for herself and her staff to hang their coats. Simple, but effective.

Tricia passed the last of the bookshelves and felt a draft. Bypassing the washroom, she hurried to the back of the shop, noticing that the rear door, which was always locked except for deliveries, was open a crack. Thank goodness her cat, Miss Marple, had been banished to her loft apartment during the signing. If she'd gotten out . . .

Tricia quickly closed the door and threw the deadbolt. Shoplifters had used the back exit for an escape route before, but the security system should have alerted her when the door was opened during business hours. It wasn't likely Ginny or Mr. Everett had circumvented the system, but whenever Angelica was around, unusual things seemed to occur.

Remembering why she'd come to the back of the store, Tricia stepped over to the closed washroom door. The little sign on it said OCCUPIED. She bent close and listened.

No sound.

She knocked.

"Zoë? Is everything all right in there?"

No answer.

Tricia leaned in closer, listening harder.

Still no sound.

Ginny approached. "Anything wrong?"

"I don't know," Tricia said. She rested her hand on the door handle. It turned. Since the room was tiny, the door opened out.

Tricia's breath caught in her throat and she backed away, bumping into the wall behind her.

Zoë Carter was seated on the lid of the commode, her dark skirt pulled primly over her knees, her mouth stuffed with paper napkins, and her face mottled a shade of purple Tricia had never seen. Scrapes marred her wattled neck, and some fingers from both hands were caught in the kelly green bungee cord that was knotted at her throat.

TWO

Sheriff Wendy Adams glowered at Tricia. "You have a penchant for finding dead bodies, Ms. Miles." She referred, of course, to the body Tricia had found in a neighboring store some seven months before.

Tricia looked away from the tall, bulky, uniformed woman who towered above her. Seated in one of the upholstered chairs in Haven't Got a Clue's readers' nook, she held a cardboard cup of cold coffee in one hand, a balled-up, damp tissue in the other. "Believe me, Sheriff, finding a body is not on my top ten list of things to do." She closed her eyes, and found the image of Zoë's distorted face imprinted on her mind once again.

"What is it with you, Sheriff? Do you find pleasure in badgering traumatized witnesses?" Angelica asked.

Tricia opened her eyes to see that her angry sister had insinuated herself between Tricia and the sheriff.

"Now, dear," Bob Kelly murmured, resting a gentle restraining hand on her arm, but Angelica shook him off. Bob had shown up—late—intending to take Angelica to dinner. Instead, he'd declined to leave once he saw the sheriff's patrol car outside and, as the head of the Chamber of Commerce and one of Stoneham's leading citizens, no one had asked him to leave.

"Back off, Bob," Angelica ordered, unaccountably surly. To Tricia's knowledge, Angelica had never said a cross word to her "good friend," as she called

him. She folded her arms across her chest, and Tricia allowed herself a twinge of sisterly pride at the sight.

"Why don't you wait outside, Mrs. Prescott," the sheriff said, her spine stiffening. "I'll get your statement in due time."

"Sure, I'll just go out on the sidewalk and stand in the goose poop that the Board of Selectmen hasn't been addressing," she growled. "And by the way, I am no longer Mrs. Prescott. I've taken my maiden name once again. You may call me Ms. Miles."

Sheriff Adams jerked a thumb in the direction of the exit. "Outside. Everyone. You'll get your turn to give me your sides of the story. Placer"—she addressed the deputy—"don't let them talk about the crime. I want to hear everyone's story in their own unique way, without them contaminating each other."

The deputy stepped forward to usher everyone outside. Dutifully they filed out, sans coats, which were hung on pegs at the back of the store, next to where the body was still located. Once the door closed, the sheriff turned her attention back to Tricia. "Well?"

Tricia heaved a sigh. "I found her. Just like—" She risked a glance over her shoulder. "Like she is."

"And you didn't kill her."

Tricia's jaw dropped. "Of course not. She was my guest."

"Did she argue with anyone tonight?"

"No." She thought about it. "Although she had a little tiff with her niece, Kimberly Peters. And Kimberly did leave in a rush. I suppose she could've come back, snuck in through the open back door and . . ." The thought was too terrible to contemplate. A family member killing for—what? Money, revenge? Weren't they the usual motives?

"Kimberly also let it slip that her aunt was being blackmailed."

The sheriff raised an eyebrow, and Tricia explained.

"Was she teasing or serious?"

"That I couldn't say."

Wendy Adams grunted. "I'll need a list of everyone who was at the signing tonight."

"I can't give you one. I mean, I don't know everyone who came. I sent press releases to the *Stoneham Weekly News* and the Nashua newspaper, and advertising circulars. We had a good crowd. Maybe twenty-five people in all."

"Give me a few for instances."

Tricia exhaled again. "My sister, Ginny Wilson, Mr. Everett, Russ Smith, and Grace Harris, of course. Then there were Deborah Black, Nikki Brimfield, Frannie Armstrong, Julia Overline—" She thought about the faces . . . but no

other names came to mind. "That's all I can think of. Ginny or Mr. Everett might be more helpful. They've lived in the area longer and are more familiar with the locals."

The sheriff's expression said *not helpful enough.* "Had you noticed anything out of the ordinary with the victim?"

"Her niece said Zoë had to take her medication at precisely eight o'clock. I thought that was a little odd, but apparently that's about the time she disappeared. I think I was on the register at the time. I sort of lost track."

"The victim didn't disappear. She died. In your bathroom, and not from taking any medication." It sounded like an accusation.

"I assure you, I had nothing to do with her death. And I don't know why anyone else would want to kill her, either."

"Do you recognize the murder weapon?"

Tricia blinked. She'd never thought of a bungee cord as a weapon before. Her insides twisted. "I . . . think . . . it could be one of the shop's. I don't know. I bought a bunch of them at the dollar store in Nashua some time ago. There were three or four in the package."

"Where would you keep them?"

"On one of the dollies in back."

Sheriff Adams bent down, grasped Tricia's elbow, and hauled her up. "Let's go have a look."

One of the deputies stood outside the washroom, taking digital photographs of the room and the victim from every angle. Tricia averted her gaze, feeling every muscle in her body tighten as they passed the tiny room and its deceased occupant.

The dollies were lined up along the wall near the back exit, two piled with boxes of books, one empty. Another deputy was crouched before the door, dusting for fingerprints, but straightened as his boss approached. "Only one or two clear prints." He eyed Tricia. "She said she touched it—they're probably hers."

Tricia swallowed her annoyance. Getting angry or protesting in her own defense would only cause them to think she could be guilty. But there was no way. This time she had witnesses.

"Where do you keep these bungee cords?" Sheriff Adams asked.

Tricia pointed to a rack of shaker pegs on the wall where a red and a yellow pair of bungee cords hung, along with an old umbrella, one of her zippered sweat jackets, and Ginny's, Angelica's, and Mr. Everett's coats.

"And you think there may have been a green one among them?"

She nodded. "Mr. Everett or Ginny might know for sure."

The sheriff's sour expression and general attitude relayed her unspoken

belief that Tricia was clueless about her own property. But honestly, was she supposed to account for every pushpin, paper clip, and bungee cord on the premises?

"Just to be clear, because Ms. Carter was a famous person, Stoneham is likely to be inundated with press from Nashua, Manchester, and probably even Boston as soon as this breaks. I don't want you talking to anyone about what you saw in that bathroom."

"Russ Smith saw Zoë's body, and he's a reporter. He's sure to write about it."

"Yes, but he won't give his scoop to another news outlet, and by the time the next issue of the *Stoneham Weekly News* comes out, the story will be as stale as week-old bread."

Tricia swallowed her resentment. "Can I reopen in the morning?"

Sheriff Adams shook her head. "Not a chance. This store is a crime scene."

"But I also live here."

"Not tonight. And maybe not for a few days."

"But I have customers. Haven't Got a Clue is participating in the book fair and statue dedication this weekend. I have to be ready."

"If the Sheriff's Department is finished with its investigation, there'll be no problem. If we're not—" Wendy Adams's smile was positively wolfish. "Too bad."

"What about my cat? Can I at least retrieve her, some clothes, and other personal items?"

"Sure. And a deputy will accompany you as you gather these things."

Did the sheriff think Tricia had already stashed some kind of evidence upstairs? That she needed to retrieve it to avoid prosecution? Tricia couldn't keep the sarcasm out of her voice. "Thank you, Sheriff."

The streets of Stoneham had been deserted for hours by the time the last of the witnesses had been interviewed by the sheriff and her staff. Standing on the damp pavement outside Haven't Got a Clue, Tricia, Angelica, Ginny, Mr. Everett, and Grace, who were finally given permission to retrieve their coats, had assembled to talk about the near-term future.

Ginny's lower lip quivered. "We aren't going to reopen? But—but I can't afford to lose even one day's pay," she said, alarm creeping into her voice. "We need a new roof. The water heater sprang a leak. And now the dryer is on the fritz—"

Ginny's newly purchased, darling little cottage in the woods—all appliances included—had turned into a gigantic money pit.

Tricia had saved the bad news about closing her bookstore until the sheriff had questioned everyone who'd remained after the signing. By then, it was nearly eleven o'clock. Zoë's body still hadn't been removed, but the sheriff assured Tricia she'd take care of securing the premises.

"Don't worry, Ginny, you can come work for me for a few days," Angelica suggested, her voice oozing with sweetness. "You, too, Mr. Everett. I'm a bit short of help this week, and it would solve everyone's problems."

"Not mine," Tricia said, and shivered. She was hanging on to her purse, an overnight bag, her laptop computer case, and the cat carrier. Beside her on the sidewalk were a bag of litter, the cat's box, and a grocery bag of food, bowls, and kitty toys.

Angelica leveled a glare at her sister. "We'll all regroup at the Cookery tomorrow at nine thirty. See you then!" She gave Ginny a shove toward the municipal parking lot. Mr. Everett and Grace Harris followed reluctantly.

Angelica looked around hopefully. "Isn't Russ going to help us with all this stuff?"

"He went back to his office. Said he wanted to get started on the story. He might even put out an extra edition if he can't stop the presses on the current issue," Tricia said, and grimaced. "Right now his top story is Stoneham's mounting goose poop crisis. What happened to Bob?"

Angelica pulled a key ring from her jacket pocket. "Damage control. He said something about calling the Chamber members to fend off any bad publicity that may come from this." She unlocked the door to her shop, turned back, and eyed the little gray cat. Miss Marple gave an indignant "*Yow!*"

"I'm not touching that cat box. I'll take your other stuff," Angelica said, and grabbed the purse, overnight bag, computer case, and grocery bag, leaving Tricia with the cat carrier, the litter, and the box.

Tricia followed her sister into the Cookery, both of them having thoroughly wiped their feet on a bristle doormat before entering the store. The Canada goose population had exploded in the past few weeks, with migratory birds joining their fellows who'd decided to winter near the open water of Stoneham Creek, local retention ponds, and the water traps in the neighboring Stoneham Golf Course. The result had been traffic snarled by wandering geese, and sidewalks littered with the birds' droppings.

Tricia followed her sister through the shop and over to the little dumbwaiter at the far end of the building. "We can put most of this stuff in there. That'll save trudging up all those stairs with it," Angelica said.

"Not Miss Marple!"

Angelica shrugged. "Suit yourself. But you'll be banging that carrier into

your knees for two flights, and probably give the cat motion sickness. And I am *not* cleaning up any cat barf."

Tricia looked up the brightly lit stairwell. What Angelica said made sense. "Okay, but don't send it up until I get upstairs and can unload her. I don't want her terrified by the ride."

"All right."

Miss Marple didn't travel light; it would take two trips on the lift to bring up everything.

Angelica pulled her keys from her pocket. "Here's the apartment key. Holler when you get upstairs, and I'll send up the lift."

"Okay." Tricia trudged up the stairs, opened the apartment door, flicked on the lights, and breathed in the ever-present smell of Angelica's perfume. She tended to use too much scent, making Tricia glad she wasn't prone to respiratory problems.

Angelica's loft apartment was completely different from her sister's next door. Where the stairs up to the third floor opened directly into Tricia's kitchen, Angelica's opened into a narrow hallway, which ran the length of the building. Near this end was the bedroom. Beyond was a spacious living room. Or, rather, it would have been spacious if it weren't stacked with cartons and furniture. Angelica had reopened the Cookery with great fanfare in time for the Christmas rush only six weeks after acquiring the property. The loft conversion had taken over three months. A rented bungalow at the Brookfield Inn had been Angelica's home during that time.

In the time since Angelica had moved in, she'd been working ten-hour days in her store, which hadn't left her a lot of time to set up her home. Retaining employees had quickly become her single biggest problem. Angelica blamed them all for laziness, but it was her own perfectionism (or perhaps anal retentiveness) that had them quitting in droves. The fact that she'd lost five employees in the past two months should have given her a clue as to what the problem was.

Miss Marple survived the trip in the dumbwaiter just fine, and Tricia had unloaded everything and sent the lift down for the rest of her baggage, which made the return trip in record time. She'd carried some of it into the living room by the time Angelica made it to the third floor.

"Throw your stuff anywhere," she told Tricia as she picked up the last few items and headed for the living room, but there wasn't anywhere to put it.

"I need to set up Miss Marple's litter box. And it's way past her dinnertime."

Angelica frowned. She was definitely *not* a cat lover. "The box can go in the bathroom. You can put her food and water bowls on the kitchen floor—some place I won't step on them, if you please."

Tricia looked around the warehouse of a living room. She hadn't seen the

apartment in at least a month, but it didn't seem to have changed a bit. "Where am I going to sleep?"

"The couch is a sofa bed . . . but I don't think there's room to pull it out. It would take too long to restack these boxes. And anyway, I have no clue where the sheets and blankets are. In one of these boxes . . . somewhere. I have a king-sized bed. You can either bunk with me or sleep on the floor."

"Ange, how can you live like this? It's so not you."

"Tell me about it. I haven't exactly had all the time in the world to sort through everything and find a home for it. And there's no one around here I can hire to do it. Believe me, I've asked."

Soon a wary Miss Marple had been freed from her carrier and shown where to find her litter box and her food. But the cat had concerns other than eating, and disappeared among the jungle of boxes to explore the confines of her temporary home.

The kitchen overlooked Stoneham's quiet main drag, but Tricia was drawn to the center island with its low-hung, Mission-inspired chandelier and its high-backed stools. Though not the most comfortable places in the world to perch for any length of time, the chairs at the dining table currently offered the apartment's only functional seating. The alternative was the bed, and Tricia was too wired to sleep. "Got any wine, Ange? After what I saw tonight, I need something."

"And I'll bet you haven't eaten all day. I'll whip you up some comfort food. What would you like?"

"Something totally bad for me. Fried chicken."

Angelica turned to inspect the refrigerator's interior. "No can do. How about I make you an omelet? At least the eggs came from a chicken."

Too weary to suggest anything else, Tricia nodded. She plunked one elbow on the counter and rested her head in her hand. "What if the sheriff keeps Haven't Got a Clue closed for a week? That woman hates me," she groused.

Angelica pulled out a carton of organic brown eggs and a half-empty bottle of chardonnay, shoving the fridge door shut with her hip. "Well, you did steal her boyfriend."

Tricia sat bolt upright, remembering the incident from the previous September. "I did not. I had lunch with him. Once. It wasn't even a real date."

Angelica shrugged, snagged a couple of glasses from the cupboard, poured, and handed Tricia the wine. "What do you want in your omelet? Veggies? Cheese? A big scoop of pity?"

"Hey, be nice to me. You said yourself I've been traumatized by finding poor Zoë dead on the toilet."

"Not where I want to be found when it's my turn," Angelica said, and

opened the fridge once again. "I've got cheddar or mozzarella. Which do you prefer?"

"Mozzarella. It's gooey and probably more fattening. Toss in peppers, onions, and anything else you'd find on a pizza."

"Right. Mushrooms, and I think I've got a tin of anchovies in the cupboard."

Tricia shuddered. "Let's not get too crazy." She tapped her right index finger on the granite counter. "The sheriff is going to make this as unpleasant for me as she can."

"Then I suggest you hold on to your temper," Angelica said, as she grabbed a knife from the block to chop an onion.

"I don't have a temper."

"No, but it wouldn't be hard to develop one if you're forced to interact with Sheriff Adams for any length of time." She waved the knife in warning. "I don't care how long she keeps your store closed. Don't rile the woman. I'll talk to Bob. We'll let him handle it."

"What?" And be beholden to him? "No way."

"Yes, way! Or do you want Wendy Adams to shut you down indefinitely?"

"She can't do that."

"Do you really want to take the risk?"

Tricia looked away. No, she didn't. Somehow, she'd have to make nice with the sheriff, or be prepared to wait a very long time to reopen her shop.

THREE

THE TELEPHONE RANG at six a.m., waking both sisters. Angelica groped for the bedside phone. "H'lo?"

Tricia rolled over onto her stomach, squeezing her eyes shut.

"What?" Angelica said, sounding a bit less sleepy. The bed jostled as she sat up. "Yes, I was." Pause. "No, I didn't." Pause. "She's my sister, why?"

Tricia opened one eye.

"Oh. Well, okay. Yes, I will. Have a nice day," she replied by rote and hung up the phone.

"What time is it?" Tricia asked. The clock was on Angelica's side of the bed.

"Six oh two."

"And what was that all about?" Tricia asked.

The telephone rang again.

"The *Manchester Union-Leader.* They wanted to know about—"

"Zoë's death," Tricia finished for her, and pulled herself into a sitting position.

"Yes." Angelica reached for the phone again.

"Don't answer that!" Tricia said, and swung her legs over the side of the bed.

The phone bleated again.

"If I were you, I'd unplug the thing. That is, unless you're willing to be interviewed again and again—and again."

"They're certainly not catching me at my best," Angelica said, and pulled at the cord, which led her to the jack just above the baseboard by the side of the bed. She unplugged the phone, but the extension in the kitchen continued to ring. "You take your shower first, Trish, while I go unplug the kitchen phone and get the coffee started."

"Deal."

Fifteen minutes later, and still toweling her hair dry, Tricia entered the kitchen to find Angelica bent over the kitchen island, coffee mug in hand, reading the morning paper.

Angelica straightened, her expression wary.

"What's wrong now?" Tricia asked.

"Why don't you have a nice cup of coffee," Angelica offered sweetly, and stepped around to the countertop to grab a clean cup from the cabinet.

Tricia hung the towel around her shoulders and moved to take Angelica's former position. "I suppose they've already got all the dirt about the murder," she said, and folded back the front page of the *Nashua Telegraph*. There, in full color, was Zoë Carter's smiling face—and the blouse she wore looked very familiar. Tricia squinted to read the photo's copyright. "Russell Smith?" she read in a strangled voice. "Russ—my Russ—sold one of the photos he took last night to a competitor? Talk about blood money."

"Now, Trish, dear, you don't know that he sold it."

"Well, I'm sure going to find out."

Tricia stomped over to the phone, which lay on the counter where Angelica had left it after wrenching it from the wall. She picked the thing up, trying to find the connector, and mashed it against the wall. It immediately started to ring. She lifted the receiver and set it down again, effectively cutting off whoever was on the other end, then snatched it up again and punched in Russ's telephone number.

It rang and rang. Either it was off the hook, or he was conversing and ignoring his call waiting.

She slammed the receiver back onto the switch hook. The phone started ringing once again.

Angelica pushed her aside, yanked the offending instrument from the wall once more, and set it aside. "How about that coffee?" she asked cheerfully.

"I don't get it. He was worried about how it would look that his paper had no news on the murder, and now his photo appears in a rival paper."

"Don't you think you ought to talk to him before making all these assumptions? And anyway, what's so bad about that? People are curious. They'll want to see the last pictures taken of a dead celebrity. Although, let's face it, she's not half as newsworthy as old Anna Nicole was when she took a dirt nap."

Tricia stared at the photo. What was she so angry about, anyway? That Russ had betrayed her trust? Exactly how? She'd known those photos were going to be reproduced in a newspaper—she just hadn't figured it would be used in such a sordid way, or that it would appear so quickly.

"How about that coffee?" Angelica asked once more, wrapping Tricia's hand around a warm mug. "I have a feeling it's going to be a very long day."

A lumbering, Granite State tour bus passed by the Cookery at nine fifty-five. Within minutes, the horde of book lovers would descend upon the village, charge cards in hand, and Haven't Got a Clue would not be their destination. The red CLOSED sign and yellow crime scene tape around the door would handle that. Any inquiries by telephone would be handled by the new outgoing message Tricia had recorded earlier that morning.

Behind the bus trailed a WRBS News Team Ten van, its uplink antenna neatly folded down the side. Tricia moved away from the Cookery's big plate-glass display window, farther into the interior of the store. She'd deleted the messages from newspapers and TV stations on her voice mail, but doubted she'd make it through the day unscathed. And she hadn't been able to get hold of Russ, either at his home or via his office or cell phone.

Across the store, a tight-lipped Ginny, clad in a yellow Cookery apron, stood beside the register, getting her orders from Angelica, who fired them off like a drill sergeant. Ginny had worked in the store under its previous owner, and it had not been a happy experience. And as for Mr. Everett, in an effort to beef up his limited culinary repertoire, he had shown up for all the cooking demonstrations under the old administration, but since he never bought anything, his attendance at these minilectures had made him customer non grata.

Tricia wandered over to the horseshoe-shaped food demonstration area that dominated the center of the store, unsure what her role was to be. Too many workers in the shop would only get in the way of customers, and as cooking was the least of her domestic skills, she wouldn't be able to make thoughtful recommendations. Still, she'd learned a lot about bookselling in the year since

she'd opened her store. Time to put that knowledge into action for her sister . . . and hope the effort would be appreciated.

But that's not what she wanted to do. She had no doubt Sheriff Adams would keep Haven't Got a Clue closed for as long as possible, just to spite her. With nothing to read—she'd forgotten to bring along the newest book in the Deb Baker Dolls to Die For mystery series that sat on her bedside table—she'd lain awake half the night listening to Angelica softly snoring on the other side of the bed. She'd spent a good portion of those hours going over her limited options. The sooner the crime was solved—or at least a suspect was identified—the sooner she could reopen. It was up to her to expedite the process.

And how was she going to gracefully exit the Cookery to do so?

Finishing with Ginny and Mr. Everett, Angelica moved her gaze, zeroing in on Tricia. Did cartons of heavy books need to be shelved, or did the washroom need cleaning? Tricia didn't want to find out. Instead, she went on the offensive. "Hey, Ange, have you thought about offering your customers cookies? You've got that beautiful demonstration area just sitting idle. Or maybe I could just nip on down to the patisserie and get some for you."

"Are you kidding? Now that I have competent help—" Angelica threw a glance in Ginny's direction—"I intend to make my own." She grabbed a book from one of the shelves, *Betty Crocker's Cooky Book*. The former owner had disdained that entire line of cookbooks, but once confided to Tricia that they were among her best sellers. Apparently Angelica had discovered the same thing. "Should I go for plain old chocolate chip, or maybe some blond brownies? The aroma will drive people nuts, and I'll sell a stack of cookie books."

Tricia resisted the urge to roll her eyes. "What ingredients are you missing? I could whip on up to the store for supplies."

"Good idea," Angelica said, still flipping pages. "But not the convenience store. I'll bet they rarely sell flour. Their stock probably has weevils. You'll have to go to Milford."

That hadn't been the direction Tricia had planned to go, but she was more than ready to make her escape.

Angelica headed for the register and grabbed a piece of scrap paper. "Hold on, I'll write up a list."

Tricia wasted no time waiting for Angelica to change her mind, and retrieved her jacket. Five minutes later, however, she was feeling uncomfortably warm as Angelica added yet another two or three items to her list. "Come on, Ange, you're making a couple of batches of cookies, not feeding a regiment."

"I know, but I'll need supplies for several days. With Ginny and Mr. Everett here, I can go back to my first love—cooking!" She checked over her list again.

The News Team Ten van rolled by the shop once more.

"Ange, if the media calls looking for me, remember I've got no comments on Zoë Carter's death."

"Right," she said, still distracted by her list. "But you don't mind if I comment, do you? Free press for the shop is free press."

"Ange!"

Angelica looked up. "Hey, there is no such thing as bad publicity. And now that I've had time to think about it, I can really milk the story."

Tricia grabbed the list before Angelica could think of anything else to add—and before she could strangle her. "Be back in an hour or so." Or longer.

Tricia headed for the back of the store and passed Mr. Everett, who was sorting misplaced books. She waggled a finger and bade him to follow.

"Mr. Everett, there's a news van that keeps circling the village. I want to avoid them."

"The hounding press," he said, and nodded. "They can be relentless."

"I can disable the Cookery's alarm, but can you reset it for me?"

"Of course. It's the same system we have at Haven't Got a Clue."

Tricia blinked. Yes, it was the same. That hadn't registered before. "Thank you." She searched the old man's face. "And thank you for showing up to help Angelica today. I know this is usually your day off, and you like to spend your time with Grace."

He held up a hand to stop her. "Grace had to leave town rather suddenly this morning."

"Oh?"

"Yes. I believe her sister has taken ill."

"Oh, I'm so sorry."

"I am, too. I must admit these past few months I've grown rather used to her company. I shall miss her."

"If you hear from her, please let her know she's in my thoughts."

"I shall. Thank you."

"Okay. I'll see you in an hour or so. And thank you again for helping Angelica."

"It's my pleasure."

Tricia disabled the alarm and watched as the door closed behind her.

TRICIA SIDLED THROUGH the narrow passage between the Have a Heart romance bookshop and the Stoneham Patisserie, turned the corner, and peered through the front window. Already tourists jammed the store, loading up on cookies, scones, and other portable pastries. Nikki brushed back a loose strand of hair and took an offered bill, ringing up a sale at the register. Harried but

happy was an apt description of her. She looked up, saw Tricia, and flashed a smile. Had she heard about Zoë's death? Probably not, but now was not the time to break it to her. It had been Nikki who had suggested Tricia invite the author. No doubt she'd feel terrible—possibly responsible—to learn of her death.

Tricia gave a quick wave and moved on. She crossed her fingers, wishing Nikki good luck with the bank loan, and headed down the street to the crosswalk. She looked left and right for traffic, waited for a green pickup truck to pass, and gave a mental sigh of relief that the WRBS news van was nowhere in sight.

So far, so good.

Frannie Armstrong was not one to gossip about the members of the Chamber of Commerce. She'd made it clear that putting her job as a receptionist in peril was something she would not consider. But none of the players in last night's drama had been members of the Chamber, except for Russ, Angelica, and Tricia herself. As the eyes and ears of the Chamber, Frannie came across an inordinate amount of useful information. From painting paneling to renting farm and other equipment, Frannie knew where to go or how to do it, and if she didn't, she could direct you to someone who did.

Tricia pushed open the bright, red-painted door and entered the charming little log cabin that served as the Chamber's headquarters. It had once been the home office of Trident Log Homes, which had gone bankrupt a decade before. Though it wasn't her taste in architecture, Tricia could appreciate the charm of the chinked walls, the timbered beams, the daylight flowing through the skylights and brightening the whole interior, and the way its designer had chosen to incorporate a soaring cathedral ceiling instead of a second-floor loft.

She found Frannie dressed in a blue and white calla lily Hawaiian shirt over dark slacks. Thanks to posters of the fiftieth state lining her workspace wall, she needed only a flower lei to look like she was auditioning for a community theater production of *South Pacific*.

Frannie was on the phone, but waved a cheery hello in Tricia's direction, then motioned for her to seat herself on one of the comfortable leather couches. On a little wooden stand near a rack of brochures was a self-serve airpot of coffee. The plate of store-bought cookies next to the pot reminded Tricia what her real mission was supposed to be. She pushed down the guilt and took one of the tea biscuits, nibbling on it while she waited for Frannie to finish her conversation.

A minute later, Frannie hung up the phone. "Hey, Tricia, I tried calling you this morning, but the answering machine kicked in saying Haven't Got a Clue is closed. Isn't it a shame about poor Zoë?"

"Yes." And about the sheriff shutting down her store, too, although she kept that opinion to herself.

Frannie shook her head and *tsk-tsk*ed. "I heard you found her. Was it too awfully terrible?" The gossip network was obviously working at peak capacity.

"It wasn't fun."

"I feel just terrible for you. And after what you went through last fall, too." She *tsk-tsk*ed again. "Have they arrested that appalling niece for Zoë's murder?"

"Not that I've heard. In fact, I haven't heard anything. I was hoping you might have."

Frannie allowed the barest hint of a smile to touch her lips. "Well, I do like to think of myself as being well-informed, but the gossip mill hasn't really had a chance to get started on this one yet. For my money, it's that nasty niece. You heard the way she talked to her aunt."

"And the way she talked to you," Tricia reminded her.

"And me," Frannie said. She shook her head ruefully. "I've lived in this town almost twenty-one years, but I never ran across that young woman before. Then again, why would I? I never had kids, so I never met many. Except the children of Chamber members, of course, at the annual picnic, et cetera."

"Had you met Zoë before?"

Frannie thought about it. "I suppose I must have, but it's nothing I remember. The people I know best are affiliated with the Chamber, or work at the library or the grocery stores in Milford. Other than that—" She shrugged. Then her expression shifted, and a sly glint entered her eyes. "Course, they say Miz Carter was mixed up in the whole Trident Homes disaster."

"Oh?"

Frannie leaned forward, lowered her voice. "Embezzlement."

"Zoë Carter?"

Frannie nodded. "I don't have the whole story, and it seems to me it was all rather hushed up. I mean, if it wasn't—wouldn't I, of all people, know?"

Yes, she would. "What happened to Zoë?"

"She didn't go to prison. Seems to me she got off with a suspended sentence. And it wasn't long after the whole sordid incident that she got published."

If Zoë didn't go to jail, there had to be mitigating circumstances. But this was at least ten years ago, and if the town gossip didn't know the details, who would? Russ had owned the *Stoneham Weekly News* only three or four years, but he did possess the bound volumes of years past. Had the former editor chronicled the story? She'd have to check.

"I wonder if Zoë was well-known at the library," Tricia mused aloud. "Her historical mysteries had to be researched somewhere."

"Lois Kerr is the head librarian. Have you met her?" Trisha shook her head. "She's a bit stern, but that's because she's old school. Still, she's the one who pushed for the village budget to include Wi-Fi access at the library. She's a real whirlwind of energy."

"I believe I've spoken to her on the phone, but . . . I haven't even had time to get a library card. I mean . . . I really only read mysteries, and I order everything I want and then some from distributors, as well as buy from people willing to sell their collections."

"It wouldn't hurt for you to talk to Lois in person. Maybe get yourself a library card. Libraries are the best value you can get for your tax dollars."

"Yes, ma'am," Tricia murmured with respect.

Frannie laughed. "Any other questions?"

"Who would know Kimberly Peters?"

Frannie frowned. "Her high school teachers, I suppose. I don't know much about her. Russ Smith might, though. I mean, if she ever got in trouble—and it wouldn't surprise me, with that attitude of hers—it would've ended up in the *Stoneham Weekly News* crime blotter." That column was often only a paragraph or two long—if it even ran.

"You might also try Deborah Black," Frannie added. "She's only a few years older than Kimberly. Maybe she remembers her from school."

"Great idea. Thanks."

Frannie craned her neck to look beyond Tricia. "There they go again," she said, and shook her head.

Tricia turned to see a line of Canada geese marching down the sidewalk, no doubt heading for Stoneham Creek. It was the only running water in the area, and it seemed to be the attraction that kept luring the geese from the relative calm of the outlying retention ponds.

"Can't the Chamber pressure the Village Board to do something about them?" Tricia asked.

"They could get the state and the federal government to approve roundup-and-slaughter operations," she said matter-of-factly.

"What?" Tricia asked, horrified.

"Yup, that's what they call it. They wait until the geese are molting and can't fly, then they herd those poor birds into boxes and gas them with carbon dioxide."

"But I thought they were protected—and that's why the population keeps growing."

"Hey, it's happened. In Washington State, Minnesota, and Michigan. I read about it on the Internet," Frannie said, her voice filled with disapproval. "I'm willing to put up with a little inconvenience—cleaning off the sidewalks—if it'll save just one of those beautiful birds."

Tricia was not fond of the job, but when she thought about it, she felt the same way.

"Is the Chamber actually considering killing the geese?"

"It's an option."

"Who told you this?"

"Bob. Bob Kelly."

The phone rang. "Break time over," Frannie said, and stepped across the room to the reception desk. She picked up the receiver. "Stoneham Chamber of Commerce, Frannie speaking. How may I help you?"

Tricia gave a brief wave before she closed the door behind her. Sure enough, she was going to have to step carefully in the wake of the geese.

The early April sunshine held no warmth, and Tricia pulled up her collar against the wind. Since she was supposed to have lunch with Deborah today, she could ask her about Kimberly Peters. In the meantime, Angelica would be hopping mad if she didn't show up with flour, walnuts, and chocolate and peanut butter chips within the next half hour.

Reluctantly, Tricia headed for the municipal parking lot and her car. Preoccupied with the search for her keys in her purse, she didn't spot the WRBS van parked at the edge of the lot until it was too late. A brunette in a camel hair coat and calf-high black boots, clutching a microphone, made a beeline for Tricia.

Panicked, Tricia dropped her keys, fumbled to pick them up, and stood, finding herself looking into the lens of a video camera.

"Tricia Miles?" asked the brunette. "Portia McAlister, WRBS News. I understand you found the body of best-selling author Zoë Carter in your store's washroom last night."

"Uh . . . uh . . ." Mesmerized by the camera, Tricia couldn't think.

"She was strangled with your bungee cord."

"I'm—I'm not sure."

"About what?" Portia pressed.

"If it actually was my bungee cord." She turned, pressed the button on her key ring and the car's doors unlocked. "I really have to go." Good sense—and Sheriff Adams's order not to talk to the press—clicked in. "I've got no more comments."

"She was found on the toilet. What was the state of the body? Was she fully clothed? Had she been sexually assaulted?"

Appalled by the question, Tricia slid into the car, slammed the door, buckled up, and started the engine. The cameraman swung around to block her exit.

Tricia pressed a control, and her window opened by two or three inches. "Please," she implored, "I have to be somewhere."

The microphone plunged toward her again. "Where are you going? Will you be talking to a lawyer?"

A lawyer? She hadn't done anything that warranted talking to a lawyer!

Tricia jammed the gearshift into drive, letting the car move forward a few inches. The cameraman didn't budge. She honked the horn furiously, edged forward a few more inches. What if he didn't move? If she hit him, then she'd have reason to speak to a lawyer.

"This is harassment. If you don't leave me alone, I'll call the sheriff!"

"Back off, Mark," the reporter said, and the cameraman immediately obliged, lowering his camera. "We'll speak again, Ms. Miles," Portia said as Tricia pulled away.

It sounded like a threat.

FOUR

The ten-minute drive to Milford helped calm Tricia's frayed nerves, and she steered directly for the biggest grocery store in town—the better to find bitter chocolate, she figured. Angelica's list of ingredients was long and varied, and Tricia had doubts she'd find everything her sister wanted.

Once inside the store, Tricia pushed her shopping cart down the various aisles until she found the baking section. She paused, scanning the bags of flour, and frowned. She didn't bake, hadn't even attempted it since she was a Girl Scout too many years ago. Should she buy all-purpose flour? Self-rising? Would wheat flour make a healthier cookie? And Angelica's list said brown sugar, but even that came in two choices. Should she buy the dark or the light?

Carts and people pushed past her as she contemplated the myriad choices. Should she take a wild guess, or break down and call Angelica? But if she did, she was likely to get a lecture for taking so long on her errand, and get the same again when she returned to the Cookery. It would be far better to get that dressing-down only once rather than twice.

"Tricia?"

She looked up at the sound of her name, instantly recognizing the voice. "Russ, what are you doing here?"

"Looking for you." Russ pushed his cart forward, pausing when he reached

Tricia's. He nudged his gold-tone glasses up the bridge of his nose. "Angelica said I'd find you here. I've been waiting for almost an hour. Do you know how boring a grocery store can be when you have an hour to kill?"

"Sorry," she said, but wasn't sure it was true. And judging by the nearly full grocery cart Russ pushed, it looked like he'd found plenty to occupy his time.

"No, *I'm* sorry," he said, and sighed. "I didn't mean to blow you off last night and run to the paper. I didn't realize the sheriff would toss you out of your home. Why didn't you call? Why don't you come stay with me?"

"I want to be near my store—my home. It's more convenient for me and my cat to stay with Angelica."

"But Angelica doesn't even like Miss Marple."

"Everybody likes Miss Marple," said a voice behind them. An elderly woman bundled up in a parka and wearing a plastic rain bonnet stood behind a grocery cart. "Can I get through please? I need to get a cake mix."

Tricia and Russ moved aside. "I tried calling you for over three hours this morning. There was no answer," Tricia said.

"Sorry. Every news outlet in the state has been calling me for an interview."

"Yes, and I see you talked with someone at the *Nashua Telegraph* last night," she said, her tone cool.

"It was too late to stop my press run. I figured I may as well cut my losses and get some exposure for the pictures I took last night."

"Did they pay well?"

"No, I gave them to a buddy of mine on staff. I owe him, and this was a way to pay him back. Now I can feel free to call upon him some other time I need a favor."

That still didn't make it right in Tricia's eyes, but at least she felt better knowing he hadn't made money from Zoë's death. It was time to turn the tables. "Russ, what do you know about Zoë Carter's part in the downfall of Trident Homes?"

He blinked at her. "Nothing. Why?"

"A little bird told me that Zoë was prosecuted for embezzlement."

"That's interesting. When did all this happen?"

"Before she became a best-selling author."

"Maybe that's a reason she never wanted publicity."

"Indeed. Would the *Stoneham Weekly News* have covered this?" she asked.

He exhaled a long breath. "Possibly. But Ted Moser, the former owner, wasn't known for printing anything that reeked of scandal. He was a real cheerleader for the village."

Not unlike Bob Kelly, Tricia thought.

"I'll have a look at the archives, see what I can come up with."

"Thanks. Meanwhile, I have to get this stuff for Angelica," Tricia said, waving the grocery list in the air. "She's going to have a fit because I've already been gone so long."

"Come back to Stoneham and have lunch with me."

She shook her head. "I'm having lunch with Deborah today."

"Then have dinner with me tonight."

"Where?"

"My dining room."

"You're going to cook?" she asked.

He shrugged. "Let's face it, I'm better at it than you."

She nodded in reluctant agreement. "Deal." She thought about her encounter with News Team Ten. "It just so happens I may need some . . . professional advice."

He leaned, as far as he was able, over the grocery cart. "I'm intrigued."

Tricia's attempt at a seductive smile was interrupted by the cake lady. "Can I just grab a bag of brown sugar? I'm making a caramelized frosting for my son-in-law's thirty-fifth birthday. It's his favorite."

Tricia forced a smile. "How nice." Then her brain clicked into PR mode, and she almost started a pitch for books as gifts before she remembered Haven't Got a Clue was closed.

"You were saying?" Russ prompted.

She frowned.

"Professional advice?" he pressed.

"Oh, how to keep the press from bugging me."

"Why, what happened?"

"A TV reporter named Portia McAlister cornered me at my car in the municipal parking lot not half an hour ago. Talk about persistent. The sheriff told me not to speak to the press—"

"What about me?" he asked indignantly.

"She doesn't consider you important."

"Thank you very little, Wendy Adams."

Tricia ignored his feigned injured pride. "Anyway, she rattled me."

"The sheriff?"

"No, Portia McAlister. Before I knew it, I'd said more than I intended."

"She got what she wanted—throwing you off guard so you'd blather. As long as the camera was rolling, she got something she can broadcast. It'll placate her boss—for a few hours. But don't be surprised if she keeps popping up to bug you. Zoë's death is big news in these parts. Unless a bigger story comes along, she's going to keep at it."

"I was afraid you'd say that."

"Now, on to more important things. Like dinner. Is seven thirty okay?"

"Yes."

The cake lady had retreated, so Russ sidled closer, planted a light kiss on Tricia's lips. "Until later, then."

ANGELICA WAS IN a foul temper by the time Tricia arrived with two paper sacks full with groceries. "Look at *this*!" she growled, pointing to the opened bakery box piled high with cookies in the shape of daisies, and frosted in pastel shades, that sat on the Cookery's sales counter.

"You went out and bought them after sending me all the way to Milford and the grocery store?" Tricia asked, irked.

"No! Nikki Brimfield sent them over for *you*!"

"Me?"

"Yes. She heard about Zoë's murder and you finding her, and felt sorry for you. So she sent these over to cheer you up."

"Why are you so angry?"

"Because *I* wanted to bake. I want my customers to enjoy *my* food, not mass-produced *bakery* food. If I use a recipe from a book in stock, I've got a good shot of selling that book. But not with *bakery*," she emphasized it like it was a dirty word, "items."

"Oh, come on. Everybody says Nikki's goodies are to die for."

"Yeah, well, I don't need a death in my store like you had in—" She cut herself off, looking horrified. "Oh, Trish, I didn't mean that . . . it's just, why does she have to sell cookbooks in her bakery?"

"It's a patisserie," Tricia corrected.

"I don't care what she calls it. She's a baker, not a bookseller."

"Ange, Stoneham is known as a book town. Can you blame her for capitalizing on it?"

"Yes! Would you feel so generous if another store sold mysteries?"

Tricia didn't answer. Truthfully, she hadn't considered the equation from Angelica's perspective.

Tricia eyed her sister for a long moment. "I think sending me cookies was an extremely nice gesture on her part, and I'm going to make sure I thank her for her kindness. And, by the way, if they were sent to *me*, why are they open on *your* sales counter?"

Angelica frowned. "You can't eat all those cookies. You don't even like sweets all that much, Miss Perennial Size Eight."

Tricia exhaled, her nerves stretched taut. She and her sister had been bat-

tling the same demons for years, and things were improving too slowly. Angelica still drove her crazy. The fact that she hadn't kept her girlish figure was just one example of the continuing conflict between them.

She glanced at her watch. "We'll have to discuss this later. I'm supposed to meet Deborah for lunch in two minutes. In the meantime, if you don't want to serve the cookies to your customers—*don't*!" She left the store and walked briskly down Main Street to the Bookshelf Diner.

The restaurant's lunch crowd never really thinned until the last bus of tourists left. But after waiting ten minutes, Tricia snagged a table in front, sat with her back to the window that overlooked the street, and perused the menu, trying not to dwell on her little altercation with Angelica. Was it a tuna salad or a ham on rye kind of day? It was definitely a hot soup day, but today's offering was cream of broccoli. Scratch ordering soup. Tricia had a personal policy against eating anything that looked as if Miss Marple might have coughed it up after a binge of grass eating.

Tricia was on her second cup of coffee when a wind-blown Deborah barreled through the diner's front door. She fell into the booth seat, scooted in, and pulled off her blue woolly hat. "So much for spring," she breathed. She signaled Hildy, the diner's middle-aged, early-shift waitress, and ordered coffee and a bowl of chili. "That ought to warm me up," she said, wriggling out of her jacket.

"I'll have tuna on whole wheat," Tricia said.

Hildy nodded and took off toward the kitchen.

"Sorry I'm late," Deborah said, "but I had to do some cleanup in front of my shop. That goose poop is slicker than black ice, and if you fall in it, you may as well burn what you're wearing. Why can't the geese just stick around the water? Why do they have to walk up and down Main Street like they own the place?"

"I agree, but I can't be outside my store all day, shooing them away, either. Have you seen how big they are close up?"

"Yes. Some of them can even look right into my shop window." Deborah leaned across the table and whispered, "Never mind the geese, everybody's talking about your murder last night."

"Don't call it *my* murder."

"Well, it happened in your store. Hey, did that pushy reporter from Boston corner you yet?"

"Yes, just as I was getting into my car to go to the grocery store. She wanted to know if Zoë had been sexually assaulted. I had to pull the old 'no comment' and drive away to get rid of her."

"I couldn't tell her much because I'd left your store before the body was found. I was hoping to put in a plug for my store, but she shut down the camera and lost all interest in me as soon as I told her."

Tricia shook her head. "Has the sheriff spoken to you yet?"

Deborah nodded. "Last night. Woke us out of a sound sleep. It took hours to get little Davey settled down again. I'll tell you one thing, I'm not voting for that woman the next time she's up for reelection."

"I've only talked to Frannie. Otherwise, no one's said a word to me about it. Is it because they think I'm guilty?"

"Of course not. It's just—"

"Don't start that village jinx business again," Tricia warned.

Deborah didn't bother to try to hide her smile. "Two murders in less than a year—and you discover both bodies."

"Don't tell me *you* think I'm guilty?"

"Of course not. Everyone's saying it's Zoë Carter's niece. Odds are, as her only living relative—"

"That we know of," Tricia corrected.

"She might be in for a lot of money. Zoë's books were *New York Times* best sellers. You don't make that list without earning a few big bucks."

The food arrived in record time, and Deborah plunged her spoon into the steaming bowl of chili. Tricia took a bite of her sandwich, chewed, and swallowed. "Frannie says you were in high school about the same time as Kimberly. What do you know about her?"

Deborah's spoon hovered close to her mouth. "I don't know what Frannie's been smoking, but she must be one very mixed-up lady. I'm not even from Stoneham. I graduated from East Hampton High on Long Island."

"You don't have a Long Island accent."

She grinned. "That's what a good voice coach will get you."

Tricia put her sandwich half back on her plate. "Whatever could Frannie have been thinking?"

"She must've gotten me mixed up with someone else."

"I guess." Under the circumstances, Tricia didn't bother asking Deborah if she'd heard of Zoë's checkered past. "Frannie also suggested I talk to the Stoneham librarian. Do you know her?"

Deborah shook her head. "Who has time to read?"

"But you're a bookseller."

"Among other things. But I also have a seven-month-old baby. I haven't picked up a book to actually read since the day Davey was born, and my to-be-read pile nearly reaches the ceiling. I love him dearly, but I can't wait until he starts school and I can have a few moments to myself again."

Tricia picked up her sandwich half again, but didn't take a bite. "I need to get my store open again. Any ideas on how I can push the sheriff's investigation forward?"

Deborah shrugged. "I guess you'd have to talk to everybody who was at your store last night."

"Supposedly what the sheriff is already doing."

"Yes, but she's so intimidating, she'll probably frighten everyone into clamming right up. You're more subtle. You'll be able to get them to tell you what they remember."

"That's the problem. Nobody seems to remember exactly *when* Zoë went to the washroom. Nobody was paying attention. The security system was down, but it might've been disabled for hours. Truth be told, I usually set it and forget it."

"Me, too. I mean, most of my deliveries come in through the front door."

Tricia nodded, her gaze falling to her plate and the small pile of potato chips on it. "I want to talk to Kimberly. She's staying at Zoë's house here in Stoneham, but the phone number is unlisted. All my contact information for Zoë is locked in my store."

"Have you tried reaching Zoë's publicist or agent?"

"No, but that's a good idea."

Deborah moved to one side, looking beyond Tricia and out through the diner's big, plate-glass window. "There goes the News Team Ten van cruising down Main Street again. I wonder who she's going to try and nail this time?"

"I'm actually surprised we haven't seen more news trucks and reporters."

"Be surprised no more," Deborah said. "There goes another one. Channel Seven from Boston."

Tricia pushed her lunch away, no longer hungry. "If I was smart, I'd write a press release saying I can't make any comments, and just have Angelica hand it out to everyone."

"Why don't you? Then again, this can only last a few days. By then your store will be open again and things will get back to normal. Until the pilgrimages start, that is."

"Pilgrimages?"

"Of course. You run a mystery bookstore. A best-selling mystery author was murdered there. Her fans—if that's what you want to call anyone that ghoulish—will flock to Haven't Got a Clue in droves. And if she signed your stock, you can ask a fortune for those books."

"She didn't sign the stock."

Deborah shook her head. "Too bad."

Just as well, Tricia thought. Selling the books for an exorbitant price, making money off a dead woman, just wouldn't sit well with her.

Hildy stopped by the table. "Want me to box that up for you, Tricia?"

She nodded. "Thanks."

The waitress took away the plate and Deborah scraped the last spoonful of

chili from her bowl, savoring it. "I suppose someone will find out I was at the signing last night and want to talk to me, too." She brightened. "Good promo for my shop."

Exactly what Angelica had said.

"At least you're still open."

"You'll be back in business in a day or so. Look how fast the Cookery reopened after the murder last fall."

"Different circumstances entirely." And besides, it had been six long weeks—a possible death for a going concern.

Deborah pushed her bowl aside as Hildy returned with a Styrofoam box and the check. She glanced at it, then dug into her purse for her wallet. "Hey, I wonder what I could get on eBay for one of the last copies of *Forever Cherished* that Zoë Carter signed?"

"Now who's being ghoulish?"

"I'm a businesswoman. It's my job to make money. For me!" She peeled off a five-dollar bill and set it on the table, grabbed her hat, then wiggled back into her jacket. "Call me later if you need to talk." And she was off.

Tricia stared down at the cold coffee in her cup, at the desolate little box with her partially eaten sandwich in it, and felt empty. *I want my store back. I want my life back.*

She put another five-dollar bill and a couple of ones on the table, donned her coat, and steeled her nerves to return to the Cookery, hoping Angelica's wrath had been soothed by the act of baking.

FIVE

SQUISH!

Tricia winced and looked down at her loafer and the gummy substance clinging to it. *Not again!* She hobbled to the edge of the curb to scrape the bottom of her shoe, cursing herself for not watching where she walked.

Mission accomplished, she started off again, but paused outside the Stoneham Patisserie. It was still crowded with customers; she'd have to thank Nikki for the cookies later.

Business was also brisk at the Cookery, and the air was laden with the heavenly aroma of fresh-baked peanut butter blondies. Nikki's box of bakery cook-

ies was conspicuous by its absence. A smiling Angelica flitted about the store, paper-doily-covered silver tray in hand, offering sample-sized morsels—along with paper napkins—to the grateful browsers. Mr. Everett helped customers while Ginny manned the cash register. Her smile was forced, but somehow she managed not to convey to Angelica's clientele her anger at being there, while exhibiting the helpful cookery knowledge she'd picked up while working for the former owner.

"Just a few more days," Tricia whispered to her as she bagged an order.

"I never want to see another cookbook again," Ginny hissed. "She *is* going to pay us, right? I mean, we haven't even filled out any paperwork."

"Angelica's good for it," Tricia assured her. "And you know I won't let you down if she isn't."

For the first time that day, the tension eased from Ginny's face. "Thanks, Tricia. You're the world's best boss."

"No, I'm not. But I've been where you are—in a new house that needs a lot of work, and with limited funds." Okay, that was a bit of a lie. Tricia had been extremely lucky and had never experienced a day of poverty or even strained finances in her life. But she had read Dickens, and that had to count for something.

"While you were gone, I sneaked a peek on Angelica's computer. There are already signed copies of Zoë's books, dated last night, for sale on eBay. With pictures and everything."

"You're kidding."

Ginny shook her head. "It says right on the screen, 'Item location: Milford, New Hampshire.'"

"Rats. I was hoping no one would try to cash in on her death. At least, not this soon."

"Hey," Ginny said, and shrugged. "It's human nature. Or should I say human greed?"

Tricia frowned. Deborah would have competition selling her copies of the book.

The door flew open, the bell over it jangling loudly. Kimberly Peters stepped inside, her face flushed in anger. "Where do you get off telling people I killed my aunt?" she demanded.

Ginny pointed to herself. "Me?"

Kimberly glared at Tricia. "No, her."

Several customers looked up from the books they were perusing, and Angelica turned so fast, she whipped her tray of blondies away from a woman who'd been about to sample one.

"Excuse me, but could you lower your voice?" Tricia asked.

Kimberly marched up to the sales counter. "No, I won't."

Tricia stood her ground, exhaled an angry breath. "For your information, I haven't accused anyone of killing your aunt, least of all you. Unless I'm very much mistaken, and that's always possible, I figured you were too smart to murder her after that display you put on last night."

It was Kimberly's turn to exhale loudly, although she did lower her voice. "I was a bit upset last night," she admitted. "But you're right. I'm not stupid enough to kill the goose that laid the golden egg. My aunt was very generous to me, and I'd be an idiot to exterminate my only relative and my employer. Now I'll probably have to go out and get a real job."

"You mean she didn't leave you everything?"

Kimberly's glare was blistering. "Not that it's any of your business, but no. She left me only a tiny portion of her estate. The rest will be split up among various charities. Believe me, the last thing I wanted was for the old girl to die."

So the bulk of Zoë's estate was going to charity. Tricia itched to know the circumstances surrounding Zoë's embezzlement conviction—if indeed she *had* been convicted. Embezzlers usually go to jail, as well as having to pay hefty fines. What about the investors who'd suffered losses when Trident Homes went under? Had Zoë's eventual plan been to give away all her worldly wealth as a final act of atonement before exiting this life?

Too many pairs of eyes still stared at them, and Tricia decided this wasn't the time to pursue Zoë's past with Kimberly. "So who's going around spreading vicious gossip about me?" Tricia asked, changing the subject.

"How do I know? I got an anonymous call on my voice mail. And they told me right where to find you."

"They? Man or woman?"

"A man."

Besides Mr. Everett and a couple of Angelica's customers, the only man Tricia had spoken to that day was Russ Smith, and it wasn't likely he'd be spreading that kind of gossip. Not if he ever hoped to woo her again.

Not knowing what else to say to that news, Tricia changed tack. "I'm very sorry about your loss, Kimberly. Your aunt's work was loved by millions."

"Yes," she said, yanking down her suit jacket—brown, and just as wrinkled as the one she'd worn the day before. "It was."

"It." Not "she."

"Were you serious when you mentioned blackmail last night?"

"Sort of."

"How can one 'sort of' be blackmailed?"

"There was no implicit threat. Just a strong suggestion that one should honor one's debts," Kimberly explained.

"And did your aunt owe someone a lot of money?"

Kimberly shrugged. "Not as far as I know. And anyhow, it's not my problem." And with that, she turned and stalked out of the store.

Not her problem? Only if the blackmailer gave up or Kimberly didn't care about her aunt's reputation, which was entirely possible.

Angelica hurried over to the sales desk. "What was that all about?"

"I don't think we need to do a rerun in front of your customers," Tricia whispered.

Angelica shoved the tray of blondies at Ginny. "Circulate the store, will you?"

"Please," Tricia admonished her.

Angelica glowered. "Just do it," she told Ginny, who followed Kimberly's lead and stalked away from the register.

It was Tricia's turn to get angry. "Ange, if this is how you treat your employees, it's no wonder they quit after only a couple of days."

"What are you talking about?" she asked, sounding truly puzzled.

Tricia shook her head. "I would appreciate it if you would treat Ginny and Mr. Everett with respect. I don't want either of them quitting on me because you've treated them badly."

"How have I treated them badly? I treat them just the same as I treat all my help."

"My point exactly."

"What did Kimberly say? What did she say?" Angelica badgered. "Denied everything, right?"

"Well, of course she would. But I don't think for a minute she killed Zoë," Tricia said. "I don't think she'd be that stupid."

"Unless that's what she *wants* you to think."

"Don't be ridiculous."

"I think you're discounting Kimberly far too easily."

"I'm not saying she doesn't have more to tell. But here in the Cookery wasn't the place for a meaningful conversation. I'll have to get her on her own—in a quiet setting. But first I need to find out more about both her and Zoë Carter."

"How are you going to do that?"

"By talking to people."

"Who?"

Tricia shrugged. "Townspeople. Her neighbors."

"You think a local person killed her?"

"Could be."

"You didn't know half the people who showed up at the signing last night. I suppose any one of those strangers could have strangled her."

"Maybe," Tricia said, consulting her watch. It was already after two. "I'd better get going."

"Will you come back to the store before closing time?"

"I don't know. It depends on how many people I can track down who knew Zoë. By the way, I hope you weren't expecting me for dinner. I'm going to Russ's."

Angelica frowned. "But then I'll be all alone with—with that cat of yours," she said with disdain.

"So? Miss Marple won't bite—unless you tease her. And you'd better not treat her the way you're treating your employees. Or else."

Angelica sniffed. "Perhaps I'll invite Bob over for dinner."

"Great. Maybe you can get him to help you unpack some of those boxes."

Angelica ignored the jab, narrowing her eyes. "Will you be coming home tonight?"

"Your apartment is not my home. And . . . I don't know. Probably." She thought about it—how she and Russ were so involved in their respective businesses that their time together was all too rare. If she stayed with him, they might finally get some quality time together. Then again . . . "We'll see."

IT WAS NO secret in Stoneham that Zoë Carter had lived on Pine Avenue most of her adult life. She was, after all, the little village's only real celebrity. But the house in question was no palace, and was in fact the plainest house on the block. Tricia parked her car and scoped out the neighborhood, looking for rogue Canada geese. Sure enough, several waddled down the sidewalk on the opposite side of the street, occasionally stopping to peck at the exposed grass, no doubt looking for something to eat. She should be safe enough.

Since she wasn't yet ready to talk to Kimberly, Tricia instead marched up the walk of Zoë's next-door neighbor to the north and knocked on the door. Almost immediately a burly man dressed in a paint-splattered blue MIT sweatshirt and jeans, and sporting a churlish expression, opened the door but didn't say a word.

Tricia adopted her most winning smile. "Sir, my name's Tricia Miles. I own the mystery bookstore in town."

"Where Zoë Carter was killed?"

"Uh, yes," she answered, already rattled. She hurried on. "I was wondering if you'd be willing to talk to me about Zoë?"

"You gonna give me fifty bucks? The reporter from WRBS gave me fifty bucks to tell her everything I knew about the old girl."

Taken aback, Tricia tried to remember how much cash she had in her wallet; a ten and a few ones? "I hadn't thought—" she started.

He waved a hand in dismissal and stepped back to close the door.

"Wait!" Tricia called, but the door slammed in her face.

She tried across the street, but no one answered her knock, despite the fact that a pale blue minivan sat in the drive. She'd canvass the whole street if she had to. But first she'd check Zoë's neighbor to the south. She crossed the street and walked past Zoë's home, once more noting that it was the least attractive house on the street. Not that it was run-down, but no spring flowers or landscaping brightened the drab exterior, its curb appeal nil. Only the green and gold FOR SALE sign gave the yard any color. No car stood in the drive. Was Kimberly home, parking whatever car she drove in the one-car garage, or was she out, possibly making funeral arrangements?

Tricia passed Zoë's home and headed up the walk to the house next door on the south. By contrast, this white clapboard house with pink shutters welcomed her. Scores of sunny daffodils waved in the slight breeze against a backdrop of well-tended yews, and empty window boxes promised more color come summer. A grapevine wreath was intertwined with silk flowers and painted wooden letters in pastel hues that spelled out WELCOME.

Tricia lifted the brass knocker and tapped it three times. The door sprang open and a diminutive, elderly woman dressed in slacks, sweater, and a frilly white apron tied at her waist stood just inside the door. "Yes?"

"Hello," Tricia said and explained who she was and how she'd known Zoë Carter. "Do you mind if I ask you a few questions?"

"Do you have some kind of identification? I mean . . . those TV people wanted me to talk about Zoë, and I don't want anything I say to end up on television or in the newspapers."

"I can assure you, it won't." Tricia dug into her purse and brought out not only her driver's license but also a business card for Haven't Got a Clue that she handed to the woman.

The older lady examined both items before returning Tricia's license. "I'm Gladys Mitchell," she said, taking Tricia's offered hand. Gladys shook her head. "It's all very sad, but I don't think I can help you. Although Zoë and I were neighbors for nearly thirty years, we were hardly more than acquaintances. She kept to herself, didn't have much personality. Wasn't interested in chatting or getting to know any of the neighbors."

"She seemed personable enough to me," Tricia said, knowing she was pushing it. On a scale of one to ten, Zoë might've mustered a four or a five on the personality scale.

"She was peddling her books at the time, wasn't she?"

Tricia nodded.

"Then I expect she learned to force herself to at least appear interested in those who showed up to buy her wares."

"Was Zoë friendlier before she was caught embezzling?"

The older lady pursed her lips. "You know about that?"

"I'm sure once News Team Ten finds out about it, that old scandal will make the story of her death even more titillating."

"I know she didn't go to jail." That confirmed what Frannie had said. "As far as I know, she had never been in trouble before that. And her niece had just come to live with her. I believe the girl had no other relatives."

"Did you ever read Zoë's books?"

The older woman shivered and crossed her arms across her chest, warding off the cold. "I took the first one out of the library. I was surprised it was so good. I wasn't expecting it to even be readable."

"Why?"

"Because *she* wrote it. It was actually interesting. The characters were believable. Look at her house. Would you think someone that talented would live in such an uninteresting house?"

No. Tricia thought about Zoë, sitting at the table in Haven't Got a Clue. She'd been dressed in a plain white blouse, a black skirt, and black pumps. She'd worn no makeup or flashy jewelry, and her short salt-and-pepper hair, cut to frame her face, would never be called stylish. But just because the outside package was unexciting didn't mean the woman couldn't have lived a vicarious life of adventure through her characters.

"Zoë wasn't a native of Stoneham, you know," Gladys offered, disapprovingly.

"No, I didn't."

"She came from some little town in New York," the woman said, as though that was somehow despicable. What would she say if Tricia admitted she was originally from Greenwich, Connecticut?

Tricia decided she'd have to make nice with Kimberly and get inside that house, see where Zoë had created her much-loved characters Jess and Addie Martin. Then again, many a famous author had decided that staring at a blank wall—and piece of paper or computer screen—was far less distracting to the creative mind than a fascinating vista or seascape.

Tricia changed the subject. "Do you know Zoë's niece, Kimberly?"

Gladys pursed her lips. "She was a mouthy teenager. I was glad when she went off to college. At least I had peace during the school year."

"I understand Zoë lived most of her time down south."

"For the last couple of years, yes. I wasn't surprised when the FOR SALE sign went up the other day."

"Why now? She must've made a fortune on her books. Why do you think she didn't take this step before now?"

The old lady shook her head. "As I said, we weren't friends. You'll have to ask her niece that. As far as I know, she's the only one in town that Zoë ever trucked with." The old woman took a step back, allowing the door to almost close. "Oprah will be on soon. I really have to go." And with that she closed the door, leaving Tricia standing on the cold concrete step, staring at Gladys's WELCOME wreath and feeling anything but.

FEW RESIDENTS ANSWERED her knocks as she visited the rest of the homes along Pine Avenue. One angry goose charged at her, hissing and flapping its wings, when she tried to walk up one driveway, and Tricia had to abandon her task. By late afternoon, she was chilled and had little left in the way of stamina. Still, she had a few more places to look for the facts concerning Zoë's background, and she did not want to return to the Cookery to face Angelica—or worse, the wrath of her two employees, who were little more than indentured servants until Haven't Got a Clue could reopen. A call to the sheriff's office had not rewarded her with good news. Sheriff Adams was not available. Her message would be relayed. Thank you, and have a nice day.

Not!

It was nearly five when Tricia pulled into the Stoneham library's parking lot, which was nearly full. The library had once been in a quaint little Cape Cod house, but with the explosion of new tax revenue from the revitalization of Main Street, the village had built a new library—complete with retention pond for containing storm water runoff—only eighteen months before. The concrete walks and beautiful landscaping would have welcomed her as she stepped out of her car, except, like most of the rest of the village, the library hadn't escaped the onslaught of the Canada geese, who had left their messy calling cards.

Sidestepping the droppings, Tricia entered the low-slung brick building and strode up to the front desk to ask the woman behind a computer terminal if she could speak to the head librarian. She disappeared behind a wall festooned with posters encouraging one and all to READ and returned a minute later with an older, bespectacled, gray-haired woman in a drab brown woolen skirt and a crisp white blouse.

Lois Kerr looked as stern as any head librarian Tricia had ever met—until she smiled; then her expressive eyes hinted at the warmth of her personality.

Tricia held out her hand. "Hello, my name is Tricia Miles. I own the mystery bookstore in the village, Haven't Got a Clue."

"Yes, I believe we've spoken on the phone several times. I'm very happy to meet you at last." Her smile waned. "I heard about the unpleasantness at your store last night."

"Extremely unpleasant," Tricia agreed. "One of the villagers suggested I come see you." She noticed several people at the checkout desk looking in their direction. "Is there someplace more private we could talk?"

Lois nodded. "My office has a door. This way."

Tricia followed the woman to a small office behind the circulation desk and took the chair the librarian offered. Lois sat down behind her desk and folded her hands on the uncluttered top. "How can I help you?"

"Did you know Zoë Carter?"

The old lady nodded, as though she'd expected the question. "Although not well," she admitted. "She'd come in here on Saturday mornings to read a week's worth of the *Wall Street Journal*."

"What for?"

Lois shrugged. "It certainly didn't pertain to her writing. And I would've thought she could afford a subscription."

"I understand that before she became published, she was a bookkeeper for Trident Log Homes." She waited to see if the librarian took the conversational bait.

"Yes, the Chamber of Commerce is now housed in what was formerly their main sales office. They went out of business . . . oh, maybe ten years ago."

Until today, Tricia had always assumed it had failed because there were so many log-home businesses located in New England.

"People seem to remember Zoë played a part in Trident's demise, but no longer remember the details. Embezzlement, wasn't it?"

The librarian lowered her gaze. "I believe so. I don't know the details, and even if I did, I wouldn't feel comfortable talking about it. It all happened a long time ago, and now the poor woman is dead."

"Yes. It wasn't long after the whole Trident affair that Zoë's first book was published."

Lois nodded, and seemed relieved to talk about something else. "That book always puzzled me . . . as did the ones that followed, if truth be told."

"Why?"

"Because Ms. Carter never came to us to help her with her research. I suppose for her later books she could have done it all on the Internet . . . but she could have read the *Wall Street Journal* on her computer, as well. If she had one, that is."

"Did she read historical novels?"

"Not that I recall. In fact, I don't think she had a library card. She never showed any interest in fiction, or books for that matter, at all."

That was odd. Most authors were voracious readers. Then again, Zoë hadn't talked about her writing much at her "appearance" the night before. She'd been cordial, and spoke about the book, reading a passage and answering questions—but only what pertained to the book itself. She'd bragged about her awards to Grace, but she hadn't really talked about the work itself, or how she approached it. And she'd mentioned more than once that the series had ended with no hope of her returning to it.

"What are you really saying? That you think she had help writing the books?"

"I didn't mean to imply anything," Lois said, spreading her hands in a placating manner. "I'm merely stating what I know, and that's the fact that Zoë Carter didn't read fiction."

"Lots of people don't visit libraries to take out books. I haven't visited a library in years."

"Is that something you're proud of?" Lois asked pointedly.

"No." Tricia quickly backpedaled. "It's just, I've always been lucky enough to have the means to buy every book I've ever wanted. And it's a large part of why my lifelong ambition was to become a bookseller—even if I embraced that career only in the last year."

"Sadly, for many people, the only means they have of reading a book—be it fiction or nonfiction—is through a library. Stoneham is lucky the Board of Selectmen realizes the importance of a strong library. Without sufficient funding, we'd have to cut hours and staff. We could lose accreditation with the statewide system, which would hamper us in many ways, one of which is that we couldn't participate in interlibrary loans. We can't obtain every book published, and without interlibrary loans, our patrons would be cut off from borrowing works owned by other libraries."

"I didn't realize that."

"Sadly, a lot of people don't. A library is more than just books. These days, we're total media centers. And that takes money."

Duly chastised, Tricia cast about for another subject. "Um, do you know Zoë Carter's niece, Kimberly Peters?"

"*Her*," Lois said with contempt. "She was banned from the library several times during her teenage years. Inappropriate behavior. She'd meet boys. They'd visit the more remote shelves and . . . let's just say they did their own brand of research on human biology."

"Oh, dear." Tricia sighed. "Zoë hinted that Kimberly had been a handful growing up. And after spending an hour or so with her last evening, I have to

say she hasn't changed. They had a bit of a tiff, but it certainly wasn't anything worth killing Zoë over."

"Pent-up resentment perhaps? It doesn't take much to snap a fragile mind."

"Kimberly didn't give that impression. She seemed more bored and . . . maybe frustrated? She asked one of my employees why she worked in retail, intimating it was beneath her. I wonder if she felt that way about her own job as Zoë's assistant."

"Why don't you ask her?"

Tricia nodded. "I think I will."

"You might also want to talk to Stella Kraft. She taught English at the high school for over forty years. I'll bet she taught Zoë, and maybe even Kimberly."

Tricia blinked. "I was told Zoë wasn't a native of Stoneham—that she came from somewhere in New York."

The librarian sighed. "Some of our citizens are very territorial. The truth is, we can't all be from Stoneham. I myself am originally from Reading, Pennsylvania."

"Yes, I have noticed an 'us versus them' bias from some of the villagers."

"It might die out—in another couple of generations," Lois said with a wry smile. "That is, if they can keep the young people from escaping en masse. Already the majority of villagers come from other places."

Tricia smiled, too. "How can I get in touch with Stella Kraft?"

"She's in the phone book." Lois swiveled her chair, reached for the slender book behind her desk. Adjusting her reading glasses, she flipped through the pages of the phone book until she found the entry, grabbed a scrap of paper, and wrote down the number, then handed it to Tricia.

"Tell her I sent you to her. She'll talk to you."

Tricia stood. "That's very kind. Thank you."

Lois stood as well. "Kindness has nothing to do with it. I'm a bit of a mystery fan myself. I can't wait to see how this unravels."

SIX

It was still too early to head over to Russ's house for dinner, so Tricia wandered the library, checking out its mystery section and finding a few books

she'd never read. Since she'd left her to-be-read pile of books by her now inaccessible bedside table, her visit had proved to be a godsend. She applied for and received a library card, and settled down to start the latest book in the Jeff Resnick mystery series.

The next time Tricia looked at her watch, a full hour and a half had passed. She stuffed the piece of paper with Zoë's schoolteacher's name and number between the pages as a bookmark, gathered up her purse and the other books she'd checked out, and headed for the door.

Tricia arrived at Russ's house ten minutes late, knocked on the door, and was soon rewarded with Russ's smiling face. "I wondered what happened to you. You're usually so punctual."

"I got sidetracked," she said, her nose wrinkling as she stepped across the entryway's threshold. She detected a kind of fishy odor. "What is that . . . aroma?" she asked.

He brightened. "You like it?" Apparently he hadn't heard the touch of sarcasm in her voice. "It's my mother's specialty: tuna noodle casserole. I figured that after what you've been through, you might need some good, old-fashioned comfort food."

Tricia couldn't quite suppress a shudder. Her life didn't revolve around food the way Angelica's did, and there were few things she found truly unpalatable. Unfortunately, warmed-over tuna was one of them. Was it something to do with the canning process that changed the flavor of the fish when it was heated? On other occasions, Russ had made barbeque or splendid seafood pasta dishes. Why had he resorted to this? And since her mostly uneaten sandwich still sat in Angelica's little demonstration area's fridge, Tricia suddenly realized how ravenously hungry she was.

"Let me take your coat," Russ said.

Tricia shrugged out of her jacket, glancing into the living room. Russ had assembled a plate of cheese and crackers on the chrome-and-glass cocktail table, and she made a beeline for it.

"Can I get you a drink? Some sherry, perhaps?" Russ asked, over the squeal of his police scanner.

Tricia glanced across the room at the hated little black box that sat atop Russ's TV. She turned back to him. "I'd love it," she said, seating herself on the leather couch and grabbing the cheese spreader, smearing some Brie onto a butter cracker. She wolfed it down, glad Russ wasn't in the room to notice. Maybe if she filled up on crackers, she wouldn't have to eat the casserole.

Russ returned with a cordial glass of sherry for Tricia and his usual Scotch and soda, setting them down on the cocktail table and taking a seat next to Tricia. She was more interested in the Brie.

"You said you were sidetracked?" he said, raising his voice to be heard over the scanner.

"Yes. I've had a very long day," she shouted in response.

"Looking into Zoë's past, no doubt."

"I need to get my store open and running again, and I'm sure Wendy Adams won't be in any hurry to help me with that. She'd drag her feet for months on this investigation if she thought she could get away with it."

"What?" he asked, over the squawk of the scanner.

"Can you please turn that down?" she practically yelled.

"Sure thing." He got up and turned off the scanner, plunging the room into silence. He took his seat next to Tricia and daubed cheese on a cracker for himself. "What were you saying?"

She sighed. "I said Wendy Adams would probably keep my store closed forever if she thought she could get away with it."

"Aren't you being a little hard on her?"

"No. You haven't heard her tone when she speaks to me. She blames me for something I never did. There's no way I can change her misperceptions of the past."

"I guess," he said, and took a sip of his drink. "What else did you do today?"

"First of all, I had to soothe my employees' ruffled feathers. They're not happy working for Angelica, and I can't say as I blame them. My sister's managerial style is more militaristic than altruistic. I'm surprised she doesn't strut up and down her shop carrying a riding crop, in case one of them steps out of line. She gives them orders, then hovers over them, waiting for them to make mistakes. Not the best way to build trust."

"I can see why she loses so many employees."

Tricia nodded, and spread Brie on another cracker. "I spoke to Frannie at the Chamber. She's the eyes and ears of Stoneham, but even she hadn't heard much about the investigation into Zoë's death." She took a bite.

"So far there isn't much to tell."

Tricia swallowed. "Oh?"

"I have a few friends in the Sheriff's Department," Russ admitted, "but they're not talking, at least not about specifics. What else did you do today?"

"I spoke to a couple of Zoë's neighbors, and Lois Kerr at the library. Do you know her?"

"Only most of my life."

Tricia picked up the cheese spreader and had another go at the Brie. She wasn't about to tell Russ about the possibility that Zoë hadn't written the *Forever* books. Shocked? Yes. Appalled? Definitely. And how could it possibly be true? Could someone get away with that kind of deception for almost a decade?

Still, both Gladys and Lois had known Zoë for years, if only from a distance, and had had plenty of time to observe her conduct and speculate what she was capable of, whereas Tricia had had only a little over an hour to observe her.

She took a sip of her sherry and noticed that the smell from the kitchen seemed to be growing stronger. She picked up another cracker and grabbed the knife again, overloading it with cheese.

"Whoa! Leave some room for dinner," Russ chided as Tricia bit into her seventh cracker.

Tricia sank against the back of the couch, swirling what was left of the mahogany-colored liquid in her glass. "At least I managed to avoid the press for the rest of the day. They just can't take no for an answer."

"I hope you're not including me in that statement," he said, moving close enough that his breath was warm on her neck.

"Can you take no?" Tricia asked, the hint of a smile creeping onto her lips.

He pulled back slightly. "Only if you really mean it."

Tricia sank against the back of the couch and exhaled, trying to coax her muscles to relax. "I didn't get a chance to see the news. Did Portia McAlister find out about Zoë's criminal past yet?"

Russ straightened. "It was the top story."

"Rats. I would have liked to have seen the report. I wonder if they'll post it on the station's website."

"Don't tell me you want to look right now?"

She did, but she didn't voice it. "Did you get a chance to look at the *Stoneham Weekly News*'s archives?"

"Yes, and as I suspected, Ted Moser brushed the story under the rug. There was a short article about Trident Homes going under, but no real detail."

Scratch an official record. Unless—"Where would the case have been prosecuted? Nashua?"

"Yes."

"I suppose I could go dig through old court reports, but I don't think I need that kind of detail."

"No," Russ said, and sidled closer once again. "What're your plans for tomorrow?" he asked, his voice almost a whisper.

Tricia sighed. "I'm going to try contacting Zoë's former high school English teacher."

"What for?" he said, nibbling her ear.

A flicker of unease wormed through Tricia, and she drew away. "Just looking into her background."

"Anything else?"

"I want to talk to Kimberly again . . . if I can track her down. Say, do you

remember her ever getting into trouble when she was a teenager? Apparently she was a bit of a hellion."

"Again, that was before I took over the *Stoneham Weekly News*. I've already searched the archives once. You could do it, if you're that interested."

"I might be, thanks. Has there been any word on funeral arrangements for Zoë?"

Russ sighed. "I talked with my buddy Glenn at the Baker Funeral Home, who spoke to me off the record. When the body's released by the medical examiner's office, it's to be cremated. Nobody's contacted me or my staff about a paid-for obit in the paper. I'll go with what I've been working on, although it's really pretty skimpy. Fact-filled, but not personable."

"That's pretty much what I've picked up, too."

His smile was coy. "You'd have made a pretty good reporter."

High praise, or something else? Some quality in his tone put her on alert.

He leaned in closer once more, his mouth mere centimeters from her ear. "Tell me," he said breathlessly, "what were you thinking when you found Zoë Carter dead in your washroom?"

Tricia sat bolt upright. First the photos, now this! "Excuse me!"

Russ straightened. "I mean . . ." He hesitated. "Come on, Tricia. Everybody in the village is wondering. Zoë was Stoneham's only celebrity. You found her. It's news. And giving me an exclusive would be—"

Using the couch's arm, Tricia pushed herself to her feet. "I can't believe it. I can't believe you'd use me like this."

"I'm not using you. I'm tapping you—just like you just asked me about Kimberly Peters, Zoë's embezzlement charges, and even her funeral arrangements."

"It's not the same thing, and you know it."

He sat forward, pushing his glasses up his nose. "Hey, you're a source. What we have together has no bearing on the story I'm working on. And it's not like I'm going to splash it over the national news. I'm a crummy little weekly. Throw me a bone, will you?"

"I've just told you everything I know." Maybe that wasn't entirely true, but it was close. "You saw her body. Can't you tap into your own feelings? Why on earth would you have to know about and report mine?" She stormed off toward the entryway, wrenched open the closet door, and found her coat.

"Tricia, wait!"

After struggling into the sleeves, she opened the front door and stalked into the night.

"I'm sorry," Russ called after her. "Come back. We'll talk about it."

She turned. "I'm so angry with you right now, I'm not sure I want to talk to you ever again." She headed straight to her car, her anger intensifying with

every step. She opened the car door, jammed the key in the ignition, and took off with tires squealing. It took nearly two blocks before her ire began to cool and she realized there was at least one consolation concerning her abbreviated evening with Russ: she wouldn't have to eat tuna noodle casserole.

Tricia parked her car in the municipal lot and walked the block to her store. It wasn't until she saw the crime scene tape still in place around the front door that she remembered she wasn't allowed in. She stepped back on the sidewalk to get the full effect of the storefront. She'd gone to considerable time and expense to duplicate a certain Victorian address in London, from its white stone facade to the 221 rendered in gold leaf on the Palladian transom over the glossy, black-painted door. The sight never ceased to please her.

She sighed, realizing she'd told Angelica she might not return that evening, and a quick glance around her confirmed that Bob Kelly's car was parked outside the Cookery.

It occurred to Tricia that although she had keys to Angelica's store and apartment, she might not be all that welcome if Angelica was . . . entertaining . . . her friend.

Bob Kelly had never been Tricia's favorite person. He looked too much like her ex-husband, albeit an older version, for her to feel comfortable around him. The fact that he could sometimes be a pompous ass had also colored her feelings in the past. She'd had to work at softening her dislike since Angelica had become romantically involved with the man.

It was with apprehension that Tricia pulled out her cell phone and punched in Angelica's number. One ring. Two rings. Three rings. *Hurry, or it will go to voice mail,* Tricia pleaded.

"Hello."

"Ange, it's Tricia. Can . . . can I come up?"

"Of course you can. Why would you think otherwi . . . oh." Her voice flattened. "Bob and I are eating dinner. Shall I set another plate?"

"Do you mind?"

"Of course not."

"I'll be right up." Tricia hung up the phone, extracted the key to the shop, and let herself in, locking up behind her. She was used to the three-flight walk and wasn't even winded as she reached the landing. Cautiously, she knocked on the apartment door.

"It's open," Angelica called.

Tricia hung her jacket in the closet and followed the lights and the heavenly aroma of garlic to the spacious kitchen. Several cartons had been flattened,

their contents stacked on the end of the counter. So Angelica *had* enlisted Bob's help for unpacking. Only another half a million boxes to go!

"Hi, guys," Tricia said and took her seat at the table. Angelica passed the pasta bowl. Scampi, which looked as heavenly as it smelled.

"Good thing I always cook enough for an army," Angelica said. "What happened to your dinner date with Russ?"

"Oh, he was busy. Working." She hoped her tone indicated the subject was now verboten.

"I talked to Wendy Adams this afternoon," Bob started conversationally, digging at his pasta and plucking a fat shrimp with his fork. "Sorry, but she insists she needs more time to collect evidence in your store. She grudgingly suggested you could be open for the weekend. I tried to push her, but she doesn't appreciate how closing for even a few days can affect your bottom line."

"Amen. You got more out of her than I did. I appreciate it. Thanks, Bob." Tricia picked at her pasta. Angelica poured her a glass of wine and Tricia found herself staring at Bob. Bob, the head of the Chamber of Commerce, someone who prided himself on knowing everybody who was anybody in southern New Hampshire. And if the owners of Trident Homes had been members of the Chamber, he might have inside information. But would he share it? She'd have to tread lightly.

"Bob, did you know Zoë Carter?" Tricia asked casually.

He shook his head. "Although it was partly because of Zoë that Stoneham became a book town."

"What do you mean?"

Bob actually blushed. "When I had the great idea to invite all the booksellers, I naturally approached Zoë. Here we had a *New York Times* best-selling author living right in the village. I figured she might be interested in lending her name to our first few celebrations. She ignored my calls and letters, and when I finally cornered her, she turned me down flat."

"Did she give you an explanation?"

"No. Just that she didn't do—" He put two fingers from each hand into the air and wiggled them to form air quotes, "'—those kinds of things.' I called her publisher and tried to get them to help me convince her. They were sympathetic. The woman I spoke to thought it was a great PR opportunity. We'd lined up press from Portland, Nashua, and even Boston, but Zoë refused to participate. Word got out that she wasn't willing to support the village. Ticked off quite a few people. I was shocked when Angelica told me you'd talked her into the signing. And just how did you do that?"

Tricia shrugged. "I e-mailed her from the contact page on her website. Got

a note back from her niece, Kimberly Peters, saying the date and time were fine. That was that."

Bob frowned. "I couldn't figure Zoë out at all. Most of the authors I've run into are always looking for a chance at free publicity. This woman actually seemed afraid of it. I wonder why?"

Time to introduce a tougher subject. "Could it have been her indictment for embezzlement?"

Bob cleared his throat and frowned. "That happened a long time ago."

"It was only about a year before her first book was published."

"But turning Stoneham into a book town was years later. She could have lent her name in some capacity. Nobody would have remembered her past."

"Oh, but they did," Angelica said. "I heard it on the news."

Tricia and Bob turned to look at her. "They compared her to some other famous mystery author who was convicted of murder when she was a teenager. It was the parallels they pushed. Both were historical authors; both were convicted of felonies."

"The writer you're talking about was convicted in New Zealand, not the U.S. Do they even have felonies there?" Tricia asked. She shook her head.

"Well, whatever. The fact is, they both committed crimes."

"But no one died as a result of Zoë's crime."

Angelica shook her head. "It doesn't matter. Crime is crime. You, of all people, should know that."

It was Tricia's turn to frown. Should she mention that more than one person found it hard to believe Zoë had written the books? And passing them off as her own . . . was that another crime?

No, it was too soon to talk about Gladys Mitchell's and Lois Kerr's suspicions. Tricia needed facts, not innuendo, and it was just plain bad manners to spread unsubstantiated rumors about the dead. Still, the thought niggled at her brain. How could Zoë have gotten away with that kind of charade? Someone would have to have read the manuscripts—critiqued them. Very few authors worked in a vacuum.

Tricia poked her fork at her pasta, toying with a morsel of garlic. Was it possible the real author had been present at the signing just twenty-four hours before? That didn't seem likely, either. As far as she knew, none of the readers who'd arrived to meet Zoë had any literary aspirations; at least, no one had asked the kinds of questions author wannabes tended to ask. Like "Will you read my manuscript?" and "Can I have the phone number of your agent?"

Tricia thought back to the night before and remembered something Grace Harris had said about being glad to meet Zoë under "happier circumstances." It hadn't meant anything at the time.

She waited for a pause in the conversation before speaking to Bob. "Did you ever hear of an argument between Grace Harris and Zoë Carter?"

He frowned. "Not an argument. Grace was the chair of a citizens committee reporting to the Board of Selectmen. I believe she approached Zoë on behalf of them and asked her to participate in one or more of the grand openings. Like me, she received a cold shoulder. I consider my persuasive skills to be top notch, but nothing compared to Grace Harris, who, like Mame, could 'charm the blues right out of the horn.'"

Tricia blinked at that analogy, while Angelica fought to hold back a chuckle. Okay.

Could the unhappy circumstances be as easily dismissed as Bob suggested? Could Zoë have been incredibly rude to Grace? She'd seemed anything but ruthless when Tricia had met her. A female milquetoast. From what she had seen and discovered in talking to others, Zoë had never mustered any kind of passion, be it love or anger.

"Speaking of the Board of Selectmen," Angelica said, "when are they going to deal with the goose problem here in Stoneham—and more importantly, how? I'm going to have to have the carpet in my shop shampooed again if this keeps up."

"It's a sticky situation—in more ways than one," Bob said, laughing at his own joke.

"I don't think it's funny," Tricia said, and took another sip of her wine.

Bob ate another forkful of pasta. "No one can decide the best way to handle the geese. The problem is, they're protected under the Migratory Bird Treaty Act. You need special permission to hunt them. We just can't dismantle their nests or break their eggs. By law, you're not even allowed to harass them. Half the citizens of Stoneham want them shot—and as you know, hunting season ended in September. The other half want them humanely removed. The problem is, doing it humanely takes time, and I'm afraid the majority of business owners don't want to wait."

"I can't say I blame them," Angelica said, and poured herself more wine. "I'm out there cleaning off the sidewalk in front of my shop two or three times a day."

"What's the humane way of dealing with them?" Tricia asked.

"Scaring them, for one. The trouble is, they get used to loud noises, so that doesn't really work. A lot of communities have hired companies that use border collies to chase the geese. This works, but it, too, takes time. They chase away one group of birds and another flies right in. You have to keep it up. Then there's egg oiling."

"What does that involve?"

"Sealing the eggs so what's in them can't develop. But that just stops the next generation of birds, not the ones you've already got. And it's very labor-intensive. What we really need to do is make Stoneham unattractive to the birds. If they don't like where they are, they'll go away."

"And bother some other community," Tricia said.

"Possibly," he conceded.

"How do you make the village less attractive to them?" Tricia asked.

"Unfortunately, that's difficult to do. Today's zoning laws require the presence of retention ponds to handle storm water runoff, keeping it from messing up the sewer system. The birds don't know the ponds aren't real. And it doesn't help when every stay-at-home mom in the village ignores the signs that have been posted and takes her little tykes out to feed the geese."

"Boy, you really are into this," Angelica said admiringly.

"I need to be informed if I'm going to represent the Chamber members' interests."

"What about the immediate problem?" Tricia asked. "Isn't there some way the village can clean the sidewalks on a more regular basis?"

"And don't forget these birds are huge. I've had more than one frightened wisp of an old lady tell me the things charged and hissed at her," Angelica said.

"I know, I know," Bob said. "They're very territorial. That aggressive behavior could become a major liability problem. If someone gets hurt, the business owners could be financially responsible for injuries incurred."

"Not just business owners," Tricia said. "I was chased just this morning over on Pine Avenue—a residential neighborhood."

"Cleaning the sidewalks takes money," Bob said, getting back to the subject, "money that hasn't been budgeted. I'm sure the business owners wouldn't like to see taxes go up to pay for it."

"Not especially," Tricia said, "since it's *us* who pay them—not the building owners."

"You all knew that when you signed the leases," Bob said.

Yeah, and he owned half the buildings on Main Street, and had stipulated that his tenants pay those taxes when he drew up the leases.

"Frannie told me that one of the options is to 'round up and slaughter' them. She said it's under consideration."

Bob's eyes narrowed. "She had no right discussing Chamber business with you."

"She had every right. I'm a member of the Chamber, too, you know."

"Killing them en masse would be very controversial. A lot of people love the damn things. Exterminating them could prove to be a PR nightmare—the last thing the village needs."

And *that* was what he really worried about.

As though to avoid discussing that very subject, Bob launched into an update on the weekend book fair and statue dedication, but Tricia only half listened, her mind wandering back to Zoë and the ramifications of everything she'd learned today. All the facts and innuendo swirled around in her mind in a disconnected mess.

"Something wrong with the shrimp?" a concerned Angelica asked, once Bob had wound down. "Maybe I shouldn't go so heavy on the garlic."

Feeling contrite, Tricia gave her sister a wan smile. "It's perfect, Ange." She took another bite and savored the taste, once again thankful she wasn't sentenced to eating tuna noodle casserole.

SEVEN

AFTER DINNER, TRICIA retired to Angelica's bedroom with her laptop and the pile of library books to comfort her. The computer looked distinctly out of place in the girly boudoir, the only room devoid of boxes, with its gilt-edged French provincial furniture and the stacks of sumptuous lace pillows lined up against the ivory velvet-covered headboard.

Angelica's vanity sported scores of perfume bottles and colorful nail polishes. One cobalt blue bottle stood out among the crowd: Evening in Paris talc. Tricia removed the cap and breathed in a much-loved memory of her grandmother. Where had Angelica found it? They hadn't made that scent in decades. A bigger mystery was the thought that Angelica might possibly have loved their grandmother as much as Tricia had. It wasn't something she'd ever considered, and yet Angelica had once mentioned that it was their grandmother's cookbook collection that got her interested in cookery. Either way, grandmother had inspired a love of books in both of her grandchildren.

Recapping the bottle, Tricia replaced it and settled on the bed, delighted that the little computer sniffed out a wireless connection—probably tapping into the signal from her own home next door. After a few minutes Miss Marple showed up from the depths of the living room's box jungle, settled herself next to Tricia, and purred deeply as Tricia Googled the News Team Ten website.

As she'd hoped, Zoë's murder was still a top story. Portia McAlister had stood in front of Zoë's home late that afternoon, judging by the shadows

behind her, and dragged up Zoë's past indiscretions, as well as her literary triumphs.

"Before her fame as a mystery author, Zoë Carter lived a life of mystery herself. A life that included an indictment for embezzlement," she said with deadly seriousness.

Tricia listened intently, then hit the reload button and played the video again. As a bookkeeper for Trident Log Homes, Zoë had participated in a scheme to defraud the investors. With phantom vendor accounts, she'd channeled hundreds of thousands of dollars to Thomas Norton's pocket. Norton, the company's married CEO, had had a brief fling with Zoë, whom he declared at the trial to be naive and delusional. Zoë, he asserted, had been under the impression Norton would leave his wife, and that it was her idea to divert the funds.

That story fell apart when prosecutors showed it was Norton who squirreled away the missing funds in an offshore bank account, not Zoë. Zoë had never had so much as a speeding ticket, and was the sole support of her recently orphaned niece. Her testimony was enough to convict Norton, while she got off with a suspended sentence, a hefty fine, and an order to make restitution. While out on appeal, Norton skipped the country and died in a car accident in the Austrian Alps—no doubt on his way to tap a Swiss bank account.

Tricia shook her head, folding down her laptop and setting it aside. It sounded like the plot of a bad movie.

Miss Marple scolded Tricia for disturbing her, but settled right back down as Tricia grabbed her library copy of *Dead In Red* and picked up where she'd left off reading some hours before. Sometime later, the sound of Miss Marple's purr lulled her to sleep.

Much later in the night, Tricia awoke to find her book removed and her cat gone, the lights out, and Angelica on the other side of the bed, once again snoring quietly. She rolled over and fell back into an exhausted sleep.

When she awoke in the morning, Angelica was gone, Miss Marple was back, and the aroma of freshly brewed coffee filled the air. Tricia found her robe, grabbed her book, and staggered into her sister's kitchen.

"Well, good morning, sleepyhead," Angelica said, pouring a cup of coffee and handing it to her sister.

Tricia sat on a stool at the kitchen island and took a deep gulp of the fortifying brew.

Angelica scrutinized her face. "Okay, what's up?"

Tricia refused to meet her gaze. "Nothing."

"You ate your dinner and snuck off to bed. And the corners of your mouth never lie. Something's making you unhappy. What did Russ do that you couldn't tell me about in front of Bob?"

Tricia ignored the question. "I'm sorry I showed up on your doorstep, especially after I told you I probably wouldn't. I must've spoiled your plans for the evening."

Angelica waved her hand in dismissal. "Don't give it a thought. I already told Bob that as long as your business is closed and you're staying with me, there wouldn't be any fun stuff going on here."

Tricia eyed her sister. More information than she wanted to know. She turned her attention back to her coffee.

Angelica, still clad in a robe, headed toward the bathroom. "I'm off to take a shower. Help yourself to anything you want. There's oatmeal, eggs—" Whatever else she suggested was lost in Doppler echo as she disappeared down the hall.

Tricia looked around the otherwise spotless kitchen, still cluttered with the booty from the emptied boxes. She missed her nice, uncluttered home. She missed her favorite blend of coffee. She even missed her treadmill.

Beethoven's Pastorale Symphony chimed from inside Tricia's purse. She whipped her head around, wondering where she'd left it and if she *could* find it before she missed the call. Aha! She located it on one of the stacks of boxes lined against the wall. She flipped open the phone and stabbed the button. "Hello?"

"Tricia. It's Ginny." Her tone was as cold as an iceberg. "What is it going to take to reopen Haven't Got a Clue? I don't think I can stand another day with your sister at the Cookery. He hasn't said so out loud, but I think Mr. Everett feels the same way."

Tricia's stomach roiled. Angelica had been so kind to her during the past thirty-six hours and yet she didn't seem able to engage that gene when it came to her—or Tricia's—employees.

"I don't think we're going to see the store reopen until at least the weekend. But I'll speak to Angelica. Again."

"Will you be at the Cookery today? She isn't as mean to us when you're there."

Tricia thought about her quest to speak with Zoë's ex–high school English teacher. She could probably do it by phone, but her results weren't likely to be as satisfying. Selfishly, she knew that if Ginny and Mr. Everett didn't show up, she'd have to stay at the Cookery all day and help until Angelica could hire yet another clueless temp from the Milford employment agency.

Another truth was that the subject of food preparation bored Tricia to tears. The colorful photos in many of the books were great, she supposed, if you were into that kind of thing, but they couldn't hold a candle to the magic of losing oneself in the pages of an enthralling story.

"Tricia?"

"Don't worry, Ginny. We'll work something out. See you in a little while."

"Bye," Ginny said, and disconnected. She didn't sound pacified.

Tricia put her phone away, then searched the fridge and found some whole wheat bread for toast. She was nibbling her second slice, her nose in her library book when Angelica reappeared in her robe, her head swathed in a peach-colored towel. "That looks good. Put a slice in for me, will you?"

"We have to talk," Tricia said, extracting bread from the wrapper and pushing the lever on the toaster. "You're about to have a mutiny on your hands if you don't treat Ginny and Mr. Everett nicer."

Angelica looked aghast. "Moi?" she asked innocently.

"Oui, toi," Tricia countered. She softened her voice. "Ange, you've got a big heart. Why do you lose it the minute you walk into your store?"

Angelica turned her back on her sister, grabbing her coffee cup and pouring the cold contents down the sink. "I'm a perfectionist. Is it wrong to demand the same from the people I hire?"

"When you're paying them minimum wage or just above—yes. If you're lucky, you've got two more days with Ginny and Mr. Everett, but if things don't improve this morning, they're ready to walk."

"But Ginny said she needs the money."

"She apparently doesn't need it that badly."

Angelica poured herself another cup, leaned against the counter, and sighed. "Okay. I'll play nice."

"Good. Unfortunately, I have some errands I have to run today, and may not be available to play referee. So make sure you keep your promise, or they *will* walk out."

"What kind of errands?"

"First off, I want to talk to someone who knew Zoë back when. Someone who might have influenced her . . . writing career."

"And who would that be?"

"Her high school English teacher."

Angelica nodded. "Makes sense. Where did you come up with the idea?"

"From the village librarian. You know, for such a small town, Stoneham really has a nice library. Cutting-edge, I'd say."

"I've only driven by it. Looks nice."

"It's the best value you can get for your tax dollars," Tricia said.

Angelica blinked, looking confused. "What?"

Tricia laughed. "Frannie told me that."

Angelica took another swig of her coffee and swallowed. "Okay. What else have you got on tap for today that's going to keep you from helping me in my shop?"

"The thing I don't want to do is run into that TV reporter, Portia McAlister. She hunted me down yesterday morning in the municipal parking lot." The memory made her shudder.

"She hasn't come to talk to me," Angelica said, sounding miffed. "I wish she would. I'd love to get in a plug for the Cookery."

"Call the station. I'm sure they'd be glad to give you Portia's cell number."

"Maybe I will. After all, I was at the scene of the murder. I'm sure I can add loads of color to her story."

"But you didn't actually see anything. Not even Zoë's body."

"Yes, but you did. Maybe I can milk that angle."

"Please don't. That'll only get her interested in talking to me again."

Angelica shrugged. "Oh, all right. I suppose two days later the story is old news anyway."

She drained her cup and put it into the dishwasher. "Better get dressed," she advised. "Time is money." She turned and headed toward her bedroom.

Tricia eyed the telephone, then the clock on the wall. It was after nine, surely late enough to call a retired schoolteacher. Abandoning her stool, she picked up the slip of paper with Stella Kraft's number that she'd been using as a bookmark, crossed the kitchen, picked up the receiver, and dialed.

AS PROMISED, ANGELICA was on her best behavior, greeting both Ginny and Mr. Everett like old friends about to begin a new adventure. They eyed their temporary employer with suspicion, but dutifully donned the Cookery aprons and began the day with, if not enthusiasm, at least not scorn.

Tricia's appointment with Zoë's former teacher was for eleven, and the four of them started the workday by restocking shelves, dusting, vacuuming, and getting ready for an anticipated glut of customers, who arrived right at opening time.

At ten forty-five, Tricia was just about to duck out when Ginny cornered her. "Tricia, we need to talk about Saturday."

"Saturday?" Tricia echoed.

"Yes, the statue dedication."

Tricia smacked her forehead. "Rats! I forgot all about it."

Ginny pulled a piece of paper from her apron pocket. "I managed to get a few minutes free yesterday and made some calls. I hope I'm not going to get in trouble about it when Angelica sees it on her phone bill."

"What kind of calls?"

"About the extra books. I hope you don't mind, but I didn't know if we'd be open. I took the liberty of ordering copies of all of Zoë's books. I had them

expressed, so they should arrive no later than tomorrow morning. I talked to Frannie and confirmed the tent, and wrestled the promise of a borrowed cash register if we can't bring our extra one. It's a shame we can't raid some of our used stock, but if you'll download the flyer from your laptop, I can get more of them and our newsletters printed before Saturday morning."

Tricia swallowed as guilt coursed through her. She'd been so caught up in learning about Zoë that she'd neglected her own business. "Ginny, you've just earned yourself a big bonus. What would I do without you?"

"Just doing my job," Ginny said shyly, her gaze dipping to the floor.

"And then some." Tricia glanced at her watch. Time to go. "I've got to leave right now, but I promise, as soon as I get back, we'll talk some more about this and make more contingency plans." She reached out to touch Ginny's arm. "Thank you."

Ginny smiled and turned back to the register. Tricia waved for Angelica's attention and promised to be back in time to give the others a lunch break. Since Stella lived only two blocks from Stoneham's main drag, Tricia decided to make up for the lack of her treadmill and walk the distance.

A carefully printed sign on the front door directed visitors to the back entrance of the little house. The woman who answered Tricia's knock looked about 108, with deeply wrinkled, leathery smoker's skin, a husky voice, and sharp eyes that didn't miss a trick. "Miss—" or was she a Mrs.? "—Kraft?" Tricia asked.

"Come on in," the old woman encouraged, and held the door for Tricia to enter. The dated yet immaculate kitchen was swelteringly hot, the air stuffy, smelling like boiled potatoes with an underlying scent of mothballs. Tricia was ushered past a worn white enamel table, but declined the offer of coffee or tea.

"I heard all about Zoë Carter's death," Stella said.

"She was a student of yours?" Tricia asked.

"Oh, sure. Until I retired, just about every kid who graduated from Stoneham High passed through my classroom at least once."

"But I thought Zoë wasn't from Stoneham?"

Stella shook her head. "Neither am I. Some people in this town think that if you weren't born here, you don't belong here. Just as many don't subscribe to that narrow thinking, thank goodness."

"Did you teach her niece?"

Stella frowned. "Yes, I had her niece, too. Now that one was a piece of work. Smart, but didn't apply herself." She padded down the hall, motioning Tricia to follow her into the living room. Every wall had a bookcase, and it was all Tricia could do not to abandon her mission and study the hundreds—possibly thousands—of titles.

Stella gestured to the faded gold couch. "Sit, sit," she encouraged. "Sure I can't get you anything?"

Tricia shook her head, but took the offered seat while Stella commandeered a worn leather club chair.

"I know it was a long time ago, but do you remember what kind of student Zoë Carter was?"

Stella answered without a moment's hesitation. "Quiet little mouse of a thing. She had excellent math skills. She won a couple of prizes or something, so obviously she wasn't stupid. But I wasn't all that interested in her." She leaned forward and lowered her voice conspiratorially. "I probably shouldn't admit this, but I always had favorites among my students. And those with a quest to learn about literature, I doted on."

"So as a teenager Zoë showed no storytelling aptitude?"

"None at all. If I may employ a cliché, she couldn't write her way out of a wet paper bag."

"And yet at her death she was a *New York Times* best-selling author."

The old woman cocked her head, her eyes narrowing. "Interesting, isn't it?"

Tricia carefully phrased her next question. "What do you think brought her latent talent to the surface?"

"That's my point. The woman—or at least the student—had no writing talent."

"You don't think she wrote those books?" Tricia asked, hoping she sounded convincingly skeptical.

Stella shook her head. "Never in a million years. Someone like Zoë, who'd never really known love, could never have written such believable and heart-wrenching characters."

And how did Stella know Zoë was unloved?

"Then who—?"

The old woman looked away and sighed. "I've been asking myself that for the last decade. I wish I'd saved the papers of some of my more impressive students; I had a few that showed promise. But who's to say the author of those books even came from Stoneham?"

Who, indeed? "But Zoë still lived in Stoneham when the first book was published."

"Yes. And it's well known she never sought the limelight. She didn't want to go on book tours, and was practically a hermit when it came to promotional activities. It was word of mouth that sold that first book—nothing Zoë did."

"Sounds like you've followed her career closely."

"Stoneham High hasn't graduated any rocket scientists. Apparently Zoë was our only star."

"Have you shared your suspicions with anyone else?"

"In the beginning I might have mentioned it to a few of my former colleagues—I've been retired for almost eight years now. But who listens to the rantings of an old English teacher?"

I might, Tricia thought.

Now to spring the sixty-four-thousand-dollar question. "Do you think it's possible the real author of those books murdered Zoë?"

Stella didn't even blink. "Why not? Stranger things have happened."

Time to play devil's advocate. "But why wait until the last book was published?"

"I've been pondering that same question. Zoë had been scarce in these parts since publication of the third book; I heard she moved down south. Rumor has it she only came back to Stoneham to sell her house."

"Yes, she mentioned that at the signing the other night. Wouldn't it be ironic if the person who wrote those books is still here in Stoneham and has been waiting all these years to take her revenge?" Tricia blurted, finally voicing the theory that had been percolating in the back of her mind.

The old woman nodded. "What makes you think it was a woman who wrote them?"

"The real author?" Tricia said, a bit surprised that Stella hadn't immediately refuted her idea.

"I assume you've read the books?" Stella paused and Tricia nodded. "Do you think a male author could've done justice to Addie's character, or the loss of her son in the mine cave-in?"

"That depends on the author," Tricia said, surprised a former English teacher would even voice such a sentiment. "But Kimberly Peters told me someone—a man—called her to say I was spreading rumors about her and her aunt. And let me assure you, I have not been."

"How do you know she was telling you the truth about the call?"

Tricia opened her mouth to protest, and then just as quickly shut it.

Stella nodded. "I'd be skeptical of anything *that* one tells you."

"But she knows more than she's telling."

"More than she's telling *you*. That's not to say she hasn't spoken to others."

Sheriff Adams in particular, Tricia thought. Still, that was good—if it meant solving the crime and getting her store back open.

"If all this is true, what could have happened that triggered the killer? If she wanted the glory, why wait until the last book was published to take revenge?"

Stella looked like she was about to say something, then thought better of it and shook her head. "I'd be careful about mentioning Zoë's lack of creative talent and the idea she might not have written the books."

"But wouldn't that be a credible motive for the killing? Giving the true author credit for those books?"

"Yes, but getting the credit will also land that person in jail. There's nothing to be gained—unless Zoë was killed out of spite." Stella shook her head. "Whoever killed Zoë will do everything she can to remain anonymous. If I were you, dear, I'd let the sheriff handle this one. You wouldn't want to be the killer's next victim."

EIGHT

IT WAS ALMOST noon by the time Tricia returned from Stella's house. She opened the door to the Cookery and Angelica pounced upon her immediately. "Big news," she cried. Tricia could practically feel the waves of exhilaration emanating from her sister.

Tricia wiggled out of her jacket. "Tell me about it before you jump out of your skin."

"Bob just called. They've decided to change the whole dedication ceremony on Saturday."

"Change how?" Tricia asked, heading for the closet at the back of the store.

"It'll now be a memorial service for Zoë Carter."

Tricia stopped. "What does that mean for the vendors?"

"Vendors?" Angelica said, confused.

"Yes. The dedication was supposed to be a celebration of books and how they saved Stoneham. It'll look pretty tacky if we're all set up around the square selling books, hot dogs, and fried dough. It sounds more like a circus than a memorial service."

Angelica frowned. "Oh. Well, I'm sure Bob thought about that. He's a genius when it comes to PR. But don't you see, this is a great opportunity for you. Ginny said she'd ordered extra copies of Zoë's books. You'll make out like a bandit."

"I don't know about that."

"Um, Bob—or rather the Chamber—was wondering if you'd be willing to call some of Zoë's publishing colleagues and invite them to the ceremony. Like maybe Zoë's agent."

Tricia was about to blurt a definitive "No," then thought better of it. What

better way to find out more about Zoë than from people inside the publishing industry? "Maybe you're right, Ange. Bob just might be a genius after all."

Since Ginny had gone out for a sandwich and was unavailable to talk about their Saturday plans, Tricia hiked the stairs to Angelica's loft apartment. A chatty Miss Marple met her as she opened the door, admonishing her for leaving her alone once again.

"I know, I know. But Angelica serves food in her store. No cats allowed."

"*Yow!*" Miss Marple protested.

"I'll relay your dissatisfaction to the Health Department," Tricia promised.

Miss Marple followed her to the kitchen, and Tricia filled her bowl with kitty treats.

With the cat placated, Tricia picked up Angelica's kitchen extension before scoping out the fridge in search of sustenance for herself. Despite its being lunch hour, Tricia called and found Bob in his office at the Chamber of Commerce. "Hi, Bob, Angelica said you wanted to talk to me about the dedication ceremony," she said, and it was no effort to keep a smile in her voice.

"Yes, the Chamber held an emergency meeting on it this morning, sorry you weren't able to make it—" Make it? She hadn't even known about it. But since she rarely went to Chamber meetings anyway, it wasn't a big deal. "Changing our focus to include a memorial ceremony for Zoë Carter is an opportunity we, as her adopted hometown, didn't feel we could pass up. And since we've already got everything set up for the dedication anyway, it's a win-win situation."

"But what about the words carved on the statue?" she asked, looking past the scampi leftovers to root around in the back of the fridge. It wasn't really a statue. Tricia had seen drawings of the proposed piece. A big block of marble with a carved open book on the top.

"Turns out they weren't able to do the engraving before the ceremony on Saturday, so we can still change what it says. How's that for luck?"

Tacky. But Tricia wasn't about to argue the point. She withdrew a bowl of what looked like homemade soup, removed the plastic cover, and sniffed. It still smelled good. "Ange said you wanted me to contact Zoë's colleagues," she said, and opened a drawer to find a spoon.

"Yes. They thought you, as a mystery bookseller, would have a better feel for who in the publishing world should be contacted."

Oops! Deborah had suggested Tricia do the same thing the day before—but with everything else that was going on, Tricia had completely forgotten about it. She put the bowl in the microwave and punched in ninety seconds. "Did you speak to Kimberly Peters about this?"

"Following in her aunt's footsteps, she declined to be involved, although she did say she'd at least show up," he said, his voice conveying his disapproval. "Will you help us, Tricia?"

"Bob, I would love to. How soon do you need to know?"

"We'd like to have the guest list set by tomorrow. Is that a problem?"

"No. In fact, I'll start making calls as soon as I get off the phone with you."

"Thanks, Tricia. This is a big help to the Chamber. And I'll see what I can do to nudge Wendy Adams about reopening your shop. She's stubborn, but she can see reason when it's pointed out to her."

"I'd appreciate that, Bob. Thanks."

She took notes as he repeated the details surrounding the dedication, which pretty much matched what she remembered from the Chamber's previous communications.

"I'll get right on this and give you an update later today."

"Thanks, Tricia."

Tricia replaced the phone on its cradle and resisted the urge to rub her hands together with pleasure. Then reality set in. How the blazes was she supposed to get a hold of, let alone assure the attendance of, Zoë's colleagues? There was only one thing to do—hit the Internet to try to find some answers.

The microwave stopped, giving a resounding *beep, beep, beep,* to let her know her lunch was ready, but Tricia was too hyped to eat. Instead, she went in search of her laptop computer, set it on the kitchen island, and connected to the Internet. Her first stop, Zoë's website. She checked out the media page and found pay dirt. Zoë's agent was none other than Artemus Hamilton. Tricia had met the short, balding man several times at cocktail parties during her years in Manhattan.

A search of the Yahoo! Yellow Pages gave her Hamilton's office number, and she eagerly dialed the phone. An answering machine picked up after the third ring, directing her to leave a message. "This is Tricia Miles, owner of the Haven't Got a Clue bookstore in Stoneham, New Hampshire. I'm sorry to say that your client Zoë Carter died in my store on Tuesday night. Stoneham is having a memorial service in her honor, and we wanted to invite—"

The phone clicked in her ear. "Ms. Miles? This is Artemus Hamilton. Thank you for calling."

The man himself. No doubt he'd received some crank calls, or possibly had been hounded by the press since Zoë's death and found it necessary to screen his calls. Or perhaps his assistant was out to lunch and he was monitoring his own phone.

"I don't suppose you remember me, Mr. Hamilton. We met several years ago at one of Sylvia Cranston's parties."

"Sorry. I meet a lot of people." Oh, well. That was no doubt true. "What were you saying about a memorial service?"

"Since Zoë was a longtime resident of Stoneham, we naturally want to honor her. We hope you and some of Zoë's other colleagues could join us on Saturday for a memorial service."

"That's odd. I spoke with Zoë's niece this morning, and she said nothing about a memorial service."

"I'm sure at the time she wasn't aware of the Chamber of Commerce's plans. You know Kimberly Peters?"

"Yes, of course. I had dinner with Zoë and Kimberly on a number of occasions. Delightful young woman." He must've seen a side of Kimberly she hadn't bothered to show to the citizens of Stoneham. "What time is the ceremony?" he asked.

"Eleven o'clock. It'll be outside, as there's also a statue dedication."

"How on earth did you get a statue of Zoë made so quickly?"

"It's actually a statue of a . . . a book." Boy, that sounded lame.

"A book?" he repeated in disbelief.

"Yes. It's really very nice," she lied. She hadn't actually seen it. "It's a big block of white marble with an opened stone book on the top." She flinched at her own words. It sounded ridiculous even to her.

"Eleven's rather early to come up from New York. Perhaps I should arrive the night before. Is there anywhere decent to stay in Stoneham?"

"I can recommend the Brookview Inn."

"Can you e-mail me the particulars? I'll have my assistant book me a room as soon as she comes back from lunch."

"Fine."

"Where can I reach you in case I need to call?"

Tricia gave him Angelica's number and that of her cell phone. "We'd also like to invite Zoë's editor. Would you be willing to share that number, or would you talk to him or her and have them contact me?"

"I'll speak to him, and if he's interested he can get in touch with you. Thank you again for the invitation. I'll be in touch," Hamilton said and ended the call.

Tricia got her facts together concerning the inn and e-mailed Hamilton's office, then checked that her phone was fully charged before heading down to the Cookery, where she found an impatient Ginny waiting for her.

"Oh, good. You're back," Ginny said, and glanced over her shoulder to see if Angelica was close by and listening in. "Whatever you said to Angelica must've worked. She's hardly yelled at us at all today. Makes me wonder when I'll feel the stab of pain in my back when she reverts to type."

"Ginny," Tricia chided.

"Oh, sorry," Ginny hastily apologized. "I keep forgetting she's your sister. Anyway, while there's a lull, we'd better go over the plans for Saturday. Did you know they were changing the focus of the celebration?"

"Yes. I've already talked to Bob Kelly about it, and he asked me to invite some of Zoë's colleagues. Her agent will be here on Saturday, possibly her editor as well. I'm waiting to hear."

"That's great. Several members of the Tuesday Night Book Club have stopped by or called to ask if we should do something special in honor of Zoë."

"You mean like flowers or something?"

She nodded. "They're taking up a collection and thought it would be a nice touch, since most of them were among the last people to see her alive."

And Tricia had been the one to find her dead. She gave a little shudder and tried not to think about it.

"On our end," Ginny continued, "Mr. Everett managed to snag the UPS man and signed for the books for the dedication on Saturday. So at least we can set up shop and get a little income for the week."

Tricia glanced around the store, spotted Mr. Everett speaking with a customer, and smiled. "I am so proud of you two. You've made this whole unpleasant situation much easier to take."

"Thanks, Tricia. It's nice to hear a kind word." Ginny leveled a pointed glance at Angelica's back.

"Has the sheriff or her team been anywhere near Haven't Got a Clue today?" Tricia asked.

Ginny shook her head. "It doesn't seem like she's doing much in the way of investigating, as far as I can see, so why won't she let us reopen?"

"Pure and plain nastiness."

"Speaking of which," Ginny said, lowering her voice, her gaze wandering to a disapproving Angelica, who waited on a customer at the register. "Did you know Angelica threw away all of the gorgeous cookies Nikki sent over yesterday?"

Tricia frowned. "Why?"

"I think she was jealous. She said she wasn't going to serve someone else's products in her store."

Angelica had made that perfectly clear the day before. "Well, they weren't sent here to be served in her store," Tricia said testily. "They were sent to me."

Ginny giggled. "I hope you don't mind, but I grabbed a few before she tossed them in the Dumpster out back. I wrapped them up for later. Do you want a couple?"

Tricia sighed. "With everything that's been going on, I've kind of lost my appetite. You enjoy."

Ginny nodded. "So how are your inquiries going?"

Tricia looked around the shop, making sure no customers were in listening range. "Don't say a word, because I have no proof . . . but several people I've talked to don't think Zoë was the author of the Jess and Addie *Forever* series."

Ginny's eyes widened. "That's very interesting. And certainly a motive for murder."

"Exactly."

"Any hints on who did write them?" she asked, eagerly.

Tricia shook her head. "Uh-uh. Not until I have more information."

"Darn! Is there anything I can do to help you?"

"Thanks, but no. In the meantime, I need to talk to Kimberly again. To see if I can pin her down." Tricia remembered what Frannie had said about Deborah and Kimberly possibly being classmates. Deborah and Ginny both had long hair. Could she have gotten them mixed up? "You weren't in high school with Kimberly, were you?"

Ginny nodded. "But I didn't know her. She was a senior when I was a freshman—a much lower form of life. Eventually we all knew her by reputation, as the class slut."

Which supported what Lois Kerr had said. "Do you think any of her friends still live in Stoneham?"

"What friends? She slept with every decent-looking guy in the school. Not many of the girls would even talk to her."

How sad. Did she act out just to get attention—attention she didn't receive from Zoë?

"I'd like to call her, but of course Zoë's phone number is unlisted, and all my contact information is locked up inside Haven't Got a Clue."

Ginny pulled a little notebook out of her Cookery apron pocket. Tricia recognized it as one she usually carried in her Haven't Got a Clue apron. "I've got Zoë's Stoneham number. Why don't you call Kimberly now?"

Tricia smiled. "Remember that bonus I mentioned earlier? It just got bigger."

Ginny positively beamed.

NINE

TRICIA WAS GLAD Kimberly answered the phone after only two rings, though she quickly made it clear she had no desire to discuss her aunt. That is, until Tricia suggested they meet for dinner; then suddenly Kimberly was only too happy to oblige. They made plans to meet at the Bookshelf Diner at seven.

Tricia adopted her bravest smile and prepared to spend the next five hours hand-selling—she nearly shuddered—cookbooks.

But before she had a chance to dive into the world of cookery, a Milford Florist Shop truck pulled up outside and double-parked in front of Angelica's store. Tricia watched without interest as the driver got out, went to the back of the truck, and opened the gate. He consulted a clipboard, then pawed through his inventory and withdrew a large white box. He jogged to the door and opened it. "Delivery," he called.

Angelica rushed forward, her face flushed with pleasure. "Oh, that Bob! He's such a sweetheart." Her grin soon disappeared as she looked at the card on the top of the box. She turned, annoyed. "They're for you, Trish. Seems to be your week to receive gifts."

Tricia stepped forward, unsure she wanted to accept the box. They had to be from Russ, and she wasn't sure she was ready to accept an apology. She took the card, opened it, and frowned. *Please forgive me. Love, Russ.*

Love? He hadn't uttered that word to her in person.

She set the card aside and removed the red ribbon that bound the box. Drawing back the green tissue, she gasped. She'd expected roses, but instead found nine perfect calla lilies—her favorite. Had she ever told him? How else could he have known?

She glanced at Angelica, who seemed reluctant to meet her gaze. Was there a conspiracy in the works?

"Ooooh," Ginny cooed, coming up behind her. "Someone thinks a lot of you."

"Possibly," she said, trying to keep her voice neutral, and lifted the card to read it once again.

"I think I've got a vase in back," Angelica said, and disappeared to find it.

"Are you going to call him?" Ginny asked.

"Who says they're from a 'him'?"

"Oh, come on, Tricia, they've got to be from Russ."

Angelica returned with a tall, clear, pressed-glass vase. She stopped at the little sink in her demonstration area to fill it with water, then set it on the counter. "You are going to call and thank him, I hope."

Tricia blinked innocently. "Who?"

"Russ."

She frowned. "Why does everyone assume these flowers are from Russ?"

"Well, who else have you been dating for the past five months?"

Tricia turned up her nose. "I have a lot of admirers."

"Not in this burg," Angelica quipped.

The door opened, and several customers entered. Angelica and Ginny both sprang into action, leaving Tricia at the sales counter with her flowers. She lifted them one by one and placed them in the vase.

Love, Russ.

She didn't love him, at least not yet, but, she admitted to herself, she was quite fond of him. She didn't like there being tension between them. Still, she didn't want him to think he could buy her affection with a vase of flowers—beautiful though they might be.

Love, Russ.

She glanced around, saw Angelica, Ginny, and Mr. Everett were busy, and turned back to her lilies, allowing herself a small smile.

It was after six, and the sun hadn't yet begun to set as Mr. Everett buttoned his coat, getting ready to leave for the evening. Ginny had grabbed her purse and jacket. "Are we coming back here tomorrow?" she inquired, her voice almost a whine.

"I didn't hear from the sheriff that I could open tomorrow—so I guess we're stuck here at least one more day."

Ginny let out a long breath and almost looked like she wanted to cry.

Since there were no customers in the store, Angelica flounced around the bookshelves with her lamb's wool duster, humming happily.

"Today wasn't so bad, was it?" Tricia asked.

Mr. Everett looked to Ginny, who seemed all too ready to speak for the two of them. "No, but that's only because you were here. You will be here tomorrow, won't you?"

"As far as I know."

"I shall say good night now," Mr. Everett said. He called to Angelica. "Good night, Mrs. Prescott."

Angelica looked up from her dusting, and frowned. "That's Ms. Miles," she reminded him. "Good night. And good night to you, too, Ginny!"

"Good night," Ginny growled, and turned her back on Angelica. "I'd better leave before she finds one more thing for me to—"

"Oh, before you leave—" Angelica said, hurrying to the front of the store.

"Go!" Tricia ordered, and Ginny and Mr. Everett quickly made their escape.

"Hey," Angelica protested, "I wanted Ginny to post a couple of bills for me."

"I'll do it when I leave to go to dinner. I'm meeting Kimberly at the Bookshelf Diner."

"You're not eating here?"

"Kimberly insisted we meet there. I want to please her. If she's happy, she might be more open with me about her aunt."

"What more do you need to know about the woman? She's dead. Seems like you've talked to everyone in town who knew her. Whoever killed her isn't going to just walk up to you and say, 'Hello, I killed Zoë Carter.'"

"Have you seen Sheriff Adams—or even a patrol car—roll by even once today, let alone enter Haven't Got a Clue?"

"No, but what's that got to do with—?"

"As long as Wendy Adams isn't breaking a sweat to investigate this murder, it's up to me to do all I can. I want my store to reopen. *Now*!"

Angelica backed off. "Okay, okay!"

The door opened and Nikki Brimfield stepped inside. "Am I interrupting something?"

"Not at all," Angelica said with relief.

Tricia remembered yesterday's box of goodies and flushed with guilt. "Nikki—I meant to drop by and thank you for the cookies. That was so sweet of you."

Nikki waved a hand in dismissal. "I just felt so bad for you. What rotten luck. And I see the sheriff still hasn't let you reopen. Are you on for tomorrow?"

"No, which is what we were just discussing when—"

The door opened, the bell above it jingling. There stood Russ.

Angelica gave Nikki a nudge. "Let me show you this marvelous new cake cookbook that just came in," she said and grabbed Nikki's arm, pulling her away, apparently willing to temporarily forget that Nikki competed for her customers.

Russ didn't even seem to know they were there. He stepped forward. "Hi, Trish," he said shyly.

"Hi," she answered.

His eyes were drawn to the flowers still sitting on the sales counter. "Oh, good. They arrived okay."

"Yes, thank you, they're lovely."

"Like you."

Their gazes held for a few long seconds, then Tricia turned to admire the flowers. She picked up the card. "I wondered about this. Did you mean it?"

He studied the card in her hand for a moment, then his gaze met hers. "I'm pretty sure I did."

"Pretty sure?" she asked.

"That's about as definite as I can be right now. How about you?"

"I'm not at all sure, but I'm willing to hang around to see if it happens."

He took her hands and pulled her forward, pressing a gentle kiss against her lips before pulling away. "Can we try dinner again?"

The thought made her throat constrict. "On one condition. No more tuna noodle casseroles—ever."

"I think I could pull that off." He smiled, and tugged on her hand. "Get your coat. Let's go."

She stood firm. "I can't. I promised Kimberly Peters I'd have dinner with her tonight." Disappointment shadowed his eyes for a few brief seconds, and then they flashed. "No," Tricia said resolutely, "you're not invited."

"I didn't say a word," he protested.

"No, but I could read the thought balloon over your head. You're still working on your story," she accused.

"It's not much of a story until something breaks. Did you notice the Boston and Manchester TV vans have left town, although they might be back for the statue dedication on Saturday? Bob Kelly has sent press releases to half the East Coast news outlets."

"Only half?"

"He's still got another day," Russ added dryly. "When can I see you again?"

"I'm not doing anything for lunch tomorrow."

"I was thinking more along the lines of dinner, remember. How about Saturday?"

"Saturday's fine."

The corners of his mouth lifted. "And then maybe . . ."

"Maybe what?"

"We could . . . become friends all over again."

She felt the edges of the card still clutched in her hand. *Love, Russ.*

Out the corner of her eye, Tricia noticed Nikki and Angelica peeking around a bookshelf, eavesdropping. She cleared her throat, and they disappeared. Turning her attention back to Russ, she said, "Saturday night it is."

• • •

THE BOOKSHELF DINER pulled out all the stops for its evening crowd, offering early bird specials and even lighting the miniature hurricane oil lamps that sat on each table. Kimberly was already seated in the last booth when Tricia arrived. She settled in the seat across from her, and shrugged out of her jacket. "Have you been waiting long?"

"No," Kimberly said, barely looking up from the laminated menu she consulted. She ran her finger down the list of appetizers. "I haven't had a cigarette in two days, and I'm starved." She looked up. "You did say I was your guest, didn't you?"

She quit smoking? Obviously she wasn't stressed about the death of her aunt. "Of course."

A nasty little smile twisted Kimberly's lips. "So what was it you wanted to know about dear Aunt Zoë?"

So much for small talk. And Tricia wasn't sure she was ready to discuss what she knew—or at least thought she knew. "Several people I've spoken to wondered about your aunt's unsold novels." Not the truth, but not a total lie, either.

Again Kimberly looked up from her menu, her expression darkening. "Unsold?"

"It's a known fact that the first efforts of most authors usually aren't up to publishing standards. And for Zoë to burst out of the gates and not only win *the* major mystery award and hit best-sellerdom, she had to have a few 'practice' or trunk novels squirreled away. You know, things that she never thought would appear in print."

Kimberly ran her tongue across her lower lip. "Not that I'm aware of."

"But you were her assistant. Didn't she confide in you about her early work? Her dreams and plans for her future work?"

Before Kimberly could answer, Eugenia, the perky blonde, college-age night waitress, approached the table. "Good evening, ladies. What can I get you to drink?"

"I'll have a glass of the house red," Tricia said, noticing Eugenia had added a pierced brow to her already pierced nose and ears.

"Me, too," Kimberly echoed.

Eugenia nodded. "I'll be back to take your orders in a few minutes."

Tricia waited until she was out of earshot before speaking again. "The unsold books," she prompted.

Kimberly's attention was again focused on the menu. "I'd have to search her files. She may have left something in one of the file cabinets. She did most of

her work in the Carolina house these past few years. Maybe I'll check when I get back home."

"You don't consider Stoneham your home?"

Kimberly looked up sharply. "This dump? Not on your life. I hate the winters. And besides, who can you meet here?"

If it was husband material Kimberly was talking about, Tricia had to agree. Most of the booksellers were married, and as Lois Kerr had pointed out, the majority of young people in the village seemed to move to Boston, Portland, or New York as soon as they could escape. "When will you be going home?"

"When I can find the gas money. All Zoë's accounts have been frozen until probate is complete. I'm not her executor," she reminded Tricia. "She didn't trust me enough for that."

"Who *is* her executor?"

"Until recently, it was her agent. Now it's some lawyer. At least he's given me permission to stay in either of the houses until they're sold. But it makes more sense to close up this one as soon as possible, since that's what she wanted. I never intend to live in, let alone visit, Stoneham ever again."

Why had Zoë changed executors? Did she have a falling-out with her agent? He'd sounded eager to attend the memorial service. She shook the thought away. If nothing else, it would look good for him to be there. But whom did he want to look good for?

Eugenia returned with their wine, and soon held her pen over her pad, ready to write. "All set to order?"

Kimberly nodded. "I'll have the twice-baked potato appetizer, French onion soup, the chicken pot pie with a side of mashed potatoes, and a slice of the cherry pie. Oh, and a Diet Coke."

Tricia folded her menu, wondering how someone as thin as Kimberly could eat such great quantities of food. She sighed. "I'll have the Cobb salad plate with peppercorn dressing on the side. Thanks, Eugenia."

Eugenia collected the menus, nodded, and headed for the kitchen.

Tricia addressed Kimberly once more. "At the signing, you made a big point of reminding your aunt about taking her medication. Why?"

Kimberly shrugged. "The old girl was diabetic. She'd been known to keel over if her sugar skyrocketed. We hadn't had dinner that night—just ran out of time. I'd gotten so I could pretty much gauge when she was going to need another insulin shot."

That sounded reasonable. Tricia thought about the big question that had weighed heavy on her mind. Despite Stella's warning, she decided to test Kimberly. "Your aunt told my customers she was done with the Jess and Addie series. Had she started another?"

Kimberly hesitated. "No. Like Margaret Mitchell and Harper Lee, my aunt only had one set of characters whose stories she cared to tell. Only in her case, instead of just one novel, it came out in a five-book arc."

"I've been talking with a number of people around the village. Some people find it hard to believe Zoë actually wrote the Jess and Addie mystery series."

Kimberly raised an eyebrow but said nothing, her expression bland.

Tricia decided to try a different approach. "You wouldn't want to tell me why you were so angry at your aunt the night of her death, would you?"

"For just that day, or do you want the full ten-year list?"

"Just that day will do," Tricia said.

Kimberly leaned forward, resting her arms on the table. "My aunt was very wealthy, but you wouldn't know it to see the way we've lived."

"But she had two houses."

"Two cheap houses. I worked my ass off on this book tour, but she couldn't—or wouldn't—acknowledge it. Good press? Oh, that was from the publisher—not from the interviews I lined up for her, or the coaching I gave her. She didn't like to fly. Who drove her ten thousand miles in the last two months?"

"Why didn't you leave?"

Kimberly hesitated. "Let's just say I had my reasons. But I was quickly running out of them. In fact, just before we came to your store, I told her I was ready to walk. She called my bluff, but not before dangling another carrot in front of me."

"And that carrot was?"

Eugenia chose that moment to set the appetizer in front of Kimberly, who plunged her fork into it with zeal.

"Would you like the soup with your entrée?" the waitress asked.

Kimberly shook her head, already wolfing down a bite. "Bring it now, thanks."

Eugenia shot Tricia a look that asked "What gives?" but Tricia could only shrug. She looked back at Kimberly. "Sure thing," she said, and headed back for the kitchen.

"What did Zoë offer you to keep you from leaving?" Tricia asked.

Kimberly shoveled in another forkful of potato before she set down her fork. She took a sip of her wine. "That's none of your business. But I'll be honest with you about one thing, Tricia. I'm broke. Flat busted. There's no food in Zoë's house, and I have no idea how I'm going to manage. I've even contemplated snagging one of those pesky geese roaming the village and roasting it. That would probably feed me for a week." She gave a half-hearted laugh, but soon sobered. "Until probate is settled, I've got a roof over my head but no

income. This food," she pointed at her plate, "will have to last me a few days. After that . . ." Her mouth trembled, and her desperation was nearly palpable. "I don't know what I'll do."

Tricia resisted the temptation to reach out and comfort Kimberly, who probably wouldn't have appreciated it anyway. Kimberly's despair wasn't grief for her aunt—more for her own circumstances. And what could Zoë have possibly offered to keep her in a situation she found so miserable?

"What about the manuscripts? Can you tell me about them?" Tricia asked.

"What do you expect me to say?"

That Zoë didn't write them! she wanted to scream. Instead, Tricia struggled to keep her voice level. "What was Zoë's writing process? Did she write them on a typewriter or a computer—or even longhand?"

Kimberly stabbed her potato with her fork, and exhaled a long, slow breath. Evidently that question had hit a nerve. "I believe the original manuscripts were written on an old manual typewriter. I wasn't around when they were actually typed, so I can't be sure."

"Are you saying all the manuscripts were written before you came to live with your aunt?"

Again, Kimberly hesitated. "I was seventeen years old when I came to live with Zoë. My parents had just died. I'd never been close to my aunt, and I didn't much care about her or her hobbies. I didn't become interested in the books until my sophomore year in college, when I changed my major from humanities to English lit. One of our assignments was to read the first *Forever* book." She paused, and took a breath. "It changed my life. Those characters were so beautifully drawn, they inspired me. And that's when I first thought that I might want to write a book, too."

Tricia raised an eyebrow, surprised at Kimberly's candor. "Go on," she encouraged.

"Zoë was delighted I took an interest. She hired me during vacations to key in her manuscripts, read over her contracts, and help with publicity. It got her publisher off her back, and it was a great way for me to learn about the publishing industry. In some ways we actually became a team."

"But there was always a bit of animosity between you?"

Kimberly's gaze dipped, and she scraped cheese and flesh from the potato skin. "Zoë was a really private person. There was a lot she never wanted to talk about, things she didn't want to reveal, even to me. She'd be pissed to know I'm talking to you about her."

But that didn't answer Tricia's question, and she got the feeling they could dance around the subject for days and Kimberly wouldn't reveal what it was that Zoë had kept hidden all these years. She swallowed, abandoning that line

of inquiry. "Tell me about those threatening letters Zoë received that you mentioned the other day."

Kimberly sobered, and then let out a resigned breath. "I only found out about it a few weeks ago, when a new batch of them came in. Apparently, she'd been getting them off and on for years."

"What made you think the blackmailer could be here in Stoneham?"

"Most of the letters were postmarked from Milford or Nashua."

"Did Zoë worry about them? Is that why she finally put the house here in Stoneham up for sale?"

"No. She blew them off as from a crank. Authors get a lot of oddball fan mail and solicitations. Someone always wants you to look at a manuscript or to give them your literary agent's name. Zoë hadn't been back to Stoneham in over a year, and she was tired of paying for utilities and for someone to look in on the house now and then."

"How did Zoë respond to these letters?"

"She ignored them."

"Did she keep the letters?"

Kimberly shook her head. "Just the last batch. Sheriff Adams asked me about them the night Zoë was killed. I had to turn them over to her. She seems to think they'll lead to the murderer."

Tricia bit her lip to keep from saying, "Well, duh!" Then again, she wasn't sure Wendy Adams was capable of solving a petty robbery, let alone a murder. "Too bad. I would've loved to have seen them."

Kimberly's mouth twitched. "I thought you might say that. I brought copies." She reached for her purse.

Talk about a surprise. But still . . . "Why give them to me?"

"Because, besides the press, you're the only one who seems to care what happened to my aunt."

"Funny. I wasn't sure *you* did."

Kimberly leaned forward. "I didn't like my aunt very much. She could've helped me a lot more than she did. She interfered with friendships I'd made and kept me from seeing people I enjoyed. But she was all I had, and I guess I feel some kind of weird twisted loyalty to her." She brought out the papers. "If you don't want them, I can always get rid of them." She pulled the little oil lamp to the center of the table, removed the hurricane glass, and waved the papers over the flame.

Tricia's heart pounded. "No!"

The old Kimberly was back, and flashed another wicked smile. For a moment Tricia was afraid she'd actually set the pages on fire. Then the smile faded. She placed them on the table and shoved them toward Tricia.

Tricia swallowed, her hands shaking as she picked up the folded stack. Kimberly had just earned the price of her gargantuan dinner. Tricia read the first note and frowned.

An honest woman repays her debts. You've found riches in your new career, leaving behind those whose financial life you helped ruin.

Tricia scanned through the several sheets of paper. They were all like that, random sentences pointing the finger of guilt, but not specifying the crime nor demanding a set amount of cash.

But worst of all, she recognized the handwriting.

TEN

TRICIA SWALLOWED, AND tried to keep her hands from shaking. "Can I keep these, or at least one of these?"

"You can have them all," Kimberly said. "I made more than one set of copies."

"Thank you."

Tricia couldn't tear her eyes from the familiar script. How many times had she seen that spidery scrawl on book requests and other forms at Haven't Got a Clue? It belonged to Mr. Everett.

She scanned the lines again. No, he'd made no mention of the books themselves, didn't accuse her of stealing another's work—just that she had unpaid debts. Why would he believe Zoë Carter owed him money? Had she known he was the one sending the letters? Was she shocked when she showed up at Haven't Got a Clue and found Mr. Everett at her signing?

Tricia thought back to that night. Mr. Everett had barely spoken to Zoë. She couldn't swear on a Bible, but she also didn't remember him being in the vicinity of the washroom at any time before Zoë's body was found. In fact, he and Grace Harris had been pretty much inseparable that entire evening—as they usually were since they'd started . . . well, dating didn't seem the right word—since they'd renewed their friendship over the past winter.

"Are you okay?" Kimberly asked, pausing in her eating marathon. "You look a little pale."

"Perfectly fine," Tricia said, but she pushed her plate away. She'd completely lost her appetite.

Eugenia paused at the table. "Everything all right?"

Kimberly pushed her plates of uneaten food toward the waitress. "You want to box these up? I'll be taking them home."

"Sure thing." She placed the check facedown on the table, picked up the plates, and headed for the kitchen.

Kimberly pushed the check toward Tricia. "Thanks for feeding me for a couple of days. Got any ideas on how I can eat for the next six months?" she added snidely.

"I'm not your enemy," Tricia said.

"Yeah, and you're not my friend, either," Kimberly said. She stood up.

"If you can stand to play the part of the bereaved, you might be able to milk brunch out of the Chamber of Commerce on Saturday. It sure wouldn't hurt you to show a little respect for your dead aunt."

Kimberly raised an eyebrow. "Not a bad idea," she said, and managed a wan smile. "After all, I did minor in drama in college." She got up from the table, intercepting Eugenia and the bag of leftovers, and left the diner.

Tricia drained the last of the wine from her glass. If she'd thought her dinner with Kimberly was tough, an even worse situation awaited her—talking to Mr. Everett. She paid the bill, leaving Eugenia a generous tip, and headed for the door, dreading what was yet to come.

Tricia had never been to Mr. Everett's home before, although, as his employer, she knew his address by heart. She drove past the darkened house and saw that his car was missing from the drive. On impulse, she turned into a neighbor's driveway and turned around, then drove across the village to another, more impressive house in a more expensive neighborhood. She well remembered the pseudo-Tudor home from her previous visits, only now spring flowers nodded cheerily along the neatly tended walk, quite a difference from the forlorn and unkempt appearance it had sported the previous fall.

Mr. Everett's car sat in the drive, and the warm glow of lights made Grace Harris's home look inviting and friendly. Tricia parked at the curb, marched up the walk, and rang the bell. When no answer came in thirty or forty seconds, she rang again. Light burst from the copper sconces on either side of the great oak door, and it opened.

"Tricia! My goodness, what are you doing here?" Grace asked. "Come in. Come in from the cold."

Tricia entered the foyer, which had also undergone a transformation. A vase of fresh flowers graced the marble-topped table, and the polished floor positively sparkled. "May I take your coat?" Grace inquired.

"No, thanks. I really came to speak to Mr. Everett, if you don't mind."

"Certainly. William is in the living room. Follow me."

Tricia already knew the way. The last time she'd seen the room, it had been in a state of dishevelment. Grace's treasures had now been restored to their former places, and a gas fire glowed brightly in the once-dark hearth.

"Ms. Miles," Mr. Everett said, and stood at her arrival. He'd donned a beige sweater with suede patches at the elbows, and held a well-worn leather book in his heavily veined hands. A pot of coffee and two cups sat on a silver tray on the coffee table.

"Can I get you—?"

Tricia waved a hand to forestall an invitation to join them for coffee. "I need to speak with you about a very important matter. May I sit down?"

"Go right ahead," Grace said, directing Tricia into one of the plush, brocade-covered wing chairs. Grace sat next to Mr. Everett on the love seat, taking his hand.

"You've come about the letters, haven't you?" Mr. Everett asked.

Tricia nodded. She reached into the pocket of her jacket and brought out the copies, handing them to the elderly gent.

His gaze met hers, his eyes worried. "Are you going to fire me?"

Tricia blinked. "Of course not! But I suspect you may need to speak to an attorney. As your employer, I would be glad to vouch for you and help in any way I can."

"That won't be necessary," Grace said, her face growing pale.

"These aren't the originals," Mr. Everett said, shuffling through the pages.

"I'm afraid the sheriff has those. Kimberly Peters turned them over to her the night Zoë Carter died. I don't for a minute believe you killed her, but the sheriff hasn't been known for listening to reason."

Mr. Everett continued to look at one of the letters in his hand.

"Would you like me to explain, dear?" Grace asked.

He shook his head. "If you will recall, Ms. Miles, I once owned the only grocery store in Stoneham. My accountant used to chide me for giving credit to customers. Over the years I helped out many people who were down on their luck. Zoë Carter was one of them. After she lost her job at Trident Log Homes, she was in need of financial help. She was proud, but she had her niece to think of. She asked for and received credit from me."

"To the tune of over two thousand dollars," Grace piped in.

"It wasn't a lot of money, but when I was struggling to keep the store open, I asked all my customers to try to pay back at least some of what they owed me. Most of them rewarded me by shopping at my competition in Milford. Ms. Carter was among them. After she became a best-selling author, I approached

her a number of times about repaying her debt. Even though the store had closed, I myself needed cash when my Alice took sick."

"I wish you'd come to me, William," Grace said, real tenderness in her voice.

"I didn't want charity. I only wanted to be repaid by someone who could now afford to do so. I never threatened Zoë Carter; I tried to appeal to her conscience. Sadly, I don't believe she had one."

"So she knew it was you who sent the letters."

"Of course. I always put my return address stickers on the envelopes—that was so she'd know where to send the money. I didn't even ask for interest—just what was owed me."

"And did you continue to send the letters even after your wife passed?"

He nodded. "Once or twice a year. Sadly, I can't live on only what you pay me. And Social Security only goes so far."

"I understand."

The silence lengthened, only the ticking of the grandfather clock in the corner and the hiss of the gas fire making any sound in the quiet room. "You should tell the sheriff about this, if only so that she doesn't waste precious time when she could be going after the real killer. And I'm sure we both want to see Haven't Got a Clue reopen as quickly as possible."

Grace patted her friend's hand. "I'll call my attorney first thing in the morning and get his advice."

Mr. Everett shook his head. "No, Grace, I can't let you—"

"This is one time I won't let your pride keep you from accepting my help. You need competent legal advice, and I'm sure young Mr. Livingston will be glad to help you."

Tricia stood, unwilling to get into the middle of that discussion. "I'll leave it to you, then, to contact the sheriff."

Mr. Everett nodded, and then he, too, stood.

"I'll explain to Angelica why you won't be at work tomorrow. Between Ginny and me, we should be able to keep her happy."

"I shall apologize to your sister myself, perhaps on Saturday. Thank you again for not firing me, Ms. Miles. I enjoy working at Haven't Got a Clue and would miss the books, you, Ginny, and Miss Marple."

"Thank you, Mr. Everett. I'm glad you feel that way."

As Mr. Everett was not a touchy-feely kind of person, Tricia restrained herself from reaching out to hug him and instead extended her hand, which he solemnly shook.

Grace led Tricia back to the big oak door. "Thank you for looking out for William, Tricia. He's a good man. He's suffered a lot, what with losing his business and then his wife."

"Yes, I know." Tricia gave the old lady a smile. "I hope your sister is feeling better."

Grace frowned, looking puzzled. "Sister?"

"Yes, I understand she wasn't feeling well."

"Tricia, where did you get the idea I have a sister? I was an only child."

"But—?" Tricia stopped herself. She wasn't crazy. Mr. Everett had told her Grace had left town the day after Zoë's murder to nurse an ailing sister.

If that was a lie . . . could she believe anything the old man told her?

TRICIA PARKED HER car in the municipal lot and walked the block and a half to her own store on autopilot, preoccupied with everything she'd learned that evening. She even had her key out, ready to open Haven't Got a Clue's front door, when the crime scene tape across it reminded her she was still shut out.

She turned, walked to the Cookery, and took out that key. Entering, she locked up behind her and walked through the quiet store and up the stairs to Angelica's loft apartment, wishing she was taking the steps to her own home.

Upon opening the door, an eight-pound bundle of gray fur pounced, meowing frantically. "Miss Marple. Did you miss your Mum?"

"*Yow!*" the cat replied emphatically.

"Angelica? Angelica?" Tricia called, but there was no other sign of life in the darkened apartment. She flicked on the switches and padded down the hall to the kitchen. A note was attached to the refrigerator door. *Having dinner with Bob. Don't wait up for me.*

"*Yow!*" Miss Marple insisted.

"We're alone! Hurray!"

But Miss Marple was not about to be placated. Her dinner was late, and she'd been left alone for yet another day. Tricia busied herself and fed the cat, who tucked in with gusto.

Tricia stood in the middle of the unfamiliar kitchen and tried to think of what she should do next. She could unpack some of Angelica's boxes, which would either anger or delight her sister, but she was tired, and the thought of hauling around a lot of dusty, heavy boxes was not enticing.

Take care of your own business, said a small voice within her. Though she didn't have access to the store itself, voice mail continued to pick up the shop's incoming calls. Although the outgoing message said the store was temporarily closed, customers and creditors were still leaving messages that needed to be answered.

Tricia settled down on one of the stools at the island and keyed in the number to retrieve her calls. Sure enough, there were seven of them awaiting her

attention. Three were from customers wanting to know the status of their orders; two were from buyers; someone was interested in selling her late mother's collection of mysteries; and the last was from Frannie. "Tricia, it's me," she said. No mistaking that Texas twang.

Miss Marple jumped up, landing on Tricia's lap, startling her, and nuzzled Tricia's hand for attention.

"Looks like Nikki didn't get the loan for the patisserie, and she is absolutely *devastated.* I've been talking to a bunch of the Tuesday Night Book Club gals, and we want to do something to cheer her up. We're thinking of going to brunch on Sunday at the Bookshelf Diner. Ten o'clock sharp. I know it would mean a lot to Nikki if you could be there, too. Give me a call to let me know if you can make it. Bye!"

Miss Marple wiped her damp gray nose across the back of Tricia's hand, demanding more of her attention. "You're not the only unhappy person on the planet, you know," Tricia chided, but Miss Marple was seldom interested in the goings-on in the world at large if they did not directly apply to her.

Tricia absently rubbed the cat's head. She actually did feel sorry for Kimberly. She felt sorry for Nikki, and despite the fact that Zoë might have misrepresented someone else's work as her own, Tricia still felt a pang of pity for the woman. Had Zoë accomplished so little of worth in her own life that she felt no qualms at passing off another's work as her own? At least at first. The fact that she had rebuffed the attention best-sellerdom could have afforded her, lived rather frugally, and left the majority of her estate to charity could attest that she had never felt entirely comfortable with the whole deception.

And now she was dead at another's hands.

"You wouldn't want to be the killer's next victim," Stella Kraft had told Tricia the day before.

No, she wouldn't. And yet someone she'd spoken to—perhaps someone she knew well—had a reason for killing Zoë Carter. And now that Zoë was gone, there was a chance the killer would go to ground and never be discovered.

Over the years more than one friend or acquaintance had asked Tricia why she was so enamored of the mystery genre. How could she actually enjoy stories that celebrated violent death? They had it all wrong. The books didn't celebrate death, but triumph for justice. Too often real-life villains got away with murder, but in fiction, justice was usually assured.

Sometimes she wished life better imitated art.

ELEVEN

Friday dawned cold and wet. Typical April weather. And, Tricia reminded herself, rain was good for retail—it brought out shoppers. Too bad none of the shoppers would be visiting her store. No sooner had Tricia delivered the bad news to Angelica that Mr. Everett would be absent for the day, than her cell phone rang.

"Tricia, it's Ginny." Her voice sounded strained.

"Are you okay?" Tricia asked.

"No. I'm calling in sick." This troubled Tricia. Ginny *never* called in sick, especially now, when she so desperately needed the money for home repairs.

"What's wrong?"

"Food poisoning, I think. Your sister made appetizers yesterday, and I had quite a few."

"Are you sure that's what made you sick?"

"I didn't have anything else all day, and I spent most of the night huddled in the bathroom with cramps and diarrhea."

Tricia winced. More information than she wanted to know.

"Would you tell Angelica I'll be in this afternoon if I can? I really hate to lose a couple of hours' pay, but I think it's better if I stay home, at least for the morning."

"I agree. Take care, now."

"Thanks, Tricia."

Tricia hung up the phone. With Mr. Everett out for the day, and now Ginny, Angelica would be depending on Tricia to help out at the Cookery. That meant there'd be no extended breaks to look into Zoë's death. No chance to get away at all.

It was going to be a very long day.

Try as she might, Tricia's heart was not into selling cookbooks. Although the bulk of her own stock favored classic mystery, Tricia had been on a "cozy mystery" kick of late. Not for the first time she found herself telling Angelica's epicurean-minded customers about Diane Mott Davidson's Goldy Schulz culinary mystery series. Did Angelica's customers like chocolate? Then a Joanna Carl mystery was just the ticket. She made a beeline for a woman checking out

Martha Stewart's Homekeeping Handbook to make a pitch for a Barbara Colley's "squeaky clean, Charlotte LaRue" mystery series.

Angelica did not approve, and more than once interrupted one of Tricia's pitches. "Will you stop trying to sell things I can't supply?" she hissed. "Heck, you can't even supply them, since you sell mostly vintage stock."

"I know, but your customers would really *enjoy* those books. It wouldn't hurt you to start stocking them, either—especially since I don't."

"Don't even go there," Angelica said, straightening up so that she stood her full two inches taller than Tricia.

The Cookery's door opened, and Frannie Armstrong strode in. "Tricia!" She waved and charged forward. "I'm glad I found you. You're the last person on my list."

"List?" Tricia repeated.

"For the flowers."

Tricia stared at her, uncomprehending.

"For Zoë Carter's memorial service tomorrow. Or will Haven't Got a Clue be sending its own floral arrangement?"

Ginny had mentioned something about it the day before. "To tell you the truth, I hadn't thought about it."

Frannie blinked, obviously startled by this gaffe. "Oh."

"Is the Chamber providing flowers?" Tricia asked.

"Of course. They've ordered a beautiful Victorian mourning wreath that exactly duplicates the one Zoë wrote about in *Forever Gone* for Addie's beloved father, who died so tragically."

"Of course," Tricia echoed. "Who came up with that idea?" Surely not Bob. For all he'd done to bring the rare and antiquarian booksellers to Stoneham, she doubted he'd ever picked up a book to read for pleasure.

"Me, silly," Frannie answered. "It was fresh in my mind, since I just reread the book a few weeks back in prep for reading the new book. I finished *Forever Cherished* just last night." She shook her head sadly. "To think of all that talent gone from the world."

Or possibly still living among them—angry at Zoë for taking credit for work that was not her own. Angry enough to kill.

"Would it look tacky if I only contributed to the group fund?" Tricia asked.

"Not at all. In fact, two displays—one on either side of the statue—would give balance. Three wouldn't look as harmonious."

Unless someone else sent flowers. Considering Kimberly's financial situation, Tricia doubted there'd be an offering bearing a ribbon with BELOVED AUNT draped across a spray of gladiolas. Would Zoë's agent think to send flow-

ers? Tricia had met Zoë exactly once—for a little over an hour—had barely spoken to her, and Frannie had offered the perfect out.

What was she thinking? She could well afford to spring for flowers. It was the proper thing to do. And yet—honoring someone who'd passed off another's work as her own just didn't set right with Tricia. So what if she didn't yet have proof? She believed it.

"So what do you think?" Frannie said.

"How's twenty dollars sound?" Tricia asked.

Frannie's eyes lit up. "That's very generous. Thank you."

"It's my pleasure."

Angelica ambled up to join them.

Frannie's gaze wandered around the Cookery. "My, you have done a beautiful job with this place."

"Thank you," Angelica said. "Would you like a tour?"

"Just a short one. I'm on my lunch break."

Tricia retrieved her wallet and extracted a twenty-dollar bill. After her tour, Frannie left with it, plus two Tex-Mex cookbooks, a miniwhisk, a nutmeg grater, and a jar of jalapeño pepper jam.

"Bye, Frannie," Angelica called as Frannie left the shop. She turned to her sister and grinned. "Feel free to invite your friends to my store any time."

GINNY SHOWED UP for work about two o'clock, looking pale, but willing. Instead of putting in hours for Angelica, though, she spent the bulk of time helping Tricia with the plans for the statue dedication and book fair set for the next day. Angelica would not be participating, and kept complaining—loudly—that she would not be able to handle the usual expected crowd that a Saturday would produce. Thank heaven Mr. Everett called to say he would return the next morning at nine forty-five sharp.

With Ginny there to help Angelica, Tricia didn't have to feel guilty about making a call she already felt was long overdue.

"Medical examiner's office."

"Yes, I'd like to speak to the medical examiner."

"I can take a message. Your name—?"

"No, I don't want to leave a message, I need to speak to someone in charge. My place of business was the scene of a crime. I've been shut down for days during the investigation. I need to know when I can reopen."

"Please leave your name and number, and someone will get back to you."

She did, but she didn't believe for a minute that anyone would.

She tried another tack and called her lawyer, Roger Livingston. He was actually available, and said he'd personally call the ME's office.

Tricia helped three customers look for books, and had rung up another two sales by the time her cell phone interrupted her. She glanced at the number on the tiny screen. "Ginny, can you finish up here? I need to take this call."

Ginny manned the cash register and Tricia stepped behind a shelf of books.

"Tricia, it's Roger Livingston."

"Thanks for getting back to me so soon, Roger. Good news or bad?"

"Good. I called in a favor and got to speak right to the medical examiner. You were right. His office finished with your store yesterday, and so have the county's crime scene investigators. He said there's no reason you weren't informed and allowed to reopen."

"I knew it. I knew Wendy Adams was just being ornery. She hates me."

"I can't comment on that, but I've got a call in to her office. It's getting late. We may not get satisfaction today, but I'll follow up and make sure something happens by tomorrow."

"Thanks, Roger, you're the best lawyer in the world."

"That's true," he said, and she could picture him smiling. "And you'll receive my bill in the mail."

It would be well worth it to reopen the door to Haven't Got a Clue and be back in business.

A much happier Tricia kept an eye on the clock, and at five fifteen announced she needed to leave to pick up Zoë's literary agent at the airport.

"Why don't you bring him back here for dinner?" Angelica said.

"What for?"

"It doesn't seem very friendly just dumping him off at the inn."

"I'm not his friend," Tricia reminded her. "I'm doing him a favor."

"Well, you could be his friend. I mean, you're in the book business."

"Yes, but I'm a book*seller*, not an author."

"You could be—you have many talents. And besides, I think we should cultivate friendships with people in the publishing world. It'll be good for business in general."

Tricia studied her sister's innocent expression. Something was going on—something Angelica wasn't being open about. A quick glance at the clock told Tricia she didn't have time to pursue it just then.

The drive to the Manchester-Boston Regional Airport took less time than Tricia anticipated, and a glance at the arrivals screen informed her that Hamilton's plane was delayed. She browsed the airport bookstore with a judgmental eye, eventually bought the first book in Sheila Connolly's Orchard series, and settled down for a peaceful read, grateful to escape the stress she felt inside the

Cookery. Half an hour later, a glance at her watch told her she'd better head for the security checkpoint and the arriving passengers. She pulled out the paper sign bearing Artemus Hamilton's name that she'd made earlier, and stood searching the faces for one she wasn't confident she'd recognize.

The crowd had pretty much thinned when a short, chunky, balding man dressed in a black turtleneck, suit jacket, and dark slacks strode toward her, his raincoat neatly folded over one arm, a briefcase in the same hand. "Ms. Miles?"

Tricia held out her hand. "Nice to meet you, again, Mr. Hamilton." They shook on it, his grip firm but not crushing.

"Can you direct me to the baggage claim? I would've preferred to travel lighter, but at least I was able to read most of a manuscript during my flight."

"A mystery?" Tricia asked eagerly.

He shook his head. "Sorry. It's a diet book. I really don't handle that much mystery."

"Then why—?"

"Was Zoë Carter my client?" he finished. He shrugged. "She had a great book that transcended the genre, and I felt I could place it for her."

Evasive, but it was an answer.

"The baggage claim?" he reminded her.

"Follow me. While you wait for your bag, I'll bring the car around and meet you out front. It's a white Lexus."

Ten minutes later, Tricia pulled up to the curb, popped the trunk button, and Hamilton loaded his suitcase into it. It seemed a big bag for just an overnight stay. He climbed into the passenger seat and buckled his seat belt as Tricia eased the car back into the airport traffic.

"How far is it to Stoneham?" he asked.

"About twenty-five miles. It only takes about half an hour to get there."

He nodded, taking in what scenery was discernible in the rapidly fading light.

Conversation was light, and Tricia waited until they were off the airport property and well on their way toward Stoneham before voicing the question that had been on her mind for the past two days. Hamilton was a captive audience, and if he refused to answer, it could be a very long thirty-minute drive to Stoneham.

"Mr. Hamilton—"

"Call me Artie," he insisted good-naturedly.

Tricia forced a smile. "Artie, there's speculation around Stoneham that Zoë never wrote any of her books." She risked a glance at her passenger, whose gaze had turned stony.

"Why would anyone even think—let alone voice—that, especially now that she's passed on?" he asked. His voice had gone cold, too.

Tricia was glad to turn her gaze back to the road ahead of them. "Her back-

ground. Her lack of interest in fiction. Her lack of interest in much of anything, really." She risked a furtive glance at the man, but he'd turned away, and was staring out the passenger window.

"It would be—" He paused. "—disrespectful of me to even dignify that question with an answer."

"Mr. Hamilton," she tried again, trying to sound as respectful as possible, "as you pointed out, Zoë's dead. Whoever wrote those books probably killed her. He—or she—deserves the credit. And they—him or her—deserve to pay for the crime as well."

He sighed, still refusing to answer.

"If you don't know who wrote them, do you know who did the rewrites?"

"Rewrites?" he repeated dully.

"Yes. I've never heard of an editor who accepted a manuscript without making a few single-spaced pages of editorial suggestions."

"You've worked in publishing?" he asked, sidestepping the question.

"No, but I've talked to enough authors to gain a good deal of insight into the process."

Hamilton sighed, still refusing to meet her gaze.

She tried again. "Kimberly Peters told me the original manuscripts were written on an old manual typewriter. She never actually *saw* her aunt write the books." Okay, that was stretching the truth a bit, but it might be what it took to get answers. "Kimberly said she keyboarded some of the manuscripts into a computer."

Hamilton still said nothing.

"She never actually called the books her aunt's, always referring to them as 'the manuscripts.' Like they were separate entities. Not really a part of Zoë, but something foreign. Did you ever have that same feeling?"

Hamilton seemed to squirm in his seat. He didn't answer.

Tricia's hands tightened on the steering wheel, and the silence went on for more than a minute, until she thought she might want to scream from the almost palpable tension. Hamilton sighed again. "I did the rewrites on the first three novels," he admitted, voice low, almost embarrassed.

Trisha exhaled a *whoosh* of air, finally able to breathe once again.

"Mind you, Zoë never came right out and admitted she didn't author those manuscripts. She just made it clear that she was not open to rewrites or promotion."

"So you took them on because they were almost good enough for publication?"

He nodded. "Just reading her correspondence convinced me Zoë wouldn't know a verb from an adjective. She couldn't talk about the research necessary to pull off a historical novel. She had no knowledge of punctuation."

"And yet you represented those books."

"They were good. I was new to the business, but I knew I could sell them. At the time that's all I—and Zoë—cared about."

"Would you have made a different decision today?"

He didn't answer.

Tricia's grip on the steering wheel tightened once more as she thought about everything he'd said. "Who did the rewrites on the last two novels?" She thought she knew the answer before he even spoke.

"Kimberly Peters."

Aha!

"Kimberly has an English degree. She's written a couple of novels—women's fiction. I've read her work. It's good. It's publishable. But Zoë wouldn't hear of it."

"Why not?"

"She thought one author in the family was enough."

Which would seem to be a motive for Kimberly to get rid of her dearly "beloved" aunt.

"Why didn't you do the last two rewrites?"

"No time. Thanks to Zoë, my agency is one of the top twenty in New York. Kimberly offered to take over the rewrites, and she was good at it. She also took over Zoë's correspondence. She approved the cover copy and worked with the publisher's publicist. Zoë hated any kind of promotion, but Kimberly talked her into a website. She put the whole thing together—coordinated the updates. She answered the fan mail. She made Zoë at least appear to be accessible. Somehow she even convinced Zoë to go on tour for the last book, coaching her all the way."

"Kimberly did all that for Zoë, and then the woman more or less disinherited her?"

"Zoë was not a logical woman. She rarely asked me for advice."

"Kimberly said that until recently you were named the executor of Zoë's will. Did you know that?"

"Yes."

"Do you know why she changed her mind?"

"Yes."

"And?"

"It's none of your business."

Touché. Time to try another tack.

"You knew there'd be no more Jess and Addie *Forever* novels. What's to stop you from helping Kimberly get published now?"

He exhaled loudly. "While Zoë was alive, it made sense to placate her. I now represent her estate. Those books will sell for another five, maybe ten, years. It

wasn't like I totally ignored Kimberly's aspirations. I gave her a few of my colleagues' names, but I don't think she's yet found representation."

"I take it that you haven't spoken to Kimberly about her own manuscripts since Zoë died?"

He shook his head. "She did phone me, but that subject didn't come up."

"Would you consider representing her now?"

"I don't know. Maybe."

"She'll be at the dedication tomorrow. I'm sure you two will have a lot to talk about."

"Possibly."

They rode in silence for a good five minutes before Hamilton spoke again. "Ms. Miles—"

"Tricia," she insisted.

"Tricia, please don't talk about this to anyone. It would be—"

"Bad for business?"

"As you said, Zoë's dead. What good would it do to drag her name through the mud?"

"I'll make you a deal. I won't talk about this until after this weekend. It wouldn't do to embarrass my colleagues in the Chamber of Commerce, but if the real author of those manuscripts killed Zoë, eventually it will come out. You *do* see that, don't you?"

He shrugged, sounded resigned. "If it happens, it happens. I'll deal with it later."

By denying everything, Tricia thought bitterly. She pulled onto Route 101, steering toward Stoneham and the Brookview Inn. She'd be glad to be rid of Hamilton. And yet . . . for some reason, she didn't think he could be as cold and calculating as he'd come across. Or, despite his part in concealing the truth about Zoë's books, was she just hoping she'd see a better side of him?

Long minutes of silence later, she pulled into the Brookview's drive and stopped the car by the inn's welcoming front entrance. She popped the trunk as Hamilton got out, then retrieved his suitcase. He walked up to the driver's door. Tricia hit a button, and her window slid down and out of sight.

"Thank you for the ride, Ms. Miles. And thank you for giving me some time to—" He hesitated. "To come up with a plausible explanation for my actions. I hope I can be as creative as the person who wrote Zoë's books." With that, he turned and walked up the steps and into the inn.

THE COOKERY HAD been closed for more than an hour by the time Tricia made it back to Main Street. Dodging the goose droppings, she ended up in front of her sister's store. After the long day, she wanted nothing more than a glass of

wine, a soak in a tub, and to escape into an Agatha Christie story. That wasn't likely to happen. At least Bob's car wasn't parked at the curb, so she'd only have to contend with Angelica tonight.

She unlocked the door, trailed through the darkened store with only the dim security lamps overhead to light the way, and headed up the stairs. She got to the top and opened the door Angelica had left unlocked. "Hello!" she called.

"In the kitchen," came Angelica's muted voice.

The patter of little paws sounded, and before Tricia could hang up her coat, Miss Marple scolded her, at the same time rubbing her head against Tricia's legs. "I'm sorry I didn't come to see you all day, Miss Marple. You must have been terribly lonely," Tricia said, and scooped up the cat, which purred loudly, fiercely nuzzling Tricia's neck.

Tricia put the cat down and headed to the kitchen.

"I'm glad you're here," Angelica said, looking up from the stove, where she stirred some heavenly smelling concoction. "That cat has done nothing but make a pest of herself since I came up an hour ago."

"Did you feed her?"

"That's not my job."

Tricia sighed, grabbed the empty and well-licked food bowl, and took it to the sink to wash. Miss Marple kept rubbing against her slacks, which were soon coated in cat hair. She selected a can of tuna in sauce, supplemented the wet with some dry food, and set it on the floor. Miss Marple dug in gratefully. Tricia rinsed and refilled the water bowl before collapsing onto one of the kitchen stools.

"You look pooped. Ready to talk?" Angelica asked eagerly.

"You bet. More than that, though, I'm starved."

Angelica abandoned her spoon, took three steps and opened the fridge, grabbed a plate and peeled off the cling wrap before setting it on the island in front of Tricia. "I whipped these up yesterday afternoon in the store. Had a few left over and saved you some. They went over real well. Sold seven books on hors d'oeuvres because of them."

Tricia wrinkled her nose. "Ginny said she got sick eating them."

"Oh, don't be absurd. Nobody else did, and believe me, if any of my customers had gotten sick, I'd have heard. People love to sue. I use only fresh ingredients, and you know how meticulously clean I keep my workspace. I'm not afraid to use my digital thermometer, either."

No doubt about it, Angelica was a hygiene hound, and was especially careful not to cross-contaminate raw with cooked foods.

"Besides," Angelica said loftily, "I ate six of them for lunch, and they were delicious."

They did look appetizing, and Tricia *was* hungry. Throwing caution to the

wind, she studied the delightful little morsels before her, choosing a baguette slice topped with cheese and what looked like homemade salsa. She took a tentative bite. Good, but probably needed time for the cheese to warm up to room temperature to truly be appreciated. "What are you making? It smells wonderful."

"Tlalpeño soup. Got the recipe on a trip Drew," her ex-husband, "and I made to Mexico City about three years back. You do like avocados, don't you?"

"Definitely."

Angelica grabbed another glass from the cupboard and poured Tricia wine from the opened bottle of Chardonnay, then handed it to her. "Margaritas would be a better choice, but I ran out of lime juice. So tell me all about Zoë's agent." Angelica wasn't above listening to gossip, and Tricia figured she could use a sounding board.

She took a sip, and sighed, letting herself relax for the first time in hours. "I had an interesting conversation with Mr. Artemus Hamilton."

Angelica resumed her position at the stove. "And?" she asked eagerly. "What's he like? Is he looking for new clients?"

Tricia blinked, taken aback by the question. "I didn't ask. He did, however, admit that Zoë Carter never wrote her best sellers."

Angelica snorted. "Yeah, and Santa comes down my chimney every Christmas Eve."

"I'm serious, Ange. I've been hearing rumors, and her agent confirmed it."

"But that's ridiculous."

"I talked to Zoë's next-door neighbor, the Stoneham librarian, and even Zoë's old English teacher. None of them ever believed she wrote the books."

"Then why didn't someone say something before now?"

"No one had proof."

"So what are you saying, that the real author stepped up and killed Zoë?"

Tricia nodded.

"But why would the author wait until now? The first book was published over a decade ago. I know. I bought it. In fact, I still have it." She waved a hand toward the stacks of unopened boxes that still littered her adjoining living room. "Somewhere in all this mess."

"I talked to Kimberly about it. She wasn't the author, but she knew Zoë didn't write them, either. Kimberly has an English degree and supposedly has some writing ability. Somehow she got Zoë to allow her to do the rewrites on the last few books. It's possible she could've felt at least a bit of ownership after she started doing that and approving the cover copy, et cetera."

"But who *did* write the novels?" Angelica asked.

Tricia shrugged. "We may never know. And speaking of books . . . why are you so interested in Artemus Hamilton?"

"Me?" Angelica said, sounding anything but innocent.

"Yes. Every time I mention him, you glow like a lightbulb. Come on, level with me."

Angelica bit her lip, looking thoughtful. "If I tell you, do you promise you won't make fun of me?"

Tricia sighed. "I promise."

Angelica turned to her pantry, opened the door, and took out a folding metal step stool. Setting it in front of the refrigerator, she stepped up to open the cabinet over the appliance. From it, she withdrew a sheaf of papers. She stepped down, closed the distance between them, and handed it to Tricia.

"Easy-Does-It Cooking," she read, "by Angelica Miles." She looked up at her sister. "You've written a cookbook?"

Angelica nodded. "Actually, I've written three. This is my latest."

Tricia flipped through the pages, noting the document wasn't formatted in accepted manuscript style. "What are you going to do with it?"

She shrugged. "I thought I might offer it to Mr. Hamilton. I kind of looked at his firm's website. Apparently they do take nonfiction. Now I just need an introduction to him."

Tricia handed back the papers. "Don't look at me."

Angelica frowned. "Why not? You did him a favor by driving him to the Brookview. He owes you."

"May I remind you, we did not part on happy terms. And"—she looked at the manuscript in her sister's hands—"you can't submit something like that without doing the upfront research."

"Are you kidding? I've been researching cooking my whole life. And during the past five months, when I've been working ten-hour days, I realized that what the world needs is recipes for delicious, easy, and quick-to-make dinners."

"Ange, have you looked at the bookshelves in your own store? There are scores of cookbooks just like that already in print."

Angelica shook her head. "Not like mine."

"And it's not even properly formatted," Tricia pointed out.

"Oh, who cares about that? The quality will shine through."

"Fine. Find out the hard way. But one more thing: if I've learned anything talking to authors, there's nothing worse than shoving your manuscript at an agent or editor at an inappropriate time. It's the kiss of death."

"Oh, what do you know?" Angelica said, and held the pages to her chest as though they were a babe in diapers. "You'll see. I'm going to sell my cookbooks. I'll be fabulously successful, maybe even land my own TV show like Rachael Ray or Paula Deen. Lord knows I've got the personality."

And the ego, too.

"Fine. Don't listen to me." Tricia sniffed the air. "But, oh fabulous sister chef of mine, I think you'll find your soup is scorched."

Angelica dropped the manuscript on the counter as though it were on fire, and rushed to the stove. Grabbing the spoon, she stirred the pot, her expression souring. She took a taste. "Oh, no," she wailed. "My lovely, lovely soup."

Tricia shook her head, got up, and walked over to pick up the phone. "Looks like it's pizza again, after all."

TWELVE

TRUE TO HIS word, Mr. Everett was at the Cookery before opening on Saturday morning, just as Ginny and Tricia packed up the last of the books to take to Stoneham Square and the statue dedication. Tricia had questions for Mr. Everett, but this wasn't the time to voice them all. Perhaps later in the afternoon an opportunity would arise.

Still, she drew him aside to ask the most important one. "How did it go with Sheriff Adams?"

"She is not a very nice woman. I was glad Mr. Livingston did most of the talking; otherwise, I'm sure I'd be staring at the walls of a jail cell right now."

"Thank heavens for good legal counsel," Tricia agreed. "There's something else we need to discuss, Mr. Everett."

"Tricia, can you help me with these boxes?" Ginny called.

"Just a second." She turned back to Mr. Everett. "We'll talk later."

He nodded, and headed for the back of the shop to stow his coat.

Tricia helped Ginny stack the boxes on two of the Cookery's dollies.

"I think I should go to the dedication," Angelica said, as she watched Mr. Everett don his yellow Cookery apron.

"You can't leave the store," Tricia said, putting on her coat.

"Why not? Mr. Everett is here to take care of things. And anyway, it's likely most of the village, and a lot of the tourists, will be at the square. The Cookery might not have any customers, anyway."

"Not if the weatherman is correct. He's predicting a high of only forty-six degrees today. That might just drive a bunch of the tourists into your toasty warm shop."

"I heard a couple of TV stations will be covering the dedication," Ginny said, and laughed. "It must be a slow weekend for news."

Angelica went behind her sales counter, came back with a big brown envelope, and handed it to Tricia. "Here, if you see Mr. Hamilton, will you give him this?"

Tricia handed the package right back to her. "I know what this is, and I already told you, the answer is no."

"What's in the package?" Ginny asked, curious.

"None of your business," Angelica snapped. She turned back to her sister. "Tricia, please? I'll make you a cheesecake—from scratch."

"I don't like cheesecake." Tricia pulled her gloves from the pockets of her jacket. "We'll tell you all about the dedication afterward."

"I can't wait," Angelica said, sarcastically.

Tricia tipped back her dolly of books and headed for the front door. "We'll probably be back about five, after striking the set."

"It's not showbiz," Angelica drawled.

"It is to me," Tricia said, and continued to the door, which Ginny opened for her. She'd already parked her car at the curb and had loaded the borrowed cash register and some boxes of books. Too bad all of it was new stock. Mystery lovers who traveled to Stoneham were expecting to find some of their long-out-of-print favorites. Curse Sheriff Adams and her stubbornness.

The atmosphere in the village square was more like that of a circus than a cemetery, considering the event had morphed from a celebration into a memorial service. As many as twenty tents lined the outside of the square, decked out in balloons and colorful wind socks madly waving in the brisk wind, while the aroma of fried dough, hot dogs, and kettle corn filled the air. Potential customers were already milling about as the vendors set up their wares.

Fifteen or twenty geese stood by, eyeing the crowd from the edges of the park's retention pond. Despite the DO NOT FEED THE GEESE signs posted all around, these birds knew that the presence of people often equaled food, and they looked ready to pounce should it appear.

Tricia stood at the opening of her three-sided tent. A gale blew through the canvas walls, threatening to make a box kite out of the whole contraption. Her generic "Thank You" plastic bags had to be weighted down with rocks Ginny found in one of the small park's gardens.

"Are you sorry you came?" Tricia asked.

Ginny had wrapped her arms around herself, the sleeves of her parka drawn over her fingers, her shoulders hunched until they touched the edges of the watch cap that covered her head and ears. She stamped her feet on the cold,

damp earth. "I'd still rather be here, freezing off my behind, than working at the Cookery. I'm sorry to say I don't feel one bit guilty leaving Angelica and Mr. Everett alone together."

Tricia stifled a smile.

"Knock-knock. Anybody home?" Nikki Brimfield stood outside the tent, holding a white cardboard cake box in one hand and a grocery bag and the handle of an airpot coffee carafe in the other. "Thought you guys could use a bit of warming up."

"Hooray!" Ginny cheered, and turned to make room on one of the tables.

"I stopped at the store first, hoping you'd be open again by now. Then I went by the Cookery and Angelica said I'd find you here. Boy, she was grumpy."

Tricia ignored the last comment, but addressed the first. "We'd kill for hot coffee now, that's for sure."

"Yeah," Ginny echoed.

Nikki set the box and carafe on the table, handing the grocery bag to Ginny. She opened the box, revealing a white-frosted cake with a large splotch of red.

"Oh," Tricia said, afraid her lack of enthusiasm would be taken the wrong way.

Nikki laughed. "You're not seeing it complete," she said and dismantled two sides of the box to reveal the entire cake. "There's a fake knife in the bag, Ginny. Want to hand it to me?"

Ginny did as she was told. Nikki removed a cardboard sheath and plunged the plastic carving knife into the center of the cake. Now the splotch of red made perfect sense: it represented a river of pseudoblood puddled around the knife and dripping down the sides. "It's a red velvet cake. It was my mom's recipe. I thought you might need some comfort food."

Why did everyone seem to make wrong assumptions about Tricia's definition of comfort food? So far they'd pretty much missed the mark. Couldn't they have just asked?

"That was thoughtful of you, Nikki. Thank you," Tricia said, trying to sound keen. Had Nikki forgotten it was less than a year ago that Tricia had seen a body with a knife in its back? The sight of the cake made the memory of that terrible evening all the more vivid.

"Now don't you go sharing that," Nikki cautioned, "it's just for you, Tricia." She indicated the bag. "I brought a couple of coconut cupcakes for you, Ginny."

"Thanks. They're my favorite."

"I really appreciate the gesture," Tricia said, taking the knife from the cake and shoving the box under one of the tables and out of sight.

"I feel so bad about everything that's happened this week," Nikki said. "Baking is my way of . . . well, coping."

"Has something else bad happened?" Tricia asked.

Nikki frowned. "Didn't you hear? The bank loan didn't go through. Apparently I don't have enough business acumen or assets or . . . anything."

Oh, yes, Frannie had mentioned the loan.

"But you have all that experience. You've run the patisserie for a couple of years, and you're a certified pastry chef trained in Paris," Ginny put in.

"I know. But it isn't good enough for the Bank of Stoneham." She let out a loud sigh, and for a moment Tricia thought Nikki might cry. But then she straightened, throwing back her shoulders. "I'm not giving up. I've already signed up for an online course on writing a business plan. I just hope Homer doesn't find another buyer before I can get my financing together."

"I'll keep crossing my fingers for you," Tricia said.

Nikki glanced at her watch. "Oh, I've got just enough time to go watch the unveiling. Are you going?"

Tricia shook her head. "We've got to stay here, not that we've been inundated with customers so far. I'm hoping that after the unveiling we'll see a few more sales."

"Okay," Nikki said, and turned to go.

"Oh, go ahead, Tricia," Ginny encouraged. "I can certainly handle things here. And I'm not all that interested in looking at a big old hunk of rock with a carved book on it, anyway."

"Come on, Tricia, it'll be fun," Nikki chided.

Fun? To go to a memorial service? Still, Tricia looked hopefully at Ginny. "Well, if you really don't mind."

"Go ahead," Ginny said, and took a Styrofoam cup from the bag Nikki had provided, then pumped coffee from the carafe.

Tricia removed her Cookery apron, stowing it under one of the tables. "Let's go!"

They left the vendor area circling the village square and headed for the center, where the gazebo sat amid a sea of short, stubby grass, still brown from its winter dormancy. This was no backyard variety structure, but a grand, freestanding granite edifice, its copper roof a mellow green with age. Mere feet away stood the short, tarp-shrouded statue, looking lumpy and ugly against such a stately pavilion. Bob had done a good job, ensuring that the sidewalk and grass surrounding the monument were devoid of goose droppings, although telltale stains still marred what had recently been pristine concrete.

A crowd had already gathered around the monument. Tricia recognized members of Haven't Got a Clue's Tuesday Night Book Club in the crowd, as well as Artemus Hamilton, standing with a subdued Kimberly Peters. She wore

the same wrinkled suit she'd had on at the signing. Didn't she know how to use an iron? Tricia recognized several selectmen, a couple of the other bookstore owners, and Chamber members, who also stood by. Lois Kerr and Stella Kraft were standing with a knot of older ladies who'd gathered to one side.

Sheriff Adams and one of her deputies stood with a number of selectmen who'd shown up for the event—no doubt invited by the Chamber to give the ceremony some semblance of official sanction. Clipboard in hand, Frannie Armstrong flitted about the front of the gazebo, checking the names against her master list of invitees.

Among the missing was Grace Harris, not that Tricia had really expected Mr. Everett's close friend to attend without him. Or was there a reason she didn't want to be seen at Zoë's memorial service? Another angle Tricia would have to investigate.

News cameramen and still photographers had gathered to the left of the monument. Portia McAlister was also among them and, as a member of the press, so was Russ, his Nikon dangling from his neck, a steno pad clutched in his left hand. The rope, which earlier had been securely tied around the white canvas at the bottom of the monument, had already been removed.

Bob looked dapper, if partially frozen, in a kelly green sport coat that he always wore while showing real estate. The crowd quieted as he stepped up to the microphone, tapped it, then blew on it. "Testing, testing." Apparently satisfied with the sound quality, he consulted his notes, then raised his gaze to stare directly into the News Team Ten's video camera. Tricia squinted. Had he had his teeth whitened since the last time she'd seen him?

"It is with great pride and affection that Stoneham's Chamber of Commerce dedicates this statue to one of our own, *New York Times* best-selling author Zoë Carter, who helped bring fame to our little village. We hope Stoneham will remain a mecca to her millions of fans for generations to come." His words were greeted with a smattering of polite applause.

"Too bad Angelica is missing this," Nikki whispered, and giggled. "She might even swoon, seeing Bob in his green jacket."

"Shhh!" Tricia admonished.

"We had hoped Ms. Carter's niece," Bob nodded toward Kimberly, "might speak, but naturally she's quite distraught at her loss."

As though on cue, Kimberly dabbed a tissue at her dry eyes.

"Is there anyone here who'd like to offer a fond memory or words of praise for Zoë?" Bob cleared his throat, looking hopefully at the assembled audience, but no one stepped forward. "Mr. Hamilton?" Bob implored.

All eyes turned toward the literary agent, who blushed.

"Go on," Kimberly mouthed, and gave him a nudge.

A reluctant Hamilton stepped up to the microphone. "Uh . . ." He cleared his throat. "Uh, Zoë Carter was my very first client." His gaze wandered the crowd, lighting on Tricia. He frowned, no doubt remembering their conversation the night before. He looked away. "Zoë, uh, never missed a deadline. The world is a . . . a different place without her."

Different? That's all he could come up with? Perhaps he was afraid to gush, leery of what the press might say about him when the truth about Zoë came to light.

He nodded at those assembled and stepped away from the microphone.

"Thank you," Bob said to the sound of weak applause. "Anyone else?"

Not a soul stepped forward.

"Anyone?" he begged.

As if on queue, the air was broken by the sound of flapping wings and the fierce honking of Canada geese as a portion of the flock took flight from the pond, making a low pass over the crowd, who seemed to duck as one.

When the cacophony receded, Bob cleared his throat, stepped away from the microphone, and moved over to the monument. He grasped the tarp with both hands and yanked dramatically. The wind caught the canvas, whipping it into the air like a sail. The crowd backed off as it came straight at them. Nikki gasped, and for a moment Tricia thought she might have been injured, but she stared straight ahead, her mouth open in astonishment. Tricia turned, and immediately her expression mirrored Nikki's.

The carving of the opened book had been shattered into several large chunks. Below, scarlet spray paint marred the brilliant white marble base, spelling out the word THIEF!

THIRTEEN

"WHAT DOES IT mean?" Nikki gasped.

"This is an outrage!" someone called out.

"What kind of security measures were taken to protect the statue?" said someone else.

Bob Kelly stood transfixed, his gaze focused on his brainchild, utterly flabbergasted at the devastation, while Wendy Adams and her deputy tried to keep the crowd away from the ruined marble.

The TV cameras continued to roll while photographers' flashes strobed. Russ scribbled madly on his steno pad.

Among those not speculating on the vandalism: Kimberly Peters and Artemus Hamilton, who stood staring mutely at the desecrated monument. Was it because they understood what the graffiti meant?

"Wendy," Bob bellowed, "how could you have let this happen?"

"You can't blame the Sheriff's Department—we never got a request to protect the statue."

"Maybe not, but it's your responsibility to keep the village safe."

The sheriff's brows inched menacingly closer. "My deputies and I have eight hundred and seventy-six square miles to protect. We can't be everywhere at once, Bob."

Bob turned to face Kimberly Peters. "I—I don't know what to say, how to apologize—" he stammered.

Tight-lipped, Kimberly replied, "Try, Mr. Kelly."

Bob stood there, mouth agape, his gaze returning to the defaced monument.

Tricia backed away. "I think it's time to go," she told Nikki.

"Yeah. To think I left Steve alone in the shop for an hour for this. Then again . . ." She let the sentence trail, looking thoughtful.

"You don't trust Steve?"

"Of course I trust him. He's got a lot of talent, and he works harder than anyone I've ever hired. But sometimes I just need a break from him. He doesn't have a lot of friends, so I'm afraid he sees me as a confidante, and I'd really rather not play that role."

"Have you let him know this?"

She sighed. "He doesn't always listen to me."

"Yet he wants to bend your ear?" Tricia nodded, knowingly. "I've met a few men like that myself."

Nikki looked to the south, toward the patisserie. "Well, I hope they find the creep who wrecked the statue and nail him. Then again, Wendy Adams couldn't find herself in a fun house mirror, let alone locate a vandal." She shook her head. "See you on Tuesday at the book club, if not before," she said, and gave Tricia's shoulder a quick pat before heading for Main Street.

Tricia headed in the opposite direction. At least she wasn't the only one in the village who questioned Sheriff Adams's qualifications.

Most of the crowd had already dispersed, deserting the square and definitely not visiting any of the vendor tents or food kiosks. Talk about a disaster. Her bottom line for the week was already red, and this event had plunged it into an even deeper scarlet.

Ginny stood at the tent's opening, arms wrapped around her, stamping her feet to keep warm. "I saw everyone leaving. What happened?"

Tricia explained while Ginny craned her neck and stood on tiptoes, looking across the square in a vain effort to see the ruined statue. "I miss out on all the fun," she groused.

"We may as well pack up. I don't think we'll sell another book here today."

"Tricia, we didn't sell *any* books today."

Tricia grimaced at the thought, bending to grab one of the empty boxes from under the table.

"What will you do with Nikki's cake?"

"I can't take it to the Cookery. Ange doesn't want to serve anything she didn't make herself."

"Can I take a slice home to Brian? He could use a treat. With the stove on the fritz, he's pretty sick of sandwiches and microwaved soup."

"Take the whole thing. I'm not going to eat it. It's very sweet of Nikki to keep giving me sweet treats, but I'm just not into them."

"And that's how you stay so thin," Ginny said, and poked at the padding on her own hip.

Tricia grabbed another couple of books. "It would also aggravate Angelica if I brought it home."

Ginny laughed. "Well, that alone might be worth it. Are you sure you can't take even half of it?"

Tricia pushed the cake box toward her assistant. "No. Until the sheriff lets me back into my store, I have to live with Angie."

"It'll be a hardship, but I think between the two of us, we can eat the whole cake." Ginny set the cake aside and started packing books.

Fifteen minutes later, Tricia pulled her car in front of the tent, and they loaded it. She waved at her nearest neighbor, who was packing up her fried dough stand. "What a bust today turned out to be," she said to Tricia, who nodded and offered a wan smile.

Ginny decided to walk back to the Cookery so that she could put Nikki's cake in her car trunk. Mr. Everett met Tricia on the sidewalk with a dolly and helped her take a case of books from her car's trunk.

"Did you notice the crime scene tape is gone?" He nodded toward the door of Haven't Got a Clue.

"When did that happen?"

"Just after you left. I tried to call, but your cell phone must be turned off."

Roger Livingston's call to the medical examiner's office must have done some good. "Are we allowed inside?" she asked, almost afraid to hear the answer.

"Yes," he said eagerly, and shot a glance at the Cookery, where Angelica stood behind the closed door, disapproval etched across her face.

Tricia flashed her a smile. "Mr. Everett, I know it's a terrible imposition, but would you be willing to stay at the Cookery, at least for the rest of the day, while Ginny and I get things going again next door?"

He sighed, as though he'd known she'd ask this question. "Yes. But, tomorrow is Ginny's day off, and you'll need me at Haven't Got a Clue." It wasn't a question; it was a statement.

"Yes, of course."

That was sure to start a fight with Angelica. But really, shouldn't she have been looking for a new employee during the past week anyway?

Tricia plucked the store key from among the others on her ring and placed it in the lock, savoring this moment. She opened the door and breathed in the scent of her store, a mix of old paper, furniture polish, and . . . *freedom*. How she'd missed days spent in the long, narrow shop with its richly paneled walls decorated with prints and photos of long-dead mystery authors, the comfy tapestry-upholstered chairs in the readers' nook, and the restored tin ceiling—the only original feature she'd been able to keep during renovation. She took in all her favorite features and sighed. She was home.

Mr. Everett cleared his throat, reminding her that he stood, coatless, directly behind her. "Where do you want me to put these?"

"Oh, anywhere. I don't think we'll be able to reopen today."

"Why not?" said Ginny, coming up from behind. "We've still got five hours. It won't take us that long to get the coffee on and the register open."

"Yes, but I need to give that washroom a thorough cleaning and I need to rescue Miss Marple," Tricia said, hearing the joy in her voice and realizing, for the first time in days, that she actually felt something other than angst.

"Come on, Mr. Everett, help me get these books inside while Tricia gets her cat," Ginny said. "It's time for us all to go back home."

Not exactly.

Angelica pounced on Tricia as she reentered the Cookery. "What are you doing with my employees?"

"*Your* employees?" Tricia said, taken aback.

"Yes. I'm paying them. At least, I'm paying Mr. Everett for today."

"And he will be right back, as soon as he helps Ginny unload my car."

"You can't have him tomorrow."

"Yes, I can. I'm going to reopen, and it's his regular day to work. It's Ginny's day off. Maybe you can talk her into working for you."

Angelica exhaled loudly through her nose, her mouth immediately settling into a pout.

"Ange, the minute Stephanie quit, you should've called the temp agency."

"I did. They . . . they've—" Her cheeks colored and she lowered her voice to a whisper. "They've blackballed me."

"What?"

"They said I have a bad reputation, and they will no longer supply me with candidates."

"What are you going to do?"

"Tricia, you've got to let me have Ginny or Mr. Everett. Just for a couple of weeks. Please. *Please!*"

"It's not up to me, it's up to them. And let's face it, you haven't exactly endeared yourself to them in the past couple of days."

"I've been a lot nicer to them than I was to my own employees."

"That's only because you were desperate."

Angelica opened her mouth to protest, apparently thought better of it, and closed her mouth once more.

"Mr. Everett has already told me he's coming back to Haven't Got a Clue tomorrow. You can try and sweet-talk Ginny, but I don't know if you'll have any luck."

"I could offer her a bonus."

"That might work." Tricia turned and headed for the back of the store.

"Where are you going?"

"Upstairs to get my cat and the rest of my things. It's time for me to go home."

FOURTEEN

The circa-1935 black telephone by the register rang. From her perch on the sales counter, Miss Marple batted her little white paw at the offending jingle.

"Not again," Ginny wailed.

"You don't know it's Angelica," Tricia said, reaching for the receiver. The ringing stopped and she said, "Haven't Got a Clue, Tricia speak—"

"It's me," Angelica interrupted.

"Stop calling. Ginny told you she'd let you know in the morning. I'm hanging up now. Good-bye." She replaced the receiver and looked at her watch. "Whoa! Look at the time." It was nearly seven. "I've got a date tonight with Russ."

"And I've got a date tonight with a paintbrush," Ginny said. "We're working on the laundry room. Hopefully Brian got the right color this time. Men!" She reached for the duster.

"Leave that. You know it's Mr. Everett's favorite job. It'll give him something to do *and* make him happy tomorrow. Now, are you going to make Angelica happy and work for her tomorrow?"

Ginny sighed. "Yes. But she's going to have to sweat for it. I don't intend to call her until at least eleven tomorrow morning. Then Monday morning, I'm back here. That is, if it's okay with you."

"More than okay." Tricia smiled. "And thank you for helping Ange. She doesn't mean to be . . . mean—"

"She just is," Ginny finished.

Tricia shrugged. "Yeah." She reached for her coat, which still lay across the counter where she'd left it when she came in, and now sported a circle of cat hair where Miss Marple had made herself comfortable for most of the afternoon. Ordinarily Tricia wouldn't have allowed it, but the cat had been cooped up for days and Tricia felt she deserved a treat. And, besides, that's why she kept a sticky lint roller under the counter at all times, although she'd left it too late to use tonight. "Grab your coat, Ginny, we're out of here."

Tricia turned off all but the security lights. "You're in charge, Miss Marple," she said, and closed and locked the door.

Tricia and Ginny headed for the municipal parking lot. "They say it might snow tonight," Ginny said.

The streetlamps made it impossible to see much of the sky overhead. "Spring snow doesn't last long."

"We hope. See you tomorrow," Ginny said.

"You're going to the Cookery," Tricia reminded her.

"Shoot, I forgot already. It's just five hours. Every time Angelica makes me mad, I'm just going to tell myself it's only for five hours."

Tricia smiled. "See you Monday."

"Bye," Ginny said, and crossed the lot to her own car.

Tricia made it to Russ's house exactly on time. She hadn't even had a chance to raise her arm to knock on the front door before it was jerked open. "Tricia!" It sounded like he was greeting a long-lost friend. His hopeful expression and the way he practically bounced on his feet reminded her of a small child desperate to get back into someone's good graces.

"Hi, Russ." She stepped forward, planted a gentle kiss on his lips, then another, before he took her hand and pulled her over the threshold and into the brightly lit entryway.

"Let me take your coat," he said.

She handed him her coat and stepped into the living room.

No dim lights, no unpleasant aroma. In fact, no aroma at all. And, once again, the sound of the police scanner contributed to the lack of ambiance. Tricia sighed. Well, what did she expect? Maybe sending the flowers a few days before was all the romance Russ could muster. He was also probably dying to talk about the statue dedication, and she wasn't sure she was up to it. "What are we having for dinner?"

"Pizza. After last time, I figured it was a safe choice."

And easy. "Have you called it in yet?"

"I wanted to wait for you. I didn't want to take a chance on ordering the wrong toppings." And, unspoken, risking her ire. Okay, they would both be walking on eggshells with each other for a little while.

"I'll eat anything but anchovies . . . and maybe those terrible canned black olives."

"Veggies?" he offered.

"Always."

Squawk! "Dispatch to Two-A."

Russ's head snapped around as he listened to the police scanner.

"Two-A," said a disembodied voice.

"Respond to a noise complaint at seventeen Wilder Road. The complainant, who does not wish contact, is a neighbor directly across the street and reports loud music coming from the house for the last three hours."

"Two-A responding."

He turned back to Tricia, risked a smile. "Let's have a drink," he said, took her hand and led her to the living room couch. Scattered across the books and folded newspapers on the cocktail table were photographs of the vandalized statue he'd taken earlier that day, along with a bottle of white zinfandel and two glasses. He poured, offering her one of the glasses.

Tricia took it, but also picked up a photo. "What made you print them?"

"I thought you might like to see them."

She studied the picture. "It's a shame someone had to ruin the statue. If only Bob hadn't decided to dedicate it to Zoë." She wasn't about to elaborate on her theories to Russ. Let him find his own answers about the so-called writer's life—and her death.

"The whole thing was a fiasco, from start to finish," Russ said, leaning back against the cushions. "First of all, Bob should never have contracted with a Vermont quarry for the marble. He should've gone with granite. After all, New Hampshire is the Granite State. And as the head of the Chamber of Commerce, he's the first one to complain when someone doesn't support local business."

"Oh, you're right. A major faux pas," Tricia agreed.

"And then they ordered the inscription too late for the dedication, which made it easy for them to change the focus of the celebration. Let me tell you, more than a few of the booksellers are annoyed the Chamber would honor a woman who refused to help the village get established as a book town."

Tricia hadn't had an opinion on that before now, but she had to admit she agreed with the sentiment.

"Added to that, a bunch of the locals are upset that the Chamber is honoring an 'outsider.' At least it wasn't public money that paid for the statue. That would've really landed the Board of Selectmen in hot water."

"You're a Stoneham native. What do you think of outsiders?" Tricia asked.

"I love them," he answered without hesitation. "You in particular." He leaned forward to kiss her nose. "They've saved this burg from dying."

She set the photo down on the table and sat back on the couch, wishing they were in her own loft apartment. Was that what was wrong? In her own home she could control the atmosphere. Play soft music, dim the lights, light a few scented candles. Okay, she'd probably served pizza way too many times herself, but that was only because she wasn't very good at—or interested in—cooking, despite Angelica's offers to teach her a few basic recipes. Maybe she ought to reconsider that decision.

And maybe she should reconsider what she wanted out of the relationship. Russ was the only man she'd dated since her divorce less than two years ago. Could what they had even be called much of a relationship? Was she afraid to risk more heartbreak? If there was any spark between them, she'd spent little effort fanning what might burst into flames.

And he had been the first to say—in writing, no less—the word *love*.

"Did you read my top story in this week's issue?" Russ asked.

Tricia looked up at him. He wasn't at all like Christopher—and maybe that was something she found comforting. "Story?" she asked.

"Yeah, in the *Stoneham Weekly News*."

It took a moment for the question to register. Tricia hesitated before answering. She hadn't. The *Stoneham Weekly News* had arrived, but what with everything that had happened, it had been shunted into the trash—probably by Ginny. "Not yet," she said finally. "Didn't you say it concerned the geese problem?"

"Yes." He shook his head and frowned. "We have a murder right here in the village, and I come out with a story on goose shit."

"You're not psychic. You couldn't know someone would die," she said reasonably.

"Of course, the geese are just another one of Bob's problems."

"Surely it's up to the Village Board to deal with them, not the Chamber of Commerce."

"Yes, and privately Bob is advocating killing them."

"Frannie mentioned that was an option. She was pretty upset by the idea. But Bob seemed noncommittal when I spoke to him the other night."

"He knows you're a bleeding-heart animal lover—despite the inconvenience of cleaning up after the birds. He's not about to say what he really thinks in front of you."

"And what do you think?"

"About the geese?"

"No, about Bob."

Russ looked thoughtful. "Four years ago he almost single-handedly brought the village back from the brink of bankruptcy. That's pretty amazing."

"You didn't answer my question."

"Personally, I think the guy's a jerk. But you won't see that opinion in the *Stoneham Weekly News* any time soon."

A smile crept across Tricia's lips. Their eyes met, and she leaned in to kiss him.

Squawk! "Dispatch to Six-B."

"Six-B," came the reply.

She pulled back, lips pursed. "Russ," she said, speaking over the dispatcher, "do we have to listen to the scanner all evening?"

"Would you rather watch TV?"

"Not really. I want to sit and converse, although not about Zoë's death," she said adamantly. "Can't we talk about . . . I don't know . . . current events? Books? Music?"

"You're so interested in crime, I thought you were entertained by it."

"I'm interested in crime *stories*—fiction—not listening to noisy neighbor reports, or—"

"Fourteen Alpha and Six Charlie, respond to a burglary in progress at thirty-six Pine Avenue. Break."

"Thirty-six Pine Avenue?" Tricia repeated. "But that's Zoë Carter's house." She leaped up from the couch, nearly spilling her wine.

"Fourteen Alpha en route," came a voice from the scanner, quickly followed by "Six Charlie en route."

"Are you sure?" Russ asked, not as quick on his feet.

"Yes," she called behind her, already heading for the front closet and her coat.

"Where are you going?"

"Kimberly's staying at the house alone. That's only two blocks away! We might be able to get there quicker than the sheriff's deputies. Come on!" she yelled and was out the door, running for her car.

Ginny's prediction of snow had already come true in the few minutes Tricia had been inside Russ's house. A dusting covered the grass and the windshield of her car.

She'd hopped in, had the engine revving, and the wipers going when Russ finally slammed his front door and jogged to the car. He'd barely closed the passenger door when Tricia jammed her foot on the accelerator and spun the tires.

The car fishtailed on the damp pavement as she rounded the corner.

"Slow down!" Russ implored.

Hands gripping the steering wheel, Tricia paid no attention to her panicked passenger, turned the corner, and took out a piece of the corner lot's grass.

"I'm going to report you to the sheriff if you don't slow down," Russ hollered.

Tricia jammed on the brakes and the car shuddered to a halt at the curb in front of number thirty-six. She yanked open the door and started running toward the house.

"Hey, you! Stop!" Russ yelled, and began running in the opposite direction.

Every light in the house appeared to be switched on, and the front door was ajar. Without a thought—and probably foolishly—Tricia entered. "Kimberly! Kimberly!"

The living room had been ransacked. Pillows and sofa cushions slashed, books dumped on the floor. The shelves on one wall had been cleared of everything breakable. Porcelain figurines and ginger jars lay smashed on the carpeted floor. Tricia cast about, but found no sign of Kimberly.

"Kimberly, where are you?"

She stepped over the detritus and headed down the well-lit hallway. The bedroom door on the left was open. She poked her head inside, saw the bed had been dismantled, the sheets and blankets in a jumble on the floor, the mattress and box springs standing against the far wall—just the metal frame and dust bunnies marked where they had once been. Except for a few clothes on hangers, the closet was empty. Not much else populated the space. Was it because the house was in the process of being sold, or was Zoë as spare with her possessions as she had been with the details of her life?

Tricia moved on. The bedroom on the other side of the hall was in much the same condition. A couple of empty suitcases lay open on the floor, the mattress stood against the wall, the box springs askew, revealing nothing had been stored

beneath it. The dresser drawers all hung open, but there was nothing inside them, the contents—socks and underwear—were strewn across the floor.

"Kimberly?" Tricia called again.

Still no answer.

Tricia hurried on. The hallway dead-ended at what looked to be a home office—no doubt Zoë's inner sanctum—and it, too, had been turned upside down. Copies of the hardcover and paperback editions of the *Forever* books were scattered across the floor; a lamp lay smashed; pens, pencils, and other office supplies were spread among tapes and broken CDs and DVDs. The screen on a little television in an armoire was shattered. The glass from every picture had been smashed, the pictures themselves punched from the frames. Likewise, holes, three or four inches in diameter—from a sledgehammer?—marred the walls. And an old, battered trunk was upended in the corner, its contents dumped over the floor. It had suffered the same fate as the walls, with holes punched through its thin exterior.

A groan came from what appeared to be a bloody mass of clothes on the floor. "Kimberly!"

Tricia crouched and pulled back what had once been a white sweater. Kimberly's face was mottled, and her cheek was sunken; her blood-coated teeth hung broken, jagged in her gums. Tricia was glad she and Russ hadn't gotten as far as eating pizza, because her stomach roiled, but with nothing to bring up, she merely gagged.

Kimberly groaned again, and Tricia forced herself to turn back to the once attractive woman.

"The deputies are on their way," she managed, her voice catching.

Kimberly's hand groped for Tricia's, found it, her fingers slippery with her own blood. "Thone," she said through swelling lips.

"I don't understand."

"Thone," she tried again, almost frantic.

"I don't know what you mean."

Kimberly whimpered. "Thone," she said again.

Thone? "Phone?" Tricia tried.

Kimberly shook her head ever so slightly, a moan escaping.

Thone?

"Stone?" Tricia asked.

Kimberly nodded. For a moment her fingers tightened around Tricia's, and then went slack.

"Can't you ever mind your own business?" came a cold, hard voice from the open doorway.

Tricia started; she hadn't heard anyone approach. She looked up to see a grim-faced Sheriff Wendy Adams looming over her.

FIFTEEN

ZOË'S TINY KITCHEN was about the only room in the house that had escaped the madman's wrath. And surely it had to be a man who'd inflicted all the damage.

Unlike the night of Zoë's death, when Angelica had thrust a sustaining cup of coffee into Tricia's hand, now she had only a damp tissue to clutch. She sat at the little Formica table under Sheriff Adams's unrelenting glare. "Let's go over it again."

Tricia sighed. "We heard the call come over the police scanner. We raced right over. Russ went running across the yard and I came into the house."

The sheriff shook her head in disgust. "A tremendously stupid act," she said under her breath.

"Russ was chasing whoever ransacked the place and injured Kimberly," Tricia continued.

"There could've been more than one assailant. You didn't know there wasn't."

That was true. Still, their showing up had probably frightened the attacker away.

At least, that was what Tricia chose to believe.

"Get on with it," the sheriff prompted.

"I hurried through the house and found Kimberly in the office. Bloodied but breathing. Is she still alive?"

"She was when the ambulance pulled out of here."

Tricia shuddered at the thought of Kimberly's bashed and bloodied face. "Where's Russ?" she asked, in an effort to distract herself.

"Talking with one of my deputies."

"I take it he didn't catch the robber."

"No. Too bad he was our high school newspaper editor. He might've caught the perp if he'd lettered in track."

Tricia blinked. *Perp?* Wendy Adams sounded like a caricature of a TV lawman . . . er, woman.

The sheriff crossed her arms over her ample bosom and leaned against the

counter by the sink. "Now what was it Ms. Peters said to you before she lost consciousness?"

"Stone." Tricia frowned. "At least I think she said stone. It was hard to tell through those broken teeth."

"What do you think she meant by it?"

"The statue that was destroyed? What other explanation is there?"

"And she said nothing else?"

"She said it three times. I think she wanted to make sure I understood her."

Sheriff Adams's lips pursed. It didn't make her look any more attractive.

"Where did they take Kimberly?" Tricia asked.

"Southern New Hampshire Medical Center in Nashua. They've got a trauma center. If she makes it there."

A boulderlike weight seemed to rest on Tricia's chest. She hadn't been one of Kimberly's biggest fans, but she couldn't imagine how anyone could inflict such damage on another human being.

"Did you see any sign of a weapon?" the sheriff asked.

Tricia shook her head. "I assumed he—"

"Or she—"

"—used a sledgehammer. What else could've punched such holes in the walls and furniture?"

Sheriff Adams made no comment.

"I'll bet it was the same tool that smashed the statue."

Still no comment from the sheriff.

Tricia glanced at the clock over the sink and wondered if she should volunteer her suspicions about why a hammer-wielding burglar would ransack Zoë's home and critically injure Kimberly. The sheriff hadn't wanted to hear Tricia's theories about the murder at the Cookery some seven months before; she'd probably be less receptive now. But how much longer could she keep her suspicions to herself?

She needed more information. But how was she going to get it?

Tricia sighed. "Are we about finished, Sheriff?"

"Not quite. I'm going to tell you this once and only once; you are never to violate a crime scene again. What did you think you were doing, playing hero?"

Heroine, Tricia mentally corrected. No way would she say it aloud and set off Wendy Adams's hair-trigger temper. "I've read enough mysteries and true crime to know not to do that. And I did not violate a crime scene. I walked through the house, and I touched nothing but Kimberly Peters's hand. Giving her that tiny bit of comfort was the least I could do for her—the very least I would expect from anyone."

Wendy Adams's expression was doubtful. "I also don't want you talking to the press about any of this."

Tricia raised her hands defensively. "No problem there. In fact, I'm glad to have your blessing *not* to speak to them."

The sheriff merely glared at her. "Go home, Ms. Miles. And stay there." She turned her head toward the doorway. "Placer!" Seconds later, a deputy appeared. "Please escort Ms. Miles to her car. And keep an eye on her. We wouldn't want her to get hurt." She ended her little speech with a sneer.

Tricia got up from her chair. The sheriff didn't budge, and Tricia had to sidle past her in the tiny kitchen. She was glad to get away from the disaster that was Zoë's former home. Glad to inhale deep breaths of the cold, invigorating air.

Glad to get away from Wendy Adams.

Tricia pulled up Russ's driveway and eased the gearshift to Park. "Are you sure you don't want me to come home with you?" he asked.

"No. I just want to go home."

"I could keep you company," he offered with a wry smile.

"Not tonight," she said dryly.

"Don't I even get a good-night kiss?" Russ asked, still strapped in the passenger seat and making no move to leave.

"Just one," Tricia said, and leaned forward, aiming for his cheek, but Russ took her face in his hands, planting a light, warm kiss on her lips before pulling back.

"Maybe two," Tricia said, and put a little more effort into that kiss, remembering why she liked to spend quiet time with Russ. But not tonight. Her nerves were too taut, and Russ would only want to rehash the evening's events for hours on end. She needed something different. Someone different to talk things over with.

Russ pulled back. "I'll call you tomorrow."

"Okay."

He unbuckled the seat belt and got out of the car, shutting the door. He stood, watching, as she pulled out of the drive. He waved as she took off down the road. At the corner, she could still see him standing in his yard.

Instead of heading home, Tricia steered for the convenience store on the edge of town. She parked the car and rummaged in her purse for her cell phone, selected one of the preset numbers, and waited as it rang, two, three, four times.

"Hello?"

"Ange, it's Tricia. What are you doing tonight?"

Angelica sighed. "Unpacking boxes."

"Alone?"

"Yes," she said shortly. "And you don't have to rub it in."

"I'm not. I'd kind of like some company, and I was wondering . . . what kind of ice cream do you like?"

"Ice cream?" Angelica asked, her voice rising with pleasure. "Oh, anything. But I especially like butter pecan, pralines and cream, and—what the heck—rocky road. Do you need more suggestions?"

"That'll do."

"Get some of that canned whipped cream. And nuts. Maybe cherries, too. If we're going to splurge, we may as well go whole hog."

"See you in about twenty minutes," Tricia said, and folded up her phone.

True to her word, she arrived at the Cookery's door precisely nineteen and a half minutes later, and let herself in.

Angelica met her at the top of the stairs to the loft apartment. No Miss Marple greeted her. In all the excitement, Tricia had forgotten she'd taken the cat and all her equipment home.

Angelica led her back to the kitchen, where the light was better, frowning as she took in her sister's face. "What happened? You look pale. Did you and Russ have another spat?"

Tricia shook her head. "I had a bit of a shock this evening."

"Hang up your coat. I'll unpack the grocery sack, and we'll talk."

Tricia handed over the bag with its four pints of ice cream and all the trimmings. Angelica had its contents spread across the kitchen island, along with spoons and dishes, by the time Tricia returned to the kitchen.

Tricia looked around the room. The long line of boxes that had been stacked against the wall for months was considerably smaller. Several pictures had been tacked up on the walls, giving the kitchen a much homier appearance. Not prints, but antique oil paintings of fruits and vegetables—succulent strawberries, dew-kissed pears, and sun-ripened tomatoes. They reflected Angelica's love of food—her joy in its preparation and the care she took with its presentation. Tricia looked into the living room. There was actually a coffee table in front of the couch! Okay, it was still covered in boxes, but it was at least visible, and she saw pots of herbs on the sills in front of the street-side windows. "Wow, you've made a lot of headway with your unpacking tonight."

"Forget the decor; tell me what happened," Angelica demanded, removing the lid from a pint of butter pecan.

Tricia recounted her evening. From the lack of romance at Russ's home to finding a bloodied Kimberly to Wendy Adams's stern interrogation.

As Angelica listened, she plopped a big scoop of ice cream into her bowl,

added some whipped cream, sprinkled it with crushed nuts, and topped it with a maraschino cherry. "Oh, you poor little thing," she cooed, not without sympathy, when Tricia finished.

Tricia scraped a small spoonful of French vanilla but didn't put it in her mouth. Suddenly the idea of all that sweetness was a turnoff. She set the container aside. "You should've seen that house. There was hatred in every swing of that hammer—sledgehammer—whatever it was."

"What were they looking for? The original manuscripts Zoë passed off as her own? Why would they think Kimberly would have them there? Didn't you say Zoë's main residence was down south somewhere?"

Tricia nodded. "And I can't imagine her keeping them. The woman was an accountant—or at least some kind of bookkeeper, which might indicate she had a logical mind. I'm sure she got rid of them years ago. Kimberly said she retyped a couple of them. And if Zoë was smart, she burned the originals so there'd be no paper trail."

Angelica shook her head, took another spoonful of ice cream. "And Russ had no clue who he was chasing?"

"Just someone in dark sweats and a hoodie."

Angelica frowned. "Didn't you say there was no sign of a hammer in the house?"

Tricia nodded.

Angelica shook her head, frowning. "That doesn't make sense. It would be pretty difficult, if not impossible, to run while carrying a sledgehammer. The handles are like three feet long."

"We're not sure it actually was a sledgehammer."

"From the way you described those holes in the walls, what else could it be? And you're no slouch when it comes to those kinds of details."

Modesty prevented Tricia from agreeing.

"So," Angelica continued, "where do you think the bad guy threw the hammer? In some bushes? Was this person already in the neighbor's yard when Russ took off after him—her—whoever?"

Tricia thought back. Everything had happened so fast. "I'm not sure. I ran straight for the open front door, and Russ didn't, so I guess maybe that could have happened. A couple of deputies followed the trail in the snow, but it petered out on the street. They talked about bringing in some dogs, but Russ said he lost the runner after about a block. He thought he heard a car start up on the next street over, but he couldn't be sure if it was just a neighbor or the person he was chasing."

Angelica added some more whipped cream to her bowl. "It's pretty cold out, but I've got plenty of long underwear and fresh batteries in my big flash-

light. What say we take a field trip to Pine Avenue and have a look for that hammer?"

Tricia pushed her spoon and the virtually untouched container of ice cream aside. "Oh, no. Sheriff Adams warned me off, and I don't intend to disobey her. Besides, I'm sure she's already combing the neighborhood for it."

"Are you afraid of the sheriff?"

"Yes! She shut down my business for four days. I'm not going to give her a reason to do it again."

Angelica stuck out her tongue. "Party pooper!"

Tricia shook her head. "I think I'm just plain pooped." She stood. "Time for me to go home. To my cat. To my *own* bed." The thoughts cheered her.

Angelica's expression was a cross between a frown and a pout. "I can't say I'm happy you're going home."

Of course not. If the store had been closed a few more days, she'd have a reprieve from finding permanent replacement workers as long as Ginny and Mr. Everett had nowhere else to go.

"I'm going to miss you, Trish. It was fun having you here. While I was alone here tonight, I realized I even miss Miss Marple."

Tricia swallowed, feeling guilty for her sarcastic thought. She felt even worse when Angelica came around the island and gathered her in her arms for a hug.

SIXTEEN

Tricia woke at seven the next morning to the sound of a flock of honking geese flying over her building. Why was it they made such a pleasant noise and such an unpleasant mess? As the sound faded, she threw back the covers and got up to revel in her usual Sunday morning routine: three miles on the treadmill, a shower, and then a satisfying breakfast of a microwave-thawed bagel with cream cheese and coffee. Miss Marple had been especially happy to return to her favorite haunts and eat her meals in her usual spot. All was right once again in Miss Marple's world, and she let Tricia know it with her continuous happy purring.

First on Tricia's agenda was tidying her shop. Although the store had been closed to customers, it had still accumulated an inordinate amount of dust.

Dusting was Mr. Everett's favorite job, so she decided that she'd give the washroom another going over. Despite all her efforts the afternoon before, she feared she'd missed cleaning all the messy black fingerprint powder, and she wanted to give Haven't Got a Clue a thorough vacuuming before the store opened.

Then she remembered Artemus Hamilton was leaving Stoneham this morning. She took a chance, phoned the Brookview Inn, and found him still there.

"Mr. Hamilton? It's Tricia Miles. I'm glad I caught you before you checked out."

"By any chance are you related to an Angelica Miles?" he asked.

"Um . . . yes," she said, taken aback. "She's my sister."

"I just had a visit from her. She brought me fresh-baked muffins, hot coffee, and a manuscript." He didn't sound pleased.

"I'm so sorry. I tried to tell her she should query you, but she's very new to bookselling and knows virtually nothing about the publishing business."

"That much was obvious. Now why were you calling?"

"I'm afraid I have some disturbing news."

"News?" he repeated, dully.

"It's about Kimberly Peters. I'm afraid there's been—" Accident wasn't the right word. "I'm sorry to tell you she was attacked in Zoë's home last night. She was taken to Southern New Hampshire Hospital in Nashua. I'm sorry, I don't know what her condition is."

"Attacked?" he repeated, sounding much more interested.

"Yes." Tricia proceeded to fill him in on the previous evening's events.

"Oh, my," he said, sounding rather shell-shocked by the time Tricia finished her recitation.

"I know she's not your client or anything, but I thought you might like to know."

"Yes. Thank you. And you say she's at a hospital in Nashua?"

"Yes."

"Perhaps—" He stopped, and Tricia was surprised to hear a catch in his voice. "Perhaps I'll send her some flowers before I leave."

"That would be nice," Tricia said, and then mentally amended—*if she survives.* "Have you got a ride to the airport?"

"Yes. The inn's shuttle will take me. Thanks for asking. And thank you for calling, Ms. Miles." Hamilton hung up.

Tricia frowned, annoyed at his abrupt dismissal. She exhaled a long breath, but decided not to worry about it. She had other things to do.

Miss Marple danced around the door to the stairwell, and Tricia was just about to head downstairs when the phone rang. She glanced at the little read-

out, but didn't recognize the number on caller ID. She picked up the receiver anyway, hoping it wouldn't be Portia McAlister. "Hello?"

"Tricia?" Whew! It was Ginny.

"You sound awful. What's wrong?"

"I'm just tired. I spent most of the night in the emergency room at Southern New Hampshire Medical Center in Nashua."

"How did you know about Kimberly?"

"Kimberly?" Ginny echoed, sounding puzzled.

"Yes, she was taken there by ambulance last night after being attacked in Zoë's home."

"That's terrible. But I wasn't there for her. I drove Brian in somewhere around midnight. He was so sick. He came over all pale and clammy early last evening. He was vomiting and had diarrhea. He wouldn't let me call an ambulance, but after three or four hours of this, he agreed to let me drive him to the emergency room."

"Appendicitis?" Tricia guessed.

"No. They think it was food poisoning. I admit I'm not that great a cook, but how can you ruin soup and sandwiches? The fridge came with the house, and I don't think it keeps food cold enough. It was probably the sliced ham. We'd had it for almost a week."

"Were you sick?"

"No. But we didn't eat the same things. I had a slice of pizza from the convenience store down the road. The doctor said it will probably be tomorrow before the lab can identify what made Brian so ill."

"I'm really sorry about this, Ginny. Is Brian home now?"

"Yes, but he's so weak, I don't think I should leave him. Will you tell Frannie I can't make it to the diner?"

"Diner?"

"Yeah, the Tuesday Night Book Club is meeting there. A cheer-up brunch for Nikki."

"Oh, dear, I completely forgot about it."

"Can you do me another favor? I was afraid to call Angelica. I know she was counting on me to come in today."

"Don't worry about Ange. I'll explain it all. And if Brian needs you tomorrow, don't feel you have to come to work."

"But I do have to come in. Especially if we're going to have to replace the fridge now, too. And I don't know how we're going to pay the hospital bill. We don't have any insurance," she said with a small sob.

Tricia could well afford to give Ginny the money she needed to buy a refrigerator or pay the hospital bill, but she also knew Ginny was proud. Too proud

to take what she hadn't earned. She'd have to think of some way to give her a bonus. But then she also knew Ginny would insist that Mr. Everett be treated in the same way. She'd been lucky in hiring two of the hardest-working, best employees in all of Stoneham. And why was it so hard to be generous and not appear to be fawning?

"Do what you have to do, Ginny. You know I'm behind you."

"Thanks, Tricia. I'm just worried that Angelica will think I'm trying to screw her. I'm not. Really. Please, make her understand."

"I will. Now you take care of yourself *and* Brian. And keep me posted."

"Thanks. I will." And Ginny broke the connection.

Tricia hung up her phone. Now the real work began. Convincing Angelica that Ginny *wasn't* just out to annoy her. The thing was . . . could she spare Mr. Everett, who did not want to work for Angelica, and since she hadn't been open in days, could she really do without any help?

Her mind raced. Mr. Everett had made it plain he did *not* want to return to the Cookery. Tricia thought of everyone she knew in Stoneham—was there anyone she could call upon to lend a hand?

She grabbed her local phone book, flipped through the pages, and came up with the name of someone she thought might help. She punched in the number and recited a silent prayer.

The phone rang once, twice, and was answered on the third ring.

"Hello?"

"Frannie?"

"Is that you, Tricia?" came the oh-so-familiar Texas twang.

"Yes. Frannie, I'm calling to let you know Ginny can't make it to the diner for Nikki's brunch this morning. Her boyfriend is very ill and she doesn't want to leave him."

"Oh, that poor thing. I hope he'll be better soon."

"She thinks so. Frannie, I also have a very, very big favor to ask of you."

Frannie laughed, a joy-inspiring sound like that of an angel. "What's up?"

"You know my sister Angelica owns the Cookery—the cookbook store."

"Oh, sure. I was in there the other day, remember? She's got the most marvelous gadgets hanging up on her north wall. I swear I could've spent an entire paycheck in there."

"Well, she's got a really big problem. She's lost her sales force." Tricia had to bite her tongue not to say why. "If you're not doing anything this afternoon, would you consider spending a few hours helping her out?"

Tricia squeezed her eyes shut, held her breath, and crossed her fingers.

"If this was football season, I'd have to say no. I watch all the Patriots games—and the Dallas games, if they ever show 'em. But right now—I'm

champing at the bit to do something I've never tried before! So, yes, I'd be glad to give your sister a hand."

"You would?" Tricia said, hoping she didn't sound too astonished.

"Yeah. I was just gonna sit around here and watch an Audrey Hepburn marathon on American Movie Classics, but it sounds a whole lot more fun to spend the day talking about food."

"So—so, you'll come to the Cookery?"

"Sure. What time does your sister need me?"

"Come about eleven thirty. That way she can give you a brief overview of the store and how she operates."

"Sure. We'll be done with brunch by that time."

Tricia winced, hoping that by Monday Frannie would not be her newest enemy. "Great," she managed. "I'll tell Angelica that you'll be there before she opens. I really owe you, Frannie."

Frannie laughed, the sound of her voice pure gold. "Not at all. I think this will be a blast. Woo-hoo! Today will sure be a lot more interesting than what I'd planned."

Yeah, and may you *not* live in interesting times, as the old Chinese curse proclaimed.

"See you at the diner," Tricia said. They said good-bye, and she hung up.

Tricia had to fortify herself with a very strong cup of coffee before she dared dial Angelica's number. She picked it up on the third ring.

"Ange, it's Tricia."

"Hey, what's up?"

"First of all, why did you take your manuscript to the Brookview Inn?"

"Because that's where Artemus Hamilton is staying. I figured this morning would be my only chance to get it to him before he leaves for New York."

"You could've mailed it to him."

"That's so tedious, and why bother when a personal visit is so much more—"

"Annoying? Presumptuous? Impolite?" Tricia interrupted.

"Personal," Angelica finished. "I think he was charmed by me and my presentation. I'll look forward to receiving an acceptance letter in the coming weeks."

She was absolutely clueless.

"Believe it or not, I didn't call to talk about your manuscript. Now don't get mad, but Ginny can't work for you today."

"What?" came Angelica's scorching voice.

"I said don't get mad. Her boyfriend has been hospitalized, and she needs to be with him today."

"Oh. Well, I guess I can understand that," Angelica said, not sounding at all convincing.

"He's going to be okay, but even better, I've found somebody willing to give you a hand for today at least."

"Who?" Angelica demanded, not in the least placated.

"Frannie Armstrong."

"Oh, Frannie?" She almost sounded pleased. "That sounds quite all right. Thanks, Trish."

Tricia resisted the urge to exhale a breath of relief. "Good. Well, I told her to show up half an hour before you open. That should give you all the time you need to train her." No, it didn't, but it sounded reasonable.

"Oh, Trish, you are a savior." No, she wasn't, because she hadn't been willing to offer up Mr. Everett as a sacrificial lamb. And really, would Frannie hate her forever after several hours of unpleasant servitude at the Cookery?

Maybe. But right now she was willing to take the chance.

MISS MARPLE BOUNDED down the stairs to the shop, eager to get back to work sunning herself on the counter, dusting the higher shelves with her fluffy tail, or just taking a nap on one of the comfy chairs in the nook.

Tricia crossed the store to open the blinds over the big display window. The sight of the News Team Ten van greeted her. Standing outside it, looking a bit windblown and partially frozen, was Portia McAlister.

Feeling a tad sorry for the woman, Tricia opened her door. "You look like you could use a cup of hot coffee."

"Could I ever," Portia said.

"Where's your cameraman?"

"At the diner. He wanted something a little more substantial."

Tricia held the door wide open and sighed. "Come on in."

Portia wasted no time.

Tricia shut the door. "Look, the sheriff says I can't talk to you about Zoë's murder or what happened to Kimberly Peters last night."

Portia frowned. "She's gotten to everyone. There *is* such a thing as freedom of speech in this country, you know."

"I'm a firm believer in it myself. I also firmly believe in not annoying Wendy Adams," Tricia said, and stepped over to the store's coffee station.

A sly smile crept onto Portia's lips. "Yes, I understand you've had a run-in with her before."

"Something else I'm not interested in talking about."

"Then why did you invite me in?"

"Because I'm tired of trying to avoid you."

"It's my job to be persistent. And you're making that job very difficult."

"Sorry. It can't be helped."

Portia straightened. "If you can't tell me about the crimes against Carter and her niece, at least tell me why you're so interested in them yourself."

"Initially I wanted to get my store open. Wendy Adams had me shut down for days. Longer than was technically necessary."

"And now?"

"Let's just say I'm not sure the Sheriff's Department is following every one of their leads." *And are clueless about some potential leads*, she kept herself from voicing aloud.

Portia leaned her elbows on the counter. "You know, I could be a big help to you. I know things about the case you probably don't."

"Such as?"

"I'm not about to spill them without getting something in return."

Tricia hoisted the coffee grounds basket into the air. "I did offer you coffee."

"I can get that from the diner."

"You do have that option."

"Come on, Tricia, toss me something. Just a crumb."

Tricia thought about it. It might be better to get someone with the tenacity of a terrier in on the hunt. Someone who could ask questions and redirect Wendy Adams's anger away from Tricia's inquiries.

"How do you feel about revealing your sources?"

"I spent a week in jail back in the spring of 2003 to protect one. I have to tell you, those orange jumpsuits are ugly as hell, and the fabric chafes, but I'd do it over again if I had to."

Tricia poured water into the coffeemaker and hit the On switch. She'd promised Artemus Hamilton she wouldn't say anything about Zoë not writing the Jess and Addie books until after the weekend. That was before someone had gone after and nearly killed Kimberly Peters.

"Okay, I'm ready to dish. Years ago, several of Stoneham's citizens questioned whether Zoë Carter actually wrote any of the books she's credited with."

Portia's eyes widened. "Interesting. Did they have any proof?"

Tricia shook her head. "No, but their suspicions got me looking into things."

"And you don't believe she wrote the books, either?"

"I *know* she didn't write them. I've had it confirmed from two sources."

"Would one of them be Kimberly Peters?"

"I'm not saying. You asked me to toss you a crumb. That was it. Now it's your turn to give up something."

Portia straightened and smoothed back her hair. "Okay. Fair is fair. Like you, I've been looking into Zoë Carter's background. It seems she was indicted for embezzlement back in the 1990s."

Tricia waved a hand in dismissal. "I saw your report online days ago."

"Ah, but I didn't tell the whole story. She got off by turning in her boss—her ex-lover. The court was lenient because she had no prior convictions and had recently taken in her orphaned niece. It was very unusual. She may have had some kind of political in, although I haven't been able to figure out the exact connection."

"It's still old news," Tricia said.

Portia chewed her lip for a moment, as though considering. "Zoë was being blackmailed."

"The person who wrote the letters has come forward. The sheriff investigated that angle and moved on to other things."

Portia frowned and sighed. "You *have* been persistent."

"I had good teachers," Tricia said, and waved a hand to take in all the mystery stories on the bookshelves around them.

"Okay, but this is the last thing I'm offering up." Portia leaned closer, lowered her voice. "As a girl, Zoë Carter wanted to be a nun."

"A nun?" Tricia repeated, surprised. Then again, Zoë dressed so conservatively, and her lifestyle was so . . . bland. But no one she'd spoken to had mentioned Zoë had deep religious convictions.

Portia nodded. "She got kicked out of the convent for improper behavior. With a little digging, I found out it was for stealing. Apparently she wasn't quite able to honor her vow of poverty. I guess her indictment for embezzlement several years later shouldn't have come as a huge surprise."

Maybe, but despite the millions she'd raked in as the so-called author of the *Forever* books, she hadn't lived the life of a millionaire, either.

"None of this seems to have anything to do with her getting murdered in my store."

"Nothing we *yet* know about. She had so many skeletons in the closet, I'm surprised no other reporters dug deep to find the truth about her before this."

"Yes, it would've been great fodder for the tabloids, especially as she was such a hermit when it came to book promotion."

"If you can't tell me about your run-ins with Zoë dead and Kimberly just attacked, tell me what you make of that ruined statue."

"Same thing as you do—that Zoë's killer did it."

"Any suspects?" Portia pushed.

Tricia shook her head. "Not so far."

"And why attack Kimberly?"

"To retrieve the original manuscripts?" Tricia suggested.

"Why?"

"To conceal who wrote them."

"Conceal or reveal?"

Tricia nodded. "Good question."

The coffeemaker stopped bubbling as the last of the brew dripped into the pot.

"If what you said about Zoë not writing the books is true, it's just another chink in her armor," Portia said.

"What are you going to do with that piece of knowledge?"

"I'm going to find out the truth. And I'm going to report it. Maybe I can even parlay it into a job in a better market."

"Better than Boston?" Tricia asked.

"Hey, winter in LA is a lot warmer than here on the East Coast."

"Can I count on you to tell me what you find out?" Tricia asked, pouring coffee for them both and handing one of the cups to Portia.

"Possibly. Can I expect the same from you?"

"Count on it."

They touched their paper coffee cups in a toast.

SEVENTEEN

TRICIA ALWAYS CONSIDERED the Bookshelf Diner's name a bit of a misrepresentation. After all, she didn't know of many diners with a function room. Whether it was a diner or a family restaurant, it did indeed offer this amenity, and it was usually reserved for private parties, baby and wedding showers, and after-funeral-service occasions. The theme of its decor was unidentifiable; no doubt its creamy walls and the nondescript purple-gray floral border that ran just below the room's ceiling were deliberate choices, so that the room could be used for any purpose. In this instance, the occasion was more supportive than celebratory.

A long table had been set up in the center of the room, with unused smaller tables and extra chairs pushed off to the side. A stab at elegance had been attempted, but the linen tablecloth, though clean, had seen its share of spilled wine.

Tricia arrived later than she'd wanted, and was seated at one end of the table. The guest of honor was seated directly opposite her at the far end of the table, with at least four book club members and several of Nikki's other friends

in between. Nikki's assistant, Steve Fenton, sat at her left, looking uncomfortable in the presence of so many women. He'd made an effort to spiff up, too. The do-rag was gone and the sleeves of his denim shirt were rolled up, revealing his heavily muscled arms.

Among the missing, Grace Harris and Mr. Everett. Tricia hadn't expected to see her employee—he never spent money frivolously—but she'd more than half expected to see his lady friend, who often acted as the book group's unofficial spokesperson.

"Glad you could make it," Frannie said, handing Tricia a menu.

"Where's Grace?" Tricia asked, noting an empty chair at the middle of the table.

"Grace Harris come to a diner?" Frannie asked, incredulous.

"Why not? I never got the impression she was a snob."

"Oh, I didn't mean that. She's the nicest woman on the face of the planet," Frannie hurriedly attested. "It's just that she's so classy, what with her lovely clothes and jewelry. I would just never expect her to get down and dirty and eat eggs, bacon, and home fries with ketchup."

Tricia had to agree with that statement. And it was also true that, gracious as she was, it was the reading and the discussion of the books that she enjoyed, not necessarily the company of the people in the group. Except for Mr. Everett, that is.

Tricia glanced at her menu. She'd already eaten a bagel, and wasn't the least bit hungry. Maybe she'd just order toast and a cup of anything other than coffee. She set the menu aside.

"Anyway," Frannie started, addressing the others, "as I was telling you, if you don't want to be responsible for the deaths of innocent creatures, you've got to contact the Board of Selectmen and tell them."

"They wouldn't really kill the geese, would they?" Julia Overline asked.

"I don't care if they do," said a woman in a blue sweater, sitting farther up the table. "They're messy and they're noisy. Think of all the homeless people we could feed with them."

Oh, yeah, that's the answer, Tricia thought, considering all the health regulations that proposed solution would violate. Some people just didn't have a clue . . . or were just woefully ignorant. She chose to think the latter.

At the head of the table, Nikki sat in animated conversation with a woman Tricia didn't know.

"Poor Nikki. I'm glad so many people showed up to cheer her up," Frannie said, changing the subject.

"She's worked so hard," Julia piped up. Of all the members of the book group, Tricia knew Julia the least. Gray-haired and plump, wearing a floral-

embroidered sweatshirt, she was a voracious reader who'd recently joined the readers group, and had bought at least ten books, which certainly endeared her to Tricia. "She's had such a rough life. The family's home burned to the ground when she was just an infant. Her father died, too, but that was years after her mother's disappearance."

Tricia blinked. "Her mother's what?"

"Disappearance—when Nikki was just a young girl. It was the talk of Stoneham for months."

"And she was never found?"

Julia shook her head.

"Did the authorities feel it was foul play?" Tricia asked

Julia shrugged. "She just disappeared. No sign of a struggle, or blood, or anything. She didn't take any clothes. Her purse was still in her home. Her car was parked in the driveway. She was just gone."

"Didn't they suspect her husband?"

Julia shrugged. "Of course. After all, it was no secret he used to hit the poor woman. But they never arrested him for it. He was at work—with witnesses—the day she disappeared."

Tricia knew that in cases like the one Julia described, the husband was always suspected—especially if the relationship had involved domestic abuse. "How old was Nikki at the time?"

"Nine or ten. Years later they had her mother declared dead in order to settle the estate so Nikki could go to that fancy pastry institute in Paris."

"They? Who's they?"

"Nikki's grandmother and her aunt—Phil's mother and sister."

Poor Nikki. Tricia had never really been as close to her mother as she would've liked. Angelica had been the child her parents never thought they'd have. Tricia's arrival five years later had been a surprise, and perhaps not as welcome as that of the favored Angelica. But Tricia had had her grandmother to love. A grandmother who'd imparted to her the love of books—especially mysteries.

"Sounds like Nikki's a real fighter," Tricia said.

"She sure is," Frannie agreed, and took a sip of her ice water. "Which is why I'm sure she'll bounce back from this loan disappointment. And speaking of fighting, just look at the muscles on that guy's arms," she said, with an admiring glance at Fenton.

"Oh, yes," Julia agreed. "It's so sad about him, too."

"Sad?" Tricia asked.

"He was once considered a shoo-in for the Olympic track team, until he hurt one of his knees."

"He used to be a personal trainer at the Stoneham gym." Julia gave Tricia a knowing glance. "You don't think he developed all those heavenly muscles lifting trays of cookies and cakes, do you?"

"Gym?" Tricia asked. There was no gym in Stoneham.

"It folded before you got here," Frannie explained.

Tricia studied the hunk at Nikki's side. He had to be a decade older than Nikki—more Tricia's age—reminding her of a younger, more handsome version of Bruce Willis. "Are they involved?"

"Not a chance," Julia answered, and laughed. "Nikki told me she was through with men after her divorce. They say she married a man just like her father—and just as abusive."

"I've seen Steve walking or jogging around the village or out on the road to Route 101," Tricia said.

"Of course. He doesn't drive, you know."

"Why is that?" Tricia asked.

Julia shrugged. "I guess because he's such a fitness nut. I've also seen him tooling around the village on a bike in good weather."

Frannie leaned closer, spoke with a hint of excitement in her voice. "I heard you were involved in some excitement last night."

"Me?" Tricia said, frowning.

"Yes, it's all over town that you and Russ Smith chased away a burglar and saved Kimberly Peters's life."

"Oh, that," Tricia said, and looked around, hoping to see the waitress and snag a cup of something hot.

"Did you really?" Julia asked eagerly. Obviously the whole town *wasn't* talking about it. Conversation around the table had stopped, all of them now looking at Tricia, waiting for her to spill the whole story.

"It wasn't that big a deal. Kimberly had already called 911. We just got there before the deputies did."

"What about the burglar?" Julia asked.

"Russ went after him, but he got away."

"Kimberly? Wasn't she that awful young woman at the signing with Zoë Carter?" Julia asked.

Tricia nodded.

"Why do you think someone came after her?" Frannie asked.

"I have no idea," Tricia lied.

"I heard Kimberly's in critical condition," Frannie said. Had she called the hospital to find out, or had she relied on her network of friendly informants to get this information?

"I didn't know that," Tricia said.

Frannie nodded. "She suffered head injuries. It's touch and go if she'll live." She shook her head and *tsk*ed. "I've been reading a lot of detective books lately, you know, and I think Kimberly's attacker was probably the same person who killed her aunt."

"Oh, that's obvious," Julia said. "But the funny thing is . . . it's probably someone we all know." Her gaze flitted around the table. "Someone who was in your store on Tuesday, Tricia."

As though she hadn't already considered that fact one hundred times. Then again, there was no one she would even think could be capable of such a heinous act.

Still, she wondered about Grace. How she'd suddenly left town either the night of the murder or the morning after. And Mr. Everett had lied about it. But there was no way Grace had killed Zoë. She'd been accounted for during the entire ten or fifteen minutes Zoë had been absent from the group.

It couldn't be Grace. Grace, who'd had some as yet unknown beef with Zoë.

But what if the killer was someone Grace knew? Someone she'd tried to shield? What if—?

"Can I take your order?" Janice, the Bookshelf Diner's weekend waitress stood by Tricia's elbow. She'd been so lost in thought, she hadn't even noticed her arrival.

"Just an order of wheat toast and a cup of tea, please."

Frannie tapped Tricia's arm. "No wonder you've managed to keep your figure. You never eat anything fattening."

"That you know of," Tricia said, and forced a laugh.

Janice continued circling the table until she'd taken all the orders, then retreated. The woman in the blue sweater tapped her water glass, gaining everyone's attention. She stood up and held her glass up in a toast. "Stoneham has, unfortunately, had a spate of serious crime. What one individual has done has shaken many of us. And yet it can't be argued that our little town isn't safe. It's outsiders that have attracted the wrong element." Her gaze momentarily settled on Tricia before moving back to the head of the table. "The real citizens of Stoneham know what true friendship is. That's why we're here this morning, to show our love and support to our dear friend, Nikki."

"Hear, hear," someone echoed.

Tricia's cheeks flushed. She glanced at Frannie to find her tight-lipped, and her complexion just as rosy.

The woman sat down.

"Of all the nerve," Frannie muttered under her breath.

Though this wasn't the first time Tricia had experienced the undercurrent of an us-against-them mentality from some of the denizens of Stoneham, she hadn't ever heard anyone voice that sentiment so blatantly.

Nikki stood and cleared her throat. "Thanks, Linda. I can't thank everyone—and I mean *everyone*—enough for coming here today." She focused her attention on Tricia and Frannie, and laughed nervously. "You guys *are* the best."

Everyone at the table broke into applause, with Frannie clapping the loudest.

IT WASN'T HARD to get back into the groove of hand-selling mysteries, and Tricia fell in love with her store all over again. Mr. Everett was back to his cheerful self, and Miss Marple luxuriated in the afternoon sunshine that poured through Haven't Got a Clue's front display window. Trade was brisk for a Sunday, and only a few people loitered around the washroom, hoping for some titillating clue about Zoë Carter's murder. The fingerprint powder had been nearly impossible to fully clean, and every time Tricia shooed away some curious gawker, she saw another spot of the stuff that needed eradicating.

She'd just shut the washroom door for the fifth time when Mr. Everett signaled her from the register. "We're out of coffee, Ms. Miles. I made a pot before the last crowd of customers came in. It won't last until closing. Shall I go get another couple of pounds?"

Tricia shook her head. "I'll go. And I'll pick up a few goodies from the patisserie. Can you handle everything here for ten or fifteen minutes?"

He nodded, always dignified. "Certainly."

"I'll just grab my coat, then."

Though the temperature was only in the forties, the sunshine felt warm on her cheeks as she stopped first at the Coffee Bean, then made her way down Main Street to the Stoneham Patisserie.

For the first time in a long time, the patisserie was not overflowing with customers. Nikki stood behind the counter, waiting on a customer who bought a loaf of cinnamon raisin bread. She rang up the sale. "Have a nice day," she said, and turned to Tricia.

"I'm surprised to see you here."

"Why?"

"Isn't Haven't Got a Clue back in business?"

"Yes, thank goodness. Mr. Everett is holding down the fort. I just came to get some cookies for our customers."

"I've got some nice raspberry thumbprint cookies." She leaned forward, lowered her voice to a whisper. "I think they're Mr. Everett's favorites."

"Then how about two dozen of those? If any are left over, he can take them home."

"Sure. Let me wrap them up."

The door opened and another customer entered. "Nikki, I need three loaves of Italian bread—now! I've got guests arriving in ten minutes, and—"

Nikki looked from her new customer to Tricia, who waved a hand. "Take care of her first. I'm not in a rush."

"Thanks," Nikki said gratefully.

Tricia wandered the store, peeking through the display cases at the bread, cookies, cakes, and pies. Pretty pedestrian fare for someone who'd trained in Paris, but if that was what the local traffic demanded, that's what Nikki had to supply.

The door from the shop to the working bakery beyond was propped open with a rubber wedge, and Tricia noted the now-silent industrial-sized mixer and bowl, which currently sported a bread hook. Angelica had a regular-sized model on her kitchen counter. She recognized a bread slicer and saw a metal cabinet filled with trays of baked goods. It was from there that Nikki gathered the cookies. Steve stood at a counter with what looked like a nail in one hand and a pastry bag in the other, magically producing a beautiful rose out of pink icing. He plopped it on the frosted cake in front of him and started another.

Tricia's bored gaze wandered, but soon stopped on the floor against the far wall, focusing on something she hadn't expected to see in a bakery: a satchel of tools. Sticking out of the top were a can of spray paint and what looked like a . . . sledgehammer. But it couldn't be. Sledgehammers had long handles, and this hammer's head stuck out of a bag that could be only nine or ten inches in height. And why did Nikki have a bag of tools in the working part of her bakery?

Nikki finished plucking cookies from the tray and brought the bakery box back into the shop, setting it on the counter and tying string around it. Tricia handed her a ten and Nikki made change.

"Thanks," Tricia said, pocketing the money.

"Are you okay?" Nikki asked, concerned. "You look kind of funny."

Tricia forced a smile. "I'm fine."

"Thanks for coming to the diner this morning. Only I can't apologize enough for Linda's rude comments about 'the wrong element' here in Stoneham. Honest, Tricia, not everyone in the village thinks like her. I tried to give Frannie a call and apologize to her, too, but she wasn't home."

"No, she's helping Angelica at the Cookery this afternoon."

"She's got a big heart."

The door opened and another customer wandered in.

"I'd better go," Tricia said, sounding nervous even to herself.

"See you on Tuesday at the book club," Nikki called, as Tricia made good her escape.

"Is something wrong, Ms. Miles?" Mr. Everett asked as Tricia closed and locked the shop door on the last of their customers. The clock read five o'clock even.

"No." That wasn't true, especially not when her suspicions about Nikki had so recently been ignited. "Yes, there are several things wrong. One of them concerns you, Mr. Everett." It was time to clear the air at last.

"Me?" he asked, puzzled.

"Something you said the other day. You told me Grace had to leave town to take care of a sick sister. When I mentioned to her that I was sorry to hear about it, she told me she didn't have a sister."

Mr. Everett lowered his head so that his gaze was focused on the carpet.

"It's none of my business what Grace was doing or where she went, but I am concerned that you—"

She hated to say that four letter word.

He said it for her. "I lied. And I'm not proud of it."

"But why?"

"I didn't feel it was up to me to discuss another's personal business."

"I understand that. And I would never ask you to betray a confidence, Mr. Everett. But I don't appreciate it when someone I work with breaches my trust. You've been a businessman, I'm sure you can understand where I'm coming from."

He nodded. "If Grace wants you to know her business, she will tell you. I can't betray *her* trust."

Tricia nodded. "I accept that. But please, Mr. Everett, don't lie to me again. Next time, just tell me it's none of my business."

He nodded. "Then I must respectfully tell you that this is none of your business, Ms. Miles."

Tricia straightened to her full height. "Thank you, Mr. Everett. We won't speak of this again."

"Thank you, Ms. Miles." Mr. Everett turned away.

And Tricia knew no more now than she had before they'd started the conversation.

EIGHTEEN

Not ten minutes after Mr. Everett had left for the evening, a knock on the door caused Tricia to look up from her paperwork. Angelica stood outside. Tricia crossed the front of the shop and opened the door. "Why didn't you use your key?"

"It's upstairs. I thought I'd invite you over for dinner."

"Bob busy tonight?" Tricia asked.

"Yes, but I also figured you might want some company. Unless you have plans with Russ, that is."

Tricia shook her head. "He hasn't called. Besides, I was thinking about going to the hospital in Nashua to visit Kimberly."

"Great idea. I'll come with you."

Tricia stacked her papers, and tucked them under the counter. "You don't have to."

"No, I insist. You don't want to be driving there all alone in the dark."

"It won't be dark when I leave—which will be any minute," she said, and headed for the back of the store to retrieve her jacket. "Besides, I'm a big girl. I can handle it."

"Oh, you know what I mean. Hey, we can stop and get a bite to eat on the way up there."

"Okay. I'll drive."

"Fine. Just let me go back to the Cookery to get my purse."

As Angelica disappeared through the door, the old telephone rang. Tricia headed back to the sales counter, tossed her jacket on it, and picked up the receiver. "Haven't Got a Clue, Tricia speaking. Sorry, but we're closed."

"Tricia? It's Russ."

"Hey, I was hoping I'd hear from you."

"You busy tonight?"

"I wasn't, until five minutes ago. But now Angelica and I are going to Nashua to visit Kimberly Peters at the hospital. What did you have in mind?"

"Dinner, of course. I was hoping the third attempt might be the charm."

"No such luck, darling. At least not tonight. Ange and I are getting a bite on the way."

"You might be wasting your time and gas by driving to Nashua. When I

checked earlier this afternoon, Kimberly was still out of it. They're keeping her heavily sedated."

"I thought hospitals didn't give out personal information on patients anymore."

"I'm a reporter. I have my sources. So why go visit? She's not your friend."

"As far as I know, she hasn't got anyone else. No family, and no friends that I know of—at least not in Stoneham. If she *is* awake, she might be grateful to see at least one familiar face. I thought I might buy a plant or something on the way. That way, when she does wake up, she'll have something pleasant to look at."

"You're hoping she's going to tell you who attacked her and ransacked Zoë's house," he accused.

"Don't be absurd," Tricia said, although that was exactly what she'd hoped, and was extremely grateful he couldn't see her face at that moment. "And what if I do? Am I supposed to call you so you can add that to your story?"

"Play nice," he warned. "If she *is* awake, I suspect you'll have to vie for her attention with Sheriff Adams or one of her deputies. If the woman has any smarts at all, she'll have a guard posted at Kimberly's door."

"I did think of that," Tricia said, not bothering to hide her disdain.

"The thing is," he said, his voice softening, "have you considered that you could be in danger?"

"What are you talking about?"

"Don't play dumb with me, Tricia. At every turn, you've been one step behind the killer. That means you're likely to be the next target."

"May I remind you I'm not the one who chased the robber?"

"No, but you were the last one to speak to Kimberly. Zoë's killer might think she said something of significance to you."

"But she didn't."

"The killer doesn't know that."

Why did he always have to be right?

"I'll be perfectly safe with Angelica."

"Only if she's packing heat in her handbag."

"Now who's been reading too many old detective stories?"

He laughed. "You have contaminated me," he conceded. "Let me come with you two."

"You just want to tag along in case Kimberly's awake and *does* tell me something. That way you can put it in your next issue."

"Tricia, there's no such thing as 'breaking news' when you publish a weekly. And could you try to think the best of me once in a while instead of the worst?"

Whoa, that hurt. But he was right.

"I'm sorry, Russ. That was uncalled for."

"Thank you. Now what about my offer to take you to Nashua?"

"I don't know. Angelica might feel the need for bonding. And she'll probably want to dish on Frannie."

"Frannie?"

"She worked with Ange today. I arranged it. Frannie will probably never speak to me again."

Russ laughed. "Angelica's reputation does precede her."

"Sadly, you're right."

"Look, why don't you give me a call when you get back? Or maybe you could drop Angelica off and come see me."

"We'll see." She glanced at the clock. "Ange will be here any minute. I'd better be ready. You know she doesn't like to be kept waiting."

"Okay, but don't forget me."

"How could I?" she said, her voice softening. "You sent me a card that says you love me."

"Yes, I did."

Tricia couldn't help but smile. "I will definitely call you later."

"I'll hold you to it. Bye."

"Bye." She hung up the phone.

The shop door opened and Angelica entered, her gigantic purse slung over her shoulder and a smile plastered across her lips. "Let's get this show on the road."

Tricia and Angelica headed down the sidewalk to the municipal parking lot.

"Cold again," Angelica said, and shivered. "Doesn't winter ever end around here?"

"Give it another month and we'll have plenty of spring flowers," Tricia said as they approached her car. She pressed the button on her key ring and the doors obediently unlocked. They got in.

"Where can I find some daffodils or a plant to take to Kimberly?" Tricia asked.

"Hey, you've lived here longer than me. Shouldn't the hospital sell some in their gift shop?"

"Possibly, but they may close early on a Sunday evening."

Tricia started the car and pulled out of the parking lot and into Main Street, steering north for Route 101.

"Do you know where we're heading?' Angelica asked.

"I looked at a map earlier this afternoon. Do you want to eat first or go straight to the hospital?"

"Visit first. Eat later. I'd like to try a new little French bistro not far from the hospital. One of my customers told me about it the other day."

"If you've got the address, I'm sure we can find it," Tricia said, as the last of the village fell behind them. Though it wasn't yet dark, the trees that lined the road cloaked it in deep shadow. Tricia turned on her headlights. Theirs was the only car on the road.

"By the way, I can't thank you enough for sending Frannie to me today, Trish."

"What?" Tricia asked, disbelieving.

"We just had the most fun all day long. And I sold a ton of books. The woman's a natural-born salesperson. Too bad she's got a regular job, because I would hire her in a heartbeat. In fact, she's coming back to work for me next weekend. She suggested I order some Hawaiian cookbooks, and we could make some appetizers or dessert and pass it around next Saturday. Have you ever had poi?"

"No. Isn't it some kind of messy, green goop from a root, that's beaten to a pulp—and looks not unlike goose droppings?"

"Frannie swears it's delicious."

"I think I'd just swear if I had to eat it," Tricia said, glancing into her rear-view mirror. A car coming up from behind flicked on its headlights, blasting her retinas with its high beams.

"You have absolutely no culinary adventure in your soul," Angelica went on.

They zipped past a deserted vegetable stand. "So says you."

"Are you kidding? I've eaten eel, whale blubber—highly overrated in my opinion—and once I even ate a box of chocolate-covered ants."

"On a dare, I'll bet."

"Of course. I was about eleven. Nowadays I can think of plenty of better uses for luscious dark chocolate."

The lights of the car following seemed to grow bigger in the rearview mirror. Tricia stepped on the accelerator a little harder, but the too-close car kept pace. A growing anxiety caused her to press down even more.

"Should we be going this fast on this road?" Angelica asked.

"Someone's playing with me," Tricia said, and eased up on the gas.

The car following them bumped her.

"Hey!" Angelica called, bracing her hands against the dashboard. "That's not playing. That's serious stuff."

Tricia steered for the side of the road, the spinning tires sending gravel flying.

The car behind did the same thing.

"What do they want from us?" Angelica cried, grabbing for her purse.

"Playing chicken. But it's not a game, and I won't play." Tricia slowed even more, and the car rammed the back end of her vehicle.

Angelica withdrew her cell phone, frantically pushing the buttons. "Why is there never a cell tower around when you need one?"

"Keep punching those buttons," Tricia hollered as the car bumped them again, harder this time. The driver meant business.

"Do something!" Angelica wailed.

"What?"

"I don't know. You're the one who reads all those mysteries. What would Miss Marple do now?"

"She never drove a car," Tricia said, and swerved to the left, hoping to shake their tail, but the car swerved right behind her like a shadow.

Tricia wrenched the wheel again, desperately hoping they wouldn't go into a spin. The road was some four or five feet above the surrounding terrain, drainage ditches running along both sides of it.

"If mysteries won't help—think of what James Bond would do."

"James Bond?" Tricia repeated, grimly holding on to the steering wheel while flashing on a sexy, young Sean Connery. Yes, James Bond would've gotten out of this easily—by dumping oil on the road, or nails to puncture the bad guy's tires. But Tricia didn't drive an Aston Martin; she'd purchased the white Lexus without the "licensed to kill" package.

As she struggled to maintain control, a dark shape came whizzing overhead—a Canada goose—and then another.

"We're going to die!" Angelica wailed, shielding her face with her hands.

Tricia's gaze bobbed from the road to the rearview mirror. The car behind swerved—and Tricia heard the screech of brakes.

"It's falling behind!" she hollered.

"Behind what?" Angelica wailed, her hands still plastered to her face.

"The car, it's—"

But their pursuer regained control, the car's headlights growing bigger and bigger.

It rammed them, this time sending the Lexus careening off the road and into a ditch with a shuddering crash.

NINETEEN

The flashing lights of the police cruiser cast weird shadows against the pines. Tricia watched as the winch on the back of the flatbed tow truck pulled her car up the makeshift ramp. The Lexus might've been drivable, but she

wasn't about to take the chance. While Angelica had called 911, Tricia had extricated her own cell phone and called the one person in Stoneham she knew would mourn her.

Russ stood beside her, collar pulled up around his neck, his hands thrust deep into his jeans pockets, his ears already beginning to go pink. It wasn't until he'd shown up that she'd stopped shaking.

"I should have listened to you when you said Zoë's killer might come after me," Tricia said.

"And I should have insisted on driving you to Nashua." He withdrew his right hand from his pocket and wrapped his arm around Tricia's shoulder, pulling her close. She allowed herself to rest her head against his chest.

If it hadn't been for that goose . . . Russ had found its remains by the side of the road some hundred or so feet behind them.

Her gaze drifted to where the Lexus had come to an abrupt halt, the tall brown grass flattened and grooves cut into the thawing earth where the wheels had dug in from being towed out. Beyond that was Miller's Pond, with a lone mute swan, silhouetted by moonlight, serenely sailing across the still water. Not a goose in sight.

"This stupid thing," Angelica growled, shattering the quiet moment. She leaned against the tow truck's bumper as she stabbed the buttons on her phone. "I still can't get hold of Bob."

"Maybe his phone is turned off," Tricia offered.

Deputy Placer ambled up, clipboard in hand, pen poised to write. "And you said you couldn't identify the make of the vehicle?" he asked, as though their conversation hadn't taken a ten-minute break.

Tricia shook her head. "I told you. The car's headlights were on bright."

The deputy turned his attention to Angelica. "What about you, ma'am?"

"I was too shook up to notice anything—except that we were probably about to die."

"Check the collision shops in the morning," Tricia suggested. "I'm sure it hit a low-flying goose. That's the only thing that saved us."

"Right," the deputy said, his voice filled with sarcasm.

"Hey, Jim, what's going on with the Carter murder investigation?" Russ asked.

"What's that got to do with this accident?"

"Tricia's the common denominator. She was there at the murder; there at the scene of Kimberly Peters's attack. And now this."

Placer shook his head. "No link that I can see," he said, jotting something down on the paper on his clipboard.

"No," Tricia muttered, "and I don't suppose Wendy Adams will, either."

Placer looked up, distracted. "Huh?"

"Nothing." It was all Tricia could do not to lose her temper.

The tow truck driver from the Stoneham Garage hooked chains to the bashed and dented Lexus, securing it to the truck. He dusted off his hands and turned to Tricia. "Just tell your insurance adjuster where to find it."

"Thank you." Tricia made a mental note to call the shop in the morning to see if anyone brought in a car needing a new windshield or other damage repaired. She doubted the Sheriff's Department would.

The trio stood back as the driver got back into his rig and pulled onto the highway.

Placer stepped forward. "Tell your insurance company to call on Tuesday or Wednesday for the accident report. We're always backed up with paperwork after a busy weekend. This is my third accident today." He shook his head and muttered, "Women drivers."

He made the accident—and what Tricia and Angelica had gone through—sound so trivial, the chauvinist pig.

"Come on, girls, I'll take you home," Russ said.

"No way," Tricia said. "I want to visit Kimberly." She turned to her sister. "That is, if you don't mind, Ange."

"Not at all. And I really do want to try out that new French bistro. I'm not letting a little thing like attempted murder spoil my dinner plans for the evening."

Tricia winced: the phrase "attempted murder" hit a little too close to home.

"I hope you don't mind, but I brought the pickup, so it'll be a snug fit," Russ said.

"I only worry about those things after I eat a fabulous meal—not before," Angelica said.

Russ opened the passenger side door and Tricia piled in, with Angelica squeezing in beside her. After buckling up, they were back on their way to Nashua.

As Russ had predicted, a uniformed deputy stood outside Kimberly Peters's private hospital room. "Uh-oh," Tricia muttered, clutching the vase filled with colorful tulips. "Do you think he'll let us in?"

"Probably not," Russ said.

The deputy's name tag read BARCLAY. His broad shoulders and imposing height made him look more like a former linebacker for the New England Patriots than a cop.

Tricia strode up to face him. "Excuse me, sir, we're here to visit Kimberly Peters."

He looked down at her from his six-four or six-five height. "No visitors. Sheriff Adams's orders."

She tried again. "The medical staff wouldn't tell us how she's doing. Privacy laws or some such. Can you at least tell us if she's regained consciousness?"

"She hadn't, last I looked."

Not very talkative, either.

"And when was that?" Russ asked, shoving his press credentials in front of the deputy.

The deputy glanced at them, but they made no impression. "Half an hour ago."

"Is there a chance she can recover?" Angelica asked.

"I'm no doctor, ma'am."

"Can we at least leave our flowers for her?" Tricia asked, offering up the tulips. The vase was clear glass, so it was evident that it contained only green stems—and nothing lethal. She handed him the vase.

He poked at the flowers and took a tentative sniff. "I'll put them on the bedside table," he said, turned, and opened the door to Kimberly's room.

What Tricia saw took her breath away: Kimberly, her face bruised and swollen, looking more like a jack-o'-lantern than a human being. Crowding the over-bed table and the windowsill were vases of flowers: roses, gladiolas, tulips, and daffodils, and at her bedside sat a well-dressed, chunky man, his hand wrapped around hers, his attention focused only on Kimberly, his expression filled with worry and grief.

"Artemus Hamilton!" Tricia cried.

The literary agent looked up at the sound of his name, just as the door to the room *whoosh*ed quietly shut.

"Zoë's agent?" Russ asked.

"Yes."

"What's he doing here?" Angelica asked, no doubt delighted that she could give her cookbook manuscript another heartfelt testimonial.

A moment later the deputy reappeared with Hamilton right on his heels. "Ms. Miles, what you doing here?" Hamilton asked, sounding incredibly nervous.

"The same thing you are." She turned her attention back to the deputy. "I thought you said Ms. Peters was allowed no visitors."

"Mr. Hamilton is Ms. Peters's fiancé," Barclay said.

Tricia felt her jaw drop—then quickly shut her mouth.

"Why don't we go get a cup of coffee or something?" Hamilton said and grabbed Tricia's arm, pulling her away from the deputy, with Russ and Angelica bringing up the rear. Down the corridor, they stopped beside an empty gurney that had been parked near a storage closet.

"Ms. Miles—"

"Tricia," she insisted.

"Tricia, I had to tell the sheriff I was Kimberly's fiancé. It's the only way they'd let me visit her. She hasn't got anyone else."

"Yes, I know. How is she?"

He let out a sharp breath. "Doing better than they'd originally expected, but she's got a few hard days ahead of her and a lot of reconstructive work to come."

"Did you buy her all those flowers?" Angelica asked.

He nodded. "I felt so bad for her. She won't want to see her face when she wakes, and she deserves to have something beautiful to look at after what she's been through."

There was no arguing that.

"I take it you'll be staying in Stoneham for another night?" Tricia asked.

"Not at the Brookview Inn. I've booked a room at a hotel not far from here. I'll pick up a rental car tomorrow."

"Sounds like you're planning on staying for the duration," Russ said.

"I've asked my assistant to clear my schedule for the next few days."

"Very generous—especially since Ms. Peters *isn't* your fiancé," Russ added.

"Kimberly and I have known each other for several years. We even dated for a while. I consider myself her friend. And isn't being with her now the least a friend can do?"

"Yes," Tricia agreed. Or had simply seeing Kimberly's battered face reawakened whatever feelings he had for her—of friendship, or otherwise? She wasn't about to second-guess his motives.

"You must be exhausted after spending the day here. We're going to dinner when we leave. We'd love to have you join us," Angelica chimed in, ever the gracious hostess.

Hamilton shook his head. "I got something from the cafeteria an hour or so ago. But thanks for asking."

Tricia nodded, understanding completely. Angelica, however, looked annoyed.

"When Kimberly wakes up, I'll let her know you came to visit—and that you brought flowers," Hamilton said.

"Thank you."

"The sheriff told me you found her. Did she tell you who did this to her?"

Tricia shook her head. "Sorry." She wasn't about to tell him what Kimberly had said—and risk Wendy Adams's wrath. Besides, the information hadn't pointed to whoever had attacked Kimberly and why.

"Look, I'd better get back to Kimberly. If she wakes up, I want to be there for her." He gave them a wan smile and turned toward the main corridor.

Tricia, Russ, and Angelica looked at one another.

"Well, that was certainly unexpected," Angelica said.

"It sure was," Tricia agreed.

"But it doesn't mean anything, either," Russ said. "I mean, so the guy feels sorry for the poor woman—or maybe he even discovered he cares about her. It doesn't give us any more information."

"No," Tricia agreed, "it doesn't.

TWENTY

The ambience at La Parisienne reflected its cuisine, from its textured plaster walls to its gilt mirrors and the shiny copper-bottomed pans that hung as decoration. Angelica had pronounced the coq au vin adequate, but assured Tricia and Russ that in her own hands it would've been magnificent. And, in fact, it would make a wonderful addition to her *European Epicurean* manuscript. Russ was about to ask her to explain when Tricia gave him a warning look. He kept quiet.

"Let's face it, I missed my calling," Angelica said, as she swirled the last of her pinot noir in her glass and Russ dipped into his wallet to pay for the dinner. "I should've opened a restaurant instead of a cookbook store. It sure would've been a lot easier."

"On whom?" Tricia asked, thinking about her sister's continuing employee problems. "And what's going to happen at your store tomorrow? You're still short staffed."

"Frannie said she'd put out the word that I need help. She has a lot of contacts over at the Chamber of Commerce, you know."

No doubt about that.

"Of course, if you don't need Ginny—" Angelica hinted.

"I don't even know if she's coming in tomorrow. It depends on how Brian's doing and if she feels she can leave him."

Angelica waved a hand in dismissal. "Oh, what's a little food poisoning?"

"I'm sure you'd feel differently if it was your intestines tied in knots," Tricia said.

"Let's change the subject," Russ said. "Like what are you going to do to protect yourself, Tricia?"

She stared at him, surprised. "From whom?"

"Exactly," Angelica quipped.

"Come and stay with me," he said.

Angelica shook her head. "Nope. It's too far from her shop. And don't forget about your cat, Trish. You can stay with me. I loved having you this past week. It was just like being back in college with a roomie."

"Sorry to disappoint you both, but I have my own home, and I have a perfectly good security system. If somebody breaks in downstairs, they've got to come up three flights. I have a sturdy door in between, and a cell phone if my landline goes dead."

"You can't count on someone having a coronary trudging up those three flights. And remember, Kimberly was bludgeoned with a sledgehammer. That could knock down a door, no matter how sturdy," Russ said.

"You're not going to frighten or bully me into anything. Either of you."

Angelica sighed and turned her attention to Russ. "Doesn't she sound like the heroine in a bad movie or novel? You know, the stupid character—usually a woman—who goes into a darkened basement or attic when there's a serial killer on the loose?"

"May I remind you that I have no basement, and whoever killed Zoë is not a serial killer?"

"Unless Kimberly dies," Russ pointed out.

For a second—and only a second—Russ's argument made sense. "But Artemus said Kimberly will recover. I have faith in the doctors at Southern New Hampshire Medical Center to pull her through, and in no time she'll be her smiling self again." She cringed. Kimberly rarely smiled, and now with no front teeth, she'd be even less apt to flash her gums.

"There's no argument. If you won't come stay with me, I'm going to stay with you." Angelica patted her massive purse. "I just happen to have brought along my toothbrush and nightie. I'm all set."

"But—"

"Good," Russ said. "Then it's all settled."

"It's not settled."

"Would you prefer we drop you off at a motel here in Nashua to stay the night?" Russ asked.

"Oh, come on, guys, you're paranoid—both of you."

"And you ought to be," Angelica said.

Tricia thought about how frightened she'd been when the car had forced them off the road. Was she being foolish?

"Okay, Ange, you can stay with me. But only for tonight."

Angelica eyed Russ. "We'll see."

• • •

A LOT HAD changed in the six months since Angelica had come to live in Stoneham. The biggest change, of course, had been in Tricia herself. They'd returned from Nashua and Angelica had made herself comfortable on Tricia's couch. They'd opened a bottle of wine, and Miss Marple had deigned to join them, even contemplating sitting on Angelica's lap, which, upon further reflection, she decided not to do.

For more than an hour the sisters had chatted and laughed, sticking to subjects that did not include murder, cookbook manuscripts, or personal criticisms. It occurred to Tricia that somewhere between their squabbles and disagreements, the two women had added something else to their ofttimes troubled relationship: they'd become friends.

Angelica acquiesced to sleeping on the comfortable leather couch, and peace reigned during the night.

Tricia awoke the next morning to the heavenly aromas of coffee and bacon coming from her kitchen. She found Angelica standing over the stove, a dish towel safety pinned to her nightgown, and Miss Marple sitting smartly at her feet, licking her chops.

"Did you know your cat likes bacon?" she asked.

"Where did you find bacon?"

"In the back of your freezer. You really should clean it out more often, Trish. This meat was on the verge of freezer burn."

"I don't cook very often," she defended herself.

"Excuse me; you don't cook at all."

Tricia grabbed a mug from the cupboard and poured herself a cup of coffee. "I've been thinking about that. I think I'd like to take you up on your offer to teach me a few simple things. Just so I could have Russ over now and then and not have to rely on Angelo's Pizzeria or spaghetti sauce from a jar."

Angelica paused in turning the crispy slices, her mouth dropping open. "You want me to—?"

Words seemed to fail her.

"If you don't mind. Maybe on a Sunday morning—before we have to open our stores."

Angelica's eyes began to fill. "I'd love that," she managed, turned away, and cleared her throat. "And as a start, I could let you read my cooking manuscripts—use you as my guinea pig."

Tricia set her cup down, not bothering to hide the smile that touched her lips. "Sure thing. In the meantime, how about I get the toaster out? I've already perfected the recipe for toast."

She'd just plugged it in and taken bread from the fridge when the phone rang. "Tricia?" Portia McAlister asked.

"I didn't give you this number."

"I'm not a reporter for nothing," she said. "Look, I thought you said you'd keep me in the loop."

"Loop?" Tricia asked, gazing into the toaster to check on the toast's progress.

"That incident last night. You know, the one that dented your car and nearly did the same to you and your sister."

"How did you find out about that?"

"Uh-uh. I told you, I protect my sources."

The police report wasn't supposed to be available until at least Tuesday. Could it have been the tow truck driver from the Stoneham Garage who'd squealed?

It didn't matter.

"We weren't hurt, just shaken up."

"Where were you going at the time?"

"Is this off the record?"

"Maybe."

Did that matter, either?

"We were on our way to visit Kimberly Peters at the hospital in Nashua."

"Did she say anything enlightening? I can't get to her, and her fiancé won't talk to me."

That snippet of information made Tricia smile. "No. She wasn't awake when we got there, so we went out to dinner. Would you like to know what we ordered?"

"That won't be necessary." The line went quiet for long seconds. "I can still use this," Portia muttered.

"How?" Tricia asked, as the toast popped up.

"I'll let you know," Portia said, and hung up.

MR. EVERETT WAS waiting at the door when Tricia came down to prepare Haven't Got a Clue for another day of commerce. The day was overcast, the clouds hanging low and threatening. Another perfect day for retail!

"Good morning, Ms. Miles."

"Good morning, Mr. Everett. Lovely weather."

"Yes, we should have a good day." Mr. Everett headed for the pegs in the back of the store to hang up his coat. "Shall I straighten up the back shelves? Someone pawed through them yesterday, stuffing the books in every which way." He shook his head in disapproval.

"That's fine," Tricia said, and bent down to open the safe to collect and count out the bills to start the day. She thought about calling the Stoneham

Garage to see if anyone had brought in a damaged car, but decided it was probably too early. And anyway, perhaps whoever had come after her the previous evening was smart enough to take their damaged car to Nashua or even Manchester for repairs. It wasn't likely the Sheriff's Department would be interested enough to make a few calls to try and locate it.

A knock at the door caused her to look up. She pushed the cash drawer shut with her hip and went to answer it. She lifted the blind; Ginny waited in the cold. Tricia opened the door.

"I think I should've brought my umbrella from the house."

"Yes, but it's too warm for snow, so that's something in our favor."

"Only if you believe the low forties are warm," Ginny said, pulling off her knit hat and stuffing her gloves into her pockets.

"How's Brian?" Tricia asked.

"Much better." Ginny took off her coat, and headed toward the back of the store to hang it up.

The phone rang. Although the store didn't officially open for another ten minutes, Tricia wasn't a stickler for such details and picked up the receiver. "Haven't Got a Clue, Tricia speaking."

"Hi, it's Brian. Is Ginny there yet?" He still didn't sound well.

"Brian, Ginny says you're better."

Ginny stopped at the sound of Brian's name.

"Lots. Can I speak with her, please?"

"Sure."

Ginny hurried to take the phone from Tricia. "Hey, sweetie, what's up?"

Tricia went back to sorting the bills for the cash drawer, trying not to listen to Ginny's conversation, which appeared to consist of only three phrases: "Oh, God!" "You're kidding?," and "I don't believe it."

When she finally hung up, she was ashen-faced.

"What's wrong?" Tricia asked, concerned.

"The lab report came back," Ginny said, her voice shaking.

"That was quick. How did you get them to turn it around so fast?"

"Brian's aunt works at the hospital. She pulled some strings. They said it was salmonella that made him sick."

"It was the ham from the fridge, right?" Tricia asked.

"No, Trish, it could only be Nikki's cake."

"What?" Tricia said. Astonished didn't begin to express what emotion coursed through her.

Ginny nodded. "Brian was so caught up working on the laundry room, he didn't eat lunch, so when I brought the cake in on Saturday night, he ate a huge piece. Not long after, he was sick."

"Salmonella," Tricia repeated. "It often comes from eggs. Nikki's been in the food service business a long time. I don't understand how she could accidentally—"

"I don't think it was an accident. Remember I took home some of those cut-out cookies she sent over to the Cookery? I didn't make the connection until I talked to Brian just now, but they made me sick. And now this."

Tricia shook her head in denial. "I just can't believe—" That Nikki would want to hurt her? Make her ill? Why? Unless what Russ had been saying all along was true. That Zoë's killer thought she was getting too close to the truth—too close to tracking down him or her. Tricia remembered the bag of tools containing the sledgehammer and the can of spray paint sitting on the bakery's floor. But what possible motive could Nikki have for killing Zoë? True, it was she who'd asked Tricia to invite the so-called author. Nikki left the signing early . . . and came in through the back door to strangle Zoë?

"What do you remember from the night of Zoë's signing?" Tricia asked.

"What do you mean?"

"I wasn't paying attention when Nikki left, but she did leave early. And neither of you remembers disarming the security system, nor does Angelica."

"It doesn't matter. It wouldn't be hard for Nikki to do," Ginny said.

"What do you mean?"

"I've worked in several stores in Stoneham. Half the merchants on the street have the identical system we do. Even the Cookery."

"You think the Stoneham Patisserie might have the same system? That Nikki disabled our system and came in the back of the store to kill Zoë?"

"It's possible."

"But what's her connection, her motive?"

Ginny shrugged. "The only way we'd know that is to ask her. And I doubt she'd say a word."

Tricia thought about the awful scene at Zoë's home on Saturday evening. "The last thing Kimberly Peters said before she lost consciousness was 'stone.'"

"Stone," Ginny repeated, looking thoughtful.

"I thought she was talking about the statue that got ruined."

"But it's marble, not stone."

"Technically, marble is stone."

"Stone," Ginny repeated again. "It seems like I should remember something about that word."

Tricia looked across the room. "Mr. Everett?"

Mr. Everett paused in straightening the shelves to join the two women. As a lifelong resident of Stoneham, he was a font of useful information. "Is there a family in the area named Stone?"

The old man shook his head. "Hasn't been for years. Stoneham was named after Hiram Stone, who opened a quarry back in the mid-eighteenth century, although the village wasn't incorporated until 1798."

"So they died out generations ago?"

"Oh, no. One of my favorite customers was Faith Stone. Wonderful woman," he said. "Very generous with her time. I occasionally saw her when my grocery store donated dented canned goods to the local food pantry where she volunteered. I believe she and Grace were acquainted. Something to do with the library."

"What happened to her?"

He shook his head. "No one seems to know. She just disappeared one day."

A shiver ran through Tricia as she remembered what Julia Overline had said the day before at Nikki's brunch.

"Her family had her declared dead so that the estate could be freed up and fund her daughter's further education," Mr. Everett continued.

"Who was her daughter?" Tricia asked, dreading the answer.

"The manager of the Stoneham Patisserie: Nikki Brimfield."

"Nikki?" Ginny repeated.

Mr. Everett nodded. "Brimfield is her married name, although I believe she's now divorced."

"And her maiden name?" Tricia asked, already knowing the answer.

"Stone, of course."

SINCE MR. EVERETT had mentioned that Grace and Faith had been acquainted, Tricia's first impulse was to call Grace. She did, but there was no answer. Grace didn't have voice mail or even an answering machine, so Tricia could only slam down the phone in frustration.

Her next thought was to talk to Stella Kraft. Unlike gadabout Grace, Stella was pretty much a homebody, and answered the phone on the first ring. "I'd be glad to talk with you again, Tricia."

"Can I come over now?"

"Now is fine. I'll put on a pot of coffee."

Tricia left Ginny and Mr. Everett with a few hurried instructions, donned her coat, and started down the sidewalk. In a moment she heard her name being called.

"Tricia, Tricia!"

Tricia turned, delighted to see Grace Harris waving to her. She waited until the older woman caught up with her. "Grace, what brings you out so early on a Monday morning?"

Grace looked down at the sticky goo on her shoe. "Oh, dear, not again," she

muttered, and tried to scrape the goose poop from her sole. "I've run out of the Coffee Bean's superior blend. When I saw you, I wanted to tell you how much I admire you for helping that Peters woman the other night."

"News certainly gets around."

"She wasn't very nice, but I can't imagine the cruelty it took to inflict those injuries."

Tricia shuddered, remembering the amount of blood that had soaked into Kimberly's clothes and pooled on Zoë's office floor. "It was the least I could do."

Grace nodded.

"Do you mind if I ask you a couple of questions?" Tricia asked.

"Of course not, dear."

"At Zoë's signing, you said you were glad to speak to her under 'happier circumstances.' What did that mean?"

Grace bowed her head. "Had I known she was destined to die within minutes, I never would have brought it up. It was thoughtless of me."

"You couldn't have known she'd be murdered."

"Yes, well, I like to think of myself as a good person. And bringing up an unpleasant incident from the past is just plain bad manners."

This was maddening. "What was it?"

"A confrontation—in public—over her not supporting Stoneham's efforts to promote ourselves as a book town."

"Oh, that," Tricia said, blowing it off. "Bob Kelly mentioned it to me last week."

"He did? Why—that—how could he?" Grace sputtered.

"Grace, it was years ago, and I'm sure everyone—everyone but Bob," she amended—"has forgotten about it."

"I hadn't forgotten it, but whatever feelings I had about it, they didn't stop me from supporting her as an author."

Finding out the truth about who actually had written the books would have done it, for sure.

"It's all in the past now. I think you should just forget about it," Tricia said.

"I have tried," Grace admitted. "I was sorry I couldn't make it to her memorial service on Saturday, but it sounds like that was a fiasco as well."

"Yes, it was."

"I had an appointment at the New Hampshire Medical Center," Grace volunteered.

"Oh, dear, I hope nothing's wrong."

Grace smiled. "Luckily, no. Thank you for your concern."

"Is that also where you were early Wednesday morning?" Tricia asked, pushing the boundaries of polite conversation, but she wanted to know what Mr. Everett felt so strongly about that he would lie to her.

"Yes. In the past I had some female problems," Grace said, without elaborating.

"I see," Tricia said, and nodded. "Well, I'm certainly glad you're all right."

"Thank you."

"I had another question for you, too. It concerns Faith Stone."

Grace laughed. "Good grief, I haven't thought about her in years."

"Mr. Everett says you were friends."

"Not really. We were acquainted. We belonged to the same book club—not unlike the one you host at Haven't Got a Clue, only this was sponsored by the Stoneham Library. A nice little group. Mostly retirees and stay-at-home mothers."

"Did you know Faith wanted to be a writer?" Tricia bluffed, wondering where the idea had even come from.

"Oh, yes. She used to carry a notebook around with her, scribbling down thoughts and ideas for some great saga she said she hoped to write one day."

"She didn't say she was actually writing it?"

Grace frowned. "She didn't talk a lot about herself, poor thing."

"Poor thing?"

"Her husband was the jealous kind. I can't say I was surprised when she went missing, although they were never able to pin anything on that brute Phil Stone. More than once she came to our meetings with bruises on her arms or legs."

"Her husband was the controlling type?"

Grace nodded. "She ultimately stopped coming to the meetings. It wasn't long afterward that she disappeared."

"And no one's ever heard from her?"

"I think her body was probably dumped in the woods somewhere. Perhaps some hunter will find her bones one day."

"Perhaps," Tricia said.

Grace put a hand on Tricia's arm. "You were obviously on your way somewhere, and I'm holding you up."

"No, I'm just running an errand."

"Well, I'll let you go. I'll see you tomorrow evening at the book club meeting. I'm grateful we won't have a guest," she said with a laugh.

"I'm so glad what happened last week hasn't scared you off," Tricia said.

"Oh, I think you'll find that we'll return. After all, don't we love a good mystery?" Grace asked.

Tricia laughed. "Yes, but I prefer mine between the covers of a book."

"Good-bye, dear," Grace said with a pleased smile, and continued on her way.

Tricia pushed forward, glad to have one more mystery cleared up . . . and another still facing her.

• • •

Stella Kraft opened her back door before Tricia could press the bell. "I knew you'd eventually figure it all out," she said smugly, her pale blue eyes sparkling.

Tricia pursed her lips, annoyed. "Why didn't you just come right out and tell me about Faith Stone?"

"Come in, come in. I'm not paying Keyspan to heat the great outdoors," Stella chided.

Once again the smell of boiled potatoes and mothballs filled the immaculate kitchen. Stella had set the table with mugs, spoons, and napkins, and a plate of gingersnaps. "Let me take your coat."

"I don't want to be a bother. I'll just drape it over the back of the chair," Tricia said, and settled at the table.

Stella moved to the stove, picked up the coffeepot, and poured. "Now, what led you to Faith?"

"A number of things." Tricia told Stella about her conversations with Kimberly and Artemus Hamilton; Nikki's tainted cookies and cake; Mr. Everett's revelation; and Grace's confirmation. "Nikki sure had me fooled. She always seemed so even-tempered at our book club meetings, always bringing the refreshments and all. Did you have her for a student?"

Stella nodded, taking her seat. "She's another one who slid through my class without making much of an impact. Such a disappointment after having her mother."

"And you lied to me when you said you had no idea who really wrote Zoë's books."

"I didn't actually lie," Stella said. "I kept the truth to myself. That's not lying. Exactly."

Tricia wasn't about to debate her. Instead, she said, "Tell me about Faith Stone."

Stella sat back in her chair, a smile lighting her face. "Faith was the best student who ever passed through my classroom. She had a real thirst for learning. Even in high school she had a wonderful gift for storytelling."

"You said you didn't keep any of your students' work."

"That was no lie, but it wasn't easy to forget her way with words, even at that age. I hoped she'd go far. Obviously, she would have, if the books had been published before her disappearance. They would have set her free." She shook her head sadly.

"But how did Zoë get hold of Faith's manuscripts?"

Stella reached for a cookie. "Near as I can figure, it was from the estate sale."

"Estate sale?"

"After she disappeared, Faith's former in-laws pushed to have her declared dead."

"Her in-laws, not her husband?"

Stella nodded. "Five or six years after she disappeared, her good-for-nothing husband, Phillip Stone, died in a work accident. He was a lineman for PSNH." The local power utility. "Faith's daughter went to live with her grandmother. I don't know if the in-laws ever legally had Faith declared dead, but they made a big show of it and had a big sale at the house. I believe Zoë got the manuscripts at that sale. Faith's in-laws wouldn't have known what they were—and would have cared even less. They considered her writing a frivolous waste of time. Her ex-mother-in-law was dead by the time the books were published. Her sister-in-law never recognized Faith's work, or I'm sure she would have tried to get her hands on some of the money Zoë raked in."

"How long after Faith disappeared was the first book published?"

"Oh, maybe ten years. I'm assuming Zoë had the manuscripts for a couple of years before she figured out what to do with them. Not the sharpest pencil in the box, that one."

"Why didn't you say something? Why didn't you let people know Zoë didn't write those books?"

"I told you, I did hint about it to my colleagues, but I had no proof. All I could do was be enraged on Faith's behalf. Eventually—" She shrugged. "I got over it."

"But what about Nikki? Didn't she deserve compensation? Imagine what she must have felt like. It's certainly motive enough to kill someone."

Stella frowned. "The only one who deserved to benefit from Faith's work was Faith herself."

"Which was impossible. She was dead."

Stella blinked, then smiled. She picked up her coffee mug and took a sip. "Faith's not dead. She just lives in Canada."

TWENTY-ONE

"NOT DEAD?" ANGELICA murmured in disbelief.

Tricia had left Stella's home in a fog. The ex-teacher wouldn't say much more, leaving Tricia with far more questions than she'd had before she'd arrived. Armed with new knowledge, she knew she'd burst if she didn't tell

someone, and her first thought was to call her sister. She had pulled the cell phone from the pocket of her jacket and dialed.

"Well, where is she? Where's she been?" Angelica asked, when she'd heard the tale.

"In Canada. Somewhere."

"And no one knows she's still alive—not even Nikki?"

"As far as I know, only you, me, and Stella know. She wouldn't tell me more. She said it wasn't up to her to out her former student."

"But what about Faith? Why doesn't she want her daughter to know she's not dead?"

"Stella wouldn't say. But if I had to guess, I'd say because it's been over twenty years. Maybe she doesn't want to intrude on her daughter's life. Maybe she's ashamed she left without taking Nikki with her. I know that would be my reaction."

"So what are you going to do?"

"Look for Faith myself."

"In Canada?"

"No, on the Internet. The only clue Stella would give me was that Faith is still writing, and has been published."

"Under her real name?"

"Apparently not."

"That's going to make finding her a little difficult, don't you think?"

"Difficult, but not impossible."

"Ha! Who died and made you Sherlock Holmes?"

"Hey, I've read enough police procedurals and true crime novels to have picked up a few tips."

"Well, all I can say is 'go for it.' And tell me everything as soon as you know, will you? I feel like I've just put down a book I can't wait to get back into."

"You and me both."

Tricia arrived back at Haven't Got a Clue just in time for the afternoon rush, which kept her from her laptop for another hour. By then she was ready to jump out of her skin. But between customers she'd thumbed through the Sisters In Crime and Mystery Writers of America membership directories she kept near the sales register. Not surprisingly, there was no Faith Stone listed. She'd searched for last names that began with S that had first names beginning with F. There were no published authors she recognized.

"What am I thinking?" she said, and gave her forehead a slap. "I'm not going to find her in a U.S.-based group."

"Find who?" Ginny asked.

"A writer," Tricia said.

"Maybe I can help."

"I need the laptop. I've got to check the Crime Writers of Canada website."

"Crime Writers of Canada? We don't carry any books from Canadian publishers, do we?"

"Not really. To make any kind of a living, most Canadian authors have U.S. publishers."

"So what's the name of this Canadian author?"

"I'm not sure."

"Then how can you look him—or her—up? Or do you have the book title?"

Tricia shook her head. "No author, no title, no ISBN."

Ginny spread her arms wide. "Then—how?"

"I'm going to take a good guess." Tricia headed for the back of the store and the stairs to her loft apartment. "I'm going to go online to check. Call me on my cell if things get hairy down here."

"You got it," Ginny said.

Miss Marple saw Tricia heading for the stairs and jumped down from one of the bookshelves to lope after her. Tricia opened the door to the stairs and the cat took off like a shot.

Less than a minute later, Tricia had powered up her computer and waited as it found the Internet connection. At the Google site, she typed in "Crime Writers of Canada," and in seconds was taken to the CWC home page. She clicked on the button labeled Member Bios, selecting S. A fast perusal came up with only one name that had the initials F and S: Fiona Sample.

Tricia was already familiar with that name. She'd read at least one, perhaps two, books in the Bonnie Chesterfield librarian "cozy mystery" series. She remembered she'd liked them, but hadn't kept up with the rest of the series—simply because she'd been preoccupied. By her divorce, by opening Haven't Got a Clue, and by the hundreds of other mystery books vying for her attention . . .

The question was: Could Fiona Sample actually be Faith Stone?

She clicked on the link to the author's bio. Fiona Sample was born in the U.S., but came to Canada in the early 1990s to live and work in Toronto. She married a Canadian citizen and lived happily outside of Kitchener, Ontario, with her two children, twins Jessica and Andre, and a house full of cats and dogs, as well as a yard full of chickens.

Chickens? Addie Martin from the *Forever* book series had kept chickens, too.

Tricia tried to remember the Bonnie Chesterfield books. They were contem-

porary novels set in western New York. Had Faith originally come from that state and transplanted herself to New Hampshire, as Tricia had done, or was the locale just enough over the border to interest an American publisher?

Tricia left the computer long enough to search her own bookshelves. It took ten minutes, but she did find the first book in Fiona Sample's series: *Death Turns a Page*, published some seven years before.

She flipped through the pages, reading paragraphs at random. The book was well written, and memories of it came back to her almost at once, but it didn't resonate like the Jess and Addie *Forever* historical mysteries. Could this be the same author who wrote the books Zoë took credit for?

Tricia just wasn't sure.

She went back to the computer and scanned the rest of the entry, then clicked on the link to Fiona's website. The site had only four pages. The About Fiona page had little more on it than the CWC site, and no picture, either. Tricia clicked the Contact button. That page gave her yet another link, which she clicked, and up popped an empty note addressed to Fiona@ FionaSample.com with a subject line of From the website.

Tricia thought about what she could write in the message area, something that would elicit a fast reply. After a few moments she erased the subject line and typed in "Nikki's in trouble." In the message area, she added, "She needs her mother." Tricia signed it with her standard signature line of her name, the store name, and the telephone number; clicked the Send button; and sent it flying through cyberspace.

WITH HER LAPTOP tucked under her arm, Tricia returned to Haven't Got a Clue, set the computer up behind the sales counter, and wondered when—or even if—she'd get a reply to her e-mail. For now, there was nothing to do but wait. And since the store was quiet, she decided to surf the Internet.

What she'd seen Sunday night at the scene of her car—chase? wreck?—had stayed with her: an open body of water with no geese. She Googled the words "swan" and "geese," and hit the Enter key. Within seconds, a list of websites appeared on her computer screen.

The first few sites weren't helpful. But on the fourth one, she hit pay dirt. It suggested that mute swans, like the one she'd seen on Miller's Pond, had been used successfully as goose deterrents. Apparently swans aggressively protect their young, chasing away any creatures—including man—that dare to intrude on their breeding grounds. Bob hadn't mentioned swans during their talk some days before. Did he even know about this?

Hitting the Compose button, Tricia keyed in a quick note, including the

website's URL, addressed the note to Bob at his Chamber e-mail address, and hit the Send key—just as a customer opened the door and entered. Tricia didn't get back to her computer for another ten minutes. The note she found waiting her attention wasn't from Fiona Sample or Bob, but from Portia McAlister.

"Did you see my latest report? Catch it online," and she gave the URL.

Tricia clicked on the link.

The report was dated that morning, and she waited impatiently while the video loaded, then hit the Play button.

Portia stood along a bare patch of road, tall pines the only backdrop. The location looked suspiciously familiar. The door opened, admitting three potential customers. Ginny sprang into action, welcoming them as Tricia strained to listen to the report.

"—on this lonely patch of road. Stoneham merchants Tricia Miles, owner of the mystery bookstore Haven't Got a Clue, and her sister Angelica, who owns the Cookery bookstore, were two sisters on a mission of mercy when tragedy almost struck."

"Is this the only Agatha Christie book you have in stock?" asked a white-haired woman in a purple ski jacket.

"Uh—" Tricia tore her attention from the laptop's screen. "No." She cast about. "Mr. Everett, could you help this customer?"

Mr. Everett signaled the woman to follow him.

Portia had continued with her report, heedless of her lack of an audience. "—Kimberly Peters, in critical condition at Southern New Hampshire Medical Center—"

"There's no more coffee in the pot," said a gentleman customer, thrusting his empty cardboard cup at Tricia.

She gritted her teeth, trying to hold her temper. "One of us will take care of that in just a minute. Please excuse me for a moment." She turned back to the screen.

"Are these three incidents linked?" Portia asked earnestly.

The old telephone on the cash desk rang.

"With murder and attempted murder," Portia went on.

The phone rang again.

Tricia clicked on the video, stopping Portia in midsentence. She grabbed the phone. "Haven't Got a Clue mystery bookstore. This is Tricia, how may I help you?" she asked, sounding anything but helpful.

"This is Fiona Sample. What did you mean by your e-mail, Ms. Miles?"

"Oh, it's you!" Tricia said, startled, and had to catch her breath. "Uh, as I said in the note, I think your daughter Nikki's in terrible trouble. She needs her mother."

"I don't have a daughter by that name."

"You did when your name was Faith Stone."

Silence.

"Did you write the five Jess and Addie *Forever* historical mysteries attributed to Zoë Carter?" Tricia asked, point-blank.

"What?" Fiona said, sounding breathless. "What did you say?"

"Did you write the Jess and Addie historical mysteries?"

"Who are you? Where did you get that idea?"

"Miss, Miss!" the woman in the purple jacket insisted, holding up two volumes in her hands. "These aren't the Agatha Christie books I want. Don't you have a back room with other titles?"

"Mr. Everett!" Tricia called.

"Ms. Miles?" Fiona Sample insisted from hundreds of miles away.

"Excuse me," Tricia told Fiona, and turned to Mr. Everett. "We may have other titles, but they haven't been inventoried. I wouldn't know where to find them right this minute."

The woman slammed the books onto the glass counter. "What kind of customer service is this? I want *Murder at Hazelmoor.* I was told your store stocked every mystery book ever written!" she said indignantly.

Was she crazy?

"Ginny!" Tricia called.

Ginny looked up from her customer, excused herself, and hurried to the cash desk.

"Ginny, I'm on a very important phone call. Can you please help this customer?" she asked, pleading.

Ginny turned to the irate woman. "How can I help you, ma'am?"

"Ms. Miles," Fiona said firmly.

"I'm sorry," Tricia apologized. "It's organized mayhem in the store today. Would you be open to me calling you right back from a more quiet location?"

Tricia heard the woman on the other end of the line sigh. "Yes." She gave Tricia her number.

"Please call me right back," Fiona said. "I want to get to the bottom of this."

TWENTY-TWO

"Wow," Ginny murmured, not for the first time. "You're practically a living, breathing Miss Marple to figure all that out yourself."

Hearing her name, Tricia's little gray cat jumped onto the cash desk, immediately nuzzling her head on Ginny's chin. "Not you," she chided, petting the purring cat.

Tricia shook her head. "I had a lot of help. And a lot could still go wrong. That's why I need your help to set this up."

"Hey, all you have to do is ask," Ginny said. "But do you really think you can pull it off by tomorrow? And what are your safeguards?"

"Good question."

Ginny beamed. "Hey, in the last year, I've read a lot of mysteries. I can't wait to see how this goes down," she said, perhaps a bit too eagerly.

Tricia shook her head. "You aren't going to be here. I won't put you or Mr. Everett in danger."

"Oh, but you being in danger is okay, right?"

"I won't be in danger."

"Doesn't that kind of contradict your previous statement?"

"It all depends on how much cooperation I can get from the Sheriff's Department."

Ginny snorted. "I think you can count on one hundred percent total noninvolvement from our local law enforcement."

"I hope you're wrong, but it will mean pulling in a few favors from friends and acquaintances."

Ginny crossed her arms over her chest. "Okay, I'll do as you ask, but if I don't get all the juicy details, I will commit serious mayhem."

"And you won't be the only one, I'm sure."

Ginny sobered. "What do you want me to do?"

"Tomorrow, late in the afternoon, you and I will call all the members of the Tuesday Night Book Club and tell them the regular meeting's been canceled."

"All but one member?" Ginny asked.

"Yes."

"And what if she calls or comes in asking about it?"

"There's only one person who could spill the beans."

"Frannie?"

Tricia nodded. "I'll handle her myself."

"Okay. That doesn't seem like much work to me."

"I'm sure I'll think of something else for you to do. In the meantime, there's a box of Agatha Christie books to shelve. I want to be ready in case our irate customer decides to come back and berate us again."

Ginny smiled. "You got it," she said, and trotted to the back shelves.

Tricia looked down at the notepad in front of her. The logistics of pulling everything off in just about twenty-four hours were frightening, but she felt she needed to gather all the players and have an old-fashioned showdown, just like in a Rex Stout Nero Wolfe story.

First up was talking to Artemus Hamilton. She called his office and was told he would be out of town for at least the rest of the week, and no, she could *not* have his cell phone number. The Southern New England Medical Center told her that Kimberly Peters's room had no phone hookup. Okay, if that meant she'd have to make another visit to the hospital to track down Hamilton, she would.

Next on the agenda: backup for herself. She didn't feel like making the lonely ride to Nashua all by herself. Another phone call later and she'd lined up Russ to ride shotgun, but only if she promised to tell him the whole story. This time she readily agreed. There were just two people she didn't want to make a party to her plans: Angelica and Frannie. As she told Ginny, although without malice, Frannie was liable to blather, and Angelica was likely to put herself in danger trying to protect her baby sister. Tricia wasn't about to put her plan at risk by telling either woman more than she needed to know.

Still, the twenty-four-plus hours until her own private D-Day seemed like a lifetime.

Tricia let out a sigh and hoped she could orchestrate her plan. If the whole thing soured, Zoë Carter might not be the only fatality.

THE ELEVATOR DOORS *whoosh*ed open. Tricia stepped into the quiet hospital corridor, with Russ right on her heels. He hadn't ridden shotgun after all, leaving that spot for her, and their trip to Nashua in his beat-up old pickup truck had been uneventful. The journey, that is. The conversation had been lively.

"Are you nuts?" Russ had asked when Tricia told him her plans for the next day. His next question had been "Can I be there?"

The answer to that was a flat "No! If you want to watch the store—either from across the street or behind in the alley, I could use someone out in the field on guard, just in case something goes wrong."

"Okay, but only because I'm getting that exclusive."

They turned the corner, passing the nurses' station and heading down the hall. The door to Kimberly's room was open, with no deputy on duty outside it. They peeked inside. The TV was switched on, with some decorating program from HGTV playing for background noise. Kimberly sat propped up in bed, her face still alarmingly swollen and bruised, a trail of bloody drool leaking from the corner of her mouth. Artemus Hamilton held a small plastic cup of dark liquid in one hand, and a spoon in the other. A blood-stained cloth lay on the bedside table. On the floor, parked against the wall, was Hamilton's opened briefcase with manuscript pages poking out of it. Angelica's manuscript?

It was Hamilton who first noticed their arrival. "Oh, look, Kimberly, Tricia and Mr. Smith have come to visit."

Kimberly blinked and slowly turned her face toward the doorway. What seemed like eons later, her eyes brightened and her lips parted into a toothless smile. "Tre-ah," she managed in greeting.

Tricia swallowed the urgent impulse to cry. She gave into emotion and surged forward to capture the frail Kimberly in a gentle hug, grimacing as she took in the fetid odor that seemed to surround her. A long moment later she felt a soft pressure on her back and realized Kimberly's free hand was patting her.

She pulled away. "Are you okay, Kimberly?"

A very dumb question.

Kimberly fell back against her pillows and a mix of grunt and laugh escaped her lips.

"She's much better today," Artemus said, his voice faltering, his eyes bright with unshed tears as he gently wiped away the bloody spittle that leaked from Kimberly's slack mouth.

Tricia braved a smile. "Yes, I can see that."

"I goh no teef," Kimberly mouthed, pointing at the stubs of knotted black suture that stuck out at angles from her scarlet gums.

"The dental surgeon came by today," Hamilton said. "He looked at the X-rays, and tomorrow he'll tell us what we can expect for treatment."

What *we* can expect?

"Kimberly could be eating steak again in just a few months," Artemus continued, his voice breaking.

Kimberly clapped her hands together like a small child, the gesture bringing Tricia close to tears once again. She cleared her throat, swallowing the onslaught of emotion that threatened to overwhelm her.

"Where's the deputy?" Russ asked.

Hamilton glowered. "The sheriff has decided that whatever danger Kimberly was in has passed, and she pulled the guard earlier this afternoon."

"Is that wise?" Tricia asked.

"I don't think so, but she wasn't interested in my opinion," Hamilton said. "That's why I've decided to spend the night. Someone needs to look out for Kimberly's interests."

Kimberly blinked, her brow furrowing as she tried to follow the conversation.

Tricia waggled a finger at Hamilton, who got up from the bedside chair to follow her.

Russ reached over to take the cup of cola and spoon from Hamilton's hands. "Hey, Kimberly, did you ever play dinnertime airplane when you were a kid?"

She looked at him quizzically. He dipped the spoon into the flat soda and waved it back and forth in front of Kimberly's face, her gaze joyfully following.

"*Yee-ow, yee-ow,*" he intoned, mimicking a small aircraft, and gently landed the spoon onto her tongue.

She swallowed and laughed. "A-gah!" she said.

Russ obliged.

Hamilton followed Tricia into the corridor, his hands plunged deep into his pants pockets, his shoulders slumped. "She's pretty high on painkillers," he said, glancing back into the room. "They're planning to wean her off them in the next couple of days."

Tricia nodded. "I'm so glad she's making progress, but it was really you I came to see."

"Me?"

"I found the woman who wrote the Jess and Addie books."

He frowned. "Why am I not surprised?"

"It really wasn't that hard. But I will admit I had some help."

"And what do you expect me to do about it?"

"Help me expose Zoë's killer."

"You know who killed her?"

"I'm pretty sure I do. And I'm pretty sure I know why, too."

"He wants a cut of the money."

"She."

He turned, looked back into the hospital room. "And you think this person is the one who attacked Kimberly, too?"

"I do," Tricia said, and nodded.

"Then, yeah, I'll help you. I'll do anything to put that bitch behind bars."

TWENTY-THREE

ANGELICA WAS ALREADY ensconced in Tricia's loft apartment by the time she and Russ returned to Stoneham. They knew this even before they opened the door because the heavenly aroma of something delicious met them on the stairs.

Miss Marple greeted Tricia at the door, looked up at Russ, and turned away in disgust. Luckily, he was used to her reaction and took no offense.

"Finally!" Angelica called from her position at the stove. Decked out in peach sweats and fluffy pink slippers, there was no doubt she felt totally at home in Tricia's digs. "How was Kimberly?"

"Awful. I mean, she'll recover, but I hope she's got good insurance. She'll be seeing a lot of her dentist in the next few months. You should've seen Russ with her. Her mouth smelled awful, but he spoon-fed her warm cola."

"*Ewww.* She's a stranger. How could you do that?" Angelica asked.

Russ shrugged. "I used to help my mom by feeding my grandmother after she had a stroke. It never bothered me."

"You're a very nice man," Angelica said, and pointedly stared at Tricia, mentally transmitting the words *Who you don't appreciate enough.*

Maybe she was right.

"Ange, you didn't have to cook for us," Tricia said. "We were going to call for a pizza."

"You two live on pizza. You need *real* food."

"I agree," Russ said. "What smells so great?"

"Chicken cordon bleu."

"Homemade?" he asked hopefully.

"Sort of not. But this shortcut version is really tasty. Now that you're here, I can pop them back in the oven," she said, and removed a plate from the fridge, transferring the contents to a baking sheet and into the oven.

"What are we having with it?" he asked.

"Caramelized carrots and stuffed baked potatoes. Is that okay?"

Russ nodded. "I'll say."

"I appreciate the effort, but aren't you tired after working alone all day?" Tricia said, already feeling guilty.

"I wasn't alone," Angelica said, and stirred the carrots on the stove. "At least not the whole day. You want a beer or something, Russ?"

"You bet," he said.

Angelica turned toward the fridge.

"You've hired someone?" Tricia took off her coat and handed it to Russ, who hung it, plus his own, on the oak hat tree in the corner.

Angelica handed Russ his beer and a pilsner glass from the cupboard. "I contacted another employment agency. They sent over a woman who'd never worked retail a day in her life," she said, and turned up the heat under the carrots.

"And she's already quit?"

"No, but I wouldn't be surprised if I have to call them to send me someone else before the end of the week. I just can't get competent help."

Tricia ground her teeth together to keep from speaking.

"Then again, I wonder if there's any way I could wrestle Frannie away from the Chamber of Commerce."

"Wouldn't that just upset Bob?" Tricia asked.

Angelica waved a hand in dismissal. "Oh, he'd get over it . . . eventually. It's just that he can offer her benefits like health care and the like." She sighed dramatically, truly the epitome of the put-upon small business owner.

"It might be a stretch, but you could offer benefits," Russ pointed out. "Of course you'd have to pay for it. I do it for my two employees through a group plan."

"Oh?" Angelica said, actually sounding interested. "Doesn't the Chamber offer insurance? I know some do in New York."

Russ shook his head. "It's not legal here in New Hampshire. But I'm pretty sure the Chamber stocks a few brochures on local group plans for their members. Ask Frannie for one. She doesn't have to know why you want it."

Angelica raised an eyebrow. "I might have to offer benefits just to keep an employee for more than a few weeks." She shook her head. "People these days have such an entitlement complex. They think everything should be done for them. Tricia—set the table," she ordered, her tone full of entitlement.

Tricia did as she was told. Chicken cordon bleu made a far better dinner than pizza. It made one more affable to commands from someone else in one's own kitchen. She only half listened as Russ and Angelica discussed the pros and cons of group health insurance plans. She needed to keep Angelica away from Haven't Got a Clue tomorrow night. Perhaps she could enlist Bob's help—get him to take Angelica out of the picture and keep her safe from any potential harm.

Or was she just getting paranoid? Was it likely Nikki would pull out a gun and shoot whoever was in the store at the time? *Don't be silly*, she chided herself, yet worry continued to worm through her. Her grand plan was hit-and-miss at best. She was counting on the element of surprise.

Nikki was the unknown, possibly explosive, factor. If she was capable of murder—and attempted murder—what else was she capable of?

"Would you like a glass of wine, Trish?" Angelica asked.

Tricia looked up, took in her sister's face. Angelica was here, in her kitchen, cooking a meal for her, because she didn't want Tricia to be alone—to possibly face a murderer with no backup. That was a form of love she'd never expected to receive from Angelica.

Tricia gave her sister a sincere smile. "Yes, Ange, I would."

The phone rang the whole next day, and tour buses disgorged hundreds of tourists looking for bargains, rare books, and the volumes missing from their personal libraries. Haven't Got a Clue hadn't been this busy since the week before Christmas. Even the weather had seemed to break, bringing warmer temperatures and a flood of customers.

Besides being kept busy by the minutiae of running her own business, when others weren't on the phone to Tricia, she was on the phone contacting the players for the little drama she expected to produce that night. Only Sheriff Adams balked at the idea. It was time to implement Plan B.

Back in her loft apartment, Tricia dialed Grace Harris's number, crossing her fingers that she'd find Mr. Everett's companion at home.

"Hello?" Grace answered.

"It's Tricia Miles. I've got two reasons for calling. First, I've had to cancel tonight's meeting."

"Oh, and I was so looking forward to it."

"I'm a little pressed for time, so I'll let Mr. Everett explain everything."

"Secrets?" Grace said thoughtfully.

"For the time being."

"Just like a good mystery. I shall look forward to seeing William tonight. But what's your other reason for calling?"

"As I think you're aware, Sheriff Adams and I aren't the best of friends."

Grace laughed. "I think the entire village knows that."

"You, on the other hand have a lot of clout in this town. I need to get the sheriff to come to my store at six p.m."

"Does this have anything to do with Zoë Carter's death?"

"Yes, it does."

"Will the sheriff be making an arrest?"

"If someone can persuade her to come. The problem is, she's already rebuffed my invitation to join us. She wasn't happy last fall when I tried to

point her in the direction of Doris Gleason's killer, and she isn't open to my suggestions now, either."

"I'll do my best to persuade her, and get back to you after I speak with her."

"Thank you, Grace. I can't tell you how much this means to me."

"Dear, it doesn't begin to repay you for what you did for me last fall. I'll call you as soon as I speak to her."

"Thank you, Grace. Good-bye."

TRICIA WAS GETTING more antsy by the minute. At almost three o'clock, when she could stand the inactivity no longer, she grabbed her coat and escaped the shop, heading for the Chamber of Commerce. This mission was too important to accomplish via telephone.

As usual, Frannie was on the phone when she arrived. She waved a less-than-cheerful hello and continued talking, her voice lower, less boisterous than usual. In fact, she almost sounded depressed—something Tricia hadn't thought Frannie was capable of.

Knowing this might take time, Tricia wandered into the cabin's main room, bypassing the free coffee and heading for the brochure rack. As Russ had mentioned, in addition to tourist material covering the bulk of southern New Hampshire, Tricia found a folder for the local group health insurance plans. She glanced through it before pocketing it for Angelica. On impulse, she grabbed one for herself, too.

At last, Frannie hung up the phone. "What brings you out to visit during work hours?"

"I had an errand to run," Tricia lied, "and thought I'd kill two birds with one stone. You're the last one on my list."

"List?"

"Of members. I wanted to personally let you know that I had to cancel the book club meeting for tonight."

"Oh, and I was so looking forward to it. I thought it might be good for all of us to get together to, you know, kind of heal after what happened last week. But maybe it's better for us to just take a break. Has something come up?"

"Yes. I've already spoken to everyone else to let them know."

"And?"

"And?" Tricia echoed.

"What came up?"

"Oh. Well . . ." Her mind scrambled. "It's . . . it's Angelica. She's had such a hard time keeping workers that she's fallen terribly far behind in her paperwork.

I felt so bad for her I volunteered to help her out this evening—what with it being early closing and everything."

"That is so sweet of you."

Tricia nodded. "Well, that's what being a sister is all about."

Frannie sighed. "I just had the best time helping Angelica out on Sunday. I wish I could do it again."

"Oh? I thought she said you'd be coming back next weekend."

"I'd love to, but Bob won't let me."

"He won't let—why?"

"He doesn't think it looks good for the Chamber's only paid employee to be moonlighting at a second job."

"But helping Ange isn't like a real job. It's helping out. Okay, so maybe she paid you—she did pay you, didn't she?"

"Oh, yes. And very well, too."

"But that isn't a regular job."

"According to Bob it is."

"But he knows how swamped she is. How could he begrudge you helping out his girlfriend?"

"I don't know. I've known Bob for over a decade, and I've never seen him so angry." Her lip trembled. "It really hurt my feelings."

"I don't blame you for being so upset," Tricia said. "Does Angelica know about this?"

"I didn't think it was my place to say anything. But I do need to let her know I can't help her out this weekend. And I was so looking forward to it."

"Do you mind if I speak to Bob?"

"That's up to you. But don't be surprised if he reams your ears out good, too."

He'd better not, Tricia thought.

Frannie let out a breath and straightened. "I'd best get back to work. I don't want Bob angry with me if I don't get the monthly flyers folded, stuffed, stamped, and to the post office before the end of the day."

"Okay. I'll see you soon."

Frannie sniffed, and for a moment Tricia thought she might cry. She reached out and gave her friend a hug. "It'll work out," she said.

"I hope so," Frannie said, and pulled back from the embrace. "Until yesterday, I loved my job. I hope I can feel good about it again in a week or so." She turned back to her desk.

Tricia left the Chamber office and marched next door to the Kelly Real Estate office. By the time she yanked open the door, steam threatened to escape from her ears.

Bob sat at his cluttered desk. He looked up at her entry and smiled. "Hey, Tricia, I was just about to call you on—"

"What have you done to poor Frannie?" she demanded, cutting him off.

"Done?" he asked, and stood, his plastered-on grin faltering.

"Yes, I just spoke to her, and she said she'd gotten in trouble for working at the Cookery on Sunday."

"Yes."

"Why?"

"Because it looks bad for the Chamber."

"How?"

"Frannie is the public face of the Chamber. She gets paid a decent salary to work for us."

"Minimum wage?"

"No. We pay her better than that. A bit better."

"A bit better? What does that mean?"

"Two dollars an hour over minimum wage."

"And you expect her to live on that? I'm surprised she hasn't had to find a second job before now. Oh, wait, you'd probably fire her if she did."

"Now, Tricia, she gets health care benefits, too."

"And how much does she have to pay toward that?"

"Fifty percent."

"Fifty percent?" she repeated, hardly believing what she'd just heard. "On two dollars an hour over minimum wage?"

"There aren't that many clerical jobs in Stoneham. Frannie's lucky to be with us. She's only got a high school diploma, you know."

"Doesn't ten years of experience with the Chamber count for anything?"

Bob shook his head, his expression insufferably patient, as if he was about to speak to someone with a low IQ. "We're paying a wage commensurate with her education and comparable jobs within the community."

"Then obviously the community isn't paying its female workers a living wage."

Bob shook his head again and looked at his watch, as though she was taking up too much of his time.

"Who's going to tell Angelica about this?" Tricia demanded.

"Angelica?" he repeated, a note of alarm entering his voice.

"Yes. She's expecting Frannie to show up to help her out on Saturday. I don't think it ought to be Frannie who tells Angelica why she can't be there. And I don't think it should be me who tells her, either. That leaves only one person."

"Me?" he asked, appalled.

"Yes, Bob, you. And the sooner, the better. In fact, this evening would be

perfect. It's early closing night. You could take her to dinner and break the news to her. Take her someplace nice, too, won't you?"

"I'd planned to take her to this little seafood place I know in Portsmouth."

"That's wonderful. And I'll make it my business to talk to her tomorrow morning to make sure this little situation has been resolved."

"You'd check up on me?"

"Yes. And if she doesn't know the reason why Frannie can't work for her on Saturday, I *will* tell her myself, and you can bet I won't put the same spin on it you would."

"That sounds like a threat."

"You bet it is," Tricia said. She turned, grabbed the handle, and made sure she slammed the door on her way out.

TRICIA WORKED OFF most of her anger on the chilly walk back to her store. She stopped off at the Cookery to find a harassed Angelica overwhelmed with customers. Whipping off her coat, she held down the register for fifteen minutes while her sister helped patrons. Thankfully, the bus that awaited most of the customers had a tight schedule, and the store soon emptied out.

"Thanks for showing up when you did. It's been like this all day," Angelica said, breathless.

"What happened to your new employee?"

"She didn't show up." Angelica studied Tricia's face. "Why are you here?"

Tricia wriggled back into her coat sleeves. "I brought you this," she said, taking the health care brochure out of her pocket. "I haven't had a chance to look at it, but you might want to study it carefully. Hiring Frannie away from the Chamber might not be as difficult as you thought."

"What do you mean?"

"That's for you to find out. I'm sworn to secrecy."

"Intriguing," Angelica said with a smile. She looked down at the brochure in her hand. "I will study it. Thank you."

The phone rang, and Angelica practically jumped on it. "The Cookery, how can I help you?" She paused. "Oh, Bob, it's you! Sure, I'm free tonight."

Tricia forced a smile and waved as she let herself out. At least one part of her plan had been set into motion. She continued down the walk to Haven't Got a Clue. It was full of customers who were in need of assistance.

As the rest of the afternoon wore on, and still no word from Grace, Tricia's anxiety multiplied. As she checked her watch for the hundredth time, she hoped Nikki had been kept as busy over at the Stoneham Patisserie. At the

same time, if she was run ragged, Tricia worried Nikki might opt out of attending the weekly book club meeting—which would spoil everything.

At T minus one hour, she dialed the number.

"Stoneham Patisserie, this is Nikki. How can I help you?"

"Hi, Nikki. It's Tricia over at Haven't Got a Clue. I just wanted to make sure you'll be attending the book club meeting tonight. I managed to line up a special guest—someone in publishing who was here for Zoë's memorial service. He stayed in town an extra couple of days just so he could talk to the group. I'd like to have as many warm bodies as possible in the store to make him feel welcome."

Nikki sighed, and Tricia flinched, afraid her plans might already be on the verge of unraveling. "I guess I can make it, but I can't pull off a cake on this short notice. Can I bring something else? Cookies?"

It was Tricia's turn to sigh—with relief. "You don't have to bring anything," she said. "I've got everything covered."

"Oh. Well, okay. I'll be there around six."

"See you then," Tricia said brightly and hung up the phone. No sooner had she set the receiver down than it rang again. "Haven't Got a Clue, this is Tricia."

"Tricia, it's Grace."

"Thank goodness. I was getting worried. Do you have good news for me?"

"It took some persuasion, but I've convinced the sheriff to arrive at precisely six o'clock."

"What excuse did you give her?"

"None at all. I just reminded her of her duty, that she's a public servant, and that it would be in her best interest to be there on time."

"And she bought it?"

"I believe she respects my reputation and the authority I used to wield. I wonder if I could use that same tactic to get the Board of Selectmen to step up their efforts and find a humane solution to the geese problem."

"Grace, I'm sure you could."

"Thank you for your faith in me. Ah, I think I hear William at the door. I'm looking forward to hearing all about the intrigue that's going on at your shop."

"And I'll be glad to update you later myself."

"Thank you, dear. Good night."

Tricia hung up the phone.

"Aha! The stage is set," Ginny said, as she wrestled into her jacket a full half hour earlier than usual. Mr. Everett had been dismissed early after flawlessly performing his part of Tricia's scheme.

"Stage?" Tricia asked, pretending she hadn't thought of what lay ahead in the same terms.

"Didn't Shakespeare say that in one of his plays?"

"Not that I'm aware of. Now scoot, will you?"

Ginny hesitated halfway to the door, her expression growing serious. "I don't like this, Tricia. I think you should cancel the whole thing."

"It's too late now. And anyway, I'm not a bit worried," she lied.

"Well, I am."

No way did Tricia want Ginny hanging around and possibly spoiling everything. She came around the cash desk and put an arm around Ginny's shoulder, guiding her toward the door. "Look, if it'll make you feel better, I'll call you at home later tonight, okay?"

"Well, okay."

"Now go home. Relax."

"I'll go back to our house, but it's not yet a home."

"It will be one day." Tricia opened the shop door, gently pushed Ginny through. "I'll see you tomorrow. Say hi to Brian for me."

"Good night," Ginny called, and shuffled down the sidewalk toward the municipal parking lot.

Tricia shut the shop door, turning the cardboard sign around to CLOSED, but she didn't lock the door. Nor did she shut the blinds along the big display window. If something unforeseen was destined to happen, she wanted Haven't Got a Clue to stand out like a lighted stage with the curtains drawn for the whole world to see.

She looked out over the street. Several of the other bookstores were already darkened. Tuesday was early closing night for most of the booksellers and other merchants. It was no joke that they rolled up the sidewalks of Stoneham a little after six p.m. If something unusual did happen, would there be anyone around to notice?

That's when she saw Russ across the street, standing in the doorway of History Repeats Itself, trying to blend in with the shadows. She raised a hand to wave, but he ducked out of sight. He'd promised he'd be there, cell phone in hand, to call 911 in case of an emergency.

There will be no emergency, Tricia told herself. And if she was lucky, this whole fiasco with Zoë's murder and Kimberly's attempted murder would be over and done with within the hour. Tricia glanced at her watch. She was still two players short for her little production: Artemus Hamilton and Wendy Adams.

A silhouetted form paused in front of the shop. The door opened and Hamilton stepped inside. "Am I too late?"

"No," Tricia said, relief flooding through her. "Let me take your coat."

He stuffed his leather gloves in his pockets, unbuttoned his coat, and shrugged out of it. Tricia took it to the back of the shop to hang with the others.

"What do you want me to do?" he asked, when she returned.

"Why don't you stand over by those shelves? I'll make all the introductions once the sheriff gets here."

Hamilton looked around the shop, his gaze resting on the nook for a moment. "Whatever," he said.

The door opened, the bell above it jangling. Angelica stepped inside, dressed to the nines in her pink-dyed rabbit fur coat, another enormous purse, and matching magenta stilettos. "Why is your CLOSED sign up?" she said, noting the two people in the store and turning it around to say OPEN again. "It isn't six o'clock yet."

"And why aren't you in your own store?" Tricia said, charging forward.

"I closed early and didn't want customers pounding on my door. I'm meeting Bob here. He's taking me to Portsmouth for dinner overlooking the harbor."

"That's all very nice," Tricia said, pushing her sister back toward the door, "but I think you should just go back to the Cookery and wait for him."

"What's the big deal?" Angelica protested, digging her heels into the carpet. She caught sight of Artemus Hamilton lurking farther back in the store. "Oh, Mr. Hamilton!" she called brightly and waved.

"Ange, you've got to go. Now!"

Before Tricia could maneuver here sister to the exit, the door opened again, but instead of Wendy Adams, it was a coatless Nikki who stood in the open entrance, still dressed in the white waitress garb and thick-soled shoes she wore at the patisserie—a full twenty minutes early. "What's going on, Tricia? Frannie just stopped by the shop and told me the meeting had been canceled. But you called me not half an hour ago to say there was a special guest coming in. What gives?"

Rats! Her worst fear had come to pass.

"We do have a guest. In fact, we have two."

"Then what—?"

The woman who'd been quietly sitting in the nook, her back to the door, finally stood. Slight, with shoulder-length graying blond hair, she turned, face taut, arms rigid, and fists clenched at her sides.

"Nikki, this is Fiona Sample. She writes the Bonnie Chesterfield librarian mystery series," Tricia said.

Nikki gave the woman a quick once-over. "Oh, sorry. Nice to meet you." She turned back to Tricia. "What's going on? What gave Frannie the idea the meeting had been canceled?" She looked around the room, her gaze settling on the only other person in the shop. Nikki took him in, and Tricia wondered if she'd remember Hamilton standing next to Kimberly at the statue dedication.

"I could've brought some cookies or cupcakes if I'd known," she said,

distracted. "I should go home—change. Where is everyone else? Will they be here at six?"

"This is a private signing," Tricia said, and turned to her guest. "Fiona, I'd like you to meet Nikki Brimfield."

Fiona held out her hand. Nikki took it, shook it impatiently. "Nice to meet you," she said again.

"But we've met before," Fiona said, her voice shaking.

"Before?" Nikki echoed, puzzled.

"Yes. I'm your mother."

TWENTY-FOUR

Nikki's jaw dropped. "My mother's name was Faith. She died over twenty years ago."

"She left Stoneham over twenty years ago," Fiona said. "But here I am." Her right hand dipped into the pocket of her long, dark skirt. She pulled out an old photograph, handed it to her daughter.

Nikki stared at the image of a little girl on a bicycle.

"I have more in my purse. Your seventh birthday. Even then you liked to bake. Remember, together we made a three-layer chocolate cake with marshmallow frosting?"

Nikki looked up from the photo to glare at the woman before her. "My mother is dead."

Fiona swallowed. "Your father's mother and your aunt told you that. Did they ever offer you any proof?"

Nikki opened her mouth to answer, then closed it again. "What are you doing here? Why now?"

Fiona's eyes filled with tears. "Because . . . I'm afraid. Afraid you've done something very, very bad."

"Me? I didn't abandon anyone. I didn't stay away for years and years," Nikki accused. "You let me believe you were dead. Where have you been all these years?"

"Believe me, I didn't want to leave. I told you—"

"But you did nothing to let me know you were alive, either."

"Your father gave me an ultimatum: leave without you—without anything—

or he'd kill me. I believed him. No one told me when he died. Many years later, I was told his mother and sister had had me declared dead."

"You could've come back."

"To what? I had no home—no one, except a daughter who probably hated me. And I had a new life, a new family in Canada. Was I supposed to abandon them?"

"Family?"

"Yes, you have a half sister and brother. Twins. They're sixteen now."

"Don't tell me Jess and Addie," Nikki sneered.

"No, Jessica and Andre. My husband's French Canadian."

Nikki crossed her arms defiantly over her chest. "So what do you want me to do, embrace you all with loving arms?"

"I came to ask you to do what's right. To give yourself up."

"What?"

"You've done a terrible, terrible thing."

"Just what is it you think I've done, killed someone?" She took in the faces of the people surrounding her, focusing on Hamilton's penetrating, hateful stare. "Good grief! You don't think I killed Zoë Carter, do you?"

Fiona's gaze swung toward Tricia.

"Tricia? What have you been telling people?" Nikki asked.

Tricia stepped forward. "I'm sorry, Nikki, but the evidence is pretty overwhelming."

"You wouldn't like to let me in on some of this *evidence*, would you?"

"You knew who the real author of the Jess and Addie *Forever* books was when you asked me to invite Zoë Carter to sign here at Haven't Got a Clue. She hadn't returned to Stoneham in several years, but an invitation to speak in her hometown as the last leg of her first and only book tour was an opportunity you could use."

"And what was I supposed to use it for, blackmail?"

"Zoë made millions off your mother's work."

The anger drained from Nikki's face, replaced by annoyance. "How was I supposed to shake her down for money? I didn't have any proof my mother wrote the books. I didn't even know they'd been published until a few months ago when I was browsing in this store."

"And what was your reaction when you found out?" Fiona asked.

"Okay, I was angry. It wasn't right that someone made money off of your work. But so what? I thought you were dead."

"So why didn't you out Zoë?" Tricia asked.

"What proof did I have? Was I going to tell a lawyer that Addie was afraid of thunderstorms? That was mentioned in the second book. I could tell them

that in *Forever Banished,* when Jess had to kill his horse, Prince, because he'd broken a leg, my mom cried buckets. But guess what? By the time I knew of the books being published, they'd been in print for years. Why would anyone ever believe some down-and-out baker in the boonies of New Hampshire? It would sound like sour grapes—or some kind of greedy envy."

"There's more," Tricia said. "The attack on the statue in the park. I saw a satchel full of tools in the patisserie on Sunday."

"So what? Steve knocked out an old closet so we could have more space for the baking trays."

"There was a can of red spray paint in the bag as well."

"Is it against the law to possess spray paint?"

"And Kimberly was attacked by someone wielding a sledgehammer," Hamilton said, finally joining in the conversation.

"Did she point the finger at me?"

"She doesn't remember what happened that night," he admitted.

"Very convenient," Nikki said.

"Someone forced Tricia's car off the road Sunday night. We could've been killed," Angelica said.

Nikki rounded on her. "What proof do you have that it was me?"

"None," Tricia said, "but you did give me poisoned food."

"Are you delusional?"

"The cut-out cookies and the red velvet cake you gave me were laced with some foreign matter that contained salmonella. A lab in Nashua has confirmed it—at least with the cake."

"You don't look sick."

"It wasn't me who ate them. Ginny Wilson and her boyfriend, Brian, did. Brian was so ill he was hospitalized on Saturday night."

"That can't be. I baked them myself, I—" She stopped short, her eyes growing wide in horror, her face blanching.

The door to Haven't Got a Clue opened, and Steve Fenton stepped inside. "What's taking so long, Nikki? I got the bakery cleaned up, but you know I can't cash out without you."

Nikki turned to face her assistant. "What have you done?" she asked, her voice shaking, frightened.

Steve shrugged. "Cleaned the bakery, like always."

She raised her left arm, pointed abstractedly at the people behind her. "They think I put something in those cookies and that cake I gave Tricia. They say they have proof."

"What are you talking about?"

"I assembled the ingredients for that cake, but you put it together and iced it. I baked those cookies, but you frosted them."

"You'd take their word that something was wrong with them?"

"Yes, because what they're saying makes a lot of sense. My God, I'm surprised the Health Department hasn't swooped in and closed me down." She clasped her head in her hands, looked at Steve in panic. "What am I thinking—they all think I killed Zoë Carter. They think I destroyed the statue in the park." She inched closer to him. "They think I attacked and nearly killed Kimberly Peters."

"You would never do that," Steve said, his gaze softening as he looked at her. "You could never hurt anybody."

Nikki closed her eyes and swallowed hard before speaking. "Please tell me you couldn't, either."

Steve looked away, his mouth flattening into a straight line, exhaling short breaths through his nose, sounding like an angry bull.

Tricia stared disbelieving at the couple before her. Steve the murderer? Not Nikki?

Then she remembered what Kimberly had told her the morning after the murder: that a man had called to tell her Tricia was spreading rumors about Zoë Carter's death, and Kimberly's supposed part in it.

With his focus still only on Nikki, Fenton clenched his fist, punched himself in the chest. "I take care of my own."

"Excuse me, but I don't belong to you. I don't belong to anyone. Not now. Not ever again."

"Nikki, it's just a matter of time," he said, oblivious of the others standing by in stupefied silence. "It's always been a matter of time before you turn to me. We were made to be together, babe."

"Why would you think that?"

"You hired me. You gave me work when no one else would. You and me. We're a team at the bakery. We can be a team in life."

"You killed Zoë Carter," she accused.

Steve didn't deny it.

"Why—why did you do it?" she cried, horror-struck.

"For you. I did it for you."

"But why?"

"I felt so bad when you told me about the books and your mother and all. The money that woman made off those books should have been yours. That woman was a liar and a thief. You could've had a better life—owned the bakery without bank loans. You wouldn't have had to work so hard."

"Stop calling it a bakery. And I *like* working hard."

"And what did you gain by killing Zoë and attacking Kimberly?" Tricia asked him.

"Gain?" he asked, blinking.

"Nikki could never prove her mother wrote those books. She'd never get her hands on any of that money. What was the point?" Tricia said.

Steve stood straight, looked her in the eye. "If Nikki couldn't have that money, I didn't want those bitches to have it, either."

The shop door opened once again, the little bell jangling cheerfully as Wendy Adams stepped inside. "What's this all about?" she asked Tricia, ignoring the others standing there like mannequins at the edges of the action taking place in the center of the store.

"What're you doing here?" Steve demanded, staring at the uniform and the badge on Wendy Adams's jacket.

"Apparently, I'm here to arrest someone. That is, if what I'm about to hear isn't yet another cock-and-bull story."

"You called the cops on me?" Steve demanded of Nikki.

"No. Tricia called them on me!"

Steve turned, his eyes blazing. He charged forward, yanked back his right arm, and punched Tricia square in the face. She fell back against the sales counter, clutching her bleeding nose as the room seemed to explode in a cacophony of noise. A raging pink blur launched itself at Steve, clawing and screeching like a banshee.

"Steve!" Nikki yelled.

"Nikki!" Fiona screamed.

"Stand back, stand back!" Sheriff Adams called, and yanked the handgun from its holster at her side.

"Angelica!" Tricia cried through the blood gushing over her lip.

The shop door banged open. "Tricia!" Russ howled, as Angelica and Steve rolled over and over across the carpet, Angelica punching him with the power of a pile driver.

"That's. For. Hitting. My. Sister. You. Stinking. Little. Coward!"

"Stop it! Right now!" Sheriff Adams ordered.

Russ jumped forward, grabbing Angelica's arms and pulling her onto her feet. She wasn't about to give up, and though she'd lost her shoes, she kicked at Steve again and again.

He lunged for her, but Wendy Adams's voice stopped him. "Don't make me shoot!" she hollered.

Fiona pressed a handful of tissues into Tricia's hand while Nikki hauled her to her feet. "Are you all right?" Fiona asked.

Angelica continued to struggle in Russ's arms.

"Stop it!" Sheriff Adams yelled once more, this time aiming the gun at Angelica.

"Wendy!" Russ yelled, outraged.

Steve lunged again, and Sheriff Adams charged up to him, planting the barrel of the gun against his temple. He froze.

"Don't make me shoot," she repeated, this time her voice low and menacing. "Firing a weapon means an awful lot of paperwork, and quite frankly, you're not worth it, scum."

Sirens screamed outside.

"Lie down on the floor. Now!" the sheriff ordered.

Fenton did as he was told as two deputies barreled through the door.

"Placer, take care of him," the sheriff said.

Another vehicle pulled up—the News Team Ten van. Portia hopped out before it came to a complete halt.

Angelica broke away from Russ, hurrying to her sister. "Trish, Trish, are you okay?"

"Ange, your coat is torn," Tricia said, her voice sounding high and squeaky.

"That doesn't matter. Let me see," she said, pulling the tissues away from Tricia's face. She recoiled. "Oh, Trish, I think your nose is broken."

The deputies pulled a handcuffed Fenton to his feet.

"Get him out of here," Sheriff Adams said.

"What's the charge?" Placer asked, as Portia stuck a microphone into the store.

"Apparently the murder of Zoë Carter and the attempted murder of Kimberly Peters. I'm sure we'll have a few more charges to add before the night is over."

"Wonderful!" Portia squealed, as the cameraman's lights flashed behind her. "Why did you kill Zoë Carter?" Portia asked Fenton. "Did you attack Kimberly Peters? Did you—"

"Get out of my face!" Fenton roared.

Wendy Adams straightened her uniform jacket, stood an inch or two taller, and prepared to meet the press.

"She's going to take credit for finding Zoë's killer," Angelica said, annoyed.

Tricia held the bloody wad of tissues to her nose and winced. "She can take all the credit she wants." She turned to face Nikki. "I'm so sorry I thought you—"

Nikki held up a hand to stop her. "Not now, Tricia. It's all too new. I need some time to think about it." She gazed at her mother. "To think about a lot of things." She moved to stand near the wall.

"Fiona, I'm afraid I've ruined whatever relationship you could've recaptured with Nikki."

Fiona glanced after her daughter, who stood, arms folded over her chest,

looking lost and forlorn. "I'm not ready to give up yet," she said, and crossed the room to stand beside her daughter. Nikki didn't turn away, so perhaps there was some hope of reconciliation, after all.

Yet another vehicle rolled up across the street from the store. The rescue truck from the Stoneham Fire Department. Two EMTs hopped out, gear in hand, and jogged across the road, headed for Haven't Got a Clue.

"I think your dates have arrived," Russ said.

"I don't need—"

"No arguments," he said, grabbed her arm, led her to the nook, and forced her to sit before he signaled the paramedics to come over.

Angelica consulted her watch. "Where is Bob? Our reservations are for seven."

"You're going to leave me?" Tricia cried, clutching for Angelica's hand.

"Of course not. Bob will have to cancel them. I hope they send you to Southern New Hampshire Medical Center instead of that rinky-dink hospital in Milford. Then we can order off the take-out menu from that little French bistro we went to the other night. At least the onion soup was palatable." She glanced down at her manicured fingers. "Oh, darn, I've broken a nail."

"Good grief," Russ said, "Tricia's gushing blood, her nose is broken, and you're worried about a broken nail?"

Angelica frowned, looked down at her shoeless feet. "I've got a run in my stockings, too."

"Angelica," Russ said sharply.

"Don't, don't," Tricia pleaded. "She saved me from Steve."

Angelica smiled. "All in a day's work, my dear sister, all in a day's work."

TWENTY-FIVE

"I THOUGHT YOU were going to call me last night," Ginny scolded Tricia before she'd even shucked her jacket the next morning. She'd arrived at Haven't Got a Clue half an hour before the store was to open—much earlier than usual. She took in Tricia's bruised face, and winced.

"It was late when I got home from the hospital. I didn't want to wake you," Tricia said, and tried to sniff. She couldn't breathe, at least not through her swollen nose. Already the skin around both of her eyes was turning a lovely

shade of purple. The concealer she'd applied wasn't meant for that degree of discoloration and failed to disguise it. "I didn't get home until nearly midnight. And I have to go back in two days for them to reset my nose."

"I had to find out all about it from the eleven o'clock news last night. You picked the wrong killer," Ginny accused. "Wasn't that really embarrassing?"

"You bet," Tricia said. "I don't see how Nikki can ever forgive me. If I was her, *I'd* never forgive me. And to make the accusation in front of her long-estranged mother . . ." She shook her head in disgust.

"So, are you okay?" Ginny asked.

"I feel like I've got a really bad head cold because of all the gauze packing my sinuses. But as I handed over my insurance card before I got treated, I remembered that you and Brian have no insurance. That's why—" Tricia reached under the cash desk and handed Ginny an envelope.

Ginny stared at it. "What's this?"

"Open it."

Ginny worked at the flap, removed the check that was inside. "Oh, Tricia—a thousand dollars." She looked up, tears filling her green eyes.

"I promised you a bonus for all your help this past week, and I wanted to make good on it."

Ginny shook her head. "I can't accept—"

"Oh, yes, you can. And not only that, I don't want you and Brian ever to be in a situation where you might put off a hospital visit because of the cost. That's why I've decided to get health insurance coverage for you and Mr. Everett through a local group health plan."

"Tricia, I don't know what to say. Thank you seems so inadequate." She threw her arms around her boss.

"It's enough," Tricia said, trying to swallow the lump in her throat.

Ginny pulled back, wiping tears from her eyes.

"I'll tell Mr. Everett as soon as he gets in," Tricia said.

"What a wonderful surprise. I can't wait to tell Brian," Ginny said, and put the check into her purse.

The door opened and Angelica burst into the shop, balancing a tray. "My poor baby sister. How are you feeling this morning?" she cooed. On the tray was a plate covered with a clean dish towel. "I'll bet you didn't have a thing for breakfast, so I've made you some muffins."

"Ange, you know I don't like sweet—"

"Who said they were sweet? These are sausage and cheese muffins." She removed the towel, allowing the aroma to escape. "Like to try one, Ginny?"

"Sure," she said, and plucked the top muffin from the plate.

The door opened again. This time it was Russ, carrying two insulated cups

from the Coffee Bean. "Hey, if I'd known you guys were here, I'd have brought some more," he said, and paused beside Tricia, bending to give her a soft peck on the cheek. "Wow, you look terrible."

Tricia faked a smile. "You sure know how to sweet-talk a girl."

"And she sounds like Rudolph the Red-Nosed Reindeer when he had the false nose on," Ginny chimed in. "I'll get the coffee going. You want a cup, Angelica?"

"I'd love one. Try one of these muffins, Russ."

"Thanks, don't mind if I do."

Tricia took a muffin as well, brought it up to her nose, and tried to sniff it. "I can't smell anything. I don't think I can taste, either."

The door opened again, this time admitting Mr. Everett. "Ms. Miles! I heard on the news you'd been hurt," he said. In his hands he held a brown paper sack. "I brought you some poppy seed bagels. I know they're you're favorite. I even brought you some dental floss to get the seeds out of your teeth."

"That's very sweet, of you, Mr. Everett, but—"

"I've already brought fresh-made muffins," Angelica broke in. "Would you like to try one?"

Mr. Everett removed his gloves. "Thank you, Mrs. Prescott."

"Miles," she reminded him. "I'm Ms. Miles again. And I think I'm going to remain Ms. Miles, no matter how many more times I get married. Did you bring butter or cream cheese with those bagels?"

"Both."

"Excellent. Give me that muffin, Trish, I'll butter it for you."

"But I don't think—" The door opened again. "What is this, Grand Central Station?" Tricia muttered, straining to turn to see who'd arrived this time.

Nikki and Fiona each held a tray as they descended on the nook. "Looks like a party," Nikki said. "And what's better than partying on fresh-baked Danish? Mom and I made them together."

"I brought bagels," Mr. Everett said, brandishing the paper sack.

"Nikki, I—"

Nikki held out a hand to stop her. "Tricia, don't you dare apologize. Mom and I talked until almost one last night. Added all together, the evidence—"

"All circumstantial—" Tricia interrupted.

"Was pretty convincing," Nikki finished. "Sheriff Adams called me this morning. Steve made a full confession. He admitted he handled goose droppings before he frosted those cookies, and when they didn't make Tricia sick, he actually put some in the red frosting on the cake."

Ginny blanched. "Oh, Lord! No wonder Brian was so sick."

Nikki nodded. "The Health Department came in first thing this morning and shut me down. I'm afraid the patisserie is closed for the time being."

"Oh, no," Tricia said.

"To tell you the truth, I'm surprised they didn't do it yesterday. Apparently there was a paperwork holdup, or they would have. And it might actually be a good thing in the long run—at least for me," Nikki added, trying not to smile. "You see, I got a call from the owner this morning. He's already lowered the price, and if the patisserie stays closed for any length of time—which means no income for him—he'll be really eager to unload it. By then I should have my new finance package assembled."

"Then at least one good thing has come of this," Tricia said.

"There are still some things I don't get," Angelica said. "Everybody knows Steve doesn't drive. So who tried to run Tricia and me off the road?"

"It *was* Steve," Nikki said. "It wasn't that he couldn't drive—he just didn't. He lost his license years ago from a DWI conviction. He never tried to get it back."

"But whose car did he use?"

"Apparently he stole one in Milford, then returned it to the same house he'd taken it from. If it weren't for the smashed windshield—"

"From where the goose hit it," Tricia piped up.

"The owner probably wouldn't have known it was even taken."

"Don't tell me Sheriff Adams figured that out."

Nikki shook her head. "Once Steve got talking, he couldn't shut up. He told the deputies *everything*."

"Can I try one of those Danish?" Russ said, dusting the muffin crumbs from his fingers.

"Oh, sure." Nikki held up the tray, offering him the pastries.

Angelica was still shaking her head. "But I don't understand where Zoë got the manuscripts. Tricia, didn't you say she got them at an estate sale? Did they come in a box lot?"

"I can answer that," Fiona said. "My husband didn't approve of my writing, so I had to hide the manuscripts. I lived in fear he'd destroy them, so I kept them in an old trunk. It sounds stupid and corny, but I put a false bottom in the trunk. If he'd ever thought to look carefully, he would've found them."

"Did you know about the trunk?" Tricia asked Nikki.

She nodded. "And I told Steve about that, too."

"The night Kimberly was attacked, I saw an old trunk in Zoë's home office. Steve did a real number on it. I doubt it can be repaired."

"I don't care about that. I left it—and the manuscripts—behind a long time ago," Fiona said.

"But aren't you furious that Zoë took the credit and made all that money from your work?" Ginny asked.

"Of course. I've got two kids who will head off to university in two years. I'll

probably consult a lawyer, but I don't have the kind of money to wage a long legal battle—and that's most likely what would end up happening."

"So no happy ending there," Ginny said.

"Perhaps not, but I'll never regret you sent me that e-mail, Tricia. It gave me a way to reconnect with my daughter." Fiona gazed at Nikki with loving eyes.

Nikki, however, wasn't as easily placated. "We've still got a lot of issues to resolve. A one-night chat-a-thon can't solve everything."

"But at least we've agreed to talk everything through and try to remain civil," Fiona added.

Nikki nodded. "Hey, it takes some getting used to, finding out the mother you thought was dead is still alive, and you've got a whole new family you never knew about. I've got a brother and sister to meet sometime in the near future."

Fiona gazed at her watch. "And I've got an interview in less than half an hour. Tricia, that friend of yours, Portia McAlister, wants to make me the feature on her newscast tonight, talking about how I wrote the Jess and Addie books, and what I think of all that's happened in the last week."

"That ought to give your Bonnie Chesterfield series a push, too," Tricia said.

Fiona laughed. "At the very least, I'm determined to prove that there's no such thing as bad publicity."

The door opened yet again, this time admitting Artemus Hamilton, whose leather-gloved hand held Kimberly's. Her face was still swollen and bruised, but her toothless smile would've brightened a cold, dark night.

"Tri-ah," Kimberly managed, "Oo loo li me."

"Not too much talking, now," Hamilton warned her gently. "Kimberly got released from the hospital first thing this morning, and we made a stop before coming here," he said.

Kimberly pulled off her left glove. "-ook!" She wiggled her hand, showing off what was probably a two-carat diamond on the ring finger of her left hand. "An Ar-ie's gonna sell my ook."

"I'm going to try," he said, glancing at her with fondness, seeing past her temporary ugliness to the beautiful soul beyond.

"Would you like a muffin?" Angelica said, proffering the plate.

Kimberly shook her head.

"For now, she can only drink room temperature liquids," Hamilton explained.

"An -oy, am I -ungry," she said, laughing.

"I have some good news for you, too, Ms. Miles."

"For me?" Tricia said.

He shook his head, then turned to look at Angelica. "I read your manuscript yesterday. It's well done. There's a market out there for time-stressed

working women who want to feed their families healthy foods. I think I could sell it—at least, I'd like to try."

"Well, of course you would," Angelica said, her smile as wide as Tricia had ever seen it, and she gave her sister an "I told you so" glance.

"We'll need to talk more about it, and you'll need to do some rewriting before I can start rounding it to publishers. But it doesn't have to happen today. I'll give you a call early next week."

"You have my number," Angelica said brightly.

"I've got a question," Russ said, directing his gaze to Kimberly. "The night you were attacked, you said the word 'stone' to Tricia. Did Steve Fenton tell you that was the name of the author of the Jess and Addie books, or were you talking about the desecrated statue?"

"Boph," she said. "He hur- me—hittin- me. Saying I wou- pay for wha- happen to Fayfe Thone."

"The thing is," Hamilton said, "Kimberly didn't have a clue who Fenton was talking about."

"I'm so sorry he put you through that," Fiona said.

"I sorry my aun- -tole you wok. Fo- a lon- time, I din know."

"Everyone thought you were dead," Hamilton added.

"That doesn't make it right, but I do understand," Fiona said.

Ginny brought over a tray of Haven't Got a Clue paper coffee cups, the carafe, sugar, and cream, setting it all down on the nook's table. She picked up a cup, raising it into the air. "Why don't we all cheer up?" she suggested. "We've got a lot to celebrate this morning."

"I sure do," Angelica said.

The door opened yet again, this time admitting Frannie Armstrong. "Come on, boss, we've got a store to open," she said, her smile so wide it showed off most of her teeth.

"Boss?" Tricia asked, in awe.

Frannie entered the store, closing the door behind her.

"In a minute," Angelica told Frannie. She picked up the carafe, poured coffee into all the cups. "Bob and I had a long discussion last night after we left the hospital." She shook her head. "Sometimes I don't know what I see in that man."

Amen, Tricia felt like echoing; instead, she bit her tongue.

"When I found out what he was actually paying Frannie, I knew I could do better, and even give her benefits. I called her last night the minute I got home. Woke her from a sound sleep, too."

"But that was one call I was glad to take," Frannie said.

"What about the Chamber?" Russ asked. "Who'll be manning the reception desk?"

"I offered to give Bob two weeks' notice, but he seemed in rather a big hurry to get rid of me. So much for a decade of dedicated service." Frannie shrugged. "I start today at the Cookery." She glanced at her watch. "We're supposed to open in twelve minutes, Angelica. Don't you think we ought to be going?"

Before Angelica could answer, the door opened once again. "It worked, Tricia, it worked!" Bob called, his voice jubilant. Then he caught sight of his former employee standing in the middle of the crowd, and his face fell. "What's going on?"

"Just a gathering of friends," Angelica answered. "And what worked?"

Bob tore his gaze from Frannie, focusing his attention on Tricia. "Wow, you look terrible."

"Thanks, Bob."

"I just stopped by to tell you your suggestion about introducing swans to the geese worked. When I couldn't come up with a live swan, I bought four or five decoys. Yesterday afternoon I installed them around the pond in the park. I haven't seen a goose since. I've called the Stoneham Golf Course and the Board of Selectmen. They're going to install swan decoys at every place the geese gather. That ought to fix them. And it's a happy ending for everybody."

Except that the geese would just move to other wetlands. Oh, well. That wasn't Stoneham's problem.

Ginny raised her cup once again. "We've all got something to celebrate this morning. I want to propose a toast." She turned and faced her boss. "To Tricia."

"Me? What for?"

"For solving a murder," Ginny said.

Fiona raised her cup, gazing fondly at Nikki. "For reuniting a mother and daughter."

Angelica handed her new employee a cup. "For helping me get a new job," Frannie said.

"And me a new employee," Angelica said. "Not to mention my new literary agent."

"For giving me an exclusive," Russ said.

"For not firing me," Mr. Everett said.

"For brin-ee Ar-ie to me," Kimberly said.

"And making me realize how much I cared for Kimberly," Hamilton confirmed.

"For telling us how to get rid of the geese," Bob said.

Tricia took in the smiling faces of all her friends, a lump rising in her throat. "Oh, well," she stammered. "If that's all, then." She raised her own cup. "I'll drink to that."

ANGELICA'S RECIPES

SHRIMP SCAMPI

1½ to 2 pounds large shrimp (about 16 to 24), peeled and deveined
⅓ cup clarified butter or olive oil
2 cloves minced garlic (I often toss in more)
6 green onions, thinly sliced
⅓ cup dry white wine or vermouth
2 tablespoons lemon juice, fresh if possible
3 tablespoons chopped fresh parsley
salt and pepper, to taste

Rinse shrimp and set aside. (If they're frozen, defrost them first.) Heat butter or oil in a large skillet over medium heat. Add garlic; cook 1 or 2 minutes or until softened; do not brown. Add shrimp, green onions, wine, and lemon juice. Cook until shrimp are pink, about 1 to 2 minutes on each side. Sprinkle with parsley and salt and pepper.

Serve over linguini or your favorite pasta.

Serves 4.

TLALPEÑO-STYLE SOUP

6½ cups chicken stock
½ chipotle chili, seeded

4 skinless, boneless chicken breasts
1 medium avocado (slightly underripe for easier handling)
6 scallions, finely chopped
14-ounce can chickpeas (garbanzo beans), drained
1 cup cooked rice
salt and fresh-ground black pepper
1 cup grated cheddar cheese
1 tablespoon chopped fresh cilantro (optional)

Pour chicken stock in a large saucepan, and add the chili. Bring to a boil. Add the whole chicken breasts, then lower the heat and simmer for about 12 minutes or until the chicken is cooked. Remove the chicken from the pan and let it cool a little.

Shred the chicken into small pieces and set it aside.

Cut avocado in half, remove the skin and pit, then chop into 1/2-inch pieces. Add it to the stock, with the scallions and chickpeas. Return the shredded chicken to the pan, add rice, and heat through. Add salt and pepper to taste.

Ladle into bowls, sprinkle with grated cheese. If desired, top with cilantro. Serve immediately.

Serves 6.

PASTRY CHICKEN CORDON BLEU

2 sheets frozen puff pastry
4 boneless chicken breasts
2 tablespoons butter
salt and pepper (optional)
8 slices Swiss cheese
4 slices deli ham (I like mine sliced medium to thick)

Thaw pastry at room temperature for 30–40 minutes. Season chicken with salt and pepper if desired. In a medium skillet over medium-high heat, heat butter; add chicken and cook until browned. Remove chicken from skillet. Cover and refrigerate at least 15 minutes.

Unfold pastry and place it on a lightly floured board; roll it out until it is 1 inch wider and longer. Cut pastry in half and layer 1 slice each of cheese,

chicken, and ham, and second slice of cheese. Fold over top half and press the sides closed with your fingers. Repeat the process, making a total of 4 pieces. Bake on an ungreased cookie sheet.

Bake in 400 degree oven 20 minutes, until pastry is puffed and golden. Serves 4.

STUFFED BAKED POTATOES

3 large baking potatoes (1 pound each)
1½ teaspoons vegetable oil (optional)
½ cup sliced green onions
½ cup butter, divided
½ cup half-and-half
½ cup sour cream
½ teaspoon salt
½ teaspoon black pepper
1 cup shredded cheddar cheese
Paprika

Rub potatoes with oil if desired; pierce with a fork. Bake at 400 degrees for 1 hour and 20 minutes, or until tender. Let stand until cool enough to handle.

Cut each potato in half lengthwise. Scoop out the pulp, leaving a thin shell. Place pulp in a large bowl and mash it. In a small skillet, sauté onions in ¼ cup butter until tender. Stir into potato pulp along with half-and-half, sour cream, salt, and pepper. Fold in cheese.

Spoon mixture into potato shells. Place on a baking sheet. Melt remaining butter; drizzle it over the potatoes. Sprinkle with paprika. Bake uncovered at 350 degrees for 20–30 minutes, or until heated through.

Potatoes may be stuffed ahead of time and refrigerated or frozen. Allow additional time for reheating.

Feel free to add other toppings, such as chopped chives, chopped mushrooms, or crumbled bacon to the mix.

Makes 6 servings.

PEANUT BUTTER BLONDIES

2 cups all-purpose flour
1½ teaspoons baking powder
½ teaspoon salt
⅔ cup butter
2 cups firmly packed brown sugar
2 large eggs, beaten slightly
10 ounces peanut butter morsels
1 cup chopped peanuts (optional)

Combine flour, baking powder, and salt in a bowl and set aside.

Melt butter in a large saucepan over medium-low heat. Add brown sugar and eggs, stir well. Gradually add to flour mixture. Add morsels and nuts, stirring well. (Batter will be stiff.) Spread batter in a lightly greased 13" × 9" × 2" pan. Bake at 350 degrees for 30 minutes. Cool completely in the pan on a wire rack. Cut into squares.

Makes approximately 30 brownies.

SAUSAGE–SWISS CHEESE MUFFINS

¼ pound mild or spicy ground pork sausage
2 cups all-purpose flour
2 teaspoons baking powder
¾ cup shredded Swiss cheese
¼ teaspoon ground sage
¼ teaspoon dried thyme
½ teaspoon salt
½ cup milk
¼ cup vegetable oil
1 egg, lightly beaten

Preheat oven to 375 degrees.

Brown sausage in a skillet over medium heat, stirring until it crumbles. Drain well. Combine sausage, flour, and next 5 ingredients in a bowl; make a well in the center of the mixture.

Combine milk, oil, and egg; add to dry ingredients, stirring until moistened. Spoon batter into greased (or paper cup–lined) muffin pans, filling ⅔ full. Bake for 20–22 minutes or until golden. Serve warm. Store leftovers in the refrigerator.

Makes 1 dozen.

NIKKI'S RECIPES

EASY-TO-MAKE WHITE-CHOCOLATE GANACHE

1½ cups heavy cream
8 ounces white chocolate chips

In a saucepan heat the cream and bring it to a boil. Remove from the heat. Place white chocolate chips in a large bowl and pour hot cream into the bowl. Let sit for 1 minute or so, then whisk until smooth. Transfer to the refrigerator to cool, stirring occasionally.

When mixture is cold and thickened, beat with an electric mixer into soft peaks, then beat the last few strokes by hand with a whisk until thick and firm. Do not overwhisk, or mixture will become grainy.

For flavored ganache, use 1 ounce less of cream (or 2 tablespoons) and add 1½ ounces (3 tablespoons) of rum or your favorite liqueur. Or add ¼ teaspoon vanilla extract, or other flavoring.

Ganache can stay at room temperature for 2 days, as long as it's kept in a cool place.

Makes about 1 cup.

BUTTERMILK SUGAR COOKIES

1½ cups sugar
1 cup vegetable shortening

2 eggs
1 teaspoon vanilla
4½ cups flour
½ teaspoon baking soda
3 heaping teaspoons baking powder
1 cup buttermilk (or commercial eggnog)

In a large bowl, cream together sugar and shortening until fluffy. Add eggs and vanilla. In a separate bowl, mix flour, soda, and baking powder. Alternate adding buttermilk and dry ingredients to the creamed mixture.

Refrigerate overnight.

Divide dough into 4 equal pieces. Roll out a portion on floured surface to ¼ inch thickness. (To keep dough from getting tough, use confectioner's sugar instead of flour.) Cut out with your favorite cookie cutters. Place on lightly greased or nonstick cookie sheets or parchment paper–covered baking trays.

Bake at 350 degrees for 8–10 minutes, until they just start to brown.

Cool in pans for about 5 minutes; transfer to cooling/wire racks, and cool completely before decorating.

Makes (approximately) 4 dozen.

FROSTING

½ cup confectioner's sugar
1½ tablespoons water
3 to 4 drops food coloring (or more as needed)
Colored sprinkles (optional)

In a small bowl, mix sugar and water to form a thick, smooth icing. Stir in food coloring to reach desired shade. Use separate bowls for additional colors. Frost cookies. Add sprinkles before icing dries.

RED VELVET CAKE

½ cup shortening
1½ cups sugar
2 eggs

2 tablespoons cocoa
1½ ounces (or 3 tablespoons) red food coloring
1 teaspoon salt
2½ cups flour
1½ teaspoons vanilla
1 cup buttermilk
1 teaspoon baking soda
1 tablespoon vinegar

Cream shortening; beat in sugar gradually. Add eggs, one at a time; beat well after each addition. Make a paste of cocoa and food coloring; add to creamed mixture. Add salt, flour, and vanilla alternately with buttermilk, beating well after each addition. Sprinkle soda over vinegar; pour the mixture over batter. Mix well.

Bake in 3 prepared 8-inch pans or 2 9-inch pans for 30 minutes at 350 degrees, or until toothpick tester comes out clean.

12 servings

FROSTING

1 package (8 ounces) cream cheese, softened
1½ cups butter, softened
3¾ cups confectioners' sugar
3 teaspoons vanilla extract

In a large mixing bowl, combine ingredients; beat until smooth and creamy. Spread between layers and over top and sides of cake.

Frosts one cake.

BLOOD GLAZE

You can color your cream cheese frosting with red food coloring, or make your own "stage" blood.

1 cup white corn syrup
1 tablespoon red food coloring
1 tablespoon yellow food coloring
1 tablespoon water (optional; it'll "thin" the "blood")

Mix well, drizzle over one side of cake.

Makes 1 cup (or ¼ pint).

Bookplate Special

. . .

For Gwen Nelson and Liz Eng,
my staunchest cheerleaders.

ACKNOWLEDGMENTS

Writing a book is always an adventure—and often I have no idea where the journey will take me until I reach the end.

I could not have written this book without Mona Durgin of the Greece Ecumenical Food Shelf. She gave me an extensive guided tour and shared her experiences, as well as other information concerning the operation and maintenance of a food pantry.

Gail Bunn of Grammy G's Café kindly let me pick her brain on more than one occasion, and even let me "play" behind the counter for a shift to get the feel of the workings of a small café.

Michele Sampson, director of the Wadleigh Memorial Public Library in Milford, New Hampshire, took me on a guided tour of Milford, and encouraged me to write about the Milford Pumpkin Festival. (And she knows all the best places to eat in Milford, too!) My Guppy Sister in Crime, Pat Remick, has been extremely generous answering my questions and offering me more "local color" to enrich my stories.

My blog buddies at Writers Plot were there to encourage me when I painted myself into corners, especially Sheila Connolly and Leann Sweeney, who were always ready for an impromptu brainstorming session. And I can't forget my wonderful first readers, Sheila Connolly, Nan Higginson, and Gwen Nelson, who pointed out the places where I tripped up.

Thanks, too, to my editor, Tom Colgan, and his wonderful assistant, Niti Bagchi, and to my agent, Jacky Sach.

Please visit my website, www.LornaBarrett.com, for news and information on the Booktown Mysteries. And if you can, please support your local food pantry—and your favorite bookstores!

ONE

"Get out of my house!"

"Get *out* of my house!"

"Get out of my house *right now*!"

Tricia Miles had always considered annoying fixtures to be expendable. Like the stainless steel sink in her last home. The key to a clean kitchen was a clean sink. Water spots became the bane of her existence. So without a hint of remorse, she'd had the sink replaced with a white porcelain one that came clean with a little bleach and very little effort.

Other fixtures in her life weren't quite so easily taken care of. For instance, Pammy Fredericks, her college roommate. Pammy had arrived two weeks before to "stay the weekend," and had since taken over Tricia's living room—and her life.

That was about to end. In fact, while Pammy was taking the first of her twice-daily, forty-minute showers, Tricia had packed one of her suitcases and placed it in the dumbwaiter at the end of her loft apartment over her mystery bookstore, Haven't Got a Clue, in the picturesque little village of Stoneham, New Hampshire—also known as Booktown.

By the time the water stopped running, Tricia had gulped down two cups of black coffee and rehearsed her speech at least a dozen times, with as many inflections.

The bathroom door opened and Pammy appeared, wearing Tricia's robe—which was at least three sizes too small for her—underwear, and a grubby, once-white T-shirt. A wet towel hung around her neck, and her damp, shoulder-length, bleached-blond hair fell in stringy clumps around her face. "Any coffee in the pot?" she called.

"No," Tricia answered, and forced herself to unclench her fists. Her nails had dug into her palms.

"Why don't you make some more while I go grab some clothes?" Pammy said, evidently missing Tricia's clipped tone, and headed for the living room.

"Pammy, we need to talk," Tricia said.

Pammy halted, though not because of Tricia's words. She took in the now

tidy living room, which had been cluttered with her possessions before she'd hit the shower. "Hey, where's all my stuff?"

"I packed it. Pammy, it's time for you to go," Tricia said succinctly.

Pammy turned, her mouth hanging open in shock. "But why? I thought we were having fun."

"We had fun the night you arrived. Since then . . . you've had fun. You have lain around my home, annoyed my cat, and interfered with my employees and my customers. It's time for you to go."

"I cooked you several delicious gourmet meals—supplied the food and everything. You said you enjoyed them."

"Yes, I did. Thank you."

"What about that box of books I gave you for your store? Haven't I always looked for books for you?"

"It was very generous of you . . . but they're not really what I carry."

Pammy's expression darkened. "If this is about what happened yesterday, I told you I was sorry," she said defensively.

Saying "I'm sorry" wouldn't have helped if the coffee she'd spilled on a customer's foot had been hot—which would have netted Tricia one nice, fat lawsuit. As it was, it had cost her one hundred dollars to pacify the woman and replace her coffee-stained leather shoes. Next up: getting the carpet shampooed.

But that wasn't the worst.

Tricia crossed her arms over her chest. She was through giving hints. "Pammy, I know about the check."

Pammy blinked. "Check?"

"Yes, the one you stole out of my checkbook and wrote to yourself for one hundred dollars."

Pammy laughed nervously. "Oh, that check. Well, you weren't around, and you've been such a generous hostess that I figured—"

"You figured wrong."

Pammy didn't apologize. In fact, she just stood there, her expression blank.

"Besides, two weeks is too long for a drop-in visit. It's time for you to move on."

"But I don't have anywhere to go!" Pammy protested.

"You have family in the next county."

"But I hate them—and they all hate me. You know that," she accused.

After sharing digs with Pammy once again, Tricia could well understand why the woman's family might not want her around. Pammy hadn't changed a bit since college. Lazy. Noisy. Freeloading. Irresponsible. And now a thief. How had Tricia tolerated living with her in that tiny dorm room for eight semesters?

This time, Tricia didn't back down. "I'm sorry, Pammy. You can't stay with me any longer."

A tense silence hung between them for interminably long seconds. Tricia waited for an explosion—or at least tears. Instead, Pammy's face lost all animation, and she shrugged. "Okay." She turned away to poke through the open suitcase Tricia had left on the couch. She picked up a blouse, sniffed under the arms, and set it back in the suitcase. She repeated the process until she found a shirt she deemed acceptable, grabbed a pair of jeans, and headed for the bathroom once again. "I'll be out of your hair in ten minutes," she said over her shoulder, with no hint of malice.

Tricia stood rooted to the floor. Her little gray cat, Miss Marple, jumped down from the bedroom windowsill, then trotted up to Tricia in the living room, giving her owner a "what gives?" look.

"You've got me," Tricia said. "But she *is* leaving."

"*Yow*!" Miss Marple said, in what sounded like kitty triumph.

True to her word, Pammy emerged from the bathroom less than five minutes later, her still-damp hair now gathered in a ponytail at her neck. "You didn't have to wait for me," she said. "Or did you think I'd steal your stainless cutlery?" Then she laughed.

"I thought I'd help you with your things."

"No need," Pammy said quite affably. She rearranged some of the clothes in the suitcase, latched it, and hauled it off the couch. She slipped her bare feet into her scuffed-up Day-Glo pink Crocs and eyed a carton on the floor. It was filled with books she'd acquired during her stay. "Can I leave this here for a couple of days—just until I get settled? I don't have room for it in my car right now."

"Sure," Tricia said, eager to do whatever it took to get Pammy out of her hair and out of her home. But then, even though her kindness had been abused, everything about this seemed so wrong, so . . . nasty . . . so unlike Tricia. "Where will you go, what will you do?"

"Today?" Pammy asked, and smiled. "I might just go to the opening of the village's new food pantry."

"The what?"

Pammy glowered at Tricia. "Don't you even know what's going on here in Stoneham? Stuart Paige is in town to dedicate the Stoneham Food Shelf."

"Who?"

Pammy gave her a withering look. "Do a Google search on the man—see what good he's done here in New Hampshire. You might want to follow in his footsteps." Pammy grabbed her purse, slinging the strap over her shoulder before wrestling the heavy suitcase toward the door.

Stuart Paige? The name did sound familiar.

"Do you need some money?" Tricia asked, the guilt already beginning to seep in.

Pammy managed a wry smile. "You already took care of that, thank you. Look, I'm sorry I told you I had nowhere to go. That wasn't exactly true. I've hooked up with some people here in Stoneham. I'm pretty sure I have a place to stay for the night—or maybe a few. You don't have to worry about me, Tricia. I've survived on my own for a long time now, although I may have to actually get a job."

For a moment, Tricia was speechless. Was it possible she could have tossed Pammy out days—even weeks—earlier, instead of fuming in silence? And what about the threat of actually looking for work? From what she'd said, Pammy had never held a job for more than a couple of months before some catastrophe would occur and she'd be asked to leave. Still, Tricia couldn't shake feeling like a heel. As Pammy brushed past her, Tricia reached out to stop her. "I'm sorry, Pammy. It just wasn't working out."

"Don't worry, Tricia. I always have a contingency plan." She dug into her jeans pocket and came up with Tricia's extra set of keys, handing them over. "Thanks." And with that, she went out the door.

"Miss Marple," Tricia called, and the cat dutifully hurried to the door. It was time for work. Tricia closed the dumbwaiter and sent it down, then shut and locked the apartment door as Miss Marple scampered down the stairs ahead of her. By the time Tricia got to the shop, Pammy was waiting for her to unlock the door that faced Main Street. Tricia retrieved Pammy's second suitcase from the dumbwaiter and carried it to the exit. Pammy's cheeks were pink, and for a moment Tricia was afraid she might be on the verge of tears. But when she spoke, her voice was steady.

"Good-bye, Tricia."

"I'm sorr—"

"No, you're not." Pammy shrugged. "I'll be back for those books in a couple of days. Bye."

Tricia unlocked the deadbolt and waited for Pammy to exit, but her departing guest stayed rooted.

"Did you piss anyone else off?" she asked.

Tricia frowned. "What do you mean?"

Pammy stepped over what had once been a carved pumpkin. Now it lay shattered on the sidewalk just beyond the welcome mat outside the shop's door.

"It didn't belong to me."

"No, carving a pumpkin is fun, and that's something I'll bet you haven't

had in a long, long time," Pammy said, stepping over the orange mess. She continued north down the street, without another word or a backward glance.

Tricia studied the shattered pumpkin; its crushed, lopsided, toothy grin looked menacing. She closed the door and went in search of a broom and a trash bag.

"Today is the first day of the rest of your life."

Never had an old saw held so much promise—and guilt—for Tricia. Though preoccupied with the whole Pammy situation, she managed to get through the store's opening rituals. Pammy's comment, that she might learn something from the likes of Stuart Paige—whoever he was—and the crack about having fun, had stung. She was a productive member of her community, pitched in at community events, and liked to think she treated her employees and customers well. And she had fun . . . sometimes.

Okay, not so much lately. She worked seven days a week, had no time for friends or hobbies, and her love life . . .

Lost in thought, she barely noticed when her assistant, Ginny Wilson, showed up for work a full fifteen minutes late.

"Sorry," she apologized, already shrugging off her jacket. "The car wouldn't start. Brian had already left for work, and I thought the guys from the garage would get to my place quicker than they did. And when I went to call you, the battery in my cell phone was dead."

Tricia waved a hand in dismissal. "The day started out crappy, so nothing could upset me this morning."

"Oh, good. Maybe I should ask for an extra day off—with pay," Ginny said, and giggled.

"You're not improving my mood," Tricia said, but didn't bother to stifle the beginnings of a smile that threatened to creep onto her lips.

"Isn't Russ back today? That should cheer you up. Have you got a date with him tonight?" Ginny asked, rolling her Windbreaker into a ball and shoving it under the sales counter, along with her purse.

Tricia's statement that nothing could upset her had obviously been a lie. Things hadn't been going so well on the romance front. Pammy's presence these past few weeks hadn't helped. "I'm not sure if he's back yet." Russ had been traveling on business a lot lately, although he hadn't exactly been candid about what that business entailed. As the owner/editor of the *Stoneham Weekly News*, why did he even need to *go* out of town, when nearly all his revenue came from local ads?

Ginny looked around the store, which was devoid of customers. "Goodness. Are we to have a Pammy-free day, or is she still in bed?"

"She's gone for good—I hope," Tricia affirmed. "After what happened yesterday, I felt I had to ask her to leave. I can't risk a repeat of her carelessness—not when it comes to my customers." She wasn't about to mention the forged check.

"Hallelujah! Now the cookies and coffee we put out will actually go to our customers, instead of being hogged by that—that—" Ginny seemed at a loss for words. She scrutinized Tricia's face. "What's wrong?"

Tricia sighed. "I feel bad about the way I—"

"Tossed her out?" Ginny suggested.

"I did not toss her out. I merely suggested that two weeks was a tad long for a short visit. Pammy wasn't the least bit fazed. In fact, she said she'd 'hooked up' with some local people."

Ginny pursed her lips and raised an eyebrow, but said nothing.

"Do you think she could've found a boyfriend here in Stoneham?" Tricia asked.

"Stranger things have happened." Ginny cleared her throat.

"Pammy mentioned the opening of a new food pantry here in Stoneham. What do you know about it?"

"Oh, yeah, I heard Stuart Paige is in town to dedicate it," Ginny said.

"Stuart Paige . . ." Tricia repeated. "I've heard the name. I just can't remember who he is."

"Some rich mucky-muck. He gives away money. That's got to be good karma, right?"

"I guess," Tricia said. The circa-1930s black phone on the sales desk rang, and she grabbed the heavy receiver. "Haven't Got a Clue, Tricia speaking."

"Tricia, it's Deborah Black." Tricia's fellow shopkeeper; owner of the Happy Domestic book and gift shop. "I just had a visit from your friend, Pam Fredericks. She wanted to know if I had a job opening. As it happens, I do. Did you know she's listing Haven't Got a Clue as her last place of employment?"

"What?"

"I thought that would be your reaction." Tricia could hear the smile in Deborah's voice.

"She never worked here. She only annoyed, and perhaps even alienated, a portion of my customer base by her presence."

"I thought so. I told her I would let her know, but with T-shirts and jeans, she doesn't dress appropriately for the image I want to convey."

And that was another reason Tricia had objected to Pammy hanging around Haven't Got a Clue. "Did Pammy list an address on her application?"

"Yes—yours; two twenty-one Main Street, Stoneham, New Hampshire."

"She is no longer staying with me," Tricia said emphatically.

"About time you finally got fed up with her."

"That happened two weeks ago. I asked her to leave only about an hour ago."

"You know what they say about fish and house guests: after three days they stink. I'd have asked her to leave eleven days sooner than you did."

"But I—"

"Felt sorry for her?" Deborah asked, sarcastically.

"I always considered compassion an admirable trait," Tricia replied.

"It is, sweetie. If you don't let people take advantage of your goodwill."

Tricia's entire body tensed at the dig. Oh, yes, she'd been a real sucker. "I'll try to remember that," she said coolly.

"Oh, Trish, don't get mad. Angelica feels the same way I do—as all your friends do. You do too much for everyone. You're just too nice. Think of yourself first, for once. You deserve it."

Talk about a backhanded compliment. At least Deborah thought Tricia was a good person. Pammy had just been upset when she'd tossed off her parting slurs. "I'd better get going," Tricia said, and glanced at the clock as though it would give her permission to end the call.

"Talk to you later," Deborah said, and the line went silent.

Tricia hung up the phone. She had better things to think about than Pammy Fredericks. And if Pammy used her name again as a reference . . . Well, she'd deal with it when and if it happened.

And it happened about half an hour later when Russ Smith walked through the door, carrying two take-out cups of the Coffee Bean's best brew. "Good morning," he called cheerfully, and paused in front of the sales counter. He leaned forward, brushed a kiss on Tricia's cheek, and handed her one of the cups.

"You're a sight for sore eyes," she said, giving him a pleased smile.

"So are you." He removed the cap from his cup, blowing on the coffee to cool it. "I had a visit a little while ago from—"

Tricia felt her blood pressure skyrocket and held up a hand to stop him. "Don't tell me; Pammy Fredericks. And I'll bet she was not only looking for a job, but listed me as her last employer, and my address as her residence."

"You've developed psychic abilities," he declared, and laughed.

"No. You're not the first person to give me this news," she said crossly.

Russ sipped his coffee.

"Are you likely to hire her?" Tricia asked.

"I asked her if she could type. She admitted to using only two fingers."

"Did you let her down gently?" she asked, hoping he hadn't.

"I didn't need to. I'm not looking for help. In fact . . . things haven't been going real well on the advertising front. I may have to let one of my girls go."

Tricia removed the cap to her coffee and frowned. "Yes, I've noticed the last couple of issues have had more filler than usual."

"Tough economic times mean tough measures." Russ took another sip and stared into the depths of his cup, his expression dour.

Time to lighten the mood. "Why are you wandering around town during working hours?" Tricia asked.

"I'm heading out for the opening of the new food pantry. You going?"

"No. I have a business to run."

"Stuart Paige will be there," he said with a lilt to his voice. Was that supposed to be some kind of inducement?

"Why does everyone think I'd care? I've met lots of famous people, especially authors. I'm not the least bit impressed by celebrity."

Russ held his hands up in submission. "Okay, don't shoot the messenger." He glanced up at the clock on the wall. "I'd better get going. Maybe I can get a couple of quotes for the next issue." He leaned forward, again brushing a soft kiss on her cheek. That made twice he'd missed her lips.

He started for the door. "Do you have plans for tomorrow night?"

"No."

"Good. How about dinner? We could go to that nice little French bistro you like in Milford."

Tricia shook her head; they'd been apart too much lately, and she didn't want to share Russ with a room full of other people. "Let's stay in. My place or yours?"

"Mine." He recapped his coffee. "Come on over as soon as you close the store. I'll have dinner waiting."

"Sounds great."

"There's something I want to talk to you about." He threw a glance at Ginny across the way. She was with a customer, but her gaze kept darting in their direction.

"I'm intrigued," Tricia said, hoping her inquisitive look would get him to give her more information.

Instead, Russ opened the shop door. "See you tomorrow, then." And out he went.

The vintage black phone on the sales counter rang once again. Tricia picked it up. "Haven't Got a Clue, this is Tricia. How can I help you?"

"Oh, good, it's you. I need a favor," said the disembodied voice of Bob Kelly,

head of the Stoneham Chamber of Commerce, president of Kelly Realty, and her sister Angelica's significant other.

Tricia had learned to tolerate him for her sister's sake, and even managed to sound cheerful when she replied, "What?"

"The Stoneham Food Shelf reopens today in their new location. The Chamber needs warm bodies to show up at the dedication."

"I'd love to go, Bob," she lied, "but I'm so tied up with the store."

Her customer had gone back to perusing the bookshelves, and Ginny joined Tricia. "I can take care of things here while you're gone. And Mr. Everett will be in here at two this afternoon. Go. Have a good time."

"That's great," Bob said, since he'd obviously heard Ginny. "It's a quarter mile north of Stoneham. That new pole-barn structure they've been building. Just head out Main Street, you can't miss it. I'll see you there in twenty minutes."

"But, Bob—!"

He hung up.

Tricia put the phone down and turned her gaze on her assistant. "Why did you say that?"

Ginny bounced on her feet, looking pleased with herself. "I thought you might like to go. Maybe Russ will take your picture and you can give the store some free publicity. Besides," she said, delivering the coup de grace, "it's for charity."

STONEHAM WAS READY for the leaf peepers—tourists who came to New Hampshire to enjoy the beauty of autumn. It seemed like every store and home was decorated with red and orange wreaths, pumpkins, and corn shocks, while big plastic spiders in imitation webs covered bushes and inflatable ghosties and goblins swayed in the gentle breeze. Kelly Realty had a stack of small pumpkins in its drive with a sign declaring FREE PUMPKIN WHEN YOU LIST WITH US.

Parking for the dedication was more difficult than Tricia had imagined. Of course, the Food Shelf's lot was meant to hold only a dozen cars, and so both sides of the road were lined with another twenty or so. Flattened in the center of the street was the remnant of another smashed pumpkin. She shook her head. Kids!

Tricia watched traffic zooming past, waiting for a break before making her way across the road to the newly constructed building. As Bob had described, it was corrugated metal with a green metal roof. According to the sign atop the long, low building, the Food Shelf would be sharing space with the Stoneham Clothing Closet. She hadn't heard about that, either. Maybe she didn't get out enough.

The heavy glass front door had been wedged open, and Tricia entered the building with trepidation. She soon relaxed when she recognized a number of other Chamber members—no doubt they, too, had been bullied by Bob to attend. She took in the space. The room was painted a flat white, and lined with chrome-wire shelving. Some of the shelves were already filled with sealed cardboard cartons. Cryptic notes in heavy black marker adorned the sides of the boxes. Colorful posters that encouraged donations helped make the interior a bit more cheerful.

Beside one of the shelves was a Lucite brochure stand filled with folded leaflets that looked like they'd been made on a home ink-jet printer. Tricia picked up one of the brochures, stuffing it into her purse to read through at a later time.

A hum of voices filled the space, and Tricia inched past several people. In the center of the room stood a sturdy, wooden workbench. It held a glass punch bowl filled with what looked like pink lemonade and several plates piled with an assortment of cookies. A little tent card announced that the baked goods had been donated by the Stoneham Patisserie. Tricia saw no sign of its owner, Nikki Brimfield. She was probably back at her bakery serving her customers—something Tricia felt she ought to be doing as well.

Bypassing the food and drink, Tricia saw Russ, his Nikon camera slung around his neck, working the room, encouraging people to stand together as he took their photographs, and then penciling their names in his ever-present steno pad.

Tricia's elderly employee, Mr. Everett, and his lady friend, Grace Harris, stood to one side, conversing with other attendees. Mr. Everett caught sight of Tricia, and gave her a cheery wave. She waved back.

Bob Kelly stood near the podium, chatting with a man Tricia didn't know. The guest of honor, perhaps? The silver-haired gentleman in the charcoal gray suit looked thin and wan, but as he nodded, taking in whatever Bob was saying, his dark brown eyes seemed kind. A group of bystanders hung on their every word, looking ready to pounce on the poor man the minute Bob let him loose.

"Excuse me," a middle-aged woman said, and sidled past Tricia. Dressed casually in navy slacks and a navy sweatshirt embroidered with red roses on white hearts, the fifty-something woman with gray-tinged brown hair stepped up to Bob, politely interrupted, and indicated it was time to get the show on the road. Bob stepped right in line. Tricia might have to make friends with the woman—anyone who could get Bob to stop talking had to be some kind of miracle worker.

The woman stepped in front of the podium and tapped the microphone. "May I have your attention, please?"

The buzz of voices quieted as all heads turned to the front of the room.

"Hello, I'm Libby Hirt, Chairperson of the Stoneham Food Shelf's Execu-

tive Committee. I'd like to introduce the rest of our board—" Tricia tuned out of the next portion of her speech as her gaze drifted to the shelving units. Canned and nonperishable boxed goods lined the shelves to her left, and were separated by type: dry cereal, pasta, canned sauces, fruits and vegetables. Pretty basic food items. Another shelf held nonfood items like shampoo, soap, dishwashing liquid, and paper goods.

Tricia studied the canned goods, her thoughts drifting to the sodium content of each unit. What about fresh food: fruits, vegetables, bread, milk, and meat? Did the Food Shelf supply those to its clients? She had a lot to learn—and suddenly she found she *wanted* to learn more about it, and was glad she'd taken a brochure.

Libby Hirt had moved on to thanking the Chamber of Commerce. "We're grateful for all their support—in terms of dollars *and* collection points." Bob positively beamed at the praise, as a smattering of applause broke out.

Collection points?

"I cannot thank Mrs. Grace Harris enough for her years of tireless work on our behalf. She has been a driving force for soliciting funds from the private sector. Thank you, Grace."

More applause. Mr. Everett patted Grace's hand, and she smiled shyly.

"But most of all, we'd like to thank our most generous benefactor, Mr. Stuart Paige. As most of you know, we've planned this expansion for a number of years. The Paige Foundation offered a matching grant, and I'm proud to say that we have met our financial match through the generous contributions of our supporters, allowing us to build this new home for the Food Shelf." A burst of vigorous applause interrupted her speech, and Russ stepped forward, raising his Nikon to snap a few photos.

"In the past twenty years," Libby continued, "we've been located in a number of churches, always outgrowing the space we've been allocated. This new building will allow us to house not only the Food Shelf, but the Stoneham Clothing Closet, which has been located in the basement of St. Rita's Church for the past two years. Having both resources available in a single location will save us time and expense, and will better serve our clientele."

Another round of applause greeted that announcement.

"Without further ado, let me introduce Mr. Stuart Paige."

The applause grew more robust, but Paige raised a hand to stave off the attention. It was only after Libby cajoled him that he stepped up to the podium. "Thank you. I'm pleased the Paige Foundation was able to help out. We're very proud of—"

A scuffling noise and sudden shouting behind them all interrupted his words. Tricia looked over her shoulder to see what was happening, and caught

sight of Pammy Fredericks outside. One of the male bystanders had grabbed her arm and was pulling her away from the open doorway. The more he pulled, the more shrill her voice became.

"No, I've got to see him," she shouted.

"Miss, you'll have to leave!"

"Not until I've seen Stuart Paige," Pammy hollered.

Another suited man threaded his way through the crowd. He kicked aside the wedge in the door and it closed, shutting out the noise.

"Er . . . as I was saying," a disconcerted Paige continued, but few faces turned back to listen. "It's been a pleasure to be here today. My continued hope is that hungry people will always find the help they need here at the Stoneham Food Shelf. Thank you."

Pammy and the two men disappeared from view, but it took Libby Hirt's voice to bring everyone's attention back to the podium. "Thank you, Stuart. I'd like to remind everyone that we're always looking for new collection points, either for nonperishable food or for putting out a can to collect cash donations. If you're interested in helping out, please feel free to speak to me or any of the other Executive Committee members. And thank you all so much for coming."

Again, everyone applauded politely as Paige and Libby left the podium. Paige paused to greet Grace like an old friend, giving her a brief kiss on the cheek.

Tricia glanced back to see the two men reenter the building, trying but failing to look inconspicuous as they melted back into the crowd.

Immediately the whispers began. Who was that woman? What did she want?

Libby had steered Paige toward the food, with Bob and a group of others shuffling along behind, like groupies at a rock show.

Tricia sidled past a crowd of the other guests and exited the building. She looked left and right, and saw Pammy's retreating figure heading back for town.

What was so important that she'd try to interrupt the dedication ceremony? What could she have possibly wanted to tell Stuart Paige?

TWO

BY THE TIME Tricia left the reception some ten minutes later, there was no sign of Pammy on the road. She arrived back at Haven't Got a Clue just in time for Ginny to take her lunch break. The next hour practically evaporated as Tricia

served a flurry of customers who were in a hurry to get back to their Granite State tour bus. A glance across the street told her that the new café's lunchtime crowd had rivaled her own. Booked for Lunch would be in the black in no time.

Ginny was ten minutes late getting back from lunch. By then Mr. Everett had arrived for his afternoon stint. He'd asked to work fewer hours for the past few weeks, and Tricia was concerned. He'd seemed tired. Was his health declining? She didn't like to ask, yet she'd come to depend on him, and she enjoyed working with someone who took pleasure in serving Haven't Got a Clue's customers as much as she did.

Mr. Everett was happily dusting the back shelves, and Ginny took Tricia's place behind the register. "Sorry I'm late," she said, but offered no explanation. Late to arrive, late from lunch. A pattern seemed to be developing. If it continued, Tricia would have to bring up the subject. She decided to wait another few days before mentioning it.

It was well after three, and Tricia's stomach growled furiously. "I'm going to slip over to Booked for Lunch to grab a bite. That is, if they have anything left," Tricia said, and donned the jacket she'd taken from the peg some twenty minutes before.

"Don't worry. We'll be fine," Ginny assured her, as a woman carrying a stack of books by Josephine Tey arrived at the register.

Though the sun had reappeared from behind a bank of clouds, the crisp October air was a bit of a jolt after the drowsy warmth inside Haven't Got a Clue, but it also felt invigorating. Any sunny fall day was worth celebrating. All too soon the winter chill would be upon Stoneham. A long, cold, gray—dull—season of ice and snow. Of course, the months before the holidays were the bright spot for retailers, but after New Year's, Tricia knew she'd find herself counting the days until spring—and the influx of tourists—would return to her adopted hometown.

Tricia waited for a lull in traffic before jaywalking across Main Street, heading for Booked for Lunch. Once again, she passed a flattened carved pumpkin. Was there a crime wave in Stoneham, or just a vendetta against small, round squashes?

Tricia's older sister, Angelica, had opened Booked for Lunch with great fanfare only two weeks before. But she hadn't given up owning Stoneham's charming little cookbook store, the Cookery. After hiring an exceptional manager six months before, she figured she could extend her entrepreneurial empire. It was her love of cooking and the long-held ambition to open a restaurant that had encouraged her to open the little bistro. "Little" was right—the storefront she'd rented was the smallest on Main Street. It had previously been used as office space. The village depended on the tourist trade and boasted only a small diner, so adding another venue to the lunchtime crunch had been encouraged by the

head of the local Chamber of Commerce—Bob Kelly, who also had been dating Angelica for just over a year.

The tourists were happy. The booksellers were happy. Everyone was happy.

Except Angelica.

"This is a lot harder work than I thought," she'd confided to Tricia after her first week in business. Now, seven days later, she looked even more haggard.

Ignoring the CLOSED sign that hung on the plate-glass door, Tricia entered the charming 1950s retro café with its chrome-edged, white Formica tables, the red-and-silver-sparkled Naugahyde booths, and the counter with six matching stools to her right. It wasn't what she'd expected in the way of decor when Angelica had first told her of her plans to open an eatery. But then Angelica was always a bundle of surprises.

Angelica stood behind the counter. Her blond hair was pinned in a chignon; crimson lipstick gave her face color, along with a matching scarf tied around her neck. A black-and-white polka dot blouse and tight black slacks completed the outfit. She looked like she'd stolen her costume from an *I Love Lucy* rerun.

"About time you showed up," Angelica said. She wiped her hands on a towel, reached for the undercounter fridge, brought out a plastic-wrapped plate, and set it on the counter. "I saved you a tuna salad plate."

Tricia settled on one of the red, round-cushioned stools. "How do you always know what I want?" she asked, delighted.

"I've known you your whole life." Angelica laughed. "I can read you like a book—you're not a mystery to me."

Tricia wasn't sure if that was good or bad.

Angelica supplied a napkin, fork, and knife. "Coffee or something else?" she asked.

"The chill in the air these past couple of days has put me on a hot chocolate kick."

"Hot chocolate it is," Angelica said, reaching under the counter and coming up with a paper packet. She grabbed a Booked for Lunch mug, which sported a stack of old-fashioned books along with Day-Glo pink lettering that matched the sign out front. After shaking the packet, she tore off the top, spilled the contents into the mug, and added hot water from the urn on the shelf behind her. "You can take off your jacket and stay awhile, you know."

"Oh. I hadn't even noticed." Tricia shrugged out of the sleeves, parking the garment on the empty stool beside her.

Angelica poured herself a cup of coffee and leaned against the rear-end-high shelf behind her. "I had to pull waitress duty again today—me, an about-

to-be famous author," she said, and blew a loose strand of hair away from her cheek.

Since Angelica's literary agent had sold her cookbook, *Easy-Does-It Cooking*, last spring, Angelica somehow managed to remind everyone—in nearly every conversation—that she was about to be published. "About" being relative, since the book wasn't slated to appear for another eight months. Tricia ignored the reminder. "What happened to Ana?"

"Immigration came after both her and José. It's too bad—he was really good at food prep, and she was wonderful with the customers. I don't know what I would've done if it wasn't for my new hire."

Tricia speared a piece of lettuce, more concerned with her lunch than the immediate conversation.

"Jake"—the cook—"was in a tizzy," Angelica continued rather theatrically. "Luckily my *new hire*"—she stressed the words—"had done salad prep before. Breaking in a new person during the lunch hour would've been too much to take. Thank goodness I didn't have to train her and handle the customers."

The tuna salad had chunks of celery mixed in, just the way Tricia liked it. She swallowed a mouthful. Angelica had seen herself in more of a hostess-cum-manager role, a raconteur more than a hands-on member of her kitchen or waitstaff. But honestly, did a café the size of Booked for Lunch need a manager and three employees? Still, Tricia didn't want to get involved in *that* conversation.

"Did you know there was a food pantry in Stoneham?" Tricia asked, thinking about her earlier conversation with Pammy.

"But of course. They dedicated it earlier this morning."

"Yes, I know. I was there. Bob bullied me into going."

Angelica ignored the assault on her boyfriend's character. "Libby Hirt is a wonder. And she can write a mean grant request, too."

Grant? "How do you know about all this?"

"I've talked with her dozens of times at the Cookery. She's one of the few locals who actually patronize my store. Like many of my customers, she's a frustrated amateur chef. Besides, your boyfriend just ran a big story about her and the Food Shelf in the last issue of the *Stoneham Weekly News*. Don't you ever read it?"

Though she usually glanced at it, the local weekly rag wasn't on the top of Tricia's to-be-read pile. Not when there were hundreds of new mysteries published every year, and thousands of her old favorites to be read and reread again.

"Stuart Paige himself was in town for the dedication," Angelica went on, sounding just a little catty.

"Everybody seems to know about this guy except me. Who is he?"

"You don't remember the scandal?"

"Scandal?" Tricia echoed.

"Yes. Senator Paige's playboy son. The guy who crashed his Alfa Romeo into Portsmouth Harbor. He saved himself and let his father's secretary drown."

Something about that did sound familiar. "When was that?"

Angelica exhaled a long breath. "Oh, must be twenty or so years ago now. Rod and I were living in Boston at the time. You were still in college."

Rod had been Angelica's husband number one.

"Paige was so consumed with guilt, he practically became a monk," Angelica continued. "And he's spent the rest of his life doing good deeds."

"Good deeds?" Tricia asked skeptically, poking at the lettuce on her plate.

"Oh, you know what I mean. He's made giving away his family's fortune into a lifestyle."

Tricia vaguely remembered the story, which hadn't fazed her at the time and had obviously had no lasting impact on her, either. Although it was refreshing to know the former bad boy had had a personality turnaround.

Thinking about Paige reminded Tricia about Pammy. "I may as well tell you; I asked Pammy to leave this morning. I mean, two weeks was way too long for a drop-in visit."

"And?" Angelica drew out the word.

"She seemed okay with it. She also put in applications around the village listing me as her last employer."

"Really." It wasn't a question.

"Pammy also showed up at the Food Shelf's dedication."

"No!"

"Yes. She was hauled off and asked to leave."

"Why?"

Tricia shrugged. "I don't know. The last I saw her, she was walking back to the village. She'd apparently been trying to talk to Mr. Paige."

"Is that so?" Angelica said thoughtfully. She glanced at the clock above her work space, then stretched her neck to look back through the swinging half-doors that separated the kitchen from the dining area. She sighed. "My goodness, my new hire's been on her break a long time."

Tricia pushed aside the orange-slice garnish on her plate.

Angelica sighed and again glanced at the clock. "It may have been a mistake to take on my new hire. It's . . . it's . . ." She stammered. "Oh, I may as well just tell you. I hired Pammy."

Tricia nearly choked on her tuna. "You what?" she spluttered, and started choking.

Angelica clumped around the counter in her black high-heeled shoes to slap Tricia on the back. "Do you need me to do the Heimlich maneuver? I learned how to do it properly at my county-sponsored safety course, you know."

Tricia pounded on her chest, and then took a sip of her cooling cocoa to help control the urge to cough. "Why on earth did you hire Pammy?"

"I felt sorry for her, what with you throwing her out and all."

"I did not throw her out!" Tricia took another sip of her cocoa. "I simply asked her to leave, and she agreed it was past time."

"Really." Again, it wasn't a question.

Tricia took in her sister's guilty expression. "What did she tell you?"

"Not much. But when she spoke about it, she sounded quite wounded." And Angelica sounded quite judgmental. Trust Angelica to take someone's—anyone's—side against her.

Tricia glared at her sister for a long moment before returning to her lunch.

"Why don't you go out back and apologize to Pammy? I'm sure she'd forgive you. And it wouldn't hurt to let her come back and stay with you for a few more days—just until she gets settled."

"I don't have anything to apologize for," Tricia said, viciously stabbing a chunk of tuna. "And I do *not* want her staying with me for even one more night. You've got just as much room in your apartment—she can stay with you, if you're that worried about her."

Angelica ignored the suggestion. "Well, then, just go talk to her. You two have been friends for way too many years to just throw it all away."

Would she feel that way if Tricia told her about the stolen check?

"I'd seen her maybe three times in the last eighteen years, before she camped out in my living room for two weeks, so it's not like we've been close."

"Yes, but it's important to maintain old friendships—especially as we age."

Tricia eyed her sister's getup; she looked like she was more than two weeks early for Halloween—hardly an example of aging gracefully. Angelica had added on years, but her outlook hadn't caught up with the inevitable march of time.

Angelica nudged Tricia's arm. "Go on. And while you're out there, you can see if they've delivered my one-and-a-half-yard Dumpster. It was supposed to arrive by this afternoon—two weeks late."

"I don't want to go out there at all."

"Tricia," Angelica said, using the same tone of voice their mother had employed when she'd tried to shame the girls into doing something she wanted.

"What?"

"Go out there and make nice with Pammy while I call my soda distributor. I think they shorted me by a case. I'm going to need it for tomorrow's crowd.

Now, where did I put the business card with their phone number?" she said, and crouched down to search the shelf under the counter.

"Okay, I'm going. But when I get back, I'm going to finish my lunch and then I'm going back to work."

"Of course, of course," Angelica muttered, her voice muffled as she leaned farther under the counter.

Tricia sidled past the lunch counter and pushed through the swinging half-doors into the narrow kitchen. For a short-order cook, Jake was fairly temperamental. Angelica had complained that he'd often leave without fully cleaning his work space. As expected, he was already gone for the day and had left the place a mess of unwashed pots and pans. Angelica, or more likely Pammy, had her work cut out for her.

The door to the back alley was closed. Tricia opened it and stepped onto the concrete pad. It was obvious no Dumpster had yet been delivered. Nestled close to the building were two large gray, bulging ninety-five-gallon trash carts. Sticking out of one of them was a pair of jeans-clad legs, with a worn pair of pink Crocs on the feet.

THREE

Yet another white-and-gold Hillsborough County Sheriff's Department car pulled up outside Booked for Lunch. A tall, sandy-haired man got out of the driver's side, then stooped down to grab his flat-brimmed Mounties hat, settled it on his head, and marched purposefully toward the café. Distracted, Tricia watched him as he paused outside the entrance and then spoke to one of the other deputies for several minutes. By the number of bars on his uniform sleeve, he outranked all the other officials on the scene. Finally, the deputy pointed at the café.

The newcomer nodded his thanks, opened the café's door, and stepped inside. He bypassed everyone else, making a beeline for Tricia. "I'm Captain Grant Baker, and I'll be handling this investigation. I'm sorry we have to meet under these circumstances, Ms. Miles."

"Where's Sheriff Adams?" Tricia asked.

"Busy, I'm afraid. I hope you won't mind dealing with me."

Tricia found herself drawn to Baker's green eyes. Her ex-husband, Christopher, had green eyes. That relationship hadn't worked out, and—

Tricia shook her head to rid herself of the flood of memories that threatened to engulf her.

"No. Not at all," she found herself saying. Any time she didn't have to deal with Sheriff Wendy Adams was worth celebrating. They'd had run-ins before, and those experiences were not ranked among those Tricia cherished.

Baker glanced around Booked for Lunch, his gaze settling on Angelica, who perched on the end of one of the booths' bench seats; a high-heeled shoe discarded on the floor, she was massaging her left foot as she conversed with another deputy. "I understand this isn't your first encounter with the law here in Stoneham," Baker said to Tricia.

She frowned. "Uh, no."

He leaned forward, lowering his voice. "Are you okay, ma'am? You look a little pale. Would you like to sit down?"

"No, thank you." Tricia studied his kind face, and her frown deepened. "Why are you being so nice to me?"

His eyes narrowed in confusion. "I don't understand."

"Sheriff Adams—"

"Ah." He nodded. "The sheriff explained there'd been some conflict between the two of you. That's why she suggested I handle this investigation."

"Maybe I *should* sit down," Tricia breathed. She'd never expected Sheriff Adams to cut her any slack. Then again, Baker could be trying to lull her into a false sense of security. He might be playing good cop in contrast to Sheriff Adams's bad cop routine.

Captain Baker ushered Tricia to one of the stools at the counter. "I know you've already told your story several times to the other deputies, but would you indulge me as well?"

Polite, too.

Tricia nodded and sobered. "Pammy Fredericks—"

"The deceased," Deputy Placer supplied.

"—was my friend. Sort of." Tricia shivered as she glanced over her shoulder to the café's back door, which had been wedged open, letting in drafts of cold air. Thankfully, the garbage cart was no longer visible. The image of Pammy's legs sticking out of it . . . Tricia shuddered involuntarily.

"Can you explain that 'sort of' comment?" Baker asked, not unkindly.

"We were roommates at Dartmouth and sort of kept in touch over the years."

"I take it you were no longer friends as of this afternoon."

Tricia's insides squirmed. "Until this morning, Pammy had been my houseguest for the past two weeks."

"And what changed that?" Baker asked patiently.

"I . . . asked her to leave," she said, her voice growing softer. "I didn't really throw her out. I swear! She'd simply overstayed her welcome. If you know what I mean."

"Go on," he encouraged.

Tricia sighed. "Pammy took it well. She said she had made friends here in Stoneham and assured me she'd be all right."

"When was that?"

"About nine forty-five this morning."

"And you didn't see her again?"

"Yes, I did see her. But I didn't speak to her."

"Where was this?"

"At the new food pantry just out of town. They held the dedication this morning."

Baker waited for her to continue.

"A lot of people were there. Apparently Pammy wanted to speak to the guest of honor. She made a rather loud fuss, and was asked to leave."

Baker looked very interested. "Who asked her to leave?"

"Someone in a suit. I think he was part of Mr. Paige's entourage."

"Mr. Paige?"

"Stuart Paige. Have you ever heard of him?"

"It would be hard to live in New Hampshire and *not* hear about his good works."

"Yes, well, apparently he gave the Food Shelf half the money they needed to open their new facility."

"And did you speak to the deceased following the event?"

Tricia shook her head. "I didn't see her again until I found her out back."

"And what time was that?"

"About an hour or so ago."

Baker checked his watch. "Approximately three fifty?"

Tricia nodded.

"And other than seeing her at the dedication, you hadn't heard from her since this morning?"

"I heard of her—but I didn't talk to her."

Baker frowned. "What does that mean?"

"She apparently spent the morning going around town putting in job applications and listing me as her last employer."

"And were you?"

"No! She hung around my store during the last couple of weeks, disrupting things—but she didn't work for me."

"Did her 'hanging around' anger you?"

Tricia chewed the inside of her lip, knowing where this line of questioning was going to lead. And what would he think when she told him about the forged check?

"I wasn't happy about it. In fact, yesterday she spilled coffee on a customer's foot. That was kind of the last straw."

"But you waited until this morning to throw her out?"

"I did *not* throw her out," Tricia said, and realized her voice had risen higher than she would've liked. She took a breath to calm down. "I asked her to leave. We had a civil conversation, and Pammy agreed it was time to go."

Baker nodded, but said nothing.

"There was one other thing . . ." She hesitated. Did she really have to tell him about the check? He—or his boss—was sure to think it was a motive for murder. No one but she knew about it—unless Pammy had gone around blabbing about it, which she doubted. Angelica hadn't mentioned it.

"You were saying?" he prompted.

"Her carelessness in spilling coffee on one of my customers really annoyed me," Tricia blurted. "I could've been sued."

Baker eyed her, waiting for more.

She could still say something about the check. She ought to say something about the check.

Why didn't she say something about the damn check?

Maybe because she knew she hadn't killed Pammy. It wasn't pertinent to her death. Baker might follow in his boss's footsteps and waste a lot of time trying to pin the crime on her—letting Pammy's killer get away with murder.

"Look, I was in my store, with witnesses, all day. That is, until I came across the street to eat my lunch and talk to my sister."

"Sister?" Baker asked.

Tricia glanced in Angelica's direction. "Yes, she owns this café. She hired Pammy today."

"Why?"

Tricia sighed. *Probably to bug me.* "You'll have to ask her."

Baker looked over at Angelica, then shifted his gaze back to Tricia—assessing them? "Tell me what you saw when you found the body."

"Pammy. Headfirst in the garbage cart. I suspected she might be dead because she wasn't moving. I had to force myself to touch her. I found her wrist, but I couldn't find a pulse." The stench of rotting food and the revulsion she'd felt at touching the dead had worked together until— "And then I threw up."

Baker nodded, his expression bland. "Yes, the deputy told me."

"I didn't mean to contaminate the crime scene. It just . . . happened."

"How do you know about contaminating crime scenes?" Baker asked.

"I own Haven't Got a Clue, the mystery bookstore across the street. I read a lot of crime stories."

"How many is 'a lot'?"

"Not as many as I used to. Only two or three a week."

Baker didn't roll his eyes, but he looked like he might want to. Something captured his attention, and Tricia looked to her left. Someone had entered through the open back door—a man Tricia recognized from her last brush with murder. A member of the county's medical examiner's office greeted Baker with a curt nod.

"Have we got a probable cause of death yet?" Baker asked.

The man had a laminated ID card on a lanyard around his neck. The name on it was Ernesto Rivera. "Suffocation, most likely. Her face was covered by a plastic bag full of trash. Looks like she panicked when she couldn't get out of the garbage cart. She couldn't reach the edge of the can. Looks like she tore the trash bags apart while struggling. Her fingernails have all kinds of debris under them. We bagged 'em, and will know more once we get her on the table."

Tricia cringed at that piece of information. Pammy—her chest and abdominal cavities emptied like a gutted deer. Her scalp peeled forward until—

Tricia shuddered again. Why had she read so many Kay Scarpetta mysteries? The knowledge she'd picked up about autopsies made for an interesting read—if not applied to someone you'd actually known.

"Did she fall into the garbage can?" Baker asked.

"No way—the thing's about four foot tall. She was on her back. Someone had to put her in there."

Tricia's thoughts, exactly.

"Thanks, Ernie." Baker turned to question Angelica. "You're the owner?"

Angelica sighed theatrically. "Yes. Angelica Miles. Soon to be published, I might add. Penguin Books, *Easy-Does-It Cooking*, twenty-four ninety-nine—available on June first."

It was Tricia's turn to roll her eyes. Much more information than *anyone* needed to know.

She leaned against the counter stool and listened as Captain Baker took Angelica through the same set of questions. His demeanor was just so different from that of his boss. If the circumstances were different, she decided, she might even like him.

"And why was it you hired Ms. Fredericks?" Baker asked.

Finally, the question Tricia had been waiting to hear answered.

Angelica sighed, looked over to Tricia for a moment, and then turned back to the captain. "I figured it would keep her out of my garbage."

Baker blinked in disbelief. So did Tricia.

"Of course," Angelica continued, "I had no idea someone would actually kill her and put her *in* my garbage cart."

"Wait a minute," Tricia said, leaning forward. "What do you mean, 'keep her out of my garbage'?"

Angelica shrugged. "She came by every day—after closing, of course—and poked through my cans to see what she could salvage."

"I don't understand," Captain Baker said.

Angelica sighed impatiently. "To take."

"But it's not like you throw out anything valuable—something Pammy could actually use or sell," Tricia protested.

"Apparently she thought I did."

Baker held up a hand to interrupt. "What am I missing here?"

"It's no secret Pammy was a scavenger. I believe she was employed as an antiques picker at different periods of her life," Angelica said.

"What's that got to do with the café's garbage?" Tricia asked.

"Pammy was a freegan," Angelica said matter-of-factly.

"A what?" Baker asked, confused.

"A what?" Tricia echoed.

Angelica frowned. "She Dumpster dived for food." Taking in the incredulous faces before her, she continued. "Of course, lots of freegans give you some lofty explanation about alternative lifestyles, bucking convention, and minimizing waste in a materialistic world. I think they're just a bunch of cheapskates looking for free food."

"Pammy salvaged food out of Dumpsters?" Tricia asked, feeling the blood drain from her face. Pammy had cooked for her—had provided the food she'd used to prepare those meals. Had she found it by—?

The thought was too terrible to contemplate.

"How do you know all this?" Baker asked Angelica.

"Pammy told me—last week when we talked, and today, in between customers."

"How long was she here today?" Tricia asked.

"About two hours. A regular little chatterbox, that one."

Baker eyed Tricia. "Ms. Fredericks told you she was a freegan—but in two weeks she didn't tell your sister?"

"Apparently not."

He looked back to Angelica. "And you didn't tell her, either?"

Angelica laughed. "Of course not. Well, just look at her. She's already a lovely shade of chartreuse."

A lump rose in Tricia's throat. "How long have you known?"

"For a week or so. I knew someone was going through my garbage the day we opened. I caught Pammy at it one day last week."

"You should have told me."

"Why? You'd have been freaked out—like you are now. Believe it or not, I don't live to just irritate you, baby sister."

It was Tricia's turn to frown. So now Angelica decided to spare her feelings. Hadn't she informed her that Pammy had cooked for her?

Right now, Tricia couldn't remember.

A wave of guilt passed through her. Here she was worrying about eating food past its prime—food that obviously hadn't sickened her—and Pammy had been killed. Where were her priorities?

"Did the deceased tell you where she planned to stay tonight?" Baker asked Angelica.

Angelica shook her head. "And I didn't have her fill out a job application, either. I needed someone right away—she walked in the door. I figured we could catch up on the paperwork after the lunch crowd had gone."

Baker turned to Tricia. "Did Ms. Fredericks tell you where she planned on staying?"

"No. But she said she'd 'hooked up' with some local people."

"Probably more freegans," Angelica said.

"Do you know any local freegans?" Baker asked the women.

Angelica shook her head once again.

"I didn't even know they existed until just a few minutes ago," Tricia said.

"Can you think of anybody we can ask?" Baker asked.

"You might try talking to the other food vendors in the area. There's the Brookside Inn, the Bookshelf Diner, the Stoneham Patisserie, and the convenience store up near the highway. That's about it. But it wouldn't surprise me if the local freegans went to Milford, or even Nashua or Portsmouth. They're much bigger than Stoneham. They'd scavenge—or, as I'm sure they'd say, 'salvage'—much more food from grocery and convenience stores than restaurants and bakeries."

"Do freegans try to hustle food from charities like the Food Shelf?" Baker asked.

Angelica shook her head. "I shouldn't think so. But it's something you could ask Libby Hirt about."

"Who?"

"Libby Hirt." She spelled the last name. "She runs the Stoneham Food Shelf."

"The one your friend crashed this morning?" he asked Tricia.

She nodded.

Baker made a note. "Did the deceased have a car?"

Tricia nodded. "She'd been parking it in the municipal lot."

"Make and model?" he asked.

"I have no idea. I don't think I ever saw her drive it the whole time she was here. In fact, when she left the dedication, she walked back into Stoneham."

"She probably couldn't afford the gas for it," Angelica added.

At least not until she'd cashed Tricia's forged check. *You should say something*, a little voice within her nagged.

"Can we narrow it down? Did she have an out-of-state license plate?" Baker asked.

"Maybe. She was originally from Portsmouth, but had lived in Connecticut for the past couple of years. I think," Tricia added lamely.

"I thought you said she stayed with you for two weeks?" Baker asked.

"She did, but we didn't spend a lot of quality time together." At his puzzled look, she clarified. "My store doesn't close until seven most nights. On Tuesdays, I host a book club. That doesn't usually break up until after nine. A couple of times Pammy didn't come in until after I'd already gone to bed."

"Didn't you ask where she'd been, what she'd been doing?" Baker asked.

Answering truthfully was going to sound awfully darned cold. Still . . . "No."

Baker turned away. "Placer." The deputy stepped forward. "Grab Henderson and scout out the municipal lot down the street. See if you can find a car with Connecticut plates. Ask around. See if anyone has noticed a car parked in the lot for the past two weeks."

"Sure thing, Cap'n."

"Captain?" Rivera waved to Baker from the back entrance.

"If you'll excuse me, ladies." He left them and rejoined the technician.

Angelica watched him go. "Nice set of buns."

"Ange," Tricia admonished.

"And wasn't he just the nicest thing? Quite a change from Wendy Adams."

"Yes," Tricia agreed. She gazed at the captain, who filled the back doorway. He did have a nice set of buns at that.

"She's dead. She's really dead," Ginny murmured for at least the hundredth time. "I admit I didn't like her, but I never wanted her dead."

"Ginny, please," Tricia implored, not bothering to lift her gaze from the order blanks before her. As it was, her last sight of her . . . kind of, sort of . . .

friend had not been a pleasant one. Was that how she'd always remember Pammy, as a pair of stiff legs?

"But I feel guilty," Ginny said, then grabbed a tissue from the box under the counter and blew her nose. "I didn't want her around, and I got my wish. But I never thought—"

Tricia sighed. She removed her reading glasses, setting them on the counter. Captain Baker had dismissed her some twenty minutes before—and it would be another hour before she closed shop for the day. It seemed like weeks since her day had begun, and she was looking forward to a nice, quiet evening, although she wasn't sure she was up to reading a murder mystery. Not just yet, anyway.

"I think I'll take out the trash," Tricia said, and then she thought of Pammy in the garbage cart and winced. Still, the wastebasket under the counter was full.

She picked up the basket and headed for the back of the store, disarming the security alarm before opening the door. The alley that ran behind this side of Main Street was a good five feet lower than the front of the store, and she trotted down the steps to the waiting Dumpsters. Haven't Got a Clue didn't really create enough refuse to warrant such large receptacles—one for cardboard boxes only, the other for other trash—and she wondered if she could trade one of hers for Angelica's two trash carts.

She emptied the basket and turned to head back into the building just as the door to the Cookery slammed shut, giving Tricia a start. With Angelica tied up at her new café, her newly promoted manager, Frannie Mae Armstrong, was in charge of the village's cookbook store. As far as Tricia knew, Frannie was still working alone at the store. Why would she have slammed the door upon seeing Tricia? And then she saw two matching bowls on the landing near the Cookery's stairs. Angelica would not be pleased.

For the past couple of weeks Frannie had been feeding a little stray orange cat that had been hanging around the alley. Tricia had seen it only once, but Miss Marple, her own cat, seemed to have stray-kitty radar. Miss Marple did not appreciate other cats invading what she considered to be her territory—even if her territory didn't go beyond the confines of Haven't Got a Clue and the storeroom and loft apartment above it. Angelica wasn't a cat lover, and had warned Frannie not to encourage the cat to come around . . . something Frannie obviously hadn't taken to heart.

Tricia climbed the steps and reentered her store. Ginny was still at the register, sniffling as she waited on a customer. "I'm going next door for a few minutes. Be right back," Tricia said, and headed out without grabbing her jacket.

The Cookery was quiet, with only one or two customers browsing the bookshelves. Now that Angelica had dismantled the cooking demonstration area,

she'd gained more retail space. The store was doing well—too well for just one employee. That was just Tricia's opinion, of course. Frannie insisted she could handle the additional work, but she did look a bit frazzled, something Tricia hadn't ever seen in the year since she'd met her.

Frannie stood by the register, waiting for her next customer to check out. Her expression darkened when she saw it was Tricia who'd just entered the store. She plastered on a fake grin and called out in her infamous Texas twang, "Howdy, Tricia. What can I do for you?"

Tricia gave her friend a genuine smile. "Hey, Frannie, I just dropped in to see how things are going."

"I'm sure surprised to see you . . . after what happened and all." Frannie nodded toward Booked for Lunch across the street, which was visible through the large display window. A sheriff's patrol car—probably Captain Baker's—was still parked outside. It might be hours before the forensic squad finished gathering evidence.

Tricia had momentarily forgotten about Pammy. Frannie's words brought the memory of her in the garbage cart back with the force of a hurricane. "Oh. Yes. It was awful. I hope you don't mind if I don't want to talk about it."

"Of course," Frannie said, and shook her head sadly.

"I was out behind my store a few minutes ago, and I couldn't help but notice—"

"Please don't tell Angelica," Frannie pleaded, her face drawn with concern. "I know she doesn't want me to encourage Penny—"

"Penny?" Tricia asked.

"That darling little kitty. She's the color of a bright copper penny, so I've taken to calling her that. But, Tricia, she's got no collar and she's as thin as a rail. I'm only setting out a little water and some dry cat food during the day. And I make sure the dishes are put away before Angelica gets back from her café."

On the one hand, Tricia wanted to commend Frannie for her compassion. But as a business owner, she wasn't sure she should encourage deceit or out-and-out insurrection—especially as the store's proprietor was her own sister. And yet . . . she'd seen that hungry little cat and her heart had ached for it, too.

"I won't tell," she promised. "But now that you've been putting out food, she'll expect to be fed. If Angelica finds out—"

"I've got it all planned," Frannie said, but a customer approached the register with a stack of cookbooks before she could tell Tricia exactly what that plan was. The shop's door opened, and another three potential customers trooped in. Rats! Tricia had wanted to ask what Frannie knew about Stuart Paige. There was always tomorrow, she supposed.

This time it was Tricia who forced a smile as she waggled her fingers in a

wave and headed out the door for Haven't Got a Clue. And true to her word, she had no intention of telling Angelica about Frannie's feline indiscretion.

Before she could make it back to the store, Tricia heard her name being called. She looked around and saw Captain Baker hailing her from across the street. He waited for a car to pass before crossing to meet her on the sidewalk.

"Sir, you are guilty of a crime," Tricia said, straight-faced. Of course, she'd been crossing Main Street at its center for weeks, ever since Angelica had rented her new property.

"I beg your pardon?" Baker said.

"You jaywalked across Main Street," she explained, huddling to keep warm in the stiff breeze.

"Ms. Miles," he said, his voice growing somber, "my men found a car several blocks from here, apparently abandoned. It has Connecticut plates and was registered to Ms. Fredericks. The trunk was open and its contents ransacked. If you could look at what's left, perhaps you can tell me what, if anything, was taken."

A wave of fresh grief coursed through Tricia. "I suppose I could look, but I really don't know what she had, other than the suitcases she kept at my apartment for the past two weeks."

"Would you be willing to try?"

She stared into his green eyes, and her willpower dissolved. What was the hold men with green eyes had on her?

"Of course. But I need to let my assistant know I'll be gone for a few minutes."

Baker accompanied her to Haven't Got a Clue, where she grabbed her coat and told Ginny she'd be back as soon as she could.

Outside, Baker bowed like a gallant knight, and made a sweeping gesture toward the cruiser parked on the opposite side of the street. Then he walked her across the pavement, opened the passenger-side door, and held it open until she'd seated herself, grasping the seat belt and buckling herself in.

As he walked around the car, Tricia took in the police scanner, the little printer that sat in the middle of the bench seat, and the cup of cold coffee in the beverage restraint device. She'd never sat inside a cop car before. How many police procedurals had she read over the years? How many scenes had taken place in such a car? But the reality was far different from fiction. There was an atmosphere of . . . tension—mixed with stale coffee and sweat and a touch of angst?—that seemed to hang inside the vehicle, and she doubted that even a prolonged airing could remove the lingering scents of stale urine and vomit from within that small space.

Baker climbed into the driver's seat and started the engine. He glanced in

the rearview mirror before easing the gearshift into Drive and pressing the accelerator.

"You should buckle your seat belt," Tricia admonished.

"The law here in New Hampshire requires seat belt use only by those eighteen years and younger," he said with confidence.

"Just because the law doesn't require you to use your seat belt doesn't mean it's not the smart thing to do."

He tossed a glance in her direction for the merest part of a second, then focused his attention back on the road. "I think I can take care of myself."

She sighed. "Just like a man."

Again his gaze darted in her direction. "What's that supposed to mean?"

"It's just that men can be just so . . . stupid. What's wrong with being safe? Haven't you read the federal highway statistics reporting the percentage of deaths due to *not* wearing seat belts?"

"Officers of the law need to be able to react—to get out of their vehicles at a moment's notice."

"Not if they're smushed into paste in an accident."

"Smushed?" Baker repeated.

"Yes. It's a variation of smashed. Smushed is when what used to be a solid becomes almost a liquid. Human flesh can be smushed when it's contained in crumpled steel and glass."

"Smushed," Baker said once again. "I don't think I've ever considered that."

"Well, you ought to. I'm sure the State of New Hampshire has invested thousands of dollars in your training. If you were killed or maimed in an accident, you'd be costing taxpayers like me a lot of money."

"Smushed," he murmured again, turning left onto Hanson Lane.

Tricia kept her gaze riveted out the windshield. "I'm sure your family wouldn't appreciate the call telling them their husband and dad was now the consistency of tomato puree."

"As it happens, I am no one's husband or dad, so you don't have to worry on that account."

Tricia glanced at her companion. "Your loss." Or someone else's.

The scanner crackled, reporting an accident on Route 101. Tricia frowned. She couldn't stand the sound of a dispatcher dispassionately reporting trouble. Too often Russ insisted on allowing his scanner to act as the background noise on their so-called dates. It wasn't the most romantic backdrop.

Baker pulled up behind a parked car with Connecticut plates. Another Hillsborough County deputy stood alongside the vehicle, apparently guarding it. His thumbs were hooked onto his Sam Browne belt.

Baker opened the car door.

"Wait," Tricia blurted, reaching out to touch his arm. Should she trust him? So far he hadn't given her a reason not to. "There's something I didn't tell you."

He settled back in his seat, waiting for her to go on.

"There's another reason I asked Pammy to leave this morning."

Why didn't he look surprised, she wondered.

"She . . . stole from me. She took one of my checks, made it out to herself for one hundred dollars, and cashed it."

"When was this?"

"Several days ago. I was online going over my account this morning and found out. It was the last straw, and I asked her to leave."

"And her reaction was?"

"She left."

"You didn't argue about it?"

"Pammy freely admitted it."

"Why didn't you tell me this sooner?"

Tricia sighed. "Because it's been my experience that Sheriff Adams likes to blow insignificant events out of proportion, trying to make them look like motives for murder. With that in mind, I figured you'd probably think I killed Pammy. Believe me, Captain, it wasn't the money, it was the breach of trust that made me ask her to leave. And as you continue your questioning, you'll find I didn't have the opportunity to kill her. As I said, I've been with people the entire day."

His green eyes bored into her. Was that disappointment reflected in them?

Without a word, Baker got out of the car. Tricia unbuckled her seat belt and did likewise.

"The tech team should be here when they're finished at the café," Deputy Bracken said.

Baker nodded. "Ms. Miles, would you care to take a look?"

Tricia moved to stand over the opened trunk, taking in its contents. "Those are Pammy's suitcases all right." They'd both been forced open, their contents dumped. Pammy's scrunched-up, dirty clothes mingled with old magazines, copies of their college yearbook, an old, colorful granny-square afghan, cassette tapes, photo albums, and a lot of wrinkled papers. A ripped-open envelope was addressed to Pamela Fredericks, General Delivery, Stoneham, New Hampshire.

Remorse flushed through Tricia once again. Could Pammy have been living in her car before she came to Stoneham?

The guilt intensified. Perhaps if she hadn't asked her to leave, Pammy might still be alive.

Might: a word that held a lot of power.

Tricia sighed, her eyes filling with tears. Maybe Pammy had left on an

extended trip and intended to eventually return to whatever she considered her home base. But she hadn't mentioned that. In fact, whenever the subject came up, Pammy had been evasive.

"Are you okay, Ms. Miles?" Baker asked.

Tricia nodded, trying to blink away the unshed tears. "Pammy's dead. I guess it didn't hit me until right now. The stuff in her trunk may be all she had. She's really dead, and then someone tried to rob her. Is there anything more despicable than stealing from the dead?"

"Yes," Baker said. "Killing them in the first place."

Tricia had to agree with that.

More letters lay scattered among the junk, as well as a sagging, empty shoebox that sat on a pile of old clothes. Their former home? Baker poked at the letters and clippings with a pen. The yellowing envelopes bore twenty-two-cent stamps, indicating their age. "Mrs. Geraldine Fredericks. Who was that?"

"Pammy's mother."

"What would Ms. Fredericks be doing with a bunch of old letters?"

Tricia shrugged.

Baker waved a hand to take in the trunk. "Does there appear to be anything missing?"

Tricia's gaze wandered over the contents. "I don't know. Pammy didn't seem to have much with her. From what I could see, she had clothes and maybe a few toiletries." Very few toiletries. She'd used nearly an entire bottle of Tricia's favorite salon shampoo. "I'm sorry I can't be of more help, Captain Baker."

He frowned. "So am I."

FOUR

Tricia's loft apartment seemed especially empty that night. Miss Marple's happy purring, scented candles burning, and even soft music playing in the background couldn't fill the void that Pammy's absence had left.

Under other circumstances, Tricia would have felt elated to have her living space all to herself again. But now . . . her once warm living room seemed chilled by a death pall.

Curled on the couch, her wineglass within reach, Tricia had read the same opening page of Frances Hodgson Burnett's *A Little Princess*, her favorite

childhood book—a story without a murder—for the eleventh time when Miss Marple's ears perked up. In seconds, the cat jumped from the couch and trotted toward the kitchen.

"Tricia? You there?" came Angelica's voice.

Angelica's drop-in visits had diminished over the past few months, as her relationship with Bob Kelly had become more serious. Thanks to Pammy's untimely death, this was one night Tricia welcomed her sister's presence.

"I'm coming," she called, and set her book aside, grabbed her wineglass, and headed for the kitchen.

Angelica had already hung up her coat and was unpacking a picnic basket of comfort food. Good French bread; sweet butter; a thermos no doubt filled with what was left of Booked for Lunch's soup of the day; a quart of vanilla ice cream; and a jar of chocolate sauce.

"You didn't have to bring me dinner," Tricia said, although she was supremely grateful Angelica had done just that. Homemade soup and buttered bread always seem to hit the emotional spot at times like this.

"We both need to eat, and you need the company." Angelica put the ice cream in the freezer, and paused. "If I'm honest, I need the company, too." She shuddered. "I'm so glad it wasn't me who found Pammy."

"And I suppose you think I jumped for joy at the prospect," Tricia snapped, and instantly regretted it.

"Don't be silly," Angelica said, taking no offense. She opened one of the cupboards and took out a saucepan. "Of course it's upsetting to me that you had to find her. But don't you see, I don't have an alibi for killing her."

"Why do you need one? Although you may have been the last known person to see Pammy alive, you certainly didn't have a motive to kill her."

Angelica emptied the thermos of soup into the pan. "That's true. But the Sheriff's Department hasn't always let facts like that stand in the way of naming someone a 'person of interest.' Once they do that, you might as well have a tattoo on your forehead that says 'I killed fill-in-the-blank.' And today that would be Pammy Fredericks."

"Captain Baker can't seriously think you killed her. He seems a lot more reasonable than Sheriff Adams."

"Yes, and wasn't it a stroke of luck the sheriff decided to delegate this investigation instead of taking it on herself? We might just see justice served." Angelica removed the paper sleeve from around the bread. "Do you want plain bread, or would you rather have garlic bread?"

"Definitely garlic bread."

Angelica knew where everything was located in Tricia's kitchen—better than Tricia herself, if the truth be told—and she went straight for the correct

cupboard, removed a baking sheet, and began to assemble everything else she'd need: garlic powder, dried parsley, and grated Parmesan cheese.

"This would really taste better with real garlic and fresh parsley, but I know better than to look for it. You never buy the good stuff," she said judgmentally.

"Garlic would sprout before I could use it. If I had any plants, they'd die a lingering death, which would be cruel."

Angelica gave her sister a withering stare. "For someone as careful about her diet as you are, you'd think you'd have learned that the fresher the ingredients, the healthier the food."

"I don't eat a lot of fat or red meat, or drink hard liquor, and I intend to live forever."

"That'll be a lonely life," Angelica said as she unwrapped a stick of butter. "Seeing as everybody you love or care a whit about will be long gone."

Everybody long gone. Like Pammy Fredericks was gone . . . Tricia glanced at the kitchen clock. Pammy had been dead for less than five hours. Already it seemed a lifetime.

"You're probably right," Tricia admitted. She settled on one of the stools at the kitchen island. "I guess at our age, we're still lucky to have Mother and Daddy. Not that we see them all that often. Where are they now?"

"Rio. I expect they'll stay until summer. They didn't want to come back for Christmas to be with us last year. I'm not holding my breath for this year, either," Angelica said, creaming the butter and the dry ingredients together in a little bowl with unnecessary force.

"I thought we had a lovely Christmas together."

Angelica paused in her assault on the contents of the bowl. "Yes, we did. I'm surprised at how many people came for Christmas dinner last year. How many of us were there around my dining room table?"

Tricia thought back. Ginny and her boyfriend, Brian Comstock, had come, as had Grace Harris and Mr. Everett, and Russ and Bob. "Eight of us."

"Well, we'll have to invite Frannie this year. And maybe Nikki—if she doesn't go to visit her new family in Canada. And—"

"Let's not get ahead of ourselves. It's only October."

Angelica sighed, and set the bowl aside. "I guess I just don't want to think about what happened today."

Tricia frowned. Neither did she, and now Angelica had brought it up again.

"Here we are thinking about our little family of friends in Stoneham, and today you lost a friend of many years, even if Pammy was a pain in the butt—almost just like family."

Tricia was sure Angelica didn't count herself as being a pain, but she kept her silence.

"That didn't mean in your heart of hearts you didn't love her in some capacity," Angelica continued. "You've got to give yourself time to mourn her, just like everyone else you've ever lost."

"I suppose right now *I'm* Captain Baker's chief suspect." Tricia told Angelica about the forged check. Somehow, she didn't seem surprised. "Why did I have to choose this morning to ask Pammy to leave? Why couldn't it have been yesterday—or why didn't I put it off until tomorrow?"

"Just one of those unanswerable questions," Angelica said. "But don't think you've got the market cornered on being chief suspect. If Captain Baker takes after Sheriff Adams, I'm probably his chief suspect. I don't even know if I can reopen tomorrow."

"Why shouldn't you? The murder happened outside the café. Did they seal the premises? Put up crime scene tape?"

"Not out front."

"Then I don't think you have a problem." Tricia sighed. "Damn Pammy anyway. Why did she have to be so secretive about her life?"

"Obviously she was in some kind of trouble," Angelica said.

"She could've confided in me."

"Would you have listened?"

Tricia didn't meet her sister's gaze. "I listened to what she had to say."

"How hard?" Angelica pressed.

Maybe not as hard as she could have, Tricia admitted to herself. "It's difficult to be a loving, caring friend when you feel put upon and your generosity is abused."

"Did you ever ask her why she stayed so long?"

"I assumed it was because she'd run out of money. You know she could never balance a checkbook. And she never worked much. She depended on the generosity of friends and relatives."

"Which was about to end," Angelica said.

"How do you know?"

"Pammy told me. She was expecting a windfall that would set her free for life."

"Did you tell Captain Baker that?"

Angelica thought about it. "I don't think so. I mean, cops aren't always interested in witnesses volunteering information."

"I agree, but that could be the reason Pammy was killed."

"What are you thinking? That she was blackmailing someone?"

"It's a classic motive for murder."

Angelica waved a hand in dismissal. "You think about murder too much."

"Well, I would, wouldn't I? My job is selling mystery books."

Angelica retrieved a bread knife from the wooden block on the counter, com-

mandeered the cutting board, and sliced the baguette into half-inch pieces, but not cutting all the way through the loaf. Then she spread the butter-garlic mixture on both sides of each slice of bread. "Turn the oven on to three fifty, will you?"

Tricia got up, turned on the oven, and grabbed another wineglass from the cupboard. She made another stop by the refrigerator to grab the already opened bottle of chardonnay. "I hope that soup goes with white, because I'm flat out of merlot."

"It's chicken pastina, so it'll go fine." Angelica set the bread on the baking sheet, wrapped the loaf in foil, and popped it into the oven, before grabbing her glass. "What could Pammy possibly know about anybody that would warrant blackmail?"

"You said she was a Dumpster diver. I suppose she could've found financial statements or something of that order."

"She was a freegan. Looking for financial papers is just not on their scavenging agenda."

Tricia sipped her wine, and frowned. "I just don't understand how anybody could eat food that's been in a Dumpster. I mean—think about all the germs. Wouldn't that kill you, or at least make you deathly ill?"

"What kills people these days is not *enough* germs in their systems. We're all antibioticed to death, if you'll pardon the pun. Between hand sanitizers and antibiotics in the food chain and water, we're at the mercy of super staph germs and the like."

"Let's get back to Pammy." Tricia bit her lip. "Do you think we ought to tell Captain Baker about our suspicions?"

"What suspicions? I don't have any."

"Well, I do."

Angelica shook her head. "Look what trouble sharing your suspicions with the law has gotten you before."

"Yes, but that was when I was dealing with Sheriff Adams. I think Captain Baker is a lot more"—she paused, trying to come up with an appropriate term—"sympathetic."

"It's those green eyes of his. You're a sucker for them."

"So are you," Tricia countered. Bob Kelly had green eyes, too.

Angelica swirled the wine in her glass. "Maybe so. But it's immaterial. I'm sure we haven't seen the last of Captain Baker—but unless he asks, keep your ideas to yourself. We'll both be better off if you do."

"Okay. But I still think I must know something that could be helpful to the investigation. I just wish I knew what it was."

FIVE

Tricia found it hard to sleep that night. Maybe it was the quiet. Pammy's snores had awakened her more than once during her lengthy stay. Staring at the ceiling for hours on end gave Tricia plenty of time to think about Pammy's visit and her untimely death.

Why had she shown up at the Food Shelf just hours before she died? Why had she wanted to speak to Stuart Paige? Maybe if she could talk to Paige, she could find out what his connection to Pammy was. That is, if she could find someone to introduce her to him.

Bob Kelly probably knew the philanthropist.

Tricia winced at the thought. Because of Pammy's death—and her link with Pammy—Bob wasn't likely to introduce her to the man. Not if it meant the possibility of straining relations with the Chamber of Commerce. Could she entice the Food Shelf's chairperson, Libby Hirt, to do so? It might be worth trying.

With that decided, Tricia was finally able to drift off to sleep.

She never heard the alarm clock ring the next morning, and awoke only half an hour before Haven't Got a Clue was to open its doors. After a fast shower, she dressed, fed Miss Marple, and dashed down the stairs to the shop. Mr. Everett was already waiting at the store's entrance.

"My, we're late today," he commented after Tricia had unlocked the door and let him in.

"I had a rather sleepless night," she admitted.

Mr. Everett headed straight for the coffeemaker. "After what happened yesterday, I can well understand that. I'll get this started if you want to get the register up and running."

"Thank you," Tricia said gratefully.

By the time she'd taken money from the safe and counted it out for the till, the aroma of fresh-brewed coffee filled the front of the store. Mr. Everett brought her a cup, fixed just the way she liked it.

"I'm afraid the wastebasket behind the coffee station wasn't emptied last night," he said. Something else Ginny was supposed to have done, but hadn't. "Shall I do it now?"

"Oh, no," Tricia said. "I know how those back stairs bother your knees. I'll do it. Would you watch the register for a few minutes?"

"I'd be delighted," the elderly gent said, and gave her a smile. Come to think of it, he'd been smiling a lot lately. He took his place behind the register, and Tricia found a cap for her cup and set it on the counter at the coffee station. She grabbed the wastebasket.

"I'll be right back."

The wind was brisk on this sunny October morning as she trundled down the steps that led to the Dumpster. On her way back she again noticed two bowls on the concrete steps leading to the Cookery's back door. She moseyed over to have a look. Sure enough, one contained the remains of dry cat food; the other contained water that had already attracted a few stray locust leaves. She picked them out and tossed them on the ground. The poor kitty shouldn't have to drink dirty water.

Poor Frannie if Angelica found out she was still feeding the neighborhood stray.

Tricia glanced at her watch. By now Angelica would be at her café, getting ready for the lunch crowd that would start filing in within the hour. Frannie was safe from detection—for another few hours, at least.

Tricia reentered her store and found that they already had a customer—or at least a guest. Grace Harris, Mr. Everett's special friend, had arrived before the onslaught of tourists. Tricia had met her just a year before, under not very pleasant conditions—at least for Grace, who'd been forced into a nursing home under suspicious circumstances. Tricia had helped extricate her from the home, and since that time, Grace and Mr. Everett had renewed their decades-old friendship.

As usual, Grace was dressed to the nines. Beautiful name-brand clothes, exquisite jewelry, and expertly coiffed hair, too. With her lovely skin and natural poise, she could have easily made a fortune as a senior citizen model, but her late husband had left her very well off. She liked to read, and she liked Mr. Everett. A lot.

"Good morning, Grace. You're here early."

"I have so much to do today, and I decided I'd best start early."

"Don't overdo, dear," Mr. Everett said kindly.

Grace reached across the counter to clasp his hand. "I won't." She gazed back at Tricia, her expression luminous. She looked back at Mr. Everett. "I don't suppose you've told Tricia our good news."

Mr. Everett shook his head, a blush coloring his cheeks as his gaze dipped to the counter.

"Shame on you," Grace scolded. "Shall I?"

Again he shook his head. "It's my duty."

Duty? That sounded serious.

Mr. Everett cleared his throat and focused on Tricia's face. "Ms. Miles, you and Ginny are like family to me. That's why we want you to be one of the first to know—"

"We're engaged," Grace announced, and pulled the leather glove from her left hand, revealing a modest solitaire diamond. "And Tricia, I want you to be my maid of honor."

Tricia held Grace's outstretched hand, admiring the stone. "I don't know what to say."

"That you'd love to, would be an acceptable answer," Mr. Everett prompted with a hopeful smile.

Tricia beamed. "I'd be delighted! When's the happy day?"

"We haven't set a firm date, but at our age we don't see much point in waiting," Grace said. "Either this Sunday or next."

"What are your plans for the ceremony?"

"Something small and dignified. We have an appointment later this afternoon to talk to the head of catering at the Brookview Inn. That is, if you can spare dear William."

"Of course you can have the afternoon off," Tricia told Mr. Everett. "And you must let me know what I can do for the wedding day. Can I provide the cake? The music? The flowers?"

"That is so kind of you," Grace said, "but I think we'll have everything in hand."

"I'd really like to do *something* for you on your day."

"Just be there. That will be more than enough," Mr. Everett said, and his eyes shone with unshed tears.

Tricia smiled and threw her arms—gently—around the old man. "You better believe I'll be there. I'll close the store if I have to."

"We chose a Sunday morning so that none of our bookshop friends would have to miss the ceremony. We thought we'd have a brunch reception, and that way we'd also have plenty of time to take an afternoon flight to our wedding-night destination." Grace actually blushed at this last announcement.

Tricia felt a lump rise in her throat. Here these two dear people—who deserved decades of happiness together, and weren't likely to receive it—were thinking more of accommodating their guests than of their own circumstances on their most joyous day. Surely no two finer people deserved an abundance of marital bliss.

Tricia clasped Grace's hand. "Do you have your dress? What are your colors? Where are you going on your honeymoon?"

Grace actually giggled. "I haven't given a thought to most of the details. I imagined we'd figure it all out this afternoon. After we get the wedding license, of course." Another titter of laughter escaped her throat. "This is so much fun. I don't remember when I've been this entertained."

Again, a wave of strong emotion passed through Tricia, threatening to engulf her as the memories of planning her own wedding—what she had always considered the happiest day of her life—gushed forth. "I wish you two many years of happiness."

"I'll take what God gives me and hope I live it in relatively good health," Mr. Everett said sensibly.

"Don't be such a pessimist," Grace scolded. "I think we've both got many years left—especially if we take care of each other." The fond look she gave her husband-to-be nearly brought Tricia to tears. Weddings—and all they entailed—had that effect on her.

"Now, Tricia," Grace said, "again, I hope it won't inconvenience you too much if William has an hour or two off this afternoon."

"Take as much time as you need. You have my blessing," Tricia said, and smiled.

"I'm sorry I can't give you more than a few days' notice, but I will need a week off work for our honeymoon," Mr. Everett added in all seriousness.

"I think Ginny and I will be able to manage for a mere seven days," Tricia said, and smiled. Then again, Ginny was already five minutes late.

A customer came in, and Mr. Everett, who took his job very seriously, excused himself to help the man.

"I was surprised to see you at the Food Shelf dedication yesterday," Tricia told Grace.

"It's long been one of my favorite local charities. And who could say no to dear Libby Hirt? Over the years she's been a guardian angel to so many here in Stoneham. She and her husband are the nicest people. They took in that sick child and raised her. Others would've been put off by the prospect of all that surgery, but not Libby. She's got the biggest heart in the world."

A sick child? "I'm sorry I didn't get an opportunity to meet and talk with her."

"She's a real asset to this community." Grace glanced at her diamond-studded watch. "Oh, my, I must dash. I want to speak to the florist. Oh, I have so many things penciled in on my to-do list—I just hope I can accomplish them all before the end of the day." The excitement in her voice was contagious.

"Well, do let me know if I can be of any help. It would be an honor and a privilege," Tricia said.

"Don't worry, dear. I will." Grace crossed the store to join her fiancé and, scandalously, gave Mr. Everett a quick peck on the lips.

"My dear!" he scolded.

Grace grinned. "I don't think your employer minds one bit."

"Minds what?" Tricia asked, and looked up at the decorative tin ceiling, pretending she hadn't noticed a breach in store decorum.

"Good-bye, dear," Mr. Everett said, and Grace waved as she exited the shop.

Tricia risked a glance at her employee. Mr. Everett's cheeks were quite pink. He cleared his throat.

"I think I shall go back to work," he said, and, with head held high, went in search of his lamb's wool duster.

The shop door opened with the soft jingle of the bell that hung over the door. A couple of women bundled in heavy sweaters bustled in, adhesive name tags identifying them as being part of an Apollo Tour.

"Good morning, and welcome to Haven't Got a Clue, Stoneham's—"

"Mystery bookstore," one of them finished. "We read all about you on the Internet." She reached into her purse. "I've got a long list of books I need to find. Could someone help me?"

"I'd be glad to." Before Tricia could even inspect the list, a breathless Ginny burst through the shop door. "Sorry I'm late," she said, already struggling out of the sleeves of her jacket. She raced to the back of the store and hung up the jacket, then hurried to join Tricia with the customers.

"Tricia, I'm sorry, I—"

"We'll talk about it later. Perhaps you could help this lady here." She pointed to the other customer.

"Sure, I'd be glad to. What author were you looking for?"

"Rex Stout. I'd like a copy of *The Golden Spiders*."

"I'm pretty sure we have that in stock. Follow me, please."

Twenty minutes and three hundred and forty dollars later, the ladies departed the store, their shopping bags bulging with books. Despite the good start to the retail day, Ginny's anxious expression kept Tricia from mentioning her tardy entrance—at least for the time being.

"That was an excellent couple of sales," Mr. Everett said, approaching the register with a tray of the store's cardboard coffee cups. "We should celebrate."

"I agree," Tricia said, grateful for the opportunity to cheer her other employee.

Mr. Everett passed around the cups. "Here's to a wonderful day."

They raised their cups and took a sip. "Mr. Everett, wouldn't you like to tell Ginny your good news?" Tricia suggested.

Mr. Everett blushed, and he ducked his head in embarrassment. "Grace and I, we're—well, we've become engaged."

Ginny's mouth drooped. "Engaged?"

"Yes, isn't it wonderful? They're going to get married in the next week or so," Tricia said.

"Married?" Ginny repeated, her voice cracking, and then she burst into tears.

Tricia grabbed Ginny's coffee before she spilled it onto the carpet, while Mr. Everett stood rooted, stricken.

"Ginny, what's wrong?"

"We can't afford to get married," she wailed. "Brian's working two jobs, I've been trying to find a second job, and somehow we have to find the time to work on the house. And . . . oh, everything is all messed up."

"If I thought the news would upset you, I never would have mentioned it," Mr. Everett apologized, obviously distressed by Ginny's reaction. His words only made her cry harder.

"I'm so sorry, Mr. Everett. I'm very happy for you and Grace," Ginny managed. "And I hate myself for being so terribly jealous, but I can't help it."

Tricia pulled Ginny into an awkward embrace. "You and Brian will get married someday, and I'm sure it'll be a lovely ceremony."

Ginny's sobs increased, and she waved her ringless hand in the air. "We're not even officially en-en-gaged."

"Oh, dear—oh, dear," Mr. Everett said.

The shop door opened, the little bell above it jangling cheerfully. Two women stepped into the store, took in the scene, and quickly retreated.

"Oh, dear—oh, dear," Mr. Everett repeated, his heavily veined hands clenched, no doubt to keep from wringing them.

"Come on, Ginny, let's go upstairs," Tricia said, and guided her employee toward the back of the shop and the stairs leading to her loft apartment.

"I'll take care of things here," Mr. Everett called with relief.

Tricia opened the door marked PRIVATE and led the way up the stairs. She unlocked the apartment door and Ginny followed her in. Her sobs had wound down to sniffling, and Tricia led her to one of the stools in front of the kitchen island. "Would you like some cocoa?"

Ginny wiped a hand over her eyes. "Yes, please." She sounded about twelve years old.

Tricia filled her electric kettle with water and plugged it in. She watched as Ginny snatched a paper napkin from the holder and blew her nose. She blinked a few times and took in the kitchen with its sparking white, painted cabinets, granite counters, and thirteen-foot ceiling. "Wow, this is a great space," she managed, and hiccuped. "And there's no drywall dust or exposed wiring. I'd almost forgotten how real people live."

"When you've finished all your renovations, you'll have a lovely home, too."

Ginny sniffed and shrugged.

Tricia took a couple of mugs from the cabinet and found the cylinder of Ghirardelli Chocolate Mocha Hot Cocoa mix. She measured out the powder. The kettle was starting to sound like an engine—a prelude to boiling. "It won't be long now," Tricia said.

"I wish I led a charmed life like you," Ginny said, and sighed.

"Me? I'm divorced, my sister lives next door, and I keep discovering dead bodies. How charmed is that?"

"At least you *have* your sister nearby. Since Mom and Dad moved south, I sometimes feel like I'm all alone here in Stoneham."

"What about Brian?"

"He works so much we hardly ever see each other." She let out another shuddering sigh.

"Seems like you need to make plans for the future. Give yourself a goal. How big a wedding do you want?"

"Not big at all," Ginny said. "I'd like to have our friends, our parents, and some of the people here in the village—like you and Mr. Everett and Grace, and Frannie and Nikki, and our friends Pete and Lisa. Nothing really big."

"Have you ever heard of a potluck wedding?"

Ginny shook her head. "No."

"You could rent a picnic shelter, invite your friends to bring a dish to pass—just like an old-fashioned wedding."

"Is that what you did when you got married?"

Tricia thought about the cathedral, the eight attendants, the five-tiered wedding cake with masses of colorful fondant flowers, and the princess gown and veil. "Not exactly," she said. "But if I had it to do over again, I'd have a much simpler affair." Easy to say, now that the marriage had failed. And, the truth was, she'd loved every minute of the preparations, the ceremony, and the reception. Ending the marriage hadn't been Tricia's idea.

"If simple is what you want, I'm sure it can be arranged. Just pick a date—preferably in warm weather—and start making plans. I'm sure all your friends would love to pitch in. I could get Angelica to help with the food. She's spoken often about starting a catering service as part of the café—once she gets established."

"Angelica would not be happy about you volunteering her services for me."

"Why not?"

"For one thing, she's angry with me because I don't patronize her café. But it costs money to do that and, besides, it's always crowded with tourists. I pack my lunch and eat it in my car."

"You can't do that much longer—it's getting cold."

"Where else am I supposed to go?"

Tricia thought for a second. "You could use the storeroom downstairs. We could put a table in there. And I'll get one of those dorm fridges and a microwave. It would give you and Mr. Everett somewhere to go on your breaks and save you money at the same time."

"You'd be going to an awful lot of trouble."

"It's no trouble. You're both valuable employees. I want to keep you."

Ginny dabbed at her nose with the napkin. "Thank you."

The kettle began to whistle. Tricia unplugged it and poured the hot water into the mugs. "I can't make it happen today, but I'll see what I can do about getting it pulled together in the next couple of days."

"You're the best boss I've ever had."

"If I was, I would've thought of this a long time ago."

"You always have a lot on your mind. Especially since yesterday."

"Yesterday?"

"Pammy dying and all."

For just a few minutes, Tricia *had* actually forgotten about it. She handed Ginny her cup.

"I'm sorry I got all weepy over this whole marriage thing. I should go down and apologize to Mr. Everett. He's the sweetest person on the earth. I feel terrible about hurting his feelings. I think it's wonderful they're getting married, and I really am happy for them." Ginny blew on her cocoa to cool it before taking a tentative sip. "Do you mind if I go down now and apologize? Can I take the cup with me?"

"Yes, of course."

Ginny slid from her stool. "Thanks, Tricia. You really are the best boss in the world." Treading carefully, she made her way to the door without spilling a drop.

Best boss in the world? Tricia didn't know about that. And where would she get one of those dorm fridges? She'd probably have to drive to Nashua or Manchester to find one. Or maybe she could find one in the ad section of the *Stoneham Weekly News*. Too bad she'd tossed out the last one. On the other hand, she was having dinner with Russ later that evening. He probably had one hanging around his house.

Tricia leaned against the counter, sipping her cocoa, and caught sight of the box of books Pammy had left behind. Setting down her mug, she circled the kitchen island and crossed into the living room. She sat down on the couch, leaned over, and ran her fingers across the book spines. Nothing here that interested her. A couple of old cookbooks, something Angelica might stock at the Cookery, a few mainstream titles circa 1970, and a few battered children's books.

Poor Pammy was dead. At least Captain Baker seemed interested in finding her killer, unlike his boss during previous murder investigations in Stoneham. But what if Sheriff Adams interfered with his investigation? What if she decided for him that he should concentrate on pinning the murder on her or Angelica?

Tricia couldn't allow that to happen. What she needed were facts. What she needed to do was to find out why Pammy had wanted to speak to Stuart Paige.

Tricia stood and glanced around her apartment, looking for and finding her purse. In seconds she'd retrieved the crumpled brochure for the Stoneham Food Shelf she'd stashed away the day before. A glance at the hours of operation made her heart sink. It was open Monday mornings from nine to eleven *only.* However, the Clothing Closet was open weekdays from nine to noon. Tricia frowned. Food would seem to be more essential than clothing . . . unless, of course, you were buck naked. Why the difference in hours?

She'd just have to ask.

The problem was that Libby Hirt was the head of the Food Shelf, not the Clothing Closet. Still, perhaps someone at the Closet could give her Libby's number. Perhaps. She might need a reason other than pure curiosity to get that number. She could volunteer Haven't Got a Clue as a food drop-off site. But that still didn't guarantee she'd get the number.

Of course, she could just look Libby up in the local phone book.

There were four Hirts listed, but no Libby; no L. Hirt. She was probably married, or had an unlisted number. Or didn't have a landline at all. A lot of people had given them up, using just their cell phones. But that seemed to be younger people, more Ginny's age. She could try all four . . . and say what? *"I'm just being nosy, asking what happened at the dedication the other day . . ."* And Libby Hirt might not have a clue, thinking Pammy was just one more pushy broad who wanted to get her money-sucking paws on a philanthropist like Stuart Paige.

Tricia scrutinized the brochure, figured what the heck, and dialed the Food Shelf's number. If nothing else, voice mail might give her an emergency number to call. Instead of voice mail, a real person answered. "Stoneham Food Shelf, this is Libby. Can I help you?"

"Oh, it's you," Tricia blurted.

"Y-e-s." The word was drawn out.

Tricia laughed. "Sorry. I was expecting voice mail. My name is Tricia Miles. I was at the dedication yesterday. I run Haven't Got a Clue, the mystery bookshop in Stoneham."

"Oh. How nice. And thank you for coming to our party. You must be a Chamber member."

"Yes. I wanted to talk about the possibility of having my store be a drop-off point for the Food Shelf. I'd also love a tour of your facility."

"We gave tours at the dedication."

"Unfortunately, I got there a bit late. I would love a personal tour—if it's not too much trouble."

"Not at all. When would you like to visit?"

"How about now?"

"Now would be fine."

"Great. I can be there"—Tricia glanced at the kitchen clock—"in ten minutes."

"Fine. I'll be waiting for you. Good-bye."

SIX

TRICIA WAS A little out of breath when she arrived at the Stoneham Food Shelf. Five cars were parked in front of the Clothing Closet's door, and a blue Toyota Prius was in the slot farthest from the Food Shelf's entrance, which sported a CLOSED sign.

Tricia pressed the doorbell at the side of the plate-glass door. Libby Hirt soon appeared and greeted Tricia with a smile. After exchanging pleasantries, she gave Tricia a complete tour of the facility, including opening the connecting door to the well-stocked Clothing Closet. Several women sorted through the racks of clothes. They didn't look poverty stricken to Tricia, and she voiced that opinion.

The twinkle in Libby's eyes, as well as her quick smile, vanished. She closed the door. "Appearances can be deceiving, Tricia. Right here in Stoneham there are families living paycheck to paycheck—living near the brink. House foreclosures, the tight economy—it all takes a toll on the working poor."

"I guess I never gave it much thought, and I feel ashamed. I've been living in Stoneham for about eighteen months, and I'd never even heard of the Stoneham Food Shelf until yesterday."

Libby managed a smile. "There are several hundred people who've lived in Stoneham all their lives and have never heard of our food pantry, so you're not alone." The smile faded from her lips. "Since the booksellers came to town, everyone seems to think that the prosperity has been shared among all Stoneham's citizens. It hasn't. And this is New England. People don't like to admit they have to accept charity."

People like Ginny.

"I'm beginning to realize that," Tricia confessed. "I'd like to do all I can to help."

Libby's smile returned. "I was hoping you'd say that. We've found a collection jar near your cash register is best for a business like yours. Often tourists feel generous with their change, and readily dump it into one of our jars."

"I'm afraid a great many of my customers pay for their purchases with credit cards."

"We realize that, but anything you collect will help local families deal with hunger. That's a big plus, in my book."

Now to pull out the big guns. "What do you know about the local freegans?" Tricia asked.

Libby's mouth went slack, the color draining from her face. "I know of them."

"Have they ever contributed to the Food Shelf?"

Libby hesitated before answering. "There's a stigma attached to such donations. Even hungry people don't want to eat food that may have been salvaged from garbage bins."

"Is the food unsafe?"

"Not necessarily. But if we were to accept such donations—and I'm not saying we knowingly do—we wouldn't know how clean the trash receptacle was. Was the food in plastic bags before it was, er, liberated? It's a question of bacterial contamination. We wouldn't want to expose our clients to any kind of risk."

"So such donations are not something you readily welcome."

"Unfortunately, we don't always know where the donations come from. If we do, we naturally screen it, as we screen everything that comes in."

"Screen it? How?"

"First of all, we accept only nonperishable items," Libby said, and seemed grateful for the opportunity to veer away from the initial question. "Next, we examine every container. Cans that are dented near the seams are not distributed, nor are rusty cans. If the product comes in glass, we make sure there are no cracks. Nothing with bulging lids is accepted, either. And we check the expiration dates on everything that's donated. We'll accept food up to two years after the expiration date."

Tricia wrinkled her nose. "But isn't it spoiled by then?"

"Not at all. Admittedly, it may not be at its best, but when you're hungry, you're not as fussy."

Tricia took in the boxes, cans, and jars of donated food that lined the shelves along the walls. "Surely a steady diet of all this processed food isn't healthy."

"We're an emergency service," Libby explained. "The Food Shelf was never intended to supply individuals for an extended length of time. I'll admit processed food isn't always the healthiest food on the planet. It's full of sodium and high-

fructose corn syrup, but when the alternative is to go hungry, donated food is literally a lifesaver. We do look out for a number of our chronically ill and elderly clients who depend upon us for food when their Social Security money runs out—usually the third week of every month. We take their dietary limitations into account and supply them with as much low-sodium and fresh food as possible."

"How many of those clients do you have?"

"Right now, ten—that number varies throughout the year."

"You mentioned fresh food?" Tricia prompted.

"Yes. Money donations buy bread, milk, cheese, fresh vegetables, and meat to last our clients several days."

"Has the Food Shelf ever run a soup kitchen?"

"No, but one of the local churches did. That was before Everett's Food Market went out of business. The owner, William Everett, donated all his less-than-perfect produce. It was a big blow when he went out of business."

"Did you know he now works for me?"

"Yes, I think Grace Harris did mention that to me. I've been told to save the date for their upcoming wedding. Isn't it sweet that two such nice people found each other?"

"Yes. Now, you were saying—?" Tricia prompted.

"Oh, the soup kitchen. Yes, they tried to solicit donations from other sources outside of Stoneham, but they were already donating to programs in their own towns. It would be nice if we could get another such service going again—but it doesn't seem likely."

Tricia nodded and looked around the gleaming new facility. "It was very generous of Mr. Paige to make a matching donation to the funds your organization has collected."

"Yes. He's been a good friend to the Food Shelf over the years. We're grateful for people like Grace Harris, and for all the Chamber of Commerce has done, too. We never could have come up with the funds if it hadn't been for the Chamber. Bob Kelly is a saint."

Tricia had never thought of him in that regard. "Can just anybody use your services?"

Libby shook her head. "We're here for individuals and families who need emergency assistance. I'm sure you can understand that some people might want to take advantage of such a program, and that's why our volunteers verify the need before our drivers make their weekly deliveries to those who've requested help."

"You make deliveries?"

"Every Monday. That's also when our volunteers make pickups from food drop-off points. At the end of the month, they collect the money from the change jars."

Which explained the limited hours the Food Shelf was open.

"It's important that we let the people who need assistance maintain their dignity," Libby continued. "And with the price of gas these days, they often don't have the wherewithal to get to us."

Tricia nodded in understanding. She couldn't think of anyone she knew who would want to advertise the fact that they needed charity.

She thought about the real reason she'd come to the Food Shelf. Time to get down to business. "It was a wonderful dedication. Too bad it was marred by that woman's temper tantrum," Tricia said, not admitting her acquaintance with Pammy.

"Yes," Libby agreed. "I never did find out what she wanted. Someone told me later she wanted to talk to our guest of honor. Harangue, more like. I was grateful that Mr. Paige's security people dealt with her. It would have been extremely embarrassing for him had she made a fuss during the ceremony. Especially since the press was in attendance."

The press? Oh, she meant Russ. Funny, Tricia never really thought of the *Stoneham Weekly News* as a serious news organ. Wouldn't Russ be furious if he knew what her real opinion was?

Too bad Libby hadn't known why Pammy had tried to crash the dedication . . . but then again, if she did, she had no reason to divulge that information to Tricia. And why should Libby speak frankly? Until today, she hadn't met Tricia, and had no reason to share anything she knew.

Too bad.

"Goodness, look at the time," Tricia said, with a show of looking at her watch. "I'm sorry to have kept you so long."

"Not at all," Libby assured her. "Let me get one of our change jars for you. One of our volunteers will visit your store to collect what's been contributed at the end of every month. We're very grateful to the Chamber members who've elected to help us out in this way."

Tricia took another look around the tidy room as Libby rummaged in a locker for a collection jar. She thought about the Clothing Closet next door, and the boxes of food ready to be delivered to the people of Stoneham who were too ashamed to let others know their circumstances . . . and felt grateful for what she had and the life she lived.

After missing breakfast and talking food for so long with Libby Hirt, Tricia was hungry enough to eat her own foot. As it was almost noon, she parked her car in the municipal lot, grabbed her new collection can, and hoofed it to

Angelica's café, figuring on grabbing a quick bite before returning to Haven't Got a Clue.

Ginny was right. Booked for Lunch was booked solid. There wasn't a seat to be had, and people stood in the entryway, waiting for an opening. Tricia did an about-face and headed north down the sidewalk for the Bookshelf Diner.

Another destroyed carved pumpkin lay in the gutter outside the restaurant. How many of the village's children were heartbroken over such vandalism? Tricia bypassed the mess and entered the diner.

Though Angelica's café had put a dent in the Bookshelf's lunchtime trade, it hadn't killed it. All but one booth was taken, and the one Tricia was given was only a two-seater. She shrugged out of her jacket, set it over her purse and the collection can, and sat down. Not thirty seconds later the waitress arrived, pouring fresh water from a frosted glass jug into Tricia's waiting glass.

"What can I get you?" Eugenia, the perky, blond, college-aged waitress asked. "The usual?"

Tricia shook her head. "Today I think I'll be daring. How about a bowl of vegetarian chili—with extra crackers?"

Eugenia winked.

"Hey, I thought you only worked evenings," Tricia said.

Eugenia smiled. "I do. But Hildy called in sick today, and since I only have a couple of morning classes, I agreed to fill in. I'm a starving college student. I can always use the extra money. Be right back with your chili," she promised, and headed toward the kitchen.

Was it Tricia's imagination, or had Eugenia lost some of the hardware she usually wore? Gone were the eyebrow rings and nose studs—although the young woman still had at least three sets of gemstonelike post earrings, in a multitude of colors, decorating each ear. Should she mention the young woman's new look, or had Eugenia taken enough teasing about her former look from the more staid villagers that acknowledging the change wouldn't be appreciated?

Eugenia reappeared in record time with Tricia's order. She settled the bowl, with the requested extra crackers, on the paper placemat in front of Tricia. "Hey, I heard you met my mom."

Tricia looked into the intense blue eyes above her. "I did?"

"Yeah, Libby Hirt. She runs the Food Shelf. I talked to her on the phone a few minutes ago. She said you'd been by to scope out the place and that you'd volunteered to be a drop-off point. That was really nice of you. Thanks."

News traveled fast. She'd left Libby only some fifteen minutes before. Hadn't Grace mentioned that Eugenia had been ill as a child? She certainly didn't look the worse for wear now. "Oh, well. Just my civic duty."

"No, it's more than that. Thanks to Mom, I grew up knowing that there were hungry people all around here. Not everyone is as enthusiastic about helping the Food Shelf. They think it encourages people to be bums or something." She rolled her eyes disapprovingly.

"Since most of my customers are tourists, I don't know that they'll feel generous toward the cause, but I figured it wouldn't hurt to try." And she intended to salt the jar to get things going.

"You're right," Eugenia agreed, "but you'd be surprised how fast loose change mounts up." She nodded toward the collection can that sat by the diner's register. It was at least a third full with quarters, nickels, dimes, pennies, and a few folded-up dollar bills. "Add up all the collection cans in town, and it makes a big difference to the Food Shelf's bottom line," she continued. "I mean, we can't depend on bigwigs like Stuart Paige to pick up the tab all the time. The people of Stoneham have to take some responsibility for the villagers who need help making ends meet."

The words didn't sound rehearsed, but they weren't the jargon of a twenty-year-old, either. Eugenia must have grown up hearing the same speeches over and over again. That she'd taken them to heart said a lot about her character.

"I'm glad I can help."

"I do what I can, too," Eugenia said, her gaze traveling back toward the kitchen.

"Hey, what's it take to get some service around here?" called a male voice from behind Tricia. The accent sounded like he was a Long Islander.

"'Scuse me," Eugenia said, and took off to take care of her customer.

Tricia turned her attention to her lunch, plunging her spoon into the chili. She had always enjoyed talking with Eugenia. She was a nice kid. Like her mom . . . although with that brilliantly blond hair, and her little pug nose, she looked nothing like her mother. Then Tricia remembered again that Grace had mentioned the girl had been adopted.

She unwrapped the first of her cracker packets, crumbling them on top of the chili.

A minute later Eugenia returned, this time with a carafe of coffee. "Sorry, I never asked if you wanted anything other than water."

Tricia shook her head. "I'm fine, thanks."

"All set?"

Tricia nodded.

Eugenia dipped into the pocket of her apron, withdrew a piece of paper—the check—and set it on the table. "Thanks for coming by today—and for helping my mom."

Tricia nodded, and the young woman headed back up the booth-flanked aisle, checking with the rest of the patrons, making offers of refills as needed.

As Tricia finished her lunch, she wondered what Eugenia had meant when she said she'd done all she could to support her mother's cause. Did she contribute some of her tips, or was she one of the volunteers who packed canned goods into cartons at the Food Shelf?

Today wasn't the day to ask.

Tricia finished the last of her chili, picked up the check, her jacket, purse, and the collection jar, and paid at the register. Minutes later she was back at Haven't Got a Clue with time to spare before it was time for Ginny's lunch break.

Tricia hung up her jacket, stashed her purse, and settled the collection jar beside the register.

"Another one of Libby Hirt's soldiers against hunger, I see," Ginny said, crossing her arms across her chest.

"Yes. I hope we can help make a difference," Tricia said. She opened the register and took out a couple of dollars in quarters, dimes, and nickels, adding it to the jar. The money made a rather shallow layer. It would take an awful lot of change to fill it.

A woman approached the cash desk and set four books down by the register. Tricia rang up the sale while Ginny bagged the books. The woman handed her thirty dollars, and Tricia returned her twenty cents change, which the woman promptly dropped into the collection can.

"Thank you," Tricia said as Ginny stifled a grin.

The woman sketched a wave good-bye and headed out the door.

"See, we're making a difference already," Tricia said. She looked around the store. "Did Mr. Everett leave?"

"Grace stopped by and picked him up. Something about talking to the caterer at the Brookview Inn," Ginny said, and sighed. "While you were gone, we had a lull. By the way, it looks like the book club is off for tonight. Grace and Mr. Everett are busy; Nikki and Julia both called to say they can't make it, either. I figured what the heck, and made an executive decision to cancel the meeting."

"It's just as well," Tricia said, and sighed. "I forgot I have a date with Russ for tonight. Does everyone know?"

"Yes, I called them all. We should be good to go next week—although Grace and Mr. Everett will be on their honeymoon. We may want to postpone the meetings until they return."

Tricia nodded.

"I also called the Board of Selectmen to see about renting the gazebo in the park for our wedding. No go."

"Have you tried Milford?"

"They've got a big gazebo in the Oval, but I'm not sure they'd rent that."

"What about that ball field next to the hospital?"

"I could try that next," Ginny said uncertainly.

"What about your own yard? It's pretty big. And you could rent a tent just in case it rains."

"I hadn't even thought of that. I'll put it on the back burner. I mean, I haven't even talked to Brian about any of this. He might not want to get married at home or under a tent."

"I think an at-home wedding would be lovely."

"I'm warming up to the idea," Ginny said. "Oh, the music's stopped. I'll go change the CD." She headed for the coffee station, which also housed the store's stereo system.

"Anything else happen while I was gone?" Tricia asked.

Ginny flipped through the jewel boxes. "Captain Baker called. He said he'd call back some other time."

"What did he want?"

"He didn't say." Ginny chose *A New Journey* by Celtic Woman, setting it on low volume. "It probably had something to do with Pammy's death, though—don't you think?"

"Undoubtedly. But I don't know what else I can tell him. She didn't confide in me all that much. And sometimes she'd disappear in the evenings and didn't tell me where she'd been. If only I could find one of the local freegans, I might find out more about what Pammy was up to."

Ginny returned to the sales counter. "What do you mean?"

"Pammy told Angelica she was a freegan. They Dumpster dive for food."

"I know what they are," Ginny said.

"I asked Libby Hirt about them, but she didn't want to talk about it. Obviously there are people in the village who know about them, but I don't know who else to ask."

"I might be able to help," Ginny said. Her voice had dropped.

"You know someone?"

Ginny nodded. "In fact, I know several freegans."

"Could you introduce me to them?" Tricia asked eagerly.

"You already know them."

Tricia blinked. She couldn't imagine anyone she knew in Stoneham who would be reduced to digging through garbage for food. "Who?"

Ginny shrugged. "Well, for one—me."

SEVEN

TRICIA'S MOUTH DROPPED. It felt like someone had just kicked her in the stomach. It took a long moment before she could speak again. "Ginny, I can't believe you dig through garbage for food."

"I never intended for you to know," Ginny said, her head lowered so she did not meet Tricia's gaze.

"Why would you do such a thing, especially after Brian ended up in the hospital last spring with food poisoning?"

"Ah, but he wasn't poisoned by anything we got Dumpster diving."

That was true. Brian had eaten tainted food meant for Tricia.

"Just answer one question. Why? And don't tell me you're making a political statement."

Ginny sighed. "I was a freegan back in college. I thought I didn't have any money back then, but now it's a matter of economic survival. Buying our house has been a lot more expensive than either of us thought it would be—that's why we can never afford a nice wedding."

"Are you sorry you bought the house?"

"When I pay the bills, yes. When I drive home from work at night and see the lights on in our little cottage, no, I'm not sorry. We both love the house. It just needed a lot more work than we anticipated, and we have to cut corners where we can."

"Have you thought about using the Stoneham Food Shelf?"

Ginny shook her head. "That's for desperate people."

"And you don't think digging through trash to get your food is a desperate measure?"

Ginny held her head high. "No, I don't. Although I don't like to advertise it," she added sheepishly.

The shop door opened, and a man and woman entered the store.

Tricia stood straighter and forced a smile. "Hello. Welcome to Haven't Got a Clue. Can I help you find anything?"

"No, just browsing," said the woman, who gave her a return smile.

"Our authors are shelved in alphabetical order. Nonfiction titles are on the

left. Please, help yourself to some coffee, and let us know if you need help or a recommendation."

"Will do," said the man, and he and the woman split up, each heading for a different part of the store.

Tricia turned her attention back to Ginny. "I don't know that we should continue this conversation."

"Agreed. At least this part of it. But you wanted to know about Pammy," Ginny reminded her.

"Yes. What was she doing in Stoneham? Did she confide in you or any of your . . . freegan friends?"

"She didn't talk to me—she didn't *like* me. The feeling was mutual. But she was friendly with some of the others. One of them told me she'd mentioned she was hanging around Stoneham to meet someone."

"Did she find this person?"

Ginny shook her head. "I don't think so."

"Who are these people? Can I talk to them?"

"Stoneham is a small town. We don't like to advertise who we are to just anyone. We don't do much scavenging here in the village. We don't want to catch the flack."

"Where do you go to . . . find . . . what you're looking for?"

"Sometimes Milford—but Nashua, mostly. But Brian and I have also been to Manchester and Portsmouth, too. We've got friends all over."

"You said I'd know some of these people," Tricia reminded her.

"I don't feel comfortable telling you who—at least not without talking to them first."

Good grief! Who could she be talking about? Fellow booksellers? Respected members of the Chamber of Commerce?

"Would you ask them if they'd mind speaking to me?"

"I'll try," Ginny said, "but I can't promise that anyone will."

Libby had mentioned the stigma attached to being a freegan. "Fair enough. But I'm not out to expose anyone. I just want to find out who killed Pammy, and why. You can understand that—right?"

"Yes. But I'm certain that none of my friends had anything to do with Pammy's death. I'd stake my life on it."

Tricia wasn't sure that was a wise bet.

IT WAS AFTER five when the phone rang. Since Ginny was at the counter, she picked up the telephone. Tricia looked up from her position at the coffee sta-

tion. She was proud of that phone, a relic from another age. She liked to imagine that Harriet Vane used the same kind of instrument to talk to Lord Peter Wimsey. The look of distaste on Ginny's face, however, gave Tricia pause. Ginny laid the receiver on her chest to muffle the mouthpiece. "It's Angelica. Does she have to remind everyone she talks to that she's"—she dropped her voice to a whine—"*about to be published,* and then give the daily countdown?"

Tricia flipped off the switch on the coffeemaker, removed the filter and grounds, and dumped them in the wastebasket before heading for the register and the phone. She took the receiver, which Ginny held out as if it had cooties. "Hey, Ange, what's up?"

"I need your help," Angelica said, her voice filled with drama. "Jake has taken off again, and I've got no one to help me, and—"

"Ange, I have a store to run—"

"Then can you loan me Ginny or Mr. Everett?"

"Mr. Everett has the afternoon off."

"Again?" Angelica wailed.

"What do you need?" Tricia asked.

"I've got the kitchen back in shape for tomorrow's lunch crowd, but I need help bringing my garbage over to the Cookery. Captain Baker took one of my garbage carts, and the other one is overflowing. I've got bags of trash I have to dump somewhere. I may even need to put some in your Dumpster. Will you help me, please?"

The last thing Tricia wanted to do was soil her pretty peach sweater set, but she couldn't very well ask Ginny to ruin her clothes, either.

"I can give you ten minutes. No more."

"That's all I need. Now get over here, will you? I've got paperwork to finish over at the Cookery. Why I ever thought I could run two businesses at the same time . . ."

Tricia hung up the phone and shifted her gaze to her employee. Ginny didn't look pleased.

"I've got to help Angelica with her trash problem," she said, and forced a smile. "I'll be back in about ten minutes."

Ginny folded her arms across her chest, but made no comment.

Tricia headed for the door without a backward glance. Why should she feel guilty? After all, they weren't exactly inundated with customers, and Angelica was her sister. She was short-staffed and—

Why was she making excuses—if only to herself?

She crossed the street and found Angelica had piled several black plastic trash bags outside the door to Booked for Lunch, and was already locking the door for the day.

Tricia came to a halt at the edge of the pavement. "You needed help for four bags? Couldn't you just make a couple of trips across the street by yourself?"

Angelica turned hard eyes on her sister. "Don't start with me. I've had a rough day. You should wait on eighty-seven customers while wearing heels and no one to do food prep."

"For heaven's sake, buy some sensible shoes."

"I don't have time to buy new shoes. I don't have time to scratch my—"

Tricia held up a hand to stave off the rest of that statement. "Never mind. I'll grab two of these bags. You get the others."

"Be careful, they're heavy," Angelica warned.

Tricia grabbed the first bag and nearly staggered under its weight. "What have you got in here? Lead?"

"I told you they were heavy. It's paper, mostly. Napkins, milk shake cups, et cetera. And food waste."

Tricia picked up the other bag, holding it at arm's length, her muscles straining under the load. "Let's hurry up. I've got my own end-of-day chores to do at Haven't Got a Clue."

The sisters hefted their bags, waited for a minivan to pass, and staggered across the street.

"Do we have to walk around the block to get to your Dumpster?" Tricia asked.

"It's too far," Angelica said. "We'll walk straight through the Cookery. But for heaven's sake, don't drop those bags. If one of them splits on my carpet—"

The cheerful bell rang overhead as Angelica opened the Cookery's door and led the way. "Coming through," she told a surprised Frannie, who stood at the register with a woman customer.

Tricia plastered on a smile as she nodded a hello to Frannie and the well-dressed tourist who clutched a Cookery shopping bag in one hand. "Hi," she said, and shuffled after her sister.

Angelica had just punched in the code to disarm the security system when Tricia caught up with her. She opened the door. "If my Dumpster's full, we can put the overflow into—" Her words ended abruptly as she gazed at the top step outside the Cookery's back exit.

Tricia remembered the two bowls that had sat on the step earlier that day. "Let's get this stuff into the trash before a bag splits. Remember your carpets," she admonished.

Angelica turned, leveled an icy glare at Tricia, and then hefted her own bags of trash before trundling down the concrete steps to the metal trash receptacle. She grunted as she slam-dunked her two bags of trash into the Dumpster, then took Tricia's from her. Tricia refrained from speaking and followed her sister

back up the steps to the store. Angelica paused on the top step, retrieving the empty food bowl and tossing aside what was left in the water bowl.

The store was devoid of customers as she stalked through the aisles of books, halted at the cash desk, and slammed the bowls onto the counter. "Frannie, I've asked you not to encourage that cat to come around, and you've gone and done it again."

Frannie managed a strangled laugh. "Done what?"

"You're feeding that stray cat when I've asked you not to."

"But it's hungry. And the nights are getting colder. I wouldn't want that poor kitty to be hungry, let alone cold."

"It's wearing a fur coat," Angelica stated.

"It's got bare feet," Frannie countered.

Angelica turned to Tricia. "Are you going to help me out here?"

Tricia shook her head and shrugged. "I think it's wonderful that Frannie wants to help this little cat."

"Well, I don't. I don't want a store cat like you've got. Can the two of you understand that?"

"I wasn't trying to catch her so she'd be the official Cookery mascot, although I think it would be a wonderful idea," Frannie said. "I want to take her home—make her my pet."

Angelica blinked. "Oh. Well. I'm sorry. I didn't realize—"

"Jumping to conclusions, eh, Angelica?" Tricia asked.

Angelica leveled a withering glare at her sister. "You stay out of this." She turned back to Frannie. "And how are you going to catch this cat? I didn't see a trap."

"I've got to gain her trust first. I've already talked to Animal Control. They're going to loan me a Havahart trap."

"When?"

"I thought I might try to trap her in the next couple of days."

"Well, make it sooner rather than later, will you? I don't want it hanging around my store. It might have fleas, or some cat disease that could infect my customers."

"Cats don't have—" Tricia started.

Angelica whirled on her. "What about allergies? I could get sued if one of my customers has allergies, enters my store, and has a seizure or something."

"Don't be ridiculous. None of my customers has ever so much as sneezed because of Miss Marple."

Angelica leveled a glare at her sister. "I believe I asked you to stay out of this."

"Fine. I'm leaving. Good luck catching Penny," Tricia said to Frannie.

"Penny?" Angelica asked.

"My cat," Frannie said, and smiled.

Tricia shut the door. The wind had picked up as the sun sank toward the horizon. She wrapped her arms around her chest and stalked back to Haven't Got a Clue. The leaves on the trees were ablaze with color, and already the leaf peepers were descending on the village. That was good for business but bad if she was going to be shorthanded, with Mr. Everett going on his honeymoon.

She was preoccupied with thoughts of the busy week ahead when she caught sight of a Hillsborough Sheriff's Department patrol car moving toward her. She paused, squinting to see who was at the wheel; it was Deputy Placer. She realized that she had hoped it would be Captain Baker.

A gust of wind made her shiver.

Now why would she want to see *him?* Because he'd called and hadn't left a message? Or was it those maddening green eyes that reminded her of her ex-husband, Christopher?

And why think about him at all when she had a date with Russ in just over two hours?

The cruiser rounded the corner as she opened the door to Haven't Got a Clue.

Don't even think about that man, Tricia chided herself as she resumed her position behind the sales counter. But for the next hour, she kept finding herself looking out the big glass display window, on the lookout for another Sheriff's Department cruiser.

EIGHT

Tricia showed up at Russ's house at precisely seven thirty. He met her at the door, looking relaxed in a beige sweater with suede elbow patches. Light from the sconces that flanked the door glinted off his glasses, and his hair curled around his ears. At that moment, he reminded her of an absentminded professor. He leaned forward to give her a kiss. This time his lips actually landed on hers, and she found herself returning the kiss with enthusiasm.

"Whoa, come on in," Russ urged, holding the door open for her, a bit overwhelmed by her greeting.

After a year of what her grandmother would've called "courting," Tricia felt

at home at Russ's house. She shrugged out of her jacket and he took it from her, hanging it in the closet. As usual, there was a platter of cheese and crackers on the coffee table in his living room. She usually had to ask him to turn off his police scanner when she dropped by, but this night the scanner was silent. Instead, soft jazz played on the stereo. Perhaps things were looking up on the romance front.

As usual, a cut-glass carafe of sherry and glasses sat on the coffee table as well. Tricia took her accustomed seat on the couch, and Russ soon joined her.

"You look tired. What have you been up to all day?" Russ asked, pouring sherry for them both.

Tricia leaned back against the soft leather. "Besides selling books and annoying Angelica? Thinking a lot about Pammy Fredericks. I even went to see Libby Hirt at the Food Shelf, to ask her if she knew why Pammy would want to talk to Stuart Paige."

He handed Tricia her drink. "And did she?"

"No. Did you know Pammy was a freegan?"

"One of those weirdos that eats garbage?"

"I don't think freegans think of it as garbage. More as salvaged food. It turns out Ginny is a freegan, too, although she doesn't want it getting around."

"I can see why."

Tricia thought about what she'd seen at the Food Shelf's dedication. "Russ, you took a lot of pictures at the ceremony yesterday. Was Pammy in any of them? Maybe—"

He shook his head. "She never made it inside the building. And honestly, why would she think Stuart Paige would want to talk to her?"

"She asked everyone in town for a job. Maybe it was that simple."

He shrugged. "Let's not talk about your ex-friend."

That was unusual. The last time there'd been a murder in Stoneham, it was all Russ wanted to talk about—and he'd especially wanted to grill Tricia on what she knew about the victim, who'd been a stranger. Come to think of it, he hadn't even called her after the news of Pammy's death broke.

Russ leaned forward, spread some Brie on a cracker, and offered it to Tricia. She shook her head. "I've been thinking about the future. How I might like to try something different," he said.

"Different?" Tricia asked, and took a sip of her sherry.

He leaned back against the cushions. "I've been thinking about writing a novel."

Tricia nearly choked on her drink. "You, write a novel?"

He looked hurt. "Why's that so hard to believe? I'm a journalist. How hard can it be? Plenty of print reporters have turned to fiction. And when I worked

at the paper in Boston, I covered a lot of stories that were ripe for a 'ripped-from-the-news' kind of book."

Tricia could think of more than a few journalists right off the top of her head who'd switched gears to become novelists: Laura Lippman, Carl Hiaasen, Edna Buchanan, Michael Connelly . . . But Russ a novelist? Ha! He was so grounded in facts, she wondered if he would be able to spin a tale and keep up the pace for eighty or one hundred thousand words. Of course, she wasn't about to voice that opinion.

"I wish you luck," she said, and raised her glass. "To your new career."

Russ laughed and raised his glass, touching hers so they clinked. Then he settled back on the couch. "I've been thinking a lot about the future and what it means for us, too."

Tricia's stomach tightened involuntarily. "Oh?"

"Yeah. We've been going out for . . . oh, just about a year now, right?"

Something inside Tricia squirmed. Was she about to be dumped? "Yes."

"We've had some rough times," he admitted.

"I wouldn't say rough," she interrupted, studying his face. "Just not exactly smooth."

"But overall, would you say you've been happy?"

Happy was a relative thing. Still . . . "Yes, I'd say so." Oh, God. Was he about to propose?

Russ leaned in closer. Could he have a velvet-covered ring box tucked inside his sweater pocket? What was she going to say when he pulled it out? She hadn't even considered marrying again. It had only been two years since her divorce. And—

"It's time we had a serious conversation about the future," Russ went on.

Tricia's spine stiffened, and she drew back. "Are you sure this is the right time?"

He nodded and gave her an affectionate smile. "I am."

Tricia leaned forward, grabbed her drink, and took a large mouthful, gulping it down.

Russ laughed. "Am I that intimidating?"

"No, but you sound so serious, which makes me think bad news is coming."

"Not bad news. Good news."

Oh, no. Here it came. And how would she reply to his proposal? *No? Yes? I'm not prepared to answer such a serious question on such short notice?*

The sherry made her flush. "Russ, don't you think you might be rushing things?"

"I've been thinking about this for the past couple of months. Seriously thinking about it. I think it might be time."

Tricia looked away, exhaled. She was not ready for this. She was not ready for this at all.

Russ captured her hands in his, looked deeply into her eyes. "Tricia, I've put the *Stoneham Weekly News* up for sale."

"What?" she asked, and yanked back her hands.

"I know this will come as a bit of a shock, but I might have a job in Philadelphia. There's an opening for a crime beat reporter. I've interviewed for it, and so far I'm their lead candidate."

"What?" she repeated, still unsure of what she'd just heard.

"It's a terrific opportunity. The pay isn't great, but I'm certainly not making a fortune here in Stoneham, either."

"But, but—" She took a breath to steady her suddenly shattered nerves. "I thought you liked being your own boss. I thought you left the rat race in Boston to have a little peace and quiet—and that you'd found it here in Stoneham."

"It's a little *too* peaceful around here."

"Are you kidding? Pammy Fredericks was murdered yesterday."

He waved a hand in dismissal. "It would be more exciting if I could write about it in tomorrow's edition—not next week's. For all I know, the Sheriff's Department will solve it before I can even report her death. I'm tired of running—and writing—stories about lost dogs, stolen laundry, and the occasional DUI, not to mention vandalism—like the mystery of the smashed pumpkins all over town."

No diamond ring. The heck with that—no Russ!

"And you say you've been thinking about this for a while?" Tricia asked, her throat tightening.

"Uh-huh."

"What about me? Did you even consider me while you were making this decision?"

He shrugged. "To tell you the truth, I was surprised to hear you say you'd been happy with our relationship. I always thought you wanted more."

She had. But he never seemed to be listening.

"When will you know about the job?"

"Friday."

That gave her only a few more days to . . . what? Hope? Mourn?

Think about Grant Baker's green eyes?

"Is there someone else?" she asked, dreading the answer.

He laughed. "Hardly. Unless you call running a dying business a mistress of sorts. The truth is, I'm bored here in Stoneham. I need something more stimulating—something this hick village can't offer."

Tricia swallowed. Apparently she couldn't offer that kind of excitement, either.

She hardened her heart. "What if the job falls through? Will you keep on looking?"

"I think so."

"It's too bad you spent time making dinner. I don't believe I want to stay."

"I figured you'd say that, so I didn't bother to make anything."

Tricia's shock at his previous announcement now gave way to anger. "You invited me here, and then you didn't even make dinner?"

He laughed. "What was the point? You're leaving, just as I thought you would."

So now she was predictable!

Tricia rose to her feet and with a supreme effort offered him her hand.

He took it, albeit reluctantly.

"It's been nice knowing you, Russ. Have a good life."

She yanked back her hand and stormed off for his front door.

"Tricia, wait!"

Tricia paused, turned. "What for? You've made your life's plans, and I'm not a part of them. I don't think there's anything more to talk about."

"You're taking this much too seriously."

"If you're talking about our relationship, I did, but I won't from now on."

She grabbed her coat, opened the door, and then yanked it shut behind her, enjoying the sound of its slam. As she stalked off for her car, she noted the door did not open. Russ did not appear, and he did not call for her to return.

Damn him!

"YOU BROKE UP?" Angelica cried, dismayed. She placed a huge slice of meatloaf on Tricia's plate, plopped down a gigantic helping of garlic mashed potatoes and a sprinkling of peas, about three times more food than Tricia was ever likely to eat. She didn't protest. Food had always been Angelica's way of coping with disappointment.

"I didn't break up. Russ did." Tricia looked down at her plate. "Meatloaf? You never make meatloaf."

"Of course I do. It's Bob's favorite meal." Bob sat across the table from Tricia, and both watched as Angelica dished up her own dinner. "I know you told me Russ was a little slow in the romance department, but dumping you and leaving Stoneham all in one go? Wow!" She picked up her fork and turned a sympathetic frown on Tricia. "You've had a rough week."

"Tell me about it."

"Can I have some mashed potatoes, too?" Bob asked, offering Angelica his plate.

"Sorry, sweetie." She heaped his plate and handed him the gravy boat. He drowned his entire meal in the stuff, making Tricia cringe.

Angelica poured wine for everyone before seating herself next to Bob.

Bob shoveled up a forkful of peas. "I meant to thank you for showing up at the Food Shelf dedication yesterday, Tricia. We had a great showing. I'm sure Russ will give it good play in next week's issue."

"Don't mention Russ," Angelica snapped at him. "Can't you see Tricia's heart is breaking?"

It was anger more than heartbreak that Tricia felt. She cut a tiny piece of meatloaf with her fork, but said nothing.

"Anyway, thanks for showing up," Bob concluded lamely.

Tricia decided to change the subject. "I went to see Libby Hirt today. I've put one of her collection jars on my sales counter."

"Good for you," Bob said, and attacked his mound of potatoes. "You ought to get one, too, Angelica, for the Cookery *and* the café."

"If you say so," she said, and took a sip of her wine.

Tricia swallowed and looked over at her sister. "Boy, there's a lot of onion in this meatloaf."

"Bob likes a lot of onions, don't you, honey? And they're good for you, too," Angelica said.

Tricia took a sip of her wine, turning her attention back to Bob. "Libby Hirt more or less told me that if it wasn't for you, Bob, the Food Shelf wouldn't have its new home."

Bob shook his head, his gaze still riveted on his food. "That's not true. It was a Chamber effort."

"Led by you," Angelica piped up.

"I think it's a wonderful cause. I had no idea there were hungry people right here in Stoneham," Tricia added.

"Yes, well, not everyone who lives here has benefited from the rebirth of the village."

Before Libby's revelation, Tricia could've sworn there wasn't an altruistic bone in Bob's body—especially because he was the one who had made out like a bandit from the village's rebirth, since he owned half the buildings on Main Street. She decided to push harder. "How did you find out about it? What first got you interested in feeding the hungry?"

"There's a need," he said simply. "Angelica, could I please have another slice of that wonderful meatloaf?"

"Of course." She cut him a big slice, sliding it onto the pool of gravy on his plate.

"Yes, but what was *your* interest?" Tricia persisted.

Bob's gaze hardened as he swung to glare at Tricia. "I grew up in a home where you never knew where your next meal would come from—or even if there would *be* a next meal. I know what it feels like to be hungry—not just for a day, but for days on end. Now, are you happy with that explanation, or do I need to elaborate further?"

Tricia was immediately sorry for her pressure tactics. "I'm sorry, Bob. I shouldn't have pressed you. I just wanted to know more about you—understand you. I took the collection jar because I want to help my fellow citizens of Stoneham—and hope I never have to know who needs that help." She said the words, but she thought about Ginny and Brian, wondering what they were eating for dinner that night.

Bob looked away, his lips pursing. Angelica put a hand on his arm, and he turned to her. She gave him a reassuring smile before he turned back to face Tricia. "Thank you."

Tricia found herself smiling back at him, wondering what it had cost him to say those two very powerful words.

NINE

MISS MARPLE GREETED Tricia at the door, scolding her for leaving her alone for the evening. To placate the cat, Tricia gave her a bowl of cat cookies, and Miss Marple happily tucked in, purring as she ate.

The light on the phone flashed, indicating a message. Tricia pressed the Play button. The call had come in at seven forty-three; caller ID indicated it was a blocked number. A deep, draggy, electronically altered voice said the same four words, over and over again: "Give back the diary."

Diary? What diary?

Was this someone's sick idea of a joke?

Tricia's finger hovered over the Delete button. Should she erase the call? It was probably just a prank. But what if it wasn't? The words "give back" indicated someone thought she had a diary. She didn't. But Pammy had been murdered. Her car had been ransacked after her death. Did she keep a diary? And if she did, why would someone think Tricia had it?

And then she remembered the box of books Pammy had left behind.

The carton was still at the side of the couch, where Pammy had left it just

the day before. Tricia picked up the box, setting it on the cocktail table. She shuffled through the titles again. Most of them were old paperback volumes with faded, cracked spines, fiction from one-hit wonders, writers who'd sold one book and nothing else. Today those kinds of authors could be found published (if that was the term) by the likes of Lulu.com. The competition wasn't as fierce back in the early twentieth century.

The only title of note was a first-edition copy of Edith Hull's *The Sheik*, which might draw a bit of notice from the proprietor of Stoneham's Have a Heart romance bookstore, but not much. A novel from the Roaring Twenties was bound to read pretty tame in this day and age.

No diary.

Miss Marple entered the living room, sat down on the rug, and proceeded to wash her face.

The books could do Pammy no good now. Tricia folded the carton's flaps back in on each other. The Friends of the Stoneham Library were having a sale at the end of the month. She could donate the books, and perhaps add a few from her own stock that were used or too shopworn to offer for sale in Haven't Got a Clue. She'd box them all up and take them to the library.

The telephone rang. Miss Marple looked at the offending noise, as though daring Tricia to answer it to stop its bleating.

Tricia picked up the extension. "Hello?"

The same draggy voice. "Give back the diary; give back the diary."

"Who is this?" Tricia demanded.

Undaunted, the voice continued reciting the diary mantra. Was it a recording? She slammed the receiver back into its cradle.

Within seconds, the phone rang again. Tricia picked it up. "Give back the diary."

She slammed it back down. Again, it rang within seconds. Tricia let it ring and went back to the kitchen. Again the caller ID registered BLOCKED CALL. She turned off the ringer, but the phone in the living room continued to trill. She stalked across the apartment and unplugged it from the wall. Now only the phone in her bedroom rang. Thirty seconds later, she'd unplugged that, too, and peace reigned.

"Now, who do you suppose thinks I've got Pammy's diary, and why do they want it?" Tricia asked her cat.

Miss Marple jumped up on the cocktail table, settled herself, and began to lick her left back leg.

"Well, I'm glad you're not traumatized by those calls," Tricia said.

Miss Marple ignored her and started on her other back leg.

Tricia's gaze returned to the carton of old books. If Pammy had a diary, she

hadn't left it here. Did someone assume Tricia had it just because it hadn't been on Pammy's person or in her car at the time of her death? Good assumption—only it didn't happen to be true. Unless Pammy had hidden the book somewhere in Tricia's apartment. But why would she do that?

Tricia turned on the stereo. One of Russ's favorite mellow jazz CDs was still in the player. She hit the Eject button, and the tray slid out. Back into the jewel case the CD went. She selected one of her favorites instead, hit the Play button, and Irish Woman began a cheery tune.

Her gaze wandered around the room. Well, she had nothing better to do, and decided she'd search the place. Pammy had had unsupervised access to the premises for hours on end while Tricia was working, as evidenced by her lifting one of Tricia's checks.

She looked through the books on her shelves, on top of the bookcases, in all the cupboards, under the bed and other furniture, even checking to see if Pammy might have attached the diary to the undersides with duct tape. Miss Marple followed her from room to room, eager to see what this new game would produce. Tricia found a few of the cat's missing catnip toys and tossed them aside. A delighted Miss Marple flew after them. But there was no sign of a diary.

Finally, having looked through the entire apartment, Tricia returned to the living room, sat cross-legged on the carpet, and scanned the titles on the lower shelves of one of her bookcases. She selected a rather beat-up copy of Agatha Christie's *The Mirror Crack'd*, and opened it to the flyleaf.

I know you've been lonely without all your books. Maybe this one will be an old friend. And maybe I'll be an old friend one day, too. Your new friend, Pammy.

Pammy had given it to her in October of their freshman year at Dartmouth. She'd never said where she found the book, but Tricia had treasured it simply because she was lonely, and their tiny dorm room had no room to house even a fraction of her mystery collection.

Old friend.

Pammy had never fit in at Dartmouth. She wasn't Ivy League material. But a family member had pulled strings with some bigwig alumni and had somehow gotten her in. But Pammy had never distinguished herself in or out of college. After graduation, she'd led a dreary, apparently uneventful life—mostly mooching off of family and friends. What could be in her diary that would cause someone to kill her?

Unless it wasn't Pammy's diary.

She'd wanted to speak to Stuart Paige. Had it been his diary? Tricia frowned. Men kept journals, not diaries. The word "diary" indicated that it was probably written by a woman.

What woman? And if it wasn't Pammy's, where would she have gotten it?

"In a Dumpster?" Tricia asked aloud.

Miss Marple trotted up to her and said, "*Brrrrurp!*"

"I think you're right," Tricia said, and patted the cat on the head.

The question was where had Pammy found the diary? Surely not here in Stoneham. It was possible she'd Dumpster dived all over New England.

Miss Marple rubbed her little warm body against Tricia's knee, head butting her for attention. Tricia reached out and absently scratched the cat's ears. "If there's a diary hidden somewhere in this apartment, I'll eat your kitty treats." Miss Marple raised her head sharply. "I was only kidding."

The CD had stopped playing ages ago. A glance at the clock told Tricia she had better wind things down and get some rest. She had a lot to do come morning. Including taking Pammy's box of books to the library.

"Bedtime," she told Miss Marple, who jumped up on Tricia's queen-sized bed.

As Tricia got ready for sleep, she found herself wondering about the diary, wondering who it belonged to, and what it could contain that had cost Pammy her life.

TEN

Despite the late night, Tricia was up early the next morning, determined to find a new home for Pammy's box of books—and do it before Haven't Got a Clue opened for business. Since the library opened at nine, that gave her an hour to drop them off before she'd have to open the doors of her own shop.

As she opened the store's blinds, she saw a white-and-gold Sheriff's Department patrol car parked outside of Booked for Lunch. "Uh-oh," she said to Miss Marple, who had jumped up to see if she could catch and bite the blind cord. "I wonder if Captain Baker is visiting Angelica."

Miss Marple batted the plastic weight on the cord.

"I'm going across the road to see what's happening," Tricia told the cat. "Now don't you bite the cord while I'm gone, or you won't get any kitty snacks tonight."

Miss Marple sat back on her haunches, duly chastised.

Tricia didn't bother getting her coat from the peg out back, but grabbed her keys, locked the store, and headed across the street, dodging the remains of another flattened pumpkin.

Inside the shop, Angelica, dressed in full fifties regalia once again, faced Captain Baker, her arms folded defiantly across her chest, her expression determined.

Tricia opened the door and entered, but Angelica paid her no mind.

"Why would I hire Pammy and then kill her? How stupid do you think I am, Captain?"

Baker didn't blink an eye. "Ma'am, I don't know you at all."

"Just for the record, my sister doesn't go around killing people, and neither do I," Tricia blurted.

Baker turned to face her. "Good morning. I'm not accusing either of you of any wrongdoing. I'm trying to find out who killed your friend, and why."

"This town has a veritable vandalism crime wave going on, and all you can do is badger honest citizens trying to make a living," Angelica accused.

"Vandalism? Crime wave?" Baker repeated.

"Haven't you noticed all the smashed pumpkins around the village? The little kids around here must be heartbroken to see their creations reduced to pulp," Tricia said.

"Smashing Pumpkins? Isn't that a rock band or something?" Baker asked, straight-faced.

"It's also mangled squash. And they're everywhere here in Stoneham!"

Baker frowned. "If this apparent crime wave bothers you ladies so much, I'll have one of my deputies look into it."

"Thank you," Angelica said.

Did she miss his condescending tone?

"In the meantime," Baker continued, "if you two think of anything that might help in this *serious* investigation, I hope you'll share it with me."

Despite his tone, Tricia considered mentioning the phone calls she'd received the night before. But what if someone was just toying with her? She had no proof the diary the person on the phone had mentioned even belonged to Pammy.

And how sincere was Baker? His superior officer, Sheriff Adams, had openly scoffed at Tricia's theories on more than one occasion. And since Baker reported to her, would his opinion be colored by his boss's?

"Is everything all right, Ms. Miles?" he inquired.

Tricia started at the sound of her name. She looked up at the captain. "Excuse me?"

"You look deep in thought. Is there something you want to tell me?"

Tricia shook her head. "No."

Not yet, at any rate.

Baker looked skeptically at her before turning back to Angelica. "Let me assure you that we're investigating every lead we have."

"And how many leads is that?" Tricia asked.

"I'm not at liberty to say. But the ME did find cat hair on the clothes of the deceased."

"Well, there would be. I have a cat. Pammy stayed in my house for two weeks."

"We may want to take hair samples—just in case," Baker added.

"Feel free," Tricia said, disgusted. Then something occurred to her. "Have you informed Pammy's family of her . . . demise?"

Baker nodded solemnly.

"Has anyone stepped forward to claim her body? Have they decided on when to bury her?"

Baker pursed his lips. "They declined to take possession of the body."

"They what?" Angelica said with a gasp.

"I have no further information," Baker said.

Tricia and Angelica exchanged dismayed looks. How could any family fail to step forward and claim their dead? "Did they offer any explanation?" Angelica asked.

Baker shook his head. "Not that I'm aware of."

"What will happen to her?" Tricia asked.

"The body will remain in the county's custody for a limited amount of time, and then they will . . ." He paused, as though considering his words. "They'll dispose of it."

"You mean bury her in an unmarked grave?" Tricia asked.

Baker nodded. "It's not like they trash the indigent. It's done with dignity—just not a lot of flash. The state contributes some funds, but often local funeral parlors donate their services. Now, if you ladies will excuse me, I have work to do." He tipped his hat to them and exited the café.

They watched as he returned to his cruiser and took off, heading north.

Angelica was the first to speak. "I can't imagine what Pammy could have done that her family would abandon her . . . even in death."

"She did say something about hating them—and that the feeling was mutual. But I thought she had to be exaggerating." Tricia tried to swallow her distress. Okay, Pammy was never what she would've called a good or close friend, but to be abandoned so profoundly . . . Suddenly, Tricia had a better appreciation for her relationship with Angelica, despite their often silly differences.

She took a breath to regain her control. "Why was Captain Baker here so early?"

"Goodness knows. He probably doesn't have any leads but wants to look busy."

Angelica headed into her kitchen food prep station, where an array of veg-

etables was spread across the counter. She picked up a knife and began to slice a beefsteak tomato. "I've got to hire some help before I go crazy."

"You didn't answer my question. What did he want?"

"I think he came here just to annoy me."

"How?" Tricia demanded, frustrated with Angelica's lack of response.

"By asking the same questions he asked the other day. He's wasting his time and mine."

"It's a cop thing. They try to catch you changing your story."

"What story? I told him the truth. I don't have any hidden agenda, and neither do you."

"Did he ask about me?" Tricia asked.

Angelica nodded, set the tomato slices aside, and started shredding a head of iceberg lettuce. "He still can't figure out why you kept Pammy for two weeks."

"Well, he's got company there, because neither can I." Tricia chewed her lip for a moment. "I've got more news. Ginny is a freegan."

Angelica dropped the lettuce. "You're kidding."

"No. She told me yesterday. I've been thinking I should give her a raise. Then maybe she won't have to dig through garbage for her food."

"Don't you go and feel guilty about this," Angelica said, waving a lettuce leaf in Tricia's direction. "We pay our employees far better than any other booksellers in town. And we give them health care coverage, too."

"And more than one of the booksellers resents us for it," Tricia agreed.

"What Ginny's doing isn't illegal, and we're not responsible if people steal our refuse and then eat it." Angelica shuddered at the thought, set the lettuce aside, and started chopping a pepper. "Grab a knife, will you? I need to get those onions sliced for sandwiches."

"Sorry, I haven't got time. I've got an errand to run before I open the store." Tricia glanced at her watch. "If I get going now, I may just make it."

"What about me? I'm shorthanded."

"Call the employment agency."

"I have—every hour on the hour. Nobody wants minimum wage jobs—or those who are willing have been rounded up by Immigration. How's a small business supposed to survive these days?"

Tricia had no answers, and bid her sister adieu.

Ten minutes later, she stood outside the Stoneham Library's white-painted doors, admiring the untouched pumpkins that decorated the entrance. They weren't carved, of course, which was probably why they'd escaped being ruined by the neighborhood hooligans.

The library's door was unlocked at precisely nine. "Tricia!" Lois Kerr, Stone-

ham's longtime head (and only full-time) librarian, greeted Tricia like an old friend. "It's good to see you. What are you doing here so early?"

"Hi, Lois. I'm dropping off some books for the Friends of the Library's upcoming sale, and I wanted to do it before I opened my store."

"That's very nice of you. The revenue from that sale is a wonderful shot in the arm for us. It seems the library is one of the first line items to go when the Board of Selectmen need to trim the village budget."

"I'm glad to help."

Lois ushered Tricia inside and showed her where to stow the books in the library's small community room. It looked like other citizens of Stoneham had been as generous, for the room was very nearly stuffed to the ceiling along the back wall.

"Thank you so much," Lois said, then lowered her voice and leaned in closer. "I'm so sorry you've had to endure more unpleasantness."

Tricia nodded, but couldn't think of how to reply. At least, with Pammy being a nobody, the press hadn't descended upon Stoneham, as they had when the author Zoë Carter had died in Haven't Got a Clue's washroom.

"I understand the woman you found behind your sister's restaurant was a friend of yours."

"We were college roommates."

Lois *tsk*ed. "You must have been devastated."

"It was very upsetting," Tricia admitted.

Lois shook her head in sympathy. "And to think, she was in here only last week, making copies."

Tricia blinked. "She what?"

"Yes. As it happened, I was the one who helped her. Margaret was helping another patron check out books when your friend came in to use the copier. It jammed, and I had to clear the machine for her."

"Did you see what she was copying?"

"Some kind of journal."

"A diary?" Tricia asked eagerly.

Lois nodded. "Yes, perhaps it was."

"What did it look like? How many pages did she copy?"

"It had a red cover. I'm not certain how many copies she made. Maybe four or five pages. Is it important?"

"Possibly. Did she say anything else?"

"She asked me for directions to the post office."

Tricia stared at Lois for long seconds, her mind racing. "I have to go," she said, and turned.

"To the post office?"

Tricia looked back to see a grin breaking across Lois's face. "You could've been a detective."

"I don't think so," Lois said. "But maybe one day I might write a book about one."

Tricia smiled. "See you later, Lois."

THE STONEHAM BRANCH of the U.S. Postal Service was located in a neat brick structure on the south end of town, its windows outlined in crisp white paint. A row of four small, cheerful-looking uncarved pumpkins sat outside the door. The Stars and Stripes flapped in the stiff breeze above her as Tricia entered the squat building.

Forty-something Ted Missile seldom wore his official Postal Service uniform. He often came to work in a polo shirt or a Patriots' sweatshirt. On the other hand, his boss, Postmaster Barbara Yarrows, could be counted on to be dressed in full regalia, from her regulation blue blouse down to her official uniform slacks or skirt. She was definitely old-school civil service, whereas Ted had taken the job after being laid off from a tool-and-die shop in Milford. Ted knew everybody in the village and greeted them by name. Barbara didn't. Tricia was glad it was Ted who stood behind the counter, and hoped he would be able to tell her what she needed to know.

Luckily, only one other person was inside the building. Tricia nodded a hello as the woman checked her mailbox, withdrew the contents, locked it again, and headed for the door.

"What can I do for you today, Tricia?" Ted asked. "Do you need a book of stamps? We've got a new 'dead entertainer' stamp out this week."

"Sure, I'll take a book. But I'll have one of those pretty flowered ones, instead."

"Coming right up," he said, and shuffled through the drawer, pulling out the correct one.

Tricia withdrew a ten-dollar bill from her wallet, which he accepted and made change.

"You want that in an envelope?"

"No, I'll just put it in my purse."

"Everything okay with you and your sister?" Ted asked, leaning across the counter and speaking low.

"Okay?" Tricia repeated, playing dumb.

"I mean, about that poor woman being found behind Angelica's new café the other day. You found her, didn't you?"

"Yes," she said, and sighed. It was expected that everybody in Stoneham knew her business and would ask about it—but sometimes it just got *old*. "Poor

Pammy. I can't believe anyone would want to hurt her." Except maybe the person she was blackmailing, if that's what she was doing.

"She came in here the other day, you know," Ted said, bouncing on the balls of his feet.

"No, I didn't," Tricia lied.

Ted nodded. "Had a great big envelope filled with papers. Two ounces' worth."

"Ted," Barbara warned from the back of the post office.

"You wouldn't happen to know who the envelope was addressed to, would you?"

Ted looked over his shoulder. Barbara was pointedly staring at him. Ted turned back to face Tricia and shook his head, but mouthed the words "Stuart Paige."

"The millionaire philanthropist?" Tricia whispered, in mock awe.

Ted nodded and whispered back, "It went priority rate. She even paid extra for delivery confirmation."

"Ted," Barbara warned.

"I understand Pammy got mail here, addressed to General Delivery," Tricia said.

"A few letters. There might be one here now," he said, and bent to paw through a stack of envelopes under the counter. "Yeah, here it is."

Tricia's breath caught in her throat, and she resisted the urge to snatch the letter from his hand. "I don't suppose you could give it to me? I was, after all, her best friend."

Ted shook his head. "No can do. It would be illegal."

"It might be something Captain Baker of the Sheriff's Department might want to see. He's in charge of the investigation."

"Oh, yeah, I hadn't thought of that."

"Maybe you should give him a call," Tricia hinted.

"Ted," Barbara said again, her voice growing more piercing. "There're several boxes that need to be taken out back. Could you do that now?"

Ted jerked a thumb in Barbara's direction. "She's a real witch, ya know."

"No," Tricia said, voice hushed.

"That's just between you and me," he whispered.

She nodded as Barbara called more stridently, "Ted!"

"See you later, Ted. Bye, Barbara." Tricia headed for the door.

AS TRICIA STARTED back to her store, she reflected on everything she knew about Pammy's activities just before her death. She'd made copies of several pages of the diary, and the diary's cover was red. Big deal. She had no clue as to where the

diary was or how to prove the copied pages had been delivered. Had Baker found a delivery confirmation receipt among Pammy's things? If not, where was it? Could it have been in her purse? Tricia could ask Captain Baker, but she still didn't feel she had enough evidence to present to him. And for all his kind words so far, was he likely to accept her word? Ted could back up her story—but so what? No one could prove that Pammy had sent Paige copies of the diary pages. The fact that Lois saw her make copies, and she asked for directions to the post office, and then Ted had weighed and stamped an envelope destined for Stuart Paige, didn't mean the two events necessarily *had* to be related. At least, Tricia had read enough legal thrillers to know a judge would likely rule in that direction.

And who had written the letter to Pammy that she'd never picked up at the post office?

The voice on the phone had said, "Give back the diary."

Again Tricia was faced with the same question: What diary? And give it to whom? The caller hadn't been clear about that, either. Maybe she was supposed to find the diary and the next call would tell her what to do with it. If that was the case, all she could do was wait and see if another call came in. And since the other calls had come at night, she had the whole day to kill before that would happen.

Unless the caller got antsy.

Tricia pulled her car into the Stoneham municipal parking lot and parked it. She was sure that the only books she'd seen in Pammy's car's trunk when Captain Baker had asked her to inspect the contents had been their college yearbooks.

Tricia had once had a little girl's diary bound in pink floral fabric with a little silver lock. Angelica had found it, broken it open, and not only read every page, but relayed its contents to the entire family at Thanksgiving dinner.

She pushed that unproductive thought away, grateful her relationship with her sister had improved since those days.

During the two weeks Pammy had been her guest, Tricia hadn't seen her friend read anything—not a newspaper, not a book, not even the back of a cereal box. In fact, now that she thought about it, why had Pammy been so keen on keeping the box of books? Perhaps to resell? But nothing in the box had been of any real worth. It was probably only the diary that had been valuable—and only to the person who wrote it, or perhaps wanted to destroy it because of its contents.

Tricia locked her car and started walking toward Haven't Got a Clue. Where had Pammy gotten the diary? Dumpster diving? Possibly. It wasn't likely she prowled used bookstores, despite the fact Stoneham was full of them. Most of the booksellers had a specialty: romance, military history, religion . . .

Ginny was waiting outside the door to Haven't Got a Clue—on time for the first time in days. She held a bulky plastic bag and stamped her feet on the concrete, trying to keep warm. "I was beginning to wonder where you were," she

said by way of a greeting. "I didn't see your car in the lot, and when I called your cell phone, there was no answer."

Tricia sorted through her keys. "Sorry. I must have it turned off. I had some errands to run." She unlocked the door and entered the store, with Ginny following close behind.

"Give me your coat and I'll hang it up in back," Ginny said.

As she straightened up the pile of bookmarks next to the register, Tricia wondered if she ought to call Captain Baker and tell him about the letter at the post office. She was sure to talk to him again sometime soon—maybe she'd just wait.

She tidied the stack of Haven't Got a Clue shopping bags, and had run out of busywork by the time Ginny came back to the front of the store.

"What's Mr. Everett's schedule for the rest of the week?" Ginny asked.

"Coming and going, I'm afraid. There's a lot to pull together fast if you're planning an impromptu wedding."

"Why don't they just elope?" Ginny grumbled.

"I'm sure they feel this will be the last marriage for each of them. They want their friends to witness it, especially since they have no family."

"I guess."

Mr. Everett knew everyone in town. Would he have known Stuart Paige? Paige didn't have a long history in Stoneham, but he was well-known throughout the state. Still, Mr. Everett was the soul of discretion; he wouldn't speak of Paige's reckless past if he knew of it . . . but Frannie Armstrong might. Frannie was the eyes and ears of Stoneham—more so than even Ted Missile.

As it happened, Frannie chose that moment to walk past Haven't Got a Clue on her way to the Cookery. In one hand she clutched her purse and a sack lunch; in the other, a bulky wire cage, no doubt the Havahart trap she'd spoken of the day before.

"Oh, look, Frannie's struggling with that cage. She's been trying to catch a stray cat. I think I'll go help her."

"I can do it," Ginny volunteered.

"That's okay," Tricia said, hurrying around the register and heading for the exit. "Be right back."

"Whatever," Ginny said, as Tricia flew out the door.

She hurried down the sidewalk to catch up with Frannie. "Here, let me help you," she said.

Frannie gratefully surrendered the cage. "Hi, Tricia. This thing isn't heavy—at least it wasn't for the first couple of blocks. But then it seemed like it weighed a ton."

"Think you'll catch Penny today?" Tricia asked as Frannie fumbled with her keys.

"I sure hope so. I hate to think of that poor little cat out in the cold at night. The weatherman says a cold snap is coming down from Canada in the next few days. We might even see a little snow."

"Not until the leaves are past peak, I hope. I'm praying for an onslaught of tourists to arrive any day now."

"I hope so, too. But then there's the Milford Pumpkin Festival on the weekend, and Stoneham will be as quiet as a cemetery at midnight." Frannie opened the door and Tricia followed her into the darkened store. In a moment, the lights were on and Frannie had removed her jacket. "Need any help setting up this cage?" Tricia asked.

"Thank you. I sure hope the first bus is late. Angelica won't be pleased if I'm not ready to open right on time." She glanced at the clock. "Which is in three minutes."

"I can get things ready here at the register if you want to go load the trap and set it up outside."

"Thanks, Tricia."

"It's my pleasure. I want to see little Penny go to her new home."

Frannie paused. "I will put an ad in the *News*—just in case some poor child is missing her kitty. But I'd be lying if I didn't admit I hope no one will claim her."

Frannie had lived alone for a long time. She deserved a little feline pal. "Go on, set up the trap," Tricia said, and gave her friend a smile.

A Granite State bus passed the store's display window, heading for the municipal lot, where it would disgorge its load. Several customers had entered the store by the time Frannie made it back to the sales desk. She rubbed her hands gleefully. "By tonight I might have my very own kitty. I've never had a cat before. My family are all dog lovers, ya see. But I fell in love with your Miss Marple, and now I want one of my own."

"I'll cross my fingers for you."

Frannie looked toward her customers and raised her voice. "Y'all just let me know if you need any help." One of the women nodded and went back to her browsing.

"Frannie," Tricia started, "you've been around these parts a lot longer than I have. What do you know about Stuart Paige?"

Frannie shrugged. "Just what I've read in the papers."

That wasn't what Tricia wanted to hear.

"Although," Frannie added, almost as an afterthought, "it's been said that he was a real womanizer when he was in his early twenties."

Now that was more like it. "Oh?" Tricia prompted.

"I'm sure you've heard about that accident where he was driving his father's Alfa Romeo, crashed it into Portsmouth Harbor, and some woman died."

Why did everyone seem to remember the make of the car more than the name of the victim? "Yes, I did hear that."

"Apparently she was the love of his life. When she died, he turned over a new leaf. Got religion, so to speak, although I don't think he joined any official denomination. But he decided to change his ways and do good in the world."

That sounded like a great plot for a 1950s movie. In fact it was . . . *The Magnificent Obsession,* with Rock Hudson and Jane Wyman. But did that sort of thing happen in the late 1980s? Tricia wasn't so sure. As her grandmother often said, "A leopard doesn't change its spots." There had to be more to the story than that.

If Frannie didn't know, then probably no one else in the village did.

Rats!

A customer ambled up to the register with several heavy volumes. Tricia wrapped the order while Frannie rang it up and made change. As soon as the woman turned her back on them and headed for the door, Frannie picked up where she left off. "I heard Mr. Paige has been staying at the Brookview Inn. In fact, he's taken a room long term. They say he's got some kind of business deal brewing. I'll bet Bob Kelly knows about it."

"And wouldn't tell me if he did."

"That's true. Bob is very loyal to Chamber members."

"But would Paige be a member? He doesn't have a business, or even live here in Stoneham."

"Yet," Frannie added. "I wouldn't know about new members since I left the Chamber. It's always possible Mr. Paige's cooking up something good for the village. Maybe he intends to help people who've lost their jobs. You know, open some kind of light manufacturing plant, or something. Bob was always trying to entice someone to locate a new business here."

That was a possibility, Tricia supposed. Now, could she get past Paige's keepers to talk to the man? "What do you know about his entourage?"

"I don't think he's got bodyguards, if that's what you mean. But I know he travels with at least one or two people—one of them is a secretary or something. Keeps the riffraff from bothering him."

Would Tricia be considered riffraff?

"I wonder if Eleanor could get me in to see him." Tricia envisioned Eleanor at her reception desk at the Brookview Inn. Plump, and in her mid-sixties, she was the soul of the place. She made sure everyone who stayed there enjoyed his or her visit.

"What do you need to see Stuart Paige for?" Frannie asked.

Should she tell Frannie about Pammy trying to crash the Food Shelf's dedication ceremony? Then again, Frannie probably knew all about it.

"My friend Pammy tried to talk to him the day she died. I was just wondering if he knew her."

"I heard about that," Frannie said.

Of course!

Frannie sighed. "But I doubt Eleanor would bother a guest just to satisfy your curiosity. People who stay at the Brookview expect exceptional treatment—and Eleanor sees to it they get it. Even though she considers you a friend, I'm sure her first loyalty would always be to her guests."

"As it should be," Tricia reluctantly admitted.

"That said, there's no reason you can't ask," Frannie said with the hint of a smile on her lips. A customer stepped up to the register. "Can I help you?" she asked.

Tricia noticed the wastebasket under the counter hadn't been emptied. She signaled to Frannie that she would take it out back. She disarmed the Cookery's security system, stepped outside, and looked around. The trap sat neatly to one side, with a heaping bowl of cat food and a water bowl inside the cage. *Come on, Penny!* The Cookery's Dumpster and her own stood side by side in the alley. There was nothing in them to interest one of the local freegans. In addition to speaking to Stuart Paige, Tricia needed to speak to the freegans as well. Had Ginny contacted any of her scavenger friends?

There was only one way to find out.

Tricia emptied the wastebasket, reentered the Cookery, reset the alarm, and saw Frannie was still tied up with customers. Replacing the wastebasket, she waved good-bye to Frannie and headed back to her own store.

Ginny was inundated with customers, and it was more than an hour later when Tricia finally had a chance to speak to her. "I was wondering, have you had time to talk to any of your"—she glanced to see if any of the customers was within earshot—"you-know-what friends about Pammy yet."

Ginny shook her head. "No. But we're meeting up with a bunch of them tonight in Nashua. Want to come along? They all agreed it would be okay."

"Definitely. Where and when?"

"I brought a change of clothes so that Brian could pick us up here at seven."

"That doesn't give us any time to have dinner."

"We'll eat on the way."

Tricia felt her cheeks redden.

Ginny laughed. "Don't worry; we're not going to eat what we find tonight. We'll stop and get something along the way."

"Okay. But I've got one question: What does one wear to go Dumpster diving?"

ELEVEN

By six thirty, business had slowed to a crawl, and Tricia decided she'd best change for her first, hopefully only, food-salvaging expedition. She slipped upstairs to her loft apartment and fed Miss Marple before retreating to her bedroom closet, where she dug out her grungiest jeans and an old sweatshirt, found a pair of sneakers she thought she'd tossed long ago, grabbed her fanny pack, and was ready to go. She and Ginny closed the store a few minutes early so they'd be ready for Brian, who pulled up outside of Haven't Got a Clue at precisely seven.

Ginny climbed into the front seat of his SUV and Tricia got in the back.

"Hey, Tricia," Brian called, "glad to have you with us. Although I have to admit I never thought you'd have the guts to do this."

"Neither did I," she agreed as she buckled her seat belt. "I'm hoping some of your friends will talk to me about Pammy Fredericks."

Brian checked his side mirror before he pulled away from the curb. "Don't be surprised if they don't."

"Where are we heading?" Tricia asked.

"Nashua. There's better pickings in a bigger city."

They lapsed into idle chitchat for the twenty-or-so-minute ride to the city closest to Stoneham. Tricia's stomach began to knot with each passing minute. Did Brian and Ginny expect her to climb into a Dumpster, paw through rotting, fly-ridden garbage in search of a few potatoes, maybe a loaf of bread, or some dented cans with no labels?

The lights of Nashua were straight ahead, and Tricia found herself swallowing over and over again as dread filled her. What about the germs—the stench? Whatever had possessed her to ask Ginny to take her along on one of their scavenging outings? Oh, yeah, she wanted to talk to Pammy's new friends.

What kind of friends picked through trash and then ate it?

Good grief, she'd almost forgotten she'd been on the receiving end of two meals made with trash, although, much as she hated to admit it, the food had been good, a testament to Pammy's culinary abilities.

Brian pulled the car into the parking lot of a convenience store.

"Is this where we're going to start"—Tricia struggled to find an appropriate word— "picking?"

"Nope. I came here to get a sub. If I get a foot-long, we can share it. What do you like, Tricia, turkey or ham?"

"Turkey, please. Although I'm really not very hungry."

"What do you want to drink?"

"Water."

"I'll have a Coke," Ginny said.

Tricia dug in her fanny pack for her wallet. "Let me give you some money for—"

Brian shook his head. "Nope. You've helped us a lot in the past year. This is on us." He opened the driver's-side door and hopped out of the car.

"This is a big night for us," Ginny said, watching Brian enter the store. "It's the only night of the week we eat out anymore."

"Eat out?" Tricia repeated dully.

"Yeah, it's a big deal for us to even get a sub these days."

In minutes, Brian was back, holding a paper sack cradled in his left arm. He opened the car door and handed the bag to Ginny, who began doling out bottles and little packets of mayonnaise and mustard.

"I had the clerk cut it up into several pieces." He eyed the rearview mirror, looking at Tricia in the backseat. "Maybe it's the lighting, but Tricia looks a little green. I don't think she's too hungry, babe."

Ginny laughed. "Tricia, you're not going to get poisoned. And you won't get sick. And you won't have to go into the Dumpster. I don't."

"You don't?"

"I do the dirty work," Brian said, and pulled at the shoulder of his sweatshirt. "I wear layers. If I get grubby, I can just peel them off, and into the laundry they go."

"We've got gloves and a big bottle of hand sanitizer," Ginny said. "Brian hands us what looks salvageable and we hold on to it until we get back to the car."

Tricia let out a whoosh of air. "Thanks for the heads-up. I feel a lot better about this."

Ginny laughed. "I thought you might. Now, have a piece of sandwich. It could be a long evening." She handed Tricia a couple of napkins and a slab of the sub.

Minutes later, Brian collected the papers, stuffed them into the sack, and deposited them in the trash receptacle outside the convenience store. Soon after, they were back on the road.

"We're meeting up with our friends behind one of the smaller grocery

stores. The bigger stores are open twenty-four hours, and they don't like us poking through their garbage."

They pulled down a side street and parked. "We walk from here," Brian said.

They got out of the car and locked it. Brian stepped around to the back of the SUV, unlocked it, and took out two big backpacks, several canvas shopping bags, and three pairs of gloves, handing them around so that they each had something to protect their hands. He and Ginny donned the backpacks. "Follow me," he told Tricia, his breath coming out in a cloud.

He turned and headed back to the main thoroughfare, leading the way, leaving Ginny to walk side by side with Tricia. Up ahead, Tricia could see several people standing under a light pole on the far side of the street, two of them with battered helmets and bicycles that sported canvas saddlebags on both front and back.

"'Bout time you guys got here," said a familiar female voice from the shadows.

As they approached, Tricia realized with a start that the voice belonged to Eugenia Hirt—Libby Hirt's daughter. No wonder the head of the local Food Shelf hadn't wanted to talk about the freegans. Her own child was one!

Eugenia looked androgynous. She was dressed in black slacks, a black jacket, and black shoes, and a black-and-white bandana covered her blond hair, which was apparently pinned up. She might've passed for a cat burglar. "Hi, Tricia," she called brightly. "Bet you're surprised to see me here."

"A little." Okay, that was a big, fat lie. She was shocked.

"Have you met my dad?" Eugenia asked.

Good grief! Her father was a freegan, too?

A slim, balding man with graying blond hair, probably in his late fifties and also dressed all in black, stepped forward with his hand extended. "Hi, Tricia. Joe Hirt. Eugenia's told me all about you—or at least your dining preferences. The cold tuna plate or cottage cheese with a peach half, right?"

Tricia shook his hand and managed a feeble laugh. "We are what we eat, eh?"

Tricia noticed the bicyclers standing behind him. "This is Lisa Redwood, and Pete Marbello," he said.

They chorused a less-than-enthusiastic hello, and Tricia nodded in greeting. She had never met Lisa before, but Pete looked familiar, though she couldn't place where she might've met him.

"What's the game plan for tonight?" Brian asked.

"We hit this Dumpster," Joe said, jerking his thumb over his shoulder, "and then we try the Italian market down the street." As the oldest, Joe was obvi-

ously their leader. The others fell into step behind him, with Tricia and Ginny bringing up the rear.

"Is there some significance to everyone wearing all black?" Tricia asked.

"Doesn't show the dirt," Ginny said. "It does give us a little anonymity, too."

They stepped from the sidewalk into a parking lot. A mercury vapor lamp overhead cast a bluish glow over the large green garbage receptacle. Tricia wrinkled her nose and sniffed, grateful for the chilly night. She caught an unmistakable whiff of something vaguely sour, but not entirely off-putting.

"Who wants the honors?" Joe asked.

"It's my turn," Pete said. Brian stepped forward and gave him a leg up, as though he was about to mount a horse, and Pete climbed into the Dumpster. He landed on a pile of black plastic trash bags, piled high, sinking down so that only the top half of his body was visible. He pulled a flashlight from his pocket, grabbed a bag of trash, and loosened the twist tie that held it closed. Next, he shone the light into the bag. "Jackpot!" he called, and lifted a loaf of bread into the air. "The sell-by date is tomorrow." He tossed the bag down to Brian, who distributed the booty among them all, including Tricia.

"I really don't want—"

"Shush!" Ginny warned her.

Pete had already opened another bag, wrinkled his nose, and twisted the tie once again. "Paper trash." He grabbed another bag, and another, until he'd gone through most of them. By the time he was done, they'd collected the bread, nearly two dozen potatoes, several heads of what Tricia would have said was questionable lettuce, eight or ten jars of pickles, eleven boxes of crackers, and half a dozen soft tomatoes.

Pete jumped down from the Dumpster and joined Lisa. "Not bad for the first hit."

Joe pointed toward the other side of the lot. "Come on. The evening's getting away from us." Everyone followed.

"This is your chance to talk to the others," Ginny whispered, giving Tricia a poke.

Pete and Joe were in the lead this time, with Brian and Lisa following. Tricia caught up with Eugenia.

"How do you like your first time out, Tricia?"

"It's . . . interesting," she said. "I wasn't sure what to expect. What will you do with all that food?"

"I don't take it to the diner, if that's what you're worried about. And my mom won't accept it at the Food Shelf, either."

"Do you eat it at home?"

"Dad and I do. Mom . . . well, she inspects everything really carefully before

she'll touch it. And she washes the jars and cans with a bleach solution in case they've got germs. She's very picky."

"What got you interested in being a freegan?"

"The Food Shelf, of course. I've always known about people going hungry. You can't believe the waste that goes on in this world—and especially this country. Did you know that grocery stores alone throw out between two and three percent of their food every week? That doesn't sound bad until you realize it's like billions and billions of pounds of edible food that ends up in landfills."

Sadly, Tricia could believe it.

"Dad and I tried to be conservationists, too. We went hunting a few times—but were too squeamish to actually kill something and then eat it. Now we just shoot clay pigeons."

"I hear Pammy Fredericks accompanied you guys on several of your . . . forays."

Although her face was half hidden in shadow, Tricia saw the frown that had settled across Eugenia's mouth. "She wasn't a real freegan—she was a scavenger. She didn't care about keeping viable food out of landfills. She didn't care about making the planet a better place to live. All she cared about was money. Getting something for nothing—or getting something she hadn't earned or didn't deserve."

"And you got all that from a couple of conversations?"

Eugenia laughed. "That's all it took."

"What made you think she only cared about material things?"

"The way she talked. She kept saying she was going to come into a lot of cash—that she'd be set for life."

"Where was she getting this money?"

Eugenia shrugged. "Beats me. I didn't really care. I told Dad I didn't want her coming with us anymore. And the next thing you know, she was dead."

Tricia stopped in her tracks.

Eugenia paused and turned. "Hey, don't look at me like that. I didn't mean he killed her. I just mean he told her she couldn't come with us on another run. And as it turned out, she was dead before we went foraging again."

Tricia's dinner sandwich suddenly lay heavy in her stomach.

"Hey, come on, guys," Ginny called, and Eugenia started walking again. Tricia followed.

Eugenia was young. She wouldn't understand what—oh, God, did Tricia dare admit that she and Pammy were on the cusp of middle age?—life could force you to do.

She didn't like to think about it. Instead, she forced herself to think outside of the box.

Lisa looked to be five or six years older than Eugenia. Perhaps she had a different perspective on Tricia's ex-roommate.

Lisa, accompanied by her bike, walked beside Ginny. They laughed about something, their canvas bags swinging as they walked. They looked happy. They were young and carefree and, for a couple of minutes at least, Ginny seemed not to be bothered by the yoke of debt that bogged down her and Brian, something that seemed to preoccupy her during working hours.

Tricia picked up her pace to shadow them.

"Do you think we'll score any protein tonight?" Ginny asked Lisa.

"We got those steaks last week. There's a chance they didn't sell out what they had, and we'll score two weeks in a row."

Eating marginal meat? The thought made Tricia cringe.

"I marinated ours overnight, and they were fork tender," Lisa went on.

"We did ours on the grill. They were pretty good, but I think next time I'll try a marinade, too." Ginny seemed to sense someone dogging her heels and looked over her shoulder. She gave her boss a nod and turned back to Lisa. "Did you know Tricia was friends with Pammy—the old girl who got killed earlier this week?"

Old girl? Pammy was two months younger than Tricia!

"She came picking with us a couple of times," Ginny went on.

"I remember," Lisa said irritably. "How could I forget? The stupid cow never shut up."

Ginny tossed an uneasy glance over her shoulder and cleared her throat. "Tricia wants to know if we remember anything she could've said or done that might've pissed someone off—maybe got her killed."

"That woman pissed off the general population simply by breathing," Lisa said. "Why Joe ever let her join us, I don't know."

"How did Pammy know how to find you guys?" Tricia asked.

Lisa shot an annoyed look over her shoulder. "I'm sorry your friend died, but she was a bitch. She didn't have a clue about what we're all about."

"Which is?"

"We're making a statement. This country is awash in waste. For example, the U.S. accounts for four percent of the world's population, yet we consume almost a quarter of the world's energy resources."

Tricia had to bite her tongue to keep from saying, *Yada, yada, yada.* "That's no reason for someone to kill her," she said instead.

Lisa stopped, turning to face Tricia. Her expression held no warmth. "Pam Fredericks was a greedy user. She wanted more than her fair share of what we found, and she didn't stop at picking up food."

"What else was she looking for?"

Lisa pursed her lips, her eyes narrowing. She glared at Tricia for long moment, then turned and resumed walking.

"Lisa, what else?" Tricia insisted.

"Never mind," she called over her shoulder.

Tricia hurried to catch up. "Ginny?" she implored.

"I can't make her talk," Ginny whispered. "Try asking Joe or Pete."

"Are they likely to share anything she told them with me?"

"I don't know," Ginny answered. "Pammy wasn't well loved by our little group."

"Could she have made contact with any other freegans?"

"It's possible, but I don't think there are any others in Stoneham. And she didn't seem to stray too far while she was in town."

Lisa caught up to Pete. They conversed in hushed tones. Was she telling him that Tricia wanted information on Pammy? If so, was he likely to clam up as well?

Joe and Brian veered off the sidewalk, down a side street.

"We're almost at the Italian market," Ginny said.

"What are we likely to find here, besides steak?"

"They don't toss out a lot of jars or cans. The meat we found last time was freezer burned, which means they tossed it in their freezer when the expiration date got too close, then they didn't end up selling it. But it was edible. It was still partially frozen when we found it. We keep a cooler in the car so we can keep perishables like that fresher."

Tricia found it hard to hide her revulsion.

"Don't let the others see you making faces," Ginny warned, "or they're likely to ask you to go back to the car."

"It's hard for me to understand why you're doing this."

"We've been over it before."

"I know. I'm sorry. I'll be on my best behavior for the rest of the evening. I promise."

Once again, a bright light shone over the Dumpster, bathing it and the small parking lot in a soft glow. This time it was Brian who did the dirty work and climbed into the large metal receptacle.

"Don't you worry about rats?" Tricia whispered to Ginny.

"Why do you think I don't jump in the Dumpster myself?"

The others stood around, waiting for Brian to make a judgment call on the contents of the trash bin. He opened a black trash bag. "Anybody want stale cookies?"

"I'll take them," Lisa said, and he tossed the bag down to her.

"Having fun?" Eugenia asked Tricia.

"It's certainly a learning experience."

"There's some skanky lettuce here, but the celery looks passable," Brian said, and tossed rubber-banded bunches down to Joe, who distributed it around the group.

"I hope we find more usable vegetables. I've got a hankering to make some soup tomorrow," Eugenia said, and stamped her feet against the encroaching chill.

"Do you guys ever worry about being chased off?" Tricia asked.

"Sometimes it happens. Sometimes neighbors will call the cops, thinking we're trying to break in or steal something more valuable than veggies and jars of pepperoncini. The grocery stores could prosecute us for trespassing, but most of them don't want to draw attention to the amount of stuff they're putting into the waste stream."

"Have you ever done this during daylight hours?"

"I have," Eugenia admitted, "but it isn't as much fun. People can be cruel and say nasty things to you, too. I prefer to do it under the cover of darkness, but you need a really good flashlight."

"Do you ever jump in the Dumpsters?"

"Oh, sure. My dad and I have been doing this for years." She watched as Brian sorted through another bag of trash. "I'm sorry if I was short with you a while back. My mom wouldn't be pleased."

"Your mom's a great lady. I really admire the work she does for the Food Shelf."

"I do, too. About your friend . . . she tagged along with Dad the last couple of times we went out—probably because they're closer in age. You might want to ask him about her."

"Thanks, Eugenia." *And I'll give you a nice fat tip the next time I'm at the diner.* Now she had to figure out how to get Joe away from the crowd and willing to talk.

"Jackpot!" Brian called, and brandished a bottle of virgin olive oil, which he held high over his head. "Looks like there're eight of them here."

"You're the one in up to your knees, so you get the extra one," Joe said.

Brian passed the bottles down to everyone.

"I think that's about all we're going to get here tonight," Brian announced, and climbed over the edge of the Dumpster.

"Where to now?" Tricia asked Ginny. "Do we go get coffee or something?"

"That kind of negates the reason we're out here," Lisa said snidely. "We're trying to leave a smaller carbon footprint—not pollute the world with more paper cups from take-out joints."

Tricia figured she'd better not mention the sub she, Ginny, and Brian had eaten before they'd joined up with this group—or the papers the sandwich had been wrapped in, the bag it came in, the plastic bottles they'd drunk from, and the disposable napkins that had all entered the convenience store's trash bin.

"There *are* restaurants that use china mugs, Lees," Eugenia said.

Lisa merely sniffed.

"We could try Hannaford," Pete suggested, changing the subject. "Last week we got those pineapples, oranges, and lemons that were in pretty good shape."

Joe shook his head. "I prefer to stick to smaller markets. Besides, I'm ready to call it a night."

"Well, I'm not," Lisa said sourly. "Besides, the gas Brian used to get here is too expensive to drive all this way and only look in a couple of Dumpsters."

"I think we'll call it quits, too," Brian said, backing up Joe.

"You guys just don't get it," Lisa said with a shake of her head, and mounted her bike. "Come on, Pete," she called over her shoulder. She shoved off and pedaled toward the main drag once more.

"Sorry, guys," Pete said with a shrug, got on his own bike, and started off after his girlfriend. "PMS or something, I guess. See you next week?"

"You got it," Brian said.

The five of them looked at one another. "Not much of a score tonight," Ginny said.

"I dunno," Eugenia said, and jerked a thumb toward the street, bidding the others to follow. "That olive oil alone was worth the trip. That size bottle retails for over ten bucks. You guys got three, and Dad and I got two—that more than makes up for the fuel we used to get here."

Ginny fell into step behind her, with Brian tagging along behind. That left Tricia right where she wanted to be—walking alongside Joe. "You've got a really great kid there," she told him.

"Thanks. We think so."

They walked for a few moments in silence before Tricia spoke again. "Did Ginny tell you why I wanted to tag along?"

"Something about wanting to see what your friend was up to. Sorry about your loss."

She nodded. "Thank you. I thought I knew Pammy. We'd been friends for a long time. But—when it came down to it, I really didn't know her at all. Did she tell you much about her life?"

"Just that she was broke, but she thought that was going to change."

"Yes, I've heard that from more than one person. Did she say how that was going to happen?"

Joe shook his head. "Seems to me she was the type of woman who always had a harebrained scheme she was working." He stopped. "Sorry, I didn't mean to disrespect your friendship with Pam."

Tricia managed a grim laugh, and they began walking again. "Don't worry. You're not the first one to think that about Pammy. She always had bad luck. Always seemed one step ahead of the repo man."

"It's sad, really. A woman like that. Very few friends, a family she was on the outs with."

"She told you all that?"

He nodded. "Do you know her family?"

Tricia thought back. In all the years she'd known Pammy, she'd never met any of her family. "No. But she always said they didn't have two nickels to rub together. I can't imagine why she thought she was about to come into money. She certainly didn't mention it to me."

He shrugged.

"And why was she hanging around Stoneham for so long?"

"The night I met her, she told me she wanted to attend the Food Shelf's dedication. The thing is, it kept getting delayed. Something to do with the HVAC systems. Libby could tell you why."

Was that why Pammy had stayed so long in Tricia's apartment?

"Libby told me Pammy was eager to see Stuart Paige at the Food Shelf dedication," Joe continued. "Coming into money—making a scene to meet a rich man. That almost sounds like a formula for blackmail."

"Yes, I thought of that, too," Tricia said. They resumed walking. "I didn't see you at the dedication."

"No, I had to work."

"And where's that?"

"A public relations firm here in Nashua."

"That's a bit of a commute—a whole fifteen, twenty minutes," Tricia said, and laughed.

"Ideally, I'd like to work in Stoneham, but there's not much in my line of work in a small town—except for people wanting freebies. And Libby would never leave Stoneham. I've got an old diesel Volkswagen that I converted to run on cooking oil. I get all I need from the Bookshelf Diner and a couple of fast-food restaurants between Stoneham and Nashua. It works out pretty cheaply, and I'm not dependent on foreign oil."

"Something I wish I could say. But then, I don't travel far from Stoneham these days, myself. In fact, I usually fill up my gas tank only a couple of times a month."

"You're a good citizen of the Earth."

Tricia laughed. "Thanks. And was Pammy? She apparently liked to recycle things. I understand she was an antiques picker at one time. My sister says she knew about and was good at restaurant food prep—not that she did it for Angelica for more than an hour or so before she was killed."

Joe shook his head. "I can't believe we've had three murders in Stoneham in the last year. It bucks the odds."

Tricia didn't want to get into the old "town jinx" discussion—especially

since she'd been the one to find all three bodies—and quickly steered the conversation away from the topic. "I just can't imagine why she wanted to see Stuart Paige. You mentioned blackmail. Did Pammy give you any hint of what she was up to?"

"Not a word. We mostly talked recipes. And don't forget, we were barely acquaintances. I only met the woman twice, when she came along on our forays."

"How did she do that? She and Ginny weren't pals, so I can't imagine her inviting Pammy along. In fact, she would've told me if she had."

"I'm pretty sure it was Pete who first invited her. I think she ran into him one night in back of the convenience store in Stoneham."

Pete—the one person Tricia hadn't had a chance to talk with on this little adventure. She couldn't even remember his last name. But Ginny would know. She'd ask her as soon as they got back to the car. If she could track Pete down, she might finally find out exactly what Pammy was doing in Stoneham. Then again, he might be as clueless as the rest of them. That thought didn't fill her with confidence.

She'd get no more out of Joe or Eugenia, and figured she might as well make small talk to kill the time until they got back to the car. "Tell me more about your job," Tricia said.

"I write press releases for a nonprofit. Public service announcements. The whiz kids get all the interesting assignments. I do a lot of volunteer PR for the Food Shelf, too."

It sounded pretty boring to Tricia.

Joe continued with his job description, but she only half listened, preoccupied with her disappointment at not finding out more about Pammy and her recycling lifestyle. Before she knew it, they were standing behind Brian's SUV. He'd already opened up the back, and he and Ginny were stowing their finds. Tricia handed him the canvas bag she held.

"You really need to get a more fuel-efficient car, Brian," Joe said.

"Yeah, yeah—but this thing's paid off. I can't afford a new loan—not with the house sucking up every spare cent we have."

"Don't start this argument again," Eugenia told her father, and gave Ginny a hug. "See you next week, if not before."

"Sure thing."

Eugenia leaned in to give Brian a quick kiss on the lips. He didn't seem startled by it, but Tricia could tell by Ginny's expression that she wasn't happy about it.

"Good night, Tricia," Eugenia called.

Joe waved a good-bye to them all, and he and his daughter continued walking.

Brian gave the button on his key ring a squeeze, and the SUV's doors unlocked. Ginny waited until they were in the car to speak. "You let her kiss you again."

"Hey, babe, we have a guest. Can't we discuss this at home?"

Ginny exhaled a snorting breath. Tricia was glad she wouldn't have to hear the argument that would probably break out the minute they dropped her off in front of her store.

They buckled their seat belts and Brian started the car, steering the vehicle away from the curb and heading for the main drag once more.

No one spoke for quite a while. Brian hadn't even turned on the radio to extinguish the tension.

The lights of Nashua were fading behind them when Tricia finally broke the quiet. "Thanks for bringing me along, guys."

"Did you find out what you needed to know?" Brian asked.

"Joe told me that Pammy started coming to these little jaunts at Pete's invitation. Of course he told me this *after* Pete and Lisa left."

"Was it Pete?" Brian asked. "I thought it was Joe." He shrugged. "Guess I'm wrong."

A number of cars whizzed by in the opposite direction.

Tricia frowned. "Is there some way I can get hold of Pete? I'd like to talk to him—without Lisa being around. I think she took a dislike to me."

"She'd dislike anybody who was Pammy's friend," Ginny said.

"Why?"

"That woman was a terrible flirt. Just like Eugenia," Ginny grated.

Pammy had never given Tricia that impression. Or maybe it was just perceived that a woman alone was man-hungry.

"Do you have a number where I could reach Pete?"

"Sure," Brian said. "But you can look it up yourself. He works at the convenience store in Stoneham."

No wonder Pete had looked familiar—he'd probably waited on Tricia more than once. Had he found Pammy digging in that store's Dumpster? "I assume he works the day shift?"

"He works whenever he feels like it. His father owns the store."

Tricia felt the SUV accelerate.

"Why are you going so fast?" Ginny asked.

"There's a car speeding up behind me."

"So, let him go past," Ginny said.

Tricia looked behind her.

Brian pulled the car closer to the side of the road, but the car didn't go around them. Instead, it rode mere feet from the back bumper.

"What's this guy playing at?" Brian asked nervously.

"We've got an SUV—outrun him!" Ginny cried.

Brian steered back onto the road and gunned the engine. The SUV took off like a Formula One car, leaving the smaller car to eat its dust, until it was a couple of pinpricks of light on the darkened road.

"Yee-ha!" Brian called.

Suddenly another set of lights pulled onto the highway. Not just headlights, but blue flashing lights.

"Oh, no," Brian groaned as he braked the SUV. "Here comes a ticket. And a couple of points on my license."

He pulled over to the side of the road and hit the button on his armrest. The driver's-side window slid down, and he dug for his wallet so he could fish out his license. The Sheriff's Department cruiser pulled up behind them, its lights eerily piercing the surrounding landscape.

Another car whooshed past them, and Tricia could've sworn she heard someone yell from its window, "Suckers!"

TWELVE

Tricia let herself into the Cookery, then trailed through the darkened interior to the back of the store and the stairway that led to Angelica's loft apartment. Then she thought better of just appearing on her sister's doorstep—or threshold, or whatever you wanted to call it.

She reached into her pocket and withdrew her cell phone. She pushed the button that autodialed Angelica's number. It was answered on the first ring.

"Trish? Where are you?"

"Inside the Cookery. I wanted to let you know I'm on my way up. That is, if it's convenient." She hadn't seen Bob's car parked outside, but she didn't want to interrupt a romantic interlude—should one be going on.

"Sure, come on up," Angelica said cheerfully. "Are you hungry? I was just going to make some cocoa and cinnamon toast."

"Cinnamon toast?" Tricia repeated, brightening. "I haven't had that since I was a kid."

"Then you're in for a treat. I'll put another two slices of bread in the toaster. Hurry on up."

Angelica had unlocked the door, which was open for Tricia. She could already smell the heavenly aroma of the ultimate comfort food as she entered the hallway and followed it to Angelica's kitchen.

"Sit down," Angelica encouraged. She was clad in a pink robe and matching bunny slippers, with her hair hanging in damp ringlets around her shoulders. She'd been letting it grow out. Tricia wasn't sure that was a good idea, since Angelica looked great in short hair, but it did suit her when she wore it up, dressed in her vintage togs while working at the café.

Tricia peeled off her jacket and settled at the dining room table just as Angelica thrust a mug of cocoa at her. She could smell the nutmeg Angelica had no doubt just grated on the top. She took a sip, savoring the taste. Before she could swallow, Angelica settled a plate of cinnamon toast in front of her.

"Hey, you made this for yourself. I can wait for the new toast to pop up."

"Don't be silly. Eat. You're too skinny."

"Hey, I work at it."

"You may as well enjoy yourself. Life is too short to deny yourself anything. Particularly diamonds."

"Diamonds. Where did that come from?"

"Oh, I've been thinking about Mr. Everett and Grace. I think I'm going through marriage withdrawal," she said, and glanced at the ringless fourth finger on her left hand. "I have to figure out what to give them for a wedding gift. What are you giving them?"

"I haven't decided yet, either."

Angelica leaned aginst the island counter and took a sip of her cocoa. "What do you give the elderly bride and groom? A membership in AARP?"

"I'm sure one or both of them already has that."

"Do you think Grace is registered anywhere?"

"No. I'm sure they don't want or need anything."

"Maybe I could make some of the food. I've never made a wedding cake before."

"And when would you have time to do that?"

Angelica shook her head. "I'd make the time. Now, weren't you going out with those freegan heathens or something tonight? Tell me all about it."

"Yup," Tricia said, and took a sip of her cocoa. This was no ordinary hot chocolate. Besides the nutmeg, something else had to have been added. It tasted too rich, too thick, and . . . extremely fattening. And for once, she wasn't going to worry about it.

"I did go along with Ginny and her friends. So far, they haven't convinced me to bypass the grocery store checkout. I prefer to buy the food I eat, thank

you. But I was surprised that some of the stuff they found didn't look all that bad."

Angelica wrinkled her nose. "Did they smell?"

"The Dumpsters? Not too bad. The chilly temperatures keep the odor down, but I wouldn't want to do this on a hot summer night. And I didn't see any rats, which was really good, because I'm sure I would've freaked out." She gazed at the little bubbles on the sides of her mug. "I feel so bad that Ginny and Brian feel they have to do this to keep their expenses down. That house they bought really turned into a money pit."

"I am so thankful I didn't end up with it. I think I've made the right decisions since I came to Stoneham, what with renting the storefront and then living above it. My accountant is pleased, at any rate."

"It's certainly been a financial drain for them. And added to that, Brian got a speeding ticket on the way home."

"What was he speeding for?"

"Somebody was fooling with us. Brian speeded up, and the next thing you know—"

"Been there, done that!" Angelica said.

"Sometimes I *do* feel like the village jinx." Tricia sighed. "I told Brian I'd pay for the ticket, but that won't help him if his car insurance goes up. I wish I could help them more."

Angelica frowned. "Tricia, will you stop feeling guilty? You've already done too much for Ginny. You pay her well above minimum wage; you pay for her health insurance; and you give her bonuses at the drop of a hat. What next? Are you going to adopt her?"

"Don't be absurd."

"Well, really," Angelica said, scowling. "Tricia, you are just too nice for your own good."

"Ginny has been an exceptional employee. She didn't know the mystery genre when I hired her, but she's done enough reading and research to—"

"Fake it!"

Tricia exhaled a long breath. "Possibly. But the fact remains, she's an asset to me. When you were having employee problems at the Cookery, you wanted to steal her from me."

"Where did you get that idea?" Angelica asked, offended.

"Ginny told me."

Angelica let out several short breaths, as though she didn't know what to say. "She must have misinterpreted our conversation."

"What part of 'I'll give you a dollar more an hour than Tricia is paying you' did she misunderstand?"

Angelica opened her mouth to answer—apparently thought better of it—and shut it again. Her scowl deepened. "She wasn't supposed to tell you."

"Sorry, but she felt no loyalty to you."

"And I paid her for a week's work," Angelica groused.

"Which she more than earned. You know your profits rose that week."

"Maybe," Angelica grudgingly agreed. "Nevertheless, your profits would be higher if you didn't share the wealth so generously with your employees. You're not running a charity, you know."

Tricia's accountant had voiced the same opinion on more than one occasion. "You're one to talk. You pay Frannie well, too."

"Well, she deserves it."

"Let's get back to the main subject."

"Which I've forgotten at this point," Angelica said. "Oh, yes, what did you learn on your little field trip?"

"Not as much as I'd hoped. Pammy was considered a flirt. Eugenia Hirt didn't like her, which makes me think Pammy might have batted her eyes at the girl's father. Ginny thinks Eugenia is a flirt because she kissed Brian on the lips. And that Lisa I met was so crabby she might turn red and walk sideways."

"Eugenia's last name is Hirt? Like Libby Hirt?" Angelica asked.

Tricia swallowed a bite of toast, and nodded. "Libby's her mom. Her dad works at a PR firm in Nashua. Sounded deadly dull. I wonder why he got into Dumpster diving. I should've asked him that. Wouldn't you know, I talked to everyone but the person who invited Pammy to come along on these scavenging trips. His name is Pete Marbello, and he works at the convenience store on the highway. I'm going to give him a call tomorrow." She glanced at the kitchen clock. "And if I want to be half awake tomorrow, I'd better get home now."

She grabbed her cup, gulped the last of her cocoa, and rose from her seat.

"I'll walk you to the door," Angelica said, and popped the last bite of her toast into her mouth.

Angelica followed Tricia down the stairs and through the darkened shop. "Come by the café for lunch tomorrow. Jake's making potato-leek soup—from my recipe, of course."

"Okay. See you then."

Before Tricia could exit, Angelica pulled her into a hug and planted a kiss on her forehead. "Be good—and if you can't be good, be careful," she said, and closed the door behind Tricia.

She walked the ten or so feet to her own store and let herself in, threading through the shop and up the stairs to her own loft apartment.

Miss Marple was behind the door, and scolded Tricia for leaving her alone for so long.

"Well, I'm home now, and it's time for bed," she told the cat.

As though agreeing with that statement, Miss Marple turned and led the way through the apartment to the bedroom that overlooked Main Street.

As Tricia reached for the light switch, she noticed the light blinking on her phone—indicating she had missed several calls. No doubt her crank caller. She didn't feel up to listening to the messages and flipped off that light, then headed for the living room to do the same.

She'd just bent to turn off the last light when she heard what sounded like a *thwok* in the room ahead of her. She extinguished the lamp. The apartment was silent. But she had heard something. Fumbling in the dark, she stayed out of the line of the row of windows that faced the street. Sure enough, several small holes dotted one of her windows in a characteristic pattern she recognized: a small entrance hole with a much bigger exit hole—classic BB shots. Not exactly a lethal weapon, but maybe the shooter had wanted to scare rather than hurt her. After all, she hadn't even been in the room when the shots had been fired. If someone had wanted to hurt or kill her, they could've done it as she walked from the Cookery to her own store.

Tricia kept to the far side of the line of windows and stared into the darkness. Lights blazed in the windows of the top floors of the buildings across the street. Like her, some of the shopkeepers lived above their stores; the rest of the space was rented out as apartments or offices. She didn't for a minute believe one of her neighbors would pull such a stupid stunt, and there were no preteen boys or even teenagers living on Main Street—just the demographic that would own such a firearm. All those buildings sported metal fire escapes, as her own did. Someone could have climbed a fire escape, broken into an office and gotten onto the roof, taken a few potshots—and was probably already long gone.

She hoped.

For some reason, she wasn't really afraid—more annoyed, perhaps. Someone had decided to crank up the fear factor. If the person on the phone could shoot at her windows with a BB gun, they certainly could have done so with a high-powered rifle. And thanks to the Supreme Court, any crank with a desire to start his own well-armed militia had the go-ahead from the country's top lawmakers.

She should probably call the Sheriff's Department and report this. But at this time of night, she'd have to deal with some deputy pulled off patrol. She glanced at the glowing numerals on her bedside clock. She didn't want to wait the hour or more it might take for one to arrive, and decided instead to just call Captain Baker in the morning.

Tricia sidled along the wall, reached for the drapery pull. Before she did, she peeked out the window one last time . . . and saw a dark shape scurry into the shadow-filled doorway of Booked for Lunch. Could it be the shooter?

Heart pounding, she watched and waited.

A car rolled by, its headlights cutting through the darkness and then receding into the gloom.

Suddenly the figure darted out—its arms raised above its head—and hurled something round into the street.

The pumpkin exploded onto the asphalt. Tricia stared at the resulting mess, entranced—and missed seeing where the figure went.

She watched and waited as another car drove past, skirting what was now just refuse.

After a good five minutes with no other sign of the vandal, she pulled the cord and the curtains closed across the bank of windows. Even with them closed, Tricia decided not to turn on her bedside lamp. As she undressed and got ready for bed in the dark, she kept thinking about the demolished jack-o'-lantern, wondering if the shooter and the vandal could be the same person. She also contemplated the holes in her bedroom window, and worried what her caller's next move would be.

THIRTEEN

"Ms. Miles," Captain Baker said firmly, "you should have called the Sheriff's Department as soon as someone shot at your windows. We're here to protect the citizens of Stoneham."

Tricia glanced out the front window of Haven't Got a Clue to where Baker's cruiser was parked. "I've always wondered about that. The other towns around here all have their own police departments. Why does Stoneham depend on the Sheriff's Department for protection?"

"The Board of Selectmen dissolved the Stoneham Village Police during the early 1990s, when the village was going broke. They never voted to reinstate it. But that's beside the point. You should have called us last night."

"What for? By the time a deputy arrived, the shooter would've been long gone." Tricia sounded a whole lot braver than she'd felt the night before, and she'd spent a good part of the night lying in bed and worrying. "Besides," she continued, "I haven't had a very warm reception from the Sheriff's Department in the past."

"I know about your past difficulties with Sheriff Adams. That's why *I'm*

investigating Pamela Fredericks's murder. I want you to call my office—day or night—if you have anything to report. If there's an emergency, they can get hold of me in a matter of minutes."

Tricia exhaled a breath. "Okay. As a matter of fact, I do have something else to report. For the last couple of days I've been receiving"—she hesitated; they weren't really threatening calls—"annoying phone calls."

Baker's eyes narrowed. "How many have you received?"

Tricia shrugged. "Eight or ten." Her voice grew softer, as though she expected a rebuke. "Maybe more."

Baker looked ready to explode. "I don't suppose you saved any of them," he managed through gritted teeth.

"Just one. It's on my home answering machine."

"Is that a different number from the shop?"

"Yes."

"I suppose you're listed in the phone book as well."

"Just under my last name and first initial. But it's a P for Patricia, not T, and everyone around here knows me as Tricia."

"It doesn't matter, if the caller knows your address. Now, do you mind if I listen to this call?"

"Not at all. I'll show you the holes in my window, as well. If you'll follow me."

Baker grabbed his hat from the store's sales counter and followed Tricia to the back of the shop. Miss Marple scampered ahead of them. She wasn't about to be left behind with Ginny when she could follow Tricia upstairs and perhaps have an extra helping of cat cookies.

Tricia unlocked the apartment door and preceded Baker inside, with Miss Marple scooting in ahead of both of them. She jumped onto one of the kitchen stools and gave a sharp "*Yow*!"

"You don't need a treat right now," Tricia told her, and the disgruntled cat sat on her haunches and glared at her owner.

Baker looked around the converted loft space. "Nice."

"Thank you." Tricia held out her hand, indicating the way. "The window with the BB holes overlooks the street."

Tricia led the way to her bedroom, glad she'd made the bed, and even dusted the nightstand, earlier that morning.

"Nice place," Baker said, eying the space, his glance landing on the queen-sized bed, where it seemed to stay for far too long.

"The window," Tricia prompted, indicating the glass across the way.

Baker shook his head, becoming all business once again. He moved to the window to examine the damage, and then shifted his gaze to take in the rooftops across the way. "The perfect vantage point."

"My thoughts exactly."

"You ought to keep your curtains shut for the time being."

"I did close them last night."

He reached for the traverse cord. "Daytime, too," he said as the drapes closed. The light grew dim, and the room seemed to shrink.

"I also saw something else last night."

"Oh?"

"The person who's been smashing pumpkins."

"When was this?"

"Just after the shots were fired. I couldn't tell if it was a man or a woman—or a teenager. Just that the person was"—she paused, realizing what it was she'd seen the night before, but that hadn't registered until this moment—"chunky."

Baker frowned. "A fat vandal? You're saying it wasn't a kid?"

Tricia shrugged. "They say that thirty-three percent of today's youth are overweight-to-obese," she offered. "The person was dressed all in black. He or she raised the pumpkin over his or her head and then—*splat!*"

"*Splat*," he repeated with no inflection.

She nodded.

"I want you to know I have looked into this pumpkin vandalism, and I can tell you that not one parent or homeowner in Stoneham has reported any stolen or smashed pumpkins."

"No one?" she repeated in disbelief. "Then why . . . ?"

"I have no answer. Now, where's that answering machine of yours?" Baker asked.

"It's actually part of my phone." Tricia led the way back to the kitchen. She stepped over to the counter and pressed the Play button.

"Tricia? It's Russ. I'm sorry about the way things went the other night. I still care about you. I think we should talk. Please call me."

Beep!

Tricia stared at the Play button her finger still hovered over. If she'd known that message was there, she would never have played it for Captain Baker.

He cleared his throat. "I take it that wasn't the message you wanted me to hear."

Tricia pressed the Delete button. "No, it wasn't."

"And this Russ is?"

"Russ Smith, the editor of the *Stoneham Weekly News*. We used to be . . . friends."

Baker nodded. "I see."

Tricia wasn't about to let on that the message had rattled her. She pressed

the Play button again. This time, the draggy voice came out of the little speaker, sounding tinny and not at all threatening in the electric light of her drape-drawn day.

"Where's this diary? Do you have it?" Baker asked when the message had ended.

"I have no idea! I don't know what diary the person is talking about, and I certainly don't have it. The caller might be referring to a diary belonging to Pammy Fredericks. But if she had one, I never saw it."

"There wasn't a diary with her personal effects in her car, either."

"She did leave a box of books here, but they were pretty old—mostly mainstream paperback fiction. I gave them to the Stoneham Library for their used book sale."

"You what?"

Tricia shrugged. "They weren't worth anything. I mean, Pammy was dead. What good were they to her?"

"You should have told me about them," Baker said sternly. "We could have gone through them, maybe found something to help us in our investigation."

"Captain, I sell used books—take it from me, they were yard-sale castoffs, or something she got from digging through someone's garbage. They weren't worth anything."

"When was the sale?" he demanded.

"It won't happen until the end of the month."

"Then maybe it's not too late. Perhaps the head librarian can help me."

"Lois Kerr is great, but there must have been twenty or thirty boxes of books in her conference room. I doubt she'd remember which box I brought in."

"Would you remember?"

Tricia hesitated. The box had been nondescript, but she might remember some of the titles. "Maybe."

Baker grabbed her by the elbow and hauled her toward the door leading to the stairs and the bookstore beyond them. "Come on. Let's go."

"But I have a business to run!"

"I have a murder to investigate, and I need your help to do it."

Tricia grimaced and yanked back her arm. "You sure know how to sweet-talk a girl."

Lois Kerr stood at the threshold of the Stoneham Library's conference room and frowned. "As you can see, Captain Baker, our patrons have been very generous with their donations for our fund-raiser."

Generous wasn't the word. Since Tricia had dropped off Pammy's box of books several days before, an additional twenty or thirty cartons of old books had been added to the small room.

"I'm afraid I don't remember which box was yours, Tricia," Lois admitted.

Captain Baker did not look pleased. He sniffed the air, wrinkling his nose at the scent of old paper and mildew. "Ladies, you have your work cut out for you."

"What do you mean we have our work cut out for us?" Tricia demanded.

"You're going to dig through this pile of books until you find those that belonged to Ms. Fredericks."

"Excuse me, Captain, but I have a meeting with Selectman Tim Powers in exactly ten minutes. And as you can see"—Lois waved a hand at her neat tweed suit—"I'm simply not dressed for the task."

"Neither am I," Tricia protested.

"I pressed this myself," Baker said, jerking a thumb at his uniform blouse, "but it looks like I'll have to get it wrinkled. Your home is right above your shop, Ms. Miles; you'll be able to change as soon as you get back, if need be. And the quicker we find that box of books, the quicker you'll get to return to your store."

Lois flashed an embarrassed smile. "I'll just leave you two to your work," she said, and backed away from the conference room.

Tricia exhaled a long, annoyed breath, her gaze traveling up and down the stacked cartons. "We'll have to move all these boxes to get to the stuff that was donated before Wednesday."

"How do you know your box isn't in the front row? I think you should look at each and every box to make sure it hasn't been relocated since you dumped it off."

"I did not dump the box here. I brought it in and placed it on the pile. I thought I was doing a charitable thing, not hindering your investigation."

Baker opened his mouth to say something, and then closed it, apparently thinking better of it.

"Why don't we start sorting through the piles? The sooner we get at it, the sooner we can both go back to work."

He was trying and—if she was honest with herself—succeeding at treating her with more respect than Sheriff Adams ever had.

Tricia pushed up the sleeves of her sweater and sighed. "Okay."

She stepped into the conference room and grabbed the first carton of books, staggering under its weight.

"Hold on," Baker called, rushing up to her and taking the box from her. "I didn't mean you should have to cart all these boxes around by yourself. I'll put them on the table and you can go through them, okay?"

Chivalry was not dead after all. "That would be fine," Tricia said.

They set to work. One by one, Captain Baker shifted the boxes, Tricia unfolded the interlocking flaps, looked inside each one, and pushed it aside.

"I'm really sorry you're losing your morning to this," Tricia said after ten minutes had gone by and they'd shifted at least as many boxes. "I really didn't think the books would hold any value for you. They're just old books."

"Is that how you feel about the books in your shop?"

"Of course not. They're mysteries."

Baker laughed. "Ms. Miles, I do believe you're a snob."

Tricia looked up sharply. "I am not."

"Then why don't books other than mysteries intrigue you?"

"I never said that." She folded the flaps in on another box, pushing it aside on the table. "I do read other genres. My sister has been working on a new cookbook. I'm helping her edit it. I can also repair books—although I haven't had the time to do it since I opened my shop. Not only have I read the classics, from Shakespeare to Tolstoy, but every Harry Potter book, too."

"I stand corrected," Baker said, the hint of a smile gracing his lips, and placed another box of books on the table beside her.

Tricia opened the box, took out several books, and looked through the contents. She spied a copy of *The Three Roads* by Kenneth Millar—otherwise known as Ross MacDonald—and flipped open the cover, thumbing to the copyright page. She froze, her heart pounding. Yes! A first edition. The dust cover had a couple of nicks and wrinkles, but it was in very good condition—something a collector, not unlike herself, would covet.

She carefully set the book aside. Would Lois let her buy some of these books before the sale? She'd have to ask . . . and, she decided, she'd pay a bit more attention as she went through the rest of the boxes. There could be many more surprises.

"You forgot to put that book back in the box," Baker commented.

Tricia feigned surprise. "Did I?"

"Yes."

Tricia met his gaze. "I don't think so. May I have another box, please?"

Baker took the box she'd just pushed aside, set it on the floor by the other cartons she'd already inspected, and picked up a new one for Tricia to look at. She opened the flaps. "And what is it you read for pleasure, Captain Baker?"

"Certainly not mysteries. They're a little too close to what I do for a living. When I read, I want to relax, not feel like I'm doing homework."

"Then I take it true crime is out, too?"

"Definitely. Don't laugh, but I actually do read cookbooks."

"Why should I laugh? Most of the greatest chefs in the world are men. Probably because it's women who have to do the drudge work at home."

"Ah, you're a feminist, too?" he asked.

She turned a level glare at him. "Some people don't like that word."

"Do you?"

"I think it's rather a tribute."

"Why's that?"

"Let's just say I don't like to see women treated as second-class citizens. How do you feel about reporting to a woman?"

The captain's expression grew somber. "My boss was elected to the job. If she'd come up through the ranks . . ." He didn't have to say any more.

Tricia finished with another box. "What do you make?"

He leaned in closer. "I beg your pardon?"

"What kind of food do you like to cook?" she clarified. "Barbecue?"

He frowned. "Now who's making assumptions?" He didn't wait for a reply, and plowed ahead. "As it happens, I'm rather good at baking. After all, my name is Baker."

"What do you bake?"

"Bread, mostly. My grandmother taught me. Do you cook?"

"Not unless I have to. My sister got all the cooking talent in our family. That's why she opened a café."

"And has a cookbook about to be published," he added. "From Penguin. In June. *Easy-Does-It Cooking*," he recited from memory.

Tricia laughed. "Exactly."

She pushed aside yet another box. The captain moved it to the discard pile and gave her another.

"By the way, Captain; did you get a call from the Stoneham post office?"

"No. Why?"

"Because, they're holding a letter there addressed to Pammy, in care of General Delivery."

"Why didn't you tell me this before?" he asked sharply.

"I only found out yesterday. I did encourage the clerk to call you. I guess he didn't feel it was necessary. I hope he hasn't had it returned to its sender."

"I'll check into it as soon as I leave here. Thank you for mentioning it."

Tricia nodded and opened the flaps on the next box. She recognized several of the titles. "This is it."

Baker whirled round. "Don't touch the books."

"Why not? I've already handled them. And it's unlikely you'll find any decent fingerprints. Besides, it was Pammy who handled these books before me, not my mysterious caller."

"Just the same," he said, taking custody of the box and moving it away from her. He carefully folded the carton's flaps back in.

"Since you intend to take those books away, don't you think you should make a donation to the library?"

"My tax dollars are my donation."

"Yes, but the library wouldn't have to hold book sales if our tax dollars better supported it."

"Hey, you're a bookseller. The library is your competition."

"I deal in mostly used, out-of-print, and hard-to-find mysteries. Collectors are my prime customers. Libraries serve a large portion of the rest of the population."

"Excuse *me*."

He lifted the box. "I'd better take these to the main desk and leave Mrs. Kerr a receipt. If we find nothing, the books will be returned."

"After the sale, no doubt."

"Possibly." He paused in the doorway. "I want you to keep me posted on your unknown caller. And if you find that diary, I want to be the first to know about it."

Tricia snapped to attention and saluted smartly. "Yes, sir!" She relaxed. "Now, may I be excused?"

Baker wasn't amused. "I'm serious, Ms. Miles. Whoever thinks you've got that diary is likely to come after it—*and* you. Next time he or she won't use a BB or pellet gun."

Much as she didn't want to admit it, Tricia had a feeling he might be right.

FOURTEEN

MR. EVERETT STOOD behind the cash register, waiting on a customer, when Tricia returned to Haven't Got a Clue. It had been a couple of days since he'd reported in, so she was surprised to see him. She waited until he'd bid the customer a cheery good-bye before she stepped up to the cash desk.

"I didn't know we'd see you today. How are things shaping up for the wedding?"

His jovial smile faltered. "Not very well, I'm afraid. Grace had her heart set on being married at the Brookview Inn. Unfortunately, they have two other

parties already booked for Saturday, and three baby showers on Sunday. I didn't realize there were so many expectant mothers here in Stoneham."

"Oh, dear. Can you wait a week?"

He shook his head. "We've already booked a cruise, and need to board ship on Monday. I'm just not sure what we'll do now."

"Can't you have the ceremony after you return?"

Mr. Everett's eyes widened in indignation. "Ms. Miles, it wouldn't be proper. I would never sully Grace's reputation in that way."

"I'm sorry," Tricia apologized. "It was a thoughtless suggestion. Please forgive me."

He nodded. "We won't speak of it again."

That still left the problem of the wedding location.

"What about Grace's house? It's lovely, and her living room is certainly large enough to accommodate all your guests."

"That's true, but we've already arranged to have work done while we're on our honeymoon. Grace is having the entire downstairs repainted and new carpet put in. They've already started preparing the rooms. We've been relegated to the upstairs parlor to read in the evenings."

Tricia looked around her store. Except for where Pammy had doused a customer's foot with coffee, the rug was in good shape. If they pushed back the chairs in the reading nook, there would be plenty of room for the wedding party and guests.

"Why don't we hold the wedding here?"

Mr. Everett's eyes flashed, and a small smile crept onto his lips. "Here? Really?"

He hadn't fooled her one bit. He'd been hoping she would offer Haven't Got a Clue. And if they celebrated with a wedding brunch, she could still open in the afternoon. Besides, Sunday was the last day of the Milford Pumpkin Festival. As Frannie had said, Stoneham would be dead while thousands of people celebrated the wonders of orange squash right down the road in the next town.

"I would be happy to play hostess for your wedding on Sunday. In fact, I think it's a marvelous idea."

"Thank you, Ms. Miles. I'm sure Grace will be especially pleased when I tell her. Do you mind if I use the telephone?"

"Go right ahead," Tricia said. "I'll just go hang up my coat."

But before he could do so, the phone rang. Tricia let Mr. Everett answer it. She hung up her coat and soon returned to the front of the store. "Ms. Miles, it's the Cookery's Ms. Armstrong, for you."

Tricia took the receiver. "Frannie?"

"I've caught Penny!" Frannie cried with delight.

"That's wonderful."

"Yes, but what do I do now? I'm all alone here at the Cookery. She's frightened, and Angelica doesn't want her in the store. What should I do?"

"Do you have things set up at your house? A litter box, bowls, et cetera?"

"Oh, yes, but I can't leave the store to take her home."

Angelica had her hands full at Booked for Lunch, so she couldn't return to take care of the Cookery. Since both Ginny and Mr. Everett were working that day, that left only one solution. "Would you like me to watch over the Cookery while you take Penny home?"

"I'd only be gone a half hour at most," Frannie said, her words a plea.

"Grab your coat, and Penny, and I'll be right over."

"Oh, Tricia, you are a lifesaver!"

"See you in a minute." Tricia hung up the phone.

"Am I to presume you'll be at the Cookery for the foreseeable future?" Mr. Everett asked solemnly.

Tricia sighed. "At least the next half hour, I'm afraid."

He nodded. "Ginny and I will take care of things here."

Tricia didn't bother to retrieve her coat, and instead headed out dressed as she was.

Frannie had retrieved the Havahart trap, with its howling occupant, and her coat, and practically flew out the Cookery's door the moment Tricia arrived. "Be right back," she assured Tricia, and took off at a trot.

No sooner had the door closed on her than it was opened again, and several customers entered. One hundred and fifty-six dollars later, they departed, and a familiar face crossed the threshold. Pete Marbello hefted a box and frowned at Tricia. "What are you doing here? This isn't your shop."

"No, it belongs to my sister."

He looked around the store. "Where's Frannie?"

"She had an errand to run. Can I help you?"

He stepped up to the register, letting the heavy box bang onto the glass-topped counter.

"Hey," Tricia protested.

"It's just books," he said. "Frannie's been buying them from me for the last few months. I don't suppose you know anything about cookbooks?"

"Not really."

"Damn." He pursed his lips, staring at the carton. "Can I leave them here for Frannie? Could you ask her to call me?"

"Sure." But she wasn't about to let him leave before she asked him a few questions of her own. "I understand your father owns the convenience store up by the highway."

"Yeah. The greenest store in the county," he said with pride. "You noticed the different trash cans out front, didn't you? For paper, glass, and plastic."

"I can't say as I have. But I'll be sure to look next time I'm there."

"That was my idea. I sort all the trash that goes into the Dumpster, too. We recycle more than the rest of the retailers around here. We only use recycled plastic bags in the store, too. If I had my way, we wouldn't use plastic or paper, but people are conditioned to expect them."

"What would you put their purchases in?"

"Customers should bring their own reusable bags. We sell them, but not enough people buy or use them."

"You're really serious about all this, aren't you?"

"Yeah, and you should be, too," he said, the weight of the chip on his shoulder coloring his voice.

"I have tried the cornstarch bags, but they aren't strong enough to hold books. The bags I use are made from recycled plastic, and for big orders, I have paper bags with handles."

"That's better than most of the other booksellers," he grudgingly admitted.

Tricia indicated the box of books. "Have you become a picker?"

"Sort of. I'm trying to get enough money together to start a recycling plant."

"That's pretty ambitious."

"You'd be surprised what can be recycled. My plan is to buy a flatbed truck, put an ad in the local papers, and offer a free service to pick up old appliances, like refrigerators, old cars, then scrap 'em. If I can hook up with the county, I should be able to clean up the environment—and financially, too."

"Tell me more," Tricia said, and leaned forward on the counter, trying to appear more interested than she was. How on earth was she going to get Pammy into the conversation?

He droned on and on. At last he mentioned the freegans, and she jumped at the opportunity to interrupt. "I understand you met my friend Pammy Fredericks digging through the convenience store's trash, and that you invited her along on several of your Dumpster-diving expeditions."

"Yeah," he admitted with a snarl. "I thought she was a kindred spirit, but it turned out she had a one-track mind. Always bitching about coming into money—or not coming into it. At least not fast enough."

"Yes, that's what Joe Hirt said, too. Pammy didn't tell me what her big plans were. Do you know?"

He shrugged. "Something about someone paying her big bucks for what she knew. She had some kind of proof."

"A diary?" Tricia suggested.

He frowned. "I dunno. Maybe. I didn't pay much attention to her. She

wasn't really one of us. All she cared about was getting something for nothing. The world is better off without people like her. Takers. What did she ever give back to anyone?"

It was Tricia's turn to frown. His plan to scoop up scrap metal and resell it didn't sound all that altruistic, either, especially given the freegans' goal of living a less material existence.

"Pammy didn't deserve to die the way she did—suffocating in garbage."

He shrugged. "One less moocher sucking up our air and using our resources."

Tricia straightened. She'd had enough of him. "I'll tell Frannie to give you a call about these books," she said, letting him know he was being dismissed.

"She's got my number," he said, a sneer entering his voice.

Tricia watched as he left the shop. She glanced inside the carton of books. They looked to be in pretty good shape. Where had he gotten them? There weren't many yard sales at this time of year. She bent lower and sniffed. A bit musty, perhaps, but they didn't reek of the soup found at the bottom of a Dumpster or trash bin.

Pammy had spoken a little too freely about her diary and what she hoped to gain from it. Despite Pete Marbello's assessment of her, she did not deserve to be killed. More and more it sounded as though she was blackmailing—or attempting to blackmail—someone. But who? There was only one logical choice: Stuart Paige.

But Tricia had nothing but suspicions. She didn't even have the diary. Without it, there was no reason to talk to, let alone confront, the man.

Whoever killed Pammy might just get away with murder, after all.

Frannie was gone much longer than Tricia had anticipated—almost two hours. "I'm sorry I'm late," she apologized as she wiggled out of the sleeves of her coat. "When I got Penny home, I called the vet to make an appointment for her. They said they had an opening, and to bring her right in."

"I wish you'd called," Tricia said, looking at her watch. It was past Ginny's lunch break, and Mr. Everett would be holding down Haven't Got a Clue by himself.

"I'm sorry, Tricia. I should have. But the only day I have off is Sunday, and the vet isn't open then."

True enough. "I forgive you. But I'd better get back to my own store in case Mr. Everett needs to leave. He and Grace have a lot of plans to make before Sunday."

"Isn't it exciting—getting married at their age? Maybe there's still hope for me," Frannie added wistfully.

Tricia scooted around the sales desk, letting Frannie take her place. "Talk to you later."

Frannie waved. "Thanks again!"

Haven't Got a Clue was mobbed with customers, and despite its being late, Ginny had not taken her lunch break. Mr. Everett stood by one of the back shelves, helping a customer, while Miss Marple observed the chaos from her perch on the shelf behind the register.

Tricia grabbed the stack of books Ginny had already rung up, and bagged them. "Here you go," she told the customer. "I'm so sorry I'm late," she whispered to Ginny.

"If you were helping anyone but Frannie, I wouldn't be so accommodating," Ginny said. To the customer she said, "That'll be forty-three eighty-five." The woman handed over her gold card and Ginny swiped it through the credit card machine.

"Anything happen while I was gone?"

"We've been very busy. Grace called to thank you. So we're holding a wedding here on Sunday?"

"Uh-huh." She hadn't offered to let Ginny get married at the store; would she feel slighted? "Does that upset you?"

"Of course not. It was nice of you to offer. But it's a good thing they're planning a small affair."

Definitely no hurt feelings there.

The credit card machine spit out a piece of paper, the customer signed it, and was on her way.

Tricia picked up the conversation where they'd left it. "I'm not sure of the logistics on this wedding. I may need your help getting things set up. I wonder if I should rent chairs, or if the caterer will handle that. If you could come in early Sunday morning, to help set things up, I'd be glad to pay you for your time."

"You'll do no such thing. Mr. Everett and Grace are my friends, too, you know. I'll do whatever I can to help make their day a happy one."

Tricia smiled. "I knew I could count on you."

Ginny glanced at her watch. "Yikes! It's twenty minutes past my lunch break."

Tricia flushed with guilt. She hadn't yet made any headway on putting together a break room for Ginny and Mr. Everett in her storeroom. Another task undone. Luckily, the day was bright and sunny. No doubt Ginny's car would be warm enough for her to endure another lunch break, but the weather wouldn't hold much longer.

Guilt, guilt, guilt.

Ginny retrieved her coat and grabbed a book from the store's paperback

bargain shelf. As she opened the door to leave, Grace stepped into Haven't Got a Clue. "Hello, Ginny!"

"Hi, Grace. Bye, Grace!" Ginny said with a smile, and exited.

Grace hurried to the sales counter. "Hello, Tricia. I can't thank you enough for letting William and me get married here on Sunday. And I promise we'll be out of your hair in time for you to open at precisely noon."

"Don't worry about it, Grace. If we have to open later, we'll open later. I want you two to have a nice send-off. Besides, Milford's Pumpkin Festival is this weekend. We'll be lucky to have any customers at all on Sunday. How are your plans coming along?"

Grace beamed. "I've engaged a caterer, a photographer, and a florist. I've got my dress, and I'm on my way to the Stoneham Patisserie to order the wedding cake."

"Nikki's going to make your cake?"

Grace nodded. "I hope so."

Angelica had mentioned she might like to do it. Oh, well. Tricia made a mental note to mention it to her sister before she started pulling out pans and recipes.

"How about the guest list? Do you know how many people you'll be inviting?"

"I've narrowed it down to twenty. Do you think the store can accommodate that many people?"

"Oh, sure. I've hosted book signings with more than that." But not by much. "We don't have a photographer here in Stoneham. Did you have to go to Milford or Nashua to find one?"

"But of course we have a photographer here in the village. Oh, I admit he doesn't do it professionally anymore, but he accepted the moment I asked. And he refuses to take any money for it. I shall have to figure out a nice gift to give him when we return from our honeymoon."

"Who is this mystery man?" Tricia asked, intrigued. Could Bob Kelly have once owned a photography business? He seemed to have his fingers in every other pie in town.

"It's Russ Smith."

"Russ?" Tricia echoed, a bit more loudly than she would've liked. The one man in Stoneham she had no desire to see, and now he was an integral part of Mr. Everett and Grace's wedding. Could her luck get any worse?

She struggled to get her voice under control. "How nice."

Grace's smile widened. "Have you two thought about tying the knot?"

Tricia clenched her fists, and hoped to keep the anger out of her tone. "No. Sadly, Russ and I are no longer together."

Grace's face fell. "Oh, dear. I hope his being at the wedding won't be too upsetting."

"Of course not," Tricia lied. "We're adults. And we parted amicably."

Ha!

Grace brightened. "Thank goodness. It could have been very awkward."

Tricia ground her teeth together, but managed a reasonable facsimile of a smile.

Grace looked up to see Mr. Everett across the room. She caught his eye and waved.

His fingers fluttered a shy wave in return.

Grace looked back to Tricia. "Aren't I terrible—distracting William while he's at work?"

"I think it's very sweet. You both are."

Tricia suddenly remembered the peck on the cheek Stuart Paige had given Grace at the Food Shelf's dedication. "Not to change the subject—but I will. How well do you know Stuart Paige?"

"Oh," she said, taken off guard. "Casually. My late husband was a good friend of Stuart's father. Of course, I saw Stuart many times over the years, but it wasn't until he started his charity work that we really became acquainted."

"I've heard about his more rebellious days. And, of course, about the accident."

The joy left Grace's eyes. "It was very unfortunate. Though the good he's done can never erase what happened, there's no doubt he's dedicated his life to trying to make amends for past indiscretions."

Should she push Grace even further?

Tricia took the chance. "So you believe he's a good man?"

Grace answered without hesitation. "Yes."

Good now. But what if what Pammy knew about the man had happened years before? Would he want to keep another incident from his past quiet—and would he do anything, including murder, to make sure of it?

"I'd best let William know that things are shaping up for our big day, and then I'll be on my way," Grace said. "If you'll excuse me, Tricia."

"Of course."

Tricia turned away, disappointed. She hadn't learned anything new—except for Russ being at the wedding ceremony, and she didn't want Grace to know how she really felt about it. But after all, they were adults, and she could be with him in the same room for two or three hours without exploding—or falling apart.

Ha, again! Fall apart? He might fall apart if she clocked him, and that's exactly what she wanted to do.

Must distract myself.

Goodness knows, she had enough to think about—Pammy's death, the missing diary, setting up Ginny's break room, as well as the impending nuptials.

She didn't need another thing to think about.

The phone rang.

Tricia grabbed it. "Haven't Got a Clue. This is Tricia; how can I help you?"

"Oh, Trish—wonderful news," Angelica said.

Tricia looked out the window to see her sister on her cell phone, waving at her from the window of Booked for Lunch.

"Wonderful news!" Angelica continued. "Grace Harris has hired me to cater her wedding. And guess what? You're going to help me!"

FIFTEEN

"ISN'T IT EXCITING! My first catering job," Angelica gushed.

"How could you even think of taking on this wedding?" Tricia scolded. "You're shorthanded. Where are you going to find the time to keep two businesses afloat *and* make hors d'oeuvres for twenty people by Sunday?"

"Oh. I hadn't thought about that. Well, I can always round up all my friends to help."

"Such as?"

"Well, Frannie, of course. Maybe Ginny."

Tricia shook her head. "Much as Ginny loves Mr. Everett, I doubt she'd be willing to spend her off hours helping you make money."

"Oh, well, I could *pay* her."

"You can ask."

"And, of course, I'm depending on you," Angelica pressed.

"In case you hadn't noticed, I can't cook."

"If you can follow directions, you can cook."

Tricia watched as a couple of tourists entered the little café.

"Gotta go now. Talk to you later!" Angelica said, and disconnected.

The bell over the door jingled as another two customers entered her own store. Tricia put her worries out of her mind, plastered on her best smile, and said, "Welcome to Haven't Got a Clue. Let me know if you need any help."

• • •

THE DAY WHIPPED by. Customers came and went, spending freely. And, thanks to Craigslist, Tricia managed to hunt down a small refrigerator, which was to be delivered the next day. Now she just needed to get a microwave and a table. And maybe a radio. And then she'd consider painting the drab room. Did she need more lighting, too? Establishing a break room was going to be more complicated than she'd anticipated. Still, she wanted happy employees.

By the time seven o'clock rolled around and Tricia closed Haven't Got a Clue, she was exhausted. Her plan for the evening was to make a sandwich, drink a glass of wine, and *read*. She would not think about Pammy. She would not think about Russ being at Mr. Everett's wedding. She would not think about Angelica's threat that she was going to have to help make hors d'oeuvres for twenty people by Sunday.

She'd just settled down with *A Graveyard to Let* by Carter Dickson when the phone rang. Miss Marple, comfortably ensconced at Tricia's side, glared at the offending instrument on the end table. Tricia picked up the receiver with apprehension. Would it be her annoying caller?

"It's just me," Angelica said. "Have you eaten yet?"

"A cheese sandwich."

"I've got leftover soup from the café, and I'm on my way up." She disconnected.

The last thing Tricia wanted was company. Still, she hauled herself off the couch and met her sister at the apartment door. Angelica held a stuffed brown paper grocery bag in her arms, and a canvas tote was slung over one shoulder, resting on her back.

"What have you got there?" Tricia asked.

"Cookbooks. I've made out a preliminary list of appetizers, and I thought the two of us could go over it."

"I don't care about that kind of stuff," Tricia insisted.

Angelica leveled a penetrating glare at her. "You wrestled over the catering list for your own wedding for over two months. Who better to help me with my sample menus? I need to have something to show Grace tomorrow if I'm going to pull the food together for this wedding on Sunday."

In a matter of minutes, Angelica had the soup warming, the aroma filling the entire kitchen. She'd also covered the kitchen island with cookbooks dedicated to either hors d'oeuvres or breakfast meals. While Angelica served up the soup, Tricia looked over the scribbled sheets of paper with lists of appetizers. "Any one of these is good, Ange. Just let Grace pick what she likes."

"As it's a morning wedding and reception, I thought I should stick to

brunch-type foods. Strudel, little bagels, miniquiches, fresh fruit, et cetera," Angelica said, and sat down at the island.

"Yeah, yeah." Tricia picked up her spoon and began to eat her soup.

Angelica glowered at her. "You could show a little more enthusiasm. I mean, this is your employee's wedding we're talking about."

The phone rang. Tricia ignored it, spooning up more soup.

It rang again. And again. Since Angelica was already present, it could be only one other caller. Okay, maybe two if she counted Russ—and she *didn't* want to count him.

"Aren't you going to answer that?" Angelica asked.

It stopped ringing.

"Um, there's something I haven't mentioned to you. Someone's been calling me, demanding that I give back Pammy's diary."

"What diary?"

"Your guess is as good as mine. She left a bunch of books here with me, but there was no diary among them."

"Where do you think she got the books?" Angelica asked.

"I don't know. An estate sale, perhaps. She could've found them in the trash on one of her Dumpster-diving expeditions. Who says she acquired them all from the same place? And anyway, it's the diary that someone wants, not the rest of the books."

"Why would anyone think you've got the diary?"

"Probably because Pammy stayed with me for two weeks. It wasn't in her car or her suitcases. I'm probably the last hope that person has of finding the book."

"But you don't have it."

"No, and I searched this apartment pretty thoroughly, too." Miss Marple jumped up on one of the stools, as though to let Angelica know that she had helped in the hunt.

"Did this person threaten you? Maybe you should tell Captain Baker about the calls."

"I already did. And besides, they haven't been threatening, just annoying."

"Still . . . they could escalate into threats. What did Captain Baker say?"

Tricia shrugged. "To keep him informed."

"And will you?"

"Of course. He seems a lot more amiable than Sheriff Adams ever was. Maybe because it's a career for him—not just politics."

Angelica frowned, looking around the kitchen. "Let's assume Pammy did hide the diary here."

"I told you, I've looked."

"Did she have access to your storeroom?"

Tricia shook her head. "I keep it locked in case any curious customers make their way up the stairs."

"Me, too. Would you believe someone peed in the Cookery's stairway on Sunday?"

"I told you Frannie should have help at the store."

"How would Frannie have stopped someone from peeing in my stairwell? The restroom was probably occupied and someone just didn't want to—or couldn't—wait."

"I hope you didn't make Frannie clean it up."

"She's managing the store now—tidying up is part of the job."

Tricia shook her head. "That's not what I would call 'tidying.' And can we get back to the subject at hand—the missing diary? How are we going to find it?" she said, and pushed her empty soup bowl away.

"Have you looked in your store? What better place to hide it?"

Tricia sprang up from her stool, the sudden movement sending Miss Marple flying. "Of course! Pammy could've ditched the diary when she left here on Monday. She went downstairs ahead of me. By the time I locked the apartment door and followed, she might've been down there almost a minute. That would've been plenty of time to hide the diary among the books in my store."

"And how are we supposed to find it? Look on every shelf, read the spines of every title you've got? There must be ten thousand books to sort through."

"It can't hurt," Tricia said, and headed for the door.

"Can't it wait until tomorrow?" Angelica begged. "I've been on my feet all day. And don't forget, I need to start making appetizers. Besides, the light isn't all that great down there."

"The light is perfectly fine in my store."

"Only if you're a mole. You ought to invest in more track lighting."

"And ruin my original tin ceiling? It was the only thing I kept during the renovation. Are you going to help me or not?"

"Well, I didn't say I wouldn't."

"Good, then let's go!"

"I'll rinse these dishes and put them in the dishwasher, and meet you downstairs," Angelica said.

An hour later, the idea of searching the shelves didn't seem like such a good idea. Angelica had brought her cookbooks back down and left them by the door before she attacked a set of shelves in the back of the store. She'd amassed a pile of books around her and was reading the cover flap on the one in her hand. "Hey, this Dorothy Sayers sounds like a good author. Have you ever read *Gaudy Night*?"

Tricia sighed and sat back on her heels. "Only ten or twenty times. I thought you didn't like period pieces."

"I'm open to all fiction, although I prefer cooking and decorating books. I'm reading this wonderful book right now—"

"We're supposed to be looking for the diary, remember?" Tricia interrupted.

Angelica poked her tongue out at her sister.

Tricia reseated herself in a more comfortable position and resumed her search. Red cover. No words on the spine. She squinted in the bad light. Perhaps Angelica was right. Perhaps she did need to add more lighting so that customers could better see the bottom shelves.

"How long are we going to keep up the search?" Angelica asked.

"Until we find it."

"What if it isn't here?"

Tricia didn't want to think about that. If the diary wasn't hidden in Haven't Got a Clue, it could be anywhere—if it still existed. And what was she supposed to tell the voice the next time it called? "Sorry, but I don't have it. Never did. Don't know where it's at. Please stop bothering me."

That and five bucks would get her a double latte cappuccino with hazelnut and cinnamon at the Coffee Bean across the street.

Tricia pulled out another two or three books, noting that none of them had any dust on them. Mr. Everett was truly serious about his dusting. Thinking of Mr. Everett reminded her that he and Grace were about to get married, and that he'd need a week off right at the peak of the fall foliage season, when Stoneham would be filled with tourists.

"Red cover," Angelica muttered. "No type on the spine." She held up a book, waving it in the air. "It's not a diary with a lock, Trish. It's a journal."

Tricia's head snapped around. "You found it?"

"I'm almost as good as Saint Anthony when it comes to finding lost items. Remember, it was me who found the missing cookbook after Doris Gleason was—"

"Don't remind me," Tricia interrupted, holding up a hand to stave off another round of "I told you so," which Angelica had probably been about to make.

Tricia crawled across the space between them until she was inches from her sister. She made to grab the book, but Angelica held it out of her reach. "Hey, I found it, I should be the first to read it."

Tricia scowled but sat back, extending her arms behind her, palms down, on the floor.

"Uh-uh-uh!" Angelica tut-tutted, pointing at the circle of books around her. "Don't get comfortable. You can put these back while I read aloud."

"You took them out—you put them back."

Angelica looked down her nose at Tricia and cleared her throat. Then she grabbed the reading glasses that hung around her neck on a chain. She stared down at the book. "Hmm. Somebody obviously wanted to get rid of this thing. Look." She held the book out for Tricia to see.

The edges of the pages had been singed.

"Looks likes someone tried to burn it and changed their mind, or someone tried to burn it and someone else rescued it. Wow, there must be some juicy stuff inside." Angelica opened the cover and turned to the first page. "The first entry is dated August seventh, twenty-one years ago." She frowned. "The author would not win points for penmanship."

"Read!" Tricia commanded.

Angelica squinted at the cursive handwriting. *"Bunny and I went shopping on Saturday, but nothing in my size fit. I knew then that I was probably pregnant. Just my damn luck."* She looked up. "Oh, Trish, this is delicious. A scandal on page one."

Tricia frowned. "Being pregnant is hardly a scandal, even in the nineteen eighties."

"How do you know? Maybe this woman was a society maven."

"We don't even know who the author is. Unless there's a name on the flyleaf."

Angelica looked at the inside front cover. "No such luck, honey." She flipped through several pages, skimming the handwriting. "Oh, my, I may have been wrong. This looks deadly dull. Here's a weather report: *Rainy and gloomy today. I think I'll clean out the kitchen cabinets. That ought to keep me out of trouble for at least the afternoon."* She pulled a face. "I've changed my mind about reading this. Here." She handed off the book. "You can have it. Pick out the more salacious parts and give me a capsule update."

Tricia flipped through the pages. "Fine. I've got nothing better to do tonight."

Angelica struggled to her feet. "Oh, yes, you have." She nudged one of the books on the floor with the toe of her shoe. "I told you, I'm not putting these away. I'm going home." She headed for the shop's front exit, and picked up her bag of cookbooks. "Good night, dear sister. See you tomorrow."

Tricia, too, pulled herself to her feet, and crossed the store to lock the door behind Angelica. She didn't want to put the books away, either, but if Mr. Everett was going to be scarce for the next couple of weeks, she didn't want to overwork Ginny.

Twenty minutes later, Tricia and Miss Marple headed up the stairs, the formerly missing journal in hand. As Tricia entered her loft apartment, the phone began to ring. "Not again," she groaned. She let the answering machine take the call. Sure enough, it was the same voice. What that person wanted, she now

had. She waited until the caller hung up before she turned down the volume on the phone. She poured herself a glass of wine and sat down on the comfortable leather couch in the living room. Miss Marple deigned to accompany her, settling herself on Tricia's lap.

The phone rang three more times while Tricia read the contents of the journal. Angelica was right: most of it was pretty dull. Its unmarried author chronicled her pregnancy—the morning sickness, the expanding waistline—and her firm determination to hook the baby's father; she wasn't prepared to settle for just child support. Not surprising, the love of her life was not about to leave his comfortable lifestyle for the likes of an unwanted lover. And not once in the hundred or so pages of rather sloppy cursive handwriting did the author ever mention the name of the baby's father—let alone her own. What good was this as an instrument of blackmail? But someone thought the journal was worth killing for. And now that someone was hounding Tricia for it.

Well, "hounding" was a strong word for the relatively benign calls she'd received so far. If so, maybe that was why the threat wasn't explicit, nor the calls all that frightening.

The author's water had just broken, but Tricia was yawning, and decided she could wait until tomorrow to read the rest and find out the sex of the baby. Miss Marple had fallen asleep long before, and was startled to awareness when Tricia's hand slipped and she nearly dropped the journal on the cat. Miss Marple stretched her legs and jumped from Tricia's lap, heading for the bedroom.

"I'm with you, Miss Marple."

Tricia set the journal aside and turned off the living room lamps. As she entered her bedroom she paused, looking over her shoulder to see the book once again.

If the journal's contents weren't worthy of blackmail, could there be something else about the book that warranted further investigation? She crossed the darkened living room to retrieve it.

In her bedroom, she turned on the bedside lamp, sat down, and examined the book in greater detail. There was nothing special about it. It hadn't been expensive and was probably purchased in a discount store. She held the book by its spine and shook it. No loose pieces of paper fell out. No secret compartment revealed itself.

She thumbed through the pages, picking up where she had left off. The next entry wasn't as drab and/or hopeful as the previous hundred or so pages. The tone had changed to hysteria.

I can't believe I gave birth to that—that thing! *All my plans—all my beautiful plans for a wonderful life—are gone. I don't even want it. Bunny talked to Social*

Services this morning, and thank God I can dump it into the foster care system. I'm signing away all my rights. If anyone asks me about it, I'll tell them it died. I'm just so disgusted!!!

Tricia slammed the cover shut and tossed the journal onto the night table. Talk about disgusted! The author's self-serving dreams of a pampered life must have turned into a nightmare when the child was born with some kind of birth defect. Or maybe it was a Down syndrome child.

It wasn't the author who earned Tricia's pity, but the poor baby. The author hadn't even mentioned if it was a boy or girl—just *it*.

Tricia rose to her feet and began to pace, Miss Marple watching her every move.

As far as she could see, Pammy had been killed for nothing. The author had never mentioned names. She'd given the child up. There was no indication where the author lived. Without more information, it would be impossible to prove if Paige—or the Pope himself—was the father of the illegitimate child.

Maybe she should just give the caller what he (or she?) wanted.

Better yet, she'd call Captain Baker and turn it over to him.

Tricia glanced at her bedside clock. It was too late to call tonight, but she'd do it first thing in the morning.

That said, she wasn't sure she was ready to give up the journal. She could copy it, but that wasn't the same as actually having it in her possession, despite whatever danger her caller represented. Yet keeping it was foolhardy. And how would she convince her unknown caller that she'd given it to the Sheriff's Department? Should she hold a press conference? Perhaps she could give the journal to Baker with the stipulation that he report his findings to the media. Would he? Well, perhaps her acquaintance Portia McAlister, from Boston's News Team Ten, would help. Of course, Pammy's murder wasn't big enough for the Boston market, but maybe Portia knew someone at the *Nashua Telegraph*.

Tricia made another circuit of her bedroom. There was no way she was going to ask Russ for a favor, not the way they'd left things. *He'd* left things, she reminded herself. She hadn't instigated their breakup, and so what if he'd called her to smooth things over? He was probably wracked with guilt over the way he'd treated her.

She considered that idea. No, he wouldn't feel guilt. He didn't seem capable of any real, *strong* emotions. And besides, what good was a weekly newspaper, when the current issue would come out the next day—and had been printed days before? Anything she could contribute wouldn't be released for another eight days.

Yes, she'd give the diary to Baker—but only after she'd made a copy of it. Just in case.

SIXTEEN

Tricia left a message for Captain Baker at eight the next morning. She glanced at the clock as the phone rang ten minutes later. A public servant who arrived at work on time—more or less—and immediately returned his calls. Very refreshing.

Tricia held the phone tightly as she considered how she wanted to phrase her situation. "I'm ready to talk," she said, expecting a scolding.

"Talk about what?" Baker asked.

"About everything I *think* I know about Pammy Fredericks's death."

"Is this new insight since we spoke yesterday, or have you been holding out on me?"

"What information would I be withholding?"

"I don't know—perhaps the names of the local freegans. I haven't had much luck tracking them down."

Should she confess she'd joined the freegans on one of their Dumpster-diving expeditions? That was probably the prudent thing to do, but would it get Ginny into trouble?

She sidestepped the question. "As a matter of fact, I've got the diary my caller has been demanding. It was here in my store, mixed in with my regular stock. I want to turn it over to you."

"I'll be right over," he said, and hung up.

"Right over" was relative, since he had to drive at least thirty miles to get there.

Tricia decided to kill time by heading down to the store. She'd had a run on best sellers and needed to restock—and that meant order forms and faxing. As usual, Miss Marple was keen to start the workday, and accompanied her down the stairs to the shop.

The phone rang at eight thirty, and Tricia picked it up. "Haven't Got a Clue. We're closed right now, but we'll open at—"

"Tricia? It's Frannie."

"Hi, Frannie. You're lucky you caught me in the store."

"I already tried your home and cell numbers. You ought to turn that cell phone on once in a while, ya know."

Tricia laughed. "Everybody tells me that. What can I do for you?"

"It's Penny," Frannie said, and her voice cracked.

"What's wrong?"

"She doesn't like me." Frannie began to sob.

"Hey, now. How do you know she doesn't like you?"

"She spent all of last evening hiding behind the couch. I couldn't even coax her out with cat food, kitty treats, or even a catnip toy."

"That's not surprising," Tricia said. "You've only had her a few hours. She doesn't know she can trust you, yet."

"Well, of course she knows me. I've been feeding her for weeks."

"You've been leaving out bowls of food for weeks. She doesn't know it was you who did it."

Frannie sniffed. "What can I do to make her like me?"

"Nothing."

"What?" she cried, aghast.

"Let her get used to her new home. Let her come to you on her own terms."

"Is that what you did with Miss Marple?"

"Yes. And with every other cat I've had. You'll see. She'll warm up to you in a couple of days."

"Are you sure?"

"Positive."

"Okay."

Tricia moved the phone away from her ear as Frannie blew her nose loudly.

"I wish I didn't have to leave her alone all day," Frannie said. "Do you think there's any way Angelica would ever let me bring her to the store?"

"Not likely. Besides, Penny needs to get used to her new home before you even think of bringing her to the store."

"But would you ask Angelica about it? I'm sure you could get her to change her mind."

No one's powers of persuasion were that good.

"I'll ask," Tricia agreed, "but don't get your hopes up."

"Oh, thank you, Tricia. You're a peach! Talk to you later."

Tricia replaced the receiver. It would be a cold day in hell when Angelica let Frannie bring a cat into the Cookery. Still, she'd keep her promise, and ask. It was the least she could do.

By the time Captain Baker arrived at Haven't Got a Clue, Tricia had finished her chores and had a fresh pot of coffee waiting, and there was still plenty of time to talk before the store opened or her employees arrived.

She handed the journal to the captain.

"And you say you found it here in the store?" he asked.

Tricia nodded. "Actually, my sister found it. Pammy must have stashed it among my stock on the morning she left—the day she died," Tricia clarified. "I read through it, and it appears to be a woman's journal through her pregnancy. Pammy told a couple of the locals she was about to come into a lot of money, and she was very interested in talking to Stuart Paige."

"Just who did she tell?"

Tricia shrugged. "I'm not sure I remember exactly who told me," she fudged.

Baker studied her face for a long moment. Was he psychic? Did his cop's intuition tell him she wasn't being entirely truthful?

Finally, he spoke. "I haven't had any luck finding any of the local freegans. I've talked with Mr. Paige, and he assures me he never spoke to Pamela Fredericks."

"Pammy may have thought he was the father of this woman's baby, but there's no way to prove it. The author didn't name names—not even her own."

Baker flipped through the pages, reading snatches of it before thumbing through to other passages.

Tricia decided not to mention she'd copied its contents on her all-in-one printer earlier that morning. Those pages now resided in the bottom of the cedar chest in her bedroom.

Baker frowned. "I don't suppose there are any useful fingerprints on it anymore. You say your sister handled it, too?"

"Sorry, but we did."

"Did she read the contents?"

Tricia shook her head. "She thought it looked pretty tame. She was right—that is, until the last entry. The author gave up the child, and from the looks of it, then tried to burn the book."

Baker continued to page through the journal, only half listening to her.

"Captain, I hope you'll announce to the media that you've got the journal or diary or whatever my elusive caller wants to call it. If he knows it's in your custody, he'll probably leave me alone."

He snapped the book shut. "Not if he thinks you read it."

Oops! Tricia hadn't considered that.

"Are we sure it's a man who made the calls? It could've been a woman. You can get those voice-altering devices at places like Radio Shack," Tricia said.

"I'll keep an open mind," Baker said, giving her a wry smile.

Tricia couldn't help but smile as well. Unlike his boss, he *had* listened to her. At least he hadn't ridiculed her assumption about Pammy and Stuart Paige.

The ghost of a smile touched Baker's lips. "What?"

"What, what?" Tricia repeated.

"You're smiling."

"I am? Oh, I'd better stop, then," she said, and tried to keep a straight face, but it was impossible. She laughed and realized she probably looked like an idiot. And heavens—what if he thought she was flirting with him?

Good grief, she realized—she *was* flirting with him. She covered her mouth with her hand, and this time she was able to wipe the smile from her face. She looked up and into his green eyes. Haunting eyes—like her ex-husband's. The man she'd never really gotten over.

"I apologize, Captain Baker. I was thinking about something funny, and this situation is anything but funny."

"I agree. But there's nothing to apologize for. I'm surprised you're able to keep a sense of humor after what you've been through—not just the death of your friend, but what you've gone through in the past year."

True enough.

"I've been reading mystery books since I was a little girl. I never, ever expected to know a murder victim, and now I've known three. It's terribly upsetting. Pammy and I weren't close, but we had history together. I'd like her killer to be found and brought to justice."

"Justice?" Captain Baker asked with a laugh. "That's not something I see too often in my line of work."

"But you're a man of the law."

He sighed. "Yes." He looked down at the book in his hands. "I'd better get back to the office and read this," he said, reaching for his hat.

"I made a fresh pot of coffee. You could sit in the readers' nook. It would at least be quiet—for the next hour, that is."

"I've got an office with a door. It'll be quiet enough. But thank you."

Tricia nodded and walked him to the door.

"Unless I have more questions, your part in this investigation is now done. Is that clear?" he said.

"What do you mean?"

"Sheriff Adams doesn't think you'll be content to . . ." He hesitated.

"To mind my own business?"

"I didn't say that."

"But that's what you were thinking."

Baker sobered. "I don't know you very well, Ms. Miles—"

"Tricia," she insisted.

"But from what I've already seen, you might be as stubborn as a terrier. I wouldn't want you to get hurt pursuing avenues of investigation better left to the Sheriff's Department."

"I'm flattered you're concerned about my personal safety," she managed, trying not to bite her tongue.

"It's my job to protect and serve." His tone was definitely verging on condescending.

She shook her head and pursed her lips. "You had to go and ruin it, didn't you?"

He looked baffled. "Ruin what?"

"Here I thought I'd been dealing with a reasonable member of the Sheriff's Department, and you had to revert to being a jerk just like your boss."

Baker straightened in indignation. "I—what?"

Tricia pointed toward the door. "Go. Now. Before we both say something we'll regret."

Baker opened his mouth to say something, apparently thought better of it, and closed it. He seemed to do that a lot. His grip on the diary tightened. "Good-bye, Ms. Miles."

He stalked off to the door, yanked it open, and exited.

Nobody told Tricia what to do. Not Angelica, not Bob Kelly, and certainly not Captain Baker of the Hillsborough County Sheriff's Department.

The problem was . . . she had no plans to defy him. There were no other avenues she could investigate on her own.

Unless . . . If Baker went directly back to his office to read the diary, she might have time to track down Stuart Paige and ask him about Pammy herself. She hadn't remembered to tell Baker about the envelope Pammy had mailed to Paige.

Tricia glanced out the store's large display window, watching as Baker got into his cruiser. There was still time to flag him down and share that piece of news.

He started the engine and pulled away from the curb, heading north. Should she call him, leave a message about the envelope?

She might have . . . if he hadn't gotten snarky.

Stubborn as a terrier, eh?

What was it Frannie had told her days before—that Paige was staying at the Brookview Inn, just south of the village?

Tricia glanced at her watch, and grimaced. Half an hour before Ginny or Mr. Everett showed up for work. It would take Baker almost half an hour just to get back to his office. She'd still have time to go to the inn and try to talk to Paige. Although if what Frannie had said was true, the inn's receptionist, Eleanor, wasn't likely to help her get in to see the man. Maybe she could bluff her way in.

It wasn't much of a plan, but it was all Tricia had.

NO MATTER THE season, the Brookview Inn always looked lovely. Since it was October, corn shocks, gourds, and pumpkins decorated the long porch that ran

across the front of the white-painted colonial structure. And no smashed jack-o'-lanterns, either. Tricia didn't linger to enjoy the view, however, and jogged up the front steps and through the main entrance.

The parking lot had been full, and the noise coming from the restaurant adjacent to the reception desk told Tricia that some kind of breakfast business meeting was still in session. As usual, Eleanor was seated behind the check-in desk. Trust her to be the most dedicated employee on the face of the planet. Didn't she ever take a potty break?

Before Tricia could make a hasty exit, Eleanor called her name.

"Tricia, it's so good to see you. What's it been, three—four months?"

"Hi, Eleanor. Yes. I've had a great summer at the store. Not much time to attend Chamber meetings or even go out to dinner."

"Yes, it's been a long time since you and Russ have been in here."

Tricia cringed at the sound of his name, and Eleanor was quick to notice. "Uh-oh, trouble in paradise?" she asked.

"Russ and I have decided to . . . cool our relationship." That sounded a lot better than saying she'd been dumped. And surprisingly, the whole village didn't know about it yet. Well, they would now.

"I'm so sorry. You made such a nice couple."

"I'm keeping busy."

"Yes, we are, too. The inn is booked to capacity. It's a real coup for us, since there aren't a lot of accommodations in Milford—we're always packed straight through the Pumpkin Festival."

"I'm sorry I have to keep the store open and will miss it."

"Me, too, for the most part. But I'm taking off a couple of hours so I can enter the pie contest. I won third place two years ago, and I'm going for first this year. But talking about the festival isn't what you came in for. What can I do for you?"

Should she offer the truth?

Why not?

"I'm here to see Stuart Paige."

Eleanor shook her head. "I'm afraid he's tied up right now."

Frannie was right. Eleanor was good at protecting her guests from unwanted visitors.

"He's in the dining room, giving a speech to the Chamber of Commerce."

"What? Why didn't anyone tell me?"

"They always meet here on the second Friday of the month. The breakfast portion of the meeting is already over. Since you're a member, I don't see why you can't go in there. Perhaps you can introduce yourself to him when he's finished speaking."

"Thank you, Eleanor. I think I will." And Tricia marched across the lobby. The French doors to the restaurant were open, and Tricia slipped into one of the empty chairs at the closest table. Paige stood at a lectern. His amplified voice sounded rather husky as it resonated through the restaurant's sound system. Tricia recognized a number of her fellow bookstore owners, as well as members of the Board of Selectmen. Sitting at the table closest to the lectern was Russ, jotting down notes on his ever-present steno pad.

Paige's tone changed ever so slightly, and Tricia realized she'd entered just as he was about to wrap up his speech.

"In conclusion, building the Robert Paige Memorial Dialysis Center here in Stoneham will bring new life to the village. New construction, new jobs, new residents, and an influx of tax revenue for Stoneham. It's a win-win situation, and I hope you'll all elect to be a part of it." He collected his notes. "Thank you for inviting me to speak here today—it's been a pleasure."

The room erupted into applause, and Bob Kelly, clad in his green Kelly Realty sports jacket, rose to lead the ovation. So that was why Paige was still in town—to drum up support for another of his pet projects.

Paige's handlers crowded around him, ushering him away from the front of the room, with Bob following in his wake. Bob would no doubt stick to Paige like glue—unless, of course, Paige's entourage interfered. They'd done so after the opening of the Food Shelf. She stood, moving to the side of the room to intercept the man. She might have to ask her questions on the fly.

The applause died down, and already other business owners were up and out of their seats, headed for the exit.

One of Paige's handlers sidled close to his boss, and whispered something in his ear. Paige listened, nodded, and then spoke to Bob, who looked disappointed.

The handler snagged Paige's jacket sleeve, and steered him toward the exit.

Adrenaline coursed through her, making Tricia feel jumpy as she waited the interminable seconds it took for Paige to navigate through the crowd.

"Mr. Paige—Mr. Paige!" she called through the din of overlapping voices. She waved, trying to draw his attention, but Paige's handler looked right through her, still guiding his employer through the thinning ranks of Chamber members.

"Mr. Paige," Tricia called again, falling into step behind her quarry. "What was in the envelope Pammy Fredericks sent you last week?"

Paige abruptly halted, his head jerking around to take her in. "What did you say?"

Tricia caught up. "The Sheriff's Department is investigating Pammy Fredericks's murder. I think they'd be very interested to know what was in the envelope she sent you."

"Envelope? I don't know what you're talking about."

"Mr. Paige," the handler insisted, grabbing his employer by the elbow once more. "We're going to be late for your ten thirty meeting."

"She made copies of pages from a woman's diary. A woman who wrote about her pregnancy and intended to strong-arm the father of her baby into marrying her—that is, until the child was born with birth defects. Pammy mailed those pages to you several days before her death."

Another gray-suited flunky stepped behind Tricia, grabbed her by the elbow, and propelled her forward. "Not the time and place for this, honey," he growled. "You're outta here."

"Let me go!" The hand on her elbow tightened. At least she was going in the same direction as Paige, heading for the Brookview's front entrance.

"Mr. Paige! Mr. Paige!" she cried.

Paige was on the top step, and turned back to look at her. Shots rang out, splintering wood and shattering glass.

The flunky let go of Tricia's arm, pushing her aside. He made a flying leap at his employer, knocking him forward, and the two of them tumbled down the inn's wooden steps.

"He's hit!" came a voice.

A stream of suited businessmen and businesswomen emerged from the inn's open doorway, led by Bob Kelly, whose green jacket stuck out like a flag, while Paige's handlers dragged the wounded man to the side of the inn and out of the line of fire.

"What happened?" Bob demanded.

"Someone fired shots at Mr. Paige—my God, at me!" Tricia cried.

Instead of stopping to make sure she was all right, or even reassure her, Bob barreled down the stairs after Paige and his entourage. "Stuart! Stuart!"

"Someone call 911," a voice behind Tricia shouted.

Russ was suddenly beside her. "Tricia, what happened?"

"Is he dead? Is he dead?" another voice yelled.

Tricia's knees felt weak as she grabbed the banister to keep from stumbling down the stairs. Somehow, she took off after Bob, with Russ right behind her.

A pasty-faced Paige sat on the ground behind a linen delivery truck, his bloodied right hand clasping his left shoulder. His crisp white shirt was stained scarlet. Although gasping for breath, he managed to speak with his flunkies, one of who was on a cell phone. Meanwhile, Bob hovered over them all like a worried mother hen.

The cell phone flipped shut. "The sheriff and ambulance are on their way," the gray-suited man announced.

"Can I get you something? Something cold to drink? Something hot?" Bob blathered.

The flunky in brown pushed him aside. "Why don't you take care of crowd control?"

Bob nodded like a bobblehead. "Sure, sure."

Again he pushed past Tricia, heading back for the inn's entrance.

Tricia surged forward, but a hand held her back. "Tricia!"

Russ! "Let go," she growled, and pulled away. She crouched next to Paige. "Had you been threatened before this happened? Who'd want to kill you? Does it have anything to do with those pages Pammy Fredericks sent you?"

Paige opened his mouth to speak, but Tricia was yanked upright before she could hear what he said.

"Hey!"

"Stand back, ma'am. Give the man some air," said the flunky in brown.

"I tried to stop her," Russ said, sounding like a tattletale.

The wail of a siren cut through the cool autumn morning, and moments later the Stoneham Fire Department's rescue unit pulled alongside the inn's entrance. The EMTs jumped out, equipment in hand, and jogged to intercept Gray Suit.

Tricia and Russ were shunted off to one side, forced to stand with the rest of the rubberneckers. Their attention was riveted on the wounded man, but Tricia stared at the wooded area across the road from the inn. It hadn't been developed. In addition to trees, the area was thick with brush—the perfect hiding place for someone with a rifle.

"Is that where the shots came from?" Russ asked.

She nodded. She was in no mood to look at—let alone speak to—him, and moved aside, skirting the crowd to stand on the other side of the inn's driveway.

Once a couple of deputies had arrived, Bob managed to wrangle his way back to the mob surrounding Paige. No doubt he was already pondering the bad press that this incident would generate, and thinking about damage control.

"He's going to be all right, right?" he badgered.

"His wounds aren't life threatening," an EMT told him, "but to be on the safe side, we're going to take him to the trauma center in Nashua."

Another Sheriff's Department cruiser pulled up outside the inn, and Tricia was surprised Captain Baker wasn't behind the wheel. Good. That would buy her more time.

She decided not to wait for the ambulance to take off, and walked purpose-

fully for her car in the back parking lot. If she could arrive at the hospital before the captain, perhaps she could sneak in to see Paige before the sheriff's deputy could interrogate the philanthropist.

"Tricia, wait!"

She turned and stopped. Russ. Again.

"Tricia!" he called again, and caught up with her. "What were you asking Paige? What's with the envelope you mentioned?"

So, he had heard her. And, typically, he was more interested in the story than in her. He hadn't been this interested on Tuesday before he'd dropped his bombshell about leaving Stoneham.

Her anger boiled over. But instead of coming up with a scathing retort, she settled on simplicity. "Leave me alone."

He reached for her arm, but she wrenched it away. "Come on, we've been friends a long time."

"A year. We were friends for a year. We're not friends anymore."

"Tricia!"

She pointed at the crowd still milling around the Sheriff's Department cruisers and the ambulance. "Go get your story. You need the practice if you're going to be a big-time crime beat reporter once again."

Russ glared at her for what seemed like a long time, and then he turned to stalk back down the driveway.

Tricia watched him for a couple of seconds before she started for her car. As she walked, she pulled her cell phone out of her purse, and punched in the preset button to dial Ginny's cell phone. She picked up on the second ring.

"Ginny, it's Tricia."

"Where are you? The store was supposed to open five minutes ago!"

"I had an errand to run. I'll be right there. By the way, didn't you once tell me that Brian has an aunt who works at the medical center in Nashua?"

"Sure. Her name's Elsie Temple. She works at the reception desk in the ER."

Bingo!

"Is there any chance you could pull in a favor for me?"

"I can try," Ginny said warily. "What do you have in mind?"

SEVENTEEN

Brian's Aunt Elsie wrung her hands nervously. A woman of fifty or so, her neatly coiffed hair was a dull jet-black, with not a gray root in sight. "If anyone but Ginny had asked me to do this, I'd have said no right on the spot," she said, bending to look beyond Tricia, checking for feet in the bathroom's four stalls, and any eavesdroppers. Finding no one there, she handed a visitor's badge to Tricia.

They'd had to meet in a second-floor ladies' room, well out of the way of any security cameras—just in case. Tricia had no desire to get this nervous wreck of a woman fired.

"If anyone asks who you're here to visit, say Smith. Seems like we've always got at least one in the ER at any given time. And for heaven's sake, don't let on who gave you the badge."

"I won't. And I promise I won't cause a disturbance. I only want a chance to talk to Mr.—"

"Don't tell me the patient's name. The less I know, the better. Holy smoke," Elsie nearly whimpered, "I can't believe I'm doing this."

Tricia peeled off the backing and applied the sticker to her jacket. "I'd better go. Thank you."

Elsie nodded, grabbing a paper towel from the wall dispenser and soaking it in cold water. She wrung it out before applying it to her forehead.

The ladies' room door closed behind Tricia, who felt like six kinds of a creep, but she had to get to Paige before Captain Baker did.

Was it possible she could find a dirty laundry bin and rustle up a lab coat? No, without a hospital name badge, she'd be outed in a heartbeat. Playing the visitor card was her best shot to get in and out of the ER without a hitch.

Head held high, Tricia made her way back to the emergency room lobby, looked around, and confidently strode through the doors into the patient-care area.

The ER reminded Tricia of a giant horseshoe, with patient cubicles grouped around center workstations filled with computer terminals. Patient names were written on whiteboards outside each cubicle. It had been at least ten min-

utes since Paige had been brought in. Since his injuries weren't life threatening, he wasn't liable to be rushed into surgery . . . she hoped.

Thanks to her visitor's badge, nurses and technicians passed by her without a second glance. Good. She passed the last cubicle on the first side, and started down the row to check out the others. Intent on reading the patient names, Tricia almost bumped into a man in a gray suit. Too late she recognized him as part of Paige's entourage.

"What are you doing here?" Gray Suit growled.

"I—I . . ." Caught—and without even finding Paige's cubicle. "I need to speak with Mr. Paige."

"Now is hardly the time." Gray Suit looked around, grabbed Tricia's elbow, and steered her toward the exit. Now she'd not only be shown the door, but probably be turned over to hospital security.

Gray Suit guided Tricia through the ER lobby, right past security, and out the Emergency entrance.

The cool air felt rather refreshing as Gray Suit kept Tricia moving down the sidewalk and away from the hospital. Finally he stopped and let go of her arm. "Paige won't tell you anything," he said at last.

"But you don't even know what I want to ask."

"I heard what you said back at the inn. You asked about an envelope from Pam Fredericks. He never saw it. I'm paid to make sure he *doesn't* see things like that."

"What happened to the envelope?"

"It was turned over to one of Mr. Paige's attorneys."

"Does the Sheriff's Department know about it?"

Gray Suit shook his head.

"Were you aware Pammy Fredericks was murdered?"

Gray Suit looked up sharply. "No, I wasn't. I don't pay attention to what happens in hick towns. But that explains why we didn't hear from her again."

"Don't you find it strange that Pammy attempted to blackmail Mr. Paige and then was found dead a day or so later?"

"Not at all. Sounds like she was bad news."

"A case could be made that someone in Mr. Paige's organization—say, a bodyguard like yourself—might be responsible for her death."

Gray Suit laughed. "Hey, lady, I ain't no James Bond, and I'm definitely not licensed to kill."

Tricia studied his face. He was probably no older than thirty; muscular, with sandy brown hair and dark eyes. Could he be a reader? No, too young. More likely a moviegoer.

"Now that you know about Pammy's death, you ought to report receiving

that envelope to Captain Baker of the Hillsborough County Sheriff's Department."

"I'll consider it."

At that moment, a Sheriff's Department cruiser pulled up to the side of the building. Sure enough, Grant Baker sat in the passenger seat.

"And here he is now. I hope you'll do the right thing," she told Gray Suit, "because if you don't, I will."

Baker got out of the car, making a beeline for Tricia and Gray Suit.

"What are you doing here, Ms. Miles?" he demanded.

"I came to see Mr. Paige after he was shot." She jerked a thumb in Gray Suit's direction. "This gentleman works for Mr. Paige. We were just discussing the envelope Pammy Fredericks sent to Mr. Paige last week."

Baker's eyes narrowed. "Envelope? What envelope?"

Tricia explained how Lois Kerr had seen Pammy making copies of the diary, and then immediately afterward she'd gone to the post office, where Ted Missile had seen Paige's name on the envelope.

"Why didn't you tell me this sooner?" Baker demanded.

"Maybe if you hadn't called me a terrier, I would have."

Gray Suit smirked.

"You know very well I meant you were probably stubborn—and now you've proved it."

Tricia balled her fists, willing herself not to haul off and smack the captain.

He'd already moved on. "And you are?" he asked Gray Suit.

"Jason Turner."

"What happened to this envelope?" Baker asked.

"She's right," Turner said with a nod in Tricia's direction. "The package did come to Mr. Paige's office. He never saw it. It's now in the hands of one of his attorneys."

"I'll need the name."

Turner gave it to him. Then he went on, "Look, I need to be inside with my employer. I'll be available for any other questions you have." He fished inside his suit jacket, came up with a business card holder, and handed the captain one of his cards.

Tricia watched him walk back through the emergency room entrance.

Baker stepped around to block Tricia from following. "Wasn't it just a couple of hours ago I told you to stay out of this investigation?"

"Shouldn't you be asking me about the shooting? I was a witness. In fact, what if those shots were intended to kill me—not Paige?"

"I doubt it," he said, and frowned.

Appalled at his disregard for her safety, Tricia felt her mouth drop open. "You're just as useless as your boss."

She turned, but Baker grabbed her by the arm. "Okay, what did you see?"

"Nothing."

Baker pursed his lips. "I'm not going to tell you again: stay out of this investigation."

She glared at him. "You're not my mother." And with that, she stepped off the sidewalk and marched toward her car—angry at him for bringing out the worst in her.

Moments later, Baker jogged to catch up with her. "Ms. Miles, please wait."

Tricia halted, still fuming.

Baker removed his trooper hat, holding it in front of him like a scolded child looking for mercy. "Ms. Miles, let me apologize. We seem to have gotten off track today."

An apology? From a member of the Sheriff's Department?

"I'm sincerely worried that you could get hurt if you continue to poke around and ask questions about Pamela Fredericks's death. As I understand it, you and your sister were nearly killed in a car accident last fall when you got involved with an unsavory character. And you were physically assaulted last spring. I don't want to see a repeat of either scenario."

Tricia found herself looking into Baker's sincere green eyes, and felt herself melting once again.

Damn those eyes!

She swallowed. "I don't know anything more about Pammy's death—or what she did in the hours before she died—than I've already told you."

"Will you please promise me that you'll stop looking into this?"

"How can I promise that? I run a store where every piece of stock involves a mystery. If somebody tells me something, of course I'm going to be curious about the implications. I can't deny my nature, Captain."

Baker exhaled an exasperated breath. "You can be curious all you want. Just don't act on that curiosity. Please!"

Tricia shrugged. "I'll try."

Baker squeezed his eyes shut, his lips pursing. Was he about to explode?

"I think you should ask Mr. Turner where he was at the time of Pammy's death," Tricia said. "How do we know he didn't decide to shut Pammy up after she'd tried to blackmail his boss?"

Baker sighed. "What would his motivation be?"

"Protecting his employer."

"I will definitely speak with him—and his employer, whenever he's available. Now, please put this out of your mind."

"Pammy Fredericks was my friend."

"You said she was 'sort of' your friend," Baker reminded her.

"Nevertheless, we had a twenty-four-year history, even if we weren't particularly close. And what headway have you made in the case?"

"I'm not at liberty to talk about it."

"In other words: none. How about the shooter at the inn? Have you scouted out the woods across the road from the inn?"

"My men are doing that now."

"What are the odds it's the same person who shot at my bedroom window?"

"Of course, we can't rule that out. Yet from what I understand, Mr. Paige was not shot with a BB gun or air pistol."

"Well, of course not. Although as far as we know, they haven't dug a slug out of him yet."

"As soon as I talk to the doctors, I'll know more." Baker set his high-crowned hat back on his head. "Good day, Ms. Miles."

"Good day, Captain Baker."

He turned away, and Tricia continued on to her car. Thinking... thinking.

Turner knew the contents of Pammy's envelope. Baker would probably know the contents of that envelope within the hour. She wanted to know, too. Pammy had wanted money to keep the paternity of the journal author's child quiet. Paige was the object of her blackmail scheme.

That explained why Pammy had been killed, but not who had done it. All attention would be riveted on Paige or his associates, as it should be.

End of mystery, at least from Tricia's point of view.

Maybe.

She unlocked her car and climbed in. It was just as well. She had a wedding to host on Sunday, and losing Mr. Everett to his honeymoon during prime leaf-peeping season, she'd be too busy to think about Pammy's death.

It was all for the best.

Why did she have a niggling feeling that she had missed something?

That niggling continued into the early afternoon. Tricia rang up a thirty-nine dollar and eighty-five cent purchase for three Rex Stout mysteries while on autopilot. She kept turning over in her mind what little she knew about Pammy's interactions with Paige and the freegans; neither Gray Suit nor Ginny's friends had been willing to share much.

Ginny staggered to the register, dumping a stack of old books, most missing

their dust covers, on the counter for what looked to be the best sale of the day. "This lady here sure is a fan of Ngaio Marsh."

"Yes, I can see," Tricia said with delight, and quickly totaled up the sale. Two hundred and twenty-seven dollars and fifty-five cents. Not a bad afternoon at that.

Ginny bagged up the books and sent the customer on her way before looking at her watch. "Almost lunchtime. I'm having celery dipped in one hundred percent virgin olive oil."

"Your take from the other night?"

Ginny laughed. "They were the best things we found that night."

"I've been thinking a lot about our Dumpster-diving expedition," Tricia said.

"Sorry you had to come on such a dull night."

"It was very interesting. If nothing else, you have a diverse group of friends."

"I wouldn't exactly say we're *all* friends. But we work together well."

"Tell me, is Lisa always so annoying?"

"Yes. Pete and Brian have been friends since they were kids. Unfortunately, Lisa now comes with the package. She's the only militant freegan in the group. Well, Eugenia thinks she is because she once ate vegan for an entire month, but Lisa wouldn't agree."

"I noticed she hardly spoke to Eugenia. They aren't friends, either?"

Ginny frowned. "It's all so complicated—like a soap opera, really. See, Pammy annoyed Eugenia by telling her she knew about her biological parents, and that for a price she might reveal that information."

"What?"

"I thought I told you all this."

"No. Please go on."

"Well, Eugenia's a bit sensitive about being adopted. Her parents didn't tell her until she was about twelve. Mrs. Hirt told her that her biological mother had died and had never named a father on the birth certificate. Eugenia never thought about tracking down her biological parents until Pammy came along and dangled information in front of her. Eugenia was all upset and told Lisa, who was a real bitch about it. She told Eugenia to hold the drama and get her head together, or see a shrink or something."

"Full of compassion, that one," Tricia commented.

"You said it. Lisa also thinks it's great that somebody's going around ruining all the kids' carved pumpkins. She said there was never such a waste of good farmland as that used for raising pumpkins. She says it's a crop that can't be used for anything but frivolity. I've got to admit that in a way she's right. Still, what doesn't get sold can always be used as compost."

Tricia rolled her eyes, and Ginny laughed but soon sobered. "Anyway,

Mrs. Hirt was—" Ginny gave a wry smile. "Well, she was *hurt* that Eugenia would even want to find out about her biological parents."

"Doesn't every adopted child at least wonder about their birth parents? And what kind of proof did Pammy offer?" Tricia asked, thinking about the diary.

Ginny shrugged. "I only got the story thirdhand. Eugenia and I aren't really chummy. But apparently Pammy knew some deep, dark secret about Eugenia, something the poor kid never told anyone about. She was practically hysterical when Pammy casually mentioned it."

"Mentioned what?"

"Lisa didn't know. Eugenia may have been upset, but she wasn't willing to share what she was upset about—at least not with Lisa."

Had Eugenia told her father all this? She'd said she'd asked him not to allow Pammy to join them on their Dumpster-diving expeditions. And conveniently soon after, Pammy was dead.

Sweet little Eugenia a murderer?

No. Tricia refused to believe it.

And yet . . .

"How did you guys get tied up with Eugenia and her father?"

"Brian and Pete have known him since they were little kids. He coached soccer . . . or was it softball?" She frowned. "I'm not really sure. But we've been going out on our expeditions with Eugenia and Joe for at least a year, if not two."

"This morning Captain Baker asked me if I knew any freegans."

Ginny's eyes widened. "What did you tell him?"

"I skirted the question. But it might be a good idea for you or one of your friends to talk to him."

"What for? We don't know anything about Pammy's death."

"Are you sure?"

"I trust those guys—with my life."

"Even Lisa?"

Ginny didn't answer.

"If he asks me again—point blank—I can't lie."

"No, I guess you can't. I'll call the others and see what they want to do."

"Maybe you could all talk to Captain Baker at once."

"Maybe," Ginny said, without conviction. A customer entered the store, and Ginny jumped to attention. "Can I help you find something?"

Tricia looked through the shop's big display window. From this vantage point, she couldn't see the Bookshelf Diner, where Eugenia worked. What deep secret had the poor girl hidden all her life? What did Pammy know about her, how had she found out, and how cruel was she to threaten the kid?

But Eugenia a murderer? No way. Tricia had met her parents and deeply

admired her—apparently adoptive—mother. Besides, Eugenia couldn't possibly have the physical strength to pick Pammy up and toss her into the garbage cart. It had to be a man who did that.

That brought her back to Stuart Paige, who also didn't look physically capable of killing Pammy. And anyway, maybe the idea hadn't been to kill Pammy at all. Someone had gotten angry at Pammy and probably decided to scare her. From what the technician had said the day Pammy died, she'd struggled to free herself from the garbage cart before suffocating.

It could have just been a tragic accident. Someone trying to scare someone who'd used scare tactics and blackmail for her own profit. Which brought Tricia back to Jason Turner. He seemed to enjoy being a bully.

Tricia sighed. She simply didn't have enough information. Eugenia might like her as a customer, but she wouldn't reveal to Tricia whatever secret she'd hidden her entire life. Nor was it likely her parents would speak about whatever it was Eugenia found so shameful.

Once again, Tricia found herself back to square one.

EIGHTEEN

Lunch came and went. The UPS man delivered the little refrigerator and microwave Tricia had ordered off the Internet. The employee break room would soon be a reality. The next steps were to find a table, something to act as a counter, and some reasonably comfortable chairs.

Ginny was as excited as a child on Christmas morning. "Do you mind if I take the appliances upstairs and get them set up?"

"Oh, they're much too heavy for you to cart up the stairs."

Ginny waved off her protests. "No, they're not. If you could see what I've lifted and carried these past few months while working on our house, you'd know I could've been a successful stevedore."

Tricia laughed. "Where did you come up with that description?"

Ginny thought about it. "I don't know—some book I read. I've been reading a lot of classic mysteries lately."

"Yes, I know. And I think it's wonderful. But there's nowhere to put them yet."

"I'll just take them out of the boxes and set them on the floor. I can come in early one day and we can set them up. When we get some furniture, that is."

"I don't want you to get hurt. If they're too heavy, don't mess with them. Maybe I can get Bob to help us take them up. He ought to be good for something."

Ginny giggled and took off for the back of the store.

Business picked up, and Tricia waited on several customers, helping them find their favorite authors and ringing up the sales. In between, she was preoccupied with thoughts of how to approach furnishing the break room. She was staring out the window, looking at nothing, when a Sheriff's Department cruiser pulled up and parked right outside Haven't Got a Clue. She watched as a tight-lipped Captain Baker emerged from behind the driver's seat, slammed his regulation hat onto his head, and marched for the door.

Ginny reappeared and stood behind Tricia. "Uh-oh. This looks like trouble."

Baker opened the door, letting it slam against the wall, stepped inside, and let it bang shut before he advanced on the sales register like an angry bull.

"Where are they?" he demanded, shoving the red-covered diary at Tricia.

"Where are what?"

"The missing pages. There are at least two sheets—four pages—missing."

"There are?"

"Would I be here demanding you return them if I didn't think so?"

"I don't know what you're talking about."

He opened the book to the middle. "Read the last sentence on this page and see if it makes sense to you."

Tricia scanned the cursive text at the bottom of the left-hand page. *I've asked him for money so that I can*—her gaze traveled to the top of the right-hand page—*and I'm not about to make waves. That would insure I never get him back again.*

Tricia frowned. She must have been tired when she originally read that segment of the journal. Otherwise she would've noticed that the sentence didn't make sense. Unless the writer had been fatigued herself, and lost her train of thought. She noticed the diary's signature threads were loose, as though pages had been ripped out. Funny she hadn't noticed that before—maybe because the lighting in her living room wasn't as bright as it could be.

Tricia handed back the journal. "What makes you think I took the page or pages out?"

"You were the last one to have the book in your possession."

"But why would you think I tore them out? Isn't it more likely Pammy would've done it herself? Or how about the diary's original owner?"

"Someone did it. If the diary was found here, perhaps the missing pages are here, too."

Tricia straightened in indignation. "What do you propose? To tear my shop apart looking for them?"

"It's an option."

She stood tall. "I don't think so."

He stood taller. "I can get a warrant."

It was all Tricia could do not to explode. "Captain, Pammy was unsupervised in my store for less than two minutes—more like one minute—before she left here on Monday. She only had time to hide the diary. My sister and I took nearly every book off the back shelves before she found it. Pammy could've had those pages in her suitcase or her purse. And don't forget, she tried to confront Stuart Paige at the Food Shelf's dedication after she left here. Isn't it likely she would've had them with her?"

"No. Because if he or his associates took them from her, she'd have no leverage for blackmail."

"No one ever said Pammy was the brightest light on the Christmas tree."

Baker had no rebuttal. Instead he turned to Ginny. "Why didn't you tell me you were a freegan?"

Ginny looked like a deer standing in headlights. "You never asked."

He turned on Tricia. "You knew I was looking for freegans. Why didn't you tell me your employee was one?"

Ginny had already used up the best excuse. "I didn't think they could help you. I've already talked to them, and—"

Baker lost it. He yanked his hat from his head and threw it on the counter, startling both women. "When are you going to get it through that head of yours that I'm running this investigation, not you?"

"How did you find out about Ginny?"

"The convenience store owner told me."

Ginny's eyes blazed. "Did he also mention his son is one of us, too?"

Baker spoke through clenched teeth. "No, he didn't." He looked down at the journal still clutched in his hand.

"What's your next move?" Tricia asked. "You've tracked Pammy's movements the morning of her death. She could've dropped off those pages at any one of her stops."

"Yes. I suppose I'll have to go back and interview everyone who spoke with her that day."

Tricia pointed to her watch. "Time's a-wasting."

This time it was Baker who looked like he wanted to slug somebody. Instead, he jabbed his index finger in Ginny's direction. "I'm going to call for another deputy to come and question you. Stay here. Don't talk to any of your friends. Do you hear me?"

Ginny's head bobbed, her eyes still wide.

"I'll talk to you later," he told Tricia, then grabbed his hat, and stormed out of the shop.

Ginny winced. "Are you actively trying to make an enemy out of him?"

Tricia shook her head, almost as angry as Baker had been. "We started off on the right foot, but things have gone downhill since Monday. Maybe it's my destiny to never get along with law enforcement. Me, who's a fan of police procedurals."

"Maybe you should have gone into police work instead of bookselling. For you, it would be just as dangerous as owning this bookstore."

Tricia chose to believe Ginny was kidding.

She glanced down the street and saw Baker enter the Happy Domestic, the first place Pammy had put in a job application. Next up would be Russ at the *Stoneham Weekly News*, and then Angelica at Booked for Lunch.

Was it possible Pammy had dumped the pages at the last place she'd visited before her death?

"Watch the shop, Ginny. I've got to go see Angelica."

"Sure thing. But what am I going to say to the deputy who comes to interview me? Do you think I need a lawyer?"

Tricia shook her head. "Just tell the truth. You'll be okay." She headed for the door. "I'll be back as soon as I can."

Tricia jaywalked across Main Street and entered Booked for Lunch. The place was a madhouse. Every table was full, as were the stools at the counter. Angelica waited on a table of four while a strident voice at the counter called, "Miss! Miss!"

Angelica looked up and saw Tricia. "See what that guy wants, will you?"

Tricia jumped behind the counter. "How can I help you, sir?"

"More coffee," he said, shoving his stained cup toward her. She reached behind her and grabbed a coffeepot from the warmer. "Not decaf, you idiot!"

Tricia looked down. Sure enough, the pot's handle was orange. "Sorry." She switched carafes and poured. "Do you need creamer with that?"

"Of course I do," he snapped. "Why doesn't the owner hire competent help? First that stupid waitress, and now you."

It took all Tricia's resolve not to pour coffee on his lap.

A little bell rang from somewhere in the vicinity of the kitchen.

"Miss, I could use a refill, too," said a voice at the other end of the counter.

Tricia poured, and offered everyone else a refill.

Angelica rushed to the counter to grab a bottle of ketchup. "What are you doing here—not that I care. I can use the help." She grabbed a jar of mustard, too.

The little bell rang again; twice this time.

"Captain Baker says there're pages missing from Pammy's diary. He'll probably be here any minute to search the place."

"Not until I close! And why would he think she left the pages here?"

"This was the last place she visited before she died. Have you seen anything that looks like diary pages?"

"Miss, where's my ketchup?" a voice demanded.

Tricia threw an angry glare at the offending customer. "Remind me why you wanted to start this business."

"I'm shorthanded, and they want their food when they want it—not when I can get it to them."

"Captain Baker also found out Ginny is a freegan. He was furious because I didn't tell him."

A little bell rang madly from the kitchen.

"What is that?" Tricia asked.

"Jake's got my two burgers and fries up. Can you go grab them? They're for table four."

"I've got my own business to run, you know."

"Please?" Angelica pleaded.

Tricia turned. If their father could see the two of them working as waitresses—after all the money he'd spent on Ivy League colleges—he'd have a fit.

She collected the plates and delivered them to table four, grateful Angelica had hung a little numbered ceramic tile above each table. After she'd collected ketchup and mustard for the table and had been assured the couple needed nothing else, she went behind the counter once again. No one was screaming for anything, so she crouched down and began her search.

Though the café had been open only a little over two weeks, Angelica had accumulated a wide assortment of junk behind the counter. Condiments, jumbo coffee filters, packages of napkins, a case of cocoa mix, coffee, nondairy creamer, order pads, a box of pens, odd dishes, silverware, and heaven only knew what else. What she didn't find were the missing pages of Pammy's diary.

"I'd like my bill, please," the counter's crab said.

Tricia looked up. Angelica was conversing with a foursome at table two. "Ange. Check needed over here."

Angelica didn't turn, but gave a backward wave.

"Miss," crabby insisted.

"Ange!"

Angelica turned, reaching into her apron pocket for her order pad. "Sorry, honey," she said, handing the patron his check. "We're shorthanded."

"I'd like to speak to the manager," crabby demanded.

"You're looking at her," she said, tearing another sheet from her pad.

"You ought to hire competent help," he said, glaring at Tricia.

"As I told you, sir, we're shorthanded. Tricia here came over just to give me a hand. Of course, if you'd like to apply for a job as a waiter, I'd be willing to look at your résumé."

The man grabbed the check, thumbed through his wallet, and yanked out a few bills, which he tossed on the counter.

Angelica picked up the money. "Hey, a fifty-cent tip. That's forty-nine cents more than I expected."

The customer stomped out of the café.

"Ange," Tricia whispered, "you shouldn't be so flip with your customers. You know the old saying, 'the customer's always—' "

"Right," Angelica finished. "Well, guess what—sometimes they're not right. Sometimes they're downright rude." She turned back to the people sitting at the counter. "Anybody need another round of coffee?" she asked cheerfully.

Nobody took her up on it.

She turned back to her sister. "How long can you stay, Trish? The lunchtime rush will be over in another fifteen or twenty minutes."

"I guess I could stay that long. But I'm totally incompetent as a waitress."

"It doesn't take a rocket scientist to bus tables. You can start with the stuff on the counter. Afterward, I'll give you a hand looking for Pammy's pages."

"Fair enough."

Tricia scooped up the dishes and took them to the kitchen. Before she could escape, Jake, the cook, had her wrapped in an apron with her sweater sleeves pushed up as far as they would go, and up to her elbows in suds, washing dishes. Just what she needed—dishpan hands.

But Angelica had been right about the lunch crowd. Within fifteen minutes most of the customers had left the café.

"Oh, Trish, you are an angel," Angelica said, swooping in with yet another load of dirty dishes. She scraped the leftovers into a plastic tub and handed the plates and silverware to Tricia.

Jake, who'd been cleaning the grill area, untied his apron. "I'm off to my second job," he said, and grabbed his jacket from the peg. See you tomorrow, Angie."

"'Bye, Jake."

The door slammed behind him.

"He's got a second job?" Tricia asked.

"I pay him better than average, but it's still not enough to make ends meet. I just hope he doesn't quit on me." Angelica handed Tricia a towel. "Dry off, and we'll see if we can't find those papers you're looking for."

Before Tricia could remove her apron, a voice called out from the dining room. "Ms. Miles."

"Oh, no," she groaned, recognizing Captain Baker's voice.

"Which Ms. Miles do you think he's calling?" Angelica asked.

"We'd better both go, although my being here is sure to make him angry—and he wasn't in a good mood when he left my store."

Angelica led the way back to the dining area. "Captain Baker, how nice to see you again." What an actress! She actually sounded pleased to see the man. "Did I tell you my cookbook, *Easy-Does-It Cooking*, is going to be published on June first?"

"Yes. More than once." He looked past her, and saw Tricia. "What are *you* doing here?"

Tricia indicated the damp apron still covering her sweater and the front of her slacks. "Helping my sister. She's shorthanded."

"Bull! You came over here to see if those diary pages were here."

"Well, you can rest assured they're not," Angelica said. "If they were, I'd have seen them in the last four days."

"I did take a peek behind the counter, but couldn't find them," Tricia admitted. "And if I had found them, of course I would have turned them over to you. I want you to find Pammy's killer before someone else gets hurt or dies."

"Do you mind if I have a look?" Baker asked.

"You'd better say yes, Ange. He's already threatened me with a warrant."

He shot a blistering glare in Tricia's direction.

"Of course you can look," Angelica said. "But if you tear the place apart, you're going to put it back the way it was." There was no arguing with *that* tone.

Baker's hostility backed off a couple of points. "Thank you."

"Why don't you start under the counter?" Angelica suggested. He moved away. "Tricia, I think you should go back to your store now. Thank you for helping me with the dishes." She said it loud enough for Baker to hear her.

Tricia untied the apron and handed it to her sister, making a show of it. "You're welcome. If you get in a jam again, you know you can always count on me."

"I'll hold you to it," Angelica whispered. "And I'll give you a full report the minute he leaves."

Tricia nodded and headed for the door.

"We'll talk later, Ms. Miles," Baker told her again.

Not a threat, a promise.

NINETEEN

TRICIA GLANCED AT her watch. She'd been gone a lot longer than she'd expected—and with nothing to show for it but chapped hands. Another Sheriff's Department cruiser was now parked outside the Cookery, but its driver was inside Haven't Got a Clue—and so was a crowd of customers, with no one to serve them. A chagrined Ginny sat on one of the chairs in the nook while Deputy Henderson grilled her.

Tricia jumped behind the register. It took nearly ten minutes before she'd taken care of those ready to pay and be on their way, before she could finally leave her post to join Ginny.

Henderson slapped his notebook closed. "Thank you, Ms. Wilson. You've been very helpful."

"I don't see how. I told you, I don't know anything."

The deputy nodded to Tricia and headed for the door.

"Are you okay?" Tricia asked once the deputy had left.

Ginny nodded. "But my friends are going to kill me for dropping a dime on them."

Tricia couldn't help but smile at the phrase. Ginny must've picked it up from one of the mysteries in stock—or was she more street savvy than Tricia had believed?

"No luck finding those missing pages?" Ginny asked.

Tricia shook her head. "I didn't think I would." She thought back to her last encounter with Jason Turner. "Only one person I know read those pages. Jason Turner opened that envelope. He read the pages that Pammy mailed to Stuart Paige. But if Captain Baker is still looking for them, Turner must not have told Paige or the rest of his entourage what they said."

"What makes you think they're so important? I mean, if she took them out, maybe she *didn't* want Paige to see them."

Tricia hadn't thought of that. The references to the baby's father were vague—maybe deliberately so. Could Pammy have concocted the whole diary-blackmail scheme by writing a fake diary?

No. She wasn't that smart.

Could the missing pages point the finger at the real father, making the

diary useless as a blackmail tool? That made a lot more sense. Had she destroyed them? Knowing Pammy, that didn't seem likely, either.

"How are you going to get this Paige guy to talk?" Ginny asked. "He doesn't know you. He's got no reason to tell you anything."

"That's true, but I've got nothing to lose by trying." Tricia glanced at her watch. Almost two o'clock. "I hate to keep asking you to cover for me, but—"

Ginny waved a hand in the direction of the door. "Go!"

Tricia went to get her coat from its peg at the back of the store. But first, she made a brief stop in her apartment to pick up something—something that might be the key to getting her inside Paige's hospital room.

The medical center's brightly lit corridors were buzzing with activity. Scrubs-clad nurses came and went, monitoring equipment beeped and buzzed, and as visiting hours were in full swing, people in street clothes seemed to be everywhere.

Tricia thought the hospital might refuse to tell her Stuart Paige's room number, but when she asked at the lobby reception desk, they directed her to the third floor.

The door to Paige's room was open. She stepped inside. He lay on the bed, which was cranked up to a semisitting position. Eyes closed, he looked pale, and older than he had a mere six hours ago.

"Mr. Paige?" Tricia called softly.

The door to the private room's bathroom opened, and a figure stepped out. "What are *you* doing here? Get out!" Turner ordered.

"Jason?" came a feeble voice from within the room.

Tricia looked back to the rumpled figure on the bed. Paige's eyes were now open.

"I'm sorry, sir, but you have an unwanted guest."

Turner grabbed Tricia's elbow to usher her out.

"No, let her come in," Paige said, his voice weak.

Turner let loose, and Tricia tiptoed into the room.

"Please, sit down," Paige said, indicating the chair next to his bed.

Tricia took the offered seat. Why was it hospitals provided only uncomfortable chairs for visitors? She clutched her purse on her lap, unsure of what to say. Paige solved that problem.

"You were at the Food Shelf's dedication. And at the Chamber of Commerce breakfast this morning."

"I'm sorry I arrived too late to hear most of your speech."

His smile was weak. "I don't think you missed much."

"I don't know—a new dialysis center could be a boon for Stoneham."

"It will certainly be a boon to dialysis patients in the tristate area. A press release went out earlier today. It'll be on the news tonight, if you're truly interested."

Which explained why Russ had attended this particular Chamber meeting.

"And you are?"

"Tricia Miles. I own the mystery bookstore in Stoneham—Haven't Got a Clue."

"And do you?" he asked.

"Do I what?"

"Have a clue?" He leaned back against his pillow. "Jason has told me about the diary and the pages your friend sent to my office. Now you'll want to know about my relationship with Marcie Jane Collins—everybody else does."

Tricia swallowed. The woman who'd died when Paige had crashed his car into Portsmouth Harbor. "Did she have your baby?"

He blinked. "That's a new one. Everyone else wants to know about the night she died."

"I read the story on the Internet. M.J. died about a year after she gave birth to a child. A child she apparently gave up for adoption. Was it your child?" she asked again.

Paige sighed, looking even more tired.

"Sir, you don't have to answer this woman's questions. You don't even have to put up with her being in this room," Turner said.

Paige waved a weak hand to quiet his employee. "It's going to come out eventually. I'd rather tell my story to this young lady than to a TV reporter."

"Sir, we can issue a statement. There's no need to—"

"Jason, why don't you go get a cup of coffee and leave us alone for about fifteen minutes?"

Turner looked ready to protest, but nodded. He backed up. "I'll be just outside if you need me," he said, then turned and left the room, closing the heavy door behind him.

"He's very protective of me," Paige said.

"I can see that," Tricia said. Fifteen minutes wasn't much time, and she didn't want to waste it. "Had you ever met Pammy Fredericks?"

Paige shook his head. "I never saw the woman, but Jason tells me she called our offices several times. She mailed us some papers, asking for money or she'd reveal something about my sordid past." The ghost of a smile crept across his lips. "As if anything else could be as embarrassing as what everybody already knows."

"You were saying about your—" Had the woman been his friend, lover, mistress?

"M.J." He smiled. "She liked being called that. Like in the Spiderman comics."

"What did the papers Pammy sent you contain?"

"According to Jason, nothing. At least nothing with my name on it. Just ramblings about hooking 'him.'"

Tricia opened her purse, took out a folded piece of paper, and handed it to him. He took it, fumbled to straighten it out on his lap, and gave a shuddering breath.

"That's her handwriting, all right. Where did you get this?"

"Pammy hid the diary in my shop. I made a copy of it before I handed it over to Captain Baker of the Sheriff's Department."

Paige nodded. He pointed to the date in the top left corner. "See this? At the time the diary was written, I was out of M.J.'s life—had been for at least a year or so."

"Yes, I understand you two had broken up for a while."

He looked at her through narrowed eyes.

"I read several accounts of your colorful past online," she explained.

He shook his head, perturbed. "I wasn't very stable in those days. I drove too fast—drank too much. She worked on my father's clerical staff." He was quiet for a moment, lost in thought. "After we started going out, Dad grew to love her. He hoped she'd straighten me out. Sadly, she only managed that in death. He didn't know she was almost as wild as I was, which was part of the reason we originally broke up. When we got back together, it was as if that wild streak in her took over. She didn't care about anything. We did a lot of foolish things together. Things I'm deeply ashamed of now." He sighed. "No matter what good I've done these last nineteen years, it will never make up for what happened that rainy night in Portsmouth."

"I read that the police theorized the car hydroplaned."

He nodded sadly. "We'd both been drinking. Truth was, at that point, M.J. drank more than I did. She said it helped her forget."

"Forget her child?"

He looked up sharply. "How did you know?"

"I read most of her diary. M.J. was very upset. I take it the child had birth defects. She called the baby . . . *it*."

"M.J. made the mistake of having an affair with a married man after we had parted ways—I never did know his name."

"What happened to the baby?"

"It went into foster care. The people who took it in eventually adopted it."

"Now you're calling the baby 'it,'" Tricia admonished.

"I'm sorry, but I don't know what sex it ultimately ended up being."

Tricia blinked. "Excuse me?"

"Didn't M.J. write about what was wrong with the child in her diary?"

"No."

"It was born with multiple sex organs. The baby needed gender assignment surgery. M.J. saw it as a punishment for her affair."

"The baby was a . . . hermaphrodite?"

He nodded. "I believe the more popular term now is intersex. To make things worse, M.J. suffered from postpartum depression. It wasn't as well understood in those days. Sometimes not understood today, either."

"You seem to know a lot about it."

"My foundation has contributed funds to study it, to find new medications that can help women in need."

Paige closed his eyes, and Tricia decided he'd had enough traumas for one day. She reached out to touch his arm. "Thank you for seeing me, Mr. Paige. I'm sorry I had to drag all this up for you again."

His smile was tepid. "I suppose I'll have to go over it with Captain Baker at some point in the future, but I don't understand what significance it can have to his case. Ms. Fredericks may have tried to blackmail me, but she never would've succeeded. I wouldn't have paid. The child wasn't mine."

Tricia shook her head. Pammy had probably figured blackmailing Paige was worth a shot, withholding the missing pages that would back up his claim of innocence. A paternity test would've cleared him in a heartbeat, but Pammy probably hadn't been smart enough to consider that, either. There could only be one reason she'd withheld those pages: they had to have named the baby's real father.

If Pammy had been smart, she would've destroyed the pages. But time and again Pammy had proven she wasn't that sharp. Unless she reserved the pages in some kind of backup plan in case Paige wouldn't pay. Could she have saved them to blackmail the baby's real father? But why? Unless that man had money or something else that would improve her life.

It just didn't make sense.

Then again, Pammy had never made sense.

Tricia noticed Paige staring at her. "Do you read mysteries, Mr. Paige?"

"Yes, as a matter of fact I do. Dick Francis is my favorite author."

"As I mentioned, I run a mystery bookstore in Stoneham. May I send you a few titles?"

"I'm missing several of his early books from my collection. Do you have a copy of *Bonecrack* at your store?"

"I sure do, and I'd be glad to send it over."

That would be very kind of you. Let me pay you for—"

"You'll do no such thing. It would be my pleasure to give it to you."

"You're very kind. Thank you." He handed her the sheet of paper.

"Would you like to keep it, as sort of a remembrance?"

He shook his head. "I don't like to remember M.J. from that last year of her life. I prefer to think about the days she worked for my father, before all the unhappiness consumed her."

Tricia nodded and rose from her chair. "Thank you for seeing me."

Turner stood outside the door, his expression dark.

"I hope you didn't upset the old man. It wouldn't be good for him."

"Actually, I'm surprised the hospital kept him here. The paramedic said his injury wasn't life threatening."

"No, but his kidney disease is. He's already had one failed transplant, and has been back on dialysis for years. So far they haven't been able to locate another donor kidney for him."

"Surely a man in his position—"

"Oh, I'm sure he could buy one from a living donor—but that's not his style."

Tricia remembered how pale Paige had been at the Food Shelf's opening. No wonder he'd stepped up his philanthropic gifts. If he felt his time was growing short, he might want to see the fruits of his generosity.

"I'm very sorry to hear that. I'll be sending over a book for him. I'll have it left at the reception desk. May I call you to be sure Mr. Paige has received it?"

Turner reached into his pocket and withdrew his business card holder once again. He handed her a card. "Please don't stir up any trouble." His concern was genuine.

"Believe me, I'm trying to stop trouble from erupting."

"Then you'd better be careful. Being in the middle of something you don't understand could get you killed."

"Is that a threat?"

He shook his head. "Just an observation."

IT WAS NEARING five o'clock by the time Tricia returned to Haven't Got a Clue. As usual, customer traffic had thinned. In fact, there were no customers in the store. Ginny leaned over the sales desk and looked up as the door opened and Tricia strode in. She'd been reading a copy of *This Old House* magazine.

"Looks pretty dead," Tricia said, indicating the lack of warm bodies in the shop.

Ginny nodded. "Thanks to the Pumpkin Festival, I don't think we've pulled in ten dollars in the last hour. How did it go at the hospital?"

"It went. I'm convinced Stuart Paige and his people had nothing to do with Pammy's death."

"How come?"

"He's too nice. And he's not well. In fact, I promised to send him a book at the hospital. How would you like to go home early tonight?"

Ginny frowned. "Didn't you say he'd been taken to the medical center in Nashua?"

"I'll give you gas money. If you go there and back, you should still be home at least a half hour earlier than usual."

Ginny nodded. "Okay. That'll give me time to slap some joint compound on the living room's new Sheetrock before dinner. Let me get my coat."

Two minutes later, Tricia had wrapped up a copy of *Bonecrack*, given Ginny Turner's card with instructions to call him when she arrived at the hospital, and sent her on her way. Tricia stared at the clock. She still had another hour and forty-five minutes before closing time. After that, she'd go upstairs, scrounge in the fridge, and settle down with a good book.

She glared at the phone. It wasn't going to ring. It wouldn't be Russ, calling to apologize for this morning. His phone message said he wanted to talk, but he hadn't called again. That meant he'd only been trying to smooth things over. To assuage his guilt, perhaps? And anyway, if he was the photographer at Grace and Mr. Everett's wedding, he could talk to her then. He probably knew about the new job by now. Maybe he'd even gloat.

Now she was being ridiculous.

Tricia glanced out the window. A light still glowed inside Booked for Lunch. Angelica was probably holed up in her café's kitchen, preparing the food for Grace and Mr. Everett's wedding. She hadn't called to tell Tricia the results of Captain Baker's search, as she'd promised. Or if she had, Ginny hadn't mentioned it.

Tricia picked up the heavy receiver on the old 1930s phone. She dialed the number and waited as the phone rang and rang. Twelve, thirteen, fourteen times before it was answered with a testy "What do you want?"

"Ange? It's Tricia. You said you'd call me after Captain Baker left your place."

"You caught me at a bad time. I'm working on the food for Grace's wedding."

"And?" Tricia prompted.

"Captain Baker didn't find a damn thing. I could've told him he wouldn't—but why listen to me?"

"I've been to see Stuart Paige. Lots to report, but it doesn't get me any closer to finding out who killed Pammy."

"Why don't you just let the captain work this out? I mean, why are you so interested?"

Tricia wasn't sure she could answer that question.

"Ginny said it's been dead here for the last hour. I'm feeling discouraged. In fact, I may even close the store early tonight."

"Terrific. Then come over here and help me with these miniquiches."

"You know I can't cook."

"You just have to assemble ingredients; I'll do the cooking."

Tricia sighed. "Why not? I'll be over in about ten minutes."

"See you," Angelica said, and hung up.

Tricia hung up the CLOSED sign on the door, pulled the shades, and put the day's receipts in the safe. She checked to see that Miss Marple was asleep in one of the chairs in the nook before she grabbed her jacket and purse, and headed out the door.

Angelica was waiting for her, and let her into the darkened café. "Come on back to the kitchen."

With only the dim security lights on, the café's usually bright and cheery interior looked dated and unwelcoming. It was far more pleasing in the light of day. Tricia followed her sister to the cramped kitchen.

The work counter was littered with bags of flour, cartons of eggs, and mounds of what looked like seaweed on a platter. "What's that?' Tricia said, turning up her nose as she hung her jacket on a peg next to Angelica's.

"Thawed frozen spinach. You can squeeze it dry while I whip up the eggs. I've already got all the little pastry shells made. See?" Angelica pointed to the stack of minimuffin pans and their contents. "I'll bake and freeze these tonight, and then thaw them and pop them in the oven on Sunday morning, just before the ceremony."

Tricia's lip curled as she contemplated the mass of wet, limp spinach. "Spinach for breakfast? What were you thinking?"

"These days, people don't eat enough fruits and vegetables."

Tricia sighed. "No matter how many veggies you put in a quiche, it'll never be a healthy food. You'll be putting Grace's guests in danger of a heart attack."

"Get on with your work," Angelica said.

"Okay, what do I do first?"

"Wash your hands. And scrub them like you were about to do surgery. There's a nailbrush on the sink. Use paper towels to dry them. And don't touch the rim of the garbage pail when you throw them away."

Tricia did as she was told, while Angelica cracked eggs into a large plastic bowl.

"Tell me all about what happened after you left here this afternoon," Angelica said.

Tricia told her tale as she squeezed cold, green juice from the spinach until her hands ached.

"I'm betting Pammy tore those pages out of the diary because they would've proved Paige wasn't the father of M.J.'s child. And knowing Pammy, if she

couldn't wring money out of Paige, she might have tried to go after the baby's real father."

"That doesn't make sense," Angelica said, as she beat eggs with a big metal whisk. "Why would the real father care about the baby twenty years later? At this point in time, he might not even be married to the same wife. Hardly anybody lasts twenty-plus years of marriage these days. We're prime examples."

"But just say he was—that news could destroy his marriage."

Angelica shrugged. "So many people harp about the sanctity of marriage—but if it's so sacred, why is this country's divorce rate more than fifty percent?"

Tricia finished squeezing the last of the spinach. She dried her hands. "I'm convinced that Pammy left those pages here in this café."

"Don't get your hopes up. Captain Baker was pretty thorough in his search. He did everything but empty the bags of flour."

Tricia's eyes widened. "Where was Pammy working before I found her in the garbage cart?"

"Here in the kitchen. She was washing dishes."

Tricia looked up at the sacks of flour and sugar on the shelf above the triple sink. Most of them hadn't been opened.

"Let's go back to the day Pammy died. Jake had left for the day. You were busy out front with the last of the customers—or cleaning up or something, right?"

"That's right," Angelica agreed.

"So Pammy was here in the kitchen, all alone. What if someone called her out to the back of the café? If she had the pages on her, and she recognized the voice, she might have stuffed them into something really fast—if she wasn't prepared to give them up just yet."

"I told you," Angelica said patiently, "Captain Baker tore this place apart."

Tricia studied everything on the shelves above her. A big glass jar held white crystals. Sugar or salt?

"Why is that stuff up there in a jar—and what is it?"

"Sugar. I had ants just after I started stocking the place. I didn't want to spray chemicals around my food prep area, so I sprinkled some borax on the shelves and put my sugar in jars. I haven't seen an ant since."

Tricia reached for the jar. The lid did not want to come loose.

"Give it to me," Angelica said. Since the opening of the café, her nails had taken a beating, but her hands were bigger and stronger than Tricia's. She wrenched off the lid and shook the container. The sugar didn't want to budge. She grabbed a spoon from the drying rack, plunged it into the sugar, and stirred it around.

Nothing but sugar. No folded pages. No nothing.

"Rats! I was really hoping we'd found them," Tricia said.

Angelica replaced the lid and put the jar back on the shelf. "Too easy. And I'm sure Captain Baker looked in every other container in this kitchen, too. Those pages just aren't here."

Tricia wasn't about to give up.

While Angelica stirred the spinach into the egg mixture, Tricia took out the step stool and moved it to the shelving. Since Angelica seemed in an affable mood, Tricia decided to broach a potentially volatile subject. "Frannie has fallen in love with Penny."

"Penny?" Angelica asked, squinting down at her recipe.

"Her new cat." Tricia climbed to the stool's top step and steadied herself by grabbing onto the shelf. It was obvious everything had been moved, for Angelica liked order, and nothing was lined up to her usual standards. Cans of vegetables, tuna, and fruit stood next to a meat slicer and a food processor—everything you'd expect to see in a small working kitchen.

"She hates to leave the poor little thing all alone at home while she's at work all day. It could make for a neurotic cat."

"Well, she's not bringing it to the Cookery. I've made that clear. And I'm assuming she'd have to lug a carrier with her to work every day. That wouldn't be good for the cat. Talk about making the thing neurotic. Can't she get it a friend to keep it company during the day?"

"Maybe," Tricia admitted, exasperated.

"If there's one thing the Cookery doesn't need, it's some kind of animal mascot," Angelica said, and it was obvious by her tone that the subject was now closed.

Tricia wasn't ready to quit. "Ange, what is your problem with people having pets? Just because you don't like them—"

"I'll tell you what's wrong with pets," Angelica said, shaking her whisk in Tricia's direction. "They die on you. You give them all your love for years and years, and then they go and die on you, and give you a broken heart." She finished the sentence with a sob, her eyes filled with sudden tears.

"Ange," Tricia said, with understanding, "have you lost a pet?"

Angelica wiped at her eyes with the edge of her apron. "Maybe."

"There's no maybe about it. Was it a dog or a cat?"

Angelica sniffed. "A toy poodle. His name was Pom-Pom. John, my second husband, bought him for me. When he left, all I had was my little Pom-Pom. He was the joy of my life. And then he got sick. Cancer." Tears cascaded down Angelica's cheeks, and her face scrunched into an ugly mask of grief.

A lump formed in Tricia's throat. "I'm so sorry, Ange. You never told me you had a dog."

"Well, why would I? It sounds so stupid to love a damn animal."

"No, it doesn't. Pets enrich our lives."

Angelica waved a hand in dismissal. "Anyway, after Pom-Pom died, I told myself I'd never put myself through it again."

"How many years did you have him?"

"Just three. He was such a tiny boy. I spent thousands of dollars on treatment, but it didn't help. It nearly killed me when I had to have him . . ." She couldn't finish the sentence.

Tricia wrapped her arms around her sister. "I'm sure he loved you. And you had three wonderful years with him."

Angelica sniffed. "Not nearly enough." Then suddenly she was sobbing into Tricia's shoulder.

Tricia patted her sister's back. "How long have you been denying yourself the love of a pet?"

Angelica hiccuped. "Fifteen years."

"Oh, Ange, I'm so sorry."

"I don't understand how you can allow yourself to love that silly little cat of yours, knowing you're going to lose her someday."

"It's painful to lose a pet. Especially for people like us, who'll never have children. But I like to think of the wonderful years Miss Marple has already given me, and I hope we'll have many more years together. Our pets give us unconditional love. Something we can't always count on with people," she added, thinking of both her ex-husband, Christopher, and Russ.

"It's been a long time since you lost Pom-Pom. And you've got a lot of love inside you. Wouldn't you like to share it with someone besides just me and Bob?"

Angelica pulled back and wiped the tears from her eyes. "Maybe. But my heart would be broken when that pet died, too."

"Yes, but if your heart breaks, at least you know it was real love that you felt." Tears filled Tricia's eyes, too. "I'm not saying this right. What I guess I mean is . . . why deny yourself any kind of love? You deserve it, Ange."

Angelica straightened up, took a stiff breath, and swallowed hard. "You know, maybe you're right. I was a wonderful mother to my sweet little Pom-Pom."

"Yes. And you could do the same for some other dog or cat. There are a lot of abandoned dogs and cats who need homes."

"I don't know if I'm ready to do this again just yet."

Yet? Pom-Pom had been consigned to doggy heaven at least fifteen years before.

"When you are, you should really consider contacting a shelter to make your choice. I'd be glad to help you with that."

"Well, I guess I hadn't thought that getting a new pet would actually honor Pom-Pom's memory," Angelica said softly. "No other dog could ever take his place."

"Of course not." Tricia patted Angelica's back one last time, and stood back. "And you know, if you gave her a chance, you might get to like Frannie's cat."

"Cats aren't as bad as I thought," Angelica admitted. "I actually kind of liked it when you and Miss Marple stayed with me last spring. She's really not a bad little cat at all."

Tricia smiled. "No, she's not."

Angelica cleared her throat and started beating the egg mixture with renewed vigor.

Tricia let out a long breath, feeling exhausted.

She let her gaze travel around the entire kitchen. Everything looked just fine . . . except for maybe the clock, which was a teensy bit crooked. No doubt Captain Baker had knocked it askew during his search of the premises.

She moved the step stool across the kitchen.

"What are you doing?" Angelica asked.

"The clock is crooked. It bugs me."

"And you always say *I'm* the picky one."

Tricia mounted the steps. As she grasped the clock, something slid out from behind it. "Eureka!" In her haste to get down, she nearly fell.

"Watch out!" Angelica cautioned.

Tricia scooped up the folded papers and spread them out on the counter. They were indeed the missing pages from Pammy's diary.

"Read, read!" Angelica encouraged.

Tricia scanned the words.

I'm so annoyed with Joe. At first he was angry about the baby, but I thought I'd wear him down. Libby can't have children, after all. Why should he want to stick with her when I can give him what he wants?

Tricia gasped. "Good Lord! Joe—Libby! She's talking about the Hirts."

"You think little Eugenia's father killed Pammy?" Angelica asked, aghast.

Tricia's mind whirled with the implications. "Oh, sweet heaven! Eugenia was the baby who needed gender assignment. No wonder she didn't want anyone to know her secret. Can you imagine how the kids at school would have teased her with that piece of news?"

"But she's been out of school for years," Angelica said.

"Public school, yes, but she's still taking classes at Daniel Webster College in Nashua."

"I'm sure she's practically anonymous at college. Unless you live on campus, most people are."

Tricia's mind whirled with the implications. "It had to be Joe who killed Pammy, don't you see?"

"That poor woman," Angelica said, shaking her head in sympathy.

"Who, Pammy?"

"No, Libby. Married to a rat. Well, what else is new? I've married four rats." Angelica nodded at the pages on the counter. "What are you going to do with them?"

Tricia sighed. "I certainly don't want to confront Joe Hirt. I'm going to let Captain Baker take care of that." She grabbed her purse from the counter and dug through it until she found the business card the captain had given her days before.

By the time the captain arrived more than an hour later, all the miniquiches had been baked and were nestled in plastic wrap in the café's large freezer.

Tricia and Angelica were sitting at the counter in the dining area, eating tuna sandwiches and spooning up Angelica's delicious potato-leek soup, when the cruiser arrived. Angelica let the captain in.

"Thank you for calling me, Ms. Miles. Somehow I had the impression you were going to try to deliver justice by yourself."

"Not me. Last time out, I got my nose broken. I'm content to stand quietly along the sidelines."

"I'm not sure I would have believed that a few hours ago."

"I'm sorry if you thought I was interfering. I simply wanted to make sure that whoever killed Pammy was found."

"Why don't you have a cup of coffee while you look them over?" Angelica suggested.

This time, Baker took her up on her offer, settling at one of the counter's stools. He quickly skimmed the pages. When he'd finished, he picked them up, waving them in Tricia's direction. "This doesn't prove Joe Hirt killed anyone. All it says is that he fathered a child, with a birth defect, out of wedlock. I'll be speaking with him concerning this, but we're still a long way away from proving he or anyone else killed Pamela Fredericks."

"I suppose you're right," Tricia said. "But at least you have one more piece of the puzzle."

He stood. "I don't want you to speak to anyone in the Hirt family until this whole thing is settled. Do I make myself clear?"

"I wouldn't know what to say. But what if I run into Eugenia at the Bookshelf Diner?"

"Stay away from her until this is resolved." Baker glanced around Angelica's café, which looked a lot more cheerful with all the lights turned on. "What's wrong with eating here? It seems like a charming little place."

"Why, thank you, Captain Baker. Are you in a hurry? I've got some wonderful potato-leek soup that's to die for!"

"No, thank you, I've already had dinner. But it does smell good."

"Suit yourself," Angelica said, and dug into her soup once more.

Tricia walked him to the door.

"It goes without saying that you shouldn't talk about the contents of the diary," Baker said.

But she already had. Ginny knew some of what the diary held. Thankfully, Tricia hadn't told her what she'd learned from Stuart Paige. And it would be best not to tell her that Eugenia was the subject of the entire diary, since the two young women were . . . kind of . . . friends. The same kind of friends she and Pammy had been? More like acquaintances stuck with each other.

Tricia cleared her throat. "Of course, Captain. I don't want anything to interfere with your investigation."

"Thank you, Ms. Miles."

"Call me Tricia."

He nodded and smiled. "Tricia." He tipped his hat. "Good night."

Tricia closed the door, lingering as she watched the captain get into his cruiser and drive off.

"*A-hem*!"

Tricia looked over at her sister. "What?"

Angelica sported an absurdly smug expression. "Methinks you're sweet on that man."

Tricia frowned. "Don't be absurd. I'm merely glad he's not as obnoxious as his boss. And besides, now that he's got the missing diary pages, I'll probably never see him again."

The thought saddened her, but she wasn't about to admit it to Angelica.

"Sit down and finish your soup," Angelica said. "After all, now you can relax. No matter what happens next, it's totally out of your hands."

It certainly was.

TWENTY

It was after ten when Tricia decided to put her book down and go to bed. Only then did she realize that for the first night since Pammy's death, she hadn't been bothered by her mysterious caller. Did that prove it had been Joe Hirt on the other end of the line? No one had shot at her windows, either. Eugenia had said she and her father shot skeet. Had Captain Baker thought to ask him about owning any guns? And had the captain spoken to Joe with Libby or

Eugenia present? She hoped not. But if Joe had killed Pammy, everything would eventually be made public. Would the community rally around Libby? She'd worked tirelessly for more than two decades to help those less fortunate. She deserved better than to be the subject of vicious gossip.

Everything will work out, Tricia told herself. But the uneasy feeling in her stomach wouldn't go away.

She turned off her bedside lamp and sat on the edge of her bed, staring at the closed curtains. Miss Marple jumped up to join her and gave a hearty "*Yow*!"

"I don't like them being closed, either," Tricia said.

She petted the cat's head and scratched behind her ears, idly wondering how Frannie had made out with Penny. Miss Marple made herself comfortable on the bed, but Tricia didn't feel as settled as her cat. She got up and nudged the curtains where they met in the center of the window. Once again she saw a figure dart along the west side of Main Street. With hands raised overhead, the figure tossed yet another carved pumpkin into the center of Stoneham's main thoroughfare.

She thought she recognized that silhouette, and grinned. It wasn't only the freegans who donned black and slunk through the shadows like cat burglars. She wasn't sure what she would do with this new knowledge.

She let the curtain fall once again. "Oh, well, there's always tomorrow."

"*Yow*!" Miss Marple agreed.

TRICIA AWOKE EARLY the next morning, and decided to make use of the time by working in the storeroom. Ginny had moved the microwave and fridge to the second floor the day before, and Tricia was determined to whip at least one part of her miniwarehouse into an employee break room.

The front of the storeroom overlooked the street, and contained shelves full of inventoried books, as well as twenty or thirty cases of books that still needed to be unpacked and sorted. The cavernous room also held the assorted furniture and bric-a-brac she hadn't wanted to incorporate into her apartment. Assessing the space, Tricia decided the back of the room could be sectioned off to make an agreeable space for Ginny and Mr. Everett to eat their lunches or just take a break.

She unearthed her old kitchen table and chairs, and a sideboard that would hold the microwave, and dragged them into place. Digging through a box of kitchen utensils, she found mismatched silverware, a napkin holder, and eight mugs. Only three of the mugs were chipped, and she tossed them. Next she scrubbed the old utility sink so they had a place to rinse their dishes.

It was nearly nine thirty when Tricia stood back to evaluate her work. The

space needed some homey touches, but it would do for now. She had just enough time to take a quick shower before opening the store.

Tricia had finished pouring water into the coffeemaker and hit the On button when she heard a knock at the door. She answered it and found a red-eyed Ginny, who'd shown up for work a full five minutes early.

"Is something wrong?" Tricia asked.

Ginny shook her head and sniffed. "No." Her voice was strained. "Yes."

"Why don't you hang up your coat, and then come back and have a cup of coffee?"

Ginny nodded and shuffled toward the back of the store. By the time she returned, Tricia had poured the coffee. She handed Ginny a cup, and they moved to sit in the readers' nook.

"Now, tell me what's wrong."

"Every Friday night I balance our checkbook. Last night was no different. But things just aren't adding up. Brian works all those extra hours, and it's not showing up in the bank."

"Did you ask him about it?"

She shook her head. "I'm not sure if I want to know the answer."

What had Angelica said about rats?

Tricia decided to push. "What do you suspect—that he's seeing someone on the side?"

"Until last night, I never would've even considered he might cheat on me. We've been together since high school."

And maybe that was part of the problem.

"What do you think I should do?" Ginny asked.

Tricia chose her words carefully. The last thing she wanted was to give Ginny advice and then have it blow up in her face if Brian had a reasonable explanation for his actions. "I've always found the best thing to do in these situations is to talk things through." The way she had talked things through with Russ? By leaping out of her seat and fleeing from his house? By refusing to return his telephone calls?

Oh, yes, she was one to talk. But then, she wasn't in the dark about where their relationship stood. Russ had made it plain he was moving on.

Tricia took in Ginny's tear-swollen eyes and decided it was time to lighten the mood. "Hey, I've got a surprise for you."

Ginny sniffed. "For me?"

"The break room. It's finished. Well, almost."

Ginny brightened. "Do we have time for me to look at it before we open?"

"Sure."

Tricia led the way upstairs to the storeroom. She threw open the door. "Ta-da!"

Ginny entered before her, her mouth opened in awe. "When did you have time to pull this together? It was a mess the last time I was up here."

"This morning. I got up a little early. The fridge is plugged in, and I even tested the microwave. It does boil water."

"This is fantastic. Thank you, Tricia. You sure know how to keep your employees happy."

Tricia glanced at the microwave's clock. "Oops! We should've opened a full minute ago. We'd better go. I hope you won't sit in your car to eat your lunch anymore."

"No way. Maybe I'll bring in my old boom box. That way I can listen to music while I eat lunch or read."

"Go for it!"

Back in the store, Tricia unlocked the shop door, turned the sign to say OPEN, and headed for the register. Not thirty seconds later, the door opened, the little bell overhead jingling as Joe Hirt stepped over the threshold. He didn't look happy.

"Hello, Tricia."

Tricia's heart sank.

Joe nodded at Ginny. "Can I have a few minutes alone with your boss?"

"No, you can't," Tricia said. "Captain Baker told me I'm not supposed to speak to you."

"I'll bet he did. When was that? Right after you gave him Pammy's diary?"

"I really should go . . . do something," Ginny said nervously.

"No, please stay. Joe, you'll have to leave. I simply can't speak to you about any of this. I promised Captain Baker."

"You're finishing what your friend tried to do—break up my family," he accused.

"I turned the diary over to the Sheriff's Department. Anything else would've been obstruction of justice—a crime. And I really cannot talk about any of this with you. If you don't leave, I'll have to call the Sheriff's Department and have them remove you from my store."

His arms hung rigidly at his sides as he clenched his fists—not unlike Clint Eastwood in an old spaghetti western, about to draw and fire. "We'll speak again," Joe said grimly, then turned and left the shop.

Tricia let out a long sigh and leaned against the counter, feeling drained.

"What's he so pissed off about?" Ginny asked. "And why does he think you're trying to hurt his family?"

"I'm not supposed to talk about it to anyone."

"Not even me?" Ginny asked, hurt.

Tricia shook her head. "I'm sorry, Ginny, not even you."

Ginny sighed, her shoulders sagging. "I guess I have enough problems to worry about anyway."

They both looked up as the shop door opened. This time it was a real customer.

Tricia spoke. "Sometimes the best thing you can do when things aren't going well is to lose yourself in work. That's what I'm planning to do today."

Ginny drank the last of her coffee and tossed the cup into the wastebasket. "You know, we ought to use those china mugs I saw up on the sideboard in the break room—at least for you and me and Mr. Everett. We're wasting a lot of paper when we drink out of these disposable cups several times every day. And it would be better for the business's bottom line."

Trust Ginny to be worried about the store's welfare—if not the entire planet's. "I never wanted to bother with washing them," Tricia admitted.

"How about if I do it?"

"That would be great. Maybe later I'll go upstairs and bring some down, unless you'd like to bring in one of your own from home."

"I do have a favorite one—it's got a little gray cat on it. It reminds me of Miss Marple." At the sound of her name, Tricia's cat appeared and jumped on the counter, giving a *yow*! for attention. Ginny petted her, but even the damp nose nuzzling her hand didn't seem to lift her spirits.

"Hey, you're not supposed to be up here," Tricia scolded the cat. She picked her up and set her on the floor. Miss Marple walked away with her head and her tail held high.

Ginny took a deep breath, as though steeling herself. "I guess I'll ask if this customer needs help."

Tricia touched her assistant's arm, and nodded in reassurance.

With Ginny occupied, Tricia took out the disinfecting spray and wiped down the counter before she headed for the register, taking the paper cup and its tepid coffee with her. The phone rang. She forced a smile into her voice that she didn't feel. "Haven't Got a Clue, this is Tricia. How may I help you?"

"You didn't do as I said," came the voice. "You didn't give me the diary."

That damn voice again. And he/she/it had called the shop line, not her personal line.

"How could I? Besides, I told you, Joe, I can't talk to you. And I've told the Sheriff's Department about these calls. I wouldn't be surprised if they've already tapped my line to catch you." A lie, but the caller didn't have to know that.

"You'll pay for this," said the voice.

Tricia hung up the phone. She wasn't about to be intimidated by Joe Hirt.

Instead, she picked up the receiver and dialed the Sheriff's Department. It took five minutes on hold before Captain Baker came on the line.

"I didn't think I'd be hearing from you again," he said.

"Neither did I, but Joe Hirt came to my shop this morning."

"That is a problem," Baker agreed. "I talked to him earlier, and I told him not to contact you."

"He also just called me with that stupid voice-altering device. This time on the shop line—not my personal phone."

"Probably because the caller knew you weren't in your apartment."

That was true. She thought about what he'd just said. "You don't think my caller is Joe Hirt?"

"It could be—but not necessarily."

"I told whoever it was that you were tapping my phones, and would catch him."

His only comment was a flat "Hmmm."

"What do you want me to do in the meantime?" Tricia asked.

"As I told you before; avoid the Hirt family—and keep your curtains closed at night."

"Yes, sir," she said with a bored sigh.

"Tricia, I mean it."

"And I'll do it."

"Thank you. And please feel free to call me with any new developments."

She thought about it. "Does this mean you don't think Joe is the one behind Pammy's death?"

"There's no proof he is."

"But the diary—" Tricia interrupted.

"Is just one piece of evidence. And don't you dare go looking for anything else."

"At this point, I'm totally clueless—and I don't mean that in a Paris Hilton kind of way."

"Well, stay that way." His voice softened. "At least in this instance. Otherwise, I think you're a very sharp lady."

Now who was flirting with whom?

Only . . . for some reason, she didn't mind.

"Thank you, Captain."

He cleared his throat, and when he spoke again, it was in his "cop" voice. "Keep in touch."

"I will. Good-bye." She hung up the phone.

Ginny wandered up to the cash desk. "What are you smiling about?"

Tricia immediately sobered, unwilling to share those particular thoughts and feelings. "Nothing."

• • •

It was a glorious fall day in Stoneham, which meant that most of her potential customers were probably in Milford for day two of the Pumpkin Festival. Still, Tricia was determined to enjoy the tiny part of the day she could access—her lunch break. She called Booked for Lunch and placed a take-out order, but instead of immediately picking it up, she decided to take a walk down Main Street.

She passed the Chamber of Commerce. Their new secretary/receptionist, Betsy Dittmeyer, was very sweet . . . in a noncommittal, bland sort of way. Gone were the colorful posters of Hawaii that Frannie had used to decorate the reception area. Instead, the walls were empty of any ornamentation. Not even a picture interrupted the stark order of Betsy's desk. Tricia missed Frannie as the face of the Chamber. Still, the Chamber's loss had been Angelica's gain, and Frannie had blossomed with the responsibility of running the Cookery.

Tricia stopped in front of Kelly Realty. The pile of pumpkins that had decorated the front of the building just days before had dwindled considerably. Surely his giveaway program hadn't been that successful. Tricia opened the door to the office, a little bell jingling cheerfully over her head as she entered.

Bob Kelly sat at his desk, the *Nashua Telegraph* propped up before him, as he spooned soup from a plastic container—the same kind of take-out container Angelica used at Booked for Lunch. No doubt she'd been feeding him lunch since the day she'd opened. Okay, she cared for him. That was her lookout. But Tricia wasn't feeling as generous.

Bob looked up, dropping his plastic spoon onto the desk blotter. He yanked away the paper napkin that he'd had draped over his suit coat and shirt. "Tricia, what brings you here?"

"Hello, Bob. Sorry to interrupt your lunch, but I have a couple of questions I'm hoping you can answer."

He smiled and waved a hand, indicating she should take one of the two chairs in front of his desk. This was where he wrote his real estate contracts—and the leases he held on most of the buildings the booksellers occupied on Main Street. Tricia had sat in the very same seat when she'd signed the three-year lease on the building that Haven't Got a Clue now occupied. Later she'd found out she'd paid far more than any of the other leaseholders. That had set a precedent, escalating the prices on all the other leases—something that had not endeared her to the booksellers who had come to Stoneham before her.

"First of all, what do you know about the person who's been smashing pumpkins for the past week?"

"Why, nothing. I'm just as appalled as the rest of the citizens of Stoneham."

"Really?" Tricia asked. "Somehow I find that a little hard to believe."

Bob's mouth dropped open, his eyes growing wide in what looked like genuine anxiety. "Whatever do you mean?" he asked, his voice the epitome of concern.

"Cut the crap, Bob, I know it's you who's been smashing those pumpkins all over town. I saw you do it on Wednesday night, and again last night. I should go straight to Captain Baker and report you. I'm sure you've probably broken more than a couple of laws—including littering."

"I don't think I understand what you're getting at," he said in all innocence.

"I'm telling you I've seen you toss carved pumpkins into Main Street on two separate occasions. Only I wasn't sure until last night that it was really you, and I mean to report you."

"You can't do that!" he cried.

She nodded. "Okay . . . give me a reason not to."

Bob frowned, but didn't offer an explanation.

Tricia waited for at least thirty seconds before she spoke again. "Okay, then answer me one question: Why are you doing this? Do you have some kind of sick squash fetish?"

"I don't owe you any explanations," he grumbled.

So, he didn't deny it.

Tricia crossed her arms. "No, but what will Angelica think when I tell her about this?"

"Why do you have to tell her anything?" he asked, panicking.

"I think she should know what kind of man she's involved with. Someone who'd destroy a child's jack-o'-lantern . . ."

"I did not smash anybody's pumpkins but my own."

"You mean to say you carved all those pumpkins before you busted them all over the streets of Stoneham?"

"Of course I did. You think I want to get arrested for trespassing or stealing?"

"But you made a terrible mess. That costs the taxpayers money."

"The village did not order a street sweeper run. I . . . talked them out of it. Besides, most of the shopkeepers have cleaned up the messes in front of their shops."

"Of course they did. They didn't want their customers to slip in the slimy mess you made, and sue them. And that still doesn't explain *why* you did it."

Bob snorted a few anxious breaths before answering. "For the publicity—what else? It got Stoneham noticed by the *Nashua Telegraph*, didn't it?"

"There was a two-inch story buried in the 'Outlying Towns' section. And do we really want to be known as a village that harbors a pumpkin smasher? Come on, Bob, what's the real explanation?"

"Okay, maybe I'm . . . jealous." The man actually pouted.

"Of whom?" she demanded.

"Not whom, what. Every year that darn Milford Pumpkin Festival gets tons of publicity. People come to the town by the thousands to look at a bunch of stupid old squashes."

Tricia couldn't believe what she'd just heard, and burst out laughing.

"Hey," Bob protested. "It's *not* funny."

"Yes, it is." Tricia covered her mouth to stifle a smirk and had to clear her throat before she could speak. "Milford is a beautiful, picturesque little town—"

"So is Stoneham," Bob countered.

"Yes, but we bring in people twelve months a year, thanks to being known as a book town. Milford has their festival three days of the year. How could you possibly be jealous?"

"We ought to have some kind of festival here, too, and drum up some national exposure."

"Then go for it. Come up with something else. There are three other seasons and a lot of other possibilities you could choose from."

"Like what?"

"I don't know. Pilgrim Day."

"Plymouth, Mass., has that covered."

"Choose another fruit or vegetable, then. Maybe we could have a cauliflower festival, or how about okra?"

"We don't grow them locally," Bob groused.

He'd missed her sarcasm.

"Then how about a 'welcome-back-geese festival' next spring? Or why don't you get that nudist camp down the road to march in the Stoneham Fourth of July celebration?"

Bob's eyes narrowed. "Now you're teasing me."

Maybe she was. She leaned forward on his desk. "Do you really want the rest of the Chamber of Commerce, the Board of Selectmen, and the whole village to know what you've been up to?"

Bob stood, pulled in his overhanging stomach, and puffed out his chest. "Are you threatening me?"

"Not at all. I just want you to stop. And I want you to clean up the mess you've made."

"And what do I get out of the deal?"

"I never tell Angelica just what kind of a nutcase you really are." She shook her head. "I still don't know what it is she sees in you. But—there's no accounting for taste. And you do have *some* redeeming qualities," she said, remembering what Libby Hirt had said about him championing the Food Shelf.

Bob stared into his cooling soup. "Okay, I'll clean up the mess and I won't smash any more pumpkins."

"Good." Tricia rose from her seat. "I'm glad we came to this understanding, Bob. I really wouldn't want the rest of the villagers—and God forbid, the organizers of the Pumpkin Festival—to know anything about this. I mean, you're a respected man in this town. If only for Angelica's sake, I don't want people to think you're a total jerk."

"Thank you, Tricia." His face screwed into a frown as he thought about what she'd said. "I think."

"We'll talk no more about this, shall we?" she asked.

"Yes. Thank you." Bob rose from his seat and walked around his chair, offering her his hand.

She took it, resisting the urge to wipe it on her jacket afterward. "Well, I'd best be on my way. I've still got a business to run."

"Yes. Me, too."

Tricia gave him a big smile. "See you later, Bob."

"You, too, Tricia."

And off she went to pick up her lunch.

It was nearly three o'clock, and once again the store was empty of customers. If Tricia had better anticipated the slowdown, she could've had Ginny start inventorying the books up in the storeroom, but it was too late in the day for that.

The phone rang, and Ginny grabbed it. "Haven't Got a Clue, this is Ginny. How can I—" She paused. "Sure thing. Tricia, it's Frannie—for you." She held out the phone.

Tricia left the shelves filled with true crime titles she'd been alphabetizing, and picked up the receiver. "Hi, Frannie. What's up?"

"Oh, Tricia—I've been meaning to call you all day, but with one thing and another—"

"Don't tell me you made headway with Penny?"

"I sure did. Just like you said. I ignored her last night. It took a few hours, but eventually she came out from behind the couch. First she sat in the middle of the living room. Then, little by little, she moved closer to me. By the time the eleven o'clock news came on, she was sitting on my lap and purring like crazy."

"See, I told you."

"Yes, you did. And I can't thank you enough."

"It wasn't me. It was you. Sometimes you just need to show a little patience where animals are concerned." And people, too?

No, she was not going to think about Russ again. He'd made his decision. He could live with it. She was determined to do so, too.

Tricia heard the soft tinkle of a bell.

"Oops—got a customer. Gotta go. See you at the wedding tomorrow."

No sooner had Tricia hung up the phone than it began to ring again. Tricia picked it up. "Haven't Got a Clue, this is Tricia. How can I help you?"

"Tricia, it's Libby Hirt."

Good grief.

"Libby, I'm not supposed to talk to you or Joe or Eugenia until—"

"Why did you give that diary to the Sheriff's Department? Why did you have to drag up the past? Why couldn't you just destroy the damn thing?"

Tricia took a deep breath. She should hang up the phone. She should do as she had been told, and end the conversation. But the hurt in Libby's voice, the anguish, was like a stab in the heart. "Libby, I'm sorry. It's evidence in Pammy Fredericks's death."

"How? It doesn't prove anything."

"Did you know about Joe's affair with M.J. Collins?"

Silence. Then, "Not until last night. I wish he'd never told me. It destroys the faith I've had in him. It makes our entire marriage a sham. And what will it do to our daughter when she finds out the truth?"

"Perhaps it could bring you all closer together."

"Or it could destroy our family."

"Everyone seems to forget that Pammy Fredericks was murdered."

"Maybe she deserved it," Libby said bitterly. "Blackmail is an ugly game. Would she have bled Joe dry? And what about Mr. Paige?"

"Libby, I know you're upset and you don't mean what you just said."

"And just maybe I do."

She broke the connection.

Tricia hung up the phone. Was there something in the Stoneham water supply causing relationships to crash and burn? First she and Russ; Ginny and Brian might be on the skids; and now Libby and Joe Hirt—who, until yesterday, had apparently represented the village's most stable marriage.

And what was she going to tell Captain Baker, now that she'd spoken to yet another member of the Hirt family? There was no way she could set foot inside the Bookshelf Diner—and run into Eugenia—until this whole mess was resolved. In fact, if she was smart, she wouldn't step outside Haven't Got a Clue.

She forced herself to think about other things. With the wedding set for the next day, she had too much to do. The store needed a thorough cleaning. Although it was last minute, perhaps she should hire a cleaning team to come in—but did cleaners work Saturday evenings? What if she couldn't engage someone to come

after store hours? And had anyone thought to rent chairs for the reception? Or maybe tall tables, so the guests had somewhere to park their plates of breakfast foods, champagne, and cake while they ate? She'd have to ask Angelica.

With less than sixteen hours to go, Grace and Mr. Everett's wedding seemed so far away—so normal and life-affirming. And Pammy was still—and forever would be—dead. Although she'd been on the outs with her family for years, it seemed doubly cruel they should decide not to claim her body. There'd be no commemoration of her life. And if Tricia took it upon herself to arrange one, would anyone show up?

Pammy had been shy and awkward when they'd met twenty-four years ago. She'd been shrewd and apparently heartless the last time they'd spoken. And she'd accused Tricia of not knowing how to have any fun. But was fun at someone else's expense enjoyable, or just spite?

Tricia preferred to think the latter.

Pammy was dead and, as far as Tricia knew, no one—and she would have to include herself—would mourn her.

A truly wasted life.

Though she had too many other phone calls to make, on impulse Tricia hauled out the phone book and called the Hillsborough County Medical Examiner's office. Maybe Pammy's family had reconsidered. Maybe plans were already in place for some kind of service, and no one had thought to call her. However, the person she spoke with at the ME's office only reaffirmed what she'd already been told by Captain Baker.

"What does that mean?" she asked, already knowing the answer.

"Eventually, the body will be buried at taxpayers' expense."

"Thank you." Tricia hung up the phone.

Buried in an unmarked grave. Did anyone deserve that?

Several customers entered the store. Tricia waited on them, all the while thinking of the phone calls she needed to make to ensure the wedding went off without a hitch. It was time to put Pammy out of her mind . . . forever.

Still, until her killer was caught, Tricia wasn't sure she could do that.

Everything felt unfinished. Like Pammy's life.

And Tricia hated that feeling of helplessness.

TWENTY-ONE

TRICIA COULDN'T REMEMBER a day that wore on as long as that particular Saturday. The Milford Pumpkin Festival really *had* cut into business. The few customers she'd had that afternoon had regaled her with tales of the Great Pumpkin contest, the pumpkin catapult, the chili roundup, and the scarecrow contest. And oh, the food!

Rats, Tricia thought. *Maybe Pammy was right. I always miss out on the fun.*

Eleanor had indeed won first prize in the pie contest—Frannie had called back with that update. No doubt the blue ribbon would be framed and hung over her receptionist's desk at the Brookview Inn by the next morning.

Grace had called with an update about the wedding flowers, thanking Tricia profusely once again for letting them hold the ceremony in the store, and promised she would arrive early the next morning to help coordinate the last-minute details.

The thing Tricia hadn't been able to accomplish was hiring a cleaning firm. That meant the job was up to her. Oh, well . . . she tried to think of it as part of her gift to Grace and Mr. Everett. With Mr. Everett in short supply these last few days, the place had become dusty, so she commandeered his lamb's wool duster and started working on the shelves.

It was ten minutes until closing. Haven't Got a Clue had had no customers for at least twenty minutes when Tricia glanced at her watch. "Don't you just hate this time of year?" she asked Ginny.

"Yes. When the sun goes down, it's like the whole world closes up."

"I've been thinking of adopting winter hours—except between Thanksgiving and Christmas, of course."

"I would hate to see my hours cut, but you have to do what's best for the store," Ginny said sensibly. "Besides, it would give me more time to work on the house. I have this vision of the living room being finished in time for Christmas. I can already imagine a crackling fire in the fireplace, and our stockings hanging from the mantel. That is, if I can find someone to tell me the chimney is safe enough to light a fire."

Tricia laughed. "We'll stay open until seven tonight, but depending on how trade is on Monday, we might as well adopt new hours."

"What about the Tuesday Night Book Club?"

Tricia shrugged. "We might have to start an hour earlier. Hey, dinner at a decent hour. Now there's a plan."

Ginny laughed and began her end-of-day chores, emptying the coffeemaker's filter of grounds, and pouring the last of the coffee down the washroom sink. She was still in the back of the store when the door opened. Eugenia Hirt entered Haven't Got a Clue, her face dark with anger. "What's going on, Tricia?"

Tricia had been counting out the day's receipts, and closed the register's cash drawer. "I'm not supposed to speak to you or anyone in your family. Direct orders from Captain Baker of the Sheriff's Department."

"That's what my mother said. But something's going on, and nobody will tell me what it is. Everyone seems to think *you* know."

"Captain Baker said—"

"I don't give a damn what any sheriff's deputy said. You know, and *you will tell me*!"

"Are you threatening me?" Tricia asked.

Eugenia threw back her head, standing taller. "Maybe I am."

Tricia tried not to laugh. "Go home." She had to fight the urge to say *little girl*. "Your mother is very upset. See if you can make her feel better."

"Not until you tell me what was in that diary."

So, she knew about Pammy's diary. Had Pammy said something, or had she heard her parents arguing about it?

Before Tricia could answer the girl, the shop door flew open. Eugenia whirled. "Dad! What are you doing here?"

"Come on, honey. Let's go home."

Eugenia shook her head. "I'm not leaving until someone gives me some answers."

Ginny reappeared from behind a set of shelves. "What's going on?"

"Nothing," Tricia and Joe said in unison.

"Ginny, why don't you go home?" Joe suggested.

Ginny's face flushed. "Why?"

"Because it looks like Tricia, Eugenia, and I have some serious things to discuss. Things that you don't need to be a part of."

Ginny moved to stand next to Tricia. "I don't think so."

Tricia was grateful for the support, but her tightening stomach told her that Ginny might be safer if she left the store—now. "Maybe he's right, Ginny. I think you should—"

"No way," Ginny said. "I have a few questions of my own. Like why did you try to run Brian's car off the road the other night, Eugenia?"

"I don't know what you're talking about."

"The hell you don't. When we left you and Joe in Nashua on Wednesday night, you came up behind us and sat on Brian's bumper, trying to scare us. Why?"

Eugenia shrugged. "It was a joke. Can't you take a joke?"

"I didn't think it was funny," Ginny said.

"Neither did I," Tricia agreed.

Joe stepped around to the front display window and grabbed the cord, lowering the blinds. Miss Marple, who'd been dozing on the shelf behind the register, got up and stretched. Closing the blinds was usually the signal that dinner was close at hand.

"Why did you close the blinds?" Tricia asked, unease creeping up her spine.

"We need privacy," Joe said. "Ginny, get your coat and go."

"No!"

"I don't care if she hears our business," Eugenia said. "I want to know everything that's going on. I'm an adult. It's time you leveled with me, Dad. What was it Pammy said to you? Please, tell me!"

Joe sighed, all the weight of the world on his shoulders. "She tried to blackmail me."

"With what?" Eugenia insisted.

"Pam said if she couldn't shake down Stuart Paige, she would come after me."

"But Dad, Pammy threatened to tell the world at large about my . . . my birth defect. That would humiliate only me. What else could she have possibly known that would hurt our family?"

Tricia said, "Eugenia's not a child anymore. Tell her, Joe. Libby told me you two have already discussed it."

"Mom knows what?" Eugenia asked.

Joe offered his daughter his hand. She took it, her own visibly shaking. "Princess, we always told you your biological parents were dead. But that's only partially true. Your biological mother died in a car accident when you were still a baby, but your father is alive."

"You know who he is?" she asked, eagerly.

"It's someone you already know and, hopefully, love."

"Who? Please tell me!"

"It's . . . me."

Eugenia's mouth fell open, and for a long time she just stared at the man she'd always known as her adoptive father. "I'm really your little girl?" Her voice was barely a whisper.

"Your birth mother couldn't handle your . . . birth defect. She gave you up for adoption. I wanted you. I talked your mother—Libby," he clarified, "into taking you in as a foster child. I knew she'd fall in love with you—as I already had, even though I'd only seen you from behind the glass window in the hospital nursery."

Eugenia shook her head, her eyes filling with tears. "But Dad, you and Mom have been married almost twenty-five years. I'm twenty-one . . . that means . . ."

Joe bit his lip, and looked like he was about to cry as well.

"I never meant to hurt your mother. It just happened. And the thing was . . . I got you in the bargain. We both got you, and it kept us together. We loved you as you were—we loved you through all the surgeries. We will *always* love you."

They fell into each other's arms, tears streaking their cheeks. Tricia hardened her heart. This was all very nice, but it didn't answer who killed Pammy Fredericks.

The door opened, the little bell below the transom tinkling cheerfully.

Ginny whirled. "Brian! What are you doing here?"

He nodded toward Eugenia. "I followed her."

"Why aren't you at work?" Ginny asked, suspiciously.

"I've got some things to tell you, Ginny. I . . . kind of lost my evening job."

"You what?"

"Two weeks ago," he admitted.

Her eyes narrowed. "And just what have you been doing every work night for the last two weeks?"

"Looking for a new job," he said, his voice harsh.

"And what else?" Ginny asked, and turned her gaze on Eugenia.

"Okay, so I hung out a few nights with Gina."

"Gina?" Ginny asked, the color rising in her face. "Is that your pet name for her?"

Joe looked confused. "What's going on?"

"Nothing, Daddy," Eugenia said.

"Apparently there's a lot more going on than I thought," Tricia said.

"Me, too," Ginny agreed. She turned back to Brian. "And I'd like an explanation."

Brian walked back to the shop door, flipped the sign to CLOSED, and pulled down the door shade. "It might be better if we weren't disturbed."

Fear crept up Tricia's spine. Nothing good would come of this conversation. They might learn the facts of what had happened when Pammy died, but she sensed lives were about to be changed—and not for the better.

Tricia swallowed before she asked her next question. "Who dumped Pammy into the garbage cart?"

"That was me," Brian admitted, turning to face them once again. "I told her to leave Eugenia alone. I only meant to scare her when I tossed her into the garbage."

"Did you know about this, Eugenia?" Joe demanded, his voice hard with anger.

"Not at first," she admitted, and turned her gaze to take in Brian. "I didn't want him to get in trouble."

"Who kept calling me, demanding the diary?" Tricia asked.

"I did it," Eugenia said. "I knew you had to have it. That stinking, evil witch stayed with you for two weeks. I figured since it wasn't in her car—"

"You broke into her car?" Ginny asked.

"We didn't have to. Brian took her keys. We drove the car over to Hanson Lane and looked through the trunk, but we didn't find anything, so we left it there. We figured Pammy would eventually find it. And then she turned up dead, and we were scared."

"What about the calls?" Tricia reminded her.

"Like I said," Eugenia continued, "we figured you had to have it, so we drove to Nashua and got one of those voice-altering things for the phone. We figured I wouldn't get in trouble if I didn't make any specific threat—and I didn't."

"It's up to the sheriff to decide if you've broken any laws." Tricia turned her attention to Brian. "And it's up to a grand jury to decide whether Pammy's death is murder or manslaughter," she said. "But either way, you're both in pretty deep trouble."

"I'm *not* going to jail," Brian said, his voice rising. "I've always liked you, Tricia, but I'm not about to let you ruin my life."

"What about *my* life?" Ginny demanded.

Tricia ignored her. "Brian, your life was ruined the moment you decided to scare Pammy Fredericks. I know you didn't mean to hurt her—but it's your fault she's dead!"

"She was a scumbag. She wanted to ruin people I care about."

"That may be true, but she didn't deserve to die."

"What about *me?*" Ginny insisted, her eyes filled with tears. "Brian, we own a house together. We're going to get *married.*"

He turned his anguished gaze toward Ginny. "Babe, I'm sorry. I never thought I'd care for Eugenia the way I do. I mean, we've known each other almost our whole lives. It just . . . happened."

Just like it had happened between Joe and M.J., only Libby had never found out.

"And were you going to leave me for Eugenia?" Ginny demanded.

Brian turned away so he didn't have to look her in the eye. "I . . . thought about it." He shrugged. "Yeah, I think so."

Ginny took a few choking breaths—sounding like a fish out of water. "And what happens now that Tricia and I know you're a murderer?"

The door opened. A breathless Angelica burst in, still dressed in her fifties

waitress costume, her feet encased in running shoes. Her eyes were wild with fear. "Are you okay, Trish?"

"You shouldn't have come here," Brian said coldly.

"Run!" Tricia shouted.

But Angelica just stood in the doorway, in shock.

Brian moved fast. In seconds he'd grabbed Angelica's arm and hauled her farther into the store, slamming the door before shoving her against Tricia.

"What are you doing here?" Tricia grated.

"I saw Joe shut the blinds, and I knew Captain Baker told you not to talk to him."

"So why didn't you just call 911?"

"You two shut up and let me think!" Brian ordered.

"Now what are you going to do?" Ginny demanded. "Throw all three of us into the Dumpster?"

"What's going on?" Angelica demanded.

Brian thrust his hand into his jacket and came out with a handgun, aiming it at Tricia and Angelica.

Ginny gasped. "Where on God's earth did you get that?"

"Brian, think about what you're doing," Tricia warned. "What happened with Pammy was an accident. If you fire that gun—"

Joe stepped forward. "Nobody's firing any guns. Hand it over, kid."

Brian shook his head. "I don't want to go to jail."

"Tricia's right. You fire that gun, and that's the end of life as you know it."

"You're one to talk. Eugenia told me you shot at Tricia's windows. You shot Stuart Paige," Brian said.

Joe's head snapped as he turned toward his daughter. "That's not true! Please tell me *you* didn't do it."

"I'm sorry, Daddy," Eugenia cried. "I only meant to scare Tricia. If Paige hadn't moved, he never would've been shot."

"You lied to me," Brian said to her, angry.

"I didn't want you to think badly of me."

Joe's face flushed, and he pursed his lips. He looked past his daughter and spoke to Brian. "You're both already in enough trouble. Enough mistakes have already been made. Don't make any more, kid."

Brian stared at the people surrounding him. The gun in his hand wavered.

"How long are we going to stand around like this?" Angelica groused. "Are you going to kill all of us? What will you do with our bodies?"

"Forensics will always nail a killer, Brian," a grim-faced Ginny piped up. "I learned that reading mysteries and thrillers."

"Shut up, Ginny! Just shut up!" Brian hollered.

Another tear slid down Ginny's cheek. "And to think I almost married you."

"We can't just stand here all night," Joe said reasonably.

Tricia swallowed. Sure they could! The best way to defuse the situation was to talk it out, not egg Brian on. But Joe took another step forward. The gun swung in his direction.

"This is insane!" Eugenia shouted. "Brian, what are you doing? Put that gun down. We'll never be together if you fire that thing."

"Quiet! Just everyone be quiet."

Joe shook his head. "I've had enough." He marched forward, his right hand reaching for the gun.

Brian shot him.

Joe staggered and fell to his knees.

Eugenia screamed and jumped forward. "Daddy!"

Mouth open in shock, Brian stared at the gun in his hand.

"Are you all right? Are you all right?" Eugenia screamed, catching her father's free arm to steady him.

Joe sat back on his heels, his face pale and sweating, his right hand clutching his left side. He took a few ragged breaths. "I think . . . I think so."

Angelica swooned, grappling for the cash desk.

As Brian turned to look, Tricia leaped forward. "Ginny, call 911!" she yelled, and lunged at Brian, knocking the gun from his hand.

It skittered across the carpet. Tricia, Ginny, and Brian all dived after it, scrambling across the floor on their hands and knees, and into the nook. Three hands snatched at it, and the gun was pushed under one of the heavy upholstered chairs.

"Get away! Get away!" Brian shouted.

"Not on your life," Tricia grated.

Their hands knocked against each other as they fumbled for the gun, but it was Tricia who came up with it. She rolled onto her backside, the gun clasped in both hands, and leveled it at Brian's chest, the way she'd seen in a hundred TV shows.

He struggled to his knees and laughed at her. "You won't shoot."

Her eyes blazed. "Wanna bet?"

"Angelica, call 911!" Ginny yelled.

The sound of a siren cut the air.

"I did that before I got here," Angelica said with a smirk.

Ginny pulled herself up with the aid of the chair's arm. "You could've said so."

"And let this bozo know it? You ought to be ashamed of yourself, Brian. Also a pretty clever ruse—me pretending to faint, huh?"

No one commented.

Brian sat in a heap, looking boneless. Joe had been right: life as Brian knew it was now over. The same could be said for Eugenia, too.

The Sheriff's Department cruiser screeched to a halt in front of Haven't Got a Clue, and Captain Baker and Deputy Placer spilled from the car. Placer kicked in the door and they sprang inside, their weapons drawn. Baker took in the scene before him: Eugenia crying, Joe bleeding, Angelica and Ginny standing guard, Tricia still flat on her butt on the floor, clutching the gun.

"What the hell?" Baker asked.

"Show's over, guys," Tricia said. "But you're more than welcome to take over."

Baker holstered his weapon while Placer kept his trained on Brian.

"What are you doing on the floor?" he asked Tricia, offering his hand.

She looked up into those mesmerizing green eyes. "Taking care of business." Her grip slackened and she handed him the gun, handle first. Then he helped her up.

She grabbed Baker's tie, pulling him close, leaned forward, and kissed him hard on the mouth, then pulled back. "You are not Christopher, and you're definitely not Russ," she declared.

Startled, Baker stared at her in incomprehension. "What?"

"I just wanted to establish that from the get-go."

"Whatever," he said, a flush coloring his cheeks, and he removed her hand from his tie. He cleared his throat. Everyone was looking at the two of them.

It was Tricia's turn to blush.

"Now, then—what the hell has been going on?"

"I think I'll put the coffeepot back on," Ginny said wearily. "This is going to take a lot of explaining."

TWENTY-TWO

It seemed like hours later that the ambulance bearing Joe Hirt took off, heading for St. Joseph's Hospital in Milford. The EMTs didn't think he needed more than a bandage and a tetanus shot.

Eugenia had been devastated when Captain Baker slapped a pair of handcuffs on her. She cried, begging to accompany her father to the hospital, but ended up in the back of the same patrol car as Brian, on her way to the county

lockup. Someone needed to call Libby and explain what had happened. Tricia didn't envy whoever ended up with that job.

Apparently Brian had learned from the mysteries Ginny had been reading that the best thing he could do was to keep his mouth shut until he could talk to a lawyer. "You're not paying for one with my money," Ginny declared.

Captain Baker had been all business as he rounded up the suspects, although he'd tried hard—and succeeded—not to make eye contact with Tricia.

Oh, well.

Once the cops and the rubberneckers had departed, Tricia, Angelica, and Ginny settled in the readers' nook. Tricia had scrounged a bottle of Irish whiskey, which they'd been adding to their coffee. Since it was a girls-only gathering, Miss Marple had deigned to join them, and had settled on a pile of old *Mystery Scene* magazines on the big square coffee table.

"There are no good men left on the face of the planet," Ginny complained, and swallowed another big gulp from her cup.

"Sure there are," Tricia said.

"Name one."

"Mr. Everett."

"Yeah, and he's already taken. Plus he's old enough to be *your* grandfather."

"Nevertheless, I haven't given up hope."

"Don't forget Bob," Angelica said with a wistful sigh. "He's a real gem."

If she only knew, Tricia thought.

"How can you be so optimistic?" Ginny said, squinting at Tricia. "Russ just dumped you—what a jerk!"

"Oh, Russ was just a rebound boy after Tricia's divorce," Angelica explained. "A nice little diversion, but I'll bet now she's ready for something a bit more exciting."

"We won't go into all that."

"No need to," Angelica piped up. "That was some smooch you gave Captain Baker. See, I told you you were sweet on him."

"It was a stupid, impulsive thing to do," Tricia said, embarrassed. "I was just grateful he arrived when he did. I really wasn't sure Brian would believe my bluff."

"Uh-huh," Angelica said knowingly.

"You should've shot him," Ginny growled. "Did you see the way Eugenia carried on when they hauled them both away?" She frowned. "On second thought, you should've shot her, too."

"You know that's the whiskey talking—not the way you really feel," Tricia said.

"No, I wish you'd shot him." Ginny thought about it. "Okay, maybe not to

kill, but you should've shot him anyway." She paused. "In the butt. Twice—once in each cheek."

"I'm just glad we're all safe," Angelica said. "But there are things that need to be settled."

Yes, several big things. Like the mess that was now Ginny's life.

"That poor Libby Hirt," Angelica said with a sigh. "Her husband shot. Her daughter arrested and in love with a murderer . . ."

Ginny leaned forward and poured more whiskey into her cup. "Nah, Brian will probably only go to jail for manslaughter. The bastard!"

Tricia leaned forward and capped the bottle. "Sorry, ladies, but we've got a wedding to put on tomorrow, and this place needs a thorough cleaning."

Angelica stood. "And I've still got food to make."

None of them moved.

"I don't know if I can go to the wedding," Ginny said, her voice breaking.

"Oh, yes, you can," Tricia said.

"But my heart is broken."

"And what better way to reaffirm that you will find someone worthy of your love one day, than to attend the wedding of two people who truly love each other? They may not have much time left in their lives, but tomorrow they're going to commit to be together—for better or for worse, 'til death do they part."

Ginny sniffed. "Does it make me a terrible person because I didn't follow Brian to the jail? He betrayed me," she reminded them.

"Honey, I've been betrayed four times, and I sure haven't given up looking for someone," Angelica said.

"Does that mean you'd like to marry Bob?" Tricia asked, taken aback.

"Hell, no." Angelica thought about it for a moment. "Well, maybe. But not anytime soon. I've rushed into too many relationships. This is *my* time in life. That's why I took over the Cookery, and why I opened the café." She nodded sagely. "I've learned from my past mistakes. You ought to think about what you'd really like to do, Ginny. This could be your golden opportunity to do exactly what you want to do—maybe for the first time in your life."

Ginny blinked a few times. "I'd like to own my own business—just like you and Tricia," she blurted.

It was Tricia's turn to blink. "You would?"

Ginny nodded. "I've seen what you've done here. I know just about every aspect of the business. I could do the same thing—I know I could. I just don't have the money to get one started."

"You might if you sold your house," Angelica said.

"I'd never be able to afford the rents here in Stoneham."

Angelica's gaze rose to the ceiling. "You might if the landlord's girlfriend could persuade him to give you a break."

Ginny blinked in disbelief. "You'd do that for me?"

"Why not? Tricia says you're the best assistant in the village. Why shouldn't you try to be the best bookseller—or toy seller—or whatever you want to be?"

"That's all very good, but then I'd have to break in someone new," Tricia complained.

"I'm not saying any of this would happen tomorrow," Angelica muttered. "But Ginny needs a goal—one that doesn't include matrimony. What do you say, Ginny?"

For the first time in hours, a smile brightened Ginny's tear-swollen face. "I'd like that."

"And we'll help you, won't we, Trish?"

"We sure will."

"My own business," Ginny said, warming to the idea. "I like that thought. A lot."

Angelica held out her hand. "Then it's all for one."

Tricia put hers on top. "And all—"

Ginny did likewise. "For one—me!"

Their combined hands bounced once—twice—three times before springing high into the air.

TWENTY-THREE

THE BRIDAL BOUQUET of white calla lilies and baby's breath looked lovely against Grace's soft pink linen suit, and the maid of honor's bouquet was made of lavender chrysanthemums, which complimented her mauve, raw silk dress. Tricia also held a wadded tissue to wipe away the tears that filled her eyes. Weddings always made her cry.

Dressed in a dark suit, crisp white shirt, and navy tie, Mr. Everett wore a solemn expression as he slipped the simple gold band onto Grace's waiting finger. "With this ring, I thee wed."

Judge Milton smiled. "I now pronounce you husband and wife." To Mr. Everett, he said, "You may kiss your bride."

A resounding round of applause broke out among the guests as Mr. Everett

landed a gentle kiss on Grace's lips—and promptly turned an attractive shade of pink.

Haven't Got a Clue had never looked as lovely. White chrysanthemums and pale pink roses decorated the counters. Ginny had arrived early that morning with a bit of a hangover and many rolls of white crepe paper, which she'd artistically draped along the bookshelves. Angelica had set up a long, linen-draped table against the wall of nonfiction titles, and lavished it with hot and cold breakfast foods. Pale pink rosettes spiraled up Nikki Brimfield's gorgeous three-tiered cake, which had taken up residence at the store's coffee station. They'd chosen their initials, G and W, in brushed silver, for their cake topper.

Half an hour before the ceremony, Russ arrived with his camera to take posed and candid shots of the bride and groom and the cake. He kept looking at Ginny, who kept her distance, and Tricia warned him that he was not to talk to her about Pammy's death, or what had occurred at the store the evening before. He frowned and instead took Tricia's picture. And he kept making excuses to be near her—asking about the food, the decorations, and any other inane thing he could think of. Tricia was civil, but soon found other places to be.

Although appointed the honorary ring bearer, Miss Marple declined to participate in the ceremony, instead watching it from her perch on the shelf behind the register, purring all the while.

While Russ snapped pictures, Tricia stepped away from the happy couple, who were receiving best wishes from their guests. Everyone from the Tuesday Night Book Club was there, including Frannie, who kept showing anyone she could corner pictures of her new cat—just like any proud parent. Nikki Brimfield looked out of place in a skirt and blouse, instead of her white baker's uniform, and Julia Overland had worn the same color as Tricia. Great minds did indeed think alike. As best man, Bob had for once forgone his Kelly green sports coat and donned a dark suit. He looked . . . weird . . . out of his usual uniform.

Tricia traded good wishes with her lawyer, Roger Livingston, and Lois Kerr from the library. Though the ceremony was over, Stuart Paige remained seated in one of the rented chairs, looking pale, but smiling, while his flunky, Turner, stood nearby, wearing sunglasses and still trying to look like a Secret Service agent.

Angelica flitted around the room with a silver tray filled with miniquiches, offering them to one and all.

Among the missing, of course, were Libby and Joe Hirt, and Brian Comstock. No surprises there.

Distracted by the crowd, Tricia was caught off guard when Russ insinuated himself next to her once again. "I've been trying to get you on your own for the past hour. Are you avoiding me?"

"You made your feelings toward me quite clear. And after what happened at the inn on Friday, I don't think we have anything to say to one another."

"I left several messages for you to call me before then. You ignored them."

"Yes, I did."

He frowned. "Okay, I admit I made a mistake in calling off—us."

Tricia turned a level glare at him. "I take it you've had a change of plans?"

Russ frowned. "Okay, so the job in Philadelphia fell through. And I've decided not to put the paper up for sale. It looks like I won't be leaving Stoneham after all." He gave a weak laugh. "I know it's asking a lot, but I was hoping we could . . . still be friends."

Tricia said nothing.

"Actually, more than friends. Is there a chance things could go back to the way they were before I opened my big, stupid mouth?"

Tricia still said nothing.

"I'd like to think we could try."

"You *are* asking a lot."

The shop door opened, the little bell overhead ringing cheerfully. A stranger entered and paused. "I'm sorry. I thought the store was open today," he said.

Tricia strode over to the door—anything to get away from Russ. "We're opening late. As you can see, we're hosting a wedding."

Tricia did a double take. The man in front of her was Grant Baker. She hadn't recognized him out of uniform. He looked . . . nice.

He also looked uncomfortable. "I don't want to intrude," he said, already backing away.

"Don't be silly. Come on in; have some coffee and a piece of wedding cake."

He shook his head. "I only came to . . . to get a book."

"I thought you didn't read mysteries or true crime."

"Maybe I decided to broaden my horizons." He let the door close on his back and stepped closer to Tricia, lowering his voice. "Or . . . maybe I came just to see you. To see if you were free for dinner tonight."

Tricia looked to her right and left. Was he actually speaking to her?

"Um . . ." At the edge of her peripheral vision, she saw Russ nearby, eavesdropping. Tricia smiled. "I think that would be very nice."

"And I also wanted to tell you what you did for Pam Fredericks was decent and noble. Especially since you were only . . . sort of . . . friends."

Tricia's spine stiffened. She hadn't mentioned this to anyone. How had he found out? "I don't know what you mean," she bluffed.

"Claiming her body, paying to have it buried. Apparently she wasn't a very good friend to you, but you proved more than once you were probably the only true friend she ever had."

Tricia grabbed his elbow, and pulled him away from the other guests. "How did you find out?" she hissed.

"You dealt with Baker Funeral Home, right? My cousin Glenn owns it."

The breath caught in Tricia's throat. "I assumed Mr. Baker would've been more discreet."

"Don't worry; he didn't say a word. Our office was notified by the Medical Examiner when the body was released."

Okay, she could believe that.

Angelica made a pass with her tray. "Hi, Captain Baker. Try one of these delicious spinach miniquiches."

"Captain Baker?" Bob repeated, worry tingeing his voice—no doubt remembering Tricia's threat to turn him in to the law. He stepped away—fast.

"Don't mind if I do," Baker said, taking an offered napkin and two of the quiches. He bit into one, chewed, and swallowed. "Hey, these are terrific."

"Tricia helped make them," Angelica said, beaming, then moved on to another guest.

"And you can cook, too," he said, impressed.

Tricia shook her head and sighed. "My helping consisted of squeezing the water out of cold, wet spinach until it was dry. I'm not bragging when I tell you that I can barely boil water."

Baker laughed, but his expression soon became serious again. He nodded toward Stuart Paige. "How did he get invited to this little shindig?"

"Mr. Paige and Grace—she's the bride—have been friends for years."

Baker nodded. "I understand you showed him a page from the diary."

Tricia felt a squirm crawl along her spine. "Yes. I wanted to verify my suspicions on its author."

"What have you done with the rest of your copy of the diary?"

"Copy?" she asked, in all innocence.

"Yes, all ninety-seven pages."

She sighed. "Nothing, yet. I thought I might offer it to Eugenia Hirt. It's not a very flattering portrayal of her birth mother—but it might give her an even greater appreciation for her adoptive mother. But I'll wait a while before I mention it to her. She's had enough upsets for now."

"It'll give her something to read while she awaits her trial." Baker wiped his fingers on his napkin. "I've had a chance to go through all those letters we found in the shoebox in Pam Fredericks's car. She was related to M.J. Collins, all right. The woman was Pam's aunt—her mother's sister."

Tricia sighed. "That made Eugenia and Pammy first cousins. Imagine that—she tried to blackmail her own cousin."

A burst of laughter came from the crowd around the buffet table, remind-

ing Tricia that this was supposed to be a happy occasion. "Do we have to talk about Pammy anymore?"

"I still want to know why you did what you did—taking care of her in death," Baker pressed.

Tricia gave another long sigh. "Because . . ."

She didn't need to say anything. Officially, he needed no explanation.

Still . . .

She looked into his mesmerizing green eyes. "It was the right thing to do."

The hint of a smile touched his lips. "Yes, it was."

"Did you ever get that letter addressed to her at General Delivery?"

He nodded. "It was from her brother. It said, in no uncertain terms, that she was not to contact him or any other member of the family again. Apparently she'd taken not only the diary and the letters we found in the trunk of her car, but she'd cleaned out her mother's jewelry box and taken other valuables the last time she'd visited."

"Oh, my. Poor Pammy."

"I'd say poor Pammy's family."

The sound of a champagne cork popping was a welcome distraction. Bob Kelly held the bottle of fizz aloft. "Time for the toast!"

Angelica worked the room, tray in hand, offering glasses that were already filled. She paused in front of Tricia and Baker, gave her sister a knowing wink, and then moved off to serve the rest of the guests.

Bob filled flutes for Mr. Everett and Grace before clearing his throat. He held his glass before him. "Friends, I'm sure everyone here will join me in wishing William and Grace a long and joy-filled life together. May they always be as happy as they are at this moment."

"Hear, hear," came the chant as everyone raised his or her glass in salute.

When everyone had taken a sip, Mr. Everett offered his glass. "To my beautiful bride."

Again, those assembled raised their glasses and cheered.

Mr. Everett raised his glass once again. "And now, I'd like to say thank you to the person who made this all possible. To my employer and my friend, Ms. Tricia Miles. Thank you, Ms. Miles. You've not only made an old man feel useful again, but if it weren't for you, Grace and I would never have"—he paused, and seemed unsure of his next words—"hooked up."

Everyone laughed and then cheered.

Grant Baker turned to Tricia and lifted his glass. "Here's hoping we can"—he paused, and did not say "hook up"—"start out by being friends, and see where that leads."

Tricia raised her glass. "I'll drink to that." Out the corner of her eye, she saw Russ frown, but then he raised his glass, never breaking eye contact. "To us," he mouthed.

Tricia sipped her champagne and smiled. The next few days, maybe weeks, maybe months—might be very interesting indeed.

She drank to that.

ANGELICA'S RECIPES

BOB'S FAVORITE MEATLOAF

1½ pounds lean ground beef
⅔ cup seasoned breadcrumbs
1 egg, beaten
1 large onion, chopped
¼ teaspoon salt
¼ teaspoon ground pepper
¾ cup ketchup
1 tablespoon Worcestershire sauce

Combine breadcrumbs, egg, onion, salt, and pepper; mix well. Add to ground beef and mix well. Shape mixture into a loaf in a loaf pan. Mix ketchup with Worcestershire sauce and pour over the top.

Bake at 350 degrees for 70–80 minutes (or until meat thermometer reads 160 degrees).

Serves 4–6.

GARLIC MASHED POTATOES

6 medium potatoes, peeled and quartered
4–6 garlic cloves
5–6 cups water

2 tablespoons olive oil (or softened butter)
½ teaspoon salt
Pinch of pepper

Place potatoes and garlic in a large saucepan and cover with water. Bring to a boil. Reduce heat; cover and cook for 15–20 minutes or until tender.

Drain, reserving ½ cup cooking liquid. Mash potato mixture. Add oil (or butter), salt, pepper, and reserved liquid; stir until smooth.

Serves 4–6.

QUICK-AND-DIRTY GARLIC BREAD

1 baguette or small (8 ounces) loaf of French bread
¼ cup butter, softened
¼ cup Parmesan cheese
½ teaspoon garlic powder (or 2 minced garlic cloves)
2 tablespoons dried parsley (but fresh is always better)

Preheat oven to 400 degrees.

In a small mixing bowl, combine butter with Parmesan cheese. Add other ingredients and mix well. Cut the baguette into half-inch slices—but do not cut all the way through. Spread mixture on both sides of each slice. Wrap in aluminum foil and bake for 15–20 minutes. (If you like it crispy, open the foil the last 5 minutes.) Serve hot.

Serves 4–6.

POTATO-AND-LEEK SOUP

2 tablespoons butter
2 cloves diced garlic
2 good-sized potatoes (or about 1 pound)
2 good-sized leeks (or about 1 pound)

4 cups chicken broth
¼ teaspoon salt
¼ teaspoon black pepper
1 cup milk or light cream

Clean and chop white part of the leeks. Melt the butter in a large saucepan and add the chopped leeks and garlic. Saute them over low to medium heat until the leeks are soft (about 10 minutes). Stir frequently; do not brown.

Add all the remaining ingredients to the pan except the milk/cream. Bring the soup to a boil and then let it simmer for 15–20 minutes.

If you prefer a smooth soup, mash the potatoes in the pan, or puree them in a blender. Just before serving, pour the milk/cream into the soup; stir well, and heat through.

Serves 4.

MINI SPINACH QUICHES

½ cup butter or margarine, softened
1 package (3 ounces) cream cheese, softened
1 cup all-purpose flour
3 slices bacon
¼ cup chopped green onion
2 eggs
½ cup half-and-half
½ cup grated Parmesan cheese
¼ teaspoon salt
⅛ teaspoon ground nutmeg
1 (10-ounce) package frozen spinach, thawed and well drained (use your hands to squeeze out the water)

In a small mixing bowl, cream butter and cream cheese. Add flour; beat until well blended. Shape into 24 balls. Press balls into the bottom and the sides of greased minimuffin cups.

Preheat oven to 350 degrees. In a skillet, cook the bacon until brown and very crisp; drain. Saute the onions in the same skillet with the bacon drippings for 5 minutes, or until tender, stirring constantly; drain. Place the onions in a

medium bowl. Crumble the bacon into small pieces, and add to the onions. Add the eggs to the bacon and onions; beat well. Stir in the half-and-half, salt, nutmeg, and Parmesan cheese. Add the spinach; mix well to combine. Divide the mixture among crust-lined cups (do not overfill).

Bake for 25–30 minutes, or until puffed and golden brown. Cool in pan on wire rack for 5 minutes. Serve warm or cool. Store leftovers in the refrigerator.

Makes 24.

Medicare Helpline

800-801-1547